'It can't be overstated how purely pleasurable *The Bee Sting* is to read. Murray's brilliant new novel, about a rural Irish clan, posits the author as Dublin's answer to Jonathan Franzen . . . A 650-page slab of compulsive high-grade entertainment, *The Bee Sting* oozes pathos while being very funny to boot . . . Murray's observational gifts and A-game phrase-making render almost every page – every line, it sometimes seems – abuzz with fresh and funny insights . . . At its core this is a novel concerned with the ties that bind, secrets and lies, love and loss. They're all here, brought to life with captivating vigour in a first-class performance to cherish' *Observer* (Anthony Cummins)

'Carefully paced, brilliantly convincing and helped along by plenty of subtle satire . . . A huge, marbled Wagyu steak of a novel that ranges confidently from humane to horrifying. It's a classic family saga in the mode of *The Corrections* or *The Sound and the Fury* . . . Murray delights in taking a stock type – the sullen pubescent, the frazzled mother – and exploding it with ambiguity and empathy . . . An immensely enjoyable piece of expert craftsmanship' *The Times* (James Riding)

'Immersive, brilliantly structured, beautifully written, so dense yet so compelling, [and] as laugh-out-loud funny as it is deeply disturbing . . . *The Bee Sting* is as ambitious as anything that has gone before, but with a focus and shape that grants it great depth as well as breadth. Seriously, all you need is this, your suntan lotion and a few days off work and you're good to go . . . I didn't see the plot twists coming. And they keep on coming. And coming again . . . I began with an ovation. I'll end abruptly, and in awe . . . Paul Murray, the undisputed reigning champion of epic Irish tragicomedy, has done it again' *Spectator* (Ian Samson)

'Expertly foreshadowed and so intricately put together, a brilliantly funny, deeply sad portrait of an Irish family in crisis . . . Murray is triumphantly back on home turf – troubled adolescents, regretful adults, secrets signposted and exquisitely revealed, each line soaked in irony ranging from the gentle to the savage . . . We live though hundreds of pages on tenterhooks, and the suspense and revelations keep coming until the end . . . He is brilliant on fathers and sons, sibling rivalry, grief, self-sabotage and self-denial, as well as the terrible weakness humans have for magical thinking . . . A tragicomic triumph, you won't read a sadder, truer, funnier novel this year' *Guardian* (Justine Jordan)

'*The Bee Sting* is the finest novel that Murray has yet written and will surely be one of the books of 2023 . . . It bears comparison to the brilliant comic writer Jonathan Coe . . . But Murray is his own writer, capable of keeping a multi-faceted and compulsive plot moving along with alacrity and confidence, while seamlessly blending drama, comedy and heartbreak . . . For thirteen years, Paul Murray has been best known as the author of *Skippy Dies*. That, I suspect, is about to change' *Sunday Independent* (John Boyne)

'An instant classic . . . Although Murray is a fantastically witty writer, his empathy with these characters is so deep that he can convey the comedy of their foibles without the condescending bitterness of satire . . . And, most impressive, while sinking into the peculiar flaws of this one uniquely troubled family, Murray captures the anxiety many of us feel living on the edge of economic ruin in these latter days of the Anthropocene Epoch . . . Every paragraph is marked by Murray's stylistic brilliance and daring . . . A masterclass in the art of narrative, *The Bee Sting* never fails to dazzle' *Washington Post* (Ron Charles)

'This bumper novel is already gaining plaudits as the book of the summer, and if it's a meaty, heart-punching, expertly executed family saga you need this August, then you can stop the search now . . . Murray delivers scarcely a duff sentence in a 600-page novel that's pure unadulterated pleasure. It's been compared to Jonathan Franzen's *The Corrections*; I'd argue it's better than that' *Daily Mail* (Claire Allfree)

'Murray is a natural storyteller who knows when to withhold, to indulge, to surprise. He specializes, like Dickens, in lengthy sagas that are mammoth in scope, generous with detail and backstory, flush with humour and colourful characters, all of it steeped in social realism . . . Ambitious, expansive, hugely entertaining tragicomic fiction' *Irish Times* (Sarah Gilmartin)

'Murray's writing is pure joy – propulsive, insightful and seeded with hilarious observations . . . Through the Barneses' countless personal dramas, Murray explores humanity's endless contradictions. How brutal and beautiful life is. How broken and also full of potential. How endlessly fraught and persistently promising. Whether or not we can ever truly change our course, the hapless Barneses will keep you hoping, even after you turn the novel's last page' *The New York Times Book Review* (Jen Doll)

'No one writes tragicomedy as good as this . . . Both brilliant entertainment and a penetrating look at the human condition, as heavy with pathos as it is rich with humour. And if 650 pages asks a lot of the reader, in this case it more than delivers' *i* (Nick Duerden)

'Delightfully rackety, raucously funny . . . *The Bee Sting* is on a par with *Skippy Dies*, Murray's most beloved book, and certainly exceeds it in ambition. A masterpiece' *Irish Independent* (Rory Kiberd)

'Stylistically it's outstanding, defined by supple, engaging prose and a preternatural sense for storytelling. Even keeping in mind the marvels of twentieth-century Irish literature, the quality of the writing still emerging from this small island is a source of wonder . . . Mr Murray has always been able to dazzle and entertain, but he has never before developed characters with this much depth or capacity for tragedy' *Wall Street Journal* (Sam Sacks)

'A coruscating return for a novelist who's been keeping us waiting for something special since 2010's *Skippy Dies* . . . A tragicomedy that never stints on great jokes – even at its saddest' *Daily Telegraph*

'Bold [and] expansive . . . Paul Murray is consistently inventive, observant and funny. He is on intimate terms with this pre-teen boy, this teenage girl, this lost middle-aged man and this semi-educated woman, and he knows how to make them vivid . . . The pages turn rapidly as farce and tragedy converge, the latter threatening to get the upper hand' *Times Literary Supplement* (Nick Clee)

'The novel, Murray believes, can help readers see clearly, listen with care, think hard. As evidence, he presents *The Bee Sting*, a novel that strives to engage with the world on every single overstuffed page . . . It's heartening to have a writer with Murray's energy devoting such attention to contemporary life . . . *The Bee Sting* is 645 pages of close observation, encouraging readers to identify the disconnections and miscommunications that plague us all, the small personal disasters that our fear and dishonesty transform into apocalypses' *Slate*

'Paul Murray's patter is so fluid, funny and clever that you'd be forgiven for pausing, from time to time, to double-check that quality of what you're being sold. For most of *The Bee Sting*, Murray seems capable of doing anything a novelist might reasonably want to do. There's laughter in every other line, but there's also a compassion and a midlife wisdom at work that suggest we aren't merely in the company of a gag merchant . . . Quirky details strike back later in the narrative, with unexpected force . . . Humane and mature, written with immense facility by an author who knows how to get the job done' *Literary Review* (Paul Genders)

'Funny, dark, moving and deeply humane. It's also driven by an inexorable tragic force, and Murray's intricate narrative dexterity makes it very easy to keep turning all those hundreds of pages' *Observer* (Mark O'Connell)

'Beguiling . . . [Murray's] prose pops from the page, precise and piquant, biting in its gallows humour. He's astonishingly versatile, tapping internet influences, stream-of-consciousness technique and social realism. Fulfilling the promise of his lauded *Skippy Dies*, *The Bee Sting* elevates Murray to the leading rank of his generation, alongside Colin Barrett, Kevin Barry and Claire Keegan' *Minneapolis Star Tribune* (Hamilton Cain)

'A family lurches into financial and emotional crisis in full view of judgemental neighbours in this astute, remorselessly funny novel about how people are invariably more complex than they first appear . . . Murray tackles some of the biggest issues facing our society in a thoughtful, tragicomic novel exploring small-town society and social class' *Daily Mirror* (Huston Gilmore)

'Breathtaking, blackly comic, Murray's style is entirely and distinctively his own . . . Handling the plot as if it were a Rubik's Cube, [he] gives each character their voice in a carousel of first-person accounts, tracking backwards and into the present . . . *The Bee Sting* is an immersion in the tragedy of what might have been' *Herald* (Rosemary Goring)

'*The Bee Sting* has resulted in Murray being heralded "Dublin's Jonathan Franzen" . . . No one does bittersweet comic novels quite like Murray – fans of his 2010 boarding school comedy *Skippy Dies* will be aching to get their hands on this' iNews (Leïla Slimani)

Paul Murray was born in Dublin in 1975. He is the author of *An Evening of Long Goodbyes*, *Skippy Dies*, *The Mark and the Void* and *The Bee Sting*. *An Evening of Long Goodbyes* was shortlisted for the Whitbread First Novel Award and nominated for the Kerry Group Irish Fiction Award. *Skippy Dies* was shortlisted for the Costa Novel Award and the National Book Critics Circle Award, and longlisted for the Booker Prize. *The Mark and the Void* won the Everyman Wodehouse Prize 2016. *The Bee Sting* was shortlisted for the Booker Prize 2023. Paul Murray lives in Dublin.

THE BEE STING

Paul Murray

PENGUIN BOOKS

PENGUIN BOOKS

UK | USA | Canada | Ireland | Australia
India | New Zealand | South Africa

Penguin Books is part of the Penguin Random House group of companies
whose addresses can be found at global.penguinrandomhouse.com.

Penguin
Random House
UK

First published by Hamish Hamilton 2023
Published in Penguin Books 2024

001

Copyright © Paul Murray, 2023

The moral right of the author has been asserted

Typeset by Jouve (UK), Milton Keynes
Printed and bound in Great Britain by Clays Ltd, Elcograf S.p.A.

The authorized representative in the EEA is Penguin Random House Ireland,
Morrison Chambers, 32 Nassau Street, Dublin D02 YH68

A CIP catalogue record for this book is available from the British Library

ISBN: 978–0–241–98440–6

Those are my best days, when I shake with fear.
John Donne

SYLVIAS

In the next town over, a man had killed his family. He'd nailed the doors shut so they couldn't get out; the neighbours heard them running through the rooms, screaming for mercy. When he had finished he turned the gun on himself.

Everyone was talking about it – about what kind of man could do such a thing, about the secrets he must have had. Rumours swirled about affairs, addiction, hidden files on his computer.

Elaine just said she was surprised it didn't happen more often. She thrust her thumbs through the belt loops of her jeans and looked down the dreary main street of their town. I mean, she said, it's something to *do*.

Cass and Elaine first met in Chemistry class, when Elaine poured iodine on Cass's eczema during an experiment. It was an accident; she'd cried more than Cass did, and insisted on going with her to the nurse. They'd been friends ever since. Every morning Cass called to Elaine's house and they walked to school together. At lunchtime, they rolled up their long skirts and wandered around the supermarket, listening to music from Elaine's phone, eating croissants from the bakery section that were gone by the time they got to the checkout. In the evening, they went to each other's houses to study.

Cass felt she'd known Elaine for ever; it made no sense that they had not always been friends. Their lives were so similar it was almost eerie. Both girls came from well-known families in the town: Cass's father, Dickie, owned the local Volkswagen dealership, while Elaine's dad, Big Mike, was a businessman and cattle farmer. Both girls were of slightly above-average height; both were bright, in fact they were consistently at the top of their class. Both intended to leave here some day and never come back.

Elaine had golden hair, green eyes, a perfect figure. When she bought clothes online, they always fitted perfectly, as if they'd been made with her in mind. Writing about her in her journal, Cass used words like *grace* and *style*. She had what the French called *je ne sais quoi*. Even when she was clipping her toenails, she looked like she was eating a peach.

When Cass came round to Elaine's house, they would sit in her bedroom with the carousel lamp on and look at the Miss Universe Ireland website. Elaine was thinking seriously about entering, though not for the title itself so much as the opportunities it might offer. The previous year's winner was now brand ambassador for a juice company.

Cass thought Elaine was prettier than any of the contestants pictured online. But it was tricky. Each of the girls competing to be Miss Universe Ireland, and from there to be Miss Universe for the world/universe overall, had an adversity they had overcome. One had been a refugee from a war in Africa. Another had needed surgery when she was a small girl. A very thin contestant had once been very fat. The adversity had to be something bad, like a learning disability, but not really bad, like being chained up in a basement for ten years by a paedophile. Cass's eczema would be a perfect adversity; they wondered, if she held her skin up against Elaine's long enough, whether she could pass it on to her. But it didn't seem to work. Elaine said the adversity requirement was unfair. When you think about it, it's almost like a kind of discrimination, she said.

The housekeeper knocked on the door to say it was time for Elaine's swimming lesson. Elaine rolled her eyes. The swimming pool was always full of Band-Aids and old people. Coming from *here*, she said. If that isn't an adversity, I don't know what is.

Elaine hated their town. Everyone knew everyone, everybody knew your business; when you walked down the street people would slow their cars to see who you were so they could wave at you. There were no

4

proper shops; instead of McDonald's and Starbucks, they had Binchy Burgers and Mangan's Café, where the owners worked behind the counter and asked after your parents. You can't even buy a sausage roll without having to tell someone your life story, she complained.

The smallness wouldn't have been so bad if the townsfolk had had a little more sophistication. But their only interest, besides farming and the well-being of the microchip factory, was Gaelic games. Football, hurling, camogie, the county, the Cup, the under-21s – that was all anyone ever talked about. Elaine hated GAA. She was bad at sports, in spite of her grace. She was always the last up the rope in gym class; in games, she confined herself to the sidelines, where she scowled, flicked her hair, and wafted reluctantly back and forth with the general direction of play, like a lovely frond at the bottom of a noisy, grunting ocean.

The Tidy Towns Committee, of which Cass's mother was a member, was always shiteing on about the natural beauty of the area, but Elaine did not accept this. Nature in her eyes was almost as bad as sports. The way it kept *growing*? The way things, like crops or whatever, would die and then next year they *came back*? Did no one else get how creepy that was?

I'm not being negative, she said. I just want to live somewhere I can get good coffee and not have to see nature and everyone doesn't look like they were made out of mashed potato.

Cass didn't care for GAA either, and she agreed about the general lack of *je ne sais quoi*. For her, though, the presence of Elaine was enough to cancel out the town's faults.

She had never felt so connected to someone. When they messaged each other at night – sometimes they'd stay up till two in the morning – they got so in synch it was almost like they were the same person. If Elaine texted Cass to say WTF was up with that jumper today, she would know immediately whose jumper she was talking about; a single, unexplained word, *bagatelle* or *lickout*, could make her laugh so loud that her dad would hear from across the landing and come in and tell her to go to sleep. In some ways, that was the best time of all – better even than being together. As she lay in bed, messages flying back and forth between them, Cass would feel like she was flying too, far above the town, in a pure space that belonged completely to her and her best friend.

Most days they went to Elaine's after school, but sometimes, for a change of scene, Elaine would want to come to Cass's instead. She liked to hang out in the kitchen talking to Imelda – that's what she called Cass's mother, 'Imelda', so casually and naturally that after a while Cass started doing it too. You are so working those jeggings, Imelda, she'd say. Oh, you think so? Cass's mam/'Imelda' would say, and she'd lean over with impossible willow-like grace to examine the back of her own thighs. I wasn't sure about the stripes. The stripes are what make it, Elaine would say conclusively, and Imelda would look happy.

Cass's mother was a famous beauty. She too had blonde hair and green eyes. It's so weird that she's your mam, Elaine said. Doesn't it make more sense that I should be her daughter?

Then we'd be sisters! Cass said.

No, I mean, instead of you, Elaine said.

Cass wasn't sure what to do with that. But the fact remained that Elaine got on better with her mother than she did. Imelda liked to give Elaine face creams to try out; they traded beauty secrets and product advice. Cass was a bystander in these conversations. Nothing works on her skin, Imelda said, because of the eczema. It's a real adversity, Elaine agreed.

Once, Imelda had taken the girls with her to Dublin for the pre-sales. The discounts hadn't been put on the price tags yet; only platinum customers knew about them. This secret elevation over the other shoppers had made Elaine visibly giddy; she watched Imelda stalk the clothes-rails, whipping pitilessly through the garments like an empress at the slave market, as if she could see the difference, like an aura around her, a platinum glow.

Cass did not totally get the Imelda-worship. In her view, Elaine was much prettier than her mother. Yeah, but your mam's got to be at least, like, thirty-four, Elaine said. I mean, she's really kept her looks.

Elaine felt that her own mother hadn't aged well, and had once confessed her 'greatest fear' was that her looks too would be transitory, and that she would spend the rest of her life as one of the lumpen potato-people she saw shuttling their shopping trolleys through the Lidl car park.

It was true: even now, as a mother of two, Imelda had an electrifying effect on people. When she walked down the street women would cock their heads and gaze at her adoringly, as if at some dazzling athletic display. Men would stop, and stammer, their pupils dilating and their mouths quivering in half-formed O's, as if trying to push out some ineffable word.

Cass's own effect was not electrifying, and when she told people that Imelda was her mother, they would stare at her a moment as if trying to solve a puzzle, then pat her hand sympathetically, and say, It's after your father you take, so.

Elaine said it wasn't just about looks. Imelda also had mystique, magnetism.

I can't believe she married your dad, she said candidly.

Cass too sometimes had trouble believing it – that her dad, who was so thoughtful, so sensitive, had fallen for Imelda's 100 per cent superficial allure like every other chump. She didn't want to devalue her mother in Elaine's eyes. At the same time, she didn't know how Elaine could think Imelda had mystique. To spend time with her mother was to get a running commentary on the contents of her mind – an incessant barrage of thoughts and sub-thoughts and random observations, each in itself insignificant but cumulatively overwhelming. I must book you in for electrolysis for that little moustache you're getting, she'd say; and then while you were still reeling, Are those tulips or begonias? There's Marie Devlin, do you know she has no sense of style, none whatsoever. Is that man an Arab? This place is filling up with Arabs. Where's this I saw they had that nice chutney? Kay Connor told me Anne Smith's lost weight but the doctor said it was the wrong kind. I thought it was supposed to be sunny today, that's not one bit sunny. Who invented chutney, was it

Gorbachev? And on, and on – listening to her was like walking through a blizzard, a storm of frenzied white nothings that left you snow-blind.

Frankly, she would have preferred that Elaine stayed away from her house altogether, that after school they only went to Elaine's, where Elaine's housekeeper, Augustina, would make them iced coffees, and they'd sit in Elaine's bedroom looking at the Miss Universe Ireland website, swapping sex tips they had never used, ranking the best-looking boys from the secondary school down the road.

At the same time, she knew she should be thankful for her mother's undeniable glamour – thankful to have something in her life that her friend envied, especially now.

The fact was that their lives were not so similar as Elaine imagined. Yes, they had the same tennis racket, the same terry hoody in peach melba. But though Elaine hadn't seemed to realize it yet, some of the other things they had in common were actually things they *used* to have in common. Both families had Brazilian housekeepers. But Marianna had been away 'visiting her family' for almost a year now, and Cass knew she was never coming back. Cass could say where the best shops were in New York City, and the best beaches on the Cap d'Antibes; but Elaine's arms still bore the tan-fade from her holidays, while if she looked at her own arms, which she tried not to, Cass would see that between the patches of eczema they were clammy white, almost indistinguishable from the fabric of the ugly school blouse.

When she first became aware that business was 'slowing down', as her dad had put it, she thought it might not be a bad thing. Elaine had confided recently that, before they became friends, she'd thought Cass and her family were stuck-up. Not just me, she hastened to explain. It's what most people think.

Cass had been horrified. She knew her family was well off, but she had never behaved like this made her special. Maybe it wouldn't hurt if they were brought down to earth a little; then Elaine would know she wasn't trying to act superior or compete for the limelight.

But the slowdown quickly became more of a freefall. An air of dread gathered over the showroom. And she used to love to visit it! From the wings she would gaze at the dazzling bodywork, the gleaming newness that was almost overwhelming. Then she would sit in the display models in turn, imagining a different life to go with each: princess, explorer, scientist, fairy. Now she couldn't bear it. The unloved, unbought cars, still dazzling desperately, reminded her of stray dogs in the pound, waiting to be put down.

Dad did his best to comfort her. Things will pick up, he said. It's all cyclical. But that only tightened the knot in her stomach.

Dickie Barnes was not a natural salesman. Often, when Cass called in to the showroom, he would be sitting in his office, reading a book. If he did happen to be on the shop floor, that was almost worse. Someone would come in looking for a new car, and he would steer them towards a used one. If they wanted a used one, he'd push them in the direction of a smaller, cheaper model. More than once she'd heard him talk people out of buying cars altogether.

When this was put to him, Dickie liked to quote his father, Cass's granddad, who had said that the key to the business was not selling cars, but building relationships. Once the customer trusts you, he's with you for life, he said. And by way of proof, he'd point out to the street, where you could see the Maurice Barnes Motors sticker in the back window of every third car that went by.

But now the customers had stopped coming.

It wasn't Dad's fault. There had been a *crash*. That was the word they used on the news: it made Cass think of something sudden and explosive, a car hitting a wall. But this crash was slow – in fact it had been going on for years – and nothing had exploded. Nothing had happened at all that you could see, yet somehow, because of this crash, there was no more money. Even the banks were out of money. Last year the microchip factory had let a hundred people go; half the shops on Main Street had an A4 page in the window, thanking customers for their many years of loyalty. Everyone was in the same boat.

And yet some people were in a different boat.

Elaine's dad had 'gone in' with a developer on a small estate of houses, carved out of the woods behind Cass's family's land. Now the developer had gone bust, and the unfinished houses were mouldering away; Elaine told her Big Mike was spending three days a week up in Dublin now, arguing with lawyers. But somehow as well as summer holidays in France, he had taken his family skiing in the autumn midterm break; they still had a standing order of lobster at the delicatessen, and every Sunday at Mass they sat up at the very front.

That man is nothing but a crook, her mother said. She couldn't stand Big Mike, with his smirk, and his investments, and his Gucci cowboy boots. And him only a yahoo, that grew up on handouts from the Lions!

But he knew how to use his loaf, which was more than she could say for some people.

Cass's mother was not handling the downturn well. She had always been an assiduous shopper. She knew every delivery man in town by name; her walk-in wardrobe was a secret paradise of unworn sweaters and shawls, boots that crowded the shoe-rails like giddy dancers, waiting to pour onto the stage. Now, with things the way they were, she couldn't even shop in the sales. For Imelda, this was like a death sentence. Other than Tidy Towns meetings, which took place in the back room of the Olivia Smythe boutique on Main Street, she had largely stopped going out.

At home, with no one to look at her, she fell into black, ugly moods. She'd lie on the couch with a magazine propped against her crossed legs, snapping the pages so loud Cass could hear it from upstairs. Then with a hiss of dissatisfaction she'd toss it aside, and go stalking from room to room, clicking her fingers – 'active', but with nothing to do, like a grounded teenager, or a supercharged pensioner in an old folks' home – before deciding on something guaranteed to make her angry, like attempting to bake a soufflé, or knitting socks.

Imelda did not listen to the news. She didn't want to hear a whole load of blather about global this and economic that. When it came to the failing business, she knew where to put the blame.

*

Imelda had long held that Cass and Dickie were 'in cahoots'. They liked books, clever talk. They had a bond, she felt, that excluded her. Now she believed Cass had 'turned' her father against the garage. Last year Cass had done a project for Geography class about climate change. With your parents' help you had to calculate how their work contributed to global warming. Dickie had thrown himself into this; he loved homework. They sat in the kitchen and made a list of all the cars the garage sold, estimated how much CO_2 it had taken to make them and ship here, worked out on average roughly how much greenhouse gas they would release over their lifetime. At the end they added the numbers up.

Cass could remember that moment very clearly. It had all been fun until then. Flippin' hell, Dad said. He looked from the picture Cass had taken of Maurice Barnes Motors to the images of sodden Bangladeshi refugees after their village went underwater. That can't be right, he said, checking the final total again.

According to Imelda, he was never the same after that. He'd started making vegetarian meals and cycling to work. Lunacy! Imelda said. What does it look like, a car dealer riding a bike to work?

Maurice himself, Cass's grandfather, had had to fly back from Portugal to talk him out of expanding the fleet to sell more electric cars. We're not selling to Björn and Agneta the Swedish architects, Dickie! he told him. People here want diesel! *Now you're suckin' diesel*, that's the bumper sticker! Not, now you're suckin' bloody soy beans.

But the damage was done, Imelda said. He never put his back into it again. And all because his golden girl made a song-and-dance. I hope you're happy, miss.

Cass couldn't deny it: she had been disturbed by the project. It wasn't just the garage; she was up to her neck in climate change too. Looking at Instagram, eating an ice cream, switching on a light: her most casual act left a toxic trace behind – as if she had a marauding shadow-self that choked the very world she lived in. For weeks she had moped around, paralysed by the inescapability of her own evil. She would stand on the threshold of the back garden, looking at the flowers and grass and the trees in the distance, imagining everything turning black, the birds and the insects falling out of the sky. Even on good days, like when Elaine gave her a bracelet she had two of, she would remember suddenly all of the animals that were going extinct and how the earth was going to flood and everything was doomed – because of the Barnes family.

Still, she was old enough now to realize that the international car trade had not been brought to a halt by her Transition Year Geography class. It's happening all over the world, Mam, she told her. It's not Dad's fault. It's a global phenomenon.

A global phenomenon and a work-shy attitude, Imelda said.

That was why it made Cass so nervous when Elaine came over. Her mother's moods swung like a ship's lantern in a storm. Who knew what she might say? It was quite possible that she would start complaining about Dickie in front of Elaine and give the game away. And what then? What would Elaine do? Would she think less of Cass? Would she still be her friend, now that their lives were no longer the same?

She tried to dissuade Elaine from visiting; she subtly undermined her mother when she could. But – although she had recently run out of toner and complained that her face felt like it had been tarmacked – Imelda was as beautiful as ever, and Elaine remained obsessed.

It was Elaine who noticed the wedding photos.

They were in the good room, where strictly speaking they shouldn't have been; Cass and PJ were only allowed in there when there were visitors, that was the rule. But Elaine wanted to look at Uncle Frank, who she thought was hot, even though he was dead; anyway, she said, technically she was a visitor.

The good room had the artificial feeling of the roped-off section of a guided tour. There was an enormous couch of turquoise velvet, a crystal chandelier, lots of little tables crowded with china ornaments. The mantelpiece was covered with pictures of the family through the years. Maurice and Peggy in sunglasses, on the deck of a yacht; Dickie and

Frank as toddlers in matching dungarees; Frank in his football gear (That's how hot he is, Elaine said, he even looks good in a GAA jersey); Cass's First Holy Communion, PJ's First Holy Communion; Dickie, Imelda and the kids on holidays past, in Malaga, in Chamonix, in Disneyland, in Marrakesh, skiing, snorkelling, sunbathing, riding donkeys.

But no wedding photos, Elaine pointed out.

Cass was sure she was wrong; there must be something tucked away somewhere. But she looked and there wasn't.

Mysterious, Elaine said, and this time Cass couldn't disagree. Having her picture taken was literally her mother's favourite thing in the world. The house was full of free newspapers and glossy magazines, in the back pages of which Imelda appeared, glowing, at the town Talent Show, or the Lions Christmas Lunch, or the new Hermès store at Brown Thomas, or the relaunch of Coady's pub, with the Mayor or the PR or one of her friends from the Tidy Towns Committee looking wan or orange or cellulitey beside her. For her mother to pass up a photo op like her own wedding was not so much baffling as genuinely shocking.

They spent the afternoon in Cass's bedroom, coming up with conspiracy theories, but nothing explained it. That night, Cass sat down on the couch beside her father while he was watching TV. Hey, Dad? Do you have any photos of you guys's wedding?

She had rehearsed this line in front of her mirror for maximum casualness.

Her dad didn't reply at first. Instead, he stroked his chin, keeping his eyes fixed on the screen, so she wasn't even sure if he'd heard. Then, just as she was debating whether to repeat the question, There are some somewhere, all right, he said at last. I must see can I dig them out. And he turned and looked at her with the same smile as when he was telling her business was cyclical.

What the fuck? Elaine said when Cass relayed this to her.

I know, Cass said.

Until then, in her heart of hearts, Cass had suspected that the answer to the riddle was something mundane – that the pictures had got lost when they moved house, or PJ had spilled paste on them, or there was some olden-days type mishap with the negatives or whatever. Now she wondered if there genuinely was a secret conspiracy.

You have to ask your mam, Elaine said.

Yes, Cass said.

I can do it if you don't want to, Elaine said.

I'll ask her, Cass said.

That was the answer. Imelda was no good at lying. If Cass timed it right, she was bound to blurt out the truth.

Right now, though, Cass was trying to steer clear of her mother, who was in a particularly bad mood. Last week Dickie had sold her car. She'd parked it at the dealership, as was her habit, and went off to do her messages; while she was gone, Big Mike had come in, looking for a car for Augustina, the housekeeper. He told Dickie he only wanted a banger; then his eyes fell on the Touareg.

It wasn't – as Cass's dad had repeatedly and vainly pointed out – *actually* her car; he'd been trying to shift it for almost a year. If he'd sold it to anyone else, maybe she wouldn't have been quite so angry. But she was convinced Big Mike had bought it out of malice. He's rubbing our faces in it – that's what she kept yelling at Dickie. Until she calmed down, Cass thought it best to avoid any provocative questions, and keep Elaine out of her way.

Elaine, however, didn't like to wait. That Sunday she ran up to Cass after Mass in a state of great excitement to say that her father had been at Dickie and Imelda's wedding, seventeen years previously, and had told her what had happened.

Something happened? Cass said.

Elaine couldn't tell her right now because she had ballet. I'll come over to you later, she promised.

Is it bad? Cass said.

But Elaine was already climbing into her dad's car.

*

When her friend rang the doorbell Cass made sure she was the one who answered it; she hustled Elaine upstairs before Imelda could see her. She'd come directly from her dance class, wearing a hoody over her leotard. She sat herself on the duvet with her legs crossed. But for a moment she didn't speak.

Cass had been a little offended that Elaine had gone ahead and uncovered a secret that rightfully belonged to her. Now she felt a sudden sting of dread. Maybe her parents had never got married at all! Maybe they weren't even her real parents! So? she said.

Elaine goggled at her with glassy eyes. Then she said, There was a bee.

What?

There was a bee, Elaine repeated.

I don't understand, Cass said.

Elaine, keeping her face very stiff, explained that as Imelda's father was driving his daughter to the church, a bee had flown in the window of the car and got trapped in her veil. She started freaking out, Elaine said. But her dad thought she just didn't want to marry Dickie.

When at last he realized what was happening, he'd pulled over, and tried to get the veil off her. But it had got caught in the seat belt, and he couldn't get it free. So he jumps out of the car, and he runs around to the passenger side, Elaine said. But just as he finally untangles it, he hears this scream.

It stung her? Cass said.

Right on the eye, Elaine said, with a certain amount of relish.

Imelda's father had tried to find a pharmacy on the way to church, but the best he could do was a little pub, where he'd bought her a Twister to hold against the swelling till they arrived. It didn't help, and Imelda had kept the veil over her face as she walked down the aisle, as she stood at the altar, as they exchanged their vows, even when Dickie went to kiss the bride. She didn't take it off right through the reception, Elaine said. And she wouldn't tell anybody what happened. Everyone just thought she'd lost the plot.

Jesus, Cass said.

Yeah, Elaine said.

So that was why no pictures? Cass said. The sting was that bad?

My dad said it looked like she had a pig bladder stuck to her face, Elaine told her.

God, Cass said reflectively.

A moment passed in silence; then, at exactly the same time, they caught each other's eye. Once they'd started laughing it was impossible to stop. Before long, they were rolling around on the floor: Cass laughed so hard that she thought she might throw up.

A bee stuck in her mother's veil! A literal bee in her bonnet! It was too hilarious, too perfect. And that she had never told her children about it, even though the whole town knew – that was the icing on the cake. Imelda was so vain, she couldn't bear to be the punchline of a joke.

That evening after she went home Elaine sent her a close-up picture of a bee with the message **Will you bee mine Cass?** Cass sent one back of a bee superimposed onto a wedding dress that said **Bee my honey Elaine**. They stayed up half the night sending each other random pictures of bees. Each one was as funny as the one before it. Putting the phone down at last, she felt exhausted, in a good way, as if she'd climbed a mountain.

When she turned out the lights, though, the scene came back to her. This time she seemed to witness it through her own eyes, as if she were seated in a pew near the back of the church. She watched her mother push through the door and make her way up the aisle, and though she was veiled Cass could see her humiliation, her confusion – and Dickie's confusion too, gaping at the mysterious figure (who was under there?) he was about to wed. They were not much older than she was now; she felt sorry for them, stranded on the altar of the church she knew so well, while everyone stared, making their judgements.

She felt sorry for the bee too. Bees were dying everywhere, all around the world: PJ was always talking about it. Nobody knew the cause, but it was bad because the bees brought pollen from plant to plant and without them, Nature itself would die. This particular bee had been humming along, minding its own business, when it was swept without warning through the car window and into her mother's world. Enveloped by her veil, by her cries, it must have thought it was lost in some vast, labyrinthine flower. All points of reference had been stripped away; there was only the veil and her mother's huge, beautiful face. It seemed she could feel the bee's panic, its desperation to escape; she could see her mother's hands pummelling the air, then, as the creature made its last suicidal effort to defend itself, the sting pulsating on her skin, pumping its futile poison. She felt the bee's life ebb away. Nature was dying, the world was ending. As she fell asleep, it was her body on the floor by her mother's silk wedding shoes, already turning to dust.

After that, Elaine's interest in Imelda seemed to wane. Cass supposed the bee story detracted from her mystique. She did worry that, without Imelda's glamour, Elaine might lose interest in her too. But that didn't happen; and before long the girls had a new obsession.

There were many things to hate about their school – the ankle-length skirts, the hospital smell, the desiccated principal, the prayers, the sports, the boredom. Their English teacher, Ms Ogle, however, was more to be pitied than despised. Also known as 'the Last Nun', she was a spinster who had stayed at home to take care of her mother. The mother had been on her deathbed for thirty years without ever actually dying. The two of them lived in a grim little cottage off Main Street; Ms Ogle's teacher's bag was full of wallpaper samples and paint colour charts that she would never use.

She was a tragic figure, but she didn't seem to see it. She had a grandiose manner, and was fond of using long, exotic words – *bagatelle*, *mellifluous, distinctive* – like weird drapey silks you might find in a box in your grandmother's attic. Her actual clothes, however, were not drapey; she wore a combination of dungarees and frilly blouses, a look that Elaine called 'Victorian petrol station'.

The girls mocked Ms Ogle unceasingly. Sometimes it felt like there weren't enough hours in the day for all the mocking. Everything about her was funny – even her name, because who would want to ogle her? But they also discussed her seriously as a cautionary tale, the danger of staying in the town and 'getting stuck' looking after a relative.

Ms Ogle wasn't aware of this either. She adored Cass and Elaine, her best students. 'My girls,' she called them.

Then one day Ms Ogle wasn't in class. She was very sick, they heard; so sick that her dying mother had risen from her bed for the first time in a decade in order to take care of her.

Was this ironic? Was it funny? On Sunday they saw Ms Ogle at Mass – waxy-pale, her eyes bulging out of her head as if it had shrunk. My girls, she said to them emotionally, reaching to hug them from her wheelchair. It was so tragic that they had to bite their lips to keep from cracking up. But they also had an obscure sense that it was their fault – that the mockery they poured on her so regularly had brought her to collapse.

They forgot about that as soon as Miss Grehan appeared; they forgot Ms Ogle existed. She walked through the door in a white trouser suit that set off her long, magnificent red hair, went straight to the blackboard and wrote, in capitals, LADY POETS.

It seemed clear just from looking at her that Miss Grehan was neither a spinster nor tragic. When they found her social media that night, their opinion was confirmed. Her relationship status was 'It's complicated . . .' In the accompanying pictures, her life looked like one continuous party, shifting from one city to another, like a James Bond film. Here she was at a club in Barcelona. Now she posed on the battlements of a castle in Prague. On the seashore in California, a sunset swirled around her like an emanation of her glorious red hair. In Dublin, she sat barefoot before an open fire. Everyone she knew was good-looking. Even the old people, Elaine said.

What on earth was she doing here? Grehan, Grehan . . . Cass's dad mused when she brought it up at dinner. I sold a Passat to a Grehan a few years back. Wait – or was it a Fabia? Hold on now till I think.

It's that long since he sold a car he can't even remember, Imelda commented tartly.

Oh Jesus, don't start, Dickie said.

Miss Grehan may have had some connection to the man with the Passat or Fabia; they never found out. In the classroom she didn't talk about her past, or indeed her present, with the castles and the sunsets. What she talked about was lady poets.

The lady poets had glamorous, impassioned lives, or torturous, wretched lives. Sometimes they had both. She told them about Anna Akhmatova, a Russian who when she was young looked like a movie star and wrote about all of her love affairs, but when she was old was banned by the government, and they shot her husband and threw her son in prison and took her pen and paper so she couldn't write. She told them about Anne Sexton and Elizabeth Bishop, two women who had been gifted, misunderstood and suicidally depressed, and whose wonderfully terrible lives seemed themselves like poems of sorts, reproofs to the world so undeserving of them. She told them about Sappho, an olden-days poet from the island of Lesbos, and when there were a few snickers at this she began to recite a poem where Sappho is jealous when she sees the woman she loves laughing with a man, and she can't speak and fire ripples under her skin and her ears are filled with roaring.

People imagined poems were wispy things, she said, frilly things, like lace doilies. But in fact they were like claws, like the metal spikes mountaineers use to find purchase on the sheer face of a glacier. By writing a poem, the lady poets could break through the slippery, nothingy surface of the life they were enclosed in, to the passionate reality that beat beneath it. Instead of falling down the sheer face, they could haul themselves up, line by line, until at last they stood on top of the mountain. And then maybe, just maybe, they might for an instant see the world as it really is.

She is incredible, Elaine said when the bell rang for the end of class.

She *was* incredible. It was hard to imagine anyone so glamorous and sophisticated could come from anywhere near their school. On the one hand, it gave them hope that they, too, might escape, and start their lives anew; on the other, it made escape seem all the more urgent, as they saw their town as it must appear to Miss Grehan, so dull-witted and unpoetic. At home, Cass looked at her parents with new eyes: Dickie losing his hair, doughy around the mouth, stooped under the weight of the failing business; Imelda caked in make-up though she had been home all day, her face like a mask she held slightly away from herself. Yes, it was easy to imagine they were falling, falling down the side of a mountain, into a crevasse.

Tonight at dinner they had had a fight about her mother's 'extravagances'. Dad had wanted Mam to move to a different, cheaper phone plan. Mam said Dad had a cheek telling anyone about plans. Now they sat in different rooms – Dad drinking a beer in front of the TV, Mam typing at her phone, her long, curved nails going click, click, click against the glass. When the doorbell rang, neither of them even seemed to notice, which was good because it was Elaine.

Her face was flushed. I found something, she said.

Cass wasn't sure she wanted Elaine here if there was going to be more fighting, but her friend had already pushed her way past her. I had to show you this in person, she said. Cass followed her up to her bedroom, where Elaine opened the laptop, then stood back for Cass to see. Cass leaned down and stared into the screen and gasped. Oh my God, she said. Yes, Elaine said. It's her? Cass asked. Elaine scrolled down the page – and there she was, wearing the white trouser suit and a mysterious smile, her red hair falling around her shoulders like inverted flames. 'Julie Grehan has a Master's from Trinity College,' it said beneath. 'She has lived in Paris and New York City.'

Cass stepped back from Elaine's laptop in a daze. Miss Grehan *herself* was a lady poet! She had written a book – an entire book! – of poems, called *Salt: A Chapbook*. It was unbelievable. At the same time, it made perfect sense. Suddenly it was impossible to imagine her *not* being a lady poet.

Salt: A Chapbook was available for €18.99. We have to get it! Elaine said. Yes! Cass said. Like, right now! Elaine said.

Elaine had her own bank card, but it was at home and she couldn't remember the number. Ask your dad to get it for you, she said to Cass. Tell him it's for school. Right, Cass said. Go and ask him now, Elaine said. OK, Cass said. She stood up. In her head was the word *extravagances*. I'll just go and ask him, she said casually.

Downstairs, a woman in a blazer was talking about the financial crisis on the RTÉ news. A giant CGI number, 3.7%, loomed behind her in the studio, and she spoke of it in terms of dread, as if the 3.7% was itself on the loose in the city, like a serial killer. The light from the screen had painted Dickie's profile a deathly blue-white. As he watched, he twisted his wedding ring around and around on his finger.

She stood in the doorway, waiting for him to notice her. If he speaks to me, I will ask him, she told herself. But his eyes stayed fixed on the screen, so she slipped quietly back out and went to the kitchen. Imelda still frequently bought things out of defiance or force of habit, and hid them from Dickie. It might make more sense to ask her.

Her mother wasn't in the kitchen, just PJ, sitting at the breakfast bar with a book.

Where's Mam? Cass asked.

Tidy Towns, PJ said. Listen to this, he said, and read from the book, *Your body sheds twenty pounds of skin every year. Just in the time it takes to read this sentence, your body has lost two thousand skin cells.*

That's disgusting, Cass said.

While you were saying that, you probably lost about eight hundred skin cells, PJ said. While I was saying that, I probably lost about two and a half thousand skin cells.

Elaine appeared in the doorway. Did you ask him? she said.

Ask me what? PJ said.

Shut up for a second, Cass said. She felt ashamed and confused, as if she were surrounded by tiny dead fragments of her body.

Did you know, PJ said, looking back at his book, that the first part of the human body to form in the womb is the anus?

Elaine looked at PJ with an expression of utter repulsion. What is wrong with you? Cass said.

It's just nature, he protested.

Did you ask your dad? Elaine said.

Ask him what? PJ said.

Would you mind your own business? Cass said.

On the table, she saw Imelda's purse. I'll just use my mam's, she said airily. But her heart pounded, and as she undid the clasp and paged through the cards, she realized PJ was watching her from his vantage point at the breakfast bar. What? she demanded. PJ lowered his eyes to his book. Cass took the card and slipped it into her pocket. You're such a little spy, she said to PJ.

Leaving the room, she felt a strange mixture of triumph and humiliation. Your family is so hilarious, Elaine said.

In class next day they learned about Sylvia Plath. She was the most famous lady poet of all; in the movie of her life she was played by Gwyneth Paltrow, and they watched a clip of her cycling around Cambridge on a bicycle with a basket. She had come from America, aged nineteen, to university in England, where she fell in love with an Englishman named Ted. He was also a poet, Miss Grehan said. She showed them a picture. A murmur went around the room. He was literally the most handsome man Cass had ever seen, with a craggy jaw and eyes that were deep and stern but kind too, and playful. They had met at the launch of a college poetry magazine called *St Botolph's*. Ted came to the party with another girl. Sylvia went up to him and bit him on the cheek. So hard it left a mark, Miss Grehan told them.

Cass glanced across the room at Elaine. If Ms Ogle had told them the story, they would probably have been cracking up. Had Sylvia Plath ever heard of shaking hands? Was there ever in history a name as ridiculous as 'Botolph'?

But Elaine was rapt: she watched the teacher, her skin glowing, her lips red as if she'd been chewing them all through class, and Cass knew her friend was thinking what it might be like to be swept up by a man like that, with a craggy jaw, and find yourself so flooded with passion that you would do things – that you would *want* to do things – that ordinarily you'd never dream of, like bite him on the cheek, or put his penis in your mouth. And watching her think that, she found herself thinking it too, and feeling it; and it seemed to her that that passion was very close, like a moon hidden in the brightness of the daytime sky, whose private gravity she could feel pulling her away from the earth.

After class Elaine told Cass she had decided that instead of a brand ambassador she now wanted to be a poet. Cass said that was crazy because she had just been thinking the exact same thing. They ran after the teacher in the corridor and asked her what to do.

Up close, she was actually only a little taller than Elaine, Cass realized; she had a splash of freckles across her nose, and her beautiful hair was more cinnamon than red.

She seemed surprised and happy when Elaine told her about their plan. She told the girls that to be a poet, all you needed to do was love poetry. Devote yourself to it! Fill your life with it!

And you would advise moving to the city, a big city, Elaine probed.

Not necessarily. Miss Grehan sounded a little bit surprised. You can write poetry anywhere, about anything.

But you lived in Paris, didn't you, Elaine said.

And New York, Cass said.

After you did your degree at Trinity, Elaine said.

Miss Grehan again seemed slightly taken aback. How do you know all this?

It's on your Facebook, Elaine said.

They had sometimes experienced this with adults – surprise that information that they had made available to be viewed by anybody at any time had, in fact, been viewed by somebody.

23

If you want to move to the city, you can, Miss Grehan said. And studying poetry at university is a wonderful thing to do. But more important is to read poetry, and write poetry, every day. It doesn't have to be for long. If just once a day people read a poem instead of picking up their phone, I guarantee you the world would be a better place.

When she had gone Elaine said that this was very good advice but she still thought that living in a major city was key. The first thing we need to do is apply to college in Dublin, she said. That's what she did. Cass agreed this was the best was forward.

Inside she was exhilarated. They had often talked about leaving town before. But this was the first time Elaine had proposed they do it together. They walked through the school gates arm in arm, Elaine making plans in her ear. Lesbians! the droopy vaping boys shouted after them from the doorway of Spar. Dykes! But Cass didn't even blush. *We!* The word resounded in her head like the singing of angels.

A door opened behind her, and light slanted out onto the landing. What are you doing? a voice said.

Uh, what does it look like I'm doing?

'Uh,' eavesdropping?

Look who's talking, Cass retorted, then realized that this did not quite work. I wanted to ask Dad something, she said.

Her brother sat down beside her at the top of the stairs. Get this, he said. There's a butterfly called the Flambeau butterfly that *drinks* crocodile tears! Like, right out from their eyes! Isn't that crazy?

Cass sighed. From downstairs the argument continued in a kind of horrible clashing drone.

Seriously, isn't it? PJ said.

You are such a child, she said.

I'm almost a teenager, he said. Technically I *am* a teenager.

Cass didn't respond to this. After a moment he said, Are they still fighting?

Cass shrugged. Through the banisters she watched her mother stamp into the living room and stand in front of the TV with her hands on her hips. Who was the crocodile, and who was the butterfly? Imelda was beautiful, and iridescent, and she had lived off Dickie's job that he hated, so at first glance she seemed like the butterfly; but really wasn't it Dickie who had the fluttery, gentle quality? And Imelda who would chew your leg off? And hadn't she crocodile tears in abundance? But did that mean Dickie was living off her?

In a lower voice, PJ said, Things are really bad at the garage.

Duh, Cass said. She sank her chin into her folded arms.

A kid in my class said it's going to close. Not the one here, the other one.

She turned to look at him. He had an elfin face, his big eyes so dark in the shadows of the landing they were almost black.

What does some kid in your class know? she said.

His uncle works there. He's a mechanic.

Cass heaved a weary sigh. She was so sick of her family and its humiliating floundering. Has it ever occurred to you that I might have other things to think about?

Right, PJ said. But he didn't move from the step. Then he said, It's just, what do you think will happen?

I'm actually going to be moving to Dublin, so I couldn't really say.

As soon as she said it, she wished that she hadn't; here in the house it sounded fanciful, a child's whimsy, no different to when PJ told her he'd been practising his telepathy all day and he thought he'd almost cracked it.

You're moving to Dublin? PJ said.

To college, she said reluctantly. With Elaine.

With Elaine?

Why is that so hard for you to understand? It came out sharper than she meant and PJ flinched. She felt bad. It won't be for a while, she said. After my exams.

Oh, he said. He sounded relieved. He got up to go back to his room, but before he went he pushed something into her hands. Here.

It was a padded envelope, with Imelda's name on the printed label.

It came right after I got back from school, he said. I picked it up before Mam could see it. They'd addressed it to her but I could tell it was a book so I knew it must be for you.

Oh, she said non-committally, and took it from his hand.

It'll still be on her credit card statement, he said. But she usually just throws those in the bin.

She looked up at him again. When they were little, they used to play squirrels in the woods: he was the grey squirrel, and she was the red. Red squirrel! he'd call. The hunter is coming! Thanks, grey squirrel! And she'd scramble into a tree as Dickie came crashing through the undergrowth. In fact, PJ's hair was coppery, closer to red; but she was the oldest, so she got to choose.

It's for school, she told him gruffly. As soon as his door closed, she ripped open the packaging, already composing a message to Elaine in her head along the lines of **Guess whats arrived OMG get here now!!!**

But when she pulled it from the envelope she paused.

It looked quite different to the picture on the website, more like a pamphlet than a real book. The cover was thick paper of an ugly maroon colour; there were staples in the middle, as if someone had made it themselves. *Salt: A Chapbook*, it said, *by Julie Grehan*.

The poems inside did not dispel her sense of unease. The first one was called 'Salt'. It began: 'Your salt on my tongue / A cause of heart disease / Yet meat needs salt / And you make me meat.' Hurriedly Cass moved on to the next, titled 'The Butcher': 'A jolly sign above the door: *Pleased to Meet You! Meat to Please You!* / Tell me, butcher, lover, does *my* meat please *you*? / Or do you leave it with the liver / As pussy carrion –'

On the pages that followed, the same words recurred, *meat, salt, butcher,* with others of a similar, unpleasantly corporeal tone, *slab, heart, slice.* She tried unsuccessfully to reconcile them to the graceful teacher, with her musical laugh and capricious wisdom. Alone in her bedroom, she felt her cheeks burn. How could she tell Elaine about

26

this? They had ordered the book in the hope of seeing into the hidden parts of her life, but they'd imagined it as a kind of extension of her Facebook, further pictures of castles and craggy-jawed men. This was literally like looking inside someone, to the gore underneath their skin. Why would anyone want to see that? She put the book down. *Eighteen ninety-nine!* she thought miserably.

Then she pulled herself together. She had taken a risk to get this book. There must be something inside it to make that worthwhile. She flicked brusquely through the poems, finding only more of the same, until she got to the Acknowledgements at the back. It was a list of people who had helped her with the book. The first line was full of other Grehans, her family, Cass presumed. But then came others, with exotic-sounding names, who had let her stay with them in Paris and Barcelona while she was writing. When Cass looked them up online, she found a couple of faces she recognized from the teacher's social media. She felt a new surge of enthusiasm. This was what she wanted: extra facts, an exclusive look behind the scenes. The very last line was more mysterious: it pledged 'undying fealty' to 'the Bitches of Beastwick'.

And when Cass googled *that*, she got a big surprise.

She did not know what to do. She did not like keeping secrets from Elaine. Yet this secret was so ugly – ugly like the book, she thought, with its gross poems and anatomical line drawing of a heart – and Cass did not want to be the one to show Elaine something like that.

Yet the evil of the book seeped out anyway. In their English class, before Miss Grehan arrived, they found a gaggle of girls listening to Sarah Jane Hinchy, who was making a big stink over something she'd found online about Sylvia Plath. Apparently before she came to England and met Ted, 'Plath' – as Sarah Jane Hinchy called her – had tried to commit suicide.

So? Elaine said. She was suicidal. She died of suicide. Everybody knows that.

She couldn't stand Sarah Jane Hinchy, who was marginally ahead of them in the class rankings, and had famously worn a rainbow badge on her school jumper last year until the nuns made her take it off.

The suicide attempt Sarah Jane Hinchy had read about was particularly horrific. Plath had taken a whole load of sleeping pills, she said, and hidden under her house – it was some sort of American house that had a crawl-space underneath it. She crawled into this crawl-space and lay down there to die. Everyone thought she was missing, Sarah Jane Hinchy said. They were searching all over town for her. But the whole time, like for three days, she was unconscious under her house, basically *rotting*.

Cass saw Elaine flinch at this, and she felt a churn of unease. Suicide was one thing: lots of famous people had done it, and it meant you didn't get old and lose your looks. Rotting while alive and then reappearing out of the ground literally like a zombie was not glamorous by anyone's definition. Elaine had strong feelings about that sort of thing. So did the other girls.

I don't think we should be learning about someone like that, Petra Gilhooley commented. Like, I'm sorry, but how is that appropriate?

It's probably not true, Karen Casey said. I don't remember it being in the film.

When Miss Grehan arrived, however, she confirmed that the story was correct. She said that that was what made Sylvia so interesting – that she was, on the surface, a beautiful, all-American girl, from a good family, but underneath, she had terrible problems.

But do you think it's appropriate to be teaching us about that kind of person? Petra Gilhooley said, unmoved.

We're all that kind of person, Miss Grehan said. We all have problems. But often instead of accepting the truth about ourselves, we cover it up. We try to make ourselves the way we think we're expected to be. So many of the bad things that happen in the world come from people pretending to be something they're not.

Writing a poem does the opposite, she said. If you look at the world, a little piece of the world, and try to see it for what it actually is, you start to see yourself more clearly too. And that can be very liberating. Sometimes it can save your life.

So, for tonight's homework, each of them was to write a poem. A groan went up at this. Miss Grehan laughed. It's not a punishment, she said. It might even be something you enjoy. Write about your life, about your world. Your world is full of *details*. *Look* at them before you write. If something is red, what kind of red is it? If you see a tree, what kind of tree is it?

After class, to Cass's surprise, Elaine didn't mention the gruesome Sylvia Plath story at all. She did, however, have strong words to say about *some people* who seemed determined to sabotage Miss Grehan's class.

You don't think Petra had a point? Cass suggested neutrally. Like, maybe it's not appropriate.

Elaine said Petra Gilhooley was just a stooge. Sarah Jane Hinchy was the one pulling the strings. And it's obvious why, she said. She has a crush on Miss Grehan. And she's jealous because Miss Grehan prefers us.

You think so? Cass said. She had got the churning sensation in her stomach again.

Oh yeah, Elaine said. She's always staring at her and trying to get her attention.

I mean, you think Miss Grehan prefers us? Cass said.

Definitely, Elaine said. Because we get the whole poet thing. That reminded her of something. Her eyes sparked and she leaned forward confidentially. Come to my house after school. I have something to show you.

Then she hurried away to Business Studies.

On the way home Elaine told Cass she was going to post her poem on her Instagram. She had discovered that there was a new generation of lady poets who posted their poems online and got millions of views. They wrote about real-life issues, like racism and homophobia, and were friends with singers, influencers and other celebrities. You could actually become seriously famous from poetry, Elaine noted.

Miss Grehan didn't seem to have got very famous from it, Cass pointed out. Elaine agreed it was strange, especially considering the way she looked. Cass asked if Elaine thought Miss Grehan was good-looking. Elaine didn't reply, apart from a strange sort of smile, as if she had a joke in mind she wasn't sure Cass would get.

What are you going to write about? Cass asked her.

I have a few ideas, Elaine said airily. They had settled in her bedroom, with a plate of Ryvitas on the floor between them. She bent her head over the keyboard so her face disappeared behind her hair. Cass looked down at her own blank screen. She didn't have any ideas. All she could think about was the book; she had brought it with her in her schoolbag in case she suddenly changed her mind and wanted to show it to Elaine. Now she was worried Elaine would somehow discover it on her own.

Elaine's head jerked up. For a moment their eyes locked. How do you spell *caress*? Elaine said.

Cass spelled it. Elaine frowned. I was sure there were two r's.

Maybe I'm wrong? Cass said. Elaine returned to her keyboard without replying. After a moment she asked about Cass's trees.

Trees? said Cass.

The trees, the fucking trees you have in your back garden, Elaine said, snapping her fingers.

There are lots of different ones, Cass said. I think most of them are oaks.

Elaine pressed her lips and typed some more. What are you writing? Cass asked.

I'll tell you when I'm finished, Elaine said coyly. Cass smiled. She had to fight the urge to wrest the laptop away from Elaine so she could read her poem. Her own page remained pristine.

Evening was falling. In the silver glow of the screen Elaine looked like a moon child. What's another word for red? she said.

Scarlet, Cass said.

No, when it's for someone's hair. Not ginger. Deeper than that.

Without knowing quite why, Cass felt uneasy, just as she had in the classroom that morning.

Cinnamon, she said in a low voice. The word was right there, as if it had been waiting for her.

Cinnamon. Elaine was happy. She typed some more, chewing savagely on her lips all the while. They were crimson, ruby, blood-red.

Cass's head buzzed. She yawned artificially. Wasn't there something you were going to show me?

Oh yeah! Elaine jumped to her feet, and without another word she ran into the en suite.

Immediately Cass seized her laptop, but Elaine had locked the screen. Where have you gone? she called after a minute. Almost ready, Elaine returned in a sing-song from the bathroom.

Cass picked up a cracker and crumbled it in her fingers. She looked around the room that she knew so well, the My Little Pony lamp sending its doe-eyed steeds around and around the walls in a pale rainbow carousel, the bed covered with teddy bears.

Check it out, Elaine's voice came from behind her.

Cass turned. Elaine was standing in the doorway of the en suite, wearing a bright white trouser suit.

What do you think? she said, doing a twirl. Do I look like a lady poet?

Cass didn't know what to say. All her thoughts slipped out of her head. Suddenly Elaine was a different person, chic, cosmopolitan, older. Not like a poet, not like a college student; more like a girl who lived in a big city, and worked in an art gallery or an advertising agency, someone who got up at 6 a.m. to do Pilates, and then went out onto a balcony in a towelling robe cupping her coffee in her hands. She was a woman already, Cass realized; her future was right there, a plush chamber at the edge of the bedroom she could step into at will.

She didn't know why that should make her feel so sad; but it was all she could do to whisper, Beautiful.

Elaine looked at her with a quizzical half-smile, then let out a laugh.

It's a joke! she exclaimed. I found it in my mam's wardrobe. I wouldn't wear this for real!

Cass laughed weakly. Again her head was full of buzzing, as if a whole swarm of bees had got trapped there, behind some invisible veil.

I've got to find some way to show it to Julie, Elaine said. She'll think it's so funny.

Julie? Cass repeated dazedly.

Miss Grehan, Elaine said. She took out her phone and handed it to Cass. Here, take a selfie of me.

It had been long established that Cass took better pictures of Elaine than she did of herself. But this time, she couldn't focus. All she could see was a white-gold shimmer that seemed to blur free from the screen.

Then from behind her she heard a knock. The housekeeper was there. Your mother is downstairs, she said.

My mother? Cass said.

What's your mother doing here? Elaine said.

I don't know, Cass said, and then, forlornly, I'd better go and see what she wants.

From the landing, she saw Imelda down below in the hall, talking to Elaine's mother. She caught sight of Cass at the top of the stairs. You're needed at home, she said.

Now? Cass said, and then, What for? But Imelda had already stepped outside. Cass took a last glance behind her. Elaine, all in white, gazed down over the banisters, literally like an angel, bidding her farewell from heaven. Laterz, she said.

In the car Cass told her mother she should have just texted her. She could have come home herself, there was no need to physically remove her from her friend's—

Enough! Imelda said sharply. They made the rest of the journey in silence.

At home, PJ was sitting at the dinner table – just sitting, motionless. He didn't look at her; he had that blinking, misaligned look he got after he'd been swimming. Cass could hear their father talking on the phone in the next room. His voice was grave. With a sudden rush of fear, Cass realized what had happened. PJ had told them about the credit card! Her heart began to knock against her ribs. Inside she wept, she cursed the book, and Miss Grehan too, whose arrival had pulled everything apart! Her father came in and sat down at the end of the table. He let out a deep sigh. Then he began to speak.

It was not about the credit card. It was about the garage – the one in the next town over. With a heavy heart, their father told them, he had made the decision to close it. He'd done everything he could to keep it alive, but the numbers just wouldn't add up. They would cease trading at the end of next week.

He spoke for a while in this oddly formal way; Cass realized he was practising the speech he would have to give to his staff. Finally he looked across the table at the two children. I wanted you to know what was coming, he said. In case you heard any of the kids talking about it in school or around town. He paused a moment. Is there anything you want to ask me?

PJ shook his head.

Can I go back to Elaine's? Cass said.

No, snapped Imelda.

Cass burst into tears.

Dickie reached across the table, awkwardly, to put his hand on her shoulder. I know this has come as a bit of a shock, he said, in the measured, implacable tone of a moment ago. But I don't want you or PJ to worry. These things are cyclical. The market is slow now, but it'll pick up again. The important thing—

Oh Jesus, Dickie! Imelda exclaimed, slapping her palms on the table. You ran that place into the ground! Into the ground!

Her relief that they hadn't found out about the card had lasted only a moment, then it gave way to rage – rage that they had dragged her away from her friend to listen to this, dragged her into their humiliating mess.

As soon as she got upstairs to her room, she sent Elaine a message. **Total fucking bullshit**, it said. A tick appeared to show the message had been delivered, then two blue ticks to show Elaine had read it. But there was no reply.

Cass let out a gurgle of fury. She made fists, and dug her nails into her palms, then beat her fists against her head. She looked in the mirror at her hateful face. Tears were running down her cheeks. Everything was ruined. When the garage closed, there was no way Elaine wouldn't hear about it. At last she would know the truth about Cass and her family. And then? Would that be the end of Trinity too? In desperation she wrote again: **U free 4 a call really need 2 talk 2 u**

This time, the message wasn't even read. She looked out the window at the drab, dead landscape – the wet fields, the power lines, the trees. The sky above was bleak and grey. She felt like she'd been buried under her parents' lives, their failures, their unhappiness. Into her head came the grotesque image of Sylvia Plath lying in her crawl-space, rotting. She sobbed in revulsion, chased it from her mind – only for another to take its place, more terrible still.

Did Elaine *already* know? Had Imelda said it to her mother earlier when they spoke in the hallway? Was that why she wasn't responding now? Was it already too late? She let out a wail – she picked up her phone, begged aloud for Elaine to call her. But Elaine couldn't hear her. She was probably messaging Miss Grehan instead. *Julie!* She had friended her on Facebook – she had DM'd her the selfie – new messages were flying back and forth between them as they soared in their matching trouser suits, hand in hand, over the town, while Cass lay buried beneath it! Image after image sprang up in her mind: Elaine crossing the cobblestones of Trinity College, with Miss Grehan there beside her, it didn't make sense but nevertheless there she was, and now she turned to Cass from the dream or vision and looked out at her and smiled a click-clack mannequin smile, before turning back to Elaine, leaving Cass alone, alone, to weep . . .

*

She told Elaine the next morning that Imelda had brought her home to Skype her granddad for his birthday. Uh huh, Elaine said. Her eye was on the door, waiting for Miss Grehan to appear; Cass knew she had a picture of the trouser suit with her, ready to share.

From her voice Cass could tell she hadn't heard about the garage. As class began she wondered whether there was some way to break it to her that would make it seem less bad – make it sound as if Dickie was closing it for dynamic business reasons, like he was planning to open another garage in a different county. Or if she told her he was planning a whole new—

Miss Grehan's hand fell on her shoulder. Do you mind, Cass?

What?

Do you mind if I read out your poem? Miss Grehan said.

Oh, Cass said, flustered. From the other side of the room, she saw Elaine looking at her. No, she said. She didn't know herself whether she meant no, she didn't mind or no, she would prefer if she didn't. But Miss Grehan cleared her throat, and there in the middle of the classroom, began to read.

Flying, by Cassandra Barnes

Hand in hand, night by night
We are flying out of sight

No one can touch us when we fly
Our words, our dreams become the sky.

Unseen, the higher up we go
The clouds themselves are far below

And our sleeping bodies, miles apart,
While we press closer, heart to heart.

And closer still, until the dawn
Returns us to our mortal form
And day, and rules – still, in your eye
I see the night dream of our sky.

Isn't that sensational? Miss Grehan said, smiling down at Cass, and then turning the smile on the rest of the class. I think that's just sensational. She turned to Cass once more. Can I ask you what inspired it?

Cass gazed unhappily at her hands in front of her on the desk. She had written the poem while lying in her bed with a breaking heart. *Twilight*, she said quietly.

Miss Grehan cocked her head, then nodded and smiled again. Well, thank you for letting me share it, she said, and then, to the others, she said, So as we can see, anything at all can be the spark for a great poem.

She moved off at last. Cass kept her eyes on her textbook. She was uncomfortably aware of Elaine looking at her still from her desk by the window. She longed to go to her side. The first chance she got she would tell her everything. But time dragged on endlessly, and when the bell finally rang, Miss Grehan called her back.

Unwilling, Cass approached the top of the class, aware again of Elaine's eyes flashing onto her and away again as she filed with the others out of the room.

At the teacher's desk, Miss Grehan regarded her merrily. Such a wonderful poem, Cass, she said. Well done.

Thank you, Cass said, looking at the floor.

I hope I didn't embarrass you by reading it out. I know poetry can be very personal.

Cass shook her head and said it wasn't personal at all. The teacher went on: there were competitions she should enter, poetry books she should read; Cass just kept nodding dumbly until at last Miss Grehan relented. Well, she said, putting her books in her tote bag. I hope you keep writing, anyway.

Cass raced out after Elaine. She found her by the lockers, deep in conversation with Sarah Jane Hinchy. Sen-*sational*! Elaine was saying.

SEN-*SATIONAL*! Sarah Jane Hinchy exclaimed, in a louder voice. They both laughed.

Oh hello, Elaine said casually to Cass, over her shoulder. Then they went back to talking, and Cass had to hover at the edges until they were finished. Maybe see you later, Sarah Jane Hinchy said to Elaine as they parted. I'll text you, Elaine said to her. Then she turned to her locker and took out her coat. Cass scrambled around for something to say. At that moment Miss Grehan passed them. She beamed at the girls as she went. Cass said, Aren't you going to show her the photo?

Hmm? Elaine said, looking into her locker.

The photo, of you in the suit. Weren't you going to show it to – Julie?

Now Elaine turned to look at her directly. Her green eyes were cool and emotionless. That was a joke, Cassandra, she said.

Yeah, I know, Cass said. She laughed falsely. She blew air through her lips. I can't believe she read out my crappy poem, she said in a blasé, Elaine type way. I wrote it literally in thirty seconds this morning.

Don't run it down, Elaine said, gazing ahead of her again. It was good. She paused, then added, as if speaking to herself, It was sen-sational.

Cass laughed again, carelessly, but she felt a deep bell-toll of dread within. Will I come to yours today?

I don't care, Elaine said, with a shrug.

They walked through the school gates together, past the droopy boys, in silence. Elaine did not seem angry. She wore a half-smile, and gazed ahead of her placidly. They were like two strangers who happened to find themselves in lock-step on a city street.

Listen, there's something I have to tell you.

Just a minute, Elaine murmured, thumbing her phone.

Cass waited impatiently. She had already opened her bag to take out the book. Wait till Elaine heard about the Bitches of Beastwick! What does it mean? she would say, and Cass would be like, Google it, and she would, and she'd see for herself, and then they'd start a new story together, a story in which they alone knew the true identity of the seemingly perfect teacher, and slowly uncovered her plot.

Listen, she said again, when Elaine finally put the phone aside. I found out something crazy. It's about Miss Grehan.

Elaine rolled her eyes.

You're not going to believe this, Cass promised.

Do you realize you talk about her a lot? Elaine said. Like – a *lot*?

Me? Cass said.

It's like you're obsessed, Elaine said.

Cass gaped. Her heart was beating hard. She didn't know what to say or do. She began to feel like she'd been trapped – as if Miss Grehan, by singling her out in class, had pulled her over to her side – as if she knew that Cass knew, and wanted to separate her from Elaine, to make her as repulsive as she was, so she couldn't pass on her secret. It's mental, I swear, she said, reaching for the book. Just look.

I'm kind of tired, Elaine said doubtfully.

It'll only take a second, Cass pleaded.

I might just go in and have a nap, Elaine said. They were outside her house.

Oh, Cass said. She remembered her exchange with Sarah Jane Hinchy. Okay, she said.

You can tell me whatever it is tomorrow, Elaine said.

Sure, Cass said. She stayed and watched as her friend walked up her driveway. She couldn't move, she couldn't speak; fire rippled under her skin. Then she turned. She did not continue to her own house; instead she went back to the school. She locked her bike in the bike stand, and walked inside, down the corridor to the Principal's Office. She left the book at the door, with the corner turned down at the Acknowledgements page.

*

Miss Grehan did not come to class the following day. In fact, for the rest of the week, the girls spent English in study hall.

No one in authority would tell them where she had gone, but there were rumours that a parent had complained. Complained about what? Here the stories became vaguer, weirder. Some said the content of the class was inappropriate. Others that it was the teacher herself who was found inappropriate. Petra Gilhooley said she'd heard Miss Grehan was in a coven. Karen Casey said no, it was some kind of dance troupe; they wore tassels on their nipples and strap-on dildos.

None of the rumours predicted she would be coming back.

You know who's behind it, don't you? Elaine said darkly. Sarah Jane fucking Hinchy.

Elaine was so distraught by the teacher's disappearance that when the news broke about the garage closing she didn't even notice. She went about in a daze, her eyes red from crying. Then one morning right before midterm she came up to Cass with a lot of wild talk about how they needed to go to Dublin and track Miss Grehan down. Her face was flushed, her hair in disarray. What if something's happened to her? she said. We need to find her!

But how? Cass said.

From her Facebook, Elaine said.

Cass was surprised, because the week before Miss Grehan had set her account to private. But before she did, it turned out, Elaine had taken screengrabs. She showed Cass her phone, scrolling through what seemed like hundreds of pictures of pubs, cafés, grocery stores, bookshops, seaside strolls. It's everywhere she referenced in the last three months, she told Cass. She zigzagged her finger over the screen and a map appeared, with all of the locations marked out and red lines traced between them. We'd start around here, Elaine said, placing her fingertip on a dense red blot at the centre.

Cass listened, nodded along, agreed that they would find an excuse to go to Dublin. Inside she felt blurred and sad, as though she were filling with a kind of acidic mist that obscured her and corroded her at the same time.

In the event, they did not go to Dublin. On the first day of the mid-term break, Elaine was whisked away to the airport; a surprise holiday, courtesy of her father. She messaged Cass conspiracy theories from the airport, from the taxi, from the hotel reception. Then she went silent.

Cass thought about going on her own. She pictured herself walking the streets, gazing at Elaine's snowflake diagram, not resting till she had tracked the teacher down. Instead she spent the week at home. The atmosphere was hellish. Her mother railed at Dickie, when he was there; when he was not, she railed to the girls from Tidy Towns, or to Dennis the postman, or to her children. He with his books, Mr Trinity College, she would say. Letting on to be some great genius! But where's the evidence of this supposed genius? Do you know? Did anyone see light of it since? And she would bring her hand up to her brow, searching the horizon for the genius that Dickie had once had and then lost.

Cass still held out hope that the rumours might be false, and the teacher would somehow return after midterm. But then something happened. Ms Ogle's mother – who had enjoyed such a spectacular return to health since her daughter got sick – slipped on a guava while shopping in the exotic fruits section of the supermarket and hit her head. She died in hospital the next day.

Elaine arrived late to the funeral – she must have just got back. She didn't see Cass, though they were standing close by, and Cass didn't approach her. But Ms Ogle, who was out of her wheelchair, made a bee-line for the two of them. She spread her arms wide and embraced them both together. My girls! she exclaimed. They looked at each other, startled, over the teacher's sobbing head. Ms Ogle dabbed her eyes. Now, she said in a more businesslike voice. Tell me everything you've been doing in class while I was away.

Cass was struck dumb. How could they begin to describe those tumultuous weeks? How could they explain the elation and the heartbreak, the sense of the future opening up before them and then closing down again? Again she looked at Elaine – ruefully, hopelessly. Elaine shrugged. She had a fresh tan and a bracelet Cass hadn't seen before, with a heart on it.

Nothing, she said. Just the stuff from the book.

When school resumed on Monday, Ms Ogle resumed with it. She stood at the top of the classroom, cheeks aglow. The supermarket had given her a huge cash payout as compensation for the tragedy, they had heard. She had already painted her front door a radiant guava-pink.

II

Since the closure of the garage in the next town over, her father had stopped saying things would get better. They knew how bad things were; the whole town knew. Old ladies would come up to Dickie after Mass, and tell him they had said a Novena for him and for the motor industry in general. Others steered clear, as if his failure might be catching. Sometimes when Cass walked into a shop now everything went quiet, and she felt shame prickle over her, like a hideous second skin, a new adversity arrived to take the place of her eczema.

The Crisis had transformed Main Street into a mouthful of cavities, businesses big and small shuttered in its aftermath. Yet the collapse of the garage was felt by the townsfolk to be of a different order. A fall as dizzying as the Barneses' couldn't come from simple economics. There had to be a moral element.

Many of them felt that Imelda was to blame. Dickie made a fortune and Imelda spent two – that was what people said. Imelda, with her cheekbones and her Italian leather boots, got up like the Queen of Sheba just to drive to the supermarket! Giving the poor manager an earful because they didn't have star anise or tamarind or whatever was supposedly all the rage in New York! It's a long way from tamarind she was reared, they told each other darkly. It's a long way from underfloor heating and orthodontists or any of that palaver. Well, look at her now.

Yes: look at Imelda. Nails chipped, roots showing, driving to Lidl first thing in the morning so she'd be sure not to run into anyone she knew; she spent her days excavating her walk-in wardrobe – laying out gloves,

42

hats, scarves, blouses, dresses, jeans, skirts, gilets, stoles, pelisses on the bedroom floor and taking pictures of them from every angle, like a cop at a crime scene. In the evening, she sat at her laptop selling them off – cursing the online vultures who haggled over every penny like farmers at a mart, and when they finally paid, drove her mad with messages wanting to know why their purchases hadn't arrived.

Admittedly, sometimes they hadn't arrived because Imelda hadn't sent them; Cass had come into the kitchen more than once to find her mother with her arms flung around the cordless Dyson or the 'old' Dyson or the forty-eight-piece bone china dinner set she had never opened, bawling her eyes out like it was a beloved pony being sent to the knacker's yard.

Their father often worked late; it was as if the fewer cars the garage sold, the more time he had to spend there. But who could blame him? Whenever he came home, he faced the same tirade from Imelda: he had ruined them, he had betrayed them, she had been duped. Cass wished he'd defend himself, fight back! But he just sat there at the dinner table, head bowed, without saying a word, which of course only made Mam angrier.

It's okay for you, PJ said – whispering, as if Imelda would hear them, though downstairs she was roaring at the top of her voice. You're going to college. I'll still be stuck here.

Oh yeah, it's so great for me, Cass said. Doing my Leaving with all this going on.

In truth she told herself the same thing – that in a few months she'd be gone. She stayed up till midnight most nights now, revising – parabolas, modal verbs, yardangs, the Land League – fact after fact, filling her up. But it had become harder to believe in the future, to see it. The problems at home were so huge and omnivorous that the idea of escaping them, of *being somewhere else*, had come to seem impossible. Her dad – who had studied at Trinity himself when he was young, who'd been so excited when she told him her plans! – no longer reassured her that it would all work out. He rarely spoke to her at all now, about anything. As for her mother, she'd only say that Dublin was full of perverts and she didn't know why anyone would want to live there; she'd read something in the news about a man caught walking around TK Maxx with mirrors on his shoes so he could look up girls' skirts.

Worst of all, Cass no longer had Elaine.

It wasn't that they didn't get on: they still chatted every day at school, and sometimes they walked home together too. But Elaine no longer invited Cass to her house to study; she no longer asked for stories about Imelda; she no longer spoke about the life they would have up in Dublin. Was it because of the garage closing? Or what had happened with Miss Grehan? Cass had no clue – she only knew that Elaine's interests, these days, were elsewhere.

She told herself she wasn't sorry. Though it hurt almost beyond description, she did not want Elaine to have to share in her family's humiliation. Better that they should just drift apart.

Elaine's interests now lay, specifically, in boys. She threw herself into the pursuit of boys with the same comprehensive determination as she had poetry the term before. Though *pursuit* was the wrong word – Elaine was too good-looking ever to need to pursue anybody. It was more about controlling their pursuit of her. Boys for Elaine were not a challenge or an aspiration or an Other; they were more like a commodity, a resource to be managed. Her love life resembled stock inventory at a warehouse. When she told Cass she was no longer seeing Ryan Doyle because she was seeing Ciaran Teeling but that was just a temporary thing until Malachy Atkins broke up with Lucy O'Neill, which she had it on good authority that he very shortly would, Cass thought of the flow charts she had drawn up that directed them to Trinity and from there to Paris and New York.

She and her revolving cast of boys hung out in a pub in the town known as the Drain, and at school she surrounded herself with other girls who went to the same place, Holly Maguire, Jane Tan, Rachel McElligott. You should come along some night, she'd say to Cass. Cass knew Elaine knew she would say no. She preferred not to go out in town any more than she could help; hellish as it was at home, being in town, with people looking at her and pitying her, was infinitely worse. Still, it was nice of her to ask, she thought.

She did wonder why her friend had chosen *now*, with the Leaving on the horizon, to start her new life as a party girl. Already her grades were down slightly. Sometimes when they talked Cass thought she detected an out-of-kilter quality to Elaine's conversation. But if something was wrong she wasn't going to confide in Cass.

Because Elaine was busy with other people, Cass found herself on her own at school. After a while, though, she realized that Sarah Jane Hinchy was often on her own with her. There was no great moment of bonding. It had just sort of happened, and at first she accepted it as another element of her fall. Sarah Jane Hinchy was a girl they had always looked down on. She was the class swot, and though she had historically been slightly higher than them in the class rankings, it was only because she worked so much harder. Being friends with her was a sort of vicious circle, because Elaine was visibly disgusted with Cass for associating with such a loser, which made her even less likely to want to associate with Cass herself. But after a couple of weeks of sitting in the park together at lunchtime, Cass couldn't remember quite why she and Elaine had disliked her so much. Yes, Sarah Jane had thick legs, and almost definitely cut her own hair. She lived on some sort of a farm up in the hills and there were rumours that her family were poor. But she was undeniably bright, and although she looked super-square, she knew about a lot of interesting things, from Harry Potter to A$AP Rocky to Xeeon. Wow, Cass said, and then, What's Xeeon?

It's like the new Instagram, Sarah Jane Hinchy said, except not run as a Zuckerberg creepshow.

She often came out with statements like that, as if she had access to a reality Cass had never heard of. It was confusing. Elaine and Cass had always agreed that the only reason Sarah Jane Hinchy knew things was to make herself seem interesting. Yet what if the things she knew actually *were* interesting? What if the things she had chosen to make her seem individualistic had actually made her into an individual? Like her rainbow badge. She still wore it, but on her blouse, under her school sweater, so you could hardly say it was for show. She told Cass that she didn't self-identify as gay, in fact she didn't believe that sexual orientation was fixed at all; she wore the rainbow as a sign of her belief in everyone's freedom to choose who they wanted to be and be with.

How had they found this problematic? Cass started to wonder whether the reason she and Elaine had thought Sarah Jane Hinchy was a loser was because *they* didn't understand what was cool – the same way the basics in the town might think Cass and Elaine were lame because they didn't wear GAA tops. It was an alarming thought.

Sarah Jane too was applying to Trinity. Have you thought about where you're going to live? she asked Cass. Cass kept her answer vague. It was one thing to talk to Sarah Jane Hinchy in school, quite another to make her part of her future. She still dreamed that after the exams Elaine would be restored to her – in college, on their own terms, far away from their families. She was not yet ready to sacrifice that.

Then one day Sarah Jane Hinchy told her about a grant she was applying for. Why would she need a grant, when college was free? Cass wondered. Rent's not free, Sarah Jane said. Food's not free. Books aren't. The grant would pay for all of that, even give you monthly pocket money. You should think about it, she told Cass.

Cass had never thought about who would pay for her accommodation, her books, her meals; she had never before thought that this might be an issue. The idea that she might need financial assistance was horrifying to her. Was that who they were now? Like the people she saw in anoraks queuing outside the post office on Wednesday mornings?

I can show you how to do it, if you want, Sarah Jane said. The application, I mean. If you come over to my house we can do it together. Then afterwards we could watch *Throne of Blood*.

It was an old Japanese film but it was based on *Macbeth*, which was the play they were doing for their exams. It might be interesting to see it from a non-Western perspective, Sarah Jane said.

Cass hesitated. Going to Sarah Jane Hinchy's seemed like a leap, in terms of their friendship. But filling in a form together and maybe watching a movie didn't tie her to anything. And it might be nice to get out of the house; last night at dinner Imelda had thrown a box of Lidl cereal at Dickie's head.

Sarah Jane lived a few miles out of town, so to get there Cass would need someone to drive her. Her parents were fighting again, and she was waiting for the worst of it to be over before she asked them. Then she got a message.

It was from Elaine. **Hey bey-atch whats up???** it said.

Cass didn't reply straight away; she wasn't sure what it meant, like if Elaine was actually saying she was a bitch or if she intended it in a friendly way. While she was figuring it out another message came in.

Am in da Drain wid a boi sez he liiiikes u

This was even more puzzling, but before Cass could figure out what or who Elaine was talking about, another, simpler, message came in.

Get down here girl!!!!

Cass didn't know what to do. Elaine clearly expected her to come to the Drain. At the same time, it annoyed her that Elaine thought that after ignoring her for literally months she could click her fingers and Cass would come running. So she put her phone away without replying, and went down the stairs to see if she could get a lift. She met Dickie coming up the opposite way. Hey, Dad? she said. But he didn't seem to hear her. He had a beer can in his hand and breakfast cereal in his hair. He was wearing a ratty old anorak she had never seen before. An image flashed into her mind, of him and her and Sarah Jane Hinchy, queuing at the post office. So she called over her shoulder, I'm going out! and headed for the road into town.

The name on the sign was Doran's, but everyone called it the Drain. The reason was clear as soon as Cass stepped inside. People said that in the days when you could smoke you barely noticed it, but now even with the yard door left permanently open the stink was inescapable. No one knew exactly where it came from; it was structural. The PA played a non-stop barrage of 1980s metal, the pool table had a rip, and the Guinness tap frequently got infested with ants. But the barman never checked ID and so, apart from a handful of genuine rockers with greasy greying locks and upside-down pentagrams on their T-shirts, the place was full most nights with underage drinkers. It had been like that for a generation, with the result that even the most strait-laced mammy in town could tell you the line-up and running order of e.g. Slayer's *Seasons in the Abyss.*

The door faced the bar, where the elderly metallers sat on tall stools. A couple of them turned and looked at Cass resignedly as she came in. The barman was staring at his phone. Behind him there were rows and rows of spirits bottles and a black-and-white photo of a Spandex-clad man with a perm. In the spotted mirror she looked like a little grey child, a waif in a forest of dust.

Cass! Elaine waved at her. She was standing in the middle of a crowd – one or two girls from school, but mostly people Cass didn't recognize at all. She was wearing earrings Cass hadn't seen before. Her cheeks were flushed, her eyes sparkled, she held a glass with ice cubes and a slice of lime in it. As Cass approached, she reached out for her and took her hand. This is Cass, she announced to the others. My best friend since for ever. She gazed at Cass with a smile of prideful approval. Then she dragged her off to the toilets to reapply her make-up.

Why does this place smell so bad? Cass said, looking into the mirror.

You get used to it, Elaine said. So Rowan Headley thinks you're hot.

Who's Rowan Headley?

He's Enda Frame's friend, Elaine said.

This threw no light on the matter as far as Cass was concerned.

Well, anyway, he must have seen you around, Elaine continued with a hint of impatience, because he said you were hot.

He used that word? Hot?

I think so, Elaine said. Maybe I said it, I don't remember.

You said it?

I might have said I had a hot friend. It doesn't matter!

Does he even know who I am?

Elaine didn't reply. She zipped up her make-up bag and regarded Cass with dissatisfaction, like a baker confronted with a not wholly successful cake.

Cass followed her out to the smoking area, where Elaine promptly vanished into the crowd; and now a guy in a duffel coat came over to her. She realized she recognized him as one of the droopy boys that used to shout things at her outside the school gates. And she did recall now that some of the things had been complimentary, not that she was hot necessarily but that she had nice tits.

He was tall and pale, with dark curly hair. So you're Elaine's friend, he said.

Yes, Cass said. Cass, she said. The boy nodded to himself while looking away, as if this was just as he'd suspected.

You're Rowan? she said. He sniffed in an irritated manner. She wanted to point out that he had come over to her. Then he said, I'm going to the bar, do you want something?

Okay, she said.

Rowan pushed himself away from the pillar he'd been leaning against and stalked off inside. Cass wondered if she'd done something wrong. She huddled against the wall; she felt cold even though she was standing under a heater. She saw Elaine now, standing not far away with her back to Cass. She turned momentarily and glanced round at her, but turned back again before Cass could wave. Cass understood cloudily that Elaine wanted her to do something, that she had been brought here for a specific purpose. She blew on her fingers, listened to the horrific screeching noise that issued from the PA.

Rowan returned with two pints of lager. The beer here is piss, he said, handing one to her.

Thanks, Cass said.

Do you play games? Rowan said.

What?

Video games.

Oh, she said. Angry Birds? He looked displeased by this, so she said, My brother's a major gamer.

Oh right? Rowan perked up. What games does he play?

Behind him, another boy, not as tall but slightly droopier, had started kissing Elaine. It was distracting; it seemed like she could hear it even over the metal, a squelching noise like walking on frogspawn. Rowan waited expressionlessly, like a soldier for his orders. Cass tried to focus. She and PJ used to play Donkey Kong together when they had the Wii. Now the games he played were like being trapped inside a food processor. Is there one about beavers? Or otters?

Otter Devastation, he said offhandedly. Yeah, it's pretty good. If he likes wipeout games tell him he should play Agents of Extinction.

Right, she said. There was a pause. From behind them, she heard Elaine make little cries of ecstatic pain.

So how do you know Elaine?

Oh, Cass said again, brightening, and she began to tell him the story of the Chemistry class. But before she even got to the iodine he had grabbed her face and was kissing her. She closed her eyes. His fingers were soft against her cheek, but his tongue was unexpectedly stiff, and thrashed around without a clear goal or direction – like something he was operating at a distance, by remote control, she thought. The wall-mounted heater was directly over her head, baking her hair but leaving the rest of her icy-cold. Every few seconds it switched itself off, then a few seconds later came to life again with a thunk, and she felt her hair fry. She told herself to stop being distracted. She leaned her body against him, and placed a hand on his chest. He had an arm around her waist; now his other hand slid up her tummy, which she instinctively sucked in, and remained there a moment, perfunctorily rubbing it up and down, before making the leap to her boob, where it squeezed happily in a way

The Bee Sting

that brought to her mind the stress ball in her father's office. One of his
salesmen had got it for him as a joke, back in the days before the crash,
when there was nothing to be stressed about. It was red and printed on
it were the words QUIT BUSTIN' MY BALLS!! He kept it on his
desk, beside a black-and-white picture of his brother, Frank, a model of
a 1953 VW Beetle, and another photograph of the four of them, that is,
her and Mam and Dad and PJ, smiling in their Christmas jumpers on a
visit to Funderland. Her mam was always saying could he not find a
better picture for his office, but they all looked happy, even though PJ
had got sick on the Crazy Cups; they *were* happy, even Mam. Cass must
have been, what, ten? eleven? In the picture her chest was flat, no stress
balls to squeeze, and her hand and wrist had a sleeve of eczema, she
hadn't met Elaine yet, Elaine hadn't spilled iodine on her and cried outside the nurse's office, they hadn't joined pony club together, or built
their Minecraft palace together, or had their adventure where they
bunked off school and went into town dressed in tracksuits with their
hair in ponytails, Elaine thought no one would recognize them because
it was so far from their usual look, but they were spotted after twenty
minutes, and grounded, and had their phones taken away, and she had
pressed her hand to the glass of her bedroom window and wondered
where Elaine was, and then known, like she knew her own name, that at
that same moment Elaine had her hand pressed to *her* window, and that
nothing would ever split them apart—

The tongue in her mouth, which had been thrashing about like a
great blind beast, suddenly retracted. I have to pee, Rowan said, and
wandered off.

Instantly, Elaine was back at her side. He's such a good kisser, isn't
he, she said.

Yeah, said Cass, though it struck her as an odd thing to say. She
started drinking the beer. It tasted like he did, or the other way around,
she supposed. The glass seemed enormous, her body felt full, like there
wasn't room in it for anything more – alcohol, tongues, even words.
Somehow she was now in the centre of the group, who had all apparently

relocated themselves outside, listening to Elaine tell a story, which she realized with a start was about Sarah Jane Hinchy, or more specifically Sarah Jane Hinchy's sister.

Oh yeah, this is hilarious, said Rowan, who had returned. He sipped his beer and checked his phone.

So Sarah Jane's sister, Denise, is really smart, right? Elaine said. She was like three or four years ahead of us. And her dad – her dad sells livestock feed or something, and he's a total cheapskate. Like, legendarily stingy. But he tells her if she gets seven A1s in the Leaving he'll buy her a car. Like, he wants to encourage her, but he didn't think she'd get it, because she was smart but not that smart, okay?

So funny, Rowan said. He put his phone away and took Cass's hand.

But Denise studied really really hard and then in August the results came out and she gets seven A1s. She was, like, first in the county. So her dad has to get her the car. He's so mean that she's *sure* he's going to break his promise. But he doesn't. One day he takes her outside and there in the yard is a VW Golf. Not new, but not ancient, like eight years old maybe.

Nice, another girl said.

Yeah but wait, Elaine said. When she looks at the side of it, like the passenger side—

It was the door, Rowan said. The balls of Cass's fingers were sweating into his palm.

Right, on the door on the passenger side it's got scratched in big letters, CUNT.

Written on her car? Cass didn't understand. Her dad wrote on the car?

Someone had gouged it into the side with a key or whatever. And they'd tried to paint over it but you could still see it really clearly. Can you imagine giving your daughter a car with CUNT written on it?

Why would he do that? Cass's head was swimming. Above her the heater clicked on and off, and from the speaker a man was screaming, literally screaming, like the music was slicing him up.

Well, he must have got it cheap. But he could say he held up his part of the deal.

I used to see her driving it around, one of the boys said. They live out near Naancross.

I didn't know Sarah Jane had a sister, Cass said.

She moved to London. She doesn't come back much, said the boy.

Who's Sarah Jane Hinchy? a girl said.

You know her, Elaine said. She's that girl with the lisp and the lazy eye and acne.

Answers to the name of Lucky, a different boy said.

She calls herself a lesbian, but it's just for attention, Elaine says.

This wasn't totally accurate, and Cass thought she should speak up: but when she tried to remember exactly how Sarah Jane had explained herself, like about fluidity and so on, she couldn't get it straight in her head, and then she realized she ought to have messaged Sarah Jane to say she wasn't coming to her house, and she felt a wave of annoyance at her, i.e. Sarah Jane, so she didn't say anything.

Didn't you say your dad said he'd buy you a car if you got your exams? Rowan said to Elaine.

Ugh, don't even mention that guy to me, Elaine said frostily.

Your dad has the garage, the new boy said to Cass. He had shaggy black eyebrows and quick eyes beneath them. You'll definitely get a car, even if you fail.

Duh, the garage is closed, you mongo, another boy said.

Elaine explained that the main one wasn't closed, only the one in the next town over. Right, Cass?

Cass nodded miserably.

Anyway, there's no way Cass could fail her exams, she's the smartest person I know, Elaine said. We're going to college together in the autumn, she added, and she took the hand that Rowan wasn't holding and gave it a firm but gentle shake, as a kindergarten teacher might ring a bell. Aren't we? she said.

Cass was too surprised to do anything more than nod; inside, she felt a rush of joy so intense she thought she might catch fire and flame away to nothing, a burning girl-pyre there on the cement floor of the pub smoking area like something from one of the rockers' olden-days metal videos.

Later in the evening, Elaine asked her why she'd been avoiding her. Cass was speechless – could Elaine really have seen it that way? She told her it wasn't like that; she confessed that she'd been too embarrassed to talk to her because of what was happening to the family business. As she did she started to cry.

Elaine put a hand on her shoulder. That's your dad's fault, she said. Not yours.

Cass began to blub – the words were practically inaudible, and she barely knew what she was saying – something about how everyone saw her as Dickie's daughter, and so they blamed her too. Elaine was wise and calm. No one blames you, she told Cass. Everyone feels sorry for you. Your dad should never have let things get this bad. He's supposed to protect you, and he didn't. She reached her arm around Cass and drew her close. Fuck him, she said comfortingly.

After that, Cass went to the Drain a few nights a week. Her mocks were coming up; still, she had no problems getting out of the house. Dad was hardly ever there; her mother was either on the phone to the Tidy Towns girls lamenting, or upstairs bagging up her possessions. After months of work, areas of bareness had started to appear in the walk-in wardrobe, like patches of earth exposed by melted glaciers. She didn't notice when Cass shouted from the hall that she was going to Elaine's.

PJ noticed, of course: he had nothing better to do than notice things.

Why are you wearing make-up if you're going to study in Elaine's? he said.

She didn't think he would tell, but she didn't like him having power over her. So she started leaving her make-up, mostly purloined from her mother, in the old stone shed in the woods behind her house, with a mirror propped on a sill, and did her face using the torch on her phone.

The shed was right in the middle of the woods. She didn't know what it had been used for originally; it was empty now. When she was little, she had played here with her brother. They would bury pine cones and dig them up again; when Dad came roaring, they would squeal and laugh and go scurrying up a tree till they were too high for him to reach. Though sometimes she would pretend to stumble, and Dickie would throw his arms around her and lift her into the air, growling all the while, A squirrel! A squirrel for my dinner!

She thought of these times on her secret trips to the woods at night; they made it marginally less frightening to be out there on her own. Anyway, the fear was part of the enchantment. She learned to do her make-up in three minutes flat: then she would run – run! – through the trees to the new road, and from there into town, under the night sky, simultaneously terrified and free, until she came at last to the Drain, and felt the now-familiar stench and the barrage of dated noise hit her as she pushed through the door, like being jumped up on by two ancient, smelly dogs, and there would be Rowan in the yard vaping, and there, turning to greet her from the heart of the crowd, would be Elaine. And she would smile, and Cass would smile, feeling like she was full of starlight, the way a firefly is full of sparks.

In the Drain she spent most of her time kissing Rowan, while Elaine, never more than a few feet away, was doing the same with Jesse Farrell, initially, and then Fiachra O'Grady, and then Malachy Atkins, who had finally broken up with Lucy O'Neill. After the Drain, if it was dry, they sometimes went with takeout to the graveyard. Once, Rowan told them that the writer Mary Shelley had lost her virginity to Percy Shelley on top of her mother's grave. He looked at Cass meaningfully. Imagine having sex with someone called Percy, Elaine said. Do me, Percy! Cass chimed in. Take me harder, Percy! On the way home they stopped at the Topaz and bought three bags of crisps each, different flavours to cover over the smell of drink; crisps were much better than chewing gum, which was like an admission of guilt.

Purely on the basis of hours spent kissing, Cass felt justified in calling

Rowan her boyfriend. But on every other basis she had doubts. If they weren't actually kissing, he was generally aloof and silent, or else he talked about things Cass knew nothing about, such as video games, or hip-hop. He had conspiracy theories about everything and got annoyed when Cass didn't know about the events that he wanted to tell her were faked.

Sometimes she wondered if she even liked him, but usually she was too busy figuring out if he liked her. She drew up lists of reasons he might break up with her: her nose was pointy, he was still in love with Elaine. He didn't bother trying to hide the porn on his phone. He rarely sent her messages, and if he did it was just links to his Soundcloud beat tapes. One time she asked him, joking but not really, if he cared about her at all, and he shot right back, as if he'd been waiting for the question, I only care about dead rappers. He seemed to find most of the things she said tiresome; he oscillated between trying to have sex with her and almost total indifference, sometimes over a very short interval of time.

That's just what boys are like, Elaine told her. The way she explained it, you weren't supposed to like your boyfriend, not in the same way you did your friends; being with boys was something you did without necessarily enjoying it, the same way you drank beer though you didn't like the taste. Cass felt better after that.

And anyway, sometimes she did like him. His hair was shiny; his duffel coat was soft. He too planned to go to college in Dublin: his ambition was to be a professional DJ, but as a fallback he was applying to study Pharmacy at UCD. He was funny too. He invented a drinking game where you had to think of a stupid name – Wanda Suckling, Ulick Flange, Antonia Bumkiss – and then google it, and if there *wasn't* a match, you had to drink a shot. But most often there was: the world revealed itself to be a treasure-house of mortally embarrassing names. Who knew?

Sometimes after he'd drunk a couple of beers, he'd come out with crazy ideas. For instance: if a dog's sense of smell was fifty thousand times more powerful than a human's, that meant that instead of humans' binary perception of There/Gone, dogs must have a *spectrum* of thereness. Like, say you're here, then you go out. To me, you're gone. But to a dog you're still *mostly* here, because your smell lingers much longer, and that's their strongest sense. So they must have a whole different understanding of time, because for them the past is literally still around. When a dog looks at the world, it must see all of these presences gradually fading out. Like a sky full of jet contrails.

That's probably closer to how things really are, he said, like with the past and everything. It's kind of good, in a way, because it means the happy moments aren't just slipping away from you for ever. He looked at her when he said that: sidelong, like he didn't want her to notice.

Elaine said the drinking game was childish; she was no good at thinking up names. And she said his theories reminded her of Cass's brother. She was starting to cool on Rowan. She told Cass there were other boys interested in her, though when pressed she said this was more a general sense she had, rather than specific individuals.

Rowan began coming out to the shed so he and Cass could walk to the Drain together. He liked the woods; deciduous forests were rare in Ireland, he told her. Most of them had been cut down by the British to burn in their factories. The shed reminded him of Hitler's bunker, where the Führer hid with his staff and their families in the last days of the war. He told Cass that when the Nazis knew they would lose, they had given their children poison before shooting themselves. Then he tried to kiss her. She laughed.

He knew a lot about Nazis. Some Nazis had fled to Ireland after the war. The big Irish schoolbook company was founded by a Nazi. That was another reason the education system was bullshit. And Volkswagen was started by the Nazis, he said. So Cass shouldn't be sorry if her dad's business closed down.

When it got less cold he brought cans to the shed, or 'the Bunker' as he called it. It was okay for some people, he said. But he couldn't afford to drink in a pub all night. Another time he asked why they had to go to the Drain at all. But Elaine is there, Cass said, confused. And the others.

Elaine, he repeated sardonically.

You don't like Elaine? Cass couldn't keep the shock from her voice.

Rowan said Elaine had a big head. She thinks she's so smart. But you're way smarter than her.

Cass told him that as a matter of fact she and Elaine got exactly the same grades.

That's because you don't want to be better than her, he said.

This conversation left her feeling conflicted. On the one hand, calling her smart was literally the only nice thing he had ever said about her. On the other, she did not want to be forced to choose between him and her friend. Elaine was going through a hard time. She didn't currently have a boyfriend, and had already kissed everyone who drank at the Drain, apart from the rockers obviously, who were old and unkissable. Cass finished her can and told Rowan they should get moving or they'd be late.

That night a new rocker appeared in the pub. He was young and handsome – properly handsome, like someone from TV, with hair so black it was almost blue, and tattoos the length of his arms. He sat at the bar, drinking by himself. When he saw the girls looking at him, he raised his glass to them. Who is *that*? Elaine said.

Cass didn't know. She hadn't seen him before; she would have remembered.

He's like a good-looking Rowan, Elaine agreed. She went to talk to him. After a few minutes of animated conversation, she waved Cass over. This is Richard, she said. He interjected a sound that sounded like Richard but wasn't quite. He's from Poland, Elaine said, ignoring this. He literally just came to town.

Up close, the man was not so much handsome as beautiful, like a girl might be, with fine, white bones from which his black eyes peered as if through spyholes in a painting in a haunted house.

Get this, Elaine said. Richard's a mechanic. And he's looking for a job! Cass looked back at her, not quite making the connection. So *I* thought, maybe he could work at your dad's garage!

Cass felt her smile falter.

Couldn't he? Elaine pressed. Work at your dad's garage?

Cass was annoyed. So that was the reason Elaine had brought her over, to use in her flirting? I don't know if they're hiring right now, she said.

It's worth a shot, though, right? Elaine said.

I don't know if it is, Cass said.

Why don't you ask your dad now?

Ask him?

If they're hiring. Send him a text.

He thinks I'm in your house studying, Cass reminded her.

So?

So, why am I suddenly talking to mechanics?

Oh Jesus, fine, Elaine said, throwing her hands up.

Cass went to rejoin Rowan. Who's that guy? he wanted to know.

Some randomer. He's trying to find a job.

He looks like a vampire from the 1980s.

He's from Poland.

Oh right.

Not long after, Elaine drifted back. Cass apologized for not being more helpful. Yeah, Elaine said vaguely. Cass, sensing some displeasure, glanced at the bar. Richard's stool was empty. What happened?

Elaine sighed and told them that Richard had tried on literally the cheesiest pick-up line she'd ever heard. She wouldn't tell them what it was; she said it was too embarrassing. Fucking weirdo, she said, and looked back yearningly at the empty stool.

Later, as she came out of the girls' toilets, Cass thought she saw the man smoking in the yard. It was dark out there, so at first she wasn't sure. Then he inhaled on his cigarette, and his face came glowing from the shadows. He was looking back at her where she stood in the doorway – staring at her, in fact, in a way that would have been creepy if someone else had been doing it. From him it wasn't creepy: it was like – what? A message in a language that no one else knew she could speak, a secret communication that jangled in her chest. His eyes were black and wet: they seemed to bore into her, making her feel simultaneously younger than she was, and also older, wanton. She wanted to laugh. It was so cheesy! Desire was cheesy, his handsomeness itself was cheesy, if Elaine was there they would be cracking up.

But Elaine wasn't there. She hung in the doorway, swaying gently. Hi, she said. Hi, he returned, softly. The cigarette-light showed the tattoos on his forearm: dice, Death, an angel weeping. She thought of Elaine gazing forlornly at his empty seat. Can I have a drag of your cigarette? she said. He held it out to her. She stepped forward into the yard, took it from his hand. She sucked on it inexpertly. Noxious smoke fumed into her lungs. She handed it back to him, twisted back and forth humming, like she didn't feel his gaze on her. Then she said, You can try the garage if you want. But make sure you speak to my dad. Dickie Barnes. Don't speak to Phil. He's the foreman, but he's a grumpy bollocks and he hates foreigners. Dad's a softie.

Richard remained silent a moment. Then he shrugged, grinned and moved fractionally closer to her. She turned her face up to him, gave him a shy smile that was actually brazen. But as he leaned closer still, she lost her courage. *The hunter is coming!* She scampered away, a squirrel in the forest.

He didn't reappear in the bar. She didn't tell Elaine what had happened.

Then the flood came. Three weeks' rain fell in a single day; the river burst its banks. It was on the national news. Schools closed; they were all trapped at home, looking out at grey lakes where the meadows had been. I am going insane, Elaine wrote. From Rowan she heard nothing at all. She wondered if he was going to break up with her, or if he actually had broken up with her and just not told her. But on the third day he appeared, saturated, on her doorstep. For a moment they stood there looking at each other. Rain dripped from his hood. Then he said, Are you coming?

Coming where? she said.

He looked at her as if she was an idiot. The Bunker? he said.

He had come by the woods, and discovered that, although the entire town was waterlogged, the old shed had been spared. They walked together through the dripping trees. He took her hand, and told her he'd been listening to a lot of Angolan hip-hop. He said he was thinking of only listening to Angolan music from now on.

The Bunker was damp, but not more so than usual. His lips were cold but warmed up after a moment. His warm body enwrapped hers. She lay her head on his chest. He looked at his phone and complained about the signal. In the doorway the rain fell and fell. He asked her what she was going to do when she went to college. She was surprised, because she had told him already, but then he forgot a lot of the things she said. English, she said.

No, I mean, like, are we still going to be going out, Rowan said. He looked pained, though she couldn't tell if it was at the thought of going out with Cass in Dublin, or because the Angolan hip-hop video kept buffering.

She didn't know what to say. Elaine had stressed the necessity of losing their virginities before college, but had also warned against getting too close. You don't want to move to Dublin and still be tied to someone from home. Cass assumed that's what Rowan was worried about too. She felt sad, but she didn't show it. She just said they would probably want to see other people.

Rowan, when he heard this, went stiff, and for a moment he said nothing, as if he too were buffering. Then he sat up, and frowned at his shoes, the way he did when he was about to make a serious statement, like the correct order for watching the *Star Wars* films. But before he could say anything:

Peekaboo! Elaine pulled back her hood, looked around in bemusement; she had never been to the shed before. Why have you got a shed in the middle of the woods? What is it, like, a bomb shelter?

A *bomb* shelter? Rowan said. It's made out of *stones*.

He sounded more irritated than ever. Cass had messaged Elaine while she was walking in the woods with Rowan – she realized now she never told him she was coming.

The others are on their way, Elaine said. Malachy's bringing beer.

School stayed closed for almost two weeks; they went to the shed every night. Sometimes there were fifteen people, packed like sardines around the portable speakers, listening to Angolan hip-hop. It was like a carnival, a damp, sodden carnival. The world had turned upside down; it was impossible to imagine it ever going back to the way it had been.

But it did go back, of course. When they returned to school, the results of their mocks were back too. I presume your parents have seen these? Ms Ogle said to them after class.

Cass didn't say anything. Her father was the one who looked at the reports, and since the flood he'd been at the garage round the clock, working on cars with damaged electrics, damaged engines, damaged transmissions; the flood was a disaster for the town, but a godsend for business, Imelda kept saying. Elaine didn't reply either, just scowled, grinding the toe of her left shoe against the floor as if she was crushing out a cigarette on Ms Ogle's face.

Ms Ogle sighed. She had left a button open on her gingham blouse; Cass could see the off-white clasp of her bra. Her breasts sat on her folded arms like the sandbags that dotted the flooded streets. Girls, she said. I understand that you may have things weighing on your minds, and that by comparison your studies may seem of lesser importance. But in twelve weeks' time you will be sitting your Leaving Certificate, and the results that you get will dictate the rest of your lives. The education system, as I have often said, is memorious. Whatever is happening in your lives now will pass. But that piece of paper will stay with you for ever. Do you understand?

Afterwards they walked down the hall in silence. Then Cass, in a funny voice, said, *Mem-ORRR-i-ous*.

Elaine said it was bullshit. It was just the mocks; who cared about those?

In the real exams we'll actually be trying, Cass said.

Right, Elaine said. Anyway, there's no law saying we *have* to study at Trinity. There are, like, a million courses in Dublin.

It was true: they had filled out their college application forms in Elaine's house a couple of weeks ago, and marvelled at the number of options on offer. Radiography? Organic farming? Possible futures swirled around them like images in a kaleidoscope.

Although Dickie would be sad if I didn't go to Trinity, Cass said, nevertheless.

Why should you go out of your way to please him? Elaine said. He ruined your life. You don't owe him anything.

The anger in her voice surprised Cass. She recalled what the teacher had said about *things weighing on their minds*. It was obvious what she meant in Cass's case. The whole town, the whole world knew about the garage. But was something weighing on Elaine? When she went to her house that time, the place had been a mess – stacks of unwashed laundry piled up in the kitchen, dishes by the sink, clutter everywhere. She had never seen it like that before.

We don't *have* to do anything, Elaine said now. We can just go to Dublin. Or somewhere else. She looked around her and rubbed her arms, as if they were out in the woods in a cold wind. All I know is if I don't get out of this place I am literally going to kill myself.

Rowan's mam was on his back about studying; he was only allowed out at the weekends. Elaine wasn't sorry. She called him Soy Boy and said he was pretentious; she said she never wanted to hear Angolan hip-hop again for the rest of her life.

She had grown tired of the Bunker too – she claimed the damp floor had given her a yeast infection. The Drain was still closed; the flood had finally overcome the ancient plumbing. We'll have to find somewhere new to drink, she said.

Cass wasn't sure. Maybe Rowan's mam was right and they should be revising too? But Elaine was sick of revision. Anyway, there was loads of time until the exams.

In town there were signs of the flood everywhere. The buildings on Main Street bore filthy tidemarks. Brackish water pooled on the floors of the closed-down businesses. You expect a flood to be clean, to wash everything away, but it was the opposite. Everywhere smelled like the toilets in the Drain.

If Cass didn't have any money, which was most nights, they would go to Clarke's, or Coady's, or Devine's, and find a group of boys they didn't know who'd buy them drinks. This was Elaine's idea: to Cass it sounded like one of the madcap schemes she'd dreamed up when they'd first become friends, like trying to get free eyeliner by telling the woman in the chemist they were models. Unlike those plans, however, it was incredibly successful. All they had to do was sit at the bar and boys would appear. Though they were probably not so much boys as men. They were rangy types in Ralph Lauren shirts and pointy boots, they were square-headed farmers up for the mart, they were sales reps, fitters, electrical engineers. They installed extractor fans or sold digital storage solutions. They had been to Australia and Alaska. They had car keys, and business cards, wedding rings and pictures of babies on their phones.

Cass never knew quite what to say to these men, but in a different way to not knowing what to say to Rowan, because in these conversations, she realized, it didn't actually matter what you said. Talking was only a kind of distraction or diversion while something else went on under the surface. She couldn't figure out if she and Elaine were supposed to be fooled by it, like if the men thought they were innocently chirruping away in apparently harmless conversation while unwittingly falling under the men's sway, or whether they were acknowledged to be in on it too, like the men knew that they knew it was fake, and this was all a strange game, simultaneously boring and exhilarating.

Elaine was good at it – at pretending not to be aware of this ulterior activity. She would tell the boys/men they were receptionists from the

Sports Centre, or trainee journalists for the local paper, or occupational therapists from the next town over, blithely prattling on while the men stared at her like dogs at a steak. Likewise, when the men bought drinks she would pretend to think they were just being generous. And they were generous. You'd ask for a beer, they'd get a vodka chaser too, you'd ask for a vodka, they'd come back with a double. Before you knew it you were shitfaced and you hadn't spent a cent.

If it was Thursday or Friday one of the Ralph Lauren shirt-wearing men might pay for the girls into Paparazzi's, where they would dance with Elaine in the same expectant, desultory way they'd listened to her story about being occupational therapists. It was hilarious to watch – these men with their biceps and their neck tattoos, jiving awkwardly to Wake Me Up Before You Go-go. Cass knew that Elaine had no intention of kissing them; she knew too that Elaine could keep dancing for hours. They thought they were closing in on a goal, but there was no goal; she just wanted to see how long they would stick it.

Even when one of them got what he wanted, and Elaine was wrapped around him on the dance floor, or outside in the smoking area, or in one of the many nooks and alcoves in the dark labyrinth that was Paparazzi's – with her knee hooked around him, pulling him in to her, and her eyes squeezed tight shut – it was quite common for her to suddenly stop and disengage herself and saunter over to Cass as if nothing had happened, leaving the fan salesman or the engineer hunched in bewilderment over his erection. Or she'd seem to be in the throes of passion, but then Cass would get a text from her consisting of something like OMG or HELP, which was Cass's cue to go over and interrupt: usually she would say something about her period, at which the man in question would beat a retreat without further comment.

Sometimes she did not want to be interrupted, however, and Cass would be left swaying vaguely on the margins of the dance floor. She did not actually like to dance; she only stayed there so she wouldn't have to talk. She wanted to be fearless, to toy with them like Elaine did; but the men seemed so big up close, even (especially) when they were being friendly.

In the end though she had to talk, that is if she wanted anyone to buy her drinks. Once she'd figured it out it wasn't so hard. All she had to do was laugh at their jokes and look interested and be ready for the moment when they would lean in to kiss her, at which point she would sidestep like a matador, a single graceful movement that hardly seemed a movement at all and left everybody's pride intact.

Sometimes she would not sidestep them; sometimes if they'd bought her a lot of drinks or at least someone had bought her a lot of drinks, she would let them kiss her. You had to kiss somebody every so often or you would get a reputation as someone who didn't kiss and then people would stop buying you drinks. Anyway, she already had a reputation. They knew she was not an occupational therapist, or a promising young reporter from the *Midlands Monitor* doing a major piece on fly-tipping. Even if they were from out of town, they knew she was a Barnes, one of that lot who had lorded it up in the good times and now were ruined. What right had she to put on airs, to push them away? So she would kiss them, and feel the rasp of their stubble grate her skin, and smell their aftershave or deodorant in her nostrils, and let their hands delve under her top and run up her back, safe in the knowledge that sooner or later Elaine would appear and poke her and the two of them would scamper off and crack up by the cigarette machine.

Although Elaine didn't always appear, and the men were not always so polite, and one time when she did the sidestep the man reached after her and grabbed her and there was a disorientating moment when she realized she couldn't remember what he looked like, even though he was right in front of her, all she could see, that is, hear, was him pushing her against the pinball machine with one hand and crushing her jaw between his fingers with the other and sliding his hand, wait, another hand? between her legs, while beneath her the pinball machine shook and pinged and announced in a spooky voice, *Out to the cemetery, come on, everybody!*

But someone usually came along and anyway it didn't matter, nothing mattered. Nothing mattered! Everything was coming to an end, everything was closing down, everything had been carried off on the flood. Her schooldays, her family, her boyfriend, the men, the drinking, she would leave it all behind, like a sloughed skin; or she was the skin, and she would be sloughed, and dissolve in the night.

That was why, though she still thought sometimes about what Ms Ogle had said, she couldn't credit that these weeks were the ones that would decide all weeks to come. She found it impossible to believe that *now*, the present, so flimsy and flyaway, whipsawing, switchbacking, should be the image the rest of her life was cast in, when she could barely see herself in it at all.

Heading out?

Cass froze. There was no point in denying it, her hand was on the latch, and she was fully made-up. She had long since stopped going to the Bunker to get changed – usually by 8 p.m. her brother and her mother were shut up in their rooms, and with her father still at the garage she could walk out of the house without anyone seeing her or knowing she was gone.

But here was Dickie, materializing from the darkness of the living room with an empty glass in his hand. Cass turned back from the door. Just going to see Elaine, she said, which wasn't quite a lie.

Dickie eased himself down into the little miniature couch by the front door that no one ever sat on; the house was full of meaningless objects like that – miniature chairs, miniature tables, Imelda had gone through a phase, as if she had run out of grown-up things to buy and so had moved on to furniture for the pixie folk. Now it was on eBay with everything else.

Do they still have the pool table? he said. In Doran's? What do you call it – the Drain?

She didn't reply. What was he doing here? He'd barely been home since the flood; he looked different, in a way she couldn't place.

There was one summer, he said, you couldn't get me off of that thing. We were working for himself above during the day, me and your uncle

Frank – clearing tyres out of an old warehouse – and then every night we'd be in there playing pool. *Money down the Drain!* your granddad used say. *You're literally throwing money down the drain!* But there was no stopping me. I'd dream about it, dream about making shots, that's how obsessed I was.

Cass said nothing. Her jaw was clenched so tight her whole body quivered. Instead of yelling at you when you did something wrong, like her mother did, Dad liked to bring you on a little journey first, up over the hills and mountains. It made it hard to fight back; you just had to follow the path he had laid out, his voice calm and even, your guilt crushing down on your shoulders, until turning a corner you would find yourself at the summit, your crime lying spread out in a panorama before you, and you and he would gaze down on it together.

I ran into a teacher of yours the other day, he said now. He had hoisted his foot up onto his knee and was examining the sole of his boot. Or not ran into at all, she called in to me at work. Ms Ogle.

He looked up at her again. She stared back at him blackly. She couldn't believe he was putting her through this, doing his dad routine on her, when for the last six months he had been hardly more than a ghost! She was so close to telling him to drop it – she so wanted to tell him the things he was accusing her of weren't even up to date! She hadn't been in the Drain for a month! Though she had been in almost every other pub in town, in much worse places, more than once passed out on the floor, what did he think of that?

Listen, Cassie, he said, and he looked earnestly into her eyes. This was the part where he asked you to see how the things you had done not only harmed others, but mostly yourself, and how you were better than that. I know it must be hard to think about your exams, what with everything that's been going on here. But it's your future. I don't want you to throw your chance away.

Something sparked in her when he said this. You don't want *me* to throw my chance away? she repeated. You don't want *me* to throw it away? *You're* the one who's thrown it away.

Dickie looked surprised. Cass found she was shaking.

How am I supposed to go to college if the money's all gone?

From his expression she knew he hadn't been expecting this. But as she spoke the words she knew they were true. Things were not up in the air. Things were underwater. Things were done and dusted, dead and buried.

Her father began to mumble about cash set aside; it was clear he was just making it up. All of his plans for her, which had been her plans too, were tumbling down about their ears. Yet it gave her a kind of black joy. Elaine was right! Imelda was right! Everything was his fault! It was almost worth losing her future to shove his guilt trip back in his face. Do you know how ashamed I am, she said, to be your daughter?

Dickie flinched. Cass, he said, in a rasping voice.

But she didn't stop; she wanted to hurt him, devastate him, so he would never think of talking to her in this way again. You betrayed us, she said. You betrayed your family.

The strangest look crossed his face when she said that, like nothing she'd seen there before. For a moment she wondered if he might hit her. She found herself hoping he would. Instead, he seemed to crumple, as if the air had gone out of him.

She felt sorry for him, but only for a moment; then it was swallowed up in anger, that she should have to feel guilty for that too, when he was the one who had ruined everything. She turned on her heel and walked out the door. She cried all the way into town.

In Coady's, Elaine bought her a shot. They're all the same, she said. They fuck it all up then act like it's your fault.

She told Cass that her mother had caught Big Mike doing the house-keeper. She came back early from golf and walked right in on them.

Cass was so shocked she forgot about Dickie. The Brazilian girl, so pristine, always so statue-still; it was hard to imagine her doing some-thing like that – like having sex. But then it was hard to imagine anyone doing it, and yet it was all people seemed to do.

It was weeks ago, Elaine said, with a shrug. It doesn't matter.

But it did matter, of course. Everything made sense now.

Elaine's mother had thrown the housekeeper out then and there. She'd told Big Mike to leave too, but he wouldn't go. Instead he was sleeping in one of the guest bedrooms. I'm sorry, Cass said. It's not so bad, Elaine replied. Ever since he got busted he keeps giving me cash. She took a roll of notes from her pocket to show her. Drinks are on Dad, she said.

After their fight Dickie didn't bother Cass again. Her mother didn't bother her either. At dinner now, without her husband to yell at, she focused her attention on Cass's brother. PJ, would you ever chew your food like a decent human being instead of some kind of water buffalo! You'd better pull up your socks, my lad, or by golly it'll be off to boarding school with you! Even PJ had stopped butting in on Cass. Though sometimes he would be out in the garden, kicking a ball, as she was going out. If she glanced over her shoulder she would see him looking back at her, bobbing along in the twilight like some child's inflatable animal that has drifted far out to sea.

Final-year students finished classes a month before the other girls, so they could concentrate on their revision. On the last day, Ms Ogle clasped her hand as she left the classroom. You're a good girl, Cass, she said. I hope things work out for you. She had tears in her eyes. This is going to be the craziest night ever, Elaine said.

It should have been. They had finished school! But when they went into town, everything was off somehow. They called in to the Drain, but couldn't find anyone they knew; it was full of different kids, a whole new cast, like in a series reboot. Even the regulars, the rockers who never even changed their T-shirts, seemed unaccountably altered. They tried another pub, then another. Wherever they went, Elaine found fault. The music was too loud; the music was too quiet; the barmen were gobshites; there were no Pringles. It was one of those nights when nothing fits together. You meet the wrong people, you say the wrong things; no matter how much you drink, you can't relax. The best thing would be to call it quits and go home, but of course you never do.

In Deasy's they caught up with some of their classmates, and Elaine finally seemed to settle. Cass went to the bar. As she waited to be served, an old-farmer type in a John Deere cap started talking to her. Who's this you are now again? he said. Cass smiled faintly and tapped her foot and looked at the barman. The farmer persisted. I know you, he said. I just can't put my finger on it.

He wasn't being lechy, he just wanted to know. The old people of the town were all like that – never satisfied until they had placed you, fixed you on their map of family trees, designated you as the latest instance of Barnes or Donnelly or whoever.

She gave the barman her order. When he turned away the farmer was still staring at her, his mouth half-open, as if to encourage hers to speak. She gave in, and told him her name.

Cass Barnes! he cried, and he slapped the bar in delight. Cass Barnes, well, well. I haven't seen you now for donkey's years. How old is it you are now? God, you must be almost doing your Leaving, are you?

She smiled wanly, waiting for him to say something about Dickie, how it was a terrible shame about the garage. But instead he said, I was a great friend of your uncle. I used coach him for the GAA. Around the time he got engaged to your mother.

She looked at him; she wondered if he was mixing her up with someone else. My uncle? she said. Your uncle Frank, the man said. When he was due to be married to Imelda.

Beneath the cap the farmer's face was open, cracked, uncalculating, the kind of face that lined the streets of the town on match days. He didn't seem insane or delusional. He spoke like he was passing on something everyone knew.

It was in this very pub they announced it, he said. There was some hooley that night, I'll tell you.

Cass smiled weakly, in the hope that might satisfy him. But the farmer kept rambling on. The room started to wheel around her, like a carousel that had just been cranked into motion, and through a wave of dizziness the farmer's voice came to her in fragments. Now, Dickie . . . of course some people didn't . . .

Finally the barman came back with her order. At the same moment, from the lounge, she saw Elaine approaching. She seized the glasses, and burbling something to the farmer, hurried away to meet her friend. Elaine took her arm, already gabbing excitably about some guy who was here. Cass nodded and smiled, let Elaine lead her back into her own life, her real life.

They got to the table with their friends, but Elaine went past it and out into the covered yard. There, slouched in a patio chair beneath a grimy parasol that dripped with rain, was Richard, the hot mechanic they had met in the Drain before the flood. He looked up at Cass with benign indifference, as if he'd never seen her before.

Elaine had been telling Richard about the man who'd murdered his wife and children. And Richard had this amazing idea, Elaine said. Why don't we go and check the house out?

Cass stared at her friend dumbly. Richard was gazing at his phone as if this had nothing to do with him.

I mean, isn't it crazy that we haven't even seen it? Elaine asked. It's literally the only interesting thing that's ever happened here.

Cass pointed out that it wasn't here, it was in the next town over.

Richard has a car, Elaine said. She seized Cass's hand. Come on! It's our last day of school. We have to do *something*.

She was hugging herself though it wasn't cold – swivelling back and forth, bouncing on her toes, dancing in the dark light of the stranger's eyes, like a lovely blonde moth.

Cass looked at Richard and he looked back at her with his cool, self-satisfied smile. Why do you want to go there?

I like dark places, he said. His voice was high and reedy, with an East European accent. But maybe you are scared?

Cass isn't scared of anything, Elaine said, taking her hand.

*

They waited under the awning out the front while Richard went for his car. The air still stank from the flood, as if there was a body rotting underneath the town. Opposite the pub, black streaks climbed the walls of the old convent.

Let's just hope he's not a psycho, Elaine said. That'd be such a sickener, if we got murdered on the last day of school. She laughed.

He didn't seem to Cass like a violent type. His affect was amused, almost feminine. Delicately, she said, Are you sure you want me to come?

Of course! I'm not going to a, like, crime scene with some guy I hardly know.

Okay, but I won't be . . . in the way?

In the way of what? Ugh, with him? Why, do you want him?

Vom, Cass said. But both the girls tingled with the same electricity, and stood on their tiptoes; and now at the top of the street a pair of headlights appeared. As it drew closer the car's wheels on the wet tarmac made a sound like a zip being pulled down slowly. Behind the glare the driver remained invisible; she imagined him looking at them through his windscreen, pale matchstick figures, the colours of their coats flaring up bright. On long car journeys she used to play a game with PJ: *red car–blue car*, one of them would say to the other, and if the next car they saw was blue, then they knew they would have a good day.

The car was red. It pulled up and the door swung open. Hop in, Richard said. Elaine did not move, she did not move. Then from behind them another voice called, Goodnight, now, Cass!

She looked back: it was the old farmer in the cap, standing on the porch of the pub to wave her off. She swore. She climbed into the car.

As soon as the door shut, the car took off and the girls were thrown back onto each other, shrieking. It was an ancient Saab; it smelled of cigarettes and deodorant. But it was fast. They went through a red light, then another one, and Cass felt a rush of exhilaration. Richard plugged his phone into the stereo, and the girls scrolled through his music for something acceptable. No offence, but your library is super-gay, Elaine called into the front seat. There was a lot of Mariah Carey and many bands who must have been Polish, with ringletted hair and pouts. At last they found some Iron Maiden. They passed their school: it looked strange at night – shrunken, insignificant. They sped out of the town on roads that were winding and slick with rain, singing along at the top of their voices to 'The Evil That Men Do'.

What was that guy saying to you? Elaine said suddenly.

What guy? Cass said, startled.

The old guy at the bar, Elaine said. You looked freaked out.

I used coach him for the GAA. Around the time he got engaged to your mother.

Oh him, Cass said. He was asking about the Leaving.

Of course some people didn't like it when she and Dickie tied the knot.

Why are people so obsessed with that fucking thing, Elaine said.

From the front, Richard asked again about the killer. Why he had done it? The girls didn't know. There were stories: that he had debts, that his wife found weird stuff on his computer, that he'd been abusing the children, that he was in a cult. Nobody likes to talk about it, Elaine said, so it's hard to get accurate information.

Actually, Cass thought, that information itself was not quite accurate. People *told* each other they didn't like to talk about the murder; then they went on to talk about it at length. But there were other things that they didn't talk about not talking about, that were simply never, ever mentioned. The laundry, for instance, right in the middle of the town. It had been part of the convent; for sixty years, girls who'd 'gone astray' were sent there, to safeguard the town from their dangerous ways. Sometimes they never came out again; they spent their lives behind the high grey walls, washing the bedlinen of the priests and the nuns, as punishment for their long-ago sins. They were all dead now. The convent was closed, and the laundry, and nobody talked about what had happened in there.

And Uncle Frank? Was he something unspeakable too? Her parents never talked about him. She didn't even know where exactly he had died. It could have been on this road.

Well, you could understand it. His own poor brother's girl!

The killer's name had been hacked off the family's gravestone in the middle of the night and was never replaced.

But if you'd seen her then. Such a beauty! Like a stained-glass window come to life . . .

In the rear-view mirror Richard's eyes met hers.

The road twisted beneath them, flung them this way and that, like it was trying to escape them.

When they arrived in the next town over they realized they had a problem. They didn't know where 'the deathhouse', as Richard called it, actually was. Richard had assumed that they knew. They had assumed that Richard knew. Elaine snapped off the music. She hated poor organization.

They pulled into a petrol station and took out their phones. Into the search bar Cass typed the name of the town and 'family murder'. Instantly images began to fill up the screen. Most were of the man, the same picture in different sizes and resolutions. He had a beard and wore a grey T-shirt. He didn't look like a killer; he just looked like a dad. As she scrolled down, there was a picture of the mam with the dad – years earlier, in her wedding dress, with red dots in her eyes, and a big smile; then the mam and the kids, two boys wearing GAA jerseys, in a sunlit garden. They had the same swing set Cass and PJ did. The picture linked to the mam's Facebook page. The wall was full of tributes from all over the world, left by people who had never met the woman or her children, only seen them on their phones, after they were already dead.

I have the house! Elaine exclaimed. She showed Richard her phone, and then Cass. Sure enough there was a picture of the house. But there was no address.

Do reverse image search, Richard said. Elaine didn't know how to do that. He started explaining in his clunky English. Elaine sighed testily. Fine, Richard said, also testily. I go ask. He got out of the car and stalked off towards the garage.

Don't call it a deathhouse! Elaine shouted after him. That's not a real word.

She climbed into the front seat and tried to get the stereo working again. Cass's phone pinged. Rowan had sent her a message:

Can i come and see u? r u home? come to Bunkr?

She wrote back:

Sorry just got this cant 2nite studying

What the fuck? Elaine said. She had opened the glove compartment and found a toothbrush and toothpaste. She delved further. There's all kinds of shit in here . . . socks . . . body lotion . . .

Richard burst through the doors of the petrol station and strode back to the car. He was angry. Is fucking bullshit, he said. I can tell he knows where is deathhouse.

Are you living in your car? Elaine said.

Why you looking through my things? He snatched the toothpaste out of Elaine's hand and replaced it in the glove compartment. Then he started the engine, and turned back onto the street. Where are we going? Elaine said.

Richard ignored her. He drove the car off the main street into an estate of houses, checking them against the picture on Elaine's phone. Seriously? Are you planning to look at every single house in the town until you find it? Elaine said. You think there'll be a giant thundercloud hanging permanently above it?

He scowled. His eyes were narrowed, his jaw was set. They went down one street after another. The estate was full of identical houses and seemed to go on for ever. Then, from the other direction, they met a garda car. They saw the cops scoping them through the windscreen. Richard cursed. As soon as they were out of sight, he hit the accelerator, taking them back to the main street and out of town.

You probably wouldn't have been able to see anything anyway, Elaine consoled him. It'd be all locked up. And they would have cleaned up all the blood and stuff.

Or it might even have been demolished, Cass said. Now she thought of it, that seemed the likeliest outcome. They could hardly just leave it there on the street? Although they had left the laundry.

He didn't reply; he was enjoying his anger. The road hurled itself under them, the dark shot past their windows. Cass had an idea. We could go to the Bunker?

What the fuck is Bunker? Richard said.

Cass began to talk it up: a mysterious old stone building in the middle of the woods, where terrible things had happened, years ago; super-creepy. Richard looked interested in spite of himself.

And there's beer there, Elaine said. Right?

There's definitely Monster Munch, Cass said.

She told him where to turn off; it looked like a gap in the wall of the forest, but there was a muddy track that led up to the estate of half-built houses Big Mike had invested in. In the moonlight their facades looked sad and wan. Any of them could be a deathhouse, Cass thought to herself; they should have just brought him here.

Who is in there? Richard said, pointing.

No one.

But there is light on.

It must be for security.

He pulled up outside one of the empty houses. The headlights dazzled in the windows, blowing up bigger and bigger as though to engulf them in light. Then they got out of the car and faced the woods. The darkness seemed to throb, pent up behind the barbed-wire fence.

You fucking kidding me, Richard said. But he had roused again: he led the way, though he didn't know where he was going. The trees were narrow and bleached in the skeletal light of his phone.

He told them about a forest near his home town where thousands of people had been executed during the Second World War. Imagine how intense: all the fucking ghosts crowded in one spot. You go there, drop acid, put on the headphones . . . He made a brain-exploding gesture with his hands.

Elaine started to giggle. Cass's phone beeped again. It was a message from Elaine. If he lives in his car where do u think he goes for no 2s??

Cass wrote back, IDK but I bet its INTENSE

When he reached the Bunker, he went quiet. He walked around it a couple of times, then shone his torch inside. No one comes here? he said. Only . . . kids? He turned the torch on the girls. Cass nodded mutely. It's abandoned, Elaine said, and then, You could probably stay here, if you wanted.

What, in the woods? Cass said. She felt the same annoyance as when Elaine offered him a job at her dad's garage.

It's more comfortable than sleeping in a car, Elaine argued, ignoring the look Cass was giving her. We could bring you, you know, bedding, she said to Richard, hooking a strand of hair over her ear.

He directed the torch around the threshold. This door, does it lock? Seeing Cass's face, he added hastily, I do not think to lock up you.

No lock, she told him. Richard considered this. Then, as if remembering his manners, Please, he said, ushering them inside.

It was strange to have an adult there. She felt self-conscious, a child suddenly aware she is playing a game. Elaine didn't seem to notice it. She handed him a beer, and as he cracked it open she caught Cass's eye and gave her a dazzling smile, like they had pulled off some incredible triumph. Richard, with his beer, grew expansive, indulgent. How about a little joint? he said. Answering his own question, he got down on his hunkers and started rolling up. Elaine watched him a moment, then, maybe feeling neglected, said, What do you think of the Bunker? I told you it was freaky.

He didn't say anything; he ran his tongue along a cigarette paper.

We never saw you again, after that night. Where did you go?

You have missed me. He phrased it more as a statement than a question; Elaine blushed.

Mystery man, she said. She nudged him with her toe. Why'd you come here, to our shitty little town?

Someone told me the girls here are so pretty. When he smiled his handsomeness exploded into a million pieces of miraculous light. It was like being showered in radiant shrapnel.

He lit the joint, took a deep pull, held it in, then released it with a sigh of ecstatic satisfaction. He passed the joint to Elaine, who sat down beside him and mimicked his motions precisely – tugging on the roach and releasing a great cloud of white smoke with the same air of luxurious completeness. Cass turned to the door, looked out into the forest. Hidden by the darkness were the trees she once climbed with her brother, Dickie chasing them with his pretend gun.

Cass. From the floor Elaine held out the joint. Richard's arm was around her now. Cass took it, inhaled. Smoke tumbled into her head. She went back to the doorway, breathed out into the night. Behind her, Elaine whispered something to Richard, and the two of them laughed. Then they went quiet.

She didn't want any more of the joint, but she didn't want to turn around, so she held on to it. She took out her phone, found the picture of the dead family there waiting for her, and more messages from Rowan. Please let me see u

He had come over to her house last weekend, unexpectedly. She'd answered the door and found him there and got a shock – though really it was more the shape of the shock, without the feeling, like the postman bringing you a letter with nothing inside it. She thought he had found out about the boys she'd kissed in Paparazzi's and that he'd come to break up with her. Instead he had told her he was in love with her and he'd started to cry.

She didn't know what to say. She was embarrassed for him – guilty, too, for how little his words meant to her, how little it meant to love someone. It was better when she thought she liked him more than he did her, she reflected. Ever since then she'd avoided him, but he kept texting. i no ur not home i no ur wit elane U tink she cares abt u???

The joint smouldered between her fingers. She took another pull, felt an agony blaze up under her ribs. Behind her – she knew without looking – Elaine was kissing Richard. She had seen her kiss so many boys, she didn't know why tonight should be different. It was no different. U tink she cares abt u??? She wiped her eyes, tried to write a reply to Rowan. Her head swam. She remembered something he'd said once, about how the past hung in the present like smoke in the air, like vapour trails, fading out slowly. She hadn't understood it then but now for a moment it seemed she could see it, literally: Uncle Frank, lying burning in a blue meadow, her mother embedded in the glass windows of the church, coloured light streaming from her body. She saw herself too, a schoolgirl, wrongness buzzing within her like a bee trapped in a veil, clutching on to her best friend's hand. Tonight would go too, fade away, like white plumes of chemicals into the blue. Her heart let out a sad mewl of grief, as if she were dissolving into the shadows, or the shadows were in her, eating her from the inside out.

Then she felt something touch her neck – so softly, barely more than a breath. At first she thought she had imagined it. But no, there were definitely fingertips grazing her own. She moved away but her body was heavy and slow, and now a hand, Richard's hand, was closing around hers. Heavily she turned to see. He was standing with his back to her, deep in an embrace with Elaine. They were locked together so tightly they looked like they'd been frozen. Elaine's eyes were closed; Richard's arm was curled around her. But his other arm reached back for Cass, and now, gently but insistently, he pulled her towards him.

Cass stumbled forward, like she was being led down a tunnel, until she was right up next to them, as if they were a door she was waiting at. Still with his eyes closed, Richard detached his lips from Elaine's. Simultaneously, his hand rose up Cass's spine to the back of her head, and gently guided her mouth towards his. She felt his warmth, his smell, encircle her, and then his lips on hers, but only for a moment; then he withdrew, and the hand returned to the back of her head, guiding her again in a new direction. Somewhere within the velvety shroud of smoke, Cass's heart set up a clatter; she heard her own breath sharp in her ears; her body seemed to course with electricity as she crossed a few inches of space. Then new lips, soft and sticky with lip gloss, covered hers. Lightning convulsed her, she spun out of control, burst into flames as she hit the wall. But she didn't move, except to open her mouth a little. Behind, Richard's breaths came heavily; he was doing something or trying to, he would take his hand away and then put it right back to make sure she stayed in place. She willed her eyes closed, she felt the forest come through the door and inspirit her, surge up through her body and into the mouth of the body whose mouth was on hers. Then her eyes sprang open again, and she saw that Elaine's were open now too, right up against Cass's, like two green moons filling the sky. For a moment neither of them moved. Elaine remained there, a quarter-inch away, gazing into Cass's eyes. Then she withdrew her lips. In a low voice she said, *Mem-OR-i-ous.*

Cass looked back at her. Then, grandly, she responded, *Mem-ORRRR-i-ous.*

Shh, Richard told her. Kiss your friend.

But Cass did not. *BAGATELLE*, she pronounced.

Elaine let out a kind of sneeze, and doubled over, and when she reappeared, her eyes were tear-bright. *Mellifluous!*

Kiss her, Richard said. But that only made Elaine laugh more, in suppressed guffaws that came out in a series of wheezes and snorts and shudders and hiccups, like some Victorian steam engine. *Now, girls,* Cass said. Elaine shrieked, put up a hand for mercy. And now Cass was laughing too, the pair of them were laughing like they hadn't laughed in for ever, so hard that they didn't have any breath left to make a sound with, and anything Richard said or did only made it worse. They were laughing so hard that they had to sit down, which made them laugh even more. Fucking bitches! Fucking children! They did try to stop, but it was no good: they curled up on the cold floor shaking, with their eyes closed, and their heads buried in each other's shoulder.

At last Cass looked up and saw that Richard was no longer there. He must have given up, she told Elaine, which set off another wave of hilarity.

Kiss the friend!
Vare is deathhouse?
I live in car!
Is fucking bullshit!

Eventually they sat up, panting with after-laugh, and looked at the space where Richard wasn't. Elaine's cheeks were wet. She wiped them with her sleeve. Can you believe he just left us here, like, stranded in the woods?

She reached into her mouth and pulled out a strand of tobacco.

He made us kiss each other, Cass said quietly, as Elaine didn't seem about to mention it.

Asshole, Elaine said, and then, You're a better kisser than he is. She stretched out to take a beer can from the dwindling supply, pulled back the ring and dipped her head forward to meet the froth that came surging out of the opening. She gasped. Oh God, that is so gross, she said. She laid her head on Cass's shoulder. I am so fucking bombed, she said.

Me too, Cass said, though actually, after the thicket of blackness that had enveloped her earlier, she now felt a strange clearness. The night arced up over them, its sheer black walls like glass; everything seemed to resonate in a single note, the darkness, the trees, the stones.

School's over, she said.

I forgot about that, Elaine said. That's so crazy.

They were quiet again. Elaine's thumb was absently stroking her hand. After a while she said, Do you remember in Chemistry class I spilled iodine on your eczema?

Mmm. She knew what Elaine was going to say next.

I did it on purpose, Elaine said. I thought it would get the eczema off. She nestled close to Cass. I wanted to help you, she said. But I only hurt you.

That's OK, Cass said. She felt Elaine's hand tighten around hers. It was the eczema hand, though the eczema had gone; it had cleared by itself that spring, she had a new skin now.

They stayed like that for a long time, Elaine's ear tucked against Cass's heart.

82

Which of them realized there was still time to get to Paparazzi's? Instantly they revived: they got up and made their way through the woods and to the road. From there, they ran all the way, hand in hand, screaming like banshees. The wind was in their hair; their heads were full of hash and supermarket beer; they ran so fast they became immemorial, amnesiac. They were racing above the town, away from their own stories, away from everyone who wanted to remember them; they were no one, they were together, and they were alive alive alive alive.

And then one day she came round to find herself sitting at a desk in the gym hall with a blank copybook in front of her and a sheet of pink paper. At the top of the sheet of paper it said *Roinn Oideachais Leaving Certificate*, with today's date.

She looked around for Elaine and found her sitting parallel to her, two rows away. She tried to catch her eye, but Elaine was busy studying the sheet.

She ran her hand through her hair, tried to collect her thoughts.

Plath makes effective use of language to explore her personal experience of suffering and to provide occasional glimpses of the redemptive power of love. Discuss.

It was the perfect question, a gift; she could see Sylvia there before her, the lady poets, Sappho, Anna, Anne, by her side. But their faces were fuzzy and when she put her pen to the paper nothing would come.

It was hot in the exam hall; light pounded through the windows, waking odours from the corroding rubber floor, making her head throb and the balls of her fingers sweat so that it was hard to grip the pen. And the poems too were slippery: she knew they were there in her head, but the lines, the exact words, kept wriggling away from her! A flush of heat broke over her neck and shoulders; she wrestled off her jumper and used the movement to glance over at Elaine again, two rows away. If only she would look up, even for a moment! If only she would meet Cass's eye, they would both probably crack up at the sheer ridiculousness of it! They were so fucked! It was hilarious!

But Elaine's head was turned away; it was lowered almost down to the desk, and her pen motored across the page, filling one line of the copybook, then another, with her neat, blue, implacable handwriting. The whole hall, Cass realized, was rumbling with the sound of pens, pouring out answers.

That's when she started to get a bad feeling.

WOLF'S LAIR

The woods of Belarus are a maze, a green snow-laden maze that switches itself around whenever he turns his back. It's winter: the cold is blistering, the enemy is everywhere, grey flashes in the branches, almost too fast to see.

Behind you! Nev calls.

PJ spins round just in time to see a rifle pointed right at him, a shadowed figure fix him in his sights—

Incoming!

He hurls himself into a hollow as the grenade comes down, rolls with the blast, crashes against a tree trunk, hauls himself to his feet and runs without looking back, into the trees, the light.

This way! Nev calls, going the wrong way.

Light slams through the branches, it twists and needles, knives of light, rivers of light, walls of light that turn and flip and bear down on him – the faster he goes, the more his chest feels like it's going to burst open.

Incoming! Another grenade lands at his feet.

Wait a second, PJ says, coming to a stop. Are you throwing those *at* me?

It was a sniper, Nev calls back. Because you're so *slow.*

Snipers don't throw grenades, PJ says. But Nev has disappeared into the trees ahead. He starts after him again but his lungs are burning, and his feet are on fire too, screaming like he's running on razors. The sky, red and purple, shrinks and darkens into a ball, a whirling black ball of pain. He drops to his knees then collapses back onto the soft earth, reaches for his inhaler.

The sky opens up again. The forest stops being on fire. He unlaces

87

his runners, pulls them off as delicately as he can. It still feels like most of his skin comes with them.

In the distance he can hear Nev crashing through the undergrowth and nearer by, something scuffling. Scuff scuff, rustle rustle, right by his head.

Holy shit – it's a squirrel, a *red* squirrel! Perched on a log, quite motionless, like it has materialized there from another world. Which maybe it has: the woods are full of greys, but he has never seen a red squirrel here before. Hey there, buddy, he says. From its log the squirrel considers him. Very very very slowly he reaches into his pocket and withdraws his phone. I'm just taking a picture, that's all, he tells the squirrel. The squirrel cocks its head amicably, as if to say, We cool.

Incoming! bellows a voice. A rock thumps down in front of him. When he looks around the squirrel is gone, like it was never there.

What are you doing just sitting here? Nev stumps up. You can't just take a break when you're on a mission. In real life I could actually shoot you for disobeying orders.

I saw a squirrel, PJ says. I was trying to take a picture of a squirrel and you scared it away.

You think in World War Two they stopped to take pictures of squirrels? Nev says. I thought we were searching for our base.

All right, all right, PJ says.

It was your idea to play this stupid game, Nev reminds him.

Okay, I'm coming, PJ says. He reaches for his runners.

Jesus Christ, Nev says. What's wrong with your feet?

In fact it's summer, not winter. For weeks the temperature's been off the charts: it almost makes PJ wish he really was in Belarus, even with all the snipers and grenades. All day long the heat rises and rises, like water in a flood. At night-time it'll fall back, a little bit, but then come morning it starts up again, and soon it will be higher even than it was the day before, leaving you submerged at the bottom.

Nobody's allowed to water their lawn. The fire brigade keeps having to go up into the mountains to put out gorse fires. In town everyone's acting happy. 'Isn't it great?' they tell each other, the butcher, the barber, standing around outside their shops in the shimmering air, but under their arms dark patches appear, and silver sprinkles of moisture break out over their scalps, and you can tell that inside they're feeling thirsty and tired and mean.

It would be fine if he could just stay indoors. One time they went on holidays to Egypt and whenever you stepped outside it was like someone was incinerating you with a magnifying glass. So they ended up not going anywhere, not even the pyramids, they just stayed in the hotel and swam in the pool and watched Egypt documentaries on the hotel TV and in PJ's opinion it was one of the family's best ever holidays.

But this summer they are not going anywhere and though the house is cool and there is a TV just waiting to be watched, fat chance of doing any of that. Instead every morning it's, *Are you kids just going to lie in bed all day?* Then soon as he's up it's, *Would you kids ever get out from under my feet!*

You kids, BTW, means him, PJ. Mam seems to have given up yelling at Cass, who if she does actually come down for breakfast brings it right back upstairs with her. But Mam makes PJ sit at the breakfast bar, then complains about the racket he's making. His chewing is too loud, his phone is too loud. One time she gives out to him for his *constant blinking*. PJ Barnes, I'm at my wits' end with you! she says. She is always at her wits' end. She's like a human tripwire, just waiting for him to set her off.

That's why the best plan, the only plan, is to get out early, and stay out as long as he can, lose himself in the suffocating airless tunnels of the forest.

They continue into the labyrinth. The ground underfoot is dry and snapping, crackles like a fire starting. Check it out, Nev says, it's your new school!

PJ looks at the phone. The screen shows a guy in a uniform with a blazer and cap though he looks too old to be in school. He is tied hand

and foot and there are three other guys dressed as teachers lined up to jizz on him. *Teachers punish naughty twink and fuck his brains out* it says above the video.

Nev chuckles to himself. Good thing you like being bummed, he says.

Under the clip there are mini-screens.

Recommended for you:
Dwarf gets busy with teen cutie
tied up twink begs for mercy from hung dwarf
real incest dwarves certified real

Can't help noticing your algorithm's generating a lot of dwarf porn here, PJ says.

Give me that! Nev snatches his phone back and stows it in his pocket. So where's this *amazing place* you wanted to show me, he says.

Hmm, PJ says. Uh, well, this is it.

This? Nev says. He looks around him in case he's mistaken. This is a *shed*, he says.

Right, PJ says. I mean, to the naked eye.

It's an *old empty* shed, Nev says. With holes in the walls.

Yeah, PJ begins, but . . . He trails off. It's weird, when he comes here on his own or with Zargham there's always kind of an atmosphere, like you can easily imagine you're in a ruin of the distant past or a shattered base in a post-apocalyptic wilderness. But with Nev sure enough it does just seem more like a small, even poky, stone shed with a rusty roof and weeds in the corners.

I thought there was going to be something *in* it, Nev says. I can't believe you brought me all the way out here to look at a *shed*.

Sometimes my sister comes out here with her friends and they have parties, PJ offers. For ages they had this big stack of beer cans, there in that corner.

Nev looks at the empty, beerless corner.

They call it the Bunker, PJ perseveres. You know, like Hitler's bunker.

Nev sighs deeply. I think you'll find that the *Führerbunker* was underground? he says. Like – that was the entire point of it?

Right, PJ says. The *Führerbunker* is where you fight Hitler at the end of Black Dawn, except he escapes in this kind of mole-machine. At least that's what PJ read on the forum – he and Nev are currently still stuck in the Wolf's Lair.

Yeah, I'm not sure why they call it that, he concedes.

Nev doesn't respond. He stands with his hands on his hips, surveying the meagre dimensions of the shed in dissatisfaction. Then slowly a light goes on. Do you think they ever *have sex* here? he says.

I don't know, PJ says.

I thought you watched them, Nev says. Didn't you say you came out here and you watched them?

I *saw* them a couple of times, PJ says, affronted. I *saw* they were having a party. I didn't *watch* them. Anyway, they haven't been out here in ages.

Nev's face darkens again. PJ realizes too late he should have leveraged the voyeuristic potential more. But he remembers something else. Then this other time? he says. Like just before the summer holidays I came out here and the whole Bunker—

Shed, Nev says.

Well, anyway, the whole shed was full of parts, like car parts. But then when I came back the next morning they were gone.

Zargham had been with him that day. They were sure it must be smugglers! They tracked through the whole forest looking for tyre marks, footprints – they thought they saw a stranger, way off in the distance! But Nev just looks at the floor with a traumatized expression, like PJ has kidnapped him and is holding him hostage here. I'm hungry, he says.

Ah! In that case! Re-energized, PJ goes to a corner and with a flourish pulls back what appears to be part of the dirt floor but is in fact a dirt-covered towel under which is a hole and in the hole is a box. Tuck in, he says, opening the box.

Nev looks into it, then up at PJ. What the fuck is this? he says. Herring fillets? Pineapple slices?

I only took stuff my mam wouldn't notice, PJ says apologetically. But look, there's energy bars too, see?

Nev turns away in disgust. I want something *cold*, he says. Like that's been in a *fridge*. He turns to PJ with a full-body plead that has undoubtedly been perfected over countless trips through the supermarket sweet section. Can't we go back to your house?

Hmm, well, uh, we could, PJ says. Though maybe not right now this second?

Nev narrows his eyes, glitters evilly. Oh, I forgot, he says. You want to stay out of your mam's way, because you're worried she'll send you to boarding school.

No, I'm not, PJ says.

I'd be worried, Nev says. You'll probably get raped there.

That's what happens at boarding school, he adds, opening an energy bar. Raping.

Last summer PJ went to camp for the whole of July. There was Art in the morning, Choose Your Own Sport after lunch – he chose Archery. Zargham was there too, in fact most of his class was. PJ won a medal for his seashell mosaic of a stunt truck and another for Best Beginner at Archery.

But this year he said he didn't want to go.

You don't? Dad sounded surprised. I thought you enjoyed it.

I did, PJ said. But sometimes it's better with things you enjoy not to do them again.

Right, Dad said dubiously.

Also it didn't leave me much time to myself. Like, I spend the whole year playing with the kids in my class. So summer's a good chance to, you know, be alone.

You won't be bored hanging around by yourself all day?

No way! PJ shook his head emphatically. Anyway, Nev will be around.

Oh right, Dad said. You like him, don't you.

I do, PJ said, I really do.

It's all part of the strategy. Lie low, act unobtrusive. A drain on our time and money? On the contrary, we barely even notice he's around! Good old PJ, why would we send him to boarding school?

Unfortunately it means that PJ's stuck with Nev. Nev doesn't go to camp: he has a tendency to rub his peers up the wrong way and the camp organizers have explained to his parents there is only so much protection they can give him.

PJ tries to accept it, think of it as the penance he would have got for his sins if he'd gone to confession, i.e. this summer with Nev is like his punishment for whatever it is he did and when he gets back to school he'll be all clear. But sometimes he cycles by O'Malley Park and sees the kids at camp and imagines he is there with them playing rounders, improving his dribbling skills, also according to Zargham they have batik this year so maybe doing batik and at lunchtime sitting beside Zargham on the bleachers in the shade, asking if he wants to swap his Capri-Sun for a KitKat.

The frustrating thing is that it doesn't have to be a punishment summer at all. With weather like this it could be an amazing summer, a legendary summer, and they wouldn't even need to go to camp! If Zargham was around they'd be in the forest morning till night and they'd never even think of going inside! With Nev by contrast there are endless complaints about poor phone signal or needles in his shorts or too many ants — it's a constant battle to keep him happy.

But mostly PJ's frustration is with himself. He could have his legendary summer if he was just able to be on his own! He does try. Banished from the house he'll go out to the roadside and work on his car log for an hour, then return to the Bunker and sit under a tree in the sun eating a pineapple slice or a herring fillet and reading *The Shining* or texting with Ethan:

WAIT A SECOND U MEAN U GOT UR OWN FOREST??!!! AWESOME!!!

I know. Check it out this is the Bunker

WOAH COOL

thanks :) Tho I guess Bunkers wrong. Its not underground

YEAH MAYBE MORE LIKE WOLFSSCHANZE

Ha ha dont remind me of that place!!!

LOL U STILL STUCK? PRETTY COOL TO HAVE 1 OF UR OWN THO!!!!

And yes, with the birds singing and the grasshoppers ticking and a couple of butterflies dancing by he will recognize that it is pretty darn cool, close to perfect, in fact, which makes it all the more infuriating when sooner or later he feels the cold damp prickling come, like a shadow falling over him, except a shadow that falls from the inside, and throwing his book down and cursing himself *Fucking shithead! You stupid fucking lamer!* for being sad, for caring he's alone, he will leave the forest to call on Nev.

Back inside, running down the twisting halls of the Nazi compound. A man jumps out, rotting face, eyes red like the band on his arm. Look out!

I see him! The gun judders, bullets hammer his torso, but the man keeps coming.

Why won't he die?! Nev cries.

He's a zombie, use the flamethrower!

It's not working!

You must be out of fuel! Go to the storeroom!

Where's the storeroom?

More Nazis rise up out of the floor to block the way; their withered hands reach and spread till they fill the screen, like bare tree branches. Then a curtain of blood falls to cover everything. I'm so sick of this level, Nev says, throwing the controller across the room.

Can I play? PJ says. Nev doesn't respond. PJ picks up the controller, respawns in a dank stone hallway.

One good thing about Nev – really the only good thing – is that he has Black Dawn. Black Dawn is probably PJ's favourite game. He was actually supposed to get it for his birthday but that didn't pan out and he decided in the present circumstances it was better not to make too much noise about it. He doesn't really need his own one anyway, seeing as he calls on Nev every day; he's a bit of a gamehog, but if you're patient you will eventually get to play.

Behind him the door opens. How are you getting on, boys?

Fine, thank you, Mrs O'Connor, PJ says.

Mam, stop interrupting, Nev says.

I'm just leaving you some cookies, Nev's mam says.

You're not *leaving* them, you're standing there talking to us, Nev says.

Thanks, Mrs O'Connor, PJ says, taking a cookie.

See what nice manners PJ has?

Nev rolls his eyes.

How's the family, PJ? she says. How's your mam? I haven't seen her in ages.

She's fine, PJ says, trying to be polite and also fight a half-incinerated Nazi who has dragged his torso over the floor on a slime trail of intestines.

And your dad? How's the garage? Any news?

News? He stabs his bayonet at the half-Nazi who WILL NOT DIE.

I thought I heard something there. I must have imagined it.

Mam, FFS!

Language, Neville!

I just said the *letters*, I didn't say the *words*.

When Nev's mam finally goes for a time there is silence, save for the whoosh of the flamethrower and the gurgling screams of dying Nazis. Then Nev says, How did you know where the storeroom was?

I must have seen it on the forum somewhere.

Pretty weird you're on a forum for a game you don't even own.

I might get BD II when it comes out, PJ says.

Yeah, Nev says, with a sarcastic little chuckle. He takes a cookie, watches PJ race down the long middle hall of Sperrkreis 1. Nazis tumble to the floor on left and right, burning. They've never got this far before! If he can only make it through the door, that's got to be the end of the level?

My dad says your dad's garage is in trouble, Nev says, without looking away from the screen. He says it's going into liquidation.

PJ ducks a bullet and parries a sword, but there must be a tripwire he didn't see. A wooden stake flies out of the wall and pins him to the pillar behind. He writhes there powerlessly: then the screen fills up with blood.

Nev holds his hand out for the controller. My turn, he says.

The Angelus bells are ringing in the distance as PJ's coming up the driveway and when he goes inside they're ringing on the TV too, slightly out of synch.

Hey, Dad, you won't believe what I saw in the wood today!

In a second, buddy, Dad says, let me just get the headlines here.

On the TV, a silver Ireland spins around then explodes into a million fragments then reassembles into a 6. The news today, a man says sternly. PJ waits. You're not going to believe this, he says to Dad. Mm-hmm, Dad says. Mam appears in the doorway. PJ, go and tell your sister her dinner's ready.

Okay, PJ says. Hey, Mam, guess what I s—

Go! she says.

Right, okay, yeah, PJ says, and hurries off upstairs.

Cass is at her desk reading a book – staring down at it so intensely it's like she's looking at it through a microscope. Now she takes a high-lighter pen and *sccrrrfff* pulls it in a line across the page then *sccrrrfff* another line below it. The sound makes him shudder and as if she senses the shudder she looks up. What? she says.

Guess what I saw in the woods today. He waits, but she doesn't respond, so he tells her. A red squirrel!

Great, vermin, Cass says, without looking up from her book.

Pretty rare to see a red one, he says. Mostly it's just greys.

What are you doing in my room? she says.

Dinner's ready.

She gets up with a sigh of exasperation. He looks to see what she's been highlighting. Why are you reading a schoolbook?

Because it's interesting?

But school's finished.

It doesn't stop being interesting just because school's over, she says. It's not like it has a use-by date like yoghurt or something.

TOP TEN REASONS CASS IS A BITCH AND YOU'RE GLAD SHE'S LEAVING #1: SARCASTIC.

What's more 'interesting': since she finished her exams Cass has barely left the house. She doesn't go to the Bunker, she hardly ever sees Rowan. All she does is sit in her room, reading her textbooks, making notes, even writing out answers in a pad. It's like she's doing it backwards, PJ thinks: all of the drinking and partying that should have waited for summer when the exams were over, she did first, and the reading and revising and staying in, she's doing now, when it's too late. It's like she believes that, because the results haven't come out yet, if she's Good enough there's still time to change them.

What does *liquidation* mean? he says as he follows her across the landing.

She stops, turns. Where did you hear that?

He shrugs.

It means— She stops again. What the fuck are you doing? Are you *limping*?

Old war wound, he says. Shrapnel.

You're such a freak, she says.

TOP TEN REASONS CASS IS A BITCH #2: DISRESPECT-FUL TO OTHER FAMILY MEMBERS.

Downstairs Mam frets in the kitchen, surrounded by smoke though they are just having cold cuts. It's hot as a furnace: the heat is coming from her, it rolls off her in waves. Dad is at the dining table with his head in his hands. The table is solid oak with pre-distressed finish and currently for sale on Bargainzz.ie for €2,000. Also available from the same seller: four pre-distressed solid oak dining chairs; one foot spa brand new with tags; one foot spa new without tags; one Lego Ninjago Training Camp, v. good condition, all pieces included, with pictures showing it fully constructed by PJ Barnes with help of D. Barnes, two Christmases ago.

PJ taking his seat is feeling pretty pre-distressed himself. He would never say it, but sometimes he almost wishes Dad wouldn't come home. At least when he's not there it's peaceful.

The fights are always the same, have been the same for months. Mam wants Dad to call Granddad and ask for money. Dad won't do it. But *why?* Mam says. He's not going to say no! Isn't it his name over the door? Just explain to me *why* you won't at least talk to him!

Dad sets down his fork and puts his hands on the back of his head and pushes down like he wants to waterboard himself in the plate of salad. Oh Jesus, he says. Am I ever going to hear the end of this?

The end is exactly where we're headed, Mam says. The end of this and everything else and you won't lift a finger to stop it!

He's an old man! All right? I don't want to burden him with our problems.

Oh God forbid he should be burdened! God forbid anything should come between him and his golf!

Beside PJ Cass has her phone on her lap and is flicking through Elaine's Instagram. He sees her add a heart for Elaine's hotel room, a flame for a pair of long white-gold legs curving down into a rockpool.

What is it you think he's going to do? Dad's face is brick-red and quivering. You think he'll take out his chequebook and everything will be right as rain? Look at the bloody news, this is everywhere!

He'll do *something*, won't he? Mam yells back. He won't just let it close!

Oh God, let it close, and be done! Dad's shouting, when Cass lets out a shriek and points to the floor.

Is it a mouse? PJ says, perking up.

No, just a pool of water that's appeared on the dining-room floor. It expands slowly as they watch it, then Dad gets up and covers it with a towel.

Only a leak, he says gruffly. Nothing to worry about. I'll get Victor to come and have a look in the morning.

*

Dad never used to get angry. Even when Mam was cross with him, he'd just sort of absorb it until she calmed down again. Now he yells right back at her, so loud that she jumps. Or worse, he's silent, twisting his ring around and around, and you don't know whether or not he's about to explode. It's like he's a totally different person. Even when he's acting like his usual self, it seems just like that, acting.

PJ knows it's business and all very complicated. Still, he can't see why Dad won't take Mam's advice and call Granddad. Granddad is rich. He lives in Portugal, beside a beach, on permanent holiday. When he comes to visit, he brings more presents than he can carry. He speaks in a firm, commanding tone, and talking to him on Skype, with the sunlit ocean behind him and his blue eyes full of calm authority, is like talking to a general, or God, simultaneously scary and reassuring. Granddad would *know* how to fix things. Why doesn't Dad just ask him?

Because he's insane, Cass mumbles. She's lying on her bed, her nose buried in *Deutsch macht Spaß!*

Granddad?

She sighs, rubs her eyes, looks up. Even if Granddad did give them money it wouldn't solve their problems, she says. Dad's through with it. He's trying to tank it. He wants out.

Out of what?

Cass shrugs.

But they won't get divorced, right?

Cass always tells him they won't get divorced because Mam thinks it's a sin. But tonight she just presses her lips together, stares into her book.

You said they wouldn't! he exclaims. You *said*!

Wouldn't it be better? she exclaims back. How would it not be better for everybody than, than *that*?

She points to the door, to the dining room, the pre-distressed table.

Because she'll send me to boarding school! he yells at her.

OMG, get a life! She covers her face with her hands.

TOP TEN REASONS CASS IS A BITCH #3: NEGATIVE

ATTITUDE. #4: NO FAMILY LOYALTY. #5: DOESN'T CARE
ABOUT ANYONE ELSE'S PROBLEMS.

There is a hissing silence. She's wrong, he tells himself. They won't
get divorced. He has sat by the roadside for an hour every day for a
month and the blue cars are leading the reds by 263 to 108. Anyway, Dad
loves Mam still. And Mam would love Dad again if he could get the garage going. If Granddad was here it could all be fixed so easily!

He wants to say to her: Remember when Dad used to be fun? Remember
when he'd spend the whole evening chasing us around the garden? He was
the best in the house at Sonic the Hedgehog, he knew everything about
animals. What's that bee doing, Dad? Well, PJ, a lot of bees, bumblebees
for instance, don't live in trees they live in nests underground so that lady
there might be a queen looking for a new home. Bees live underground?
Some kinds. Will we dig her a nest? Great idea!

When Dad was fun everything was fun. Not just holidays, not just
Christmas. Going to the supermarket! Cutting the grass! At bedtime
they had pyjama races, they read *Lord of the Rings* cover to cover, they
put a torch under their chins and told each other ghost stories, he wants
to say it to Cass, Remember?

But he doesn't, in case she says, No, that wasn't how it was. You've
got it wrong, that's not how it was at all.

In his room he takes off his runners and his socks. The blister on the
right foot has gotten bigger, and one on the left has burst, but blisters he
can deal with. The real issue is the toes, the little toes. The skin's been
rubbing off them and now they keep bleeding. He put plasters on them
this morning but they came off. Thing about plasters anyway is that they
make it even harder to squeeze into his runners.

He looks down at his feet, raw and red and sorrowful. His feet look
back at him like, *Please don't put us back in those runners, PJ!* He sighs.
I'm at my wits' end with you, he whispers.

It's not their fault, they can't help growing. But he only got these
runners two months ago and it was a really big deal then and he can

imagine what Mam will say if she has to go and buy more. So he's keeping quiet about it, only it's not that simple because his socks have started to get blood on them which doesn't come out in the laundry. He's been hiding them in his locker so Mam won't notice but sooner or later he's going to run out, and what will happen then he doesn't know, except that it won't do him any favours if they end up getting divorced. Who would want a boy with infinitely expanding feet?

The funny thing is he *knows* they won't send him to boarding school. Cass has explained it several times. Boarding school is expensive, and the whole reason they're fighting is that they have no money. But though this all makes sense in his mind, he just can't seem to *believe* it, in his heart. Instead he just keeps thinking of Jamie Cavendish, who sat beside him and Zargham in school until his parents split up and he was sent off to God knows where and nobody ever saw him again. In boarding school you don't even get summer holidays – that's what Nev says. Parents pay extra because neither of them wants you at home.

He adds today's socks to the sock stash, takes out his phone. On her Instagram Elaine has added a picture of a plate of shrimps or something, captioned #Langoustines, then a long crescent of beach studded with tanned people in swimsuits, and finally one of Elaine herself on a sun-lounger, peeping over her sunglasses with a half-smile and sipping from a tall glass #holidaybliss.

PJ puts a flame beside this then adds a smiley face in case the flame is too intense then takes out the flame completely and puts in a heart. She won't know it's him anyway, his Instagram is under the alias Max Winter, a mathematician and surfer.

As soon as he puts it down his phone pings. It's Ethan: YOU SEEN THIS YET? NEW TRAILER FOR BDII!!! He clicks the link. Out of a grey fog a figure slowly appears. It's the Statue of Liberty, only instead of a torch she's holding a dagger and on her outstretched arm is a swastika and piled up around her feet are bodies – men, women, children with blue faces. Then a hand bursts out from them holding a gun, then the words in turn emerge out of the image: *Black Dawn II.*

GOT MINE ON PRE-ORDER I CAN'T WAIT!!!

Awesome!

HOW'S THE WOLF LAIR GOING

Not so good there's a trapdoor we can't open we keep getting annihilated

U NEED THE KEY DID U FIND THE KAPO?

What's a kapo?

HE'S IN GUARD ROOM ON LEVEL 3 THIN GUY IN THE GREY CLOTHES?

Nev shot him. Thought he was a guard?

LOL U DIDNT NOTICE THE CHAIN AROUND HIS ANKLE? LOL

HE'S THE KAPO DON'T KILL HIM HE'LL GIVE U THE KEY

HEY CHECK THIS OUT

BUGATTI VEYRON TOP SPEED 220 MPH

Woah nice wheels

MY DAD MIGHT BE GETTING ONE

WE'RE GOING FOR A TEST DRIVE 2MORO!!!

Awesome! Hey guess what I saw today in the woods a red squirrel!

OMG!!!!! SO CUTE!!!!!!

I almost got a picture but he ran off

IVE NEVER SEEN A RED SQUIRREL IRL! NOT EVEN IN THE ZOO!

SO COOL THAT U LIVE BESIDE A WOODS!

Yeah

It is I guess

WANT 2 PLAY SOME MARIO KART?

Dad knocks on the door. Lights out, pal. Phone off.

Cant 2nite, gotta go!

OK SWEET DREAMS! GOOD LUCK WITH THE KAPO!

Liquidate: wind up the affairs (of a company) by ascertaining liabilities and apportioning assets.

When he turns out the light he imagines the water pooling on the floor downstairs, and away in the town the showroom too, filling up like Cian Conlon's parents' basement during the massive flood. Around him the house cracks and creaks and clanks, like a ship at sea.

Q. What kind of ship has no masts or crew or engine?

A. A dealership.

Q. What kind of ship can't stay afloat in the water?

His ship. PJ is dissolving, he is sinking into the deep. From above, Elaine's white-gold legs dangle over him. She leans in, whispers to him soft as a kiss, You are *liquidating*.

The next morning Victor's in the kitchen, staring into a hole he's made in the kitchen floor. He's wearing a flak jacket and two types of camouflage – grey and white for his pants, green and brown for his top.

Is it the Viet Cong you think are behind it, Victor? Mam stands to one side with her arms folded, staring at him staring. Or ISIS maybe?

I'd say you've a blockage, Mrs Barnes, he says.

All coming home to roost now, isn't it, Mam says darkly and sweeps out of the room.

Victor turns his doleful pink head to PJ who's sitting at the breakfast bar eating breakfast.

Well, he says.

PJ's mouth is full of granola so he just nods.

Mam does not like Victor. He is the man who renovated their house. The dripping pipes, the lumpy floor, the gappy tiles, the sockets that sometimes work and sometimes don't – all of it is Victor's work.

In fairness – Dad says – he always tries to make it right. If there's ever a problem he'll be here that same day.

That's because no one else will hire him! Mam says back. You're the only eejit will let him in the door! Running around in his camouflage get-up – who does he think he is, Rambo?

Victor is in the Civil Defence: at the weekend you see him on manoeuvres, slogging up and down Ned's Hill with a rucksack and a plastic rifle.

He has a good heart, Dad says.

He's a headcase, Mam says. It's the paint is all that's holding this place up.

Victor opens his bag and rattles around in it. Dad comes into the room. Well, Victor, he says. What way are you?

Keepin' goin' anyhow, Victor says, nodding dolefully.

We've a blockage of some sort, Dad says.

That's how it looks, all right, Victor says.

The two men stare into the hole.

It wouldn't be anything to do with the flood, would it? Dad says. That was a few months ago.

Could well be, Victor says. It's all connected. He wipes his nose. You'll be seeing more and more of this sort of thing, he says.

Is that right, Dad says.

This town's sewage system is two hundred years old. It was never meant for the kind of use it's getting now. New estates, building on floodplains. Then add global warming to the mix? No, he says, and he starts screwing a thin rod into another thin rod.

You're saying it won't last? Dad says.

I'm saying it's being put under enormous pressure, Victor says. Enormous pressure.

The tone is doomy. But Dad's eyes are alight. Dad likes talking to Victor. Victor is one of the few people in town who knows about the things Dad knows about – Nazis and Napoleon and the fall of the Mayans, the terrible roll call of genocides that is the Past. PJ suspects that's why Dad doesn't mind so much when something goes wrong with the house, because it will give him a chance to talk to Victor.

I suppose people don't realize, Dad says. How fragile these things are.

People have no idea, Victor says. No idea.

But simply look at history, Dad says.

Oh, history's a write-off, Victor says.

He has connected his rods so they look like a long metal tapeworm which he now feeds into the bowels of the house. I'm seeing a big surge for the future-proofing these last few months, he says.

Future-proofing? Dad says.

Solar panels and what have you, Victor says.

That's a service you'd provide, is it?

Oh God yes, Victor says.

Something to think about, all right, Dad says.

It's a start, Victor says, speaking to his rods. But as I always say to people – I tell it to them straight: solar panels will only get you so far. He grimaces, shunts the rod forward. Say the you-know-what hits the fan, saving the child's presence. No money in the ATMs, three days later the supermarkets are empty, the government's gone. What do you think a few solar panels will do for you then?

Divil a bit, he says. He sets his jaw, heaves the rod. There is a gurgling beneath the floor. No, he says with satisfaction.

When the floor has been put back together Victor takes them around the perimeter of the house, looking at places the future might get in. He explains how you'd install a grey-water system, a heat pump, a rain harvester.

And then you have the woods here, he says. That all yours?

For what it's worth, which isn't much, Dad says. You're thinking of fuel? Firewood?

No, Victor says. He puts his hands on his hips, regards the forest on the far side of the meadow. It's on an incline, he says.

It is? Dad says.

Victor sniffs. Did that land get flooded during the rain?

Dad scratches his head.

No, PJ says.

Victor strokes his chin and nods to himself. Goldenhill, he says. That must be it, so. Dad and PJ look at each other; it's somehow never occurred to them the house might have been named for a reason. A hill's a good place to be, Victor says, when the rain comes.

Dad's phone rings; he excuses himself and heads back towards the house. PJ follows Victor to his van. Inside it's piled with tools, pipes, fuseboards.

What's that thing? PJ points to a blocky unit with switches that looks a bit like a toppled-over Astromech droid.

Backup generator, Victor says. Eight thousand watts. If the grid goes down that should give you enough juice for your cooking, heating, light.

Why would the grid go down? PJ says.

There's a hundred and one things could bring it down, Victor says. Ageing infrastructure. Storms. Solar flares. Nuclear attack. Unforeseen black swan event.

Why would it stay up? he says. That's the question you should be asking.

PJ supposes that's true: if Maurice Barnes Motors can go down and no one's able to stop it, then a grid can probably go down too.

Things are going to change, Victor says. You've got to be prepared.

Right, PJ says, and then, I guess once you're prepared it won't be so bad. Like, things probably won't be that different.

Victor looks at him, a funny kind of look, because both of his eyes go in different directions, and neither of them is actually pointed at PJ. Still, he *is* looking at him, PJ can tell: an indescribable, sightless looking from the creased pink hairy place between his eyebrows.

It'll be different, Victor says. It'll be bad.

Back in the *Wolfsschanze*. *Wolf* was Hitler's nickname. Ethan has been to the real-life Lair, he says the game's pretty close to what it was actually like.

Right except they probably didn't have zombies and demons and stuff
fighting for them

LOL WHO KNOWS??? :)

Bounding through a door now comes a dog with the head of a man, or no, the face of a man that it looks like has been sewn on to the dog's head. His teeth are a man's teeth, they fix in your leg. You club him off, run down the corridor, it's pitch black.

Go through the door there, PJ says.

There are two men inside but this time you see that the first man with the gun in his hand is pointing it at the second, not at you.

Don't shoot him, PJ says. That's the kapo.

Who told you how to do this? Nev says. Ethan?

PJ doesn't respond.

Kind of cheating using other people's tips, Nev says.

Don't use them, so, PJ says.

Nev clams up, shoots the guard. The kapo cowers in the corner, hands over his face. How did they not spot this guy before? Even without seeing the chains it's obvious he's different. His clothes are in rags, his eyes are popping out of his grey, starved face.

Give him your gun, PJ says.

Seriously?

PJ checks his phone. Yes, give it to him. Nev does what he's told. Slowly the kapo lowers his hands, gazes at you like he's looking up from the bottom of a lake. You will need this, he says. He clasps something into your hand.

The key! Nev can't help exclaiming.

DONT DELAY THERE ALREADY COMING FOR U

Why doesn't he come with us?

U CANT HELP HIM

The kapo looks out of the screen with dark empty eyes. I am ready to die, he says. My only fear is that I am already dead.

This guy's a barrel of laughs, Nev says.

Get out of there, PJ says.

You leave him in his corner, hear the single gunshot as you close the door.

Surviving in the wilderness: difficult but not impossible. In dry terrain, simply gather dead leaves from the ground, seal them in a plastic bag and leave in the heat of the sun. In a few hours condensation will gather on the inside of the bag that you can safely drink. You can also eat wild plants, while taking care to avoid poisonous ones, such as plants with white berries, plants with thorns, plants with shiny leaves, plants with fuzzy leaves, and plants with a bitter taste. Ants are edible as are beetles though you need to remove the wings and legs—

What are you talking about? Nev says. Eating ants? What the fuck are you talking about?

I'm saying if you were living in the forest, PJ explains.

Why would I want to live in the forest? Nev says.

Well like if you needed to leave home for some reason, PJ says.

Like . . . your parents are sending you to boarding school? Nev says with a swift malevolent grin. So you try to run away?

No, PJ says. Like say if the grid went down. Or if there was a swan attack.

A what?

Like a, uh, black swan attack?

What the fuck? Nev says again. Where are you getting this shit?

Victor, PJ says.

That guy's a loon, Nev says.

He knows a lot of stuff, PJ says. About survival.

Didn't he drive a JCB through the wall of your house?

That was years ago, PJ says. Anyway, he fixed it.

Well, good luck with your new life eating beetles and licking condensation off a bag, Nev says. Frankly it sounds worse than rape school.

They're walking through the woods again. Heat rises in green waves from the ground, falls from above in slabs of light. PJ's feet are in agony, he can almost hear them cry out. Around him the forest feels vast. It's not so big on a map, but once you step inside it, it goes on for ever, and the thought comes to him, *could* he live out here? Like, could *he* live out here? Imagining Mam adjusting his tie, Well, PJ, all set for your first day of boarding school? And he's all, Sure thing, Mam, just going outside for a second – and that's it, boom, gone, they never see him again, except maybe some time in the Future when he's a millionaire aged twenty-five and he pulls up in his sports car to the petrol station Elaine is working in, and she's like, Don't I know you from somewhere? and he takes off his sunglasses which are the mirror kind and says, Yeah, a little place called the Past.

Or no, she says, Don't I know you? and he says, Maybe you thought you did.

Or, You were the only one who ever did.

Or, she doesn't say anything, he just reaches out his hand and says, Coming? and they both get in the sports car, it's a Bugatti like Ethan's dad's going to get, and they drive away.

Inside the Bunker the air is damp and cool though you can feel the heat building round the walls outside. Nev plops down on the mattress and sighs bitterly. He's always like this after he's been playing Play-Station. Sometimes PJ can re-motivate him by getting him to think of the forest as a specialized mode of the video game, like Black Dawn IRL. Today, though, Nev is too depressed.

I ASKED THERES NO RED SQUIRREL IN THE WHOLE ZOO!!! BUT CHECK THIS OUT!!!! A BABY MARMOSET JUST BORN!

Oh wow he's adorable!

THERE'S A COMPETITION TO NAME HIM! ANY IDEAS? WIN A TRIP TO DUBLIN!!!

What about Marmolade?

I LIKE IT!

Is that Dublin Zoo? You live in Dublin?

YEAH U?

Like 2 hours away. My sisters moving there for college!

How come you've got a signal? Nev says.

It comes and goes, PJ says.

Nev sighs, leans his head back against the wall. Do you think your sister had sex on this mattress?

I don't know, PJ says. Nev sits up, considers the mattress. She *must* have, he says. She *must*.

You know how dragonflies have sex? PJ says. It's really weird, they make this kind of heart-shaped—

Stop telling me science! Nev exclaims, covering his ears. It's like being in school, being with you!

Sorry, PJ says. Nev lapses into a bad-tempered silence.

YOU SHOULD COME VISIT!!!! WE HAVE A SPARE ROOM WE CD GO TO
THE ZOO + THERES A NEW VIDEO GAME SHOP!!!!

Wow that would be cool

SERIOUSLY ASK YOUR MOM!

Maybe. She's always complaining I'm getting under feet

:) MINE TOO!!!

Nev, who has been lost in thought, speaks up. Have you ever fucked
your sister?

Jesus Christ, PJ says.

Yes or no?

Of course not, he says. She's my sister.

But if you had the chance you would, right? Nev says. If I had a sister
I'd totally want to fuck her.

No, you wouldn't, PJ says. Look, we've been through this. You
think you'd want to fuck her, but if you actually had a sister, you
wouldn't.

I would, Nev says. Especially if she was hot like your sister.

She's a bitch, PJ says.

How about your mam?

PJ does not reply to this. He is trying very, very hard to stay chill.
Or u could visit me! he types.

Hey, can I check something on your phone? Nev asks.

Okay, PJ says. He's about to hand him the phone then stops. Wait,
when you say check something, do you mean, look at porn?

Oh Jesus! Nev exclaims. He takes out his own phone again and tries
unsuccessfully to connect. I would *pay,* he says. I would pay money to
right now see actual people having sex.

Well, we're in a wood, I don't know what to tell you, PJ says.

Nev throws his phone across the dirt floor. This sucks, he says.

Yes, PJ thinks, yes it does, but then Nev gets up with unusual pur-
posefulness and picks up his phone. Where are you going?

Home, Nev says.

PJ experiences a surge of panic. Wait, he says.

Nev does not wait. He strides off through the trees, holding his phone up and out like it's a lantern and he's deep underground in a pitch-dark tunnel. PJ, seeing the rest of his summer unfolding in a green spiral of loneliness, hurries after him. His feet scream with every step. Wait, he says, you can use my phone. He catches up with him and grabs his arm. Wait, he says. There's a girl.

She lives in one of the unfinished houses on the other side of the forest. Hers is closest to being done, it has a sink, a cooker, a couch. Some of the others don't even have floorboards and there are all cables coming out of the walls. He discovered her quite by accident one day when he was making his way through the undergrowth surrounding the houses and saw his mam's car parked there. That's what got his attention. By the time he'd crept up to the window he'd already remembered that Mam had sold that car, or rather Dad had sold it, which Mam had been upset about. But he'd looked anyway, and seen her.

What, she's living there? Nev says. In the middle of the woods? On her own?

I don't know if she lives there, PJ says. She's only there sometimes.

Doing what?

Nothing. She mostly just sits around reading a magazine or looking at her phone.

Have you seen her naked?

PJ doesn't reply, just blushes.

You *have*?! Nev shouts.

There's no curtains! PJ shouts back defensively.

Nev wags a warning finger. If you're making this up, he says.

The heat is intense now, swaddling them in thick invisible bands as they continue through the woods, while midges hang just over their heads like vindictive mini-rainclouds. Nev huffs and puffs with strain and excitement, and as they reach the edge of the forest, breaks into a run. PJ dreads what will happen if she's not there, though he also to a certain extent dreads what will happen if she is. But there is the car outside the house. Red, a bad-luck colour; he was glad when Dad sold it.

Drawing closer, he finds that Nev, demonstrating a hitherto unsuspected and somewhat disquieting capacity for stealth, has discovered the best vantage point in the undergrowth. The expression on his face is like a kind of religious awe. This is incredible, he murmurs.

The girl is sitting on the couch with a towel wrapped turban-style around her head, a white robe cloaking her body.

She's just had a shower, Nev says huskily.

Yeah, she does that a lot, PJ says.

Incredible, Nev repeats. Then turning to PJ, I can't believe you never told me about her! We could have been here all summer, looking at real-life actual tits, instead of running around some crappy forest like idiots!

Well, we're here now, aren't we, PJ says.

It's pretty selfish of you, Nev says frankly.

PJ bows his head. The fact is that he doesn't feel 100 per cent comfortable with staring at the beautiful girl, but it's a lot easier to sell to his conscience if it's just him on his own. Like if he just happens to glimpse her through the window as he's passing, and she happens to be sitting there in her underwear reading Brazilian *Vogue*, that all seems to him quite innocent. In fact, over time he's sort of come to believe that the girl on some level knows about it and is okay with it and even that they are in an albeit unconventional way friends. Squatting here in the undergrowth while Nev tries to get the zoom function working on his phone seems like a different proposition and in some respects a betrayal of the sacred trust he and the girl have, without her being aware of it, established together.

Wait a second, Nev says, lowering his phone. I *know* her.

She's Elaine's old housekeeper, PJ says.

Elaine Comerford's housekeeper, Nev repeats. What's she doing here?

I think Elaine's dad was building these houses, PJ says. Though that doesn't explain it.

Unless . . . A slow smile spreads over Nev's face. He's keeping her here, he says.

PJ feels a spasm of disquiet in his stomach. Maybe, he says with a shrug.

That's what it is, Nev says. He's keeping her here as his *secret sex slave*. A new thought occurs to him. Holy shit – maybe he'll come over and bang her!

PJ allows that that might be a possibility, although he's never actually seen Big Mike out here, who anyway he's pretty sure is on holiday right now with Elaine and her mam. He's about to add that they've probably got as much as they're going to today spying-wise and they should probably start thinking about moving on when inside, the living-room door opens and a man comes in.

Who the heck is this guy? Nev says in a low voice.

I don't know, PJ says.

He's not Big Mike, Nev says. That's for sure.

No, PJ says. This new guy has the lean, villainous look of a movie terrorist. His hair is jet-black, his eyes blacker still. His chest and arms are bare, and muscular, and covered with tattoos: Death, zombie woman, rolling dice and a spiral design that PJ can't quite— Holy shit.

Holy shit, Nev says. He's going to bang her!

The man has walked over to the girl, he runs the backs of his fingers over her cheek. The girl closes her eyes, leans her head against his hand like a cat.

I never stopped believing, Nev says emotionally. You said we wouldn't see sex in a wood, but I never gave up hope.

Now the man is taking off his trousers. The girl is taking off her robe. The man sits on the couch, his enormous penis pointing at the ceiling. The girl clambers over him.

Yes, it's been quite a day, PJ says. He checks the time, gets up, stretches his arms. Well, probably ought to start heading back.

What? Nev says incredulously. He stares at PJ like he's lost his mind. Maybe PJ *has* lost his mind. It's just that watching people have IRL sex seems several orders of magnitude wronger than just watching someone in a towel looking at their phone – seems, in fact, exactly the kind of crime that gets a kid sent to boarding school. And that guy: PJ doesn't know who he is, but he's willing to bet he would not appreciate being spied on.

You go! Nev says. I'm staying. This is actual sex! This is – let *go*! Because PJ is now tugging his arm – Get off me! he hisses, punching back unseeingly at PJ while directing his gaze to the window, then shouts, Get *OFF*!

Oh shit. Now the man has detached himself from the girl and is squinting out the window. Don't move, PJ whispers to Nev. But he's too late: Nev, with an immense crashing of leaves, has bolted. The man runs to the window, then to the door he came in – PJ turns and sprints into the trees.

Safely back in the Bunker, Nev is capering from foot to foot. That was unbelievable! he exclaims, like a character in a Roald Dahl book. Stupendous! Outstanding! Phenomenal!

Then, abruptly, he switches to anger. Why did you make me leave? he says accusingly.

Me? PJ says. You're the one who yelled out.

I *yelled* because you were making me leave.

Go back if you want, PJ says. Go back and get beaten up by a Nazi. I'm sure if you explain that you just wanted to film him banging his girlfriend he'll be totally cool with it.

Nazi? What are you talking about?

Didn't you see his tattoo?

No, says Nev. What were you looking at the guy for?

He had a Sonnenrad tattoo, PJ says.

That wasn't a Sonnenrad, Nev says. That was just a spiderweb.

I'm pretty sure it was a Sonnenrad, PJ says.

Well, so what, Nev says. It's just a tattoo. It doesn't mean he's a Nazi.

PJ drops this line of argument, and just says that either way, they'll probably be winding up by now. From porn the boys both know that sex tends to come in around the twenty-minute mark. He proposes that they leave it to tomorrow, when the tattooed man will have relaxed his guard again. Nev agrees reluctantly, and says he will bring his dad's camera with the telescopic lens. I'll tell him I'm studying nature, he says. Ha ha!

They walk into town, discussing the sex. Nev thinks that while the guy was totally nailing Elaine's housekeeper he (Nev) would have given it to her doggy-style. PJ feels the guy could have spent more time on foreplay, which women appreciate.

Despite these reservations they are both in high spirits. In fact, it's turning into a great day. For the first time this summer Nev actually seems glad to be with PJ and to hear what he has to say. Plus, PJ gets a free ice cream in Hourihan's newsagent's because the man behind the counter says he is the spits of his uncle Frank who was a great fella for the GAA, God rest him. They go into Dingo's and play pool without having to wait, before moving on to the arcade games which Nev uncharacteristically pays for, and as he sits in his car-shaped booth licking his ice cream and mowing down pedestrians PJ thinks to himself how a couple of hours ago he was all set to run away but now he feels brilliant and you never can tell how life's going to go, and it's in this mood of upswing, again uncharacteristic, that he remembers that they have one of those *Are You Ready to be Rich?* pub quiz games.

Over the years many people have told PJ, often in a dry sardonic tone, that with his love for and enormous collection of facts, he should go on *Are You Ready to be Rich?* In truth, he has had fantasies about being on it and winning it and saving his family like the kid in that film, and although the arcade version doesn't promise the same kind of money as the TV show – in the early rounds it pays out 5c and 10c coins, so you have to do well to even make your money back – the rumour has always been that if you get to the end, the jackpot is huge: maybe even the full million. No one has ever got that far on this machine, but right now PJ is feeling lucky.

Nev agrees, after some persuasion, to lend him the initial €1 to play. A few minutes later he's already on the fourth round. It's like the questions were designed for him. What genus is the common bumblebee? Where might you find a dendrite? Who discovered Baffin Island? He knocks them down one after another, boom, bam, boom. Soon a small gaggle of kids has gathered around him, some trying and failing to keep up by smartphone, some just observing his trivia knowledge in awe. ARE YOU READY FOR YOUR NEXT QUESTION? the presenter asks.

PJ has a quick glance left and right, hits OK. Yes get on with it.

THE NAZI CONCENTRATION CAMP FOR WOMEN WAS IT:

RAVENSBRÜCK BUCHENWALD SOBIBOR FELSENNEST

The kids watching groan but PJ is confident. Felsennest was a HQ obviously so not that. Sobibor wasn't a concentration camp, it was a death camp, though Ethan says all that stuff was faked. It comes down to Buchenwald or Ravensbrück. He feels like he knows this, people talk about it in the Black Dawn forum. They should have kept that one open! I know plenty of bitches who should go there!!! I'd send my ex-girlfriend! That sort of thing but what's it called?

YOU'RE ALMOST OUT OF TIME

Okay screw it RAVENSBRÜCK

The presenter appears doubtful. ARE YOU SURE?

No, it just sounds the most Nazi, they always liked animal names YES

The presenter looks sorrowful. He gazes out at Nev sympathetically like he knows how PJ's life has gone lately, though of course he doesn't, he's just a digital image of a recording made years ago for a company to use in their machines –

IT'S THE RIGHT ANSWER!

Money cascades out of the chute. The kids behind him cheer, Nev asks for his original coin back, the digital image of the long-ago presenter smiles, as if letting them enjoy the moment, and PJ really starts to feel – for the first time in how long? – like things could be turning round. Just in the last hour he's got, first, a free ice cream and now at least €2 in 5c coins! But these are only symptoms, it's more a sense he has inside that after the last couple of shitty years this is the beginning of a new phase, maybe just for him, but maybe for all of them, like maybe things will suddenly come right with the garage too, in a way that no one ever expected, and he sees himself and his family laughing, then he sees himself with Nev and Zargham outside the beautiful housekeeper's house and her smiling and waving, Come inside, and making them smoothies and reading to them from Brazilian *Vogue*, and although this last part seems like a long shot still as the sun gleams through the scuzzed-over windows of the arcade, and the presenter asks, WHAT WAS THE NAME OF CONSERVATIVE PRIME MINISTER TED HEATH'S WIFE? PJ's thinking that maybe just maybe this could end up being the best summer ever when he finds himself detaching from the joystick then rising unaccountably into the air over the purple gum-stained carpet to crash against Pac-Man Battle Royale.

The kids squeal and scatter. From the floor he sees two grimy Nike Airs stomp towards him, then two meaty fists descend to grab him. It's the guy from the house, the guy with the Sonnenrad tattoo, he's been following them all along, waiting for his moment—

But no, it's not him. As PJ's hauled to his feet it's a different face that stares into his, with normal-coloured eyes, a downturned mouth, and two ears so enormous they make the head look like a trophy, like the award given out for Ugliest Caveman. He knows this guy: he was a few years ahead of PJ in school, he got expelled for throwing a compass into a crowded classroom. He lives in one of the council estates behind the park. His name is something Moran – Henry? Hugo? – but everybody always calls him Ears because of his ears; PJ and Zargham have done this on dares, shouted, *Ears!* from around corners or behind a car and then run for it as he came charging after them in a fury. Is that what this is about? Very belated revenge? From over his shoulder he glimpses Nev looking on white-faced. Then he's dragged to his feet and thrown against Aliens: Extermination. You think you're smart? the jug-eared guy yells. You think you can steal from my family?

Steal? When he hears this, PJ feels a sense of – relief is too strong, but it's obvious there's been some sort of mistake, because PJ is many things, a sex-watcher, a sock-hider, a low-lier, but he's never actually stolen anything, and he's ready to explain this as soon as the boy's forearm isn't blocking his throat. Ye're one of them thieving Barneses, aren't you? the boy demands.

Yes, but— Well, no, I mean— PJ begins.

Your da's crooked garage ripped off my ma! You owe my ma a hundred and sixty-three quid!

What? PJ says, mystified. Your ma? But there are no more explanations; instead a fist descends and for a second everything goes black, then another punch sends sparks showering through the blackness. In the distance he hears someone saying, Out! Out! G'wan, away with yis!

And looking up from the floor, which is where he is again apparently, PJ sees the arcade manager waddling over like a nicotine-stained egg on two stumpy little legs, waving his arms, also stumpy, at Ears. None of that fuckery in here, off you go! Go on, fuck off!

But before he goes Ears looks down at PJ on the ground and says, You'd better get me that money or I swear to Jesus I'll batter ye spastic.

Can you see with your eyes like that? Nev says.

I can see, PJ says tightly. It just hurts.

They look like squashed tomatoes, Nev says, then adds, in a tone of admiration, The way he just picked you up and *threw* you! Like you were a Beanie Baby!

They're back in the Bunker, having safely escaped through the fire exit of the arcade. Heat pulses through his eyeballs, heat and shame. He can't help feeling that this is his punishment for spying on the girl.

He's a real psycho, Nev says. I know we say that about a lot of people. But with him it's true, he's a genuine, authentic psycho.

He nods contentedly to himself, brushes a leaf from his sleeve. So what are you going to do?

What do you mean? PJ says.

Are you going to give him the money?

Where am I supposed to get a hundred and sixty-three euros?

Nev shrugs, looks wistfully in the direction of the sex house.

That guy is a liar, PJ says. My dad would never steal from anybody.

He might do it out of desperation, Nev suggests. Because his business is going down the toilet?

He wouldn't, PJ repeats. He doesn't steal.

Nev doesn't say anything.

Anyway, I don't have a hundred and sixty-three euros, PJ says adamantly, as if that settles it.

Okay, Nev says. Though I suppose that means you can't go into town again, unless you want him to batter you spastic.

You can never, ever go into town, as long as you live, he reflects. I suppose that's all right for summer, but what will you do when it's back to school?

He reaches into his mouth and pulls out a bit of herring fillet that's got stuck between his teeth.

Maybe you should run away after all, he says.

He goes home, tells Mam he got the black eyes from borrowing Nev's swimming goggles, shuts himself in his bedroom.

The shoebox under his bed contains the money he has been saving for Black Dawn II. It amounts to €38.33. So I'd need to make a hundred and twenty-four euros sixty-seven cent, he says to himself out loud, trying to make it just sound like a sum instead of something impossible. If Granddad was back, it wouldn't be impossible, of course: €124.67 is nothing to a man like Granddad. PJ once personally saw him spend €25 on a block of French cheese. But he has already spent months wishing for Granddad to come back.

The obvious thing is to tell Dad, because clearly the whole thing's just a mix-up, like Ears's ma must have got the wrong bill or the wrong change or the car needed extra work and the mechanic didn't explain beforehand, that happens all the time. Or else, of course, Ears is making the whole thing up completely. Yes, if he told Dad in the right way – didn't mention the throwing and the threatening, just said something like, *I had a curious exchange today with an acquaintance regarding the pricing structure typically used in automotive repairs* – everything would probably be sorted out in five minutes.

But he does not want to tell Dad.

Because even though he knows Dad would never ever steal from a customer or anybody else, there is still the terrible thought at the back of his mind that he might be wrong. Haven't the last two years been a slow, methodical undoing of everything he ever thought was true? A slow transformation of his father into someone else, someone different? Looked at that way, doesn't the very impossibility of Dad stealing – of Dad being anything other than wise and smart and good – make it inevitable? The last great reversal, the catastrophic final step?

After dinner he gets a message from Cian Conlon asking if it's true Ears is planning to beat PJ with a hammer and livestream it. He hadn't heard about the livestreaming; up till then he'd allowed himself to hope that Ears, having got his feelings out of his system in the arcade, might be content to leave it at that. It's good in a way, he reflects, in that he's totally clear now about where he stands. He lies face down on his bed for a while. But then he sits up. Wallowing won't help. He needs to be *proactive*, come up with a plan. Opening up his phone, he makes a spreadsheet.

TARGET 124.67

MONEY RAISED SO FAR 0

He looks at it a moment, then changes 0 to 0.00 so it looks more like a regular number. Then he goes to his contacts. Hi, Mrs Salehi, is Zargham there?

Who's this now? Zargham's mam says.

Uh, it's PJ?

Does he imagine it or is there a slightly disapproving pause at the other end of the line?

Then she says, Well, hold on there, PJ, and I'll see can I find him.

What's the point your parents giving you a mobile if they never let you use it? he says to Zargham when Zargham comes to the phone.

Why are you calling me so late? Zargham says.

It's eight-thirty, PJ says.

I have to get up early for camp, Zargham says. He doesn't sound extra-pleased to be hearing from PJ. PJ's concerned they're starting off on the wrong foot here. He cuts to the chase. I'm selling my games, he says.

You are? Zargham is surprised. How come?

I'm buying a Switch, PJ says. (One of Granddad's Art of Salesmanship rules: The best way to get money is to seem like you don't need it.)

Really? Zargham says.

Yeah, so I'm getting rid of all my old games, PJ says casually. Thought I'd give you first dibs.

There is a complex, protracted silence at the other end of the line.

So it's not because you owe Ears a hundred and sixty-three euros?

Ha ha, you heard about that? PJ says lightly.

My *mother* heard about it, Zargham says with regret. She heard you were fighting in the street.

That's not what happened, PJ says. It was a simple crossed wire. We've already patched it up. So what do you say? Are you interested?

How much? Zargham says.

Twenty each? PJ says like he hasn't really thought about it.

There's silence on the other end of the line. Zargham is thinking and calculating, and all PJ needs to do is hold his nerve but he hears himself blurt, Okay, ten. FUCK, exactly the wrong thing to do because now Zargham is all, I don't know, I already have a lot of games.

Do you want to look at them at least? PJ says. Come over tomorrow, I can give you a demo.

I'm pretty busy with camp, Zargham says.

Come after camp, PJ says.

Zargham wavers, breath huffing from his nose. Then he says, I don't think my mam wants us to be friends any more.

A little dagger in PJ's heart. Because of the Ears thing?

I don't know. That. Other stuff.

Yes, he knew it. But he pretends it's not a big deal. What if we just happen to run into each other? Then it wouldn't be your fault, right?

I don't know, Zargham says again, sorrowfully.

Okay, no biggie, PJ says. But he is sorrowful too.

He gets a grip, makes some more calls. But the market is difficult. Most of the kids he talks to have heard about his encounter with Ears, which prompts them either to try and drive the prices down even lower, or to steer clear of whatever he's offering altogether, as if his possessions might be cursed, the relics of a dead man. He sells his skateboard that cost €100 for €5, a handheld game console for €3, his beloved *Calvin and Hobbes* collection for 50c. Chump change; it's like being beaten up all over again.

Any luck? Nev texts.

No, he writes back and then, Could u lend me it maybe?

Nev famously got €1,000 for his First Holy Communion and equally famously still has not spent any of it.

I don't think so, Nev says.

Come on dude ur my best friend, he says, which he hadn't thought of till now but it's probably true, which is pretty depressing.

I'd like to, Nev says. I just don't know if I'd get it back. Like, with your family going into liquidation and everything.

You would get it back. I'm going to sell my games.

Please, he says.

. Two ticks appear beside the message to show Nev's received it then turn blue to show he's read it. But a few moments pass before his response comes. **Perhaps we can come to an arrangement**

OK, PJ says, trying to overlook the slight Emperor Palpatine vibe from this.

I cud give u a temporary loan, Nev writes. **TEMPORARY.**

PJ's heart temporarily soars.

But I want something in return

OK what

I want to fuck ur sister

What? PJ exclaims out loud in his room at the phone and then, **Be serious.**

I am serious, Nev says. **I'll give u € all of it but first I want to fuck her**

FFS. Fine go ahead fuck my sister whose stopping u

no u have to get her to fuck me also full sex not just a BJ

how the fuck am I suppost to get her to fuck u

Thats ur problem, Nev says.

And then a moment later, **ok a bj so**

whats wrong with u

whats wrong with YOU oh wait I remember ur family is fuct and ur garage is liquidating and ur dad stole from his customer and ur going to get all ur bones broken

fuck urself, PJ writes.

A tick appears, then another.

But there are no more replies.

Tonight Cass isn't looking at her books, or at her phone. She's just lying on her bed. Her eyes are open but she doesn't seem to notice him come in. He clears his throat and she jumps. Jesus Christ, she says. Why do you keep *appearing* in my room?

I just wanted to talk to you about something.

Has it ever occurred to you that I'm in my room because I *don't want* to talk? she says.

It'll only take a second, he promises.

Cass sighs in exasperation, sits up on the bed. What happened your eyes?

I ran into a tree, PJ says.

Nice job, Cass says. So?

Right, yeah, PJ says miserably. He clears his throat, looks at his shoes. *Have you ever met my friend Nev? With a winning personality and a wide selection of PlayStation games, it's hard to believe this go-getter could possibly be single—*

I was wondering about Elaine's housekeeper, he says instead.

Her housekeeper? Cass says, looking at him sharply.

Yeah, remember that housekeeper she had? They had? I think she was from Brazil or something.

You came in here to ask me about Elaine's housekeeper? Cass says.

Did she go, or . . .?

Yeah, she says shortly. She went.

Hmm, he says, pretending to be thinking about this. There's one other small thing . . .

I can't talk to you with your eyes like that, she says, and lies back down on the pillow.

TOP TEN REASONS CASS IS A BITCH #6: INCAPABLE OF EVER HELPING ANYONE EVER.

As he's leaving, though, she calls out, Wait!

He turns around again. Has Dad ever said anything to you about Uncle Frank? she says.

Uncle Frank? he repeats.

Did you know he was engaged to Mam? she says.

PJ blinks at her. Who was?

Uncle Frank. But then he died and instead Dad married her.

PJ turns this over. It seems like a sensible solution. But there's more.

I was born five months after they got married, she says.

Interesting, PJ says, nodding. *A hundred and twenty-four euros sixty-seven cent*, goes his brain.

Imagine if the person, she says slowly, that you thought you were your whole life wasn't you.

She gazes at him with dark eyes. He senses she's looking for a reaction here, but he's not sure what. You mean . . . sorry, who are we talking about?

Cass rolls her eyes. Never mind, she says.

What, he says. Tell me.

It doesn't matter, she says. She picks up her phone to show the conversation is over.

Again he trudges away, feeling very childish and silly which is frequently how he feels when he's talking to Cass, though he can remember a time when it wasn't like that, when she, in fact, was his best friend, even if he knew that he wasn't hers, and remembering this time, he stops in the doorway and tells it to her straight: Listen, I wouldn't ask but I really need some money, because this guy Ears thinks Dad stole from him and now he's coming after me—

Oh my God, Cass says.

Yeah, he says, it's pretty intense. If you had say fifty euro—

But she is staring at her phone. Elaine's back!

Or twenty, even?

Sorry! She jumps to her feet. Gotta go!

He can't sleep. Every time he closes his eyes he hears someone outside, someone at the window. Eventually he gets out of bed, opens the door, steps out onto the landing. Everything is silent, everything is dark. He remembers how when he was little and got scared he'd go in to Mam and Dad. They seemed so much larger in sleep, bloated out in their bed like great slumbering sea beasts, walruses or whales. You could just tuck yourself in under a fin, and it felt like the world and its monsters had disappeared.

The sperm whale is the world's loudest animal. It speaks in squeaks and clicks, each one louder than a rocket taking off. Just talking to it would shatter your eardrums.

He goes to the bathroom, looks at his small sad face lit up by the white humming light. He thinks of Zargham, Elaine, Cian Conlon, everybody he knows, watching as he is beaten up, and laughing and posting FAGGOT, or thinking how sad, what a sad unlucky boy. And for ever more, there he will be, on the internet, on the ground in his hoody with a hammer falling on him.

Downstairs, Mam's purse is stuffed full of shopping lists and scratched-out lottery scratchcards. After digging around without success, he empties it out on the counter. At last he finds a tattered grey-green €5 note. He picks it up, stands for a long time just holding it, there in the dark kitchen. Then he puts it back, starts cramming the other junk back too, the receipts and parking tickets, until among the loose change he finds something else. It looks like a coin at first, but it's not: it's lighter, and oval-shaped, not round. Printed on it is the image of a woman in robes with her hands spread out and stars coming from her. It is a Miraculous Medal. He has one too. Out of the blue an idea comes to him. He runs upstairs, back to his room, and hunts around in his locker, dislodging comics and a wodge of bloody socks, until he finds a box. Inside the box is an identical medal, this one on a thread. Rose gave it to him, the last time he saw her. Wear it at all times, she said. And when you are in great need, say this prayer three times, it is never known to fail.

Never known to fail! Exactly what he wants! But where is the prayer? He remembers she'd folded the medal in it, printed on a piece of newspaper, he thought he'd put them away together. But it's not there. He turns out the whole locker onto the floor. Old Pokémon cards, a rubber shuriken, attempts to draw Wolverine, unfinished letters to Elaine – no prayer. Fuck! he says, out loud, then apologizes. He racks his brains. Didn't she mention something about a flower? A sacred flower? It's hard to be sure, he can only ever make out 50 per cent tops of what she says.

Aunt Rose is extremely old. He has never understood whose aunt she is exactly. She used to be a fortune teller, Cass told him that. Once, long ago, they went to visit her where she lived, a tiny cottage with a hen-house in the yard and a shed piled with turf, which PJ slid down and burrowed into while Mam and Aunt Rose talked in low voices in the kitchen. Now she is in a nursing home. She has hairs on her lip and she calls Dad Frank and PJ, for some reason, Lar.

But she used to have strange powers, Cass says.

It was in the nursing home she gave him the medal: she pressed it into his hand as they were leaving. Her voice was low and raspy, up close she smelled like cauliflower. For direst need, she said. It's like she knew, he thinks – like she knew all this would happen.

He googles 'sacred flower prayer'. There are 12,000 results. The top one looks pretty authentic to him, though he can't tell if it's the same as the prayer that she gave him.

Putting the medal on over his head, he begins to read: O Most Beautiful Flower of Mount Carmel, Fruitful Vine . . .

It feels weird reading a prayer off his phone, where he has looked at so many unreligious things. He hopes the Virgin Mary knows it's meant for her, that he's not praying to e.g. Candy Crush or Pornhub.

Splendour of Heaven, Blessed Mother of the Son of God, Immaculate Virgin, assist me in my necessity. O Star of the Sea, help me and show me herein you are my mother. O Holy Mary, Mother of God, Queen of Heaven and Earth, I humbly beseech you from the bottom of my heart to succour me in my necessity:

[Insert your personal petition to Our Lady here.]

Okay, here we go. He doesn't think God would be happy with asking for money directly so closing his eyes he whispers into the shadows, Please bring Granddad home.

He opens his eyes again, reads the last part of the prayer. O Mary, conceived without sin, pray for us who have recourse to thee. O Mary, conceived without sin, pray for us who have recourse to thee. O Mary, conceived without sin, pray for us who have recourse to thee.

Holy Mary, I place this prayer in your hands.

Amen.

The instant he finishes the phone vibrates in his palm. Granddad!

HEY DUDE U AWAKE??

No, it's just Ethan. Disappointment floods through him. But the prayer isn't going to work straight away, he chides himself, it's not like a spell. He writes: **Hey yeah**

U WANT A QUICK RACE?

Can't do it I'm supposed to be asleep!!!

THATS COOL, Ethan returns, with a GIF of Pikachu wearing shades rolling along on a skateboard.

PJ smiles, in spite of his disappointment. Of course it's cool, it's always cool with Ethan.

HEY GESS WHAT I ENTERED THE MARMOSET COMPETITION IF WE WIN MY MOM SAYS U CAN STAY

Wow that's awesome

OR EVEN IF WE DONT WIN IF U JUST WANT TO VISIT WE LIVE REALLY NEAR MCDONALDS :)

Thanks dude, PJ says. He thinks, not for the first time, how amazing it would be if Nev was Ethan. **I wish you lived closer,** he says.

ME TOO :)

EVERYTHING OK WITH U? U DIDTNT POST 2DAY

PJ doesn't reply straight off. Usually they keep their chat focused on the game, they don't talk about their home lives. But there's no rule against it, is there? Just because Ethan lives somewhere else doesn't make him any less of a friend. Isn't he in fact *more* of a friend? Than the ones he has here? The ones he supposedly 'knows'?

Oh yeah had some stuff going on

OH NO :(

Yeah. For a moment that's all he says. In the corner of the screen is Ethan's profile pic – goofy smile, tufty hair, straddling his bike on a sun-lit driveway in a Man U jersey which PJ has frequently teased him about. (**It's your only flaw! NO FLAW RED DEVILS 4EVER!!!**)

Then he writes, I have this friend I'm worried about. He's parents are always fighting n he thinx theyre going to get divorced n that he;ll be sent to bording school

:(

Yeah + now this guys looking for money from him too and wants 2 beat him up

WOAH THATS TERRBLE

Right so he's been saying thes ecrazy things like that he wants to run away

IDK what to do

I don't want to betray him or tell his parents but running away thats crazy right?

There is a long, long pause.

At the top of the screen it says *Ethan is typing*. But nothing appears, as if he's writing something but keeps crossing it out before hitting Send. Then:

TAHT DEPENDS

WHERES HE PLANING TO GO???

The woods, PJ says.

DA BUNKER WERE U PLAY??

Yes

Another pause. Then:

THATS THE FIRST PLACE THEYLL LOOK

As soon as he says it PJ knows he's right. It's obvious, only a kid wouldn't have seen it. They will find him straight away and bring him home and then Ears will smash him up more for trying to escape him.

Right, he says. Stupid idea anyway I dont think he ever wud of really done it.

NO NOT STUPID

I RAN AWAY ONCE

WHEN THINGS WERENT SO GOOD @ HOME

Not so good? That comes as a shock, life has always sounded pretty sweet at Ethan's house. But he doesn't ask why, just, Where did you go?

I STAYED WITH A FRIEND

But they found you?

THEYLL ALWAYS FIND U IN THE END

BUT WITH ME THEY WER SO WORRIED THAT WEN THEY DID FIND
ME THEY FORGOT ABIUT ALL THE STUFF THEYD BEEN BOTHERING
ME WITH AND THE STUFF THAT ID BEEN IN TROUBLE ABOUT
TEHY WERE JUST SO HAPPY I WAS BACK

SO IT SOLVED MY PROBLEMS SO EVEN THOUGH I DIDNT ESCAPE I
DIDNT NEED 2

MAYBE THAT WOUD WORK FOR YOUR FRIEND TOO????

PJ's mind is blown. So you don't actually have to run away – not for good. All you need is a safe place to bug out to, and your parents will be so freaked that they'll fix whatever it is that made you do it. No more fighting, no divorce, no more talk about boarding school. No chasing him out of the house, no complaining because he keeps growing. Everybody treating him respectfully, considering his feelings, even Cass. Granddad coming back on a private jet. Elaine running up to him and embracing him, with a sob. *I was so frightened!* Ears, vilified, outcast, his livestream plans in tatters.

BUT HE NEEDS TO GO SOMEWERE THEY WONT FIND HIM FOR A
WHILE

IF THEY FIND HIM STRAIGHT AWAY IT WONT WORK

HE NEEDS THEM TO BE SCARED

How would he do that? PJ asks. Like, my friend.

DOES HE NO SOMEONE WITH A SPARE ROOM SOMEWERE? THATS
THE BEST WAY THE SAFEST

I don't know, PJ says. I'll ask him.

I'll tell him.

Downstairs next morning Mam and Dad are arguing. Letting it go to rack and ruin, Mam is saying. How is it my responsibility? Dad replies. I pay for the upgrade and then I'm on the hook for it the rest of my life? I'm just telling you what people are saying, Mam says. Christ, Dad says.

A few minutes later Dad knocks on his door. How are the eyes? he says. Are you up to giving me a hand with something?

He wants to go and look at the clubhouse and see what needs fixing. Why do you have to go? PJ says.

We've all to do our bit for Tidy Towns, Dad says. Come on.

PJ hates the clubhouse; the one mercy of the flood is that it has been closed ever since and he has not had to go with Dad every Saturday morning to set up for under-10s football training. Because of his asthma, PJ mostly does not play football (also because he is no good), and being dragged along to help has always felt like a punishment, or at least a moral lesson, as if Dad was forcing him to observe from the sidelines all the team spirit and taking-part and general wholesomeness he was missing out on. What made this particularly galling is that Dad didn't play football either when he was a kid. He tries to hide it at training, but he can barely kick a ball. The only reason he trains the under-10s at all is that Uncle Frank had been coach, and when he died Dad took over. So it feels like a betrayal that he acts like he cares about it and wishes PJ were good at it, especially when he has passed on exactly zero of the skills PJ would need.

PJ has often thought how strange it is that once Dad had a brother, that they grew up together in the same house he lives in now. At home he rarely talks about Frank, but sometimes when they're cleaning up after training – taking down the nets, gathering the shin guards – he will start telling PJ stories about him: how amazing he was at football, how everybody liked him, how he scored this goal or that goal, played for this team and that team, and the whole town came out to cheer him on. PJ has never been quite sure what the point of these stories is, but the net result has been to make him hate sports even more, and also hate Uncle Frank. He feels bad about that, seeing as he never even met Frank. He just finds it depressing that this is the most Dad ever says to him any more, and it's stuff that PJ's not even sure he believes himself.

Today the sky is a brilliant cloudless blue and it's hard to imagine there ever having been a flood. From the car window, PJ looks out at the forests and the fields, the bungalows with their dogs and their cobble-lock driveways, their swing sets and satellite dishes, their washing hanging unmoving on the line. They pass Creaghan's Stores with its little army of yellow gas cylinders in the forecourt, and then the brown Bord Fáilte sign for Cantwell House Fishing and Golf, rated number eight on Tripadvisor's list of Midlands Must-sees despite PJ and Zargham spending a whole weekend posting one-star reviews complaining about ghosts (BEWARE) and other supernatural events (HEADLESS GHOUL IN BREAKFAST ROOM HOW IS THIS FOUR STAR???) after the manager had given out to them for walking across the fairway. What would it feel like, looking at all this for the last time? But it *wouldn't* be for the last time, he reminds himself, it would only be temporary – a week, two weeks max, then he'd let himself be 'found', and then he'd be back, only now everything would be better!

A NEW BEGINNING

And not just for him, but the whole family.

WHEN U RUN AWAY IT MAKES UR PARENTS REMEMBER THE THINGS THAT R REALLY IMPORTANT

Cass will stay too maybe and she'll go back to how she used to be, they will all go back to how they used to be.

MAYBE UR FRIEND CAN STAY WITH ME!!!!

Wow really that would be awesome

IF HE'S A REALLY GOOD FRIEND OF YOURS ;)

The clubhouse is in a worse state than Dad expected. The walls are saturated still and the lights won't switch on. Well, that's beyond our skill set, I reckon, Dad says. They get back in the car without having done anything. Let's have a look in the hardware store, he says. He pulls out, whistling to himself.

Dad does not like the Tidy Towns girls. He calls them the Comintern. They are always asking him to clean the petrol stains from the dealership lot.

Going to see your friend today? he says now.

What friend? PJ says.

Whatshisname. Nev.

PJ responds with a meaningful silence, which Dad does not pick up on. I hear you two lads are getting great mileage out of those woods, he says.

Immediately PJ feels a knot form in his stomach. Dad turns to him with a smile. Oh yeah, he says.

Dad turns back to the road. The old shed out there, he says. It was an ice house originally, I believe. Victor thought we could convert it into a cabin or something like that. Wouldn't that be fun? A mountain retreat, right there in the back garden.

Mm-hmm, PJ says. He's worrying about Ears, whether he might meet him in the hardware store. It's unlikely though, right? Unless he's in there buying hammers?

Your uncle Frank and me used to use it as a base, Dad says. Out there night and day, we were. Playing Star Wars and what have you. This was before Frank got serious about the football.

Right, PJ says.

One time, Dad says, we decided we were going to run away.

In the passenger seat PJ freezes. Does he know?

It was your uncle Frank's idea, Dad says. He was the one came up with the plans. I forget now was there some reason for it. Did one or both of us have a grievance, or was it only for the adventure. Anyway, somehow or other your granddad got wind of it. We went out to the shed in the woods in the middle of the night and there he was waiting for us. That was the end of that.

He laughs. Probably no need. I doubt we'd have gone far once we'd our rations eaten. And your uncle was always a homebird.

I was the one wanted to get away, he says.

He is silent for a moment. Trees, buildings, swoop towards the windscreen and at the last second swoop away. He turns again and smiles, to show this is the end of the story. And PJ realizes that he doesn't know, and this isn't a trap. More: looking back at him he sees that he is Dad again – that he is there in his face, in a way that he hasn't been for ages, though PJ couldn't explain how. And he finds all of a sudden he wants more than anything to tell him – all of it, about the secret girl in the unfinished house, about the man with the Nazi tattoo, about Ears in the arcade and the €163. About Ethan and boarding school and his plan to run away and reunite the family. He doesn't just want to tell him – it seems like he can see the two of them after he's told him, both roaring with laughter. Then he, PJ, telling Zargham how it had all been a mix-up, crossed wires. Can you believe I was actually thinking of running away?!

He sees it so clearly that it's like it's already happened. Relief courses warmly through his body as though everything has worked out without him needing to say anything at all. But he will tell him. If the next car that passes is blue then he'll tell him. Okay, once they get over the hill. Okay, as soon as they park. Okay, when they're inside the store.

The Hallowe'en stock is already out. A zombie granny with out-stretching arms, an olden-days phone that screams when you lift the receiver. A doormat that when you step on it lights up and says in a gravelly voice, *Welcome to Your Doom*.

Such tat! Dad says with a laugh. He puts the doormat into their basket. He picks up some bleach for the clubhouse. Then he calls Victor and asks about some bit of equipment Victor had mentioned and the two of them go in search of that. *Tell him now!* PJ urges himself, but as they search up and down the aisles it's Dad telling him how the last time he was here they had a beanie with a built-in LED which would be handy for Mam when she's running come winter and PJ knows this is the moment but he doesn't want to ruin the good mood, though it is being ruined anyway, he's ruining it for himself.

And now they're back in the car heading for home. *TELL HIM TELL HIM TELL HIM*, goes his brain. The unwatered lawns are turning from yellow to brown. They pass the microchip factory, the lake, Crea-ghan's stores again. They meet a garda car coming the other way, Dad gives him a nod, the guard raises a finger from the steering wheel, and there's not much time left and squirming in his seat PJ forces it out: Dad, I have to ask you something.

Yes, PJ, what is it? Dad says.

Well, I know it's crazy but this guy I met in the arcade said . . . PJ begins. Then from the back comes a WHOOP.

The garda car is now following behind them. It must have done a U-turn. Dad puts on the hazards and pulls in to the side of the road.

Well, Ken, Dad says.

Well, Dickie, says the guard. He looks in the window at PJ. Well, youngfella, he says.

Have I a tail light gone or something, Ken?

No, no, nothing like that. The guard has a pasty freckly face like 95 per cent of the people in the town but icicle eyes, like he's a robot peering through a town mask. Didn't mean to alarm you, just when I saw you there something came to me.

Oh ah? Dad says. Very good.

Yes. Do you have a Ryszard Brankowski in there with you in the garage?

Ryszard? Oh we do, yes – that is, we did.

He's not there any more?

No, he's gone, he went.

Any idea where? the guard says.

I'm not sure now, let me think did he say. It's a while ago now, he was only with us a couple of months. Why, is he after getting in trouble?

If you do see him you might let me know, the guard says. He pats the bonnet with the flat of his hand. Good luck now.

All the best now, Ken, Dad says. He starts the engine but waits for the garda car to turn around again behind them and speed away in the opposite direction before pulling back onto the road.

What was that about? PJ says. But Dad doesn't reply. Instead, after only a short distance he draws in to the side of the road again.

Why are we stopping? PJ says.

But again Dad doesn't answer and when PJ turns to look at him his face is death-white. His eyes are as wide as plates, his teeth are gritted, his knuckles on the steering wheel look like they're going to pop through his skin.

Dad? PJ says. Dad? Are you okay? Dad? He shakes his arm but there's no response, it's like he isn't there, he's gone again, totally this time. PJ gets a sick feeling. He looks out at the road in case someone's coming he could flag down but there's no one so he takes out his phone and starts to dial 999 but then he drops the phone and it goes under the seat and as he's bent over looking for it Dad begins to make a noise, a horrible croaking, or a reverse-croaking, like he's trying to suck in breath but he can't and on the road there is still no one, no cars on this road that is always busy, like everyone's deliberately staying away. From somewhere under the seat a voice answers but when he tries to speak PJ realizes he doesn't know what to say. *Hello?* goes the voice. *Hello, are you there? Hello?* It's my dad, PJ gurgles into the empty space. It's my—

When with a sharp intake of breath Dad lifts his head, looks left and looks right, then turns to PJ and says, Might pop into Lidl's first and get some sausage rolls for the lunch, and drives on *like nothing has happened* –

Were you about to ask me something? he says.

Hello hello goes the voice on the phone. PJ retrieves it, hangs up, puts his phone back in his pocket. He looks straight ahead at the road. It's not important, he says.

He makes one last effort at shifting his stuff. He sells his iPod to a kid in Subway who looks like he has literally never had a haircut while the kid's friend listens to Drake on his phone and eats mayonnaise out of the sachet. A boy from the class below him buys a rake of games for a euro then when he actually gets them becomes scared or spooked, insists PJ takes them back, lets him keep the money. A guy Cian Conlon knows promises to buy his drone for €20 then doesn't show up, ghosts him, though he's still on his Twitch channel streaming himself playing League of Legends, so PJ sells it to a dude coming out of the pub for whatever is in his wallet (€5). Rowan messages him out of the blue, says he's interested in looking at PJ's *Yu-Gi-Oh!* collection, but when they meet in the garden in front of the library, he just wants to talk about Cass. PJ tells him she doesn't have a new boyfriend, and that she seems depressed. Rowan is clearly cheered by this, and buys the whole case of cards. Then it's back on his bike to meet the kids finishing camp. A pump-action water shotgun, a slime kit, a mind-reading Poké Ball: everything must go. It's weirdly exhilarating, like jumping out of a plane and freefalling through space. When he comes home he puts the money in his locker under the socks, adjusts the spreadsheet. Then feels his heart sink because it's not enough, not even close.

He tells himself it wouldn't have helped anyway, not in the long run. He might pay off Ears, but it'd still only be a matter of time before the next problem, the next disaster. The trouble is coming from *inside*; from his family. And unless something happens to stop it, it will keep billowing out, worse and worse, like black clouds of oil from a stricken tanker, till everything is coated in it, suffocating from it.

He logs on to the forum. A couple of seconds later the message comes.
HEY STRANGER!

Hey, he writes back. **Remember we were talking the other day about my friend?**

After that everything moves very quickly. Ethan knows exactly what to do. The first thing is to pack his bag and stow it in a safe hiding place, away from the house. That means i) there's no chance of discovery ii) he's ready to leave at any moment. He fills a backpack with money, food, charger, two changes of clothes, and is just about able to squeeze it into the hole under the floor of the Bunker.

Next: covering his tracks.
FROM NOW ON EVERYTHING IN UR ROOM IS A DECOY
Leave a note showing times for the ferry, or flight numbers.

FERRY IS BETTER BECAUSE THERES NO PAPER TRAIL

Write out a list of far-off destinations. That's what they'll find, once you've gone.

THEYLL THINK UR MILES AWAY

Anything that slows down their search will help you.

He confessed last night that there was no 'friend'.

LOL YEAH I FIGURED THAT OUT!!!!! :)

So I can stay with you?

OF COURSE!

But will I need to hide from your parents? Like it'll probably be on the news

LOL MY PARENTS NEVER WATCH THE NEWS THEY'RE SUPER BUSY WITH WORK THEY;;LL JUST BE HAPPY IVE SUM1 TO PLAY WITH

MY MOM HAS MADE COOKIES ILL SAVE SOME FOR YOU!!!! :)

Wow that's amazing, thank you

Ethan is really a great friend, he thinks. In fact he could be his best friend. Like it's weird he could have a best friend he's never actually met but there it is. Just as he's thinking it, the message comes back: NO PROBLEM DUDE

UR MY BEST FRIEND ON THE FORUM

MAYBE MY ACTUAL BEST FRIEND!!!!

Thanks dude, PJ says. You are too.

The last part of the plan. They go through it together. There is a bus to Dublin four times a day. He will wait at a stop outside the town so there's less chance of being seen. Once he gets to the city, Ethan will meet him at the bus station and bring him to his house.

You'll be there, right? PJ is suddenly nervous at the thought of being in Dublin on his own.

LOL DONT WORRY

He gives PJ his number. PJ gives him his.

+ DOWNLOAD THIS

It's an app, a friend-finding app, so if they miss each other Ethan can find him.

Wow that's so pro, PJ says.

ITS ANNOYING IF U PLAN EVERYTHING OUT + THEN IT GOES WRONG BCOS OF SUM LITTLE THING

PJ doesn't see that happening. It seems like they have it all figured out. It's so simple – you'd expect something so momentous to be more complicated, to take longer. He wants it to take longer. But everything is ready to go. Lying in bed that night he gets that running-out-onto-thin-air feeling. Tomorrow yawns beneath him like a chasm.

You don't think it's cowardly? Like, running away from my problems?

YOU'RE RUNNING AWAY TO SOLVE YOUR PROBLEMS + TO HELP YOUR FAMILY!

SEEMS PRETTY BRAVE TO ME!!! :)

BUT ALSO FUN!!! U GET A 2-WEEK HOLIDAY!!! AND WHEN YOU GO BACK EVERYTHING'S BETTER!!!! :)

ANYWAY DOESNT SOUND LIKE U HAVE ANY OTHER CHOICE!!!! :)

Look, PJ, Mam says, there's one of your pals waving at you.

PJ turns and sees Ears, standing on the traffic island, his eyes trained on PJ in the car.

He's waving at you, PJ. Would you ever wave back to him like a decent civilized human being?

And PJ, with a hand that feels weightless, boneless, waves to Ears, who pulls back his jacket to reveal a hammer tucked into his belt. As the car goes by, painfully slowly, he gloats like a gladiator standing over the disembowelled carcass of a vanquished enemy.

I'm just going out for a bit, he tells Mam when they get home.

Mm-hmm, Mam says, wiping the counter.

He hovers in the doorway. I'll be back later, he says.

Very good, she says, and then, when he still hasn't moved, PJ, whether you're coming or going would you ever shut that door! Honestly, I don't know what they teach you in that bloody school.

The sun is bright. He steps outside. From beneath his feet, a voice rises up: *Welcome to your doom.*

Crossing the field towards the woods. Birds fly overhead. Golden light floods the blue sky.

HEY LOOK WAHTS JUST ARRIVED!!!!!

Black Dawn II sitting in blue light in its box on the table. OMG it's out?

WE CAN START IT AS SOON AS U GET HERE!!!!!

Woah perfect timing! I'm on my way!

You look at the picture again. Is that your room?

OH THAT'S KIND OF A JUNK ROOM

THAT'S NOT THE ROOM YOULL BE STAYING IN

THATS JUST WHERE I TOOK THE PICTURE

LET ME KNOW WHEN UR ON THE BUS!!!!

At the edge of the woods he stops. The socks! He has left the bloodstained socks balled up in his locker. If, when they discover he's gone, his parents search the room, they will almost definitely find them, and it will ruin the effect of his disappearance. Who would pine for a kid who secretly hoards bloody, unwashed socks? They might stop wanting him to return!

He looks at his phone. If he goes back to the house now, he probably won't make the 11 o'clock bus. But there's another one at 2 o'clock. He turns around, hurries back. Forgot something, he says to Mam.

Is that right, she says. Is that right. She nods to PJ, points at the phone: she's talking to someone.

On his way to his room, he sees Cass sitting on her bed with a maths book. What, she says.

Nothing, he says. Just saying hi.

Mm-hmm, Cass says.

TOP TEN REASONS CASS IS A BITCH #7: LITERALLY CAN'T EVEN SAY HELLO.

She'll be sorry when he's gone. They'll all be sorry.

That makes him think of something. Did you say Elaine is back?

Cass lets out an exasperated sound.

Do something for me, will you? Tell her Max Winter says hello.

You are such a psycho, she says, looking at her maths book.

In his room he looks one last time at the books and the toys, at the posters of Skulduggery Pleasant and Fish of Iceland. Goodbye, *Beinhákarl* (basking shark), goodbye *Marsíli* (lesser sand-eel). The fish look back at him indifferently. Everything is indifferent, everything feels thin and flat, when he wants it to be charged, emotional! It's as if, to the room, he's already gone; like it's a level he's completed and will never come back to. Embarrassed, he opens the locker, takes out the socks, puts them in a pillowcase. When he returns, he tells himself, they will buy him as many socks as he wants. But he doesn't believe it: the future too feels thin, flat, a fish eyeing him glassily from an Arctic sea.

Something is shining on the carpet. It's the Miraculous Medal, he must have dislodged it with the socks. He picks it up, for a moment grasps it in his fist. He can't remember the prayer. He just says silently: *Please.*

Downstairs, he's on his way out the door when Mam calls out, Hey, mister. That you?

PJ freezes, the pillowcase of socks dangling from his hand.

Come back here a second, please.

What was he thinking? How did he think she wouldn't notice? He trudges back over to her, and now the future is absolutely visible, it parades itself before him, scene by unbearable scene – sock discovery/ Mam's horror, plan ruined, PJ grounded, Ears arriving to confront him, boarding school, etc., etc.

That was Marita Scanlon on the phone, she says. This name means nothing to PJ, but he tries to look receptive, while slowly moving the pillowcase behind his back.

She's on the board of the Lions Club, Mam says. Their annual dinner was supposed to be this Thursday, with Paddy Wall the guest of honour. But Paddy Wall's after falling off a ladder and he's going to be laid up in bed for the next three months. So guess who they're going to have instead?

PJ doesn't have a clue what any of this means, but there's a twitchy, gleeful energy about her. If it was anybody else, you would say they were trying not to laugh. Who? he says.

Maurice! Mam exclaims. They're bringing Maurice back from Portugal to be guest of honour!

Granddad's coming back!

Isn't that great news? I asked Marita would he come because it's such short notice and he's fierce busy with the golf club over there as we know and she said yes, he's a game the next day but he told her he'd be able to fly in for Thursday and fly back the next morning.

Granddad's coming back, he repeats, in a daze.

The man himself, she says. I'd better tell your father, she says, and dances off to the breakfast bar.

Granddad is coming! Holy shit!

Back in his room, first thing he does is pull out his medal and kiss it. Thanks, God! Thanks, Our Lady the Sacred Flower, for asking God! And thanks, Aunt Rose, most of all. Wow, she wasn't blowing smoke about that prayer. He feels bad for the guy who got knocked off his ladder and starts saying a get-well-soon prayer for him but halfway through he gives up, he's too excited. Granddad is coming! The day after tomorrow! In his imagination he's at the door right now, arms loaded with presents! He will give Dad money – Dad will fix whatever is wrong with the garage – Mam will get her proper moisturizer and stop being angry about her complexion – Cass will go to college – PJ will pay off Ears and not get his bones broken – everyone will be happy and there will be no more talk of divorce or boarding school and everything will be all right again from now on for ever! Hurrah hurrah!

*

Ethan's the first person he tells.

    AMAZING!

    I know, I was just about to get on the bus!

    ???

    WHAT ABOUT PLAN?

    Well that's just it, I don't need to run away now!

    U DONT??

    R U SURE UR GRANDDAD WILL GIVE U THE $$$ U NEED?

    Pretty sure. I mean, he's pretty rich.

    AWESUM!!!!

    So funny I was literally 30 seconds from leaving.

    LOL WELL IF IT DOESNT WORK OUT U HAV A BACKUP PLAN

    RIGHT??? :)

    Thanks dude 4 everyting

    DONT MENTION IT BROS 4EVER

Isn't it fantastic? he says to Cass.

She's at her mirror putting on make-up. Ever heard of knocking? she says.

Yes, right, sorry, he says. It's cool though, isn't it?

Oh yeah, the Lions Club dinner, sitting in a hotel room with two hundred old people, *cool*, she says.

TOP TEN REASONS ah screw it who cares, he's in too good a mood for Cass to ruin it.

Mam has gone on a cleaning blitz. She's like a whirlwind, tearing up and down the whole house. It's a good thing his money and bugout stuff are hidden in the Bunker because she does his room too and yells at him when she finds a yoghurt he'd forgotten about.

What are you cleaning in here for? PJ says. It's not like Granddad's going to be coming into his room. But Mam just gives him a Medusa look. Then she hands him a scrubbing brush. Bathroom, she says.

The next morning as soon as they're finished breakfast she packs him and Cass into the car. They are going to Dublin to get new outfits for the Lions Club dinner.

I thought we didn't have any money, Cass says.

Stop asking questions, Cass, I've enough on my plate, Mam says.

It's not a question, it's a sentence.

CASSANDRA BARNES! Mam exclaims, then in a lower voice she says, I will tell you this once and once only. There's a lot riding on this dinner. It's very important we make the right impres—

Look out! Cass wails. Mam has been driving blind while turned to lecture her and now a truck blares and swerves and she gets out of the way just in time, honking her own horn and yelling, Ah beep yourself, Ollie McGettigan, bad cess to you, you old pervert, go back to staring at little girls' arses at the Feis Ceoil.

Mam always has a stream of insults ready to go at all times, it's something he's always admired about her.

Granddad has money though, doesn't he, Mam? PJ says, just to make sure he's not backing the wrong horse.

Maurice has money, she says. And he'll want to help us *if* we look like we've been making a go of it and this whole palaver isn't our fault. So we need to dress the part.

The best way to get money is to look like you don't need it, PJ says.

Exactly, Mam says.

Why isn't Dad coming? Cass says. Doesn't he need to look the part?

Don't talk to me about that man, Mam says.

I think he's doing something with Victor, PJ says. Future-proofing.

Future-proofing, Mam says. Victor-proofing, that's what we need in this house.

Dad wasn't as excited about the news as PJ thought he might be. When Mam told him at dinner, for ages he just kept chewing his lettuce, like he was going to chew it for ever. Then he said something like, That's grand, so, though it might have been, That's that, so.

PJ felt a bit sorry for him, because obviously it's going to be awkward with Granddad coming over and seeing everything he's done wrong with the business. At the same time he could understand why Mam was angry when Dad went out to meet Victor instead of helping with the clean-up.

He said they were going to do something in the woods, he tells Mam. They had to seal something or something? Mam shakes her head. It's well for them, she says, standing around jawing about the end of the world while everyone else is frantic trying to dig themselves out of the hole they're in right now.

The pair of them, she says. Doom and Doomer.

They get on the motorway and before long the local radio begins to crackle and then the voices disappear and Mam switches to RTÉ.

The big blue motorway sign flashes up DUBLIN and PJ starts to get excited. He sends Ethan a message: Guess where I'm going!

And then when there is no response: Dublin!

W/my mam, he goes on, but maybe I can sneak off for a while? We can check out that game shop?

Though he knows she probably won't let him meet up or sneak off. Anyway, Ethan doesn't reply.

Cass, who has been quiet, bent over her phone, lets out a little gasp. Elaine says her dad's taking her to Dublin tomorrow to look at apartments, she tells Mam.

Is that right, Mam says.

She wants to know can I go?

She looks at Mam hopefully. Mam looks back at her, then at the road and then at Cass again like she can't believe Cass is asking. How would you go to Dublin tomorrow? Isn't that the day of the dinner?

But can't I go anyway? Like if we went in—

NO, Mam says.

No, but if we went in the morning we'd be back in time for—

Cass! No! I said, No!

You're not even listening to me! We're only going to look at a couple of places—

Cass, what am I after telling you? We're going to the dinner! It's a very special occasion for our family and we need to be organized for this.

But why do I even have to go to—

But but but, Mam cuts in, why can't you just go with Elaine on a different day? You can go any time! You could have gone today, aren't you going to be in Dublin in half an hour?

Because tomorrow's the only day her dad is free and he needs to pay the deposit.

Oh of course, lest we forget, the whole world revolves around Big Mike and his schedule – no, Cass, you heard me! She raises her voice over Cass's protests. I won't tell you again! Elaine can take pictures, can't she, and send them to you, it's the twenty-first century, let you figure it out between you.

Cass starts to cry. You hate me, don't you, she sobs. Just admit it, you hate me.

Oh merciful hour, Mam says.

You hate me, because you think I'm going to have the life you never had and you can't stand it.

The car's engine lets out a high-pitched roar. Careful, Mam says in a low voice, and PJ in the back seat shivers, because Mam never talks in a low voice. Careful what you say, miss.

And Cass doesn't argue any further, just bows her head and swipes at her phone.

Lookit, girl, Mam says after a few miles. I don't know what your father's told you. But if your granddad doesn't come through for us, there'll be no college and no apartments. You'll be spending next year scrubbing toilets in Supermac's, do you hear me?

Cass nods.

Good, Mam says.

PJ is confused. He heard Cass tell Rowan she didn't think she'd even get into college, so why is she making a fuss about an apartment she'll never live in? But nothing is ever 100 per cent clear with Cass. Maybe she just wants to be with Elaine while she still can, he thinks, and he slips into a fantasy where he and Elaine are viewing apartments together. Let's get one with a hot tub, baby, she croons in his ear. He doesn't say anything. He's still wearing the mirror sunglasses.

It's a couple of years since Mam came to Dublin on a shopping trip. But as soon as she steps into Arnotts you can actually see her powers returning. She walks taller, speaks louder. Random men do double-takes over the aisles, a make-up girl asks her if she's interested in modelling. She pays no attention, she is 100 per cent focused on shopping. It's just like in a movie where the hero's been living in a cabin in the mountains and then they come out of retirement for one last job and they're still amazing at safecracking or ninjutsu or flying a dragon or whatever it is: she can scan a whole wall of clothes in a minute, then strike and pluck out the one perfect thing, like she's spearing a fish. A dress, a cardigan, tights for Cass; a shirt, a jumper and trousers for PJ.

Shoes too while we're here, maybe, she says.

That's when PJ panics. What's wrong with these ones? he says. I haven't had them long.

They're not formal, she says. I've said it before and I'll say it again. If there's one thing people will judge you on, it's your shoes.

He has no choice. They go together to the shoe section. Mam picks out a pair. Those look fine, he says. I don't need to try them on. Sit, Mam says. The assistant takes one shoe off.

Mam and the assistant look at PJ's foot.

My God, Mam says.

After a moment the assistant forces a laugh. Think you might have outgrown these ones! he says.

But Mam is not laughing. She is kneeling down with PJ's heel in the palm of her hand. She looks up at him with a kind of sorrowful wonderment. These shoes are much too small for you, she says.

PJ nods slowly, dumbly, like he hadn't noticed till now.

Why didn't you tell me? Do they not hurt?

Not really, he says.

Your foot is bleeding, she says. It's bleeding.

It's not actually that sore, he says. I mean, I know it looks bad, but . . .
He trails off.

Mam starts to say something then stops. Her eyes linger on his. For a
moment she looks so sad.

And PJ hangs his head, feels his face turn red. It isn't important, he says.
But she is still holding his foot and looking up at him, and now his own eyes
well up, because it's like she really had been away living in the mountains
but now she's here beside him again with all of the love from years ago
flooding back like the dragon trainer's powers. And it is too much, too much.

The assistant comes back with an expression like, Please be normal.

We'll take these too, Mam says.

At the till she watches the card in the reader as if she thinks it might
explode. Her fingers dig into his shoulder, both of them ready to turn
and run.

Well, she says as they get back into the car. As my aunt Rose used say,
if it doesn't pan out, we'll be the best-dressed lags in the workhouse.

By that evening the house is transformed. The smell of drains is finally
gone. There are flowers in the vases, there's fruit in the bowl. Every
surface sparkles. PJ's got to admit it's pretty impressive. And they are
transformed too, stiff and scrubbed in their new clothes.

There was no need to go to all that trouble, Dad says. He said he
didn't want a big fuss.

That's what he *said*, Mam says. Your own father, have you no clue at
all how his mind works?

At night in his room he looks at his spreadsheet: €50, that's what he still
needs, €50 exactly. A few days ago it seemed an astronomical figure,
impossible. Now it's just a case of asking Granddad the right way.

But what if he doesn't come? He lies awake, imagining all kinds of things that might go wrong. A bomb in Portugal, fires raging through the country, Granddad's plane dropping out of the sky, exploding on the runway. A stranger coughing on him, passing on some fatal germ. Granddad in his bedroom, sound asleep and oblivious to the cloud gathering in his bedroom mirror, Death getting ready to stretch his claws through the glass and pull him away.

In the middle of the night his phone pings. He has a message.

U KNOW WHAT UR PROBLEM IS PJ

UR A DIRTY LYING JEW

U RAT I HOPE U GET FLAYD LYING JEW FUCK

U THIK UR SMARTER THEN ME I KNOW WERE U R

I WILL FIND U I WILL TAKE U CHAIN U UP DISSEMBOWEL U

I WILL EAT UR ENTRAILS RAPE UR SOUL U WILL BEG TO DIE

On it goes like that, for pages and pages.

Then in the morning he can't find the medal. He turns the room upside down, it isn't anywhere. Could Mam have thrown it out on her blitz? She wouldn't throw out something holy, would she?

But if she did? What happens if you throw out something holy? What happens to the prayer?

He goes downstairs to ask her if she's seen it, but she's in the middle of an argument with Dad.

Granddad has sent Dad a message to say he won't be staying with them after all. Instead he has a room at Burke's hotel where the dinner is being held.

And he only tells us now? Mam says. After me running myself ragged cleaning the place?

The Lions Club booked it, Dad says. They only told him now.

Mam presses her lips together. He's onto us, she says. He's keeping his distance. She picks up a rag and starts polishing the already-sparkling counter again. Oh, he's a sly fox that one, she says. He's not going to let himself be caught up in our shite.

We're still going to see him, right? PJ says, trying not to sound worried. Like – aren't we?

Of course, Dad says. He'll come out here to us before the dinner then we'll all go in together.

He's managed to turn a blind eye this long, Mam says, scrubbing. You watch, he'll have his dinner eaten and be turned tail back to Portugal before anyone can lay a finger on him. I can't say I blame him. She looks up, then jumps back from the counter with a shriek. What in the name of God?

Victor is standing at the window, looking in at them.

Mam turns to Dad accusingly. Now? Today? Are you joking me?

We just need to finish up on a few small jobs, Dad says.

PJ can actually hear Mam grind her teeth. When Dad has left the room to join Victor, she says, It's no bloody secret why we're going out of business, is it.

It is not a good day for being unobtrusive. Wherever he goes in the house, Mam is somehow there before him. She tells him to make himself useful, gives him tasks and then is unhappy with the way that he does them. When there are no tasks left to do, she tells him to try on his new clothes so she can see what he looks like. By the time he gets changed, Mam has moved on to a fresh crisis. A cake! They have no cake for Granddad. There should be cake, and there is none.

Aren't we going for dinner? PJ says. Won't he get cake there?

We have to have something to offer him when he comes out here, Mam says. Jesus, Mary and Joseph, we can't just give him a couple of Jacob's Cream Crackers! Her face is red, she pulls at her hair and exclaims, Am I the only one in this house who understands what's going on here?

He volunteers to go into town and buy a cake.

It's good to get out of the house. The day is hot and still but the air streams through the vents in his helmet and roars in his ears. He locks his bike in the main square and walks down towards the supermarket. Granddad will be here in a couple of hours, he tells himself. It's all going to work out. Mam thinks it won't, but that's what Mam always thinks. Your stomach thinks it won't, but stomach cells are replaced every two days, so by the weekend you'll have a whole new stomach. As he waits in line with the cake he visualizes a successful outcome in which Granddad hands him €50 and then he himself hands Ears €163. He's so busy visualizing that returning to the square he forgets to take the long way round and as he walks past the arcade two hands seize his shoulders and he's dragged down an alleyway and thrown to the ground behind a skip. Cake? Ears is really angry. You're buying fucking cake?

It's not for me! PJ cries.

Shut the fuck up! Ears kicks him in the balls. PJ squeals, writhes around on the damp concrete. Do you think I'm messing around?! I told you to get me my fucking money!

PJ tries to explain that he's actually about to get Ears's money, but he can't speak, and anyway Ears is not listening. They're in a yard behind one of the pubs, it looks like. There are kegs stacked by a door and steam is coming out of a vent. Ears has gone to the back wall where a couple of steel barriers have been left from last match day. He picks one up and lifts it over his head.

Where's my fucking money? he shouts with the barrier ready to throw it down on top of PJ who squeaks, I have it! I have it!

Then where is it?

PJ shrinks himself up. It's at home, he says. And then, in the interests of honesty, I just need to get another fifty euros.

KLANNNGG! The barrier crashes down mostly on the ground but somewhat on his head. Please! he says. I'll get it! I'll get it!

Ears kneels down. He is kneeling on PJ's head. You had your chance, he says.

PJ's head feels like it is about to crack open. I'll get it, he whispers. Something is pouring out of his nose. My granddad's coming, I'll get it.

Ears grabs PJ's ear, twists it around, drags him to his feet. Look, he says.

He is holding out his phone. On the screen is PJ's kitchen seen from outside. It is night-time. PJ is in the kitchen at the breakfast bar talking to Mam. The camera zooms in on PJ's face then it moves from the window to the person with the camera's other hand which is holding a hammer.

Today, he says.

Where were you? Mam demands when he gets home. He's going to be here any minute! She steps back, looks him up and down. My God, what happened to you?

Oh, PJ says. Yeah, I fell off my bike.

Your new trousers, PJ! That you haven't even had a week!

I know, yeah, sorry.

Mam stares at him with a mixture of frustration and despair, like a painter at an unsalvageable artwork. There's no time to wash them, she says. You'd better go upstairs and change.

In her room Cass, still in her pyjamas, stares into the mirror as if gazing into a lake of sadness.

PJ continues to his own room, takes off the muddy trousers. His head pounds where Ears kneeled on him, where the barrier fell. But thankfully nothing left a mark. He smiles into the mirror. Hey, Granddad, would you like to support me in a sponsored run for a new school roof? It's ten kilometres, people are mostly giving five euro per kilometre.

He looks like he needs a blood transfusion and a heart transplant. So much for the best way to get money is to look like you don't need it. He stretches out his glassy smile. Sponsored run. School roof. Ten kilometres. Whenever he closes his eyes, he sees fires, explosions, the air unravelling. He takes a deep breath, beats them back.

You can do this, he tells himself. You're going to get through this.

The sound of a car. Oh Jesus – he's here! Mam shrieks from the hall. Fuck.

*

He comes downstairs as the taxi is crunching up the drive. Mam has already rushed outside. And now here is Granddad climbing out of the car, silver hair gleaming in the light, shopping bags hanging from his arm like candy-canes from a tree. Straight away PJ's heart gladdens. How silly it was to think anything could stop Granddad coming! Just one look at him and he knows that his plan will work because this is a man who can fix everything.

Granddad's here! he calls, not to anyone in particular, just out of joy.

Granddad comes inside and stands in the hall, looking up and around. Place looks well, he says. Seems more spacious than I remember.

Mam blushes because probably the reason for that is she has sold a lot of the furniture but Granddad has already moved on. There's the boy! he exclaims. PJ smiles but hangs back, suddenly feeling shy. Well, Granddad says. Come here till I have a look at you. He puts his hands on his hips and stares hard at PJ. His eyes are the same blue-white as the bars of the Insectocutor and when you look into them you get a ZAP like a tiny part of you has been annihilated. But then he'll smile and that little piece is resurrected again all in a moment. When he smiles you can see his gold tooth. He used to tell PJ it was the seed he was grown from. PJ would reach into his mouth and try to tug it out. These days instead of a seed Granddad likes to say it's in case he forgets his bus fare and everyone laughs because they all know that Granddad would never take the bus. But it still makes him feel like Granddad's made of different stuff to the rest of them.

How's my boy, he says. You look more and more like your uncle Frank, do you know that?

Yeah, people are always telling me, PJ says.

Granddad looks pleased at this. How's your game coming along? Where do you play? Your uncle was a forward. And a kicker! My God, that boy could kick.

PJ blushes. I'm not that good.

Granddad musses his hair. Well, I'll tell you his secret. It's the secret of anybody who's successful. He used practise day and night. Every spare moment he'd be out there kicking the ball against the wall. He'd have your poor grandmother driven demented, God rest her.

He rises to his feet. And where's my girleen?

Cass appears at the top of the stairs in her new dress. It is long and tragical and she comes slowly down the steps like she's wading into the sea.

Hasn't she grown! Granddad says. Look at you, he says.

I'm the same height as the last time you saw me, Cass says. I've been the same height since I was thirteen.

It's not the height, it's the face. Granddad reaches out and grips her chin between thumb and forefinger and studies her. Yes, he says. You're a woman now, he says. Have you been breaking the boys' hearts? I bet you have.

No, says Cass, her cheeks going bright pink.

What about Rowan? Mam says.

Oho! Rowan, is it, Granddad says.

She's growing up all right, Mam says. It's only a couple of months now and she'll be off to college.

I haven't even got in yet, Cass mumbles.

You will get in, Mam says. Yes, we're very proud of her, she says to Granddad.

Rightly so, Granddad says. She'll be the first member of this family to graduate from college. Of course your father had a stab at it, he says to Cass, but it didn't pan out. On his very first day in the big city the poor fellow stepped out of the college gate directly into the traffic and got himself mowed down by a bus.

His gold tooth, his blue eyes, his silver hair all twinkle together as he tells this story, which they have heard many times. I shouldn't laugh, he says, composing himself. He was in a desperate state. Back home for months. So, he says to Cass, it'll be up to you to right the old wrongs.

He bends down, and picks up the shopping bags pooled at his feet. Now, he says. Gifts!

Oh, you're an awful man, Mam says, as he hands one to her.

It's just a few small bits, he says.

Inside the bag is a tiny box. Opening it, Mam gasps. Oh Maurice, it's breathtaking! God, it must have cost an absolute fortune.

That's the trouble with buying a gift for a beautiful woman, Granddad says. It must be exquisite too, or next to her it will look dowdy. For you too, miss, he says, presenting Cass with an identical bag.

You're a rogue, Mam says. She looks at herself in the mirror with the necklace pressed to her throat.

And for you, young man, he turns to PJ. Don't worry, it's not jewellery.

Thanks, PJ says, as Granddad presses another shopping bag into his hand.

A little bird told me you might like this, he says. Is it the right one?

PJ peeps into the bag. Can't stop the goofy look from crossing his face.

Ha! It's the right one, Granddad says and musses his hair. Then he pauses, narrows his eyes. Did you hit your head? You've the makings of a bruise.

He fell off his bike, Mam says.

Is he all right? Granddad says. You always need to watch out for concussion. Any headaches? Nausea?

He's grand, Mam says. He's excited about seeing you, that's all.

Granddad squints at him. Are you grand? PJ nods. Granddad watches him a moment, then rises to his feet. Now, where is that scapegrace calls himself my son?

Oh, he's out in the yard somewhere with Victor, Mam says. They're installing something or updating something, I don't ask.

Granddad tilts his head. Victor McHugh? You've let him back in, have you?

Well, I'll tell you, Maurice, it's like rats that man, once they get in at all you'll never be rid of them. Here, I'll take you out to him.

No need, no need, Granddad says, patting her hand, I'll dig him out myself.

He exits through the patio door and Mam looks after him as he crosses the yard, dreamily kneading the hand he has just held. PJ looks after him too. Is this the moment? It seems like he's in a good mood. But just as he's about to set off Mam spins around on the two of them. Well! she barks. What kind of a performance was that, might I ask?

Cass doesn't say anything. As she stands there with her gift in her hand she looks like she is now fully underwater, her eyes vacant, her hair floating in a hundred different directions.

It's bad enough your father doesn't see fit to show himself. What's all this mealy-mouthed business of I haven't got into college? You're sulking because you couldn't go to Dublin with Elaine, is that it? You're getting your own back?

I haven't got my results, Cass murmurs.

You'll get in, Mam says, and now it's she who has the bug-zapper eyes. I'll tell you this, miss – you'd *better* get in. It's hard enough to hold my head up in this town as it is. And as for you – now it's PJ's turn – what's the matter with you all of a sudden?

Nothing, PJ says. I'm fine.

Good, Mam says. Because you're going to this bloody dinner if I have to carry you in on a stretcher, do you hear me? You can wait and die till after it's finished. She steps back, her hands on her hips. Listen, lads . . . She tails off, hangs her head. She looks like the music teacher at school right before she had to go on a career break. Then from behind her comes the sound of laughter.

Granddad reappears with Dad in tow. Both of them are laughing. Beside his father Dad looks younger, boyish, a freshness about his mouth and a wideness to his brow.

I found him out in the woods, Granddad says. Building himself a fort!

Well, I'm here now, Dad says, and then to Mam, Can we offer the man a drink itself?

Where are my manners at all, she says.

No need, no need, Granddad says, and then, Scotch. A single malt if you have it.

Yes, he says. This is a real treat. To be back and see you all again. Shame I have to go to this bloody old dinner.

It's a great honour, Mam says, handing him a glass. For the whole family.

Don't feel under any obligation, Granddad says. There's no need for you all to be dragged along. It'll just be a load of old geezers like myself making speeches.

We wouldn't miss it for the world, Mam says. Isn't it a celebration of everything you've achieved?

Aye, Granddad says with a chuckle. Better do it quick so, while there's still any of it left. Isn't that right, Dickie? He claps Dad on the back, raises his glass. Cheers!

From his bedroom PJ listens to the hilarity below. He can't remember the last time he heard Mam and Dad laugh. Now there's no stopping them. It's like they've saved up their entire annual store for today.

He takes off his new jumper, new shirt, new shoes, old trousers, pulls on his school PE kit.

What are you doing? Cass is in the doorway. We're going for dinner in like twenty minutes.

Oh yeah, he says.

She looks at him and then when he doesn't say anything else she rolls her eyes. I feel like I'm living in an insane asylum, she says.

PJ laces up his new shoes. Goes to check himself in the mirror. Puts on a hearty laughing smile like Uncle Frank has in the photograph. He takes a deep breath, heads out to the stairs.

New strategy. This one's much better than the roof idea, because it's personal. Still, the next moments are crucial. He waits on the landing till he hears the dining-room door open, Granddad humming as he walks down the hall. That's his cue to go bounding down the stairs, football under his arm—

Whoops!

Whoa, sorry, Granddad.

No harm done, he laughs. Where you off to? You know we're leaving for dinner shortly.

PJ nods. Yeah, I thought I might practise my kicks for a few minutes before we go, he says.

You know, like Uncle Frank did, he adds.

Good man, good man, Granddad says. He turns for the toilet. *Come back!* shrieks PJ's heart, while his head goes, *You idiot, you should have stuck with the roof plan!* What kind of boots did he use? he blurts.

Boots? Granddad says. He pauses in the hall, then turns around and looks at PJ's feet.

You're not wearing those, are you?

Hmm? says PJ, looking down at his new shoes.

Have you no proper boots?

PJ looks sorrowful. Well, no. See, my feet have had a growth spurt and the old boots don't fit.

Granddad scratches his magnificent silver head. Well, you can't kick with those.

They have boots for sale in Elverys? PJ says. They're marked down to fifty euro but the sale ends today so if you happened to have fifty euros cash I could go and get them before we go in for dinner.

Or that's what he means to say but it all comes out in a jumble, and right in the middle of it Mam appears and starts yelling, PJ, what in God's name are you doing in that get-up? We're going out in fifteen minutes!

I just want to go and practise my kicks, he says in a low voice.

Your what? Mam looks blank.

We're discussing a new pair of boots, Granddad explains.

Oh, those bloody feet of his, you'd need a bank loan to keep up with them, Mam says. Go back upstairs you and get changed and stop bothering your granddad.

She hurries off to put on her make-up. Granddad chuckles.

Your uncle Frank was always looking to me for a digout too, he says. He takes out his wallet. P J's heart thuds. At last, at last, this nightmare will finally be over—

However, I don't actually carry cash much any more, Granddad says. Wait what—

I find it bulky and inconvenient, Granddad says. I mostly use the card.

P J stares at him in horror.

However, after dinner, you and I will take a little trip into Elverys, and we'll find the best boots they have, Granddad says. Will that do you? He twinkles down at him like God, infinitely able to do everything except understand what you need from him. P J nods, tries to smile though he feels like his skull has pre-emptively turned to ice and is about to fall through his—

Oh wait, there's a fifty, Granddad says. He takes a note from the wallet and puts it into P J's hand.

P J, for the love of God! Mam on her way back.

Yes, Mam, P J says, and this time the smile is real.

Back in his room he starts stripping off the jersey and putting on the new clothes, but he's so happy! He's so happy that he can't resist taking his phone out from the locker where it's hidden and switching it on and taking a photo of the cover of the game with the Statue of Liberty wearing a swastika and sending it to Nev.

Look what my granddad brought!

Nev gets the message but doesn't reply. P J pictures him in his room, scowling, jealous, and takes a moment to exult before sending the same photo to Zargham.

Check it out!!! Black Dawn II!!!

Woah! Zargham says.

Want to come over and play it later?

Im busy later, Zargham writes back.

But then right after: **OK maybe**

Kids! Dad calls from downstairs. P J throws on his weird new clothes, keeping the €50 note bunched in his hand the whole time, then runs downstairs and is all set to get into the car when he realizes – just in time! – that the rest of the money is still hidden in his rucksack out in the Bunker. He can sneak out during the dinner and pay Ears off. Back in a second, he shouts over his shoulder. Dad makes some sort of sound of protest or mystification but PJ's already gone through the garden into the field.

It's a beautiful day, the sunlight so strong that even when he enters the woods it's almost blinding. In the far distance he hears Dad calling him again, he shouts back something meaningless, hurries on. It's hard to run in the new shoes, but already his feet hurt less. He takes the left fork at the fallen oak, skids down the slope into the gully and out again. He is not worried about the tattooed man, Nev says he staked out the house for three days and there is no one there. See, everything is working out, everything is going back to normal.

HEY DUDE DID U GET A BUNCH OF WIERD MESSEGES FROM ME YESTERDAY

He passes the log where he saw the red squirrel. In his head he's at the hotel, handing Ears his €163, bringing this whole sorry saga to an end. *That everything?* he says with a touch of haughtiness. *Yeah*, Ears says, then grudgingly, *Thanks*.

HEY MI PHONE SENT OUT A BUNCH OF MESSEGES SORRY IF U GOT SUM

And PJ walks away unbeaten unlivestreamed back to the dinner which is a success. What a lovely time they have! Everyone is so happy. Why did we ever fight or worry? Dad says. Just because of money? Money? Granddad repeats. I have loads of money! You can have as much as you want! But one condition – you can't get divorced! Mam and Dad look at each other and burst out laughing. Did you seriously think we'd get . . .? and then the same conversation over again only this time it's, Boarding school? Did you seriously think we'd send you to . . .?

SUM1 HACKED INTO MY ACCOUNT SUM WIERD NAZI SICKO

And next thing you know everyone wants to buy cars again and Dad's chasing him and Cass laughing through the woods like when they were little then Cass goes to college in Dublin but frequently returns to see them then PJ goes to college too and studies AI + robotics, lives with Cass has a lab in the attic

I ASKED MY DAD 2 FIND OUT WOT HAPPENED!

That is a brilliant invention Elaine coos at his shoulder as he works with his lab coat on. Stand back it's highly dangerous he tells her

SORRY DUDE I HOPE EVRYTINGS OK WIT U

PJ's so busy with these happy envisionings of the future that it isn't till he's almost at the Bunker that he realizes the forest is silent.

The birds aren't singing, no squirrels scurry out to check who's coming.

Light wheels through the branches but suddenly it feels freezing cold like panes of ice breaking over him.

Someone's been out here and now everything is still and watching.

He walks on slowly, fallen leaves crackling conspiratorially under his feet, and when the Bunker appears through the trees he grows tense in case someone is hiding inside, someone who'll come lunging from the doorway.

It's only when he draws nearer he realizes that there is no doorway.

In its place stands a slab of metal.

He puts his hands on it, pushes it to see if it's real. It's real. He puts his shoulder to it, shoves hard as he can. It doesn't budge. There is a whimpering sound, it's coming from him. How? What? Why? Push it again, nothing. He turns away from it, mouth open, scouring the ground, scouring the sky for an explanation.

And now the forest comes to life with a chorus of caws and croaks and clicks and tweets and screeches, the wind in the leaves a mighty multi-tongued *hissssss* from every direction, as if to laugh at his predicament, as if to say, *Well, little boy, what now?*

*

Jesus, PJ, what are you at? We need to get going!

Dad's standing at the car's open door. In the white sun he looks simultaneously young and old, like a boy who hasn't slept for a thousand years.

Dad. PJ's voice is faint in his ears like it's blown in on the wind. Dad, what happened to the Bunker?

Come on now, PJ, we're all waiting for you, Dad says. From inside the car faces look out, blue-grey, half-invisible.

The Bunker, the shed out there, there's this metal door on it, I couldn't get it open.

Yes, we sealed it up. We're going to do some work on it.

But I – how do you open it?

You're not supposed to open it. It's not safe to go into.

Okay, but it's just I left some stuff, I had some stuff in there . . .

We don't have time for that now. We'll talk about it after.

It's just I need to get—

Later, Dad says. After the dinner.

But I really need it now – it'd only take a second—

Will you get in the car? Will you please just get in the damn car?

What a glorious day! Granddad says as Dad starts the engine. Of course in Portugal it's always like this.

His face appears between the seats to peer back at them. How are we all?

Oh, thrilled to bits, Mam says. Her face bone-white though it's covered in make-up.

You've never been to a Lions Club dinner, or you'd know there's not much to be thrilled about, Granddad chuckles. The speeches! God! They go on and on!

R U STIL THERE?

I THINK U MITE BE IGNORING ME :(

No

No I just had some stuff going on. My granddads here

OH COOL! gREAT!

U NO I DID'T SENT THOSE MESSAGES RIGHT? :) I WOUD NEVER DO
THAT WE'RE BESTFRINEDS

sure :)

Granddad is telling Dad what the roads are like in Portugal. Dad is
driving. Beside PJ Mam's hands are white on her purse. On the far side
of her Cass lets out a sound between a gasp and a sob: she brings a hand
to her mouth, he sees the colour drain from her face. Her phone raised
up before her like a dagger.

Listen

Would the plan still work? If I came today?

UR GOING TO COME TODAY???!!!!

Im trying to figure it all out. Would it still work?

!!!! GREAT NEWS O WE WILL HAVE SUCH FUN

He says he will come and meet PJ at the station. He says his mam will
be there too now, she has come back early, he has told her all about him.
He says the video-game shop is having a sale. He says they have got a
new puppy.

Wow that's great awesome PJ says.

There's a bus leaving the town square one hour and forty-five minutes from now, fifteen minutes before PJ said he'd meet Ears. He will
be in Dublin before the Angelus rings.

INCREDIBEL SO YOURE DEFINITELY GOIUNG TO DO IT???

Yes but

His thumb hovers over the keyboard. There's just one thing he needs
to know. But how to put it, how even to ask. Something like:

Ethan, are you real?

Are you real, like, are you really a boy? With a mam who makes cookies and a spare room with a skylight and a friend who works in the zoo?

The moments pass, his thumb hovers. There is no way. The car slows,
arriving into town.

Ethan writes ????

And still PJ doesn't reply.

THE WIDOW BRIDE

I

On the way to the hotel she thinks she will shit literally shit

It's only a ten-minute drive She went to the toilet before she left Still passing Creaghan's it comes on her suddenly so strong she's on the point of telling Dickie to turn the car around and take her back home but then thinks would she even make it back Should she just say to pull over let her run out to the grass My God That would be about right wouldn't it On the side of the road with her knickers down and the whole town gawping at her as they pass That would about put the tin hat on it

No She grits her teeth Clamps her legs together Recalls someone PJ probably telling her the sphincter is the most powerful muscle in the human body

In the front meanwhile the two men father & son cool as can be Maurice primping himself in the mirror Giving a little nudge to the silver hair at the back of his head Dickie watching the road expressionless as if none of this has anything to do with him Sitting on the speed limit though there's not another car in sight

Will he say it to him at all or will he let him slip off back to the Algarve He still doesn't get it does he Born with a silver spoon in his mouth he still doesn't see what's coming at them

You're a martyr to that man That's what the girls say The things he's put you through Imelda!

Beside her the kids both buried in their phones till Maurice turns in his seat You're awfully quiet he says Are you there at all?

Imelda nudges PJ No point talking to the other one Your granddad's speaking to you she says

PJ looks up wild-eyed like he's just been pulled out of a dream

How's that game? Is it the right one? The fellow in the shop said it was the latest instalment

Yes no it's definitely the right one thanks a million PJ says

What is it World War Two? Fighting the Nazis?

Right only this one's set in the present so like if the Nazis had won the war It's an alternative reality

Alternative reality is it Maurice says He turns back around Well they couldn't do much worse a job than the current shower He reaches into his jacket pocket Takes out a small bundle of notecards and leafs through them then satisfied looks out at the road again The world rushing to greet him

Dickie was hoping to have a word with you after the ceremony she pipes up because if she doesn't he never will Weren't you Dickie?

Dickie doesn't say anything

A quick word about the shop she says Before you go flying off again Because he's told her ten times if he's told her at all how he's leaving first thing tomorrow for a golf game *A fourball* he called it At first she thought he was saying he'd a *furball* like a cat She wondered if that was something rich people get like the gout

Of course said Maurice the whole world's pal Nothing the matter I hope?

No no she says thinking He knows well what's the matter Sitting by the pool in his Portuguese golf resort watching Dickie make a bigger and bigger mess of things and not lifting a finger to help Does he take her for a fool

Now she's said it the pressure eases a little She takes a deep breath takes out her phone Someone off *Strictly* caught doing the dirt Balenciaga runners on special those are nice The 38 best cures for puffy eyes Someone off *X Factor* caught doing the dirt She scrolls and scrolls It will be okay People never have to shit by the side of the road It just doesn't happen but then the car slows She looks up sharply What's going on Why are we slowing down

Tractor says Dickie Yes An ancient old jalopy chugging along in front of them An oul lad up in the cab swaying back and forth giving no sign of knowing they're there Can you not go around him? she says

There's no overtaking for the next two kilometres he says

Oh Jesus Dickie! We'll be late! Would you just pass him out?

But no he will not Instead he waits patiently as the orange tractor judders along at a snail's pace And looking behind her she sees a line of cars has appeared and her bowels lurch Back worse than ever She clenches her whole body But she can't hold it in any longer She can't she can't They will have to stop here at the side of the road where there is only a field and not even a bush you might hide behind and every bloody car in the county lined up to bear witness Is that Imelda Barnes they will say What is she doing Squatting in the grass with her knickers down shitting her guts out The final humiliation Forget about a digout after that But she has no choice She reaches out to tap Dickie on the shoulder Tell him to stop the car thinking It is hell to be alive hell to be a person Hell—

The tractor turns off the road

Dickie changes gear speeds up Air streams in through the window The wave subsides

She sits back Unclenches It is going to be okay she tells herself It is only a hotel Only a place There is nothing there now that can harm you

A martyr That's what the girls say Honestly Imelda we don't know how you can stand it

It's not till they've parked that she realizes Cass is crying

Dickie and PJ and Maurice are already on their way up to the entrance where the bigwigs have assembled But Cass won't get out of the car She stares up at Imelda white-faced Tears dripping all over the dress that's brand new and she not even in the door of the hotel yet

What is it? Imelda says

Sarah Jane Hinchy was at the viewing she whispers

What? Imelda says What viewing? Sarah Jane who?

She was looking at apartments with Elaine Cass says She covers her face What if they end up living together

Well on another day Imelda might have indulged her a little though she can't make head nor tail of it because clearly the girl is upset But the fact is that if she doesn't find a Ladies immediately it is going to be Ragnarok so she grabs her daughter's chin between finger and thumb and twists her face round to look at her

Not now she says Do you hear me?

Cass's teary eyes look back with a mixture of grief and defiance

Do you? she repeats

Cass nods

We have made it this far she says speaking to herself as much as to Cass All we have to do now is get through this dinner and then please God things will start looking up

But when she climbs out of the car Sees the hotel facade shimmer in the heat it all comes in on top of her once again and she thinks *I cannot do this I cannot*

Then she feels an arm slip through hers It's Maurice You won't mind if I borrow your wife momentarily he says to Dickie Leads her away without waiting for a reply Through the grand entrance past the Mayor and the other old men in their black coats Bending in to her he murmurs I have never seen you look so sublime Oh God you're as full of it she says back to him But she lets him carry her onwards through the lobby past the sweeping staircase to the doors to the ballroom at the end of the hall and there she is glad of his arm because for a moment that is all that's holding her up

She had told herself that it surely would be different now After eighteen years it would have to have changed! But no it looks exactly the same Same carpet on the floor Same paintings on the wall Same flock of white napkin-swans floating on the tables and smell of soup in the air and the same red curtains behind the stage where they had the band All of it comes rushing at her at once All of these details she doesn't even remember noticing Roaring up to her like a horde of ghosts like they've been waiting all this time for her to come to make her look at them *remember-rememberrememberremember* And she feels sweat trickle down from under her arms It was hot that day too She was sweating in her dress The straps of the corset dug into her Her eyelid throbbed like it might explode The air was like the air of a tomb Through the white mist of the veil her breath came back at her damp and warm making the stuffy room warmer still stuffier still and she felt in her lace heavy as lead concrete A girl in a concrete dress sinking down through the floor

Applause breaks out as the guests realize Maurice has arrived Then around the room others turn and join in and the noise builds Maurice suave and magnificent receives it graciously modestly and leaning on his arm Imelda smiles and smiles When in doubt smile That's what Clara Langan says When it hurts smile

He has a good turnout for it at least Dickie says as Maurice relinquishes her to meet his audience

He has it's true He'll be in good humour afterwards You'll be sure and talk to him won't you Dickie? she says to her husband

Dickie doesn't reply He looks pretty shook himself Is it the thought of speaking to Maurice or does he remember it too that day He must But before she can ask him someone comes over to shake his hand and Dickie pastes on a smile of his own and gets to work

It seems endless the parade of well-wishers Taking her hand and kissing her cheek Many of them had been here then too Men on the up as they were then Influential men that Maurice calculated it would be good for Dickie to know That's how he had thought even then Even after everything that had happened A businessman to the core And he was right wasn't he for eighteen years later they are installed in the Chamber of Commerce the Cumann the Dairy Council for all the good any of them ever did for Dickie They laugh and laugh and call her a darling while their wives look her up and down with unconcealed distaste Their eyes like needles unpicking a stitch

Yes she knows well how they talk about Dickie hereabouts After everything he's done for these selfsame Lions For the Rotary Club and the Winnies and the football club As well as giving jobs to half the lay-abouts in the town Gombeens who wouldn't be let stack a supermarket shelf let alone run a cash register who was it had taken them in and paid them good money to sweep the shop floor only Dickie even when times got tough out of pure kindness! Not to mention the others The ones even he couldn't employ but who'd shuffle up to him regardless with their tales of woe I fell out of a digger I did in my back I lost me job because money was robbed from the till but it wasn't me took it And Dickie out with the chequebook Out with the cash slipping tens and twenties and fifties even

You're a soft touch she'd tell him You think Maurice got where he is forking out money to every sad sack that tries it on with him? But he couldn't say no though she knew as soon as the money ran out they would turn on him Rich and poor alike And so they did They call him a fool now and they are right

And what do they call her? What is she in their eyes only the biggest sob story of all? They look at her no doubt and they see where it all went wrong for Dickie Barnes In this very spot they tell each other This is where it started

People Could you be up to them She takes out her purse and tells Cass to go to the bar and get her a gin and tonic

And get a Coke for yourself and your brother too PJ put that phone away or I'll take it off you I won't tell you again

Can we have crisps? Cass says

Crisps? Imelda says Aren't you about to have dinner?

But then her eyes fall on PJ pale as a ghost He is not himself these days It is all this worry You try to keep it from them but they always pick it up O jeepers all right she says

Cass goes off with a scowl with PJ limping after her Every time she looks at him now she sees his poor foot as it was in Arnotts blue-white and cut to ribbons she could have died of shame God if it will only come off with Maurice Imagine having money again! Imagine not worrying!

But it will come off He is not an unkind man And they were right to wait till they saw him in the flesh and not be asking him on Skype It's harder to say no to someone if they're right in front of you Anyway isn't it his fault they are where they are Landing them not just with the garage but the bloody house? He sticks them with a dying business and a million euro of negative equity then he fecks off to the Algarve?

The parade continues She greets the Monsignor and Phil the head mechanic and the Cronins and the Woodleys and some bigwig or other from the microchip factory She smiles her brightest smile over and over a lighthouse blinking into the indifferent ocean Wondering are they ever going to sit down when who slooches up to her except Big Mike Comerford

Well says he

Well Mike she says back as politely as she can manage

You're looking very well says he

Thank you indeed she says Peering about for someone to rescue her But the entire room has its back turned it seems so she's stuck there with Big Mike saying Well at her

That's a lovely dress he says

Thank you she says again looking off in the other direction

It suits you he says The cut or whatever The fit

Mm-hmm says Imelda

It's Clara Langan isn't it he says

Imelda in spite of herself does a double-take

I recognize the leaves he says touching the patterned sleeve of her dress The oak leaves She puts them on everything Because she's from Kildare It's a whatdoyoucall A motif

Well you could knock Imelda down with a feather at this point It's as if the postman's dog had suddenly come up to her and struck up a conversation And though she never has been able to stand Big Mike even before he bought her beloved Touareg to give to the housekeeper that he was having it off with Or left his half-built houses there on the land at the back of the woods with the doors open for any rat or tinker that might want to stop by Still the fact remains that the motif or the fit or the cut were not things that Dickie had chosen to comment on Nor how well or otherwise she might have looked in it Instead he'd just stood there biting his lip as she took it out of the box and she could tell he wanted to ask how much it had cost but he didn't dare because he knew she would have picked it up and literally stuffed it down his throat

I saw her on the *Late Late* Big Mike says She's a mighty woman Started out as a model and now she has her own fashion line

And furniture Imelda says And she does wholefoods too Gluten free

Is that so Big Mike says Well well He shakes his head a moment and then Did you ever consider that line of work?

What she says Making furniture?

You think Clara Langan is there in her shed knocking wardrobes together? he says with a laugh She's the face of the brand The one people recognize You'd be well able for that he says A woman like you

A woman like me twenty years ago she snaps back You may get along now Mike Comerford with your old blather

Though it's true the girls have said similar things to her With your looks Imelda! You could still do it! Start off with your picture in the *Sunday Independent* posing in a bikini with a box of dishwasher tablets Next thing you know you're an entrepreneur!

They mean well she knows But how it sounds in her ears is Look what you *could* have done Imelda Look what you *could* have been if you hadn't stayed here If you hadn't reached for the first lifebelt thrown to you In this very room she thinks And again everything seems to swirl around her

So it's a mercy when Cass reappears walking hunched forward with the drinks clasped together in her hand Imelda turns away from Mike and takes her glass and mixer before they all go crashing to the ground

Cass gives her back the money They were free she says Aha a free bar thinks Imelda That explains the crowd

Have you met my granddaughter? Maurice says to the Mayor Everything he says he makes it sound like he's donating a Ming vase to a museum Cassandra will shortly be commencing her studies at Trinity College Dublin Studying English Literature

Big Mike takes out his phone Let's get a picture of you all together says he Smile!

Where's PJ? Imelda says but Mike is already taking the picture He looks down at his phone Lovely he says and then Give us your number there Imelda and I'll send it on to you

What can she do but give it to him? A moment later the photo duly arrives with Imelda's hair like a bird's nest Dickie looking like he's about to have a stroke Cass with a face on her of purest Misery and Maurice and the Mayor beaming in the midst of them like they're paying a visit to a mental hospital

We met a friend of yours up in Dublin Big Mike says to Cass Sarah Jane Hinchy She has a sister who's an estate agent who's on the lookout for a flat for the three of you

The three of us? Cass repeats

Oh you're going to have a ball up there Mike says A ball

I told you we would have been back in time Cass mutters at her when he finally shambles off

What's that? Imelda says

If we'd gone up for the viewing We would have been back in time Cass says And she gives her a look Murderous As if this whole dinner had been engineered by Imelda herself specifically to torment her daughter and stop her from getting to view flats with her friend When the *whole reason they're here* practically is so they can get her to Dublin And though she regrets speaking to her sharply in the car she thinks she may nonetheless blow her top When somebody prods her in the back and a voice says I've my eye on you Imelda Barnes

She turns around Geraldine and Maisie with her The cavalry Thank God

Where have you been? she says I didn't think you'd come

Are we late? says Geraldine We went for a glass of wine in Bojangles You look gorgeous she says

I do not Imelda says I'm a state

Isn't this brill Maisie says looking around her It's like a wedding only everyone's old

I see he's sniffing around after you now is he? Geraldine nods to Big Mike on the other side of the room with his arm around his wife

The brass neck on that man Imelda says How he can show his face here among decent people Though it strikes her that people are probably saying the same thing to each other about herself and Dickie and their debts

Have you heard the latest? Geraldine asks

What says Imelda but then she notices Cass of course long-ears drinking all this in Go and find your brother she tells her And Cass stalks off with the usual roll of the eyes sighing etc.

What's she so down in the mouth about? Maisie says peering after her

Oh don't talk to me Imelda says

She's your penance Geraldine chuckles For whatever you were yourself at that age

Who else is here? Imelda says

Una had to go up to Dublin for her radiotherapy Geraldine says Roisin's on her way

Here she is now Maisie says That's gorgeous eyeshadow Roisin What's it called

Maniac Roisin says She looks around her There's not one single man here under fifty

The girls meet once a week in the back room of Una Dwan's shop for Tidy Towns but much of their time is spent discussing Big Mike and his doings The consensus among the girls is that while he is undoubtedly at fault Joan the wife had a hand in it too

How she could have let a woman like that into her house! Geraldine says Blonde bombshell Thin as a whip apart from a set of knockers you'd give your eye teeth for It was hardly a mystery how that would turn out

The mistake was to get a Brazilian Maisie says She should have got a Pole The Brazilians are too sexual The Poles are better-looking but they're frigid

Sexual or not Geraldine says She had gold-digger written all over her Who would trust a woman like that

He's lucky Joan took him back Maisie says

He's signed ninety per cent of his business over to her to stop the bank getting hold of it Geraldine says That's what woke him up in the end I'd say Big Mike's an eejit but he's no fool However nice Miss's Brazilian knockers are he'll be damned before he gives all that up

He'll never give up that fella Maisie says He'd try it on with anyone

Joan'll be keeping tabs on him Geraldine says And her spies too You know what this bloody place is like Everybody sees everything

There is a silence for a moment then Maisie says Are you not afraid *you'll* get seen?

No because I'm careful says Geraldine Her eyes dart left and right then in a lowered voice she says He might be here right now

What? Mystery Mickey? Here? The girls all clamour at once then start looking over their shoulders Who is it? Tony Daley? It's not the Mayor is it?

Geraldine wears a cat's smile then whispers Will I show you a picture of him?

She takes out her phone and swipes through it then passes the phone to Maisie who lets out a sort of yelp then stops her mouth with her hand then passes the phone to Imelda

What do you think of that now says Geraldine

The picture is of a penis An erect penis

Look at her face! She'd love to get a hold of that wouldn't she!

Oh our Imelda's far too pure for anything like that

She's not pure at all she just prefers teasing them don't you Imelda God the amount of wanks the men of this town must have had over you Thousands literally thousands!

Mam can I have a euro for the video game PJ says appearing out of nowhere Imelda whips the phone out of sight then reaches for her purse then drops the phone Geraldine laughs and laughs

Geraldine is having an affair She is what's the word *unrepentant*

Lookit girls she says I've been married twenty-two years and I'm done trying to con myself I backed the wrong horse and that's all there is to it

At the same time she doesn't want a divorce Why put yourself through that at this stage of the game? she says Why put the kids through it? No this is much better and when I get tired of him I can chuck him and no hard feelings

What happens if you fall in love with him? Imelda asks

Geraldine just laughs and says she'll take her chances

What Imelda wanted to say of course was But it's a sin Just like when Roisin is waving her white band around and telling them how wonderful it is being Swingle as she calls it she wants to say But it's a sin But she doesn't because she knows what they will say back Honestly Imelda Do you still believe in all that stuff after everything you've been through?

People are starting to take their seats There must have been some signal The girls run off to the bar to stock up before the speeches start Imelda goes to look for her table

Big Mike winks at her as she goes past She pretends not to see The nerve of him after all his carry-on! Although sometimes she wonders could you blame him The girl was a real beauty The housekeeper Augustina was her name And he meanwhile stuck with a woman like Joan Dull as dishwater and uptight to boot One of those types that speaks with her jaw clenched as if her teeth are loose in her gums and if she opens her mouth they'll go tumbling to the pavement

But he didn't have to marry her did he Only she had money Her family had money That was why he did it Though no one ever calls him a gold-digger

Yes if she could have talked to that girl she would have told her straight Forget Big Mike Forget cleaning houses Forget about little towns like this one You need to act quick Use those looks God gave you so by the time they're gone you have your next life ready to step into

Designer Influencer Nutrition Expert Otherwise you'll be no more than a former beauty waiting to be betrayed The wrong horse The horse who became old The one people will tell each other *You'd never know it now but she was once*

Roisin is by the seating plan looking put out I spent a full hour getting into a backless dress and they've stuck me with a table of nuns she says Someone's having a fecking laugh

And maybe someone is because when she looks herself she sees they've been given the very same table they were at before Just when she thought she was getting used to it being here again The selfsame table and the selfsame seat Looking back over the guests looking back at her It's as if someone or something is determined to make her see that it has been here all this time The hotel The past Waiting for her as long as it took That's where the cake was There was the band Dickie sat on her right And across the table Rose Yes she remembers staring over at Rose through the veil Trying to catch her eye Rose looking away

Of course she is the only mug who has bothered to sit down The rest of the guests have drifted halfway to the tables and then stopped Are they all looking at her? Are they thinking That's the very place she was sat then that day too? She wishes she had the veil again Takes out her phone instead Clara Langan and her family having a picnic in a park in France The kids so gorgeous in their frocks spooning strawberries out of little polka-dot bowls #summerfun Clara Langan is wearing the same Balenciaga runners that are in the sale and now a pop-up appears Treat yourself Imelda! Additional 10% off! And she's thinking she almost would just as revenge for being dragged back here when a waiter swoops by and sets a tureen of soup in front of her Then suddenly the room is full of waiters swooping back and forth like seagulls Four identical tureens have appeared at the unoccupied places around her Dickie sits down beside her Well he says

She doesn't reply at first Gives him a moment to see if he'll realize Look over his shoulder say *Jesus Melds am I going mad or is this the very selfsame table we were at for the wedding*

Can you believe it she'd say and they'd laugh And the ghosts would fade away shaking their bony fists

Tony Daley's after getting one of them self-cleaning ovens he says

Is that so Imelda says

That's right He says it's the business

A martyr to that man Imelda You are a martyr

Next Cass hoves up at the table Slings herself into her chair Plonks a full glass of Coke down in front of her and sits there scowling at it Where's your brother? Imelda asks her Cass doesn't even look at her How would I know?

Imelda feels rage fizz up into her head like the bubbles in the glass Everything handed to her on a plate and none of it means a thing to her! God but she'd love to bring her back in time Back to her own childhood That would put some manners on her What's for breakfast Nothing What's for dinner Nothing The sheriffs knocking at the door The guards the social the galoots from this selfsame Lions Club with their cardboard boxes of tinned sweetcorn and Terry's Chocolate Orange a week past its expiry date gawking in past you with looks of horror like they'd stumbled into a crypt Learning to sew by putting stitches in your brother's head after Daddy hit him with a claw hammer How about that for starters?

But where *is* PJ?

Most of the guests are sitting now, but she still can't see him Wasn't he playing video games? Dickie says But there is the video game cabinet over by the bar unattended

Maybe he met someone he knew?

Who would he know? she says He's the only child here Dickie presses his lips together twists his ring He couldn't have gone could he? she says and a sudden panic rises up in her

Gone? says he How do you mean gone?

Gone gone she snaps without knowing exactly what she means Except that out of nowhere her heart is battering against her chest and amid the sunlight streaming through the broad windows everything has gone dark and in her mind wherever it has come from is the terrible certainty that *he is no longer here* That the room has devoured him as the price for what happened that day The life she should never have had Now she will never see him again nor will anyone even know who she means when she speaks his name—

There he is Dickie says Look There by the fire exit And he points to the back of the room where PJ stands fixated on his phone leaning into the long curtains Probably texting his pals Dickie says I'll round him up

Relief flows into her No need she tells him but he goes and she keeps her eye fixed on their son as Dickie weaves his way through the tables towards him as if otherwise he might disappear He looks so small among the gabbing fatsos and yet his expression older than it should be Harrowed is that a word Anguished This summer she feels like she's barely seen him Can't get a word out of him The bloody garage it's fucked everything The bane of her life that bloody place

He arrives at the table with Dickie's hand on his shoulder Sits down and starts mechanically spooning the soup She resists the urge to interrogate him Waits instead to catch his eye Everything okay? she says He gives her a smile And she flinches For what is it but her own lighthouse beam being shined back at her

A moment later Maurice picks his way through the crowd Whispering greetings and shaking more hands along the way like he's Frank Sinatra And the moment he sits down as if everything has been waiting on him Tommy Shiels head of the Lions Club gets up onto the stage

Chicken or beef? a waiter murmurs at Imelda's ear then turns to Dickie Chicken or beef?

A few points of business first Tommy Shiels says and starts pointing out fire exits Imelda lifts the lid from her tureen What did she eat that day or did she eat at all It would have been hard with the veil on but if she didn't what did she do during the meal Stare at Rose? Search the shadows?

To her right Maurice has put on his glasses to look over his notecards To her left Dickie twists his ring round and round readying himself to make his own sad speech Across the table from her where Rose once sat Cass leans back in her chair sips her Coke gazes aloofly into space soup untouched Last week she'd suddenly taken a vagary that she wanted to visit her Rose that is Kicked up a stink when Imelda told her no Typical For years you practically needed a bulldozer to get her out to the nursing home Then as soon as you don't want her to you can't keep her away

Poor Rose It's been God knows how long She must get out to her Once this is over if it's ever over

Now Tommy Shiels is rehearsing the good work the Lions have done this year The hampers given out Coal and firewood delivered to the town's neediest And they are not always who you think they are he says

From around the room the faces of the guests are arrayed before her Gazing past her at the stage as they tuck in to their soup and soda bread Monica Chambers Odette O'Leary Angela Batt The dentist the school principal the kids' G P

For months now she has been having the same dream Of a flood that sweeps through the house Carries off clothes from the wardrobes Toys from the cupboards Food from the table In the dream she is trying to stop it She is wading around pulling things out of the water But there's too much to hold in her arms and it overcomes her The current grows stronger Pulls away the appliances the kitchen island tiles from the floor paint from the walls The clothes are tugged from her body Till she too is carried away The townsfolk gathered at the edge of the water watching her go Staring down as she's swept past In their eyes she is old Her youth is gone too It has all been washed away by the water

Then as if he can hear her thoughts from the next seat he reaches out a hand to cover hers and clasp it A voice whispers in her ear You have never looked more beautiful

Dickie? No are you joking It's Maurice Never in a million years would it even occur to Dickie to say something like that

I mean it he says You look sensational

I don't she says My hair's a disaster

You're perfect he says You've outdone yourself Then squeezing her hand again he whispers Will you run away with me Imelda? Will you come back with me to Portugal? I'm an old man I won't wear you out

She pulls her hand free and slaps his Would you go 'way! Maurice Barnes!

She has never minded his flirting She knows that it doesn't mean anything to him no more than it does to her They understand each other They are the same in some ways

Here we are he says This is my send-off My carriage clock Makes you wonder what it all was for doesn't it

Don't say that she tells him Across the table Dickie's ears are practically lepping off his head trying to make out what they're saying You're in your prime yet I've a couple of girlfriends now I'll name no names but they'd eat you up so they would

Maurice smiles to himself She bets he has a little señorita back there in Quinta do Lago and that's why he wasn't home at Christmas

I'm glad you could come he says It means a lot to me

I wouldn't miss it for the world she says It's a testament to you

Now our guest of honour today is truly a man who needs no introduction Tommy Shiels is saying

It's strange being back here Maurice says Isn't it

She says nothing to this

I haven't been back since that day he says The— I was almost about to say the funeral God forgive me The wedding I mean

Mention the name Maurice Barnes to anyone in this town and they will respond with words like *selfless caring munificent* Tommy Shiels says

It must bring back memories for you he says She just smiles

He embodies the spirit of generosity that is what the Lions Club is all about Tommy Shiels says

That bee! Maurice says shaking his head Peggy thought it was a sign

But I never doubted that it was the right thing That you did the right thing

He looks away into the middle distance The smile lingering on his lips like a keepsake he has forgotten and for an instant she sees him again by the graveside in his black coat His eyes closed as if he would never open them again His face emptied as if that was where they had dug their hole

Get up here you old so-and-so! Tommy Shiels booms from the stage

Maurice's eyes reopen He jumps to his feet shoots his cuffs and bounds up the steps of the dais Approaching Tommy Shiels he bows his head in the manner of one well used to being given medals and Tommy slips the ribbon over it Around her everyone's getting to their feet Clapping and cheering

Mam PJ whispers urgently

Imelda turns sees that Cass is crying Slumped back in her chair tears flowing down her cheeks as if from a tap As if all the grief in the world were flowing through her

The whole room is standing now The roar of the applause something thunderous like a river in spate Dickie stoops trying to persuade Cass to get up You have to he's saying You have to Cass pushes him away

Watching the tears fall Imelda thinks of herself crying behind her veil It is as if she is looking at herself Looking into the past As if that day had been waiting here locked up for her to come

So that as Dickie reaches down to tug Cass to her feet she turns her back on the stage Gazing through the sea of faces that look in turn through her A tiny fragment of that old hope alight in her heart To the back of the room where she had waited for him to appear Her beloved her betrothed

Frank

II

Who was it told her the story It couldn't have been Daddy he only talked about himself And Mammy didn't tell stories just liked to brush Imelda's hair It must have been Rose so She remembers Rose was there in the house when she was little And it was the type of story she'd tell A warning before either of them knew there was anything to warn about

The tale was of a traveller making his way home after a long journey One night he finds himself out in the fields after the sun sets with no house nor inn to be seen where he might ask for lodging It is a bitter night but what choice does he have except to lie down where he is on the side of a hill and spread his cloak over him to keep off the cold A white moon hangs overhead He shivers on the grass It takes him a long time to get to sleep But sleep he does in the end only to be woken by the sound of music

He lifts up his head The moon is gone the sky pitch dark Not a soul to be seen wherever he looks yet still he hears the music A fiddle a squeezebox a bodhran playing a tune for dancing to

He gets to his feet and he moves towards it and then sees on the other side of the hill is a door

The door is open a crack and through that crack light is coming and music

The traveller pauses having heard tales himself of the Sídh the fairy folk who live side by side with us invisibly but from time to time may be glimpsed near a particular tree or a well or a hill that is theirs Fair to look upon but masters of cruel magic If you rub up against them there's no knowing what they'll do Kill your cattle for sport Steal your baby Make you sick Or play a trick on you so your face trades places with your arse or a tree is set growing inside you till the branches reach out of your mouth and your eyes and your ears

Stay away from them that is best he knows And yet the night is so cold! The night is so cold and the music so merry and surely nobody who makes such music would want to do him harm? So he finds himself edging towards the door He will stop just inside it he thinks Listen to the music Stay just until he is warm He need never speak to the ones inside whoever they are Though who's to say they are the fairy folk at all and not simply people living inside a hill?

So he tells himself and he steps through the door

And he finds himself not in an earthy hollow but in a mighty hall A feast is taking place On the table are plates of every kind of meat Jugs of mead wine and whiskey The people around the table are comely like no one he has ever seen before Their hair is yellow their eyes are blue and as soon as they set eyes on him they let out a cheer as if they have been waiting for him before they begin They sit him down Put a goblet in his hand Tell him to eat his fill Which he does And when he is full they take his damp old cloak and put a fine robe on his shoulders and on his head a circlet and on his finger a ring all of gold The goblets too the plates are gold Gold chains around each feaster's neck Gold lines the walls A maiden takes his hand Her hair golden as a summer's day

The music restarts though he can't see who's playing The maiden dances him round and round Kisses his forehead his cheek his lips He tells her he has a wife waiting for him and she laughs Those things don't matter here she says This is a place without care So he dances and he drinks and every time his goblet is empty it's filled again without his ever seeing how and the feast goes on but he doesn't get tired and the kind people who have brought him into their feasting hall stand in a circle around him as he dances with the maiden and they clap and they cheer Such friends he thinks And then he wakes up

It is morning He is lying in the grass on the side of the hill His old cloak spread over him damper than ever With a groan he gets to his feet His bones ache In the daylight he can find no sign of the door in the hill however he searches Till he gives it up as a dream nothing more Continues on his way back to his village

Along the road he notices differences An inn he didn't see before A wood where he remembers a farm When he reaches his village things are stranger still Someone has made off with his house and left in its place only a pile of stones And his wife his children are nowhere to be found

He asks the villagers where they could be But those villagers too are changed It is another man now who calls himself baker Another man who calls himself priest And none of them knows where his family have gone to

Till at last they bring him to a man An old old man with a long grey beard Yes he says He knew a woman of that name When he was a child But she was very old Old as I am now he says And today lies buried in the churchyard That is not she the traveller says for his wife is young and bonny Tell me says the old man where did you get that ring And the traveller sees on his finger still the gold ring that was given him by the kind people beneath the hill And he begins to tell his tale but before he is done the villagers rise up seeing that he is cursed and they drum him out of the village

And he takes to the roads and for the rest of his days he goes alone A hundred years away from his wife and children and everyone he once knew Searching in vain for a door in a hill so he might beg the kind strangers to set him back as he was before he met them

But who knew why that should even have stayed with her for she didn't live in a hall of feasting fairies nor in a village either with a baker and a priest but on a street of little houses squashed up against each other like in a big city with all around them open fields Over one field was the Texaco that did sausage rolls and over the other was the Statoil that had pies though you would have to cross the motorway for that Their house was at the end of the terrace so there was space in the yard for the car and the van and the swings and for Daddy's sheds There were six sheds though one was full of rubbish still from when he had his garbage collection business He was after the council to come and clear it but they would not and that was out of spite he said Of the other sheds four contained his wares though Mammy said that no one but he could tell them apart from the rubbish Two hundred dolls without heads Two pallets of five-year-old teabags A load of radios that only spoke French Cracked Tupperware and dusty disposable BBQs Some of the stuff had been lying there for years It was older than she was

Imelda and Lar played in the sheds when Daddy wasn't around only not the rubbish one because of the rats And the sixth shed he told them they must never go into That was where he brought Butch after the council came out about the barking What am I supposed to do? she heard Daddy say to the man from the council The kids love it I can't just kill it

Nobody's saying to kill it the council man said Just don't keep it tied up in the yard all day

When are you going to pick up that garbage Daddy said but the man was already getting into his car

It was Noeleen dobbed them in Daddy said She was always giving out about the barking She wrecked his head worse than the dog Well she could plug her effing ears so she could But then on St Patrick's Day they were all watching the parade on TV There was a girl on the milk float Miss Premier Dairies who was the prettiest girl she'd ever seen and Butch was barking out the back barking barking till finally Daddy roared out Fuck's sake He got up and went outside and grabbed a brick in one hand and with the other pulled up the stake from the ground and dragged the dog into the shed the sixth shed She and Lar tried to stop him but he sent them back in It was Noeleen next door they should go crying to he said After that they didn't speak to Noeleen again nor she to them

Yes Daddy could be very hard when he got in a rage He was on disability now but he used to be a fighter and his arms were like the carcasses she'd see hanging in the butcher's van with the heads still on them She often watched his videos with him He'd have a beer in one hand and the other he would put on her shoulder and he'd say to her Watch this fella now that he's about to try and snake up on me with a left and she'd hide her face away because she thought Daddy might die Lookit lookit see him! he'd say tugging her head up Getting excited as if it were all happening again and he'd half-rise off the couch bringing his fist up Pow! he'd shout as the other man fell down on the tarmac and Daddy descended on him with the fists like hammers

It was no joke when those fists fell on you the older lads said When they took off their shirts you could see the marks You think he's bad now youse have it lucky they said Back then you wouldn't know if he might kill you for real back then when he was drinking But he is drinking Lar said and they laughed That's not drinking

With her though Daddy was always gentle as a lamb The boys were jealous because she had her own room and she got new clothes while they wore hand-me-downs But most of all because Daddy would never hit her no matter how bad she was though she was never bad with him Nor would he let them lay a finger on her nor anyone else She was too good for the scuts and savages that lived around these parts he said A natural beauty Some day she'd win the Rose of Tralee Some day she'd marry a millionaire

In the meantime she had to be careful He was careful too Keeping an eye out after school in case some boy should start trying to put the chat on her Pulling up in the van they'd peg it before he even got out the door shouting after them None of you mongrels will ever get near a thoroughbred like that so put it out of your head And the brothers too that as soon as she started getting breasts would always be mocking them Tits they called her Here Tits Always trying to grab her grope her Pull the towel off her when she came out of the shower till Daddy put the fear of God into them with a wire coat hanger or the heel of his shoe

But not her She remained untouched An untouched beauty like a princess in a fairy tale And she combed her golden hair and dreamed of the day that her prince would come for her

Mammy said she was vain

Keep looking in that mirror miss and the Devil will appear That was what she said

She had been beautiful once herself and Imelda was like her doll She used dress her up in little smocks and frocks and berets so the women would coo over her on the steps of the church But now Mammy was sick and she did not go to Mass or anywhere else There was no more dressing up for either of them Instead she sat in her bed and called down to the brothers to bring up her dinner Though she was sick she was huge A mountain of fat half-sunk in the bed but she spoke in a small high-pitched voice like there was a little girl trapped inside the blancmange of her body

When Imelda was born Rose had told her she'd be her last And so it turned out She had tried to have more babies but they never took *The gowl is banjo'd on her* Imelda heard Daddy tell Nat O'Neill *The curse never stops* Yes The gowl was broken and Daddy's heart was broken too When he did wrong on her it was from the grief he said of the children he would never have

Mammy thought Imelda was to blame She thought Imelda had done something to her while she was inside in her womb Making sure none would follow after her Scheming to take Mammy's place even before she was born

I see through you Mammy said You might have your father fooled Not me

She called her a troublemaker She kept tabs on her Whenever Imelda was alone with Daddy downstairs watching a video on the couch sooner or later she would hear the groan of the bed above and the thud of the feet on the floor Then five minutes later Mammy would appear in the door Too out of breath to speak Just staring in at her like an enormous fleshy ghost till Daddy turned from the telly and yelled to stop letting in a draught and Mammy without replying would turn and huff and plod her way back up the stairs and the bed would creak and groan again like a coffin lid closing I'm wise to you she would say when Imelda brought her up her tea I'll tell the nuns about you and they'll lock you away for a hundred years

Don't mind her Daddy said It's just cause she's sick

But Imelda was not so sure What if Mammy saw something he didn't? What if there was something bad inside her Something that made people want to do bad things Pulled them like a magnet to chase after her on the way home from school Grab her as she passed on the stairs That made the Devil stir in the depths of the mirror?

All she could do was try her best to be good And she was good she told herself because wasn't she untouched? While the brothers had black eyes or split lips and Mammy even sat with an ice pack in her bed before the TV Imelda was untouched and that was the proof and she felt a glow of specialness And she would stay untouched she vowed For though Daddy had plans for his thoroughbred the truth was that she had no wish ever to be touched by anyone

Then one day some men came to the house

She was on the couch with Lar watching *Neighbours* when the van screeched up outside At the same moment JohnJoe burst through the door and hollered There's two of them! meaning vans The second one they'd driven fifty yards on to block off the road but she didn't find that out till later Right now she was looking at the Hiace out the front which three lads came piling out of One with a lump hammer one with a car jack one with a slash hook A second later two more appeared to join them a gingery fellow with a bat and a boggle-eyed type that she couldn't see what he had with him and they all went running out of sight down the front lane trying to knock down the door

But it was the wrong door they picked It was poor Noeleen's door their neighbour which was pretty thick of them because any eejit could have told which house was which Noeleen had her yard full of gnomes and wishing wells and climbing roses and little shrubs in pots while theirs had a Datsun up on blocks and a load of parts strewn over the grass and a ripped sofa with Lar's pony eating the stuffing out of it and a clatter of broken-down sheds

But Imelda thought maybe it was Noeleen they were after That maybe she had complained to the council about them like she had about Butch And she turned to the boys to tell them but then she saw Lar looking back behind him with his mouth open and when she looked back too she saw JohnJoe sprinting off down the back garden and jumping over the wall Then she looked at Lar and Lar looked at her

Run Lar said

Outside Noeleen was shrieking that she'd called the guards and the men must have realized their mistake because now through the frosted window of the front door she saw a shape appear

Go on Go Lar said pushing her up the stairs because he mustn't have thought she could make it over the back wall but anyway she wouldn't have left him

Who is it? Mammy called from the bedroom Who's at the door?

She didn't reply Downstairs she heard a thudding at the door then Lar opening it and saying Daddy wasn't home No one's home except me he said

The man at the door mustn't have believed him because next thing the house was full of thundering steps Men's voices as they crowded into the hall then the front room and the kitchen

What's going on Mammy said sitting up in her bed *Neighbours* on her telly too Who is in the house? Where's Daddy?

Shh Imelda whispered to her from the landing Stop talking!

But Mammy did not hush On the contrary I'm a sick woman! she exclaimed I can't have all this commotion! Imelda ignored her ran into her own room and slid under her bed Through the floorboards she heard a din of shouting to and fro and things falling to the floor and then a clatter of feet on the stairs and a moment later closer to her Mammy's voice saying quieter Who are you?

She held her breath but if there was a reply she didn't hear it and after a moment she breathed out again

Then slowly the door creaked open From under the bed she saw a pair of muddy boots Then hairy hands Then a pair of wolfish black eyes

Well he says Isn't this a nice surprise?

Downstairs the men were taking the house apart Tipping out cupboards chucking the cushions off the couch then turning the couch over If you're looking for money there isn't any! Mammy shrieked from her room but they paid no attention until Imelda appeared on the stairs Then they all stopped and looked up

One had pulled out the phone One had the TV in his arms Lar was there among them waving his hands They all of them stopped and looked up at her

See what I found said the wolfish man from behind her

Ringed below her the men grinned up at her like she was a prize they'd found in a cracker barrel The lanky one was Golly's age The ginger one about Christy's The one with the slash hook about JohnJoe's The boggle-eyed one Lar's

The wolfish man was older He'd dragged her out by the hair He pushed her from behind and she started down the stairs Maybe there's another way to settle this he said

Lar looked at her with his big white turnip of a head and his dark eyes as she came down and she looked away The men or boys stood aside like she was the guest of honour being escorted to a ball What's going on? Mammy yelled from her bed but no one answered her They all followed Imelda and the wolfish man into the kitchen

There were plates on the table with half-eaten sausages and cups of cold tea On the radio Larry Gogan playing Boyzone on *The Golden Hour* like everything was normal and in her mind she tried to hook on to those normal things and not see the rest of it

Let's have a look at you so The wolfish man turned her around and beheld her Well he said Haven't you grown into a fine thing?

She said nothing After a moment he gave her a shake Haven't you?

I don't know she said

You have he said Your daddy was right about you He stared at her and it seemed like his eyes were covered in gunge like your teeth when you don't brush them Not the eyes themselves but the look from them Where is your daddy? he said

She didn't reply because she didn't know the answer

Has he gone and left you he said His breath rolled up in her face On the radio the Just a Minute Quiz and away off upstairs Mammy yelling and Lar from out in the hall in a fake grown-up voice saying Now boys can we not settle this reasonably and outside glass still tinkling from Noeleen's smashed window and the engines of the two vans that they'd left running All of it piled up together like a garbage heap of noise but inside her silence where she remained untouched

And in the silence the wolfish man close to her

Have you nothing to say to me

She didn't reply She breathed through her nose trying to tamp down the fear for she knew it would only get him going but she couldn't stop it The fear Flaring off her like the steam from a horse on a cold morning and it did she was right it did get him going got all of them going The fear or was it whatever was inside her the magnet the badness But she could tell though they didn't move she could feel them drawn to her She could feel something opening up inside each of them and in their hands the slash hook the baseball bat the car jack the lump hammer and a Stanley knife which she only saw now but which scared her the most A Stanley knife in the hand of the boggle-eyed boy in a Superdry hoody who had not said a thing so far and she shivered though it was June and warm stifling even with all of them crammed into the tiny kitchen The quiz still going on the radio The picture of Jesus on the wall looking down sorrowfully pointing at his heart and the fear flaring off her and the magnet tugging out of her and coming back to her as a glistening in their eyes and terrible thoughts going through her head of the girls in Daddy's magazines with their gowls so red like wounds from touching and Mammy's own gowl that was busted and the Rose of Tralee committee that would want to check you and the knife twitching in the hand of the boggle-eyed boy that made her think all of a sudden that they would not only do what they would do but afterwards leave her marked for ever a punishment for all those hours mooning at herself in the mirror And in fear she tried to make herself smile at the wolfish man to please him But it had the opposite effect He darkened his mouth twisted and he said to her You must think you're God's gift

From upstairs Mammy started squealing like it was her they had taken and the wolfish man shouted over his shoulder Someone take care of this cat fuckin' yowling in my ear then raising his voice I'll give you something to yowl about you old bitch when we're done with this one And one of them goes off up to Ma and with his arm the wolfish man swipes away everything that's on the kitchen table plates cans bottles a carburettor they all went crashing to the ground and that too exploded in her head No! Lar shouts and he takes a swing at the ginger lad who just blinks like he's walloped in the head ten times a day then hits Lar a smack that knocks him to the floor Lifts his bat over his head but the wolfish man says No let him see this And there is a screaming coming from somewhere then a hand clamps over her mouth and she knows it's from her The hand tastes of grease Inside her head the screaming continues Mixing with the judder of the vans the still-falling glass Ma banging on the door of the bedroom upstairs And the hand twists her head back and other hands grab her arms and pull her back onto the table and others too take her ankles holding her down and she thinks of Daddy's horses white-rolling their eyes Tugged onto the van by their blue ropes and then the wolfish man steps forward and pushes his fingers into her thighs and says By the time we're done no one will ever want to look at you again and he squeezes his face up like the Devil come at last out of the mirror and pushes her thighs apart and then

And then the back door opens and Rose comes in

The wolfish man freezes with his hands on Imelda's thighs and with the rest of them turns and stares while Rose waddles huffing and puffing right past them to the hall where she hangs up her coat Then back again by the table where they're holding Imelda down to the counter where she heaves up two striped plastic bags and starts unpacking them Plants herbs of some kind One by one she lays them out on the draining board Only then when the bags are empty does she turn and look at the men Who's this we have? she says and she screws up her eyes at them The Finlay boys is it Francis Bernard William Patrick John

The men don't say anything to this

Is your mammy's ankle better? says Rose I was out to her yesterday fortnight

The lanky fellow begins to say something but the wolfish man cuts him off

We'd be obliged if you would move along Rose he says We've business to attend to here

Rose does not reply Humming to herself she takes a cup from the draining board and rinses it then another cup Behind him the others are confused The wound-up energy of a moment ago slipped away though they're still gripping her wrists and ankles

We've no quarrel with you Rose the wolfish man says It's Paddy Joe we're here for that done us out of a grand When she doesn't reply he says impatiently Get her out of here

Before any of them move though Rose filling the kettle says over her shoulder Is that ye're dog lads that's out there barking in the front street?

The boys look at each other We've no dog with us Rose the lanky one says at last

Well that's mighty strange Rose says because as I come in I seen a black dog sitting in the front street barking his head off like he was calling for somebody

There is a moment of silence while they think about this Silence yes because somehow the noise of the van engines has gone and the glass and everything else Mammy the radio But just as she realizes this a new sound breaks in A dog barking A savage sound like nails hammered into stone over and over

The wolfish man gives a nod and the gingery lad lets go her ankle and she hears him open the front door And for an instant the barking is louder than ever Seeming to shake the whole house Then the door closes and the gingery lad comes back again He is pale He says something that Imelda doesn't hear One by one the lads go into the hall and finally the wolfish man unhooks his fingers from her and he goes too After a moment Imelda sits up on the table She doesn't know should she get down or what She rearranges her skirt and she waits

Rose has put the kettle on and opened the cupboard She knows where the tea's kept in every kitchen for ten miles round Mammy said once

The men come back into the room They seem disturbed It's not ours says the lanky one

Rose pours water into the cups Well it's looking for one of you boys it sounds like she says

Is it ye're? the lanky one says to Imelda She shakes her head They've had no dog since Noeleen wrote to the council and Daddy had to take Butch into the shed

Is it a black dog? she asks

The men don't reply It's just a fucking dog! the wolfish man shouts like he's lost his temper But the others don't say anything to that either Maybe like Imelda they are thinking of stories they have heard Such as the black dog by the lake the day before the Gallagher boys fell through the ice Or the black dog Harriet Maguire saw when she was sick with the cancer though it was Rose who saw it first and told her and Harriet smiled for the first time in months And the black dog that appeared one night under Cawleys' window and when Mary-Jo Cawley woke next morning their little girl that was bright as a button was stretched out cold

The men know like Imelda knows that as well as healing Rose sees things Looking in the patterns of tea leaves or birds flying or frost in the well she sees what will happen And sometimes what she sees is death

But does she only see it Or is it her seeing it makes it happen? There's a question

Here's what Lar said he saw when he went out to the hall The five lads were gathered around the open door which looked outside to the front street on which there sat Nothing

But the barking she said You could hear it

No nothing he said Not out there But they could They saw it They heard it That was the thing

Well you wouldn't know with Lar who liked to tell stories himself but something clearly had passed in the hall which was why when they came back to the kitchen the boys were quiet and their hooks and their bats and their knives hung by their sides like they'd forgotten about them

You'd best be on your way lads Rose said gently and the back door was now mysteriously open and like they'd just been waiting for someone to tell them what to do they turned and filed out and did they go over the back wall to avoid the dog or round the side and over Noeleen's Imelda didn't know But when she looked out the front the van was gone and the other was too Rose pressed a cup of tea into her hands and gathered the plants she'd brought and went upstairs to Mammy

Imelda didn't know what to do now When she went to the toilet she could still see the finger marks pressed into the insides of her thighs but apart from that she felt okay Lar had a big lump where the ginger-haired lad had hit him a smack Maybe you'll start talking sense now Imelda said

When the guards came Rose told them it was men from out of town and Noeleen next door said the same Paddy Joe will get them breakages fixed for you Rose told her then off she went

It was the lanky boy that died six months later after getting a punctured lung from a screwdriver outside a lock-up in Gort

She must've known they were coming Lar said when Rose was gone It takes an hour to walk to ours from her place She must've left before the vans even got here

Wasn't she coming to see Mammy? Imelda said It was just good luck But Lar shook his head and Imelda didn't believe it either

They were out in the yard in the twilight JohnJoe had come back and then gone out again for chips for them

It was a shame Daddy wasn't there Lar said He'd have taught them fellas a thing or two

And the brothers too Not JohnJoe who'd run for it which was just like him but Golly and Christy Can you imagine Lar said Them lads coming in and meeting Daddy and Golly and Christy? It'd be a massacre

Yeah Imelda said and then Where do you think they were?

Who said Lar

Daddy she said And the boys

Lar thought about it They must of gone out on a job he said

As soon as he said it she knew that's what it was When Daddy hears about it he'll be raging she said Right Lar said Them lads better get out of town if they know what's good for them

But it was Daddy who had gone away she learned Over to England with Golly and Christy He did not come back for weeks and in that time something else happened which is that Rose came back to the house and told her to pack her things because she was coming to stay with her

Imelda was surprised Does Mammy know?

But Mammy did know Rose said Mammy needed a room of her own now and she would go into Imelda's when Imelda was gone

What about the boys? Imelda said What about him? she said pointing to Lar who was asleep in his clothes on the couch

He can look after himself said Rose So can they all

So Imelda packed her bag and went outside with Rose where there was a man waiting she had never seen before and she never saw him again after that and the only thing she remembered about him was that he had a car that the seats went up and down when you pushed a button and he drove them to Rose's cottage

She had been there before of course when she was sick It was a proper little cottage like something from a story with snowdrops in January and daffodils in spring and a patch for vegetables and another for herbs to put in spells and remedies There was a rain barrel and a henhouse and a jam jar full of water and wasps that had drowned in it and a tiny scrap of land behind with a cow that would come over to the gate and lick your face There was an Infant of Prague in the windowsill and a crow's wing nailed over the door

The cottage was far from anyone but Imelda was never afraid there Rose put her in the room where the lodger had been She said he was a teacher but under the bed Imelda found a suitcase full of parts of old phones or that's what they looked like She showed it to Rose who said to leave it there in case he came back Where is he now? she asked and Rose said he had gone to England Have you ever been to England? Imelda said She had never been there and in her mind it was not a place at all but a kind of grey mist that people disappeared into and sometimes never came back out of But Rose just told her to stop her talking and chop the carrots

Rose was a healer Every mother in the county came to her when their baby had colic or wouldn't go down She told fortunes too She knew people's secrets Visitors called to the house at all hours with maladies or questions or just to talk Many of them called her Auntie as Mammy did too though whether she was all of their aunt or nobody's Imelda couldn't tell She had grey eyes and grey hair and it was impossible to imagine her ever being young She might have been there for a hundred years doling out poultices Laying hands on the dying

Well of course as soon as Daddy was back from wherever he'd been he came looking for her The van pulled up outside and he got out and banged on the door and though it hadn't been so long since she'd seen him Imelda was struck by just how big he was Big and red with sunburn and filling up the doorway He told Rose she had kidnapped his daughter and he wanted her back

But Rose stayed calm and kept her arm across the door and said very coolly that the girl's mammy had given her permission to take her from the house where it was not safe for her

Not safe? Daddy said How is it not safe?

Rose just looked at him She did not mention what had happened at the house with the Finlays

Who's going to cook? Daddy said

So from then on Imelda lived with Rose

It wasn't always easy Rose was strict Although she never locked her in her room she always made her go to school do her homework go to bed at half past ten The TV had only RTÉ and if no one called to have their fortune told or play cards they often sat there listening to the wind whistle through the holes in the roof

She often wondered was it really Mammy's wish Rose take her Hard to imagine seeing as Mammy always took Daddy's side But maybe she knew she was dying and that changed it Or maybe Rose knew and it was she decided and Mammy just went along

When she died Rose would not let Imelda go to the wake At the funeral Daddy's face was red and sagging like a bag of mincemeat and JohnJoe wore his sunglasses inside the church Lar told her that none of them had slept and that Daddy had hit a bollard parking the van in town After they buried her they all went back to the house Daddy was drinking and started getting angry at Rose Told her it was time for Imelda to come back Didn't care what promises she had made to Mammy A house needs a woman he said We'll see Rose told him But when they got home to the cottage she shook her head and said to Imelda What woman needs a house like that

Still she started going back more often Every time the place looked worse Everything tipped everywhere as if the Finlay boys had come again and this time stayed Daddy in the middle of it He had barely left the house since the funeral Barely moved from the couch not even to go to the bookie's just sat drinking in front of the TV watching his wedding video over and over Sit sit he'd say to Imelda when she came in Look look just as he did with his fights Only now it would be Mammy and him arriving at the church or kissing on the altar or dancing together at the reception Mammy from a distance chatting with her friends Checking her make-up Looking over her shoulder and smiling at whoever held the camera My Molly he would say tears rolling down his cheeks My Molly and then You filthy bleedin' lowlife as the video player sent white lines up through everything O you rotten piece of junk LAR! as it groaned and spat out the tape and her brother would come scurrying in and try and get it working again

She knew he was beating Lar The marks were all over his face Golly and Christy too though they were bigger than him now and could surely have knocked him down if they'd wanted She alone could soothe him That's why she came Then he turned on her too

They were sitting together watching the video and she said without thinking how beautiful Mammy looked Because she did You could see it even through the fuzz and the white lines It was just something she said every time they watched it Hadn't bothered him before why would it But this time the moment the words crossed her lips she felt him stiffen and her heart sank

He leaned forward with a hiss Reached for the remote paused the video Then he turned and he looked at her and said Well of course she was Do you think you licked it off a fuckin stone

There was nothing she could say to that Still he waited like he expected an answer staring at her with bulging yellow eyes Then at last he turned back in disgust Picked up the remote Unpaused it but only for a second then paused it again

You have a lot of nerve he said and she blushed though she didn't know what he meant For another long moment he stared at the screen at Mammy's frozen face muttering to himself as if he was suddenly discovering something that had been hidden for years

She knew he was like this because he was grieving Just as Mammy had said the things she said because she was sick But she wondered So she had to keep coming to show him she was good Not one of the glamourpusses It didn't work The more she did for him the worse he got As if he saw it all as a trick You showed your true colours when you moved into that cottage he said Abandoning your homeplace your family What kind of child does that I didn't abandon you she said I'm here now amn't I But that was not the same Daddy said She'd been bespelled he said That old witch She'll turn you into a crone like herself and good enough for you

The brothers stayed out of his way lifting weights in the shed They were always saying they would leave or they would kill him One day he threw the frying pan at Lar and the grease burned his arm right up to the elbow One day she came and found the television on its back on the floor with the video recorder stoved through the screen

Rose forbade Imelda to visit It's not safe she said Lar said it too Don't come He's not himself When she went to bed at night she found herself remembering Things she'd forgot had ever happened People running up and down and up and down the stairs in the middle of the night Lights flashing in the yard She remembered playing with her doll on the floor of a strange room Her brothers standing around or sitting on the beds A woman with her hand on Mammy's shoulder speaking into her ear While from downstairs came a roaring The walls shaking like someone was trying to batter them down

No not safe Still she kept going Who else did he have with Mammy gone and anyway she knew he'd never harm her She knew he knew deep down that she was still his untouched princess

Then one day Lar called her up and said to come over What is it? she said She was alarmed because usually he would call to tell her not to come and this was the opposite But he wouldn't say anything more

When she got to the house it was dead quiet Where are they? she said Gone said Lar Gone? she said Gone where? But he didn't know He had come back from the shop and found the place deserted The van was gone and the washing off the line You think they're off on a job? she said Dunno Lar said shrugging with his hands in his pockets

There was something off about him What's up with you? she said Nothing says he But a big grin broke out across his face For a second the thought came to her that he might have done them in as they slept and they were lying upstairs with their heads split open but no that wouldn't be Lar

What is it? she said again but still he would only keep giggling and not telling her till she got angry and turned on her heel to walk back to Rose's but at the gate he called her back Look he said

He took his hand from his pocket and there was a wad of purple notes the size of a brick

Where'd you get that? she said and he shrugged and giggled again then when he saw she was about to lose it he pointed to the shed In there he said

In the shed? she said You went in there? She started towards it but he grabbed her arm

I want to see it she said She had never been in there It was the shed where Daddy had taken Butch that time But Lar shook his head not giggling now What's in there? she said but he wouldn't answer She looked again at his hand with the wad of notes How much is it? she said

Three thousand three hundred and twenty pound he said

She stared at him like he was winding her up but there it was in his hand How? she said and that was all she could say for a minute She was thinking of all the times there was nothing to eat All the times they stayed shivering in their beds because the heat was cut off Their shoes full of holes the roof full of holes the van half rust and with no reverse gear on it Mammy getting sick and not going to the doctor because there was no money to pay him

What will we do with it? Lar said

Put it back she said Her head was swimming The sight of it made her sick

Back? he said

He'll find out she said She didn't need to say what he would do

He left the lock off Lar said It could be anybody gone in and took it

But that didn't matter He'll have you in that shed like poor Butch she said Put it back Please Lar He could be on his way back this minute

All right all right he said But first he peeled some notes off the top We're getting a night out from it at least he said

They bought ice creams in the garage then walked into town The evening was warm still The tar was soft under their feet Lar kept taking the money out of his pocket to look at it and then laughing His face was lit up like he'd been huffing polish When they got to town they couldn't decide would they go to McDonald's or to Burger King so they went to both After that they got a pack of John Player and a naggin of vodka and sat on the riverbank passing the bottle back and forth The sun was setting and the river reflecting it like a bonfire and watching the midges dance around in the fiery light over the water Imelda felt that there was some enchantment going on like the man that finds the door into the hill Or maybe it was just she was outside and free For when in her life had she ever been out with money and no Daddy or brothers to keep an eye?

Maybe they'll never come back Lar said She laughed because they always came back

Imagine though Lar said Imagine not seeing him again He turned to look her in the eye as if he was asking her to really imagine it and her blood quickened because she knew what he was going to say

What if we took it

Took what she said though she knew

We could be gone he said We could take it and get away from here

Her heart pounded What are you talking about? she said Get away? Get away where?

England he said

She looked him in the eye He was grinning at her but behind it was something else and it dawned on her that he meant it

You wouldn't dare she said

I would if you came with me he said

He'd come after us she said He'd kill us

He'd kill me Lar said I don't know about you

He raised the bottle to his lips She saw the scar there on his arm from where the grease had burned him England's big he said Much bigger than here We could go to London Change our names

Instantly ideas came into her head Crystal Scott Megan St James Ivy something she had always liked that name Ivy She looked at the river invisible now in the darkness and imagined Lar and her getting away and it being like this for ever The two of them free with no one to be afraid of And she felt a rush like the milkshakes and the cigarettes and the vodka all together all at once They could do it! The lock was off the door they had only to go through But then she saw it all yawn up in front of her London like a dark river The names like midges dancing in dizzying specks and disappearing I need to think she said

Right said Lar Only we'd need to do it soon To be sure we had a head start

Yeah she said

And if you went he said you couldn't ever see him again

Right she said Suddenly she was tired talking about it Here she said are we going out or what? Will we go to Paparazzi's? And they did and that as it turned out was the end of the London plan

She had never been to Paparazzi's before Only heard the girls at school talk about it Pap's they called it for short It was packed to the rafters and roasting hot with a smell of Lynx that would knock you down Inside her everything was dancing around from the naggin and all she knew now was that she had to keep the buzz going They bought Jägerbombs and necked them then Lar found a purse that had another fifty in it so they bought more Jägerbombs then went out onto the dance floor It was heaving She had to push her way through the bodies The townie girls wore so much tan it smeared your clothes if you brushed up against them while the lads all had shirts on tucked into their chinos because you couldn't get in wearing a jersey Some of them were real slick but others had the crazed look of boggers from little far-flung villages Places Daddy would drive the van through without stopping Nothing you can sell to these people Daddy would say which was his greatest insult

Lar's eyes were on stalks looking at the townie girls with their jabs hanging out and sweat pouring off them because it was melting in there A song came on she knew Wonderwall A cheer went up She closed her eyes and it was like she fell backwards into the music and it rose up to meet her then she opened them again and then there in the lightening darkening shifting mass of dancing bodies she saw one body was stood stock-still It was a boy Standing there looking at her Not in the gawping way of the chino lads and the boggers More like she was a puzzle he wanted to solve

He was handsome like a knight in a storybook

She looked to her left then to her right There was no Daddy No brothers Only Lar wearing the face off of some fatso in white jeans Nothing to stop the boy as he came towards her

It seemed the crowd parted to let him through Heads turned to follow him Even in the gammy light of Pap's his eyes were clear blue like mountain pools and when she looked into them everything around seemed to dim to nothing like it had turned to steam

What's a girl like you doing in this kip he said

Ha? she said not understanding because to her Paparazzi's was like Buckingham Palace and the MTV awards rolled into one

He smiled asked her her name she told him Rachel Rice-Parkinson said she was from England London She didn't know why she lied He smirked like he didn't believe her He had a high opinion of himself she could tell And she found it hard to talk She kept thinking Daddy would reappear And she couldn't help noticing all the townie girls making sheep's eyes at him They were looking at him the same way the boys were looking at her though in fact the boys were looking at him too now and as they talked lads kept interrupting wanting to say something to him or buy him pints

Are ye some kind of pop star she said

He told her he'd scored the winning point in some match or other last week

Oh she said None of them at home followed the GAA Daddy had the racing on all the time

It's not important he said though he liked that everyone else thought it was she could tell

You're gorgeous he said I suppose everyone tells you that He made it sound like it was very boring of her She stared at him thinking how if her brothers were there he'd be on the ground now with three pairs of size ten boots stamping on him and he wouldn't be smirking then but then he kissed her Very gently and she stopped thinking of anything She had disappeared turned into steam mixed in with the dry ice while her body careered pell-mell into sin

Then Lar was there yanking on her arm Eyes wide We've to go he said The security was after him for taking the purse

She pulled away from the boy Wait he said Give me your number but there wasn't time Two big lads in Puffas were wading through the crowd towards them Please he said sounding desperate It was very romantic Lar tugged at her Come to the match! the boy called after I've a match next week in town Will you come Okay okay she said over her shoulder Promise? he cried but they were running already weaving through the tunnels of sweating bodies like rats till they escaped into the night

She didn't say anything to Rose about him though she wondered if Rose knew already The day of the match she was still saying to herself would she go or wouldn't she Even putting on her make-up she was debating it though she knew all along that she would

It was on in the next town over She didn't want to go on her own so Lar said he'd come and they would get the bus together But the time came and Lar never appeared and when she called him he didn't answer

Maybe he was angry at her for slowing down his plan she thought because he was still talking about that Going to England

If we're doing it we can't hang around that's what he'd said

And he was right she knew Daddy could come back any day But she'd made a promise to the boy that she'd go to his football match Can we not wait till after that she said

What boy The fella you were shifting in Pap's?

I wasn't shifting him I didn't shift anyone she said Just wait till Saturday After that I'll go with you

What if after Saturday there's another match Lar said His voice was low and sorrowing She thought again of the scars on his arm

After Saturday she said Just that one match I promise And she meant it even though in truth since meeting the boy she had thought very little about England or how they would get there or what they would do

But now Saturday was here and Lar was nowhere to be seen and if she didn't leave now she would miss the bus She finished her make-up then looked in the mirror and took it off again then went outside to the gate to see could she see Lar but there was still no sign of him so she went back put her make-up on again then set off on her own for the bus stop Thinking of the boy Imagining the things she would say to him *Darling I must leave here and you cannot follow me* Enjoying the sadness of it When she felt coming over her a kind of a chill a shadow then realized it was more of a sound Then knew what it was and who as it slowly drew up alongside her And the window rolled down

Where are you off to done up like a brasser? Daddy said

His arm was rested on the rolled-down window There was a new tattoo of a woman's face that she realized was supposed to be Mammy Behind him one two three brothers staring out at her Oh she said trying to sound glad to see him Just doing some messages

Hop in Daddy said I'll give you a lift

The van was dark Stinking of damp though the weather had been sunny for days When she got in she saw Lar was in the back Sitting in the shadows looking at his hands No one was talking The door slammed shut Where is it you're going? Daddy said

She had to tell him then What choice had she Either she lied and never saw the bonny boy again or she told the truth and opened the door to who knew what

I was going to a football match she said She looked straight ahead to avoid Daddy's eye

A football match? he said What has you going to a football match?

She wondered if he already knew If Lar had told him out of spite or to save his own skin What difference did it make anyway It was all ruined The boy and the plan both Lar was right They should have gone that day as soon as they had the money

A friend of mine is playing in it she said I told him I'd go see him

There was silence She could feel the brothers' eyes glow like jackals in a forest

But Daddy said only A match is it Sure we'll all go Why not?

The grounds when they got there were small and smelled of pee But there were lots of people making noise Singing songs and letting out roars Rowdy in a good-natured way Everyone was wearing jerseys and scarves Some had braided strings in the team colours around their heads too and there were girls that had those same colours daubed on their cheeks which actually looked quite well she thought You had to pay in which when Daddy found that out he sent the brothers back to the van

The teams came out and her heart skipped when she saw her boy She wondered would he look for her among the crowd but in fact he did not lift his eyes away from the pitch the whole length of the game Still she flushed whenever he came close to where they stood and when the crowd cheered him When they called out his name she felt a pride in her heart even though she didn't know what was going on

Nor did Daddy He kept asking questions Who's that fella now? Why's your man blowing his whistle? Was that a goal? But he noticed her boy God he's a fair turn of speed that wiry fella he said That's him she said That's my friend That's Frank Christ but he's fast Daddy said Then he cupped his hands around his mouth and he bellowed Go on Frank! Around them everyone was shouting the same thing Go on Frank! She shouted it too He had already made it to the far end of the pitch So fast so graceful That's Maurice Barnes's boy people said to each other

Afterwards when the whistle blew he stood at the sidelines in a welter of people The crowd was moving for the gate She told Daddy she was going to the toilet and she'd meet him outside Then she slipped down and waited for her moment

They had won the match There was a mob of supporters wanting to talk to him and shake his hand Girls too but none you'd look twice at He was in the middle of them Covered in mud Breathless laughing His eyes so bright Next to him the fans looked pale and wispy even with their meaty chops and their hay hair and the lipstick scrawl on their cheeks Just like that night in the club when everything around him had turned to steam But here he was real in the daylight and she knew that she had been wrong to make her promise to Lar because she could never leave now after seeing him again

But there were so many people crowding around him and she began to think who was she to talk to such a person She who lived in a cottage with an outdoor toilet He hadn't seen her yet Next time she thought and she bowed her head and ducked away

She wanted nothing more than to go home then and cry in her room for a while but Daddy had decided he wanted a pint People were heading to Coady's he said She told him she was tired Begged him to take her home but he said they'd just stay for one and she had no choice but to go along hoping to God Coady's wasn't one of the places he was barred from because sometimes he'd forget though the barmen never did

The pub was jammed full of people in the scarves and jerseys of the two teams Daddy sent Lar up for the drinks and they stood together in a little ring Daddy banging on at the top of his voice about the game So loud that even in the packed pub people kept looking over and she was ashamed How could one man not know so much And if he didn't know why couldn't he stop talking about it Her head ached She was realizing then what she'd known in her heart That it was impossible It could never have worked There would be no next time She would not see the boy again

Then a hand gripped her arm and she turned and it was him

And like that night in the club everything melted away His eyes were like stars There in the crowd It was just the two of them You're here he said You came

I thought you were gone he said I saw you after the match I was calling your name didn't you hear me?

Oh yeah no she said Now that she thought of it someone had been calling Rachel She'd forgotten that was her She blushed she laughed he laughed He was perfect

Then from somewhere very far away it seemed she heard a voice Daddy's voice You look very familiar he said peering down at the boy Are you not that lad that was playing in the match

The boy looked up in shock Seeing for the first time the lairy faces ringed around him The brothers with their gobs stuffed full of chips She could have sunk into the ground But he kept his cool I am he said Frank he said and stuck out his hand

Good game Daddy said Wish I'd stuck a few bob on it Horse racing would be more my line

Sport of kings Frank said and Daddy liked that and started gabbing away to him about the Gold Cup

She had never seen Daddy like this Usually any man came within ten feet of her Daddy would be rolling up his sleeves ready to put the frighteners on him But it was like he thought Frank was there for him not her He never stopped to wonder why the brilliant athlete the miraculous young sportsman beloved of the whole town should be there hanging on his every word and buying him pints That was Frank's gift That's what she learned about him He'd talk to anyone A duke or a derelict And when he did he made them think they were the only ones in the world A gift yes A curse too because all of those people thought they had a claim on him But she didn't know that yet and listening to the two of them she would have begun to think that it was in fact Daddy Frank had come over to talk to only that every so often he'd steal a glance at her and there would be a shock ran through her and he'd smile and she'd smile and she knew

But then the crowd parted and a man appeared

He looked like something out of *The Godfather* A head of silver hair slicked back An enormous coat you could fit two or three people in A pink tie A polka-dot handkerchief poking out of his top pocket Someone who had made money it was plain and wanted you to know it He comes up to them this fella and fixes them with an eye like he'd caught the servants drinking his sherry And Daddy's speech that he's making dies away in his mouth and there's silence

Howdy Pops says Frank

Pops who was Maurice of course doesn't reply at first Just looks at the bloody rogue's gallery of Imelda and her family clearly thinking to himself Who in the name of Christ is this shower and why are they talking to my son Then he huffs at Frank Finish up now as we will be dining shortly

Ah hold your hour says Daddy and he reaches out a hand to stay him Come and have a drink with us first

Maurice looks down at the hand Daddy's hand on the expensive wool coat and if he'd been sprayed with toxic gas he couldn't have looked more disgusted Frank meanwhile is grinning away to himself as if this is the height of comedy and in that moment she sees how it is

Now no one at that point in time would have called Imelda canny or shrewd or anything of that nature Far from it But there in Coady's pub beholding them both father and son a voice in her head said to her Here's where your work is girl This is the one who calls the shots He's the one you've to get on your side

Clear as a bell she heard it and that was before she knew who he was or anything about him She didn't know anything about anything then But she could see well enough he was a self-made man A man on the up who would most definitely not let the likes of Imelda Caffrey drag down his family's good name His son might find it romantic or entertaining to associate with outlaws He did not no sir And if there was a battle over it he would win

Outside the clouds had parted The sun fell crookedly through the window showing up the thinning crowd Maurice got impatient That's enough now he said sharply Let's get going And she could tell that he was all set to yank his son out by the ear and that that would be the end of it

And she stepped out into the light

She lit off her stool and over to Daddy Started adjusting his shirt collars Fussing at him O Daddy you've this buttoned all *wrong* As if it was something she did all the time Not heeding the other man the other father But knowing he heeded her Watching without looking as he drank her in As the sun snared in her hair and blazed up gold As she moved through the light falling through the dust-streaked window Then she turned to him and smiled with a roll of the eyes And Maurice was caught He was a ladies' man A connoisseur She found she knew that too

Well he says in quite another tone of voice And who is this

This is my daughter Imelda says Daddy That is the Sunday in every week to me and the image of her poor mother that we buried in the spring

Maurice took her hand Charmed he said Gold watch looming up from his hairy wrist like a shining mechanical eye Then glanced at it I suppose we have time for a quick half

Yes they both understood it right there She and Frank though they barely knew each other they could see that if they were ever to have a chance they needed to keep the fathers happy And so they did Frank beguiled Daddy Just as Imelda beguiled Maurice Both knowing it bound the two of them together too But that was good Though they hardly knew each other They wanted to be bound

And that was how it went from then on Frank took care of Daddy She took care of Maurice A little was all it needed Then they were left free to fall in love

And love was what it was There was never any doubt about it Though it wasn't the falling-off-a-cliff feeling she'd always expected Not a plummet More like a leaf dawdling down to earth in swoops and circles They were always happy That was how it felt Pure and simple when they were together they were happy and from that first day they were together all the time Drinking in Coady's or in Finnegan's or in the Banister She could match him pint for pint the one good thing she got from Daddy Or else just drunk on each other Kissing in a car parked down a wood path Walking through the shopping centre eating crisps Every day a blur a haze of laughs and kisses He'd carry her on his shoulders She'd try and cut his hair All the time the two of them laughing laughing It felt like an enchantment but it was real From out of a shift in Paparazzi's she and he The rich boy and the girl from the back arse of nowhere It should have been impossible It was all so easy

After that first time they did their best to keep Maurice and Daddy apart Sometimes nonetheless at a match the two men would meet and her heart would be in her mouth that Daddy might start gassing about for instance his *experiences as a horse breeder* meaning the poor nags he'd bring over in the van from his cousin in Lincolnshire Or his *interest in classic cars* meaning the Datsun he'd had up on the blocks since forever waiting on parts But Maurice would always have a dinner reservation or something like that so he never had a chance to get going And though he was always saying they should all get together and though Maurice always made a point of asking her about *her father* as he might say *the chairman* or *the Monsignor* it never happened The fact was that Maurice didn't want to see Daddy and Daddy wasn't quite fool enough to want to rock the boat

Because here at last was the millionaire he'd been dreaming of

Frank's father had a car business right in the middle of town It had his name on it Maurice Barnes Motors and on any day of the week you'd walk past and see him in the showroom with his gold cufflinks on and his silver hair swept back Talking to a customer like a king to a peasant Frank worked there too in Sales They were raking it in he said Everyone was falling over themselves buying new cars all he had to do was open the shutters in the morning and he'd have half the fleet sold by lunchtime There was that much money about he said it was almost like the cars were driving out by themselves

Frank was always taking the mick out of the old man for his ways but he liked to flash the cash himself Always wore designer jeans designer shoes designer sunglasses A Tommy Hilfiger jumper out of Shaws with a good shirt underneath Had his own little phone he carried around in his pocket If you didn't know him you'd want to give him a puck in the gob At work he wore a suit and he looked like an FBI agent from TV She could see him in there too In the showroom talking to customers Talking to people was all they ever seemed to do That's the job he said

She couldn't figure that but they must have been good at it him and Maurice because they lived in the biggest house she had ever seen It had no number only a name Goldenhill It used to belong to an earl or a lord or something like that There was a meadow behind it and a big woods like you'd have in a story

Inside the house just went on and on Maurice took her round one day Everywhere you looked there were things Shiny things china things little tables to put the things on Ornaments and knick-knacks and picture frames A family portrait A stuffed fox Couches and chairs and ottomans covered with throws and blankets and cushions Layers and layers of everything in a way that reminded her actually of Daddy's sheds though that was wrong because this was all the very best And furthermore they wouldn't just have the one of whatever it was they'd have a load of them just lying around or piled up in a cupboard or one of the rooms upstairs More ottomans More Air Maxes More tennis rackets some still with the tags on If you liked red wine this bottle was sixty years old If you liked cartoons they had all the films on video and a framed photograph on the wall of the boys holding Mickey Mouse's hand at Disneyland That's before you got into the watches and bracelets and necklaces because they had all that too Her eyes were on stalks even if she didn't know what most of it was

Not bad for a lad from Piggery Lane Maurice said That was one of his catchphrases He'd point to his trophies and say with a shrug Decent enough for a lad from Piggery Lane

Peggy didn't like it when he said that She was not from Piggery Lane

But you had to hand it to him For all his grand talk and show-offery he'd done it He'd come from nothing and made all this He hadn't sat around moaning about the bad hand life dealt him Instead he had seen his opportunity and he'd taken it She respected that

She always liked Maurice in fact She understood how some people couldn't stand him but the two of them always got on She knew he thought she was trying to get her hooks into his son and she knew he knew she knew But with a man like that the knowing was part of the game and the way that she played was to pretend she was trying to get her hooks into him instead and he into her Oh Maurice you're a scream! she'd say when he made a joke Or Maurice Barnes you're wicked! and she'd slap his hand when he held on to hers too long Other times like if there was a GAA reception Frank had to go to or some other grand event she'd look into his eyes and say But Maurice you'll be there too won't you? Or if they were in a restaurant Maurice what does this word mean? And point at the word in the leatherbound menu with her eyes wide and vacant and he'd gaze into them with delight like a miser at his treasure Langoustine darling he'd say with his face lit up gold by her Langoustine it's a type of lobster

Where had she learned to act that way? How did she know what he wanted her to say? A sophisticated man like that and she who was always the quiet one The only girl in a house full of cavemen farting and punching each other? Sometimes it would worry her that she knew how She would think of what Mammy said about her *I see who you really are* But none of it meant anything It was only pretending Except that it made Maurice like her So it meant an awful lot Because he did like her she could tell Whatever else he made of her

Peggy was different

Peggy was complicated Speaking to her was like a game of chess Frank had taught Imelda draughts and now he was doing chess with her and so she knew Maurice was draughts Black v white Man v woman A battle that was fast and only for the crack Peggy was chess A game that Imelda didn't know why would anyone even want to play it

It was Peggy who had invited her to the house that first time After they'd been together a couple of months When Frank told her she felt like she'd swallowed a bucket of ice What for? she said That made him laugh She wants to meet you that's all Why wouldn't she

She couldn't sleep all week She asked Rose had she a potion or a spell she could cast on her On Frank's mother Rose just pursed her lips To be honest Imelda didn't know that Rose was all that gone on her seeing Frank

Maybe she just wouldn't go she thought Say she was sick or Daddy was sick But even then early on she knew there were countless girls Frank had gone through and forgotten about They would sidle up to him in the pub looking bashful ashamed though it was he who had dropped them She felt sorry for them At the same time determined she would not be like them They had never been invited to Goldenhill for dinner

Peggy hadn't come to the match that first time In fact she never came to Frank's games She got too anxious Frank told her They made her physically sick Imelda thought that was incredibly glamorous So the first time she met her was there at the house

She was grey-haired though she was not old Quiet Kept herself off to the side or in the background

At dinner Maurice did most of the talking Telling Imelda about his successes and the places he'd been while Frank horsed down food and Dickie the brother sighed and sniffed and Imelda kept smiling and tried not to drop anything But then like a shark Peggy would swim up out of the deep

So what are your plans Imelda?

Imelda clamped in her shark's jaws just gaped Plans?

Now that you're finished school What do you intend to do

Oh I gotcha Imelda said nodding in the hope this might be enough But Peggy waited with her bird-head tilted gazing at her and her fairy-godmother smile while Imelda turned redder and redder

Mam don't be interrogating her! Frank said laughingly As though it was all a joke

I simply want to get to know her Peggy protested Is she thinking of college Has she a career in mind I'm interested that's all in how she imagines her future How do you see it dear?

Plans the future yes they loved all that talking about what would they do Where would they go Next week next month the Christmas holidays The best hotels best beaches best resturants Talking talking Piling it up like more stuff in boxes to go in the spare room And when she listened she realized that this was what made them different Because in her house there was never a plan No thought for the future Life just came at you like a gang of lads getting out of a van

From the hall the grandfather clock ticked like the slow beat of a drum She looked from one pair of eyes to the other and she thought *Who are you? What am I doing here?*

Then at last Maurice stepped in Imelda lives in the moment don't you darling he said And I can't think of a better place for her to be

And he kissed her on the top of her head and got to his feet Now he said Dessert!

So that's how it was She needed Maurice to like her not just for himself but to ward off Peggy Maurice never asked her about her background or her plans anything like that He knew that if he disapproved of her it would only encourage Frank Also he liked flirting with her so he had decided to let Frank sow his wild oats

But Peggy could see there was more to it than wild oats She was keeping a watchful eye And of course Maurice liking Imelda turned Peggy against her all the more

It was all lost on Frank The questions the little digs *You'll stay safe won't you* as Imelda was getting in the car for Frank to drive her home *Seat belts I mean These roads are very treacherous*

Treacherous yes Such a beautiful house so warm such lovely food and hospitality She always dreaded going there Always such a relief when she could leave

But maybe he saw it too The first time she brought him back to her home she warned him It's not like yours mind With all fuckin' turrets and what have you

And he laughed and said Thank God for that

She didn't want to bring him at all The thought of him seeing even the front yard gave her the chills But Daddy was starting to nag at her Are you hiding him away from us? Is it ashamed of us you are?

Frank didn't care about the front yard He liked it there Sitting down in the kitchen with Daddy and the brothers and cracking open a can He said it was like the shebeens he'd drink in sometimes up in the hills And

Daddy liked it too of course because Frank would always come over in some new car he'd taken off the lot He'd roar up outside and the neighbours would peep out their windows to see And Daddy would come huffing down the drive looking very important and start talking to Frank in a loud voice about specs and camshafts and then loudly Come in come in! And in they would go and sit at the table and the brothers would come and join them there as if it was a normal kitchen in a normal house and tell stories about high-jinks and characters they'd met just as normal people might until as she had at Goldenhill with Frank's parents she found herself looking at them and thinking Who are you Where am I

Your brothers are real characters Frank would say afterwards They're gas

Only Lar hung back While they were sitting drinking he'd be around but doing something Making sandwiches or tidying or something

After the first match when Daddy was just back she'd told him to go himself Take the money before Daddy noticed the lock was off the shed and get out of there to London or wherever But she knew he wouldn't not without her And he hadn't And since then they didn't talk so much

But it was Daddy who was most changed that had been in a slump ever since Mammy died but now was in the best form she'd seen him And it was all thanks to Frank! Daddy couldn't get enough of him Just thinking about him made him happy He'd be sitting back in his chair Quiet then suddenly he'd say something like You know what That Frank's a real gent then go back into his thoughts Smiling to himself He'd started shaving again Taking care of himself in case Frank might call round

It wasn't only the money either that he thought might be coming his way They had a connection as he saw it They were sportsmen

Sportsmen Yes It had never crossed her mind But Daddy was keen that Frank know all about it He'd tell long stories about his fights The pressure How you'd be that close to giving up You know how it is Frank he'd say I do sure enough Mr Caffrey Frank would say

So when Frank came to whisk her off in his fancy car with dealership plates there wasn't a meg out of him The lovebirds he'd say and he'd chuckle The same man who kept a crowbar in his van to show to any fella who might think of walking her home Lads are only after one thing he'd say

Well maybe it was the money he was thinking of and that's why he left her go off with him or maybe he thought Frank the gent was too saintly ever to dream of such a thing If that was it he could think again that boy did not stop

He liked to drive down to the lake with her in the big A6 saloon That was his favourite because you could push down the seats and it was like being on a double bed there by the waterside She'd know whenever he pulled up in the A6 he was looking for it though the fact was she told him he'd have a better chance if he took her out in the TT even if there was less comfort

Yes in the TT by the water with the sun going down in his eyes and her hand in his hair and his head on her heart Then it was hardest Everything in her wanted to give herself to him Her boy her beloved

But she kept remembering what Mammy said The badness inside her If she was touched would it come out

Soon she said

It's okay he told her We've loads of time

Yes time the future The world to him was a palace of wonders Every nook full up of treasure adventure Just waiting for him to find it

He was working in the garage but he didn't plan on staying there I don't want the old man breathing down my neck the rest of my life he said He'd made a business plan with his friend Dolly Some kind of Fantasy Football thing they were going to put on computers She could never make head nor tail of it but Frank was convinced they were about to hit the jackpot

Dolly was the numbers man A genius Frank said It was he had the computers sussed out She never figured out why he was called Dolly He wore a woolly hat the whole year round and the one time he took it off she saw his hair was going in tufts like a dog with mange He didn't look like a doll or a genius either But that was Frank He saw the best in everyone

Still and all she couldn't see why he wanted to get out of the garage when he was doing so well out of it Maurice won't be there for ever will he she said He'll retire some day Hasn't he his money made

But Maurice wanted Frank's brother to take over when he stepped down It had all been arranged Right now Dickie was home for the holidays but in October he'd be going back up to Dublin studying Business for to get ready for it

And there'd be nothing for you? she said Once he took over?

There might be a job but it wouldn't be the top job and Frank didn't want to be under anybody's thumb

Not that he held it against Dickie This was Maurice's plan not either of theirs Frank idolized his brother He was always talking about him How clever he was The smartest man you'd ever meet though that didn't cut much ice with her after him telling her Dolly was a genius Who had set himself on fire once doing a bong Dickie mightn't be as bad as that but he'd never made much of an impression when she met him at the house Two years older than Frank but it was Frank who seemed the man of the world while Dickie barely even opened his mouth Had his nose in a book most of the time Never came to Frank's matches even because supposedly he had an ear condition that was set off by the crowd noise

You mean he gets sick when he hears people cheering for you she said but Frank didn't seem to find anything strange about that And in the end it was none of her business Families One's as mad as the other you can't interfere And who knows they might have worked it out between them Frank Maurice and Dickie The garage was not the problem in the end nor was it Daddy nor Peggy It wasn't even she herself

The problem was the football

Everyone said Frank's team was the best the town had had in years

They had won eight matches in a row Racked up a record number of points And though people said it was too early to talk about the All-Ireland they talked about it nevertheless

Now Imelda didn't know one end of a ball from the other and until then she'd never imagined how obsessed an entire town could be about lads playing football Wherever you went you heard the same conversation Would Joe Blah's knee hold up Did Seanie Whatshisface deserve another crack at a starting place Had they a chance of making it to the next round

It was like a fever that had driven everybody mad and she thought they were all crackers till she caught it too and then she was just like the others tossing and turning at night over cruciate ligaments and points per game

Every weekend there was a match and they would go herself and Daddy in the van to the bockety stadium in town or some other even more godforsaken prison-yard of a place off somewhere beyond Frank said the rules were too boring to explain to her but she copped on quick enough herself Figured out the teams and rounds and bainisteoirs just like she'd figured out langoustines and cashmere coats and she stood on the sideline and screamed until she had no voice left at all

People said Frank had a gift

They talked about his *stamina* and his *technical mastery* His *precision kicking* and his *ideal physique* What they meant was he was fast Tricky to catch When he kicked the ball it went where he wanted He'd slip by his markers without seeming to try It was a joy to watch people said and it was A joy too to see the town lifted up and thrilled by this boy Her boy The doleful old mugs bursting out with smiles Yes when he was on the pitch everything was perfect

The problem was the game didn't end with the final whistle Everyone had an opinion they needed to pass on to him Everyone wanted to buy him a pint or shake his hand In the pub On the street They would come up to him they would crowd round him

Everybody wanted a little piece Their share of the magic

It surprised her to find herself playing second fiddle She the great beauty But that's how it went The lads lining up stammering and blushing it was for Frank not her and as for the girls well they wished her dead in a ditch And personally she wouldn't have minded But for Frank it was hard Talking and talking Drinking and drinking Though he loved to talk and he loved to drink it took its toll All the love All the hands slapping his back

There was a time when none of these people wanted to know me he told her once He didn't explain and she couldn't work out what it meant Did he want them slapping his back or did he see through it or did he think both things at once But it struck her for the first time that for all that he liked everybody and they all liked him he was lonely Maybe that's why the two of them got on so well she thought that had never had friends either In school the other girls jealous of her or looking down on her or scared off by her family

He was happiest she knew when it was just the two of them and she learned how to tell when he'd enough of his fans and find a way to pull him free

There were some people though he could not slip away from

Why did you kick for a point when you had a clear shot on goal? Why did you go for a goal when you had two men free in the centre? Why did you let their defence close you down like that the whole second half? Yes everyone had an opinion But Maurice had an opinion twenty-four hours a day At work Frank was getting it At home too Gameplans Strategy Training he was always on about that I suppose in training they've got you working on your kicking? I imagine they've said to you in training about building up your core?

Frank never responded except to nod or mumble and look about for something to distract himself with The only time she ever saw him pick up a book was when Maurice started talking about training

I know he thinks I'm going hard on him Maurice would say to her I just want him to make the most of the opportunity he has here He thinks life will be full of moments like this It won't

Let's face it he said Frank is a great lad But he's a waster A kick up the hole does him no harm at all

And it was true indeed Frank could be lazy How many times did he miss coaching his under-10s because he was lying in bed with a hangover With his own training too he'd be late or skip sessions Knowing he'd get away with it because he was their best player Maybe Maurice was right and he did need a kick up the hole But when he said he only wanted Frank *to excel* his two favourite words that wasn't the whole truth for it was Maurice who loved the cheers and victories The glasses hoisted The car horns honking in the street It was he cared who was man of the match or if the county manager was there in the crowd When people said *That's Maurice Barnes's son* he'd swell up As if Frank's speed and his kicks and his ideal physique were just another part of him Like the enormous coat and the enormous car and the enormous house with its breakfast room and its *sessile oak forest* and its piano that no one played

Well so what? she said when Frank complained He's your father He's proud of you Isn't that only normal

It's got nothing to do with him Frank would say Or he'd curse or change the subject

But once he said If he's so proud of me why won't he give me the job at the garage

The garage she said What's that got to do with it?

But it had everything to do with it

The dealership was the club's sponsor Maurice's name was on every shirt When Frank *excelled* on the pitch he was advertising the business The same one Maurice had decided he was not good enough to run himself Because Frank was the athlete and Dickie was the brains

She tried to talk him out of it Who cared about Maurice? Wasn't he playing for himself For the team? Because Frank lived to play football Was never happier than when he was out on the pitch But the more that Maurice nagged at him the more Frank came to feel like he was only doing it to please his father And he didn't want to please his father

The team was doing well now the best they'd ever done They beat the county favourites Clonabree handily Had a record score against Oolagh Frank was at the heart of each win Though by now the opposition thought they had him pegged Had sussed out his tricks and his moves He'd just invent new ones each time New tricks new moves Breeze past them as he always had and the team cruised along in his wake to the county final against St Fursey's where he scored a goal and could have had two or three

That was the first time they'd been county champions There was a parade with the team waving out the back of a flatbed truck The whole town out on Main Street all going balubas Jaysus lads we'll make Croke Park yet that's what they were saying But not him

He made it look easy but it wasn't she knew The youngest on the team carrying all that weight it took its toll and the dossing the messing skipping his practice all that was only a way of hiding how hard it was Now they were through to the provincials he couldn't hide it any longer If people came up to him and started in on their theories he'd cut them short We'll see he'd say We'll do our best And then he'd shuffle off

But from Maurice there was no escape

The provincial championship he'd say over dinner This is the big time all right

You've had an easy run of it so far he'd say This will be your first time facing a team of real ability

Imelda did her best to change the subject Hasn't it got awful warm she'd say or Are those begonias Peggy those blue things but it didn't work

The cream of the crop The best in their county he'd say Yes this'll sort the men from the boys all right

And Frank in response would say nothing at all just stare at his plate Turn his mashed potatoes over and over

As the day drew closer he started acting strange Going in on himself She couldn't say anything to him for fear he'd bite her head off For instance if she told him not to worry that those lads out of Ballyray were only a bunch of posers he'd turn on her Start telling her that Ballyray

were in fact probably the best club in the country right now Better prepared Technically more advanced On and on wagging his finger at her
like a guard giving her a ticket

But if she told him on the other hand that if he lost it wouldn't be so
bad because at least the two of them would have some time to themselves
he didn't like that either Jesus Christ Imelda are you trying to demotiv-
ate me? he'd exclaim and throw his hands in the air

He stopped going to Coady's He ate his lunch in the workshop in the
garage and if she wanted to see him she had to go in there or up to the
house She could understand that Wanting to have his space but then he
stopped going to training He'd disappear for hours she didn't know
where He'd got her a phone like his but he never answered when she
called him He was off in another world and she started to think was there
more going on here than the football The thought came to her that he
was seeing someone else on the sly One of the moony sidling girls from
the pub who'd give him the ride She felt sick Heartbroken at the same
time She'd been so busy worrying about Maurice and Peggy she never
thought anything could go wrong between the two of them She didn't
know what to do She couldn't ask him So she tried asking Rose Is he
cooling on me? Is there someone else?

But Rose if she knew anything wouldn't tell her I'm not getting into
that stuff with you was all she'd say Instead she found out from Dolly

Imelda had forgotten all about Dolly and Frank's supposed business
She hadn't seen him in months But he came to her now and told her how
a few weeks ago he'd met a lad from Sligo who was selling a load of hash
It was the deal of the century he told her He'd gone to Frank and
together they went in on a kilo and the plan was to sell it on and use the
money to invest in their business Only instead of selling it they'd been
smoking it themselves

Dolly's skin was coming off in patches When he told her that she
wanted to hit him a smack but she stayed cool

There was an old shed in the woods behind Frank's house he said They
kept the hash there in a hole in the floor Went out together to smoke But

what had started to happen was that Frank was going there on his own I'm getting worried about him he said That's why I came to you

Well thank you kindly for that she said knowing that Dolly's main concern was that there'd be none left for him The worst of all the false friends he was Still it explained where Frank had been and about his moodiness He never smoked usually because it made him depressed But he didn't want to go to the pub she supposed and have to listen to half a dozen gobshites explaining tactics to him

There was a great big forest behind Goldenhill that had belonged to the lord or whoever it was back in the day Maurice was very proud of it He liked to walk around it Pointing to 'notable trees' with his stick

The shed was right in the middle A tumbledown stone hut barely more than a ruin Frank had brought her out there once 'for a picnic' he'd said which she knew well what that meant Here? she'd said Are you mad? It was a strange sad little place with holes in the walls and a dirt floor Cold and dark even in the sunshine Some places are like that Always with a shadow on them

The thought of him sitting there alone hour upon hour made her sick But if she went down and dug him out of there herself she knew he'd only give out to her More nagging he'd say the last thing he needed

That's when she thought again of Rose

Rose could tell him she thought Rose could see How the game would go Would they win or lose He'd know what to expect It would ease his mind

Tricky enough to arrange all the same Frank and Rose didn't get on Maybe she was shy of him because of his fast cars and his Ray-Bans or maybe she knew he made jokes about her Called her Gypsy Rose Whenever he was over anyway she'd clam up look away Wander out to the turf shed and leave her tea to go cold Which made Frank awkward in turn Frank who could talk to anybody Guards gougers nurses nuns Whatever eejit he found propping up the bar of Coady's With Rose he was tongue-tied Clumsy After a while he stopped coming into the cottage at all If he was picking Imelda up he'd stay outside in the car and honk the horn

So when she said it to Rose first she knew well she'd try and put her off and she did But Imelda kept chipping away

To Frank she didn't reveal her plan at all Only told him Rose needed a dresser moved Even then he was full of excuses I'm up to my eyes he told her when she knew for a fact he'd been off in his shed the whole day

At last though he came over and he did shift the dresser from one side of the room to the other That part worked out well enough all right Then as they were on their way out the door she said it as if it had just popped into her head

Oh here Frank she said Why don't you ask Rose about the match?

Rose was rattling about in the background pretending she wasn't listening

Ask her he said Ask her what?

Ask her will you win What'll happen just ask her she said Go on for the laugh

Frank looked like he didn't think this would be a laugh but she kept at him Go on seeing as you're here She won't do me All right all right he said

She bustled him over to the table then called to Rose and asked if she'd read his palm Rose didn't want to do it though she'd agreed It took Imelda grabbing her by the shoulders and steering her over to the table and there finally they were sitting across from each other

On the TV the lottery was on Ronan Collins pulling balls out of the drum and Frank said Forget the match Why don't you give us next week's numbers Rose

Rose pretended not to hear kept her eyes on the television

Hush Imelda told him Give her your hand she said

He stretched his arm across the table Rose with a face on her took it turned it over looked at his palm

I'm afraid those blisters are from self-abuse he said But your niece is the one to blame there

Frank for Jesus's sake Imelda said That's not funny

I'm only teasing

Well stop teasing Ask her something

Like what? Frank said

The match you gobdaw Ask her will you win

Well Frank says to Rose

You have to ask her yourself

Frank rolled his eyes but then he took a deep breath For a moment there was silence and he sat there with his hand in the old woman's There's something else I want to ask her he said His voice was different now About the future There's only one thing I really want to know

And Imelda's heart began to dance

He leaned closer across the table and he said Will I meet a tall dark stranger

With a sigh Rose let go his hand Got up from the table and stalked outside He's only joking! Imelda said Rose! She turned to Frank Why are you being such a prick? she said It only made him laugh more She swore went out the kitchen door Rose was in the yard scattering grain over the paving stones He was joking Imelda said It's cos he's worried about this match

Chuck chuck chuck Rose said to her hens not looking up

Did you see anything? she said Are they going to win? Will you come back in?

But Rose wouldn't answer or even meet her eye

Christ she thought Stamped back into the kitchen What is your problem she said to Frank

Look I'm sorry he said But I've things to do What are you doing dragging me over here when you know I don't believe in this nonsense

It's not nonsense she said

You seriously believe your aunt can see the future Frank said Look at where she's living It's like a hundred years ago

Couldn't you have asked her anyway What harm would it have done

Imelda He rubbed his face I've a match coming up It's the biggest match I've ever played I don't have the time for this

Oh right because you're so busy preparing she said Sitting in the woods smoking hash like a tramp

That got him all right Didn't think she knew about that

If you're so worried about the match why don't you train for it?

She should have stopped there Maybe if she'd stopped there it would still have been all right But suddenly she was so angry Do you actually care what's going to happen at all she said Or do you just want to bum around the town the rest of your life drinking Getting wrecked

Where's all this coming from he said

From knowing you she said Your father's right You're a waster You'll waste your whole life away

He got up from the table so quick the chair crashed over Well I won't waste any more of it here that's for sure he said

Fine so right fuck off be on your way she said She followed him out the door and threw her phone at him the one he'd got her It clattered against the car as he got in and gunned the motor and screeched off

And she went back inside to Rose's kitchen The lottery was still on though it felt that years had passed She sat at the table her head spinning round like the Wheel of Fortune What had just happened? Why had they fought? It had all been so quick it made no sense to her

But of course it made sense to her Of course she knew why She wanted to see the future That was her plan, wasn't it Her secret plan Rose wouldn't tell her fortune but she would tell Frank's Once she had his palm in her hand she'd see it all And then Imelda would see it too Know the truth Would they be wed Would he be hers for ever

Because she loved him He loved her too she had no doubt They had been so happy! Hanging around town drinking in Coady's kissing in the car by the lake But was she the story of his life that she did not know

And at the back of her mind was the fear that he would let it go Let it slide wither away Out of not thinking Or out of wanting to prove that he was just as Maurice said he was Lazy feckless a good-time Charlie To live all that out just so Maurice would know that nothing he'd told him had changed his mind And where would she be then?

That's what she had wondered in her secret heart of hearts That's why she'd cooked up her plan that she'd thought was so clever Getting a big clodhopper of a GAA player in to have his fortune told Now he was gone

When she went back out to get her phone she saw it had been crushed in the dirt He must have driven over it as he was leaving

She shouldn't have said that about Maurice Now he knew they had been talking about him behind his back

For all that day and night she sat in the cottage watching the television with Rose It felt very far from anywhere like the world might have ended and they wouldn't know

Then JohnJoe came and said he'd seen Frank drinking in town with a bunch of lads

What lads said she but JohnJoe didn't know them He'd gone over and had a pint with him Did he mention me Imelda says What JohnJoe says then like it'd just come to him What was he at drinking hasn't he a match on Sunday?

Afterwards there were many more stories like that About Frank Barnes in this pub or that sinking pints with three days two days one day to go before the match though she knew well the people telling these tales were the very same that had been buying him drink and bending his ear with their statistics and play-by-plays instead of sending him home to rest

If she'd known she could have talked sense into him She could have brought him home He would have listened to her if she'd known

Then maybe everything would have been different Their whole lives His life

But she didn't know Not where he was nor what he was doing nor whether she should care because was it a fight or were they broken up she didn't know that Didn't know even whether she'd go to the match or so she told herself Right up until the moment came and Daddy pulled up in the van hollering out the window We're late Come on to fuck

*

Rose was in the kitchen window drying a plate as Imelda clopped down to the gate She'd asked her if she would come but Rose did not like big crowds All that hurly-burly

The bloody roads were clogged up the whole way and Daddy was in a jock Kept honking the horn at the unmoving cars then complaining about his headache STOP HONKING THE HORN THEN she yelled at him but he didn't hear Her own head was full of chaos She had a bad feeling A few times she almost jumped out the door and started running back home

When they got there they had to park half a mile from the ground and as soon as they got out of the van it started to rain A real ha-ha kind of rain that swept in under the sunshine and didn't look like anything but drenched her from head to toe Hold on till I see have I an umbrella Daddy said and started rummaging around in the back of the van though she knew there was no umbrella Fifty electric sanders with the wrong plugs and instructions in Polish yes Two petrol lawnmowers missing their rear axles certainly But something a person might actually want or need no way She had to drag him out of it then she nearly sprained her ankle trying to run in platform heels through streets jam-packed full of opposition supporters in cowboy hats drinking pints But they got inside to the ground and the game hadn't started Come on says Daddy We'll call in to Frank

Where he had got the notion to do that she didn't know She tried to put him off Look at me she said I'm like a drowned rat which she was but Daddy had his mind made up and she couldn't tell him the real reason she didn't want to because if he thought they were split up she didn't know what he would do except it would be bad He took her hand and dragged her along She was sick to her stomach She passed the players' girlfriends all together but didn't look at them so as not to see if they were avoiding looking at her All around her people were singing shouting blowing whistles letting out catcalls *Yeee-owwww!* And the sounds and the smells Burgers chips spilled cider came piling in on top of her with the colours of the jerseys the faces the grass and the sky like a huge house of cards collapsing And it was all so much she stopped hearing anything so didn't realize at first the steward at the tunnel wasn't letting them through till Daddy started shouting at him

And that was the state they were in Daddy roaring his head off and she looking like she'd been pulled out of a drain when who appears out of the tunnel only Maurice dressed up to the nines as usual Wearing leather gloves and his big wool coat in spite of it being about a hundred degrees in the ground

His face was sombre He didn't even see them at first Walked right past them till Daddy called out And then he turned very slowly and he looked them up and down

And from the jumble in her head one very clear thought appeared which was Now we're seeing the real man at last Now we're seeing what he really thinks of us

There was no charm or flattery none of that He literally looked down his nose at them and even Daddy caught it and had the wind knocked out of his sails It was as if some crime had occurred and now he had the culprits right in front of him

Is he in there she said stupidly just to say something and stop Maurice looking at her

He is said Maurice with mock politeness They are trying to sober him up

And with that he turned and walked off The poor steward in the middle of this didn't know what to do so he turned away too and they went through

There was not a word out of Daddy as they went down the tunnel to the changing room It was like going down into a sewer with the mould and stench and piss and every step brought her heart lower and lower until they arrived at the changing-room door rotten with the paint peeling off it

And Daddy knocked and opened it and what did she hear only
Laughter

Gales of laughter the whole changing room whoever was in there cracking up

And then Frank in a stuffy grand voice like some Navy admiral saying Lads ye face today a Baptism of Fire You must fight with every atom of your being I will be there beside you in spirit drinking a glass of 1976 Cabernet Sauvignon

Taking off Maurice he was Then he stopped suddenly as Daddy went in and she heard the rumble of Daddy's voice then all the lads went WHOOOO! as they always did and shouted to bring Imelda into the changing room and they'd show her what a real mickey looked like and so on

Standing outside in the dingy stinking tunnel it seemed to her an hour went by a day a lifetime

Till the door opened again and he appeared

Well he said

And all thoughts went out of her head and she threw her arms around him

He gripped her tight It was like they'd been apart for months on different sides of the world I didn't know if you'd come he whispered into her hair I called you and you never answered

You drove over the phone she told him and as she said it she could feel a smile well up from her heart and break across her face You feckin' eejit she said and he laughed and bowed his head and she draped her arm over it He told her he loved her it was the first time he'd said it she kissed him the love rushed up inside her like she was literally going to die of pure happiness No one could be as happy as this and live

Here he says You'll never guess who I saw on the way up here only a tall dark stranger

Oh you're very smart she said Then she remembered Maurice what he'd said She drew back and she looked at him Was he pissed? She didn't think so She could tell he hadn't slept much nor shaved and there was a smell of fags and booze off him that would knock you down but pissed right at that moment no It was something else He was pale so pale His eyes glittering with a sort of strange electricity so it was like you couldn't see into them She'd never seen him like this so charged up though he acted like it was all a joke

The manager came to the door and called his name I've to go he said He hugged her and kissed her I'll see you after he said There'll be some hooley tonight when we win this thing

She walked back up the tunnel towards the light and the noise feeling so relieved so happy! Her worries had disappeared She was filled instead with excitement For the match for the future for their love and their lives together!

That boy's not himself Daddy said and in an instant it all went away again The happiness the relief disappeared and the fear came back worse than ever

She didn't say it or show it She found the brothers and went down the front with the other girlfriends and families and she was all smiles to them as they were to her and as the teams came out onto the pitch she clapped and screamed so much that Daddy gave her a dig of the elbow and told her to save her voice for when she might need it Everyone was there The whole town it looked like Only Maurice was nowhere to be seen She heard someone say he hadn't stayed And Peggy of course hadn't come nor Dickie What a family she thought They made hers look almost normal Then the whistle blew and a cheer went up as the game began

It was clear straight away that these Ballyray boys were a different class to the teams she'd seen before

Though you could hardly even call it a village Ballyray two pubs and a combine repair shop still every year they were contenders It wasn't only that they had the clever players that'd slip by you and the strong men that would cripple you There was something more that bound them all together So even when things went wrong they paid no heed just kept coming at you like a machine It was the mental preparation she supposed the psychology that Maurice was always banging on about

And they'd drawn them in the first round away the first real bad luck they'd had

But her boys though they were looser gave as good as they got Matched

them point for point And Frank playing like he was possessed Darting
back and forth everywhere at once Chasing every ball Facing down the
biggest bruisers they had All of the joking and clowning and casualness
dropped away You could see the passion Maurice was always complaining
he didn't have Though he didn't let it run away with him When someone
tried to niggle him with the elbow or a jab in the eye when the ref wasn't
looking he kept his head

She had never seen him play like this before She wondered had whatever happened between him and his father fired him up Was he throwing
Maurice's rules and advice back at him Saying I'll go and get hammered
then I'll play the best I've ever played He had scored a couple of points
early on and now on the mark of half-time he scored again to draw level
so as the whistle blew they were still in it though by rights Ballyray should
have been home and dry As he disappeared into the tunnel the girlfriends
turned and smiled at her She felt a glow she was proud and when someone behind her said he'll never be able to keep that pace up she pretended
that she hadn't heard and when she remembered the strange look in his
eye the electricity she told herself that was just the focus the passion

And during the break it was their supporters singing the songs
because Ballyray were getting frustrated you could see and starting to
make mistakes and it might just be that they'd be able to nick it out from
under their noses But that's not how it went

He'd told her once how the half-time break was like a game in itself
and when they came out after it they were different All of a sudden they
looked tired You could see how it was taking more and more out of them
just to stay in it Ballyray were tired too no doubt But they didn't show
it They kept coming and coming like water flowing downhill And point
by point they started creeping ahead

Around her in the stands the crowd were doing their best Give 'em
plenty of it lads! they cried Don't spare it! But their voices were ragged
and on the pitch the boys were ragged too Being outrun Making mistakes
Frank lorried into the Ballyray half-back and got a card for that and he
was lucky not to be put off after kicking the legs off the same fella five

minutes later Meanwhile Ballyray kept the head and went on nicking points here and there and as the clock ran down it was the fans at the Ballyray end were dancing in the stands while their half of the ground was silent Even Daddy Even the girls were silent

And then guess what Didn't Ballyray give away a goal It was the same ginger bruiser Frank had fouled who now miskicked the ball and sent it straight to Brian 'Pints' Coady son of Patrick J Coady the publican Who with a burst of speed from God knows where hares off from the halfway line till it's just him and the keeper Hammers the ball past him like he's knocking a nail into a coffin and now with three minutes left there's only a point in it

The rain is falling again in soft sheets and the sun through it makes the pitch glitter like broken glass Everyone's on their feet Beside her Daddy's bellowing so loud his eyes look like they'll pop right out The thick veins on his neck snaking up and his head turned purple and she takes his arm she can hardly bear to watch

And Maurice nowhere to be seen long gone

But if he'd stayed! Oh! If he'd only seen Frank's face at that moment! Streaked with sweat and mud and carved with deep lines like a warrior Throwing orders left and right shouting and pointing and the team falling in behind him like in that moment he had fully become the man he was always meant to be And Ballyray meanwhile like a routed army Running left and right up and down not knowing what to do Hang on to it! Their coach is yelling from the touchline For if they can just keep possession for a few minutes more the match is theirs and they'll be going on to the semi-final instead of having to slog through a replay with their confidence shook

But Ballyray are at sea They don't hear the coach's words And instead of running down the clock one of them has a try at a point from way up field that doesn't even make it to touch and now Joe Daly has the ball again and there's a roar from all around her that is not just a sound but a wave of energy she feels rising up from under her Lifting her and Daddy and everyone else all together like there is some power at work here

And she who had thought it was only a game feels in her stilled heart that her whole life rests on this moment

The pitch is silver in the rain shining almost too bright to see As the last seconds tick away she buries her face in Daddy's shoulder then peeps out again

To see Ciaran 'The Bollox' O'Neill puck the ball to Pints Coady

As the ref looks at his watch

And Pints kicks a long ball diagonally across the pitch and everyone groans because there's no one waiting there

Except suddenly there is Frank has appeared there out of nowhere and he catches it up and once more they feel that wave and pitch their voices together as if they can carry Frank in it too

And Frank pivots sprints The goalposts forty yards away Then thirty twenty as the seconds go down from twenty to ten the roar around her is deafening an ocean

A point If he can get a point They'll have earned a replay on their own ground

Kick they're screaming kick

But he takes his time the last seconds that are left to get in close Taking no chances

Till right in front of the posts he looks up looks down again The whole place is holding its breath and he draws back his foot to kick

But he slips

On the wet grass he slips and falls to the ground

And the ball goes rolling out of his hands

And throughout the stand there is a kind of shattering sound a wave crashing down and turning back into nothing

Then the Ballyray half-back the same red-haired bruiser grabs the ball and boots it out of play and the ref blows for time

These things happen people said afterwards It's all luck in the end they said It'll go your way one day and the other the next

It could have happened to anyone they told him in Coady's that night and in the Banister the night after and in Devine's the night after that It's only a game they said You can't get too hung up about it Sure if you'd got the point who knows but they might have hockeyed us in the replay

You've got to take the long view they said Anyway there's always next season

People were decent about it They were at pains to make it clear they didn't blame him

But they knew

They knew that he'd been out drinking the night before and the night before that Hadn't they seen him themselves? In this place everyone sees everything You might as well be conducting your business in the middle of the town square So it was a known fact that he Frank Barnes had been out till all hours downing pints and God knows what else the night before his big game

Now Frank was a young man and strong and fit as a fiddle and some made the argument that a man like that might well go on the rip the night before and it would make only a very slight difference to his game

But sometimes a very slight difference is all it takes isn't it

On another day without the burden of a dozen pints the night before might he have stepped on that patch of wet grass and kept his balance? And got the point? And won the replay?

Someone said they'd heard he'd thrown up on the bus on the way to the ground though all the same it could have been nerves

Someone said the coach wanted to take him off at half-time but he'd argued so fiercely to be left on that he'd got his way

Someone said he'd had a big bust-up with his girlfriend the night before Imagine they said picking a fight with him and he about to play a game of that stature

His poor father was in tears they said Someone had been standing beside him at the game and he was heartbroken

Holding no one to blame and making no accusations On another day could it all have been otherwise that's what people wondered and Imelda wondered it too

If she hadn't had her stupid plan If they hadn't fought If instead she'd kissed him goodbye and he'd gone home and slept deep and dreamless and woken refreshed might he have kept his feet and scored the point and saved the match and proved Maurice wrong and been carried through the town a hero instead of sitting in a half-empty bar taking the long view?

She wondered She would wonder for the rest of her life

She asked him if he blamed her He just laughed You mad yoke he said Where did I get you

Daddy of course took his side For weeks after he was fuming about poor Frank having to play in those conditions where he might have broken his neck As for Maurice Well you can guess He had been proved right and nothing gave him more pleasure than to wag his big silver kingly head in disappointment For a full week after the game he would not speak to Frank at all Not a word imagine and the two of them looking at each other in the showroom and in the house from one end of the day to the next

He's just in a sulk Frank said He probably had money on the game He'll snap out of it

And if he had? If he had snapped out of it? If after the slip the fall Maurice had reached down to lift Frank up? Said to him You are a gob-shite and a waster but you are my son and I'm going to teach you to be a bloody man Would that have made all the difference? So years down the line Frank would remark that that fall was the best thing ever happened to him? But no he shook his head over his chateaubriand and at the showroom took Frank off the floor and set him to work cleaning out oil sumps And when customers started to discuss the match he'd sigh heavily as if the town itself had been lost and swept away as in a battle

And that's really where things went off the rails because Maurice making a song-and-dance about what a disaster it was meant that Frank had to make a song-and-dance about how much it didn't matter and so to that end he went on the mother of all benders Taking up residence in

Coady's and drinking till closing She went there with him though he didn't ask her and as she matched him pint for pint she could feel how he was getting people's backs up Could feel too people watching her and saying amongst themselves that she was to blame for the wrong turn that his life had taken That she was the root of the wildness that she'd led Frank Barnes astray A mad thing from some estate in the next town over She had ruined his life and now was up at the bar sinking pints on his account

But if she hadn't of drank she would never have seen him at all and better that she was there she thought where she could at least try to keep some grip on him before he lost the run of himself completely

The problem then though was he'd turn up hungover for work and Maurice would send him home and he'd go directly back to the pub and a whatdoyoucall vicious circle started up where the angrier Maurice got the more Frank wanted to provoke him which made him angrier still and at times she thought they would actually kill each other that Frank would grab Maurice by the lapels one day and throw him through the showroom window Instead what Maurice did was to go round to Patrick Coady and some of the other publicans in the town and tell them Frank was having difficulties and ask them not to serve him That started Frank going to shadier pubs sometimes in other towns altogether and now he wouldn't let her go along These sessions might go on for days while she was left sitting in the cottage with Rose watching *Nationwide* and not knowing what had happened to him

He's fine the brothers told her because sometimes it was they he was with He's letting his hair down is all He's been training all season doesn't he deserve a break Though even they found him hard to keep up with By God they said that lad is a hoor for the coke

When she saw him he'd act like he hadn't a care in the world Laughing at nothing All to show her and everyone else how little that match meant to him who could clearly think of nothing else And though she knew the truth the others believed it And they didn't like it

It was all right for them to pat him on the back and say it wasn't his fault That didn't mean they wanted *him* thinking it They'd had their dreams dashed by this liúdramán They wanted *him* to be sorry Inconsolable They wanted sackcloth and ashes Instead here he was carousing and acting the goat acting like he'd won not just the match but the cup itself single-handed

She could see it herself how quickly in those weeks he became a different person to them From a hero to a messer Harmless perhaps but not to be trusted not to be got too close to lest you find yourself caught up in his chaos

If they'd given it some thought they'd have figured out what was really going on but people will only go so far to understand you and she began to wonder how all of this would end

Then he got dropped from the team

The manager whose name was Peter Eglantine was a decent man and had given him a long rope He didn't want to punish him for what had happened But with the drinking Frank was not only missing practice but putting on weight and slowing down Not to mention driving his teammates mad that did in fact blame him for what happened He must have known that What would come of it Maybe he didn't think they'd drop their best player Or maybe he wanted to prove to himself they'd stick by him even when he was at his worst And they did for a while But then one day the team sheet went up and he wasn't even on the bench

That came as a shock all right For the first time he saw that this wasn't just a bust-up with Maurice it was his life A couple of days went by where he was raging at Peter Eglantine Calling him every name under the sun Saying he'd get his father to pull the sponsorship on them Then he went quiet very quiet

For weeks he barely left the house He'd stopped drinking No pub Not even a can watching the game on TV But he was still suspended from the garage What was he doing all day? She saw less of him than she had when he was off on his benders When she did he was pale and uncomfortable and full of talk about *getting his head together* and *figuring out his next move*

It made her nervous If he was taking stock of his life where did she fit If he was saying to himself it was time to stop the messing and fly right did she go on the flying-right side or was he stacking her up with the messing because she had been there on so many of those wild nights

To make things worse something had happened to his brother He'd been knocked down by a car up in Dublin now he was back at the house recuperating When she saw him he was black and blue with a gash on his forehead where he'd fallen Frank told her he was scared to go outside Kept bursting into tears The house when she went there now was quiet as a church and everybody spoke in whispers They were trying not to have visitors as he didn't like strangers being there Frank said How am I a stranger? she said

Then one day he told her Dolly and him were thinking of going to London in the New Year

They were down by the lake The fields on the far side were bright with frost They were in the A6 but Frank hadn't put back the seats so she knew something was coming

For a match? she said

He looked at her shamefacedly like a little boy No they were thinking about a longer spell Her head burned and swam in spite of the cold They wanted to get their business off the ground he was telling her London was the place to network and look for investors

There were tears in her eyes but she didn't give in to them I thought you wanted to get back on the team she said How will you do that if you're off in England?

I have to be practical he said and when she laughed because only he could possibly think Dolly's Fantasy Football computer thing was practical he said Imelda I can't keep going on like this

The frost burned in the fields the sun burned on the water the same birds as always circled in the sky

What about me she said She tried to stop herself but she couldn't

It wouldn't be for ever he said A year that's all

A year! she repeated

And I'd be back here every few weeks he said It's not far

She shook her head A year she said again sadly

He sighed and pressed some buttons on the CD player though it wasn't switched on

I could go with you she said

I suppose you could yes he said pressing buttons We haven't planned it out at all but I mean you could come with me if you wanted

But she couldn't come he knew that Daddy would never allow it Unless they were wed she couldn't come he knew and she knew he knew and that wasn't even the point The point was he didn't want her to come For a moment there was silence Do you still love me she said

Of course he said This is for both of us

She didn't say anything more

Nor did she tell a soul about the conversation Who could she tell? If Daddy heard who knew what he might do Already he was asking questions because Frank hadn't been answering his calls Rose then? Yes Rose she might have told Might have said Rose he is leaving me what will I do! And Rose would have said something wise like Let him go If he returns it is for ever

But that was exactly what she did not want to hear To let him go Because Frank though he loved her was haphazard Careless Might mean to return but just not get around to it Miss the boat Lose his ticket something like that And how could she ever explain that to Rose Who had never taken to him always suspected him Imelda's fine young man from the good family that now wanted to leave her

No Instead she decided she would take matters into her own hands

It all came back to his father she thought The drinking the fall this stupid London plan Everything came back to Maurice not thinking Frank good enough to take over the business But if she could convince him to think again Or even just to tell Frank he hadn't made up his mind Wouldn't Frank be happy then to stay on at the garage? Stay on with her?

And so one night she knew Frank was out she put on her best dress and called Lar to ask would he drive her over to Goldenhill

It was freezing cold December Lar pulled up in the van She'd seen him only a week ago but he looked thinner smaller or as if she'd got older but he hadn't She waited for him to ask why hadn't Frank picked her up but he didn't He didn't have much to say at all She thought again of their own plan that never happened They had never spoken of it since Maybe that was why she told him Frank's talking about going to London she said

He looked at her without much interest The way a taxi driver would that didn't want to talk With you he said

No she said With his buddy Some idea they have for a business A football thing Only on computers The more she said about it the crazier it sounded like something made up on the spot

Lar just said Is he coming back

I don't know

Lar didn't say anything to that Looked back at the road She wondered was he thinking It could have been us Only for him you changed your mind Now look where it got you

Don't tell Daddy she said

Lar put on the indicator We're here he said

The driveway had never seemed so long so dark The Christmas wreath on the door dripped and bulged with berries and frosted pine cones She waited for Lar to turn the van around and go back down the drive Then on the step she pinched her cheeks pushed up her breasts and rang the bell

But it was Peggy answered the door He's out she said

It's Maurice I'm here to see Peggy Imelda said

There on the doorstep she waited a beat then another as Peggy looked her up and down

She wasn't beautiful Peggy she never had been Imelda knew that from the pictures in the house But somehow she made it seem like her own personal choice Like beauty was a trashy showy thing fit only for trashy showy people She looked at Imelda in her dress out of Topshop and it came to Imelda that she probably knew or could guess why Imelda was

here and that she at least would be glad to see Frank part ways with her
It seemed a long time that the two women stood there on either side of
the threshold The cold bit at her through the thin fabric of the dress and
she thought to herself that Lar was gone and if Peggy didn't let her in
she would have to walk back down the long dark driveway alone

But at last Peggy said Hold on there now till I see where he is and
leaving the door open for Imelda to come in she disappeared into the
house's warm crowded interior

She had never been here without Frank As she waited in the hall
everything seemed to look out at her The grandfather clock the paintings the golf clubs and it made her afraid for you only notice things the
first time and the last time Then Maurice appeared with his reading
glasses as he called them in his right hand and a turtleneck sweater

I wonder if I could have a quick word she said like she'd practised In
private

Of course of course he said and showed her the way to his den and
plonked himself in a big leather chair like a judge watching her do her
bit in the Rose of Tralee

She had it all worked out what she would say Maurice she'd say I
know you and Frank have not always seen eye to eye He has not always
been a good son in the way of Dickie who attends to his studies and is a
credit to you But if you would give him a chance then I'm sure he will
settle down get his act together There is no need for him to be going off
to London

But whether it was Peggy threw her off or something else anyway as
soon as she began she forgot it all and burst into tears Oh Maurice she
sobbed I don't know what to do

Who knows? Maybe that served her better than any speech would
Maybe she knew that somewhere within her or something within her
knew It certainly got his attention for he leapt out of his chair and put
his arms around her not in a creepy way but that made her feel safe
protected a dad way she supposed And his hands gently stroked her back
until her sobs had calmed

Then he drew her back from him and gazed in her eyes Now he said What's all this?

She didn't have the heart then to mention the garage Instead she just told him about England Dolly The plan From his reaction she didn't think he'd known about it He only sighed

Frank he said Frank was always a wilful boy headstrong He acts like nothing matters He's as casual as can be But beneath it there is a will of steel And woe betide whoever dares cross him

Which is usually me he said Through no design of my own that seems to be my role He likes to cast me as the ogre he said But the one he is fighting has always been himself

There is only so much a father can do he said At last he must let his child learn his own lessons

As he spoke he drew circles in the air with his reading glasses like he was conducting an orchestra while Imelda blinked at him wondering what any of it meant

She had never been in the den before It was even more full of stuff than the rest of the house You could hardly move without knocking into a wine decanter or a signed rugby ball The smell of leather and dark wood deeper here and stronger than in the rest of the house like it had come from here and spread outwards And as he went on *Where am I even* she thought again *What is this place* and from long ago the story came back to her of the traveller who falls asleep on the hillside Wakes in a wondrous hall full of golden-haired maidens princes treasure feasting but then the next morning it's all gone he's out on the hill again with just the clothes on his back and when he goes home it's a hundred years later and everyone he knows is dead

Would that be her she thought Out in the cold her life crumbled away Frank far beyond over some impossible sea

As though he had never crossed the dance floor of Paparazzi's but only ever smiled at her and then vanished into the dry ice a hundred years ago

Maurice put his hand on her shoulder I'll talk to him he said He was taking his leave but the hand remained She looked up at him She was beautiful when she cried which not everyone beautiful is It had been a comfort to her in the past such as when Daddy sold her horse For weeks after she'd be in floods but then she'd see herself in the mirror and the beauty of her tear-stained face would distract her Like a princess in a fairy tale

Yes beautiful golden-haired tear-stained she gazed up at Maurice A prize he would not want to lose from his lovely hill His hand lay on her shoulder He stood there not speaking bathed by her glow

And then Peggy was in the door

She left feeling lighter lifted but uneasy too like she'd done something wrong

And afterwards she would think in the long hours of married loneliness in the new-built house with Cass in her belly she would think was that when it all changed? Was that the moment after all? Not Frank slipping on the wet grass Not Maurice refusing to help him up but now there Was it she If she had never gone to Maurice with her tears and her speech would Frank have gone to England and lived

So she thought on the new couch in the new house in all those hours alone

That was later though Now as if by magic all their problems vanished Everything got better almost overnight

A few days after she'd seen him Maurice brought Frank back in to work in the showroom She didn't know if it was because of what she'd said or just that they were out the door busy Christmas right through January was crazy in there with customers crowding in looking to get their cars with the next-year reg From spending the whole day with nothing to do only brood in his shed suddenly Frank was doing ten- or twelve-hour shifts six days a week

And he was happy The thing about Frank was he loved to sell cars Loved it almost as much as he loved playing football When people came into the showroom he knew how to talk to them Not like Maurice with his tricks and his mind games learned out of a book He just connected with them Whatever good was in there he'd find it The meanest stupidest person you would see them come to life like a dried-up old plant given water They liked Frank Liked to make him happy Drove off their new cars with great big smiles

That was the best quarter the business ever had From his commission Frank told her he'd made enough for a deposit on a house When she saw him he was giddy and exhausted at the same time but the gloom of the autumn was lifted His brother had finally returned to Dublin and when she went back to Goldenhill he and Maurice were the best of friends again Frank was making so much money for them that Maurice had forgiven all his sins

As for Dolly and their plans she never asked about them and Frank never mentioned them It was like he'd forgotten as you would an illness once you are through it

He was back training with the team too Peter Eglantine had rung him up Asked him back He'd stayed off the booze till he had his full fitness again which was hard when they were going out For her because she didn't like to drink when he wasn't Didn't bother him a whit He was still the life and soul Talking a mile a minute and he drinking only mineral water That was the form he was in then Full of energy

The only thing they'd argue over was going out to the homeplace It was funny because in the past he'd always been happy to visit Now he complained He had little enough time between work and training he said It's such a trek to get out there She thought it was because he was off the drink When he'd come out before he'd always have a few cans Now he was doing it cold It must have seemed like a madhouse But Daddy was always calling her up There were only so many excuses she could give

Because it had been so long since they'd been out to see him Frank brought him a present A new VCR so he could watch his old fights Daddy was thrilled When they had it set up he made Frank sit down with him just like she had when she was a little girl

The fights shook him up Till then all he'd seen of Daddy was the show of politeness that was put on for him and Maurice Now he was getting a look at the real man The one they knew Pummelling strangers in a car park Hammering a fella on the ground till his jaw cracked He turned pale Didn't say a word Daddy didn't notice Look at this lad snakin' up on me he said then jumped to his feet clapped his hands shouted Get him get him get him get him get him

He'll be feeling that tomorrow won't he? he said as on the TV screen he rose up victorious from a bludgeoned body laid out on the tarmac

But was it safe? was all Frank could think to say I mean was there not a danger you could get brain damage?

Oh! Wait till I show you the one with the Spic said Daddy and he started hunting around in his tapes

He was quiet on the way home then as they reached the edge of town he said He's some man for one man your father

You don't know the half of it she said

He doesn't do it any more does he? Fight

Only if someone provokes him she said

He must have wished he never thought of bringing out that VCR because now whenever they went out there Daddy would always put on a tape Which made Frank want to go even less Only now he was that rattled he didn't want to say no to him

Well that made her laugh The thought that Daddy would ever lay a finger on Frank that adored him more than her practically

And that was the only thing The rest of the time it was perfect They went up to Dublin for a show Stayed in a hotel and went out for a pint with Frank's brother He came over to Rose's more than before He'd started bringing over groceries for her though she never asked and she never thanked him But mostly what time they had they spent together walking in the hills Or around the lake scoured by the cold wind that came off it They were happy She was happy in a new way to before They didn't talk about the future She didn't think about their wedding day That would all take care of itself she knew There was no need to force it And no sense there was anything wrong till one day she gets a text from him to say he had to go out of town

Where to Why How long he'd be gone he didn't say Only that he had to go That was all

Which pissed her off because they were supposed to go to a twenty-first in Burke's hotel that night but she didn't think any more of it than that until a second text arrived which said

No matter what happens I want you to know Ill always love you

She didn't go to the party She sat at the table with her phone at her side in case he might ring though he didn't Didn't answer when she called him or reply to her texts She felt sick to her stomach *No matter what happens I want you to know Ill always love you* What did it mean Where had he gone What could happen that might make her think he didn't love her?

She lay in her bed stared at the ceiling with a terrible feeling she was never going to see him again So she was awake when the sound came of an engine outside and then a car pulled up so sharply in the yard it sent a slew of gravel up to hit the window And there he was climbing out of a roadster that he'd driven over a clump of bluebells in his hurry

She ran to the door but he was already hammering at it Urgently like he was shipping off to sea that same hour and this was their last goodbye

And she opened the door so full of Dread

Well he said

Well yourself she said He looked like he'd been drinking Unshaven pasty with a wildness in his eyes but his breath was clear Where were you? she said Where did you go? Your message I thought I didn't know she said and trailed off Oh yeah sorry about that he said and he told her he'd had to go and see his brother up in Dublin What for she said thinking it was something to do with the garage I needed to ask him would he be my best man he said

She looked at him dumbly She didn't get it Though she'd pictured this moment But then he gathered her wrists together in his hand bunching them as you would a bouquet of flowers Listen he said I've a mad idea he said Will we get engaged

Yes in the long hours afterwards she would think of this too that he'd said engaged not married but not now Now there was only joy Rose! she called Rose did you hear that? and Rose came blinking out of her room in her nightgown and she grasped his wrist in her hand just as he grasped hers in his She had tears in her eyes Rose did it was the only time Imelda saw it May God and all his saints and angels keep you and preserve you she said and later that night she gave him something a Miraculous Medal to put round his neck That was her engagement gift to him

Well the next spell was pure madness It was the end of the not drinking anyhow instead there was a solid week of it as Daddy and the brothers dragged him off God knows where to celebrate Then a smaller affair in Goldenhill where they drank champagne that Maurice said was regarded as one of the best and Peggy smiled quietly to her as if to say Well my dear Checkmate Then in to Coady's where Frank bought rounds for everyone He was in great form the best he'd been since before the match And everyone glad for him For both of them Peter Eglantine the manager was there His teammates The Bollox O'Neill Dec 'The Bun' Dunne Pints of course Mickey 'Swamp Thing' Sullivan The girls hugging her and kissing her and seeming to mean it She was one of them now at last though no doubt they were sorry for look at him his arms his smile his beautiful face

And such crack they had The whole pub in stitches with his jokes his songs

And she too She more in love with him than ever because he was more himself than ever More natural than ever So bright he seemed about to burn right through the world

When the parties ended theirs seemed only beginning They were in love They could tell each other now It was madness how much they loved each other Every day cascaded into the next Every colour was ultra-bright Deeper and deeper Faster and faster Forever on the crest of a wave

He had this midnight-blue roadster special import he'd taken from the lot They'd go hammering down the N7 in it and he'd turn to her lean over and kiss her Watch out she'd scream she'd laugh but still kiss him You fuckin' mad eejit

Or down by the lake in the twilight he'd push the seats back wedge his face between her thighs Your stubble's itching me! she'd squeal There's no room! He paid no attention and a moment later she'd have her legs spread back till they were practically over her head pulling him by the ears deeper into her twisting them like wingnuts like she could fasten him in there for ever The birds breaking from the trees when she cried out She almost kicked a hole in the roof that time

Imagine on our wedding night

Are you really going to make me wait still he'd say he'd smile Would you not let me now

I don't want to *let* you I want us both to *want* it and then *do* it

Though even the words made her breathless made her want him inside her She thought she'd go mad with it And that car It was sinful letting something like that on the roads She'd imagine their wedding day Driving back from the church to the reception Pull in here I can't wait any longer Push back the seats Do me in the car Riding inside it like being fucked or that's how she felt about everything then it was all one crazy riot of feeling

Yet didn't it seem even then like he was fading

For all the noise the sex the drinking the celebration All the brightness

Visiting the church planning the honeymoon looking at a little house in the town so happy

Didn't it feel like they had the TV on mute

And try as they might they couldn't turn up the volume

It was just from the drinking she told herself The drink and the coke We'll go on a detox once the wedding's over

Or maybe it was just she couldn't believe it That she would marry him that everything would work out so perfect

It was like a dream or more the opposite of a dream where it's real but you can't believe it

That was why she asked Rose wasn't it though she said it was just for fun

They were in the cottage Frank came over more since the engagement He and Rose got on better now She trusted him or at least he thought she trusted him It was a bright cold day in spring They were just back from somewhere or on their way somewhere sitting there laughing over cups of tea Everything was hilarious then While Rose peeled potatoes in the sink And that's when she asked her

You're joking Rose said meaning after what happened last time

But last time you didn't do it! Imelda said Go on Rose Just for us

A quickie Frank said For the crack She'll never stop badgering you otherwise

Rose sighed Imelda could tell she didn't want to Knew she shouldn't have asked But Rose was pissing her off She'd done her best to get her excited about the wedding What'll you wear Rose? she'd say We'll have to go into town one of these days and look at dresses But Rose would only humph and turn her back Just as she did now And Imelda felt herself get angry She wanted to hear her talk about it She wanted to hear her say the words *Bride Church Ring Wedding* She wanted to know Rose believed it so she could believe it too Seriously she said You'll tell everyone else's but not ours?

You could just tell us the weather Frank said

Yes Imelda said Just tell us will it be sunny Rose Tell us will we have a sunny day for the wedding That's all I'll ask you I promise

And Rose groaned and sat down and poured her tea leaves in a bowl and squinted into them

Frank winked at Imelda he was off his head so was she

Outside in the yard the wind frisked about She heard the tin bucket go over on its side

I can't see Rose complained Wait till I turn on the light so said Imelda

It's not the light Rose said She bent her head lower and squinted Imelda had never seen her make such a song-and-dance

I see mist she said

In the summer? Imelda said

Rose made a gesture with her free hand She saw what she saw and she said it and that was all Then she sighed and swirled the cup again and grumbled

I see a hay bale she said

A hay bale? Imelda said

I see a hay bale in a field she said and then It's burning

As long as it's not burning in Burke's hotel said Frank

Stop Imelda told him getting frustrated She'd heard her tell fortunes many times and it was never like this where you had to drag it out of her What about the wedding Rose she said Is there anything there about the wedding?

Rose took the cup in both hands and bowed over it and fell silent and all of them were silent

On the wall the clock ticked The hens clucked in the yard The electric candle glowed under the picture of Our Saviour Everything was as it always was

Then suddenly something was in the room with them

Over the table or behind it A something that she could put no name to or was not even a thing to see or touch but she could feel it And around them the wind blew up though nothing moved and there was nothing to be heard Only the hens and crows outside the potatoes bubbling on the hob

I see the sun Rose said

A sunny day Frank said and from his voice she could tell he felt it too That's it That's all we wanted

But there was more What else Rose she said What do you see

And Rose fell silent again

I see a ghost she said At the wedding I see a ghost

The invisible unhearable wind blew up around them The something that was not a thing pressed down screamed in their faces and there was silence silence silence

Then Frank let out a great guffaw and said Will it be wanting dinner

Imelda didn't laugh She was raging She banged the table with her palm and stood up and said to Rose You're a mean spiteful old woman

Rose goggled back at her helplessly like she'd just woken up

Easy take it easy Frank said

She is Imelda said

Leave her Frank said It doesn't matter

She took her coat and stamped out to the car and sat there blood boiling till Frank came out to her Why would she do that she said

She just says what she sees isn't that how it works Frank said He didn't seem too bothered by it

I've never heard her say anything like that Imelda said She's been like a wet weekend since the engagement and now this Fucking ghosts

Well think he said Think of what this means to her I'm sure she's happy for you and all But you're going to be leaving She's going to be losing you

She doesn't care about that Imelda said She's not like that whatdo-youcall sentimental

He shrugged People can surprise you he said She's getting old She's on her own Who else does she have to take care of her

It was true because she had no children nor had she ever a man no for all her spells and gobbledegook no one wanted her Well she can get used to it Imelda said She can sit by her fire all alone because I'll not be back and so on till Frank literally put a hand over her mouth Why are you so angry? It was only for fun you said so yourself

He was laughing and everything that had happened around the table The thing that had come The ghost at the wedding began to fade away

She had just to say it would be sunny she said That was all I asked for

One of you's as mad as the other Frank said and he started the car and they drove up to Dublin where Frank bought cowboy boots and she bought a belt that cost €200 just because and a hat for Rose to make amends

And all was well again until three weeks later she started awake in her bed with a terror inside her like she couldn't believe Not just the usual that came with the coke no it was like something had taken possession of her or was stuck inside her like a freezing skeleton someone else's skeleton inside her and it was scrabbling and going mad trying to get out while she herself could hardly move In a panic she reached for her phone and she called him in case he might be awake and when he didn't answer she went out to the yard in her bare feet to see could she see him

And there was the mist

It rose in a wall around her and grew thicker as the sky paled Clinging to her in cold skeins Wrapping itself round her like a dress A wedding dress that stretched off in every direction to cover the whole world

And she stood unshod and she stared into it

And Rose came out of the cottage and stood beside her on the walk

And they both waited there as the grey mist swallowed up everything around them

And then from inside the phone began to ring

Sometimes hay bales catch fire by themselves If the hay when it's cut is too wet or too green It's to do with fermentation It can happen months after That's something she learned Something someone must have told her in that awful run of days

The farmer when he saw the flames thought first it was a hay bale burning That's why he didn't go out they told her Why he didn't call for help He thought it was a hay bale and that the rain would stop it

Too late to help him anyway they told her It would have been instantaneous

He wouldn't have suffered they told her Take comfort in that

Black ice most likely they said that spot's a divil for it

They told her and told her things and more things to fill the endless unfillable hours

Let me tell you something

He used to love running his hands through her hair

It was curly then she was still on the tabs

Rapunzel Rapunzel let down your hair he would say

And she would untie it and it would fall down over him and around his face making a little cave with her face the ceiling and his face the floor she the sky and he the ground beneath her

His head on a rolled-up hoody on the back seat on the edge of the lake and she would gaze down into his eyes and he would gaze up into hers and he would whisper

Hello

Hello he would say

And she would say back to him in a whisper

Like they only had just met the sky and the ground

Like a stranger had come up and said to you hello and you looked in their eyes and saw they were your true love for ever it was that simple

Hello she would whisper back

Hello

And she thought she would burn up into cinders for love of him

But it was he who caught fire who burned in his car in a field in the rain

And now he lay beneath her eyes shut whispering not a word in the coffin in the living room in the suit he would have married her in

As they filed around him everyone knew everyone thought That must be the suit they thought

Though she did not wear her wedding dress It hung in her wardrobe it was made of mist She sat on the bed stared at the open wardrobe door waiting

For what?

For its arms to rise for it to step free of its hanger Dance around the little room in his invisible arms And then for her to wake and find herself once more in his life with her on their way to their wedding so happy

But it did not he did not she did not

There was only the empty dress the endless hours her weeping devil face in the mirror till a car came to collect her

She was still wearing the same pyjamas and Rose's coat over them At the house someone took her aside gave her a black dress to wear It must have been Peggy who else could it have been

The wake at the house among the gold candlesticks the lads from the team all twenty of them lined up Peter Eglantine Patrick J. Coady the teachers the principal Phil the head mechanic Every old biddy for miles around crowding in saying rosaries Daddy beating his chest and bawling his eyes out for his son My son he called him and she lost in this madhouse full of strangers who kept coming up to her not knowing who she was only that she was the girlfriend from the next town over so they would tell her things black ice hay bales suffering Didn't the undertakers do a lovely job one woman said to her You would hardly know what had happened and pouring her whiskey Glass after glass until she had to throw up stumbling outside falling down in the dark then heaving all over Peggy's marigolds not able to get up nor wanting to on her hands and knees howling like a dog wanting to die when someone came up put an arm round her scooped back her Rapunzel hair helped her to her feet it was Dickie

Dickie the brother blinking at her with his mild round face that was so stupid and so clever at the same time

He looked like a blasted moon a doughy white nothing

I'm so sorry he said I'm so sorry

She turned to him and she cried and cried

He was the only one who didn't tell her anything just held her

She always remembered that

She cried for who knew how long she drew back she'd left a puke stain on his lapel this poor man who'd lost his brother

It's all right he said he smiled

She drew back she looked into his eyes she saw Frank there in fragments

She stayed at the house that night not by plan just never left She slept in Frank's bed with the pictures of the two of them looking down at her She slept in the black dress it had puke on it too and in the morning

Peggy tried to wipe it clean Then the car came for them The driver wore a cap They drove in silence She wished they could just stay in it driving never get out

At the church the gawpers with their sad faces carefully prepared all massed about the car park

The coffin closed now waited at the altar between the polished aisles of pews

She thought her legs would give out from under her Rose pressed her hand

On it they had laid his football jersey and his binoculars Later Dickie told her when he was younger he used be mad into nature Always trekking around the woods right up into the mountains coming back to say I saw a pine marten I saw a hawk

They might have laid her heart there too and buried it with him

Her heart and her hair that he loved to run his hands through her eyes he would gaze into her mouth he kissed her ears full of his words her lungs that breathed him her gowl she never let him into her guts too why not Bury it all burn it all who cared what was any of it without him

The priest said Mass people snuffled and blew their noses Her head pounded sun beat through the glass saints Maurice got up and made a speech In the row behind her Daddy shook and sobbed and burped out Frank! Why? A muscle jumped in Peggy's cheek

Four boys from the team helped carry the coffin Pints Bunner The Bollox John 'The Gent' Gurry white-faced hungover stuffed into their suits like lads going up to court after a fight outside the chipper In the church car park people milled about Queued to shake hands with the family and to her too they came the strangers with their polite careful faces and their condolences A stóirín they said My dear girl the Mayor said Ah pet the girls said lining up with streaming mascara to embrace her To each other they said The poor thing she has nothing now Nothing

Where will you go? a woman asked her What will you do? But there was no answer A hundred years had passed She had woken in a field in the dawn Going doing All that was finished

At the house she helped to pass around sandwiches and when the people had finally gone home she went again to his room Dickie knocked as she was gathering up her belongings

They both slept there when they were very young he told her We had a bunk bed he said That's how he stuck up the stars And he pointed to the ceiling

He was different now Dickie than he had been before Softer gentler Didn't hide off in his room Maybe he had learned that in college she thought

I just wanted to get a few bits I'd left here she told him in case he thought she was snooping

You're not leaving? he said

I suppose I'd better she said It's late and at the same moment he said It's late

He smiled gently The day had worn creases into his face like one of Maurice's leather chairs You might as well stay for tonight he said

I should leave you in peace she said The family

You're part of the family Dickie said

Your parents though she said They will want to be alone

I don't think they'll notice to be honest he said

So she stayed that night the next day too and the next Dickie was right no one noticed Sometimes she would come upon Maurice motionless in the hall like a ghost and as if it was part of a game he'd jog to life Start to tell her some story about Frank Never with any point just a chance to say his name One time Frank was having trouble with his computer at work Frank was never much good with technology God knows so he called up Gareth Flynn in town and Gareth said Frank what you have here Frank is a Trojan

Or wandering in the garden she would find Peggy with her green gloves on and her kneepads but not moving either only gazing at the flower beds Her skin stretched tight across her face puckered at the edges The light already seeming to fall through her

They didn't sleep They didn't eat All the dinners the neighbours brought over were going off in the fridge It seemed to her she had passed through a looking glass where the riotous engagement party was continuing only reversed Underwater The days cascading sleeplessly into each other Empty in roaring silence She didn't notice herself either Didn't notice the days disappear and the world with them so quiet so calm that it didn't feel like madness

Dickie hadn't left either He kept saying he'd go back to college and that's when she'd go too she thought but then he didn't so neither did she

He was the one kept some grip on the world When well-wishers came it was he who spoke to them He'd go outside with a coat and scarf for Peggy Make scrambled eggs and spoon them into Maurice's mouth Sometimes as she lay on the bed he'd knock on the door come in and sit beside her

They mostly didn't talk they didn't need to She could feel the loss echoing through him The hole in his soul answering hers He must have felt it what was coming Though Peggy was still hale then Though Maurice still ran the garage He must have known that he would never return to Dublin and his life there

Sometimes they'd go for a walk and he'd tell her stories about when he and Frank were kids Running around these same woods with bath towels safety-pinned to their shoulders being Jedis

Or things he knew things he'd learned How trees communicated underground using chemicals though not what they said How a hundred years ago the forest would have been much bigger Part of a grand estate where the lord used to go hunting Till in nineteen-something the big house where he lived was burned down by the tenants The horses killed in their stables

The thoroughbred she said without thinking

How's that? he said She just smiled Sorry he said I didn't mean to upset you

She wasn't upset Everything came to her from a thousand miles away He could have said he was Jack the Ripper and she would have just nodded

Sometimes at night she'd get incredibly horny Ravenous with it and she'd go out into the house fantasizing that she'd meet Maurice in the kitchen also unsleeping and she would lift her nightgown and without a word he would flip her around twist her arms behind her back fuck her silently against the island crushing her tits into the cold quartz of the countertop She had a wild notion he could get her pregnant and she could have another Frank Make one of her own

Or she would go through the cupboards looking for matches so she could burn down the house

Often she dreamed the bed was the car That it slipped on the grass of the pitch and she and Frank went tumbling through space then it was a coffin he lay in but she was outside and could not get back in He wouldn't let her in though she was burning though she screamed and screamed

Then Dickie was there in the door

Was I doing it again she said

It's okay he said I wasn't sleeping anyway

Will you stay there a little while longer

Of course

And he would sit there at the end of the bed in the dark until he thought she was asleep

He was so sad Up next to him you could feel it Coming from him like heat You could feel it If you knew what it was

Every day was the same They never went anywhere It might have been a week It might have been a month or even more It felt like the world had disappeared so when one day Lar pulled up in the van and asked her to come back with him she could say in all honesty Back where

He told her Daddy wanted to see her He was in a bad way Lar said Will you come and talk to him at least

So back she went with him to the homeplace because she needed a few things out of her room anyway and it was true Daddy's face was purple His chin was covered in a dirty beard He hadn't changed his clothes since who knows when and he stank It was the smell of her childhood of her whole fucking life

He was sat on the couch watching a cookery programme How to make a roux He didn't move or speak to her when she came in but then she went to her room to get what she came for and he appeared in the doorway his belly sagging out from under his shirt

It is time for you to come back now he said

She was turned away from him rooting through a drawer Pulling out knickers socks and so on though everything in there seemed like it belonged to some other girl from long long ago

It is time for you to come back out of that he said again Your place is here not there

She did not reply It was a top she was looking for in particular

You have duties he said

The way he said it That dark warning edge that when they heard it as kids made them scatter because it meant he'd lost a bet or a job or some one of the many other parts of his life they knew nothing about had gone wrong and now he was looking for one of them to start a fight with A fight they would lose

I have duties there too she said quietly

You do not he said You've no more to do there You had your chance No point hanging around the kitchen door now waiting for scraps

Yes there it was The blame the anger The thoroughbred had fallen The race had been lost His millionaire was gone

She found the top Shook it out

It's only a matter of time now before you're fired out of the place he said

It was the one she'd worn to Pap's the night she'd met Frank She had never worn it since nor washed it When she pressed it to her nose she smelled What Dry ice Jägerbombs Bronzer Three hundred lads wearing Lynx That's the smell of falling in love

By Christ Daddy said His voice gave way She turned in surprise to look at him His fist was clenched He was pounding it gently against the top of the door frame He had tears in his eyes You let him go How could you do it

Did I let him go she said as if she couldn't remember Maybe she had

Daddy's cheeks were wet now and his face screwed up like a little child's Your mother always said there was no love in you he said Only the imitation of it that would lure a body in

I defended you More fool I for when she died I knew it to be true What loving daughter would leave her family that was in mourning and move in with a witch

And to poor Frank no doubt you showed the same cold heart

God rest his soul I thought he might change you But you drove him away

I loved him she said again and then in a pleading voice Daddy!

But Daddy had covered his face with his hands and his belly shook with sobs

Drove him away Yes that night she dreamed it was her in the car at the wheel untouched while on every side of her he burned

She woke burning too Her body crying out for him that had denied him while he was alive And she burned too to wreck it to ruin it to punish it for its wanting and not-wanting Smash it into powder so she was empty at last and nothing and free

It was unbearable Still to be here To be alive still

The door opened The bed dipped as Dickie sat down She pulled back the sheets He climbed in beside her Spoke to her as she lay turned away

Frank used to do this Come and sleep next to me I mean After we got our own rooms If he had a bad dream or he was scared he'd come in to mine

I can't imagine Frank ever being scared she said

This was when we were still quite young Dickie said He thought there was a monster in his wardrobe

And it wouldn't come after him if you were there?

I suppose it doesn't make much sense he said He laughed But I was his big brother after all

She forgot that sometimes He'd always seemed younger Dickie but now she could see it Now that he was the only brother left

The grey-green mass of stars glowed down through the darkness

Did he ever talk about me to you

Of course

What did he say

Are you wearing Lynx?

It's just this old top What would he say about me

He said you were beautiful That he loved you

Did he ever say I was cold to him Did he ever think I didn't love him

He started beside her as if the question surprised him then was silent and she imagined him staring up into the dark thinking Then he turned in the bed and though she couldn't see him she knew he was gazing into her eyes or where they would be

He loved you Imelda You were the only woman he ever loved

He was happy with you he said He would have been happy to spend the rest of his life with you

He turned his head to look at the ceiling again then said Are you okay?

Was it happiness Was it sorrow She couldn't even tell She only just managed to gasp to him Hold me And he wrapped his arms around her and she didn't have to think what kind of feeling it was She shook in the darkness and the shaking went into his body and the sadness came from him and went into her

Her tears his tears

Her mouth his mouth

The next morning she felt such horror she couldn't look at herself let alone look at him But later that day they did it again

Then for a time they couldn't stop it They'd lie all day in Frank's room in his bed Funny when he was alive she hardly even came in here now there they were with Maurice in his den yards away or Peggy outside in her garden

In the mornings she could barely lift her head Dickie would go with his father to the garage and she would lie there the whole day Or find herself in the kitchen not knowing how she got there Or in the garden barefoot on the grass

You must leave here Peggy said It is no good for you

She stood a little smaller every time she saw her Winnowed away by the light the rain Her fingers bone-white amid the green shoots

There are too many memories here Peggy said It will be too hard for you to stay

I would leave myself if I could she said

Not the house But the town

Or maybe the house too

The light falling through her She was dying then Quietly piece by piece so no one would notice her go

She put her hand on Imelda's hand You are young You can start again

Yes Imelda said She knew it herself She had to leave She wanted to leave She told herself when Dickie returned to college she would go The garage was open for business again It wouldn't be long now

Then one night he told her that Maurice had asked him to take over

Take over? she said

Maurice couldn't do it any more Dickie said Couldn't be in that office where Frank's coat still hung on the door Couldn't be on the shop floor where they'd spent so many hours side by side

Around cars all day long after what had happened

He should never have gone back he said I could see it myself

But what about you she said

It was always the plan that I would take over Dickie said It's just happening earlier that's all

It could be worse he told her He was sitting on the bed Frank's bed At least it'll mean we'll still get to see each other

His big round face like a child's face smiled at her She jumped to her feet She ran to the bathroom reached it just in time

In the cottage Rose gave her fennel and rosehip tea She knew from one look what was up with her

A baby she said

What? Where? Imelda started looking around her on the ground for a baby someone had left there Then the penny dropped The truth rose up in a bitter flood to fill her mouth and she jumped up to run outside again

A baby Well that put the tin hat on it didn't it

What could you do only laugh and she did she laughed in the out-house then laughed her way back into the kitchen and sat herself down beneath the picture of Our Saviour

Is it Frank's Rose said

Imelda shook her head The old woman didn't ask any more only looked at her the way she did at letters from the bank as if she couldn't make her out at all

She didn't go back to Goldenhill

For a day and a night she didn't speak but lay on the bed in her old room feeling her body conspire against her and thinking of Frank How betrayed he must feel Enough to rise up from his grave and accuse her Tears running down his white face *Why*

Then in the morning got up and went out to Rose and told her what she wanted to do

Imelda had learned in her time in the cottage that Rose didn't only tell fortunes and heal sprains

Girls came sometimes Not just girls but women Grown women Wives Mothers From her room Imelda would hear them weep Rose would put on the kettle Take out a box from beneath the sink

But that's as much she knew because next thing Rose would call her Press money in her hand and remember something she needed urgently from town Go now good girl she would say and even if it was raining Imelda would see the box on the table smell the strange sharp smell in the air and do as she was told

As she went to the door she took care not to look at the girl the wife the woman snuffling in the corner Instead her eyes would always fall on Our Saviour His red heart glowing outside his body And horrible pictures would flash into her mind Stories so evil and terrifying they couldn't possibly be true The consequences of being touched

But by the time she came back all would be peaceful The fire lit The TV on Our Saviour still looking out tranquilly from his frame the electric candle buzzing beneath him The girl or the woman would be gone In a way that made it seem she'd never been there Like it was she Rose had made disappear not the baby

Once she'd made up her mind she didn't feel bad Or she felt bad but it just mixed in with all the other badnesses

Rose did not want to do it Hung back just as she had before with her fortune You should know there's a danger she said If you ever in the future

Imelda didn't care about that Told her if she didn't do it she'd go over to England Get it done there and never come back

Rose shook her head Oh child she said She looked old then old and frail

But Imelda felt strong Strong and evil This must be her true self she thought that Mammy had seen hidden inside her

When? Rose said

Now she said

Dear dear dear Rose said shaking her head And she went to put on the kettle

Who knows would she have done it Maybe the kettle was only for tea Life at that time was like walking on a path made of spinning tops You took a step you were spun off one way The next step spun you off another Every moment was the moment when everything changed

There was a knock on the door She called not to answer it but Rose already had and there he was

He stepped inside but at first he didn't speak Stayed looking at nothing his hands groping the air like a blind man's

You didn't answer your phone he said finally

She said nothing How she had prayed she might never see him again

I didn't know where you were he said I had to ask about in town for your address Fortunately your aunt it seems your aunt is a bit of a celebrity

Then remembering Rose he turned and introduced himself Dickie We met at the ah

Rose nodded and smiled and then slipped out past him through the open door to her hens He turned back to her He looked anguished You just disappeared he said You just went Are you gone? Are you not coming back? What happened?

She shouldn't have told him If she'd kept quiet he would have gone off Only there was a note of accusation as if he had a right to know that made her angry

I'm pregnant she said

He tugged out a chair and dropped down onto it

My God he said and then nothing more for a moment Gazed at the candle on the table that was stuck in an ancient bottle of Guinness Extra

It must be a shock when your whole life is in books to find out you have actually done something in the world for real

It's all right she said I will destroy it

He winced He hated harming anything He'd told her once he felt bad putting bleach down the toilet because he felt sorry for the bacteria That's why she said it to throw it in his face He sat there a minute staring at the candle his lips pressed together then suddenly jumped up

I have to go he said I have to think I'll come back later

And off he went frowning to himself

Once he was gone Rose came in from the yard and Imelda tried to get her to do it now but she wouldn't Not till he had come back and they'd heard what he had to say

There was nothing he could say Imelda told her but Rose wouldn't be budged She knew of course she'd seen it all

For when he returned his mood had changed He was changed He had an excitement about him He sat down in the same chair as before He took a deep breath

I have a proposal for you he said That was how he put it And indeed a proposal was what it was though she didn't realize straight away

It may sound strange on the face of it he said It is strange But life is strange! What we've been through Who could ever have imagined it

Yet isn't it possible that from this tragedy something good could still come?

No one can replace Frank for you he said Or for me either I'm not talking about replacing him But that doesn't mean you have to be alone To go on suffering Don't you think he'd want someone to take care of you? Don't you think given the circumstances this is what he would want? For you to be with someone who understands?

And then the baby I mean you don't want to start talking about signs but isn't that what it feels like? That it's happened for a reason? That we're meant to stick together?

He gazed at her in kindly wonderment smiling like a scientist who has just described his miraculous new invention that will change everything for everyone for ever But she couldn't follow She just stared Her head spinning as it did in her dreams when she was tumbling through the air with the ground and the sky flashing past her round and round

He reached across the table Put his hand on her arm

Marriage he said I'm asking you to marry me

The car hit the ground and burst into flames

Imelda rose from the table and staggered back from it She saw his smile fade His face darken eyes widen with anxiety Then she heard herself start to bawl

You don't have to decide right away! he called from behind her Imelda!

She howled like a baby her tears splashing on the lino around her and filling up her eyes so all the room swam

Imelda he was there at her side now Listen to me All I'm saying is that if you want me to take care of you I will

I haven't said it yet because I don't think it's what you want to hear he said But I love you

The circumstances are strange but the love is real and I don't need you to say you love me back Just let me take care of you

He held her still He looked into her eyes His face kind white round like a moon

She pulled away from him ran to the outhouse where she sank to her knees crying and vomiting It was as if he had died all over again

When she left the outhouse she did not go back inside but instead to the gate One way was the river the other was England Go now she thought Choose one It does not matter which I cannot bear any more

She reached to lift the latch but before she passed beyond she looked back

Through the window she saw Dickie at the table with his head bowed and Rose setting down a cup in front of him And all of a sudden something came to her The thing from before The time Rose read his tea leaves The future Here it was again

At the wedding

Isn't this what Frank would want?

I mean you don't want to start talking about signs but

I see the sun

It came It crowded in on her so furiously she had to throw her arms around the gatepost Clasp on to it to keep from sinking to the ground

Then when she was ready she walked back into the house

From then on her one concern was that someone would stop them Someone would keep it from going ahead But who would that be? If he'd been in his right mind Maurice might have stepped in but he was deep in a hole of grief and guilt and what he should have done As for poor Peggy the fight had gone out of her When they told her she closed her eyes turned her face away though at the same time she reached her hands out for theirs As though the hands were doing it while the face wasn't looking Clutching them tight with the last of her strength

No doubt she thought that Imelda had beguiled him turned his head with her ways It was the only explanation That Dickie for all his brains was too foolish to evade her charms

That was what people were saying in the town she knew That she had shown her true colours That she'd never loved Frank it was clear now Marrying his brother while he was not cold in his grave Dickie you could forgive He was grieving the poor man Vulnerable and she comes along shaking her blonde tresses at him But she A gold-digger that was about the nicest thing you could say about her And plenty of people were happy to say worse

She didn't care Every day brought the day closer that was all that mattered It was destiny She had seen it Who could stop it now? Who could stop her?

What about your father Dickie said

What she said

Your father Shouldn't I meet him beforehand

She just looked at him

I don't mean to ask for your hand he said More as a courtesy

Given the circumstances we really ought to discuss it with him beforehand he said

She did not say anything She had not told Daddy nor even thought of telling him Hadn't spoken to him since that day at the house The less he knew the better at least till it was done

But Dickie who had said yes to the church wedding and everything else kept at her about it and in the end she gave in Who knew Maybe he'd be pleased his thoroughbred had come through after everything If not well Dickie once he'd seen the place would never want to go again So off they went to the homeplace to talk to Daddy

On the way Dickie was talking about a nursery building a nursery

A nursery she repeated

For the baby he said Oh yes yes she said

Your father might have a few tips He's handy isn't he

He looked at her She looked at him didn't say anything

She realized he thought Daddy was a regular person like a carpenter or someone like that who did things Thought he lived in a little village full of turf smoke and donkeys

Frank used to call her homeplace the Badlands His name for Daddy was Garbage McCrowbar

She imagined him cracking up thinking what kind of a nursery Daddy would build Made out of car tyres he'd say Or one of his old mattresses from the back yard

Dickie was driving Peggy's car The road was clear but he stayed just under the speed limit He had never been out this way before though it was not so far from the other garage the new one

The closer they came the quieter he got

Left here she said He turned left

In the estate the council had painted the wall over and someone had sprayed DONIE CULLEN IS BACK BEWEAR and someone else RATS OUT DEATH TO RATS and someone else TORI IS WET FOR ANTO

She remembered Tori a little girl playing on the street with her dolly

This is it she said

This one? Dickie said hopefully pointing at Noeleen's house with the gnomes She just laughed

Imagined how it must look to him The bits of engines laid to rust The car up on blocks from before she was born A bag of old clothes spilling out onto the grass Seven yellow gas cylinders that he must have lifted from somewhere

That one she said to Dickie and saw him flinch And suddenly it wasn't funny any more Suddenly she could see it too All the badness that was there in that house like it lay strewn among the garbage and she turned around about to tell him Look Forget it It's not like you think it is Let's get out of here while we have the chance

But then the door opened and there was Daddy in a string vest with a Mars Bar in one hand and a can of Harp in the other Come out of the house to see who was in the car and when he saw it was her he went down to the gate

Daddy wasn't happy at being disturbed she could tell But he brought them inside sat down at the table cracked open another can set it down in front of Dickie

Thank you I'm driving actually Dickie said Daddy stared at him like he had two heads

There was a silence Dickie looked at her to say something but she didn't know what to say She was wondering how she had ever thought this was a good idea

Dickie cleared his throat Well Mr Caffrey it's like this he said and Daddy's face darkened because the only people to call him Mr Caffrey were the social and the guards

Now the brothers came into the room leaning up against the counter as Dickie continued his speech arms folded staring at him JohnJoe Golly back from England Christy Lar who looked thinner meaner than before

Dickie swallowed but he kept going

What happened was a tragedy he said But is it possible that from it some good may still come?

What's he saying? Daddy turned to Imelda while Dickie was still talking I can't understand a word out of him

It's Dickie Daddy she said You met him at the wake Frank's wake

Nothing can replace Frank Dickie said As his brother I know that better than anyone It must seem strange but life is strange

Daddy goggled at him He could not make head nor tail of him She kicked Dickie under the table that he might shut up and they get out of there with their hides but on he went But the truth is I love your daughter

And this Daddy caught

You what? Daddy half-rose to his feet Placed his hands flat on the table While the brothers all leaned forward uncrossed their arms You done what now? And in an instant he had Dickie by the throat with his fist raised ready to start laying into him while in the same instant the brothers closed in around him and her own screams rang in her ears like echoes of all the times this had happened before To the boy who had walked her home To the drunk outside the bookie's To the black salesman who had called to the door and told her about his great deals on electricity

Stop she cried Stop He's Frank's brother

Daddy froze His face untwisted

Didn't you tell him Dickie gasped in a high-pitched voice

Tell me what Daddy said Then again Tell me what?!

Reluctantly she said

We're getting married she said

Very slowly Daddy lowered his fist He stared at Dickie Then he turned and stared at her in total incomprehension

She stood up Come on she muttered to Dickie

For a moment he didn't move Only gaped back at her and her brothers and her father helplessly like a deer watching a pack of wolves draw in Then he fumbled his way to his feet Squeezed out of his chair

I know it must seem strange he said again

Daddy and the brothers didn't speak nor did they move as she edged towards the door It was like they'd been frozen But when she'd got him outside and was walking down to the gate with him she knew without looking back that they were there on the step all of them and though they weren't moving she could feel them ready to move Braced to move like an arrow drawn back

So they walked very calmly and slowly down the concrete path to the gate past the car on blocks and the dog on the back seat that lifted its head to watch her go by

Beside her Dickie's breath came in a weird hissing He walked stiff and upright like a toy soldier

As they passed through the gate he said to her Should we ask your father if he wants to do a reading

She said without looking at him Get us out of here for Jesus's sake

And they both got in and for the next what seemed like for ever Dickie reversed and turned reversed and turned bringing the car around

While from the step without moving without speaking Daddy and her brothers watched

For a long time they drove in silence Dickie's face deathly white He clung on to the wheel like without it he'd keel right over then outside Belfinin where it was quiet he stopped the car at the side of the road

He said That didn't go so well

Don't mind him she said He's like that with everyone

He seemed *surprised* Dickie said It was like he didn't know

He didn't know we were to be wed he said and turned to her looked at her with wide eyes

She looked back at him She didn't know what to say

Dickie was looking at her still in a way he hadn't done before as if she was a person instead of a holy ideal a saint in the stained glass

Is this mad he said Are we doing something mad

She felt a pulse of fear in her throat

Do you not want to do it she said

He looked back at the wheel still in his hands His face was white and clammy They had not lain together since she left Goldenhill

I'm not saying that he said

But maybe we should postpone it a few months Give people a chance to get their heads around it There's no sense rushing it

The fear rose up to her head grabbed hold of her mind shouted NO NO

But she just said to him very serenely But there's the baby

She turned back to look at the road If Daddy knew about that she said

Dickie's face turned greenish It *was* mad The penny had dropped A girl he barely knew from Adam now he was going to marry her Have a baby with her It was lunacy pure lunacy Now he was going to call the whole thing off

She knew she had to say something It all depended on him To him this was a real wedding

She reached out her hand put it on top of his which was on top of the gearstick He's just overprotective she said I'll talk to him

Don't worry darling she said

He seemed comforted At least he started up the car again

She should not have let him go out there He was not the kind of person Daddy would like It would have been better if Daddy had not found out till afterwards Better for everybody

But too late for that

That evening the van pulled up outside the cottage She watched from a crack in the curtain as the door opened but it was Lar

He didn't come in Instead stood smoking in the yard the hens pecking around his feet Don't do this he told her

What did he say? she asked Did he say he'd go after Dickie? Did he say he'd hurt Dickie?

Lar shook his head You he said

And she knew then it would be okay For Daddy in all these years had never laid a finger on her She was his untouched beauty And no matter what happened he would never let her come to harm

He can't stop it she said simply and as she did she knew it was true He couldn't No one could Rose had seen it For her it had already happened For everyone else there was no more to do but to wait

Will you come she said to Lar

Lar didn't reply He put out his cigarette then said he had to go She wondered would she ever see him again

She told Dickie Daddy had called over to apologize and was looking forward to the big day

That's good Dickie said We wouldn't want there to be bad blood

That was the last she heard from Daddy till the day of the wedding but in the final run-up Peggy invited her over for tea Just us girls she said

Imelda put on her good dress only to find Peggy in an old cardigan and hardly had she served the tea than she took Imelda outside to the garden where she went around the flower beds telling her the name of each plant and the care that must be taken of it This is phlox This is hellebore This one only likes ericaceous soil while a blackbird hopped about the earth

It made no sense to her then to Imelda Outside in the air amidst the bright flowers and the birdsong you could not see she was sick Only slow only old It wasn't till she had died Imelda remembered it and realized she had been asking her to take care of them Her flowers when she was gone

These peonies Peggy said They did nothing for years she said I was on the verge of scrapping them Now look

Imelda looked at them Huge pink-white blossoms Not even like flowers more like some magician's illusion made out of tissue or coloured ice

It just goes to show Peggy said Things take their own time

Then bending down as if she were showing Imelda another flower in the border she said When Dickie was a little boy he wanted more than anything to be like his brother

Though Frank was younger Dickie idolized him

No She caught herself He didn't idolize him In fact I'm not sure he even liked him very much But everyone else liked Frank and that's what Dickie wanted for himself He wanted to be the boy that everyone liked But he was very clever and very complicated and you can't be clever and complicated and have everyone like you That is just not how it works And he ended up making himself very sad

She moved along the border with slow shuffling steps clinging to Imelda's arm In school he tried to play football she said Oh my Lord it was a disaster I was so happy when he went off to college and started figuring out his own way to be

I never wanted him to come back here she said Running a garage Dickie Can you imagine anything more absurd

And yet here we are she said

She stopped looked Imelda in the eye You see Dickie still wants to be the boy that everyone likes He wants to be a local hero like his brother was Stepping up Saving the day But that is not who he is And

I fear he will end up making himself and the people around him very unhappy

Look at that she said bending down and clasping a green stem between her fingers Acanthus bear's breeches we called it a lovely thing but it will take over the garden if you let it

From her hunkers she looked up at Imelda sidelong

I know what people say about you she said And I know it isn't true

I know you loved Frank I know how hard it has been for you these last months Maybe I am the only one who knows it

We have all done what we had to in order to survive It seems clear to me that that explains your relationship with Dickie

I just wonder what kind of a life you see the two of you having together

Imelda had no answer

Peggy rose to her feet Let out a little gasp as she did so She turned to face Imelda She was smaller than her now lost inside her old gardening coat There's no need to rush into this she said quietly You can wait Live together Times have changed No one will judge you for that Not after what you've been through

She took Imelda's hand in hers rubbed the back of it with her fingers Take the time to get to know each other Then decide what you want to do Don't let a date on a calendar decide the rest of your life That makes sense doesn't it?

Imelda nodded

So will I tell him to postpone? Peggy asked gently Will I tell Dickie to call the church Tell them that you want to postpone?

The wind went ssshhhhhhhh At the feeder birds went tweet-tweet

Her fingertips made circles and circles on the back of Imelda's hand

Imelda looked into her eyes That were grey-blue clever complicated like Dickie's eyes like chessboards And just for a moment she thought What if none of it was true What if he was not going to be there What if the wedding was only a wedding and after it I would be married with a baby like anyone else

But only for a moment Then gently she took back her hand

Peggy didn't speak didn't move only held her gaze there among the flowers then at last said We should go inside

It had started to rain she hadn't realized

Peggy turned and walked ahead of her to the house grey as a ghost the spring light paring her away

She was sorry Imelda was sorry But how could she explain it to Peggy when she couldn't explain it even to herself When even to herself she hardly dared think it except in her most secret heart of hearts

No she must be quiet for a little while longer And so she was until the day came at last

The day came she could hardly believe it Jumped out of bed ran to the window and there it was A sunny day *Yes the sun I see the sun*

And it shone all morning Shone through everything Through the bridesmaids fussing round her in Rose's cottage Through Daddy at the door letting bygones be bygones with a car in the yard to take her to church

Shone through the car stopped in the lane The farmer in his tractor asking was something the matter Daddy telling him it was a bee Didn't a bee get in there under her veil Even that paled to nothing the sun burning through it so there was only the light like she was looking right into it

Looking into the sun all the way to the church In case it might disappear out of the sky

Till there she was The moment had come she stood at the top of the church hardly able to breathe Every face turned to her Through the veil scanning them and casting them aside looking only for him Him

But there was no sign of him

Nor was he at the church door nor at the gates among the gawpers though she had not expected to see him there

Churches were not his thing in fact it would more likely be the hotel

They went straight there Skipped the pictures Out on the lawn Inside in the ballroom Searching through faces eye throbbing behind the veil till she thought it might explode

Through the crowd back and forth So intent on finding his that she barely recognized the faces that stopped her to talk to her Joe Daly Antoinette Corrigan Billy Farley barely heard the words spouting from their mouths Back and forth over and over Till the time came for dinner and she had to sit down Won't you eat something Won't you lift up the veil Dickie said in her ear Then the speeches began and he had to be silent

Words Each of them Maurice Dolly the best man Dickie himself with tears in their eyes each speaking his name Dear friend Beloved son Only brother His name passing through the air over her head like a quick bird fluttering by her unseen to roost up in the shadows in the eaves and she thought Will that bring him? Will he come now? Looking at Rose across the table who only nodded and grinned her gap-toothed grin as if to say Patience

But she could hardly bear it any longer Every time there was a flicker in a far corner she'd be half out of her seat But it would be only an aunt come back from the toilet or a waiter clearing plates or somebody lighting a fag or a reflection of the silverware or nothing just nothing

She told herself Wait She knew he was there all this time she could feel him Trying to reach her To speak to her

And this was the moment The wedding The magical union The transformations that God made His own self Water becomes wine Two become one Girl becomes woman Widow becomes bride Her life that was gone today she'd get back again

Yet the hours went by and there was no sign And now the best man raised a glass for the final toast To the bride and groom he said and they all stood with their drinks And her heart raced not with joy this time but dread

He would come! Rose had seen it! She had said it all those months ago *A ghost At the wedding I see a ghost* He had laughed he was alive It made no sense then But now it was clear *A ghost at the wedding* Who else could it be?

Yet the panic rose inside her And as the crowd cheered and the applause went off like machine guns in her ears she looked up and down right and left and into her mind came all those nights before that he had not appeared

In the graveyard kneeling in the earth talking to him begging him Come

Climbing out the window walking barefoot to Naancross

Lying on his bed on his sheets in his room Wearing his clothes his jeans his jacket

Drinking his bottles smoking his hash one time in his pocket she found a wrap of coke snorted half of it rubbed the rest on her gowl then threw open the window and spread herself out on the bed for him to come and lick it off her Telling herself it was him when she tingled

The crying the weeping battering her head against the tiles of the shower so he might witness her misery and take pity and come He did not

Lying with his brother *his own brother* in his own bed doing what she had never let him do so he would be enraged and come How could he not come then but he did not

Because he was waiting for this she had told herself

Waiting for the wedding day their wedding day *It's what Frank would want* Dickie said Yes

But now the lights went down The floor emptied The band leader announced the first dance Dickie took her hand and brought her onto the dance floor

Where is he? she screamed back at Rose Where is he?

Rose only goggled at her

You said! You said! through her veil over her shoulder You said he would be here!

But no A ghost at the wedding that was what she said She did not say whose

Then as Imelda stepped onto the floor they had left clear for dancing she saw something flash through the back of the room

Fleeting white faceless Drawing closer Coming straight towards her through the dark A shimmering bright haze As it rose from the guests

At last she thought for what else could it be And her heart rose too soared sang she made for it it made for her *At last* she thought for one blissful instant

Till she saw Dickie there at the apparition's side and she realized

It was her reflection

Her own self in the mirror at the back of the room In her veil and white haze of lace That's all it was Then she understood

She was the one Rose had seen in her vision She was the ghost

A leftover from another life A remnant of something that was no more That was her Haunting the feast

And Dickie placed his hands on her hips and the band began to play

III

Well I ask you is it any wonder the girl turned out so strange

How's she doing now Geraldine asks

Oh much better she says Pretty much fully recovered Only a bump really Just gave us a scare

Is this Cassie? Una says Did something happen her?

Imelda says nothing pretends to be occupied with her net Una Dwan knows well what happened

She took ill at the Lions Club dinner Geraldine says In the middle of Maurice's speech Fainted clear away

Oh says Una

It was nothing Imelda says She hadn't eaten And then the heat in there

Ah yes Una says and they are silent a moment except for the splash and swoosh of the nets in the water

She's her exam results coming out soon doesn't she Una says

Thursday Imelda says

That would be on her mind too I suppose

But Cass is so clever she's bound to do well Roisin says I'm sure she's worrying over nothing

I don't see why they're all so mad to go up to Dublin anyway Geraldine says All it is is a rat race

I never went to college and I did all right she says dropping a takeaway box into a black sack You didn't go either Imelda did you

Dickie went though didn't he Roisin remembers Did he like it Dublin

That was before we knew each other Imelda says and lowers her net once more

They have been there for hours the Tidy Towns Steering Committee On the banks of the river fishing out burger wrappers beer cans a sunlounger It's dusk but it feels like midday Warmth coming off everything The reeking water The black sacks of garbage piled up beside them All in their overalls except for Roisin who's dressed up as usual in case she meets someone Who? says Geraldine Fly-tippers? You never know Roisin says Maybe the guy with the sunlounger will come back Geraldine says Well someone's been here Maisie says now peering into a ditch under a scraggle of brambles The amount of condoms Is there nowhere else these people can find to have sex than a pile of rubbish in this day and age I mean seriously

They keep wanting to talk about Cass The Leaving Pushing on it like it's a bruise

You'll miss her Imelda Maisie says I'm telling you When my Timothy went up to Galway we were bawling for weeks

It won't be like that with Cass Imelda says Unless it's tears of happiness

That's what you think Maisie says I remember well my Timothy waiting on his results he was an absolute Antichrist We couldn't wait to be rid of him Then the day came and it felt like being hit by a truck

Don't mind them Imelda Geraldine says You'll have your life back it'll be brilliant

I don't know Una says Mine are left years and I still miss them

You spend so long wanting them gone she says then they leave and you're worse off than ever It's like the menopause

Exactly Maisie says It's only when they're gone you realize they're never coming back

Yes in the middle of Maurice's speech the girl picked her moment all right One minute she's in floods of tears the next her eyes roll up in her head and she tips over backwards taking the tablecloth with her and half the glasses

They didn't know had she had a fit or a brain haemorrhage or what She had to be carried out of the hotel on a stretcher Taken to the county hospital In the ambulance Imelda sat at her side stroked her hair it was all she could do The siren blared The lights on the computers flashed It seemed like a long time since she'd seen her asleep She looked so young like that When she was a baby she would never go down Imelda could rock her till she was blue in the face then as soon as she laid her in her crib she'd be roaring again The only way to get her off to sleep was the car The engine noise it must have been or the motion It was funny after what had happened to Frank neither she nor Dickie liked to drive Now they were in the car every night tooling round the back roads half-asleep at two in the morning Lucky they weren't all killed Though would she even have noticed She was that tired Didn't put on make-up for a full year More than once she went to the supermarket and realized she'd tied her hair up with a pair of knickers In the pram the girl screaming wanting to go back in the car

Now she was the age Imelda had been when she'd met Frank and all of that had begun Her great love her life

It went by in a flash didn't it A little squalling baby to a full-grown woman It seemed to take no time at all

But she still looked no more than a child How could you ever let her go

It never even occurred to them she might have been drinking not till the nurse asked Then when they pumped her stomach they thought she'd had eight or nine shots at least Later Dickie heard from the barman at the hotel she'd been ordering martinis which she must somehow have conspired to drink herself with no one seeing Why God who knew Who knew why Cass did anything

It could have been worse the doctor said She'll be sore for a few days But she's not in any serious danger

In these circumstances however we would recommend she has a

psychological evaluation he said We would classify something like this as self-harm Has Cassandra a history of alcohol abuse?

They didn't answer Didn't look at each other Sort of shrugged She's usually very good Imelda said eventually

I see Has she been under stress recently?

She's waiting for her exam results Dickie said

Ah the doctor said in that way doctors have Looking at the two of them figuring out was it one or both of them at the root of it

Dickie stayed at the hospital Let Imelda go back with Maurice Only as she got into the car did she realize why he'd been so gallant that he'd left it to her to explain to his father what had happened Why Cass had ruined his big day For ruin it she did let there be no question about that

She thought of making something up but she knew the truth would come out sooner or later Better he heard it from her she thought So she told him straight on the way home in the car She was drinking she said She's been drinking

Cassandra? Maurice said He looked more surprised than if it had been a haemorrhage His little girl He thought butter wouldn't melt in her mouth Ha

I never thought she'd be the type he said

It's all tied up with these bloody old exams she said

Ah yes he said These kids are under so much pressure I remember well with Dickie Not so much with Frank He could have used a bit more pressure

It's harder for the clever ones he said Because of people's expectations But she'll do brilliantly I have no doubt

Well there's more to it than that Maurice I'm afraid she said And she told him how Cassandra as he knew was dying to go off to college in Dublin only in the last few months she was scared there wouldn't be money for her to get because of the situation with the garage *Situation* That was the word she used And she watched his face as she said it to see how he would react but his face didn't change It was as if he hadn't heard of the situation and he continued not to hear of it even as she said it to him But behind that of course he was doing his calculations and drawing up his plans

Yes probably better all things considered that she was the one said it to him and not Dickie who would only have made a hames of it Turned it into a conversation about sales strategies or electric cars or something that Maurice could just dismiss His own worst enemy sometimes But with her Maurice was always at pains to show what a gentleman he was

I didn't realize he said

I'm sorry Maurice she said There's no sense dragging you into our mess Cass will be fine There's a grant she can get We'll figure something out You've got your golf game to think about

I wish you had told me he said sounding humbled

I didn't want to worry you she said

Yes better to have done it this way She and Cass Damsels in distress Leave Dickie out of it And that was all it took in the end After so much worrying Month after month The very next morning she got a message from him to say he had cancelled his flight Booked himself in at the hotel That he was going to roll up his sleeves and help them get this sorted out

She asked him would he not stay with them but he said he didn't want to be a burden with Cass unwell And she was grateful for that because he could be a difficult house guest The last time he visited he'd brought his own hard-boiled eggs wrapped in clingfilm and four cans of Campbell's soup in his case like he was worried he was going to starve there

She waited till Dickie came back from the hospital to tell him the news But he didn't have much to say Just nodded As if this was just some little fancy of hers and not the last remaining chance of keeping their heads above water It made her angry Though it was true she'd have preferred if Maurice had just written them a cheque Instead all this talk about *helping out* and *digging in* and *coming up with a plan* What exactly did that mean

But it's good she said I mean whatever he does It'll be better now won't it We're out of the woods

Of course Dickie agreed It's great news altogether He was just exhausted after the night on the hospital floor That was all

As for Cass who had come back with him she was delighted with herself Sat up in her bed like an Empress Had everyone waiting on her hand and foot Her little friends all flocking to see her Elaine Rowan the boyfriend or ex-boyfriend Sarah Jane is it Hinchy Various girls from her class with Get Well Soon cards and hand-picked flowers All of them making a fuss as if she'd survived a shipwreck and not just got blotto and hit her head off a chair leg Drama It's catnip for those girls

Not a trace of remorse needless to say for spoiling Maurice's dinner and embarrassing the family in front of the whole town Instead Imelda got the distinct impression Cass believed it was *their fault* Hers and Dickie's As if they'd poured those martinis down her throat themselves Barely a word for them And when Dickie went to her with news that Granddad had offered to help with her college expenses she told him she wasn't going to go

She's not?

She thinks she's failed her exams Dickie said looking very morose

Failed? But how would she have failed? Imelda said She's always got good marks

Unless she failed out of spite she thought But even Cass wouldn't do that Would she?

Dickie just sighed and went to put on his work boots Not long after that Victor McHugh's van appeared in the yard and she saw the two of them stumping off into the forest She almost felt sorry for him For so long he and Cass were thick as thieves with their books and their nature walks and their online petitions Now he was getting a taste of what she had had from her from day one arriving out of her womb jabbing her little elbows all the way

The Tidy Towns Committee has its work cut out this year The flood having been all over the national news Forget your dirty linen this was raw sewage flowing down the street for all to see Plus the murder still hangs over them That man who did for his family Even though it was in the next town over the Dublin newspapers are always getting it wrong saying it was here

Geraldine knows their neighbour from her jam-making course

It's still there the house she says Imagine being stuck next door to that Her kids've been having nightmares for two solid years

What was he like Maisie says

Oh the usual story Geraldine says Seemed fine Took the kids to football No trouble ever then next thing you know

God knows what's going on inside any of them Maisie says Men

I know Roisin says Trying to get two words out of Martin was like blood from a stone Until the day he turned around and told me he'd stopped loving me

Same with my Derek says Maisie Like a block of wood he is except when the Premier League is on That's where he lets out all his emotions Him and Sky Sports It's the romance of the century

They are beside the train station scrubbing at graffiti with old toothbrushes

The things people write Una says staring at the wall N-words out Up the Ra What is it they're hoping to achieve?

A lot of people looking for gay sex too Putting up their phone numbers though who knows is any of it genuine or is it people playing pranks

There could hardly be that many gays in the town could there? Maisie says Even secret gays?

Ring them up and see Roisin says Ask them if they'll make do with a straight woman

It can't be as bad as that Geraldine says

It is Roisin says It's worse

Are you not on the apps

I have all the apps and it doesn't make any difference Roisin says

You must be doing something wrong Una says

It's been so long Roisin says sadly I couldn't get Martin to look at me the last year and a half

Sure mine's as bad Geraldine says That's why I got Mystery Mickey

I have it worse Maisie says He's at me all the time looking for it

How is that worse? Geraldine says

Maisie draws in a long breath through her nose You would have to be there she says

How about you? Do you still do it? Geraldine says

Who, me? Imelda says

Who, me? Geraldine parrots with a laugh

The odd time Imelda says It's always very—

She tries to think of a word other than *neat* but she can't

Neat she says

I'll take neat Geraldine says

I would have taken neat Roisin says In a heartbeat

I haven't felt much like it lately Imelda says Neither of us has

Married with children – the ultimate unphrodisiac Geraldine says I wish someone had told me that when I was forking out two grand for a wedding dress

The night before the results come out she dreams she has a pain Cass's little elbows jabbing into her again

She can't get back to sleep so she goes downstairs Dickie's already there She turns on the radio It's on every station Inescapable

Sixty thousand students will be biting their nails this morning

For students across the country the wait is finally over

Then Cass appears Unbidden Dressed in black She tells them she wants to go in to school to pick up her grades there before they go online

Even though I know I failed she says

Oh says Dickie with false heartiness as if he hasn't heard this last bit Why not sure?

So what if she failed she thinks when they are gone What's all the fuss about But then on her phone the Tidy Towns girls have all sent her messages wishing her luck and she thinks again of that word *Failed* Imagines telling them *Oh yes she got her results she failed* Then telling Maurice seeing him think *It is she dragged Cass down It is she cancelled out Dickie's brains What is the sense of helping these people* The first day of the rest of your life she thinks then like in a vision sees Cass in the future fat and pasty in a top out of Penneys and make-up robbed off a pallet doing scratchcards in the forecourt of the petrol station while her streel of kids feck pennies at the Plexiglas to get a rise out of the lad working behind the counter Or ironing shirts while some lunk of a man with arms like sides of meat watches telly A car up on blocks in the yard a dog asleep on the bonnet

Then they are home Suddenly there like a whirlwind Cass laughing and clamouring As happy as Imelda's ever seen her We got them! she exclaims and hugs her.

You did! Imelda says reaching for the phone to tell the girls Wait who's we? she says

Elaine and me Cass says and starts reciting grades though are they hers or Elaine's? Imelda looks in disarray to Dickie who hands her a printout and there is Cass's name at the top and then her grades all As and Bs

Brilliant! Imelda says So you both passed

With flying colours Dickie says

We got almost exactly the same marks Cass says

And how about Sarah Jane Hinchy? Imelda says To which Cass just rolls her eyes Why would you even ask that? she says

Right no yeah Imelda says

That's like asking about some completely random stranger Cass says Dickie winks at Imelda behind her back Yes right of course Imelda says as she types **She did it!!!!!!** and taking comfort from the pings of congratulation that come back as Cass continues to complain about her mentioning Sarah Jane Hinchy

What's all the racket? PJ says coming in though the very fact he asks shows he knows the answer And when Dickie tells him he appears pleased but slightly embarrassed the way he does in fact when he gets a good report himself Don't look so surprised! Cass laughs then so does PJ and then Dickie joins in then Imelda too Here is the relief at last Those bloody exams hanging over them for how long Now they are done at last She has passed They have passed The family They have done it together

I am so out of here says Cass

So they go for lunch in the town to celebrate and Maurice comes from the hotel to join them and makes a big joke of tasting Cass's drink to make sure it's Coke and not something else and they sit out on the terrace at Genevieve's in the sun and the neighbours pass by and Dickie gives them the good news and Cass says stop *telling* everyone and Imelda feels a kind of worn happiness like they are normal

Then Dickie goes back to the garage and Cass goes off to see Elaine and Maurice fishes a fiver out of his pocket and sends PJ down to the square to get himself a Cornetto even though he's just had cake and the two of them are alone Her and Maurice

She says to him again how wonderful it is about Cass and how grateful they are for his help setting her up in Dublin all that

Yes he says and then Don't mention it please

And she apologizes again for the ruined dinner and again he is very courteous and says frankly he was glad to get out of there

She sits back for a moment absorbing the heat and thinking could Tidy Towns fit hanging baskets to those street lamps and just generally how long has it been that she's not been worrying about something Then idly she says Will you go back to Portugal now do you think

Well as a matter of fact Maurice says I wanted to have a word with you about that

And he looks at her and though the sun is still blazing down it's like there is a shadow and she sits up and says Oh?

I meant to go back the day after the dinner as you know he says But the extra week has been a great opportunity to get the lay of the land

At the garage she says

At the garage he says And having looked around and talked to Phil and a few others I think it might be wiser for me to stay on a little longer until it's properly back on its feet

Oh she says and then Do you think that's necessary?

I do he says and for a moment that's all he says He looks into his cup Casts about for the waiter and signals for another coffee Before turning back to her

The truth is I knew Dickie was having some problems he says But I had no idea how bad things had got

Bad's not the word she says The recession has been a nightmare here Maurice an absolute nightmare It hit everyone the whole town

But he waves this away as he might a wasp making eyes at his cake The recession is over he says

He takes off his sunglasses rubs his eyes examines something on his fingertip he has evidently found there I simply can't be confident handing back the reins to Dickie he says That's what it comes down to I can't just write a blank cheque and ride off into the sunset Not if I don't feel he has things in hand

He does she says I mean he will He just needed getting over that hump is all

Maurice slowly shakes his head I'd like to believe that he says I would But it's not what I'm hearing

Hearing from who

Hearing from everyone he says Even as I walk down the street people are coming up to me and telling me the problems they've had

Like what she says

Well since you ask I'll tell you he says People are coming up to me saying they left in their car for a service or an oil change or a broken tail light or whatever and then when they got it back it was making a noise

A noise she says

Yes a noise And some of them that's as far as they got Some of them brought the car back in and the problem went away But a few of them went elsewhere Over to Joe Mulcahy or to Forrest's and what they found was the cat converter was gone out of the engine That's the thing behind the exhaust that converts the toxic gases

I know what a catalytic converter is she said You mean someone had taken it? Out of these cars?

There are valuable metals in it Maurice says Platinum Palladium Rhodium know what that is? It's the most expensive precious metal An ounce of it will cost you twenty grand Gather enough of these converters in short and you might make a few quid

He squints at her across the table Are you familiar with an employee named Ryszard Brankowski?

She starts Then in her most imperious tone replies I do not take an interest in the doings of the mechanics

Well I'll tell you who's taking an interest and that's the Gardaí he snaps back

This time she can't hide her shock She raises her cup but her hand is trembling so she puts it back down again and looks about instead to see is there any sign of P J

You think this Ryszard fellow took the converters she says

I don't know what to think Maurice says Or how long it's been going on There could be dozens of cars affected People who haven't noticed anything is wrong Or they didn't want to say anything because they knew Dickie was having trouble

From the other side of the street Georgie Moran hollers out There's the man! Howya Maurice!

Ah eh hello Georgie Maurice waves back at him

There's a case in point he says to her in a whisper though Georgie has moved off to the lights Came up to me yesterday and ate the face off me for what we supposedly did to his wife's old Nissan! I had to give him a hundred and sixty quid out of my own pocket just to get him to go away The whole bloody car isn't worth that much Didn't even have a cat converter it was that old Still it won't stop him going around blabbing to everybody he meets

This business is about relationships You get a bad name it takes years to rebuild that trust In short you can see why I'm reluctant to hand back over to Dickie

Now it's Imelda who doesn't know what to think She looks down the road after Georgie who waits at the pedestrian crossing Enormous ears pink in the sunlight The wife's ears are huge too she recalls And they've a boy PJ's friend with a head like a hang glider

The guards are involved? she says at last

They're after this fellow for being part of some ring over in England he says This Ryszard

But he's a mechanic Imelda says They're Phil's department

Phil told me he complained to Dickie about Ryszard Maurice says And Dickie didn't do anything

Phil complains about everyone Imelda starts to say but Maurice raises his voice over hers It happened on Dickie's watch Imelda That's the point It's the same as at the dinner If his daughter passes out drunk—

Cass? How was that his—

Because he is the head of the family! He is the captain of the ship and if that ship runs aground If his daughter should fall down drunk in front of every bloody bigwig in the town Christ I've never been so humiliated

The waiter arrives with his coffee Maurice tails off Raises his hands to his head Kneads his scalp with thick fingers

Well it's all coming out now isn't it she thinks But she says You don't think he's mixed up in this? Dickie? You don't think he's behind these missing converters?

Maurice sighs Turns his hand over and inspects the garnet on a big ring as if he can see his face in it I should never have left him in charge he says Dickie has no judgement Frank now someone would walk in off the street and he'd have them sized up in thirty seconds Dickie can never understand anything unless it's in a book

She waits till he's finished tamps down her fury So you're going to stay and keep an eye on things she says trying not to make her voice too icy

I don't want to see the place go under he says I can't afford to Everything else I lost in the crash My savings The money from the house This is all I have left So yes I'm going to monitor it until I'm happy that it's functioning as it should

He looks down at his ring again There is something he does not want to tell her

But I can't do it alone he says Not at my stage of life So I've been talking to a local businessman who's offered to come on board and help get the place back in shape

A local businessman? she repeats Heat rises up through her body Pools in her head Who is this businessman?

A local man he says You know him Michael Comerford

Big Mike she exclaims Are you joking Sure he's only a crook!

Maurice regards her patiently across the table The way a doctor might look at a little girl who won't take her medicine Dickie will still— he begins

A crook is all he is! Isn't he in debt to every Tom Dick and Harry in the county! Talk about the captain of the ship Didn't he go bust with his houses and his animal feed and everything else he touched! If he hadn't signed it all over to his wife he'd be locked up! The same wife he cheated on with the bloody housemaid!

Maurice lowers his eyes People are looking now from the other tables from the street People! This bloody town is full of people!

What about Dickie she says

Dickie will still be involved Maurice says There are no plans to dislodge him This is a temporary arrangement He's still welcome to come into the garage and—

Welcome? she says The heat returns whirls through her head He's welcome to come *in?*

I'm just proposing he step back for a little while Maurice says Frankly I think he'll be happy to

Who'll be happy? PJ has reappeared on the other side of the canvas divider licking a Twister

We all will Maurice says turning his grandfatherly smile back on We all will

She's raging all the way home Isn't that the size of Maurice Barnes That's how you get ahead in business obviously Shaft the people closest to you and replace them with conmen Shaft your own son who gave up his dreams to run that bloody garage Who could be in Dubai now an architect an engineer building skyscrapers only that Maurice dumped it on him Just like he dumped the house on them that they'll be paying off the rest of their lives Millstone after millstone that he left them with The great benefactor!

It's spite is what it is Pure spite for what happened at the dinner Can you believe it? she says to Dickie expecting him to hit the roof

But Dickie already knows

We talked about it a couple of days ago he says Dad came into the garage

She is speechless He knows! And there they were in the restaurant together The two of them all smiles! So you're just going to accept it she says Accept that he's fired you Your own father

He hasn't fired me Dickie says untying the laces of his good shoes He just wants the place to himself for a couple of weeks It's pretty standard if you want to do an in-depth review

But he won't have the place to himself she says He's bringing in Big bloody Mike!

He shrugs It makes sense to have a fresh face if you're looking for new investors he says

It makes sense? she repeats Your own father turfs you out for Big Mike? He's punishing you after him not lifting a finger to help all these years?

He doesn't reply He takes off his shoes tugs on his boots

Dickie?

This is what you wanted he says It was your idea to drag my father into it

Don't pin it on me she says I didn't want this

Well then it's no one's idea It's no one's fault I'm sorry but what do you want me to say?

She wants him to say I'm angry Imelda! I'm raging! After all that I did to keep that place going After everything I put you lads through!

Or Jesus Imelda it's a knock to my pride no question but the God's honest truth that place was killing me Maybe this is just what I need To step back and think about what I want from the future Especially now the kids are getting older

But no there's none of that He doesn't seem angry or upset particularly to have his business taken away from him She watches as he ties up his boots Criss-crossing the laces and fitting them into the metal hooks Not looking at her

What about these catalytic converters? she says

Dickie puts his coat back on Mumbles that it's the first he's heard of it Whoever had a problem he wishes they'd just come to him instead of going behind his back to Maurice

She hesitates before saying it and then And this fellow Ryszard? What about him?

Ryszard? he says vaguely

Maurice said the guards were looking for him she says Is it he took the converters? Is that what they think?

I don't know what they think he says If it was him he's long gone

She pauses again then Who was he?

Who was he?

Yes yes The one they're after Do you remember him What was he like?

He thinks Tall fellow he says Wasn't he? Polish? I don't know Imelda There's that many fellas go through there And we were so busy then during the flood

Right she says

Probably gone back to Poland he says Especially if the guards are after him

Yes she says

I really don't remember he says

But she remembers

The girls couldn't stop talking about him Roisin had brought her car in and seen him and then Geraldine had gone in with hers even though there was nothing wrong with it just to have a look

Gorgeous they agreed

Imelda ask him if he does call-outs

Tell him I need a full service

Tell him to bring his grease gun

She didn't know who they meant Even at the best of times she steered clear of the workshop A troll cave full of leering youngfellas and lumpy old-timers like Phil

Then one day not long after the flood the fuel light had started flashing on the Camry and she'd decided to bring it in then and there

The workshop is a big dark barn of a place No sunlight and whenever she goes in she gets the feeling that she's interrupted something Because it's always weirdly quiet instead of full of hammering and welding as you might expect she'll find herself in this sudden silence calling out Hello? like in a horror film until the mechanics all come lurching out of the shadows like bugs

And that's how it was that day Out they came But not him He did not appear just yet He stayed in the shadows like someone who knows you will see him in time Who knows your eye will search him out before you even know you're looking

It was Phil she talked to first Stumpy little Phil like an ancient Teletubby and you'd get more satisfaction out of one of them She told him what was wrong and he started in with the usual It could be this It could be that till she cut him off It's definitely this she said

All right he says throwing up his hands like she's some whimsical old biddy asking him to turn it into a Roman chariot and he calls out Ryszard he shouts Come and set up the Camry there

And the boy rolls out from under Murt Fegan's old pickup and as he comes over he's smiling to himself because he knows she's spotted him already and he knows she knows he knows Because it's obvious before he even comes into the light that this is the boy the girls were talking about

When she was young she had a cat once called Dancer Well it was probably called something else It was someone else's cat but one summer it started coming into their garden and that's what she called it The most gorgeous black fur it had So black it looked like a hole in the universe A gorgeous cat-shaped black hole with glowing green eyes

This boy was like that His hair so black like nothing could be blacker and his eyes black too and his body so lithe in a T-shirt also black that made her think too of that cat that would slink along the narrow back wall between their yard and the neighbour's that was full of gnomes and then in a bound come through the window to find her on her bed and it would already be purring as it climbed onto her and stretched out its paws and started kneading her breasts Pricking them with its claws through the cotton of her T-shirt and purring and purring like it was saying Yes yes so she didn't stop it even though it hurt because she liked how it was purring and could feel the purrs buzz against her tummy and she liked how much it was enjoying digging its claws into her new tits that hurt anyway but now extra-hurt but she liked it

That is the kind of man he was He moved just the way that cat did Like he would hurt you but just a little bit and you wouldn't stop it because you liked how he was enjoying the hurting Frank had been a little bit like that just a little Black but less black and pretty too but not as much as this one who if Imelda was a girl still she would have been lost

But she was not a girl and she knew well that someone that pretty has their eye out for one person Themselves Especially if it's a man So she gave him a brief unfriendly look as if to say I've got your number pal and his smile just widened because obviously that is what they all do The women with their flurrying heartbeats The mams with their strollers and sunglasses Designer jeans splashed with pureed carrots

Well now he said – he spoke with an accent Polish mostly but also a bit of Dublin and maybe some London in there too – Don't you worry missus we get this sorted out for you

He had tattoos all up his arms which ordinarily she didn't care for but his wound in and out of the hard curves of his muscles in a way that might hypnotize you The air stank of grease and metal Smelled of heat without actually being hot and when he held out his hand to her at first she thought he wanted her to take it Then she realized and blushed and gave him her key

Don't you worry he said again but added that they were very busy after the flood so it might be a few days

This surprised her I'd appreciate it if you could look at it now she said and then I'm the boss's wife Dickie's wife

Well if she expected special treatment or bending the knee she didn't get it He just smiled as if this amused him There was more green to his eyes than she had noticed at first and little flecks of gold

I didn't know Dickie have such a beautiful wife he said

It was like he'd slapped her as strange as that She couldn't quite believe it had happened She looked at him as if asking What?

But he just smiled back at her A sparkling innocent smile to let her know he wasn't being serious That was the way with a man like that It was all a game and you played along and didn't let him know that for you it had stopped being a game but of course he knew anyway

I have new respect for Dickie he said How has he get a woman like you?

I think I must have misheard you she said slowly and meaningfully

His smile fell away and he held up his hands Please I don't mean disrespect he said In my country it is polite to tell a woman she is beautiful Here maybe not

Let me take your car in I get to work on it right away Please he said again

Somehow as they were talking he had got the Camry onto the lifts without her being aware of it Now he pushed a button and it rose in the air until it was hanging above them It was strange to see it like this separated from the ground Powerless with its underside exposed

What is your name? he said and then hastily So I can put in book

She told him He laughed A quick bark of surprise What's so funny she said

It's nothing he said grinning to himself

What she should have said then was I will be back at five on the dot to pick it up Make sure it's ready

But she did not He had a pull this boy Like a whirlpool or a riptide that sucked you out of your depth Tell me she said

He shook his head haplessly It's a crazy thing he said

What is she said Her nostrils were full of the scent of oil A salty bodily smell

Your name he said

My name she said back

Your name – I have it tattooed on my . . . how do you say On my . . . And he pointed to his behind

Now she looked at her watch and gathered her bags and this time she did make to go

I mean it he said Don't be angry You are boss's wife I know I shouldn't tell you But is a hundred per cent true Your name . . . I have tattoo on my . . . on my arse

He was laughing But then he stopped laughing and looked into her eyes and she knew that this was some sort of a routine he was doing on her and yet a part of her still seemed to see a door open and through it to glimpse something magical What you thought it would be like to be a grown-up to be married to be loved when you were a girl locked in a boxroom on a summer's day with a cat's paws kneading your chest

Come I show you He was back to being jokey Come and look I promise And if is not true then you can fire me okay? Tell Dickie He can fire me today I will leave No argument

And if it was true? He left that part unspoken Held out his hand again and this time she took it Let herself be pulled along Only a bit of fun she told herself though at the back of her mind the thought blazed Could he really? And if he did?

They crossed the garage past the sad carcasses of the cars The boy was talking all the time A steady stream of chatter to keep her distracted Then they came to the little hut in the corner where the mechanics went in winter to smoke He opened the door She looked over her shoulder but there was no one else around and she followed him in

The smell of ashes and stubbed-out fags would nearly knock you down There was a Premiership fixture list from last year stuck to the wall and some girl with her top off cut out of a magazine Barely room for the two of them in there she thought but he was still talking and laughing like it was a game they were playing Then he closed the door

You are very beautiful he said

Let's see it so she half-snapped back like she didn't have all day though inside she was thinking of words like *fate* or *destiny* and her heart was pounding for although she had often been tempted like anyone and though the girls were always accusing her of it in jest she had never been unfaithful Because it was wrong and a sin but also because she had never especially wanted to not really She did not believe it would ever again be like it was with Frank who at the same time it had never been like that with either so in that way she did not want to open that door she had kept closed to him But there was something about this boy you couldn't argue with only give in to And if what he said was true what could it be only a sign?

So she watched as he turned away from her and unstrapped his overalls and shucked down the straps then hitched his thumbs in around the waist and wriggled down his trousers and jocks in quite a girlish way she thought to reveal

𝔜𝔒𝔘ℜ   𝔑𝔄𝔐𝔈

tattooed on his arse One word per cheek in big black spiky letters

He grinned back at her over his shoulder Now you he said

Imelda was lost for words For a moment she could only stare – could not tear her eyes away Then she blinked Bundled past him out the door of the hut To find of course everyone who'd been missing from the workshop before had now reappeared and they all stopped to watch her hurrying out of the hut trying to keep her face composed and your man coming out after her pulling his pants up and calling her name that is to say Imelda not Her Name but she did not turn back nor look left nor right only clip-clopped as quick as she could out of that garage and onto the street and away cheeks still blazing praying she wouldn't run into anyone and thinking how in God's name did she let herself be brought into that little hut How

Was she so desperate she who Daddy used lock in her room to keep the men away Now she was just another housewife to be propositioned Another willing fool for a randy mechanic to do his little trick on

In her anger at first she had thought of telling Dickie But then she imagined the questions What exactly did he do? Insolent how? But what was it he actually said? And then he'd start going on about employment law and how he'd need to set down in writing the precise nature of the complaint or he'd expose himself to legal action down the line etc. etc.

So she never did and she did not return to the garage for a long time and the boy Ryszard she never saw again She'd heard somewhere that he'd left but she can't remember who it was told her

It hits her now that if she'd told Dickie what he was up to Insisted he fire him like she wanted then maybe there wouldn't have been this mess with cat converters and maybe Dickie wouldn't be getting replaced by

Big Mike So angry as she is at Maurice and at Dickie she is angrier still at herself And the next day when Dickie does not go to work but instead sets off into the woods with Victor McHugh bright and early she doesn't complain because in the end it's her own fault

Lord above though imagine getting that tattooed on your arse Men Could you be up to them?

That same day Cass gets her exam results she starts to pack her bags

From lying in bed supposedly too depressed to eat suddenly she's hauling things down from the attic Emptying out her wardrobe and this all before she even has a college place

Boxes and suitcases start piling up in the hall It reminds Imelda of the dream she kept having of the flood pouring through the house Washing everything away She's run ragged digging rucksacks out of the outhouse Scouring the cupboards for the so-called favourite top that Cass hasn't worn in four years

She reads on Clara Langan's blog that this is a time of transition It's important to be supportive *Often the only way your kids can tell you they need you is by pushing you away* But it is not easy

You hardly want all those shoes do you? she says

Mam I told you already If it's in this pile then it's stuff I'm bringing

But these are ski-boots Imelda says You're hardly going to be skiing in Trinity College It's not built on a slope as far as I recall

Cass who is carrying a stack of herbal teas lets them drop to the floor Is this all a joke to you? Is my life just a joke?

What? Imelda says

But Cass has already huffed off

Every conversation they have goes like that It's like the worst of the teenage years all over again Like she's determined not to be even a little bit happy until she's gone Dickie's given up trying to talk to her He just makes himself scarce Goes off with Victor into the woods whatever they're at in there Brings PJ with him too which means it's she who's left to deal with Cass all day Helping her as she takes apart her room

Listening to her rehearse her grievances Driving her back and forth to Elaine's at least once sometimes twice a day while the girl complains beside her literally as she's getting a lift in it that the car is bad for the environment

Why don't you go on your bike if you're so concerned? Imelda says

It's too hot to cycle Cass says with an unspoken *duh*

It's hotter still in the Camry even with the air conditioning turned up all the way The old Touareg had a sunroof that was a godsend in weather like this The Camry is an icebox in the winter and in the summer it's like driving a furnace

I don't see why you need to see Elaine every single day of the week Imelda says You're going to be living together You'll be sick of the sight of each before you even get moved in

I could never be sick of Elaine Cass says

Imelda is wearing sunglasses so it's safe to roll her eyes Elaine Comerford A right little madam she turned out Small wonder given her lowlife of a father Well the perverts of Dublin will make short work of her Probably wind up at the bottom of a river

When do you find out about your college place she says

I told you Two weeks Cass says

You know you don't *have* to do the same course Imelda says Books or whatever it is

Books repeats Cass sarcastically

Well literature then The point is you don't have to do it just because Elaine is doing it

I *want* to do it Cass said I've planned to do it for *years*

The windows of the Camry are down too but somehow it only becomes hotter Imelda's fingers are sticking to the steering wheel It just seems a long way to go to read a few poems she says

Mam! Cass puts her hands over her ears Please don't do this!

I'm not doing anything I'm just saying What will you do at the end of it? How will you get a job? These are things you need to think about

You've never even had a job Cass returns So maybe you're not the person who should be asking me

Well when Imelda hears that she nearly drives the car into the ditch But before she can say anything Cass goes on Are you even happy for me?

Of course I'm happy for you Imelda half-shouts

Are you sure? Cass says Because you sound like you don't want me to go to college at all

I am happy for you Imelda insists But the more she says it the less true it sounds

Oh she's just excited the girls say She's young! Off to the big city with her best friend! Such an adventure!

Right yeah Imelda says

The opportunities they have now! the girls say She can go anywhere Do anything Isn't it wonderful!

Oh yes it's brilliant says Imelda

Just a little appreciation would be nice that's all she says

I'm sure you were every bit as hard on your mother when you were that age Una says

My mother was dead when I was that age Imelda says

Geraldine laughs Well get used to it Imelda It's her time You'd better just move over and be thankful for what crumbs of affection you get That's your forties Your kids hating you is just the tip of the iceberg

I'm not forty yet Imelda says startled and then Is it that bad?

It's worse Geraldine says Everything turns to shit

Your looks go Maisie says Your body turns into cellulite You start getting aches and pains everywhere You keep thinking you have cancer

Your parents get old Roisin says Then they get sick Then they die

Your marriage goes up in smoke Maisie says He meets someone younger or starts banging the secretary

Or he disappears into his shed or his golf club or some mad hobby

Roisin says gloomily Martin got into online Scrabble He'd rather play Scrabble with some randomer in Arizona than make love to his own wife I mean I'm sorry

Josephine Toomey's Colm tried to get her to go swinging Geraldine says

Like dancing? says Imelda Swing dancing?

Ah our poor innocent Imelda says Geraldine with a laugh What was God thinking giving you a body like that at all

You think the forties are bad Una says I've said it before Wait till the Change hits you You wake up and don't know whose body you're even in

All the more reason we shouldn't grudge the girls their freedom Roisin says It's all just beginning We should be happy for them We had our turn Didn't we?

And they all say Yes yes because what kind of mother would envy her daughter's new life

The Balenciaga runners are still on sale One pair left in her size Thirty-three people watching A flame to show how excited everyone is She knows she shouldn't buy them She isn't going to buy them But she puts them in her basket to see how much the shipping is and she's that fucked off that she might actually just do it she thinks only the doorbell rings and when she goes down to answer it who's there only Big Mike Comerford

Howdy Imelda he says howdy like that like a cowboy and what she should do of course is slam the door closed again in his face but she's so surprised he'd even show up here the jackal in chief she doesn't she just gapes while he stands there beaming with his thumbs hitched in his jeans and his great big head tilted back like he's taking in his kingdom then Is the boss around? he says

Who? Imelda says

Dickie I mean he says

The boss! Who does he think he's kidding No she says He's not

Do you know where he might be Big Mike enquires

No I don't she says then adds And he's nothing left for you to take so you might as well be on your way

Don't be like that Imelda he says

You have his job You have his business You have his father's ear You'll be after the house next I suppose

Ah Imelda A pained look crosses his face It's not like that he says

Good day to you Mike she says

No listen he says and he puts his foot in the door I want to get this straight Maurice came to me Maurice asked would I help out and I said yes because I don't want to see a business of forty-odd years go under

I'm sure that's why she says It's everything she can do not to reach up and smack the bloody Ray-Bans out of where they're perched in his big bush of hair

It's the truth he says I have no interest in displacing Dickie I've enough work of my own to be doing But that garage is failing You might not like to hear it but it's a fact If it's going to survive it needs some major changes I consider Dickie a friend and that's why I agreed to help and that's why I've come here today to explain the situation

Her rage dies down a bit But only for a moment Then she sees what's parked there in the driveway behind him What is it only her old Touareg! Her beloved Volkswagen Touareg that Dickie sold it to him so he could give to his mistress!

You never miss a trick do you she said You never miss a chance to twist the knife

Oh yes Big Mike says glancing back at the car I wanted to have a word with you about that I'm not using it at the minute so I thought you might like it back The road tax is paid on it and the insurance

Imelda just looks at him

A little bird told me you still had a grá for it he says Think of it as a long-term loan Seeing as we're in business together now so to speak And he gives her a big dopey grin delighted with himself

Well she has to brace herself against the door frame so as not to physically launch herself at him Trying to buy her off with her own car! That Joan no doubt told him to get rid of! I don't need your charity Mike Comerford! she bellows Get out of here! And take your bloody whore-mobile with you!

Big Mike doesn't know what to think How is it charity? he says

That's how! she says punching him on the arm He backs away slowly rubbing his arm as she advances out towards him Everyone in this town knows the kind of man you are! she shouts Everyone knows about your carry-on! You may have pulled the wool over Maurice's eyes but you won't fool me! Now go!

But Dickie—he says then thinks better of it and pitches back to his car

But the next day doesn't the doorbell ring again And it's Larry the florist with a huge bunch of flowers for her

There must be some mistake she says

He checks the card No mistake he says

But I didn't order anything she says He just laughs and gets back into his van

Is it from Dickie? But it's not their anniversary or her birthday or Mother's Day Maybe it's to say sorry she thinks Sorry for everything But Dickie would never go for a bouquet this size It's enormous The biggest one she's ever seen

She hovers in the doorway Calls back over her shoulder Dickie? And then: Cass? And then: PJ? Then she brings the flowers inside and puts them in a vase and puts the vase on the kitchen table then sits down at the table and looks at the flowers composing herself and only as an afterthought does she lift the envelope that's nestled among the blooms and take out the little card inside it

Dear Imelda it says in blue handwriting *I hope you will accept these flowers as a sign of my sincere apology for my conduct yesterday. Please believe me Imelda that when I offered you the use of the Touareg I meant no Harm or Offence of any kind only that it might be useful to you as I am not*

using it myself any more. *I can see in the light of present circumstances of
Maurice's asking me to be his temporary Consultant at Maurice Barnes
Motors that my offer was poorly timed and insensitive. I am most sincerely
sorry Imelda. I have the utmost respect for you Imelda if you only knew. I do
hope you will accept this apology as our girls are to be Flatmates together in
Dublin very soon!! And so I hope we can put this incident behind us.*

Sincerely, Michael Comerford ("Big Mike")

Well

Who would ever have thought it?

What a lovely note so sincere and thoughtful And what a gentlemanly
touch to send the flowers You would never have expected it from him
People can surprise you

She folds the card up and puts it back in the envelope and puts the
envelope in her purse and goes about her business

Then a little later she gets a text message

Did u get flowers??

It's from him She forgot she gave him her number at Maurice's dinner
She stands there looking at the message **Did u get flowers??**

She doesn't know what it means Is he just checking they arrived? Or
is he pretending to check because he expects her to say thank you? She
hopes not because if someone sends you flowers to say sorry it ruins the
gesture if they then turn around looking to be thanked

She writes back **Yes**

Almost instantly a message pings back **Do u forgive me**

She frowns at the phone She had forgiven him when she got the
flowers but now she feels like he's leaning on her This is more the Big
Mike she knows all right **We'll see** she writes

Do u think we could meet up sometime and talk

When she reads this she feels herself blush and she looks over to the
chair where Dickie sits to watch the news But it is not news time for
several hours yet She looks down at the message again Talk? Talk about
what? The Touareg? Did she not make herself clear?

She decides she will not answer now She will wait till tomorrow then say Oh I never realized I didn't reply to this

She leaves the phone upstairs so it won't be distracting her and tries to go back to what she was doing

But what she was doing was looking at her phone And the unanswered question nags at her Needles her As well as the thought of all the other messages from other people that might be piling up unread Until finally she marches back up to her bedroom grabs the phone and writes **I do forgive you Now lets put it behind us**

Im glad he writes **:)**

She holds the phone in her hand Waits in case there is more but there is no more Good she thinks Leaves the phone down determined this time not to look at it again But it buzzes while she's still in the room so she picks it up again so quick she fumbles and it falls to the floor **IMELDA DON'T MISS OUT** But it's only the online store telling her she has the Balenciaga runners waiting in her shopping bag And in place of her panic of a moment ago she feels disappointment Confusion too because what's she disappointed about but before she can answer herself another text comes through from him

It wud be good to meet before the girls go off to Dublin + talk about arrangements + there are some documents for you to sign too

She looks at the words Businesslike He's got the message finally she thinks Now they're on the same page She writes back in the same tone **VG lets discuss soonest**

But that seems a bit cold so she deletes it and writes **All right** then deletes that and instead just writes **Yes** then deletes that too and puts **All right** back

How's tomorrow? His response comes immediately She feels a surge of irritation and writes back **Tomorrow no good Busy** though in fact she is not

Day after? Again the reply comes right away Now she feels like she's being pursued Downstairs she hears the door open Footsteps cross the floor Why is he hounding her? Why can't he talk to Dickie? Hello?

comes a voice from below Mam? Up here she calls She puts the phone down Hastens away Comes back Writes quickly again All right

Wow nice flowers says Cass coming in

Oh yes Imelda says absently

Where'd they come from Cass says

Oh just, the garden she says

The garden? Cass standing by the open fridge stares at the flowers *Those* came from the garden?

Mmm Imelda says

I don't remember seeing flowers like those in the garden Cass says *Our* garden?

That's what I said isn't it Imelda snaps and then Jesus Mary and Joseph Cassie what have I told you about leaving the fridge door open? Do you want everything to go off?

Right because *that's* going to happen Cass says and stomps out clutching a Gatorade

She should have told her the truth but she knows she would never have heard the end of it *Why* did Big Mike send them *What* had he to be sorry about That girl God almighty Won't speak a word to you all week and then suddenly she's like Columbo over a bunch of flowers

She puts on the TV for Dickie's news already annoyed at the thought of the muddy boots But it is PJ who comes through the sliding doors Wow nice flowers he says

Hmm Oh these she says

Where did they come from?

Oh one of the girls sent them she says

What for he says

What do you mean what for She just sent them People are always sending each other flowers

Oh he says

Hush now she says I want to watch the news

An earthquake somewhere People are being pulled out of the ground white with dust like ancient babies being delivered It was decent of Mike to send the flowers she thinks A nice gesture He was in the wrong he was first to admit it She admired that

There is still no sign of Dickie She glances at the bouquet wondering should she move it Not that there's anything out of the ordinary about someone sending someone flowers Just that she doesn't want to get into the whole story about the Touareg with Dickie

But as she gets up to move them Dickie comes in walks right past the flowers and plops himself down in the armchair opposite the TV Whatever he's been doing out there he is covered in mud Covered in it and before she can stop herself she says Dickie for the love of God would you ever change your clothes before you sit down on the soft furnishings? And without a word Dickie gets up and leaves the room and she feels bad but it's his fault And if you were going to write a book about their marriage that's what you would call it

The weather comes on Big orange suns all over Ireland The shower roars upstairs like an air raid Her phone pings with a message from Cass **WHERE IS MY FJALLRAVEN RUCKSACK DID U SELL IT????** Clods of mud scatter the floor I think my athlete's foot is back PJ says hopping in with his foot in his hand

But on the table the flowers shimmer serenely red gold and blue

She said she could call out to the house as she'd more than likely be dropping Cass over anyway to see Elaine but he said if she wouldn't mind the farm would be better because he had a few deliveries and things coming in There's a little office where we can talk he said Oh that's perfect she agreed kicking herself even as she said it How about midday Oh that's perfect

But then that morning she gets caught up cleaning the house Scrubs it from top to bottom in fact On her hands and knees with the hard brush Houses get so filthy Anyway she loses track of time and when she finally catches on it's too late to have a shower though she smells of detergent Well he'll just have to put up with it she thinks Sends him a text to say she's running slightly late then throws on a skirt and a blouse and ties back her hair then a quick stripe of bright red lipstick which contrasts with the blouse then looks at herself in the mirror and wipes off the lipstick

Just going out! she calls to Cass Her voice sounds high and sort of musical in her ears No response from Cass So she goes upstairs knocks on the door pushes her head in Just doing a few errands she says I'm going to run in to the supermarket and the butcher and I have to call to Big Mike to sign some forms

You don't have to tell me EVERY SINGLE DETAIL of your life Cass's voice returns from beneath the duvet

In the meadows the cows kneel in the dry grass exhausted Outside Creaghan's Stores Bart Creaghan sits on a deckchair in only his shorts He won't get much custom like that she thinks as she gives him a wave The Camry is like an oven She puts the fan on cold Full blast hoping it'll blow away the smell of Cillit Bang

Mike's farm is away over on the other side of the lake with no landmarks to look out for beside a Concealed Entrance sign and even with the satnav she spends some time going in circles Light beats through the windscreen Her blouse is soaked through with sweat there would have been no point having a shower She tries calling Mike but he doesn't answer and she gets so fucked off with him for dragging her out here that when the sign does finally appear for the turn-off she's tempted for a moment to go on home anyway

The car judders down a long twisting sun-baked mud path that leads to a circle of barns and byres and haylofts and in the middle of this circle stands Big Mike with a youngfella by the side of a flatbed truck loaded with sacks of feed Both of them staring at a piece of paper in the young lad's hand and then at the back of the truck So caught up are they with their piece of paper and the bags that Imelda is sat in the car a good five minutes before Mike notices her and then it's only after she beeps her horn because your man in the truck is about to reverse right into her

He jogs over to her and puts his forearm on the open window There you are he says I'll just be another minute You can wait inside if you want pointing at one of the barns

I'm all right here she says

But instead he is a full fifteen minutes talking first to the youngfella with the truck then another who comes out of one of the barns in a Hitachi backhoe While Imelda is stuck in the car getting hotter and hotter and hotter

Finally he comes back though he doesn't apologize Now he says

He opens the door for her then turns on his heel She follows him into a barn piled high with more feed bags and heavy with farmyard smells Cow shit and diesel At the back there's a Portakabin set up on blocks It makes her think of the smokers' hut the boy had brought her to at the back of the garage and for a moment she's grateful for the heat because she's red-faced already otherwise she would blush Isn't it crazy how the same things come back and back just pulled out of shape

Inside the cabin a desk and a filing cabinet Take a seat there Imelda Mike says pointing to a chair with a split cushion He puts on a pair of glasses and from the mess on the desk fishes out a sheaf of documents bound by a giant paperclip and starts talking to her about deposits and guarantors and utility bills and pointing out places where she is to sign

Very good she says and Oh yes and Put my name here? Then for a moment there is silence while she bows her head and signs her name and signs again her body dampening in the heat-clouded air of the baking cabin while an animal bleats somewhere and beads of sweat push insistently to the surface of her skin

Hard to believe we're letting them go isn't it he says Makes me feel He trails off

Old she says

I was going to say proud he says with a laugh But that too I suppose It certainly brings it home that time is passing

He sits back Puts his hands behind his head I mean with the kids you know it's passing because you can see them grow he says And yet one day follows the next and it all feels like it'll last for ever Then something like this happens and you realize it's gone They're gone The time you had with them be it good be it bad It's over And everything you wanted to do everything you were still planning to fix it's too late

She hears something in his voice Looks up from her signatures He gives her a half-smile

Don't mind me he says It's great that they're going A great achievement God I'm so proud of them Elaine and Cassandra too They're such brilliant girls They're the future aren't they

On his black T-shirt is a beer bottle playing a banjo He wipes his eye

She finishes her signing sets down the papers looks up at him again Businesslike

Listen he says I'm sorry again about the car I didn't mean anything by it

That's all right she says

I thought you might want it that's all he says But I've put it up for sale on the internet

Oh very good she says and there is a silence again in which she wishes him dead for dragging her out here in the heat to sign leases when he could have just dropped them over

Well she says because it seems they are done here Is that everything

Big Mike doesn't reply Instead he lowers his eyes to his hands as they rest on the desk and he says I know you don't think much of me Imelda

She starts to protest but he cuts her off I know it he says You said as much the other day At least you were honest I appreciated that Most people only say it behind my back

That's the worst of the whole bloody thing all this gossip he says I have it coming but for Joan and Elaine He shakes his head Sometimes in this town you feel like you're caught in a bloody net

She doesn't say anything to this though she has sometimes thought the same thing

He takes a deep breath purses his lips to breathe out

I can't defend what I did Imelda I'm not going to make excuses for it I love Joan and I know I did wrong

You don't have to explain yourself to me Mike she says

True enough he says But between the garage and the girls we're going to be seeing a fair bit of each other and I don't want you thinking ill of me Or if you're thinking ill of me I want it to be for the right reasons

Anyway the therapist says it's good to get the feelings out he says with the same wan half-smile If I'd spoken my feelings more maybe I wouldn't have made such a mess of things with Joan

His big pink head is glistening and his heavy shoulders rise and fall From fearing he might try it on Imelda worries now that he might have some sort of an episode

I loved her Imelda I still do But the fact is the spark is gone That doesn't excuse what I did but nevertheless that's why

He looks at her across the desk I know that won't make much sense to you he says You and Dickie have always been rock-solid Anyone can see how much you love each other It must be hard for you to understand how lonely a person can be in a marriage

His eyes shimmer at her and Imelda who was half-rising from her chair stops and sits back down

That's not to defend it he says again I hurt Joan I hurt Elaine and yes I hurt Augustina too with my selfishness and I will never forgive myself And loneliness is no excuse for anything still that's what it was even if I couldn't see it myself

He falls silent From over his ear a cow peers out of a calendar from the National Ploughing Championship Mike shrugs holds up his hands Looks into her eyes as if to say That's it

And Imelda gets up I have to go she says

Imelda he says

I have to go she repeats and she turns for the door of the cabin

Wait he says I'm sorry I shouldn't have dumped all that on you

But she darts out the door and down the little stairs and then runs runs runs all the way to the car and takes off so fast she nearly crashes into the man in the backhoe

In the mirror she sees Mike rush out Stop short in the doorway of the barn

But a moment later she rounds the bend and he vanishes behind a stand of trees

That is the mercy of this part of the world The roads have that many twists and turns You never have to go far to disappear

Back in the house she shouts up the stairs for Cass but there is no answer nor when she knocks on her door So she rings her Are you here she says

Obviously I'm *here* Cass says

In the house I mean says Imelda

I'm in Elaine's Cass says

Oh Imelda says Starts to ask if she's coming back for lunch but Cass interrupts her Mam I'm in the middle of something I'll call you later okay bye

Okay bye she returns but Cass is already gone She calls Dickie Ah no we're grand here he says Are you not hungry she says I could take you down a sandwich That's great love thanks I brought something with me Oh she says For PJ too? Yes he says For Victor too? Yes he says Oh she says Okay so I'll see you at dinner time so

Ends the call Stares for a moment at the phone in her hand

While the house spick and span after her deep clean extends around her white and gleaming in the summer light like an Arctic glacier the kind you see on a nature programme with a polar bear trudging through it a tiny dot of white on the white They are all starving the bears PJ told her Starving to death

It must be hard for you to understand how lonely a person can be in a marriage

Feeling like it doesn't matter whether you sit or stand Come or go

Live or die It will all disappear in the silence a tiny speck of white on white Bouncing off the walls like an echo of yourself

Big Mike All this time Who would ever have guessed she thinks Who would ever

And now the doorbell rings

Her heart pounds From nowhere it pounds like it'll knock right through her chest

And as she walks up the hall it pitches her left and right so hard that she can barely keep her feet

She gulps She walks She thinks Don't let it be him Don't let it be him Is it him Is it him

She opens the door

What lovely flowers Maurice says Where did they come from?

She doesn't reply to this concentrates on making the tea From across the room she can sense him staring at her with his hawk's eyes Will I do you up some lunch Maurice? she calls over her shoulder I've some gorgeous cherry tomatoes I could make you a salad?

No thank you he says I ate at the hotel Then sitting down at the table he says Imelda I'm afraid this is not a social visit

It's not?

No he shakes his head I'm afraid I have something I need to discuss with you Something rather serious

Oh? she says with a fixed smile

Yes he says You'll remember I asked Michael Comerford to come on board as we're restructuring

Of course she says Inside she turns to ice He couldn't know How could he know? There's nothing to know Nothing happened

Well Mike has found something Maurice says

The converters? she says

No he says No we're way beyond a few stolen converters here

He sighs clears his throat dabs his lips with his handkerchief

It seems there's a hole in the accounts he says

A hole? she repeats

Yes he says

I don't understand she says What sort of hole

Well it's quite simple he says There's a sum of money A large sum of money missing from the company accounts

He presents her with this and then falls silent

And where's it gone to she says at last

That's what we want to find out he says

In the midst of her confusion she is aware that he is watching her Observing her movements

Could it be she says then stops That fella you mentioned before? The Polish fella?

Maurice shakes his head Other than myself the only person with access to the account is Dickie

She turns on him A tea towel in her hand What are you saying to me Maurice

I'm not saying anything Imelda I'm simply asking whether there's any light you can shed on it

No there's no light I can shed on it Only that someone's obviously made a mistake at the bank or something

No mistake Maurice says

Excuse me but clearly there is Because Dickie if you're suggesting it's Dickie He's a lot of things but he is not a crook God bless us Dickie won't even break the speed limit On a clear day on an open road not a soul in sight he'll sit there on eighty kilometres an hour not a hair above It would drive you mad

Mmm Maurice says But he has been under pressure hasn't he Enormous pressure

He has it all worked out already hasn't he In the instant she feels her blood boil Come here to me Maurice We're all very grateful for what you did helping us out with Cass and the money and so on and I know he's made a bit of a hames of things but if you think you can come in here to my house and accuse my husband of being a thief

No no I don't mean that he says waving his hands at her like she'd stepped out into his prize begonias I only mean

He pauses pinches his nose between finger and thumb In his fine splendid white shirt and silk tie and his rings and swept-back silver hair he looks at that moment old An old frail man

Is it possible he's had some kind of breakdown he says

We've all been having a breakdown Maurice she snaps While you've been off playing golf in Portugal that garage has been one big unending breakdown If you want holes there's a hole we've poured our bloody lives into

Yes he says But my question is might that have pushed him to some form of extreme behaviour Gambling say?

Gambling?

Or whatever it might be he says with an air now of desperation I'm asking you have you noticed anything Has he said anything to you

Dickie she says

Yes he says He gazes at her quizzically You are his wife after all he says

She looks back at him without reply

Give it some thought anyway he says Maybe you'll remember something Or maybe he'll let something slip If you get him talking Obviously if we can solve the problem among ourselves that would be preferable

I'll see you out she says

Yes Maurice says He rises from the table reaches down to button his blazer But he's not wearing one He looks down in surprise This heat he says

It's something else she says

She accompanies him to the door He pauses on the step Let's keep this between ourselves for now he says No sense in alarming him There may be a perfectly simple explanation Human error as you say

He turns to go Then turns back to her suddenly urgent Where is he? he says then answers his own question He is out in the woods?

Yes she says He and PJ they've been there all week with Victor McHugh

He starts to say something but it dies in his mouth Why he says

She shrugs Future-proofing she says

Even when he's gone she can still hear his questions Little paws raking at the ground *What have you noticed What has he said He must talk to you You're his wife after all*

No no no Maurice You don't understand Dickie doesn't *say* He doesn't just *talk* If he tells you something it's only so you'll stop asking

She used to think it was because she was stupid Because she hadn't been to Trinity College that's why she didn't understand him Frank she could always see right through He'd felt up the lounge girl He'd put two hundred quid on Arsenal and they lost She knew she always knew

But Dickie no Dickie who seems so simple and straightforward Ask him a question it's like walking into a hall of mirrors Why are you back so late Who were you with Where have you been till now Well you see it's like this and off he goes

Yes no Frank was draughts Dickie is chess Chess in a fog in the dark

But for all that she knows there are some things he'd never do He wouldn't steal just wouldn't Wouldn't commit a crime Not in his nature

Yet still the little claws go dig-dig-digging in her mind

And then she hears something explode

The sound takes over the whole sky Loud as thunder But it's not thunder And at the same time that she's wondering what it is she finds she's out the back door and running Running through the field towards the woods As she reaches the treeline it happens again Huge sound Like the sky's been ripped open Noise breaks against her like a wave knocking her back leaving her ears ringing PJ she calls but can't even hear her own voice and she plunges on into the wood not knowing where she's going the trunks seeming to throw themselves in front of her The light shattering the forest into a green-gold kaleidoscope And in her head that one word *Breakdown* Till suddenly she finds herself teetering on the edge of a darkness

A hole A hole dug in the ground and down at the bottom of it is her son

Hi Mam he says

She drops down onto a tree stump She laughs wipes the sweat from her face cries a little bit clears her throat

Hiya she says

What are you doing out here

Just came down to see what you lads were up to she says That's a mighty hole

It's going to be a well he says For when the floods come and there's no water

How would there be floods and no water she says

I don't know that's what Dad said

Come out of there a minute love would you she says and he flips a bucket over and stands on top of it and his white fingers grip into the black edge to haul himself out

They are in the clearing around the old shed Frank's old shed She hasn't been out here in years Not since the kids were young It looks like a building site One wall has been knocked and the floor dug up Piled on a pallet outside are pipes coils of cables slabs of grey something that might be insulation all covered with plastic sheeting

What do you think PJ says proudly

You've been busy right enough she says

He starts telling her more Plans for when the Bunker as he calls it is done Latrine over there Generator Underground food storage Polytunnels Pointing and explaining All very grown up Wonderful she says over and over Wonderful It is so strange like a dream that she's forgotten the reason she came out here at all when Dickie steps out of the trees

Out here he is different too In an old check shirt with frayed hems and work boots caked in forest mud He doesn't look like a man with a crime hanging over him No Caught unawares he looks like someone else *Someone happy* she thinks with a pang

Then another figure appears A warped green mess for a face She flinches back But it's only Victor she realizes Victor McHugh wearing some sort of a net which is a mercy to everyone

There you are now Dickie says to her Surprised but not displeased as if at a visitor from an old life

What's going on out here she says

Do you like it Dickie says turning back to survey the works It's early days yet but we're making progress Especially since we got our helper here And he musses PJ's hair who's pleased as can be she can see

But what is it? she says What is it?

Well it's a shelter I suppose you'd call it says Dickie

For if there was an emergency PJ says And we needed to hide?

Hide she says

Right if the grid went down or if there was a war? Or a nuclear attack?

Imelda looks at Dickie darkly

Well we'll probably never need to use it for that Dickie says It's more of a forest retreat You know somewhere the kids can come out and be in nature

I've often thought it was a shame to have it just mouldering away he says And we've been learning some new tricks And having fun which is the main thing isn't it?

Yeah! PJ exclaims waving his cap and doing a Cowabunga jump And it all seems so wholesome and happy just three guys hanging out in a forest building a bomb shelter that she starts to feel like she's the one at fault for coming out here and spoiling it When she sees what's laid across Victor's shoulder

I heard a shot she says

Oh yes says Dickie While we're here he says

It's an EU initiative Victor McHugh says

Is she dreaming? What's an initiative she says

Squirrels Dickie says Grey squirrels there's a cull

Ten euro a pelt Victor says

She looks from one to the other You're shooting squirrels?

Just the greys Dickie says

They're an invasive species Victor says

You're the invasive species Victor McHugh she snaps back I'm talking to my husband if you don't mind Then to Dickie

But PJ she says What are you doing firing guns and a child present

And Dickie starts in with the explanations How Victor has a hunting licence so it's perfectly safe and they're only shooting upwards and it's for the good of the forest because the greys eat the oak trees etc. Facts facts he knows them all but he doesn't know or care that another man is sitting in his chair in his office He doesn't know his own father has him as number one suspect for embezzling the company accounts Jesus man do you not realize

She stops herself PJ is looking at her

You're a fool Dickie Barnes she says You're a bloody fool

Your relation to the client? the receptionist says She is new Every time she comes out here they are new and she has to explain herself again I'm not a relation she says She doesn't have any relations I'm the one paying for this place My husband I mean

The receptionist looks at her computer Makes a face They are behind on their payments And your name again?

On it goes They always act like they're guarding Fort Knox like they'd die before they'd let anyone interfere with their precious 'clients' Then when you go inside you see they treat them like boxes in a ware-house Drag them over here drag them over there stick them wherever is convenient

Finally a nurse comes through the double doors You're here to see Maura? she says

Usually she's with the others in the day room they call it More like a classroom an ancient classroom with no teacher just the TV Thirty of them staring up at it But today Imelda's brought straight to her room Or the nurse says it's hers though it's different to last time and nothing hers in it Not even an *RTÉ Guide* But there she is by the window so it must be her room though why have they got her in a wheelchair?

Why indeed says the nurse She's well able to walk but she's being stubborn Aren't you Maura

Her name is Rose Imelda says Maybe she'd be less stubborn if you called her her right name

They get like this when the mind starts going the nurse says It's fairly common

She says it just like that Right in front of her Imelda is shocked Looks down at Rose who purses her lips turns to the window Why ever did they leave her here She doesn't like it Never did

I'll be outside if you need me the nurse says sunnily

Imelda sighs Sits herself at the end of the bed Says what she always says That she's sorry it's been so long That she's just been so busy

Rose doesn't reply Outside there are trees and a view of the car park Starlings perched along the boundary wall

You won't believe what's been happening Imelda says Maurice came back And the Lions had a big dinner for him You'll never guess where Burke's hotel The very same room we were in for the wedding I nearly had heart failure

Just sitting there all this time she says Though I suppose where else would it be

She doesn't know quite what she means by this which makes her embarrassed for couldn't she say the same of Rose too She folds her hands in her lap Rose I need to ask you something

She glances over her shoulder checks the door is shut

It's Dickie I'm worried about him

Dickie Rose says

That's right I think he may have done something Or I don't know Maurice thinks he has

Rose peers at her She was always old or so Imelda thought but now!

Her face barely a face at all More a mass of wrinkles like a crumpled page that's been lying in a ball for who knows how long Though the eyes peering out of it are as keen as ever See through everything straight into your soul

That's not all Imelda admits She takes a deep breath looks down at her hands Do you remember Mike Comerford? Big Mike?

Rose narrows her eyes Big Mike

Yes he's a farmer from the town Farmer and businessman but he's She pauses I want to know Do you think Can he be trusted she says and then hopelessly I mean I don't know if you ever met him So maybe there's no sense asking It's just there's so much going on and I can't get it all straight in my head and I don't know who else I can talk to only you and I'm sorry I didn't come before but if there's anything you see any light you can throw on any of it because I feel like I'm going out of my mind

Rose bows her head shakes it Grouses to herself deep in thought

Then she raises her head again Looks Imelda in the eye

Are you new she says

What says Imelda

New are you new here says Rose

No says Imelda It's me Rose Imelda Paddy Joe's Imelda

Oh says Rose Paddy Joe's Imelda

That's it Imelda says Rose listen I need your advice

The other girl was from the Philippines Rose says

No Imelda insists Rose it's me Imelda Dickie's wife remember Dickie?

Dickie's dead Rose says He died in a wood

No that was Frank Imelda says Frank his brother

Frank and Imelda are to be married Rose says

Let's stop talking about it Imelda says trying not to lose her temper

At the wedding Rose says

Stop Imelda says

I see the sun And I see

Please stop

There will be a ghost Rose says I see the sun and I see

Please Rose please! she exclaims

The old woman turns to the window She has food spilled down her front Her socks have rolled down around her ankles She doesn't know who Imelda is Who any of them are Dickie Cass PJ Maurice Mike They are merely names popping around like the coloured balls in the drum in the lottery

Stupid to think this would work Every time she sees her she is worse Last year Imelda was sat in the car park for an hour afterwards Cass trying to comfort her It's okay Mam She's happy It's nice there She couldn't be at home like that

Did she know it would happen Imelda wonders Did she see it back then That she'd end up on her own with food stains on her robe surrounded by omens from long ago signs meaning nothing

Unbearable What an unbearable thing is a life

From her wheelchair she is looking at her

The flat grey eyes sit on her own like coins the withered jaw is still

Your girl is not with you this time she says

No says Imelda

She is going away says Rose

Yes Imelda says To Dublin To college Next week

That is hard Rose says She is a good girl

Yes Imelda says or tries to Rose gets up from her chair and plods over to the locker by the bed and takes out a tissue and passes it to her

She passes it to her and she stands there by Imelda's side stroking Imelda's hand with her own hand which is like reeds bound together like the Brigid's cross that hung over her door when she had a door And in a whisper like wind through the reeds She will come back she says She will come back to you

Then she frowns Blinks her eyes and again like she can't see straight No she says She mustn't come back And the reed bones snatch at Imelda's hand So tightly that Imelda cries out though more for fear that they will break that Rose's old dry fingers will break But the grip only tightens and her voice rises She mustn't She mustn't! Over and over until the nurse who must have been listening is there at the door How are we getting on?

Grand Imelda says faintly while Rose still holding her hand just gapes Eyes popping at Imelda as if she is drowning

Now Mrs Brennan the nurse says Time for your nap And gently but firmly she turns the old woman by the shoulders Sets her onto the bed Starts adjusting pillows and counterpane and Imelda finds herself squeezed out of the room Not deliberately It seems like a natural process Back into the corridor with the gleaming blue floor

A giraffe tongue is blue PJ told her once

The door is closed now Through the little window with the wire mesh she sees Rose speaking urgently All of the prophecies meant for her All the answers to the questions that she never asked Poured into the ear of the nurse who nods without listening as she arranges the bed

Did Dickie take that money Is Big Mike a liar What happened to Daddy How do you lift a curse

Are we bad people Did I do the wrong thing

What will become of us

THE CLEARING

I

Why do people say the birds and the bees? the boy said. When they're referring to sexual intercourse?

Dickie paused, confused – though he'd been confused since he arrived. Are you talking to me? he said.

If they mean it as a euphemism, the boy went on, they clearly don't know much about either birds or bees. In both cases their mating habits are quite baroque. Although perhaps that's what the expression's getting at – that nature is almost never natural. Do you think that's what it is? When people say the birds and the bees, do they mean – the orgiastic?

Students were drifting by, dawdling over the cobblestones, which had grown warm in the unseasonable sunshine. It would be so easy to join them! To say he had an appointment, hurry off – or not even speak, simply nod benignly and continue on his way.

But he didn't know what was the correct thing to do. For a week he hadn't known; he constantly felt on the verge of committing some terrible faux pas, even when doing something ostensibly quite straightforward, like checking his coat at the cloakroom, or walking, as he had been a moment ago, through the square. Simple things baffled him; conversations were unfathomable. To begin with, every facet of life at Trinity was known by some archaic code name. The Buttery was the bar, the Lecky was the library, Michaelmas Term was this, October, and he was a Junior Freshman, he'd figured out that much – but countless other referents remained obscure to him (House 6? The GMB? The 1937? DURNS?) and he only ever understood a tiny portion of what anyone said to him. Worse, even when it seemed like he did understand, he still found himself

337

at sea, because people here habitually said the opposite of what they actually meant and expected you to be able to tell. Irony was the university's lingua franca; it made it impossible to know if someone was being serious, or making fun of you.

Take this boy who had accosted him. Dickie had no idea whether the absurd language and preposterous manner was something he was putting on, or if it was what he was really like; if he was putting it on, whether he was doing it to be funny, i.e. to signal that it was exactly what he was *not* like, or whether he thought it was impressive; in that case, or in the case that it was what he was really like, whether he was regarded generally as a freak, or whether others also found it impressive, and so Dickie should too.

It was too much to figure out then and there; he should just have kept walking; but he found himself pinned to the spot by the boy's question and the boy's questioning gaze, like a bested sailor held at the point of a sword by some swashbuckling buccaneer.

Bees, for a start, the boy said, releasing him, at the very least, from the necessity of answering. The mating habits of the honeybee are a case in point. The virgin queen – is that baroque enough for you? – the virgin queen sets out on a flight, during which thousands of drones try and have sex with her. Thousands! Though only a dozen or so manage actually to mount her. Of those dozen, each will have at it ten times – this is all happening mid-flight, by the way – and when he finally drops off he leaves his guts behind. His penis is barbed, so it's ripped out of his body when he withdraws. Now *that's* hardly what your parents meant when they told you about the birds and the bees, is it? Cripes, if you heard that as a child, you'd be traumatized for life! No one would ever have sex again! The species would come to an end! It'd be like Japan!

The boy was quite conspicuously ugly. He had hair the colour and texture of the stuffing of one of Dickie's old teddies – a sort of beige that looked as if it was never intended to see daylight – ruddy cheeks and pale eyebrows dominated by a pair of enormous tortoiseshell-rimmed glasses. His eyes were large and cobalt blue; his nose was large too, and blunt, set over a pair of bow lips that were unnecessarily red and shapely, almost as if he'd been wearing lipstick. The lips would probably have looked very nice on someone else, Dickie reflected, but here the fragment of perfection just added to the overall sense of chaos.

The lips were moving again. As for birds, they were saying.

At the next stall over, a girl had stopped to talk with the two boys seated behind the little makeshift counter: there was a brief exchange, the girl gave the boys a pound note, signed her name to a list on a clipboard, then went on her way. Everyone seemed satisfied. Why hadn't they spoken to him, instead of this oddity? What did he want from Dickie? A banner over his head said, in an august, slightly old-fashioned font, *The Historical Society*. Dickie liked history; even if he didn't, he would have been happy to join, if only to escape from the boy. But the boy didn't seem to have any intention of asking him.

The fact is that the vast majority of male birds don't have penises, he was saying. Instead, the female has to extract the sperm from them. All the males can do is flash their plumage and hope to catch her eye. Most of them never get a shag their whole lives long. But the birds that *do* have penises, he went on, tend to have absolute whoppers. There's a duck in Argentina whose cock, when erect, is *longer* than his *body*. Can you imagine? But nobody ever says, *hung like a duck*, do they. Why is that, would you say?

Dickie opened his mouth and closed it again. The heat had risen from his feet through his body to mass in his head, and as a consequence he felt a sudden and vehement impatience with the boy, who seemed to see Dickie simply as an audience on whom he could try out his sophistries.

Sophistries – there was a word that might give him pause, if Dickie could summon the courage to use it. *Enough of your sophistries! I grow weary of these sophistries!* That would show him who he was dealing with! That would show him that Dickie was not just another of the gormless culchies up from the country to do Engineering – lectures from 9 to 5 at the far end of the campus, living in digs, home every weekend with their jocks in a pillowcase for Mammy to wash. No! Dickie was studying

Business, meaning his days were spent amid the cashmere-clad Dublin girls and public-school transplants who paraded about the Arts Block (one of whom had asked Dickie yesterday, apparently in all seriousness although who knew, where he *summered*).

Though the reason that Business should be included in the Arts Dickie didn't know, unless it was simply more wilful Trinity College perversity; and the fact was he did live in digs, and he did fully intend to go home this weekend with his laundry. He had heard people laugh at his accent, on the few occasions he'd spoken; he'd seen them look disdainfully at his shoes (Dubarry) and his jeans (Wrangler) – which were expensive, but nevertheless, apparently, wrong – or perhaps they were right, but on him only highlighted his own intrinsic, essential wrongness?

It had been stupid of him to assume that, simply because he didn't fit in at home, he would fit in here. What was it, after all, but the very small-town naivety he thought he was above? His momentary surge of rebellion dwindled away; shame pulsed in his cheeks; at that moment a tingling set up at the edge of his nostril, and he realized miserably that the spot he'd successfully extirpated that morning had returned with a vengeance.

The boy was staring at him, waiting for a response to a question Dickie, marinating in his embarrassment, hadn't heard.

I'm sorry? Dickie said.

Which are you? the boy said. A bird or a bee? He issued a particularly hideous open-mouthed smile that revealed bockety, yellowish teeth. Dickie felt a brief flare of superiority: the straightness of his own teeth was hard won, the result of three years of train-tracks, and he couldn't help seeing his interlocutor's crooked orthodonture as a sort of moral failing; but then he thought morosely that having bockety teeth was probably another sign of being posh, and straight teeth by contrast meant you were bourgeois, and vulgar. The thought of another four years of this loomed up before him, and it was to that prospect as much as to the boy's question specifically that he returned, What's the point of all this?

Excuse me? the boy said, amused.

Isn't this the Historical Society? Dickie said in a reedy voice, pointing to the banner of the stand the boy was supposedly manning. What has any of this stuff got to do with history?

History, the boy scoffed. He waved a hand at the Elizabethan grandeur surrounding them. History's just a pair of knickers. Pull 'em off and what do you find?

Dickie had no response to this. The boy's eyes, bloated through the thick lenses, gleamed at him gleefully. Nature, he said, answering his own question. Nothing but nature. The repulsively perfect lips smirked with satisfaction, and he added in conclusion, And it's absolutely *filthy*.

II

The hole is four feet wide and almost as deep as a man. They take turns digging – PJ too, in the beginning, though after they get to a certain depth Victor puts a stop to it: if the walls collapsed, they would bury him. At first the soil was light and springy, little more than tree roots and dust. Now it is dark and claggy and sticks to the spade. Dickie digs, or Victor; PJ stands at the edge of the hole ready to receive the bucket and empty it.

Access to water is the first and most crucial requirement of self-sufficiency. According to the 'Three threes', a body can last three weeks without food, three days without water, three minutes without oxygen. All things being equal, oxygen shouldn't be an issue. Food you can store and forage for. But water: that's the tough one.

The rule of thumb is a gallon per person per day, Victor says, and that's just for drinking and cleaning. A gallon is roughly four litres, so a two-week supply for a family of three—

Four, Dickie says.

But Cass, PJ says. Cass will be gone.

Dickie hushes him, motions Victor to continue. Family of four, you're going to need two hundred-odd litres of water, he says. And that's just for two weeks. Who's to say everything'll be back up and running after two weeks?

What about floods? Dickie says. I thought the whole problem was there'd be too much water.

There'll be extremes, Victor says.

Extremes of everything. Drought, followed by floods. The former will make the latter worse because the ground's become too hard to absorb the rain. So there'll be water everywhere, but nothing to drink, because the flood'll overwhelm the sewage system so it spills over into the public supply. If the grid's taken out, the pumps, the treatment plants will shut down altogether.

No, he says. There's only one serious answer – a well.

It was Victor's idea to dig the well by hand. Expense was one reason. Logistics was another: Victor can get his van most of the way to the clearing, but a truckload of equipment would be another matter.

Anyway, they don't want attention – so he says. That's the third and most important reason. The more you go hiring drills and diggers, the more people know what you're up to. Even if it's just the fella at the plant hire, he tells his boss, his boss tells a friend, now there's a whole raft of folks know there's a lad out in the forest dug a 50-foot well if things turn bad. People will come, sure as eggs. You might as well send out hand-written invitations, he says.

People will come: this for Victor is something like a worst-case scenario. Dickie doesn't argue. He's happy to keep the costs down – they're not actually planning to live out here, after all – and digging it by hand seems more in tune with the spirit of the enterprise. The whole point is to get away from machines and technology, do something for themselves.

Still – how slow it is, and hard, a thing as simple as digging a hole! You forget how resistant the earth is, how much lies packed beneath every footstep. The ground has been baked solid by months of dry weather, and the heat is merciless. By the end of every day Dickie's muscles ache so he can barely move; often he's asleep before the light's left the sky, and when he wakes – before sunrise usually – he feels like he's paralysed. He lies there in the grey pre-dawn, PJ still dozing beside him, listening to the birds and smiling at the pain.

In an outhouse, he discovers a camping stove and a Kelly kettle, as well as sleeping bags, air mattresses, other equipment, none of it used before now; in fact he can't even remember buying it. From then on, they cook their food on site: this avoids the awkwardness of deserting Victor, who Imelda has made it clear she does not want to set eyes on, let alone make dinner for. There's a tent too, but they haven't used it. At night they lie curled up side by side in their sleeping bags; above them, set in a black spiky frame of treetops, the endless twilight, a deep magical blue punctuated by a handful of ice-bright stars. It feels like they're at the end of the world, the edge of the universe.

How can a drought cause a flood? PJ whispers. How can everything that happens just make something worse happen?

Don't mind him, Dickie says. That's only what he tells his customers so they'll spend more.

A few yards away, Victor sits on the log, a silhouette except for his face, lit up blue by the screen of his laptop. This is how he likes to relax in the evenings – cleaning his gun while watching American survivalists give tours of their own bunkers, show off their equipment, air their conspiracy theories. Sometimes their voices weave their way into Dickie's sleep: he finds himself dreaming about George Soros, wire cutters, deals on Amazon Prime.

Imelda doesn't think PJ should be there. Day in, day out, digging around in the mud with you and that headcase, she says. It's not right. He should be playing with his pals.

He doesn't want to see his pals, Dickie says. He wants to be out with us. He's enjoying it. And he's learning things.

What things? How to shoot feckin' squirrels? What else, make pipe bombs?

Woodcraft, Dickie says. He does not know exactly what the word means, but it has a pleasing, self-justifying sound. Anyway, he adds as innocently as he can, it keeps him from getting under your feet.

He only came back for duct tape; he emerged from the shed just as she was getting out of her car. She jumped, clutching her chest, as if she'd already forgotten he lived there.

How's the Touareg treating you? he says, tapping the bonnet. Has he kept her in good nick?

Ach, she says, waving her hand dismissively.

Big Mike has given her the car back as a long-term loan: a peace offering. Decent of him, Dickie says. You always did love it.

She sighs, points her fob at the car. The locks snap shut obediently. What's the point of all this Cowboys and Indians, Dickie? How long's it going to go on for?

It's just a bit of fun, he says. It's all being done at cost. Sort of a trial run, for Victor's business.

She winces at the sound of his name.

He'll be back in school soon anyway, he says. Let him stay out in the fresh air while he can.

She presses her lips together, is silent for a moment. Then she says, Maurice was here looking for you.

Oh, he says, and then, He was here?

He said you were supposed to come and see him, and you didn't show up.

Ah, now, he says. That was a very informal arrangement. Did he say what it was about?

Imelda shrugs, staring at the point of her shoe.

Probably can't find a file or something, he says. It's ridiculous. He can't demote me and then expect me to be at his beck and call. He didn't say what it was about?

She raises her green eyes to him, and looks at him.

Ridiculous, he says.

Back in the clearing, Victor sits on the log in a beam of sunshine, smoking a rollie and drinking a cup of tea. He likes to leave the teabag in there; by dinner time, his cup will contain four or five of them, accumulated over the course of the day.

Where's the boy?

Victor nods towards the trees. Listening, Dickie hears him, rattling off imaginary rounds. He parks himself on the log beside Victor. There is silence for a moment. All good? Victor says.

Dickie turns. Victor's sheep's eyes veer off to either side of him. For some reason, he has always found the effect of his non-gaze oddly personal, as if instead of looking it created a deeper attention, a kind of sanctified space.

Oh, the usual, he says. He laughs, emptily. I swear, even if you moved out here for good, there'd still be someone after you, wanting a word.

Victor slurps from his cup, turns his face back to the sun. Then you move out further, he says.

He can understand Imelda's concerns. No one could accuse Victor of being one of the town's more eligible bachelors. His neck is a welter of tattoos, he squints, he pauses in the middle of almost every sentence to spit. His views are eccentric. He smokes unfiltered cigarettes but he won't drink tap water because of the fluoride. He keeps his phone wrapped in tinfoil when not in use, with the battery in a Ziploc bag, carried in a separate pocket. He is bow-legged, and moves in a lurch, as if his bottom half has been frozen. When they were little, the children used to ask if he was a troll.

Yet out here all of that strangeness seems to fall away. Out here he no longer looks ungainly, misshapen, as he does amid civilized folk; instead his bow legs and stooped shoulders seem perfectly suited to his work, as he digs holes, jumps in and out of them, totes bags of gravel from his van. Behind the unintelligible eyes lies an endless store of practical wisdom: how to use an air compressor, how to sheet a roof, how to filter water with a nylon stocking. He can skin a squirrel and cook it in an hour; in a single morning, he digs a latrine and rigs up an antenna to boost the Wi-Fi.

But he has more than just know-how. To Dickie and PJ, he appears almost a kind of magician, with deep connections to ancient forces. On the first day of the dig, Dickie had wondered if the clearing was really the best place to try. Didn't the ground seem awfully dry?

There's water everywhere, Victor said. Even in the Sahara desert, dig down far enough and you'll find it.

Right, Dickie said. But if we're doing it by hand, I mean . . . there's a limit to how deep we can . . .

He trailed off. Victor had turned his back to rummage in his toolbox. He took out what looked like a couple of wire coat hangers, grabbed the hook of each and untwisted it, then re-twisted it till both wires were in the shape of an L. He held them out to Dickie and asked him to make a fist around the short end of each.

Seriously? Dickie said.

This way's been used for thousands of years, Victor said. If it was an app on their fucking phones people would be all over it. He glanced at PJ. Sorry, he said.

Reluctantly Dickie opened his hands. Not too tight, Victor said. Firm but gentle. He undid Dickie's fists, refolded them around the hangers, one in each hand, then arranged Dickie's arms so they were held rigidly in front of him. His own hands, Victor's, were bright red, as if they'd been boiled, then left out in the sun.

Now, he said. Walk.

Dickie looked at him questioningly. Victor waited. Dickie gave in. Stretching his arms out in front of him, the long ends of the rods pointing forwards, he walked with slow, deliberate steps over the floor of the clearing.

Water is everywhere, Victor repeated. And it's always moving, trying to get to the sea.

It was early but the sun was hot. Victor was topless, a red mantle of sunburn covering his neck and shoulders. PJ watched uncertainly from the log; Dickie put on a half-smile, to show that if this was a joke at his expense, he was in on it.

All these trees have found it, Victor said. He pointed up at the huge sycamores surrounding them. They've dug their roots down till they've found the aquifer. For people it's no different. If they have roots in the land, they can communicate with it. The land wants you to survive.

Wishing he'd stop talking, Dickie walked east into the light, over-heated, half-blind. The joke was wearing thin, the idea of there being water anywhere in the vicinity seemed ever more absurd—

And then the rods swung out, like double doors parting in unison. Dickie stopped, stared in disbelief at his hands. From being parallel, the rods now made a single line.

PJ jumped off the log, exclaiming, Holy— Did they do that by them-selves? Let me try. Did they do that by themselves?

Dickie didn't say anything. He continued to gape at the rods, lined up with the invisible current.

Here's where we dig, Victor said, and went to get the shovels.

Days later PJ is still talking about it. In the evening, when they've fin-ished their work, he'll go and sit at the edge of the hole, looking down expectantly. When do you think the water will come?

According to Victor it won't be long now.

Before I go back to school?

You can still come down here after you go back, Dickie says. Once your homework's done. And at the weekend, obviously.

PJ doesn't reply to this. It's hard to believe autumn is on the door-step, when it's warm enough still to lie out under the stars. Dickie folds his hands behind his head. We won't know ourselves then, he says. We'd almost be able to live out here.

Live?

Well, you know what I mean.

The moon above is sword-bright. PJ turns about in his sleeping bag, around and around like an animal nesting.

When me and your uncle Frank used come out here, we dreamed of having a base like this, Dickie says. In the summer we'd spend the whole day exploring. But eventually we'd run out of water and we'd have to trek back to the house and once we were home we'd be sent off to bed.

If you had a well you'd hardly need to go back at all, he says. He looks up into the dark infinite sky.

Imagine, he says.

But his son is asleep.

The night before Cass leaves they have a farewell dinner at the house. After much agonizing, Dickie gives her wine with her meal. It's not as if she's an alcoholic, he reasons to Imelda. No sense pathologizing it.

But Cass doesn't want any wine. She barely eats the food he's cooked. It's as if she's determined to carry as little of the place with her as is feasible, as if she doesn't want anything weighing her down.

His father is unusually quiet – brooding over his salad bowl, emerging only intermittently to ask self-aggrandizing questions of his granddaughter. *And in your literature course, will you be studying the novels of Joyce? I always enjoyed the work of Joyce.* It's the first time Dickie's seen him since he asked him to 'take a break', as he put it, from the business. Could it be that that Maurice Barnes – who is never embarrassed by anything he says or does, who revels in every word and deed that issues from his personage – feels awkward for sanctioning his own son? Or is it something else?

After dinner they find themselves together in the kitchen, stacking plates by the dishwasher. It's late, only the lamp on the cooker hood is on; in the dark light, Dickie can hear his father breathe, drawing in air in through his nostrils, inflating his chest in the way that he does before a speech. But no speech ensues; in the end it's Dickie who breaks the silence.

How's life in there inside? he says, meaning the garage. Have you it straightened out?

Oh, early days, early days, his father says, scraping broccoli into the bin. We'll get there.

How's Big Mike getting on? Dickie persists.

Still finding his feet, his father says, continuing not to look at him. But he's very capable.

Well, listen to me, if you want me to come in and help out, Dickie says.

Oh, that's very good of you, his father says neutrally.

I won't deny it's in a bit of a state, Dickie says. I had to let Gerard go so I was doing the accounts myself on top of everything else. If you need me to walk you through anything, say the word. Not to have Big Mike tearing his hair out.

No, indeed, his father says. That's good of you.

He seems to mean it, to lighten somehow. When would you be free to come in, in that case?

Well, I'm free most of the time now, Dickie says, with just a little twist of the knife. I could swing by tomorrow, even.

But tomorrow he is driving Cass to Dublin, his father reminds him.

Of course. Stupid. He bites on his knuckle. Well, why don't I give you a call the day after next? See how you're fixed?

Very good, very good, his father says.

Leave those, I'll do them, Dickie says.

Very good, his father says again, and abandons the stack of plates on the counter. A moment later, he appears on the patio, smoking a cigar. From inside Dickie can see him, eyeing the night sky, counting the stars like a miser totting up his pennies.

He's been looking forward to the drive to Dublin – the two of them swapping stories, funny things she did as a baby, his own memories of college.

But when the day comes she tells him she doesn't want him to take her. She's going with Elaine; it's all been arranged, she says.

He knows better than to show his hurt feelings. Instead he points to the small mountain of cases, electronics, soft toys at the foot of the stairs. There's no way you'll fit all that in one car, he says. Not with Elaine's stuff too.

Her dad's taking the SUV, she says, as if that settles it. But Dickie stands his ground, stroking his chin and shaking his head and frowning at the pile, till finally she throws her hands up.

In the car she does not take her eyes off her phone from Kilcomery to Chalkstown. He might not be there; she might be in a taxi, on a bus.

When the radio drops out, just for something to say, he starts to tell her about the Bunker.

Why do you call it that? she says.

He's not sure. I must have got it from PJ, he says. He was using it as a base for some game. You used to play there too when you were little, do you remember?

That was a million years ago, she says.

Well anyway. If they put solar panels on the roof, and then a few others around the clearing, Victor says it could basically power itself. Get a rain butt to irrigate the raised beds and they'd be some way to feeding themselves too. Then there's a thing called a cob house—

She lets out a sigh and lifts her eyes from the phone to the window. Then she turns to him and looks at him frankly and says, When you go back to the garage is Elaine's dad going to be your *boss*?

They have arrived at a point, he and his daughter, where she can only be happy in his company if she feels like she has bested him. Doing things for her, giving her things, 'being there' for her – that is no good any more. It's only when she imagines she has exposed some weakness in him that she can be satisfied – some proof of his obsolescence, the uncovering of some embarrassment from his past, anything that can serve as ammunition in what she seems to perceive as a permanent war between them. It doesn't matter that the war is entirely one-way. She won't accept a ceasefire, or even discuss terms; the only way she'll allow him to relate to her is to let her continuously defeat him.

She has been angry with him before. When she was very little, anger was her dominant mode.

She had a pirate costume, and refused to wear anything else, even the identical replacement costume they'd bought in desperation; she stormed around the house – the first house, in Glenteelin – waving her cutlass and emanating rage. For a while Imelda had got the worst of it, but then she had turned on him. Every time he came down the stairs she'd scream, *Not you! Not you!* and run over to push him back. For months, that was how every day began.

Before he became a father, he imagined the relationship as being like an intensive version of owning a pet. The child, he thought, was essentially passive, a vessel into which you poured your love. On TV that's how it looked. Children were silent, dormant; you went into their bedrooms, gazed down at them fondly, drew the blankets over them as they slept.

But in life, he discovered, parenthood was like – it *was* – living with a person. A new person, with strong opinions, strong tastes, arbitrary swings of emotion, all of them addressed at you. *You* were the passive one: the work of care was primarily to endure, to weather the endless, buffeting storms of unmediated will.

Now they are at war again. The garage, the fights, the endless anxiety of the last two years: there is so much to be angry about. All he can do is take it, in the hope that eventually it will pass; like an old *Rocky* film where Sylvester Stallone wins because the other guy tires himself out punching him. But if they're not even in the ring together? If she's not even there any more to punch him? What then?

The girls have rented a little artisan cottage on a treeless street not far from the river. Elaine is there already; she greets Cass with a squeal as Dickie unloads the boot. Cass would have left him there, on the street, but Elaine asks him to come in. Her bearing is that of someone elevated overnight by fiat or revolution to a position she has been silently expecting all her life. It's a lovely place, he tells her. You did well.

Thank you, Dickie, Elaine says warmly, making it clear she does not care what he thinks.

He carries the luggage upstairs. The room is clean and bright, the net curtain billows gently.

Well, he says. I hope you'll be very happy here.

Yeah, Cass says. She put her hands in her pockets. Thanks, she says.

A new life, he says. You've had a hard enough time of it these last few years, God knows. But you made it. *We* made it.

She looks at him levelly, hands still in her pockets. You think you can just wave a wand and make it all disappear, she says.

So this is Front Square, he says. He has persuaded her to come for lunch in town before he goes back; they've called in to Trinity en route, so he can take in his alma mater, the setting of her new life. They pause at the edge of the square, still in the shadow of the arch that leads in from the street.

Even on a normal day, he remembers, passing beneath that arch had always felt like going through a portal – like you were leaving one city and entering another that lay in its midst, a place of pure past. Yet looking at it now he feels as if no time has elapsed at all – as if his own life were still there, continuing somehow untouched by the years, in some eternally resonating present. He puts his hands on his hips. Well, well, he says.

Cass raises her phone, takes a selfie. In Fresher's Week the square is where the societies have their stalls, he tells her. The debating societies, the Phil and the Hist, all the others. Kayaking, Sci-fi, all kinds of stuff. It's great crack, there's a great buzz about the place. I mean, I presume that's still how they do it.

What's over there? She points across the cobblestones to the cabbalistic tower on the far side.

The Campanile, it's called. It's a bell tower. In his time there was a legend that if you walked under it in your freshman year you'd fail your exams.

No, behind it, she says. That red building. He realizes that she is staring not at the tower, but past it. The Rubrics, he says, feeling his voice fade, as if someone has turned down the volume.

What are they? she says.

Just rooms, he says.

Rooms? she says.

Yes. Rooms. Apartments. Where people live. Students.

Is that where you lived when you were here?

Yes, he says.

Can we look at them?

There's not much to see. You won't be able to go in, I wouldn't think.

But Cass has already set off towards the terrace of red-bricks. He hurries after her. Which one was yours? she says.

Let me see now, he says, affecting not to be quite sure. This one, I think.

She climbs the steps, stares at the door, the battered bell with its myriad buttons. I can't believe you lived here, she says, placing her fingers on the rusty-red brick; and he has the sense that this is not just hyperbole: that she literally cannot conceive there had been a time when he was young, when he had been what she is now: or that she has never conceived it until this moment.

It was a long time ago, he says meaninglessly.

What was it like? she says.

He laughs. Fairly grotty, now. Wouldn't be up to your and Elaine's standards, I wouldn't think. She keeps staring at the building, from the doorbell up to the windows, and Dickie feels himself torn: not wanting to speak about it, at the same time glad to have her attention at last. To have something she wants him to tell her. Supposed to be haunted, he says.

She looks at him. Really?

I'm quite serious. You know this is regarded as being the most haunted building in Ireland. On the doorstep, coming out as he was going in. The autumn sky, his bag full of books. *What room are you in? I'm on the second floor.*

I never saw a ghost, he says. Come on, let's look at the Long Room.

He starts to walk away, but she stays a moment longer, there on the top step, as if waiting for the door to open.

The Old Library is full of tourists with bucket hats, carrying shopping bags that bear the college crest. The past for sale. He marches Cass around the exhibits in their glass boxes. By the time they get back outside, he feels composed again.

We should have some lunch, he says. Let me see can I remember where is there to go.

You don't need to remember, Cass says, showing him her phone. There's like five hundred cafés around here.

There's a nice place in the George's Street arcade, or there was, he says. Let's see if it's still there. She rolls her eyes, and they cross back over the square. Approaching Front Arch, she says, I didn't think students could get rooms on campus. Elaine asked.

In second year you can do an exam, the Schol exam, he says. And if you do well enough, they give you Rooms for the rest of your time there.

She looks at him sidelong. You must have been smart.

Well . . . he says with a deprecating shrug. He is about to expand when he sees her expression. She does not want to hear about his past here. This is her fresh start, her new life: what good would it do her to know that he had been here already, and done well, and still ended up where he is, as he is?

It's all different now, I'm sure, he says, and then, more generally, You're going to have a great time here. The big city, the excitement, you can't beat it. He nudges her, grins. Our little town will seem very small when next you come back. As he speaks he remembers too late how he'd hated it when people at home said this to him.

Did it feel small to you?

Well, I mean, it's still home, after all, he blusters. I hope you'll always feel that way.

Would you have come back? If Uncle Frank hadn't died?

Caught off guard, he turns to look at her. I was always the one supposed to take over the business, he says. That was always the plan.

She gazes at him impassively; not so much looking as watching, like a cat.

If I hadn't come back, we'd never have had you, he says.

Sounds like a win–win, Cass says.

They have passed through Front Gate, back into the real world. He turns his attention deliberately back to the present. Now, he says. George's Street I think is this way—

Her hand whips out to yank him back from the kerb as a motorbike roars by.

Oh, he says. Yes, bit of a tricky intersection, he says.

Cass stares at him, mouth slightly open; her eyes remain on him, and for an instant he is reminded of the way she would stare as a baby – the implacable gaze ranging over his whole face, inch by inch, pulling out information. Now she nods slightly. This is where you had your accident, she says. On your first day of college, this is where it was.

He doesn't reply, merely hangs there, suddenly exhausted. Cass presses her lips together. Whatever shadow he cast has been entirely dispelled by the invocation of his famous mishap. The day is saved; she has bested him again.

Now the walk-light flashes, and he watches as, pleased at her prize, she trots off in front of him, in silent communion with her phone. His daughter, an autonomous agent on a city street. You can't stop me being proud of you, he thinks to himself. Then he steps – glancing carefully left and right – off the kerb, and follows her up Dame Street.

What do you think she's doing now? he asks PJ. She said she'd call, but he didn't expect her to, and she hasn't.

Check her Facebook, PJ says, without looking up from his phone. At the end of each day he makes a video of their progress and posts it to his YouTube channel. Dickie takes out his own phone, wanders around the clearing till he can find a signal. This will be fatherhood from hereon in, he thinks: just another anonymous consumer of her brand. He logs in, finds a wall of selfies of the two girls unpacking, vamping in each other's clothes, making dinner together in the new house. In every picture Cass is smiling or laughing. She seems like a completely different person here; he supposes the person she wants to be.

Then he opens his gallery, the photos he took at Trinity: sees her on the step of the haunted red-brick, beneath the college clock, at the site of his accident. In these pictures she is the girl he knows again – scowling, tenebrous, a furious concentration of self-abnegating energy. He wonders if that version of her will disappear entirely now, replaced by the eternally smiling girl from Facebook; if he will look at this picture not so very far from now and think, *That was a million years ago*.

Dad? Are you awake?

The clearing is filled with blue darkness, with Victor's snores and the smell of bleach.

Yes, buddy, I'm awake.

Dad. The whisper has a hard metallic edge. The bleach is to sanitize the well. Beyond the clearing, the moon is gone, everything is swallowed in night. Dad, who turned the rods?

The rods?

When you were looking for the aquifer, and you had the metal rods, who turned them?

Are you still thinking about that?

Yeah. Was it you? Or?

The boy's outline is visible, his silhouette rather, but his voice seems to drop out of the trees, land by Dickie's ear like a soft black monkey. That doesn't mean the body beside him isn't real, is a fabrication of some kind. Well, it was the water, he says. The underground water.

Really?

I was as surprised as you.

PJ falls silent, thinking this over.

Dad?

Later still. All black now, the edges of the clearing no longer visible. The snoring stopped or rather it seems vanished, as if the perpetrator has been spirited away.

What is it?

Are there ghosts here?

Ghosts?

Here in the forest, are there? Ghosts? Are there bad things?

In the darkness the trees press closer, through the trees the darkness seethes, in and out, like the breathing of some vast edgeless beast stealing ever nearer, laying silent siege to the little clearing, the little stockade that he will never finish – he knows that, suddenly, in a flash, how? Why?

No, he says, into the unsleeping night. No, there are no bad things. No, there are no ghosts.

III

It wasn't an accident. And it didn't happen on his first day of college. He was a Junior Sophister, beginning his third year; not only that, he was a Scholar. The previous spring, while his classmates were shifting each other in Peg Woffington's and sleeping off their hangovers, Dickie had cloistered himself in the library, studying for, and getting, the Schol exams. His reward was an apartment on campus – 'Rooms', in the Trinity parlance. That capital R was by far the grandest thing about them. The reality, or Reality, was a dingy suite with furniture that smelled of mildew and a revolting green rug that a previous tenant had, to judge by the scorch marks, made a serious attempt to build a fire on. Still, after two years languishing amid the bongs and jockstraps of the boys in his digs, he was looking forward to having a place of his own.

Does that mean you won't be home at weekends any more? his mother asked when he told her the news.

Of course not, he said. True, he wouldn't be obliged to clear out every weekend, as he was with his digs. But the few friends he had went back to their own towns directly after the last lecture on Friday. He was hardly going to hang around the city on his own, just because he had Rooms. They were more of a symbol, he explained to his mother, a sign of his achievement. Anyway, he wouldn't be moving in till October; there was summer to get through first.

When he was away at college he always remembered home as different than it was. He'd get nostalgic for the most ridiculous things – pine for a glimpse of Suddz laundry, Dingo's arcade, become misty-eyed over people he knew, he *knew*, couldn't stand him. Holidays magnified the

359

illusion. When he spoke to his mother that May, he could hardly wait to spend four whole months at home!

Then in June he'd gone back and the illusion evaporated the moment he stepped off the bus. How had it ever deceived him? He'd always hated summer here: the imperative to be outside, to be bodily; the endless days and nights, with their gauzy promises of romance, significance, never made good. This time his father had prepared for his return by 'setting aside' – that was how he put it, as if he was doing Dickie a favour – 'a few things for him to do', meaning that for the next eight weeks Dickie would spend his days alternating between back-breaking manual labour – e.g. clearing a yard of three hundred crates of gone-off chickenfeed in preparation for the new dealership in the next town over – and stupefying data entry in the office, which had no air conditioning, and entailed not only constant exposure to Maurice's theories of the psychology of car sales, but also the risk of being asked to help out in the workshop, where Dickie knew the mechanics mocked him behind his back, and Phil always scowled at him for being the boss's son.

The nights, if anything, were worse – in Coady's or Devine's, trudging through desultory conversations with his ex-classmates, who welcomed him home with double-edged comments: 'You're getting the accent up there,' they'd say, or, 'That's some get-up you have on, it must be the fashion there in Dublin?' Or, the favourite, 'Our town must seem very small to you now.' Some of them knew enough about the university to mock it – oh, yah, Trinners – but no one actually wanted to talk to him about what he did there; nobody knew about his Schol exams, or cared that he would be getting Rooms. Even the well-intentioned ones, who were trying to be nice, struggled painfully to find anything to say to him; they'd try this topic and that, as if testing keys in a lock. Then either they'd admit defeat and wander off; or their faces would light up, and they'd start talking to him about Frank.

Frank, yes: it hit Dickie that, when he was away at college and having his nostalgic spells, the fundamental thing he was forgetting about his life here was how the townsfolk felt about his brother.

The two boys had always been quite different. When people asked Dickie, aged seven, what he wanted to be when he grew up, he would invariably answer, A priest. He meant it. He had memorized the Mass, and used to recite it to himself (although not out loud, because that, he thought, was probably a sin); he would spend hours kneeling by his bedside, conducting long, telepathic conversations with God, who spoke, in his mind, in a sonorous basso, like a benign Darth Vader, and encouraged him, in suitably biblical language, to further acts of holiness: HONOUREST THOU THY PARENTS AND ALSO THY TEACHERS. He had bought rosary beads with his own money, and he would get up before school to say Hail Marys, clasping the beads between his fingers, imagining he could feel grace accruing, a laser-bright light building in his chest.

When people asked Frank what he wanted to be, he would say, A criminal, and everyone would laugh.

Dickie felt overshadowed by Frank. Frank was their father's favourite; Frank was everyone's favourite, apart from their mother, who obviously preferred Dickie only out of pity and so didn't count. There was no mystery to it. Frank was bonny and boyish, with an open, sunny face, a snub nose, freckles, buck teeth. He was full of mischievous energy: 'You couldn't be up to him!' the mothers would tell each other in adoring exasperation. He was eternally getting into scrapes: putting a ball through a window, falling out of an apple tree, throwing bangers at Mrs Ogle's front door. When they started going to confession, Dickie, who didn't have any sins of his own, would compile lists of Frank's, to remind him to tell the priest. But the priest didn't mind – nobody seemed to mind when Frank did something wrong. They would just wag their heads and say, 'That Frank – he's a real *boy*!'

'And Dickie is very good too,' they would add sometimes as an afterthought, and pat him on the head; and Dickie would grind his little teeth, and realize that he had sinned after all, that Frank had tricked him into the grievous sin of envy, which made him grind his teeth even more.

Being good, he discovered, was no good. No one loved you for being good, except God, presumably, and even there he was beginning to have his doubts. At school, while Frank excelled on the football pitch, Dickie was trapped in lockers, blockaded in the toilet, wedgied, walloped, dragged through nettles, rolled in mud. If it weren't for Frank it would have been a hundred times worse. People liked Frank, they wanted Frank to like them; though he was happy to throw punches at boys much bigger than him, often his mere appearance would be enough to deter them. In fact he didn't even always need to appear. More than once, as Dickie lay on the ground with a boot about to connect with his head, he had heard somebody remark to the boot's owner, Isn't that Frank Barnes's brother? And they would pause, and confer among themselves, and then withdraw, leaving him sprawled in the mud.

Being saved by his little brother only sent his own stock lower, and eventually his father must have become aware of it, because he got it into his head to teach Dickie to fight, or 'how to stand up for yourself', as he put it. Years later Dickie's skin still crawled when he thought of it: he would rather be bogwashed a thousand times over than go through that again. He had just turned ten, or was it eleven? He remembered that it was summer: no homework to take refuge in, or rain, only endless hours of sunlit evening, so that after Dad came home and had his dinner there was still plenty of time for the lesson. In the garden the azaleas were in bloom, midges shimmered like golden static around them. Come on, his father said. Let's see what you've got. Dickie, of course, didn't have anything; his father dodged his half-hearted attack with ease, and punished him with a slap on the cheek. In reality it was more of a pat, really, barely a touch: yet it hit Dickie like a bolt from the sky. He felt astonished, violated; as if he had been stripped of some armour he didn't know he'd had. While he was still reeling, a second slap landed on his other cheek. And on it went, his father dancing around like Muhammad Ali, while Dickie lunged and swung and pummelled the empty air, the place where he was not, until he was exhausted and staggering, and Dad jogged from side to side, delivering light taps to either cheek, both of them now wet with tears: 'Tears won't stop a bully!' – tap, tap.

Even then he'd known what his father was trying to do. He wanted to push Dickie past the tears, to a point where he became so enraged he forgot himself – forgot his clumsiness, his cowardice, tapped into some hidden vein of rugged fury within him. But Dickie didn't, couldn't: he could only lumber, flail, in a hideous ballet of failure. And he never did run out of tears – he cried and cried all the while until he was a disgusting, soggy mess, and his father could no longer conceal his horror. Jesus Christ, Dickie, he said. Jesus Christ, lad. And Dickie, in the face of his disgust, wept more, till his mother – at last! where had she been? – came rushing out of the house and asked his father furiously what he thought he was doing?

Without waiting for an answer, she shepherded Dickie, bawling, back indoors, and wiped down his cheeks, and embraced him and comforted him, then led him to the playroom where Frank was placidly watching *Knight Rider*, and gave them each a little bag of chocolate buttons. And when she had gone, Frank said, unprompted, that Dickie could have his too, if he wanted; and Dickie, still jerking and heaving and shuddering, silently accepted Frank's chocolate buttons, and ate them, silently, and stared at the talking car on the TV and dreamed of driving it away, into the desert, with Frank, behind him, dwindling swiftly to an ant-man, then a dot, then nothing at all.

Frank adored Dickie, that was the kicker. Frank was probably the only person in the world who looked up to Dickie; he would have done anything for him. He even volunteered to fight Dad on his behalf. It wasn't fair to make Dickie do it, he said. Some people aren't fighters. Some people are good at other things. Dickie learned about this later from his father, who was charmed. 'See what a kind brother you have,' he said.

It was so unfair! Anyone would have a sweet disposition if they were good at sports, and handsome, and people cheered everything they did! *Everything Frank did* was seen in the light of what people thought he was – a simple, brave boy, who sometimes through sheer exuberance overstepped the line.

There was one brief period of respite. Frank had been playing football almost since he could walk – a natural, that's what everyone said. But in his mid-teens nature betrayed him. His teammates, as they hit puberty, were sprouting up; Frank was not. For a while he managed to compensate in other ways, but eventually it didn't matter how skilled and how fast he was – he simply couldn't compete. The tremors from this hammer-blow echoed through his whole life. His grades, never stellar, declined sharply. He began drinking with other stragglers in an underage pub in the town, and when their father put a stop to that, going into the woods with his friend Dolly – a tragic case whose only accomplishment to date had been starting to go bald aged sixteen – to smoke hash in the old shed.

Gratifyingly, this meltdown had coincided with Dickie's finest hour, in the form of his Leaving Cert results, 5 As and 2 B1s, which had been featured in the town newspaper ('Local Boy's "Barnes-storming" Achievement'). How sweet it had tasted, to be praised by his father, to be held up, to his wayward brother, as an example to be followed; to take Frank aside, in the moments before he left for the big city, and say, in the same equable tone Frank had so often used with him, that things were bound to pick up. He left for college in the belief that a new era had begun.

But the new era had turned out to be very like the previous era. He was just as unpopular at Trinity, only people here called him a culchie and a sheepshagger instead of a brainbox and a Protestant. And before long he was hearing disturbing news from home: Frank's hormones had woken from their long slumber, and prompted a late, and astonishing, growth spurt. *Spurt*: how many times did Dickie hear the word?

By the time Dickie returned to town at the end of his Senior Freshman year, his brother had grown six inches in eighteen months; he towered over Dickie, and was playing a starring role in what everyone said was the local team's all-time best season. Dickie chose not to attend their matches; it didn't matter. More than ever before, his life in the town felt like a bit part in the Frank show: suffocating, inimical.

When the time came at last to take up his Rooms and begin his third year at university, he felt he had well and truly conquered his homesickness. The loneliness of the city no longer scared him; on the contrary. From now on, he resolved that he would do things differently. On the first weekend of the autumn term he went home as normal. It was his mother's birthday. The weekend after, however, and without thinking too hard about what he was doing, he stayed.

At half past eight that Friday evening – just when he would usually be getting off the bus in the town square, after enduring the extended gridlock of the weekend rush hour – he was sitting instead at his desk in his Rooms, reading. The bell tolled in the nearby tower. He set down his book. His window was part-open; a breeze stole in and circled speculatively through the little room, like a dog on the qui vive, sniffing about.

The air seemed suffused with a strange energy. It was autumn, but it felt like spring. And he, too, found himself feeling an odd and uncharacteristic vitality, a sort of mischievous happiness. He wondered for a moment what it was, then realized. It had struck him for the first time that *no one could see him* here. No one knew where he was, or what he was doing. He found this idea immensely gratifying. He sat back in his chair, and breathed in and out expansively. Then he rose from the chair, put on his coat and went outside.

He crossed the square, passed through Front Arch and the iron gates of the university, and found the city humming in the twilight. He waited for the walk-light – the intersection at College Green was tricky – then hurried past the cigar shop and the book shop and the kebab shop. Around him people, strangers, were laughing and talking as they made their way down the crowded street. Four lanes of traffic, like a jerking, honking river; over them a pale moon hung in a pale-blue sky; and a voice in his head told him as he strode, *You are free, you are free, you are free.*

He had paused on George's Street to look in the window of a second-hand shop – it was closed now, but he could just make out the titles of the books on the wall to the side – when he was seized, roughly, from behind. He turned, startled, to be met by a familiarly hideous grin.

Looking for a discount wedding dress?

Dickie was too startled to think of a witty response. Willie released his arm. Come for a pint, he said.

Oh, Dickie said. There were two boys with him – one he knew to see from the Hist, the other a stranger, with a goatee and an outlandish mulberry-coloured waistcoat.

Come on, come on, Willie said. You can't spend Friday night standing outside Oxfam.

All right, Dickie said, but then, Wait – here?

For the little group had set off only to stop again a few yards down the street, at a pub with purple doors and gilt letters over the windows that spelled out *The Butterfly*.

Why not? Willie said.

Dickie stared dubiously at the door, where a bouncer stood with his arms folded, chewing gum and staring vigorously out at nothing. Sounds of laughter and gaiety could be heard from within. All right, he said again, with a shrug. As they entered, however, a hand appeared to block their way. Regulars only tonight, lads, the bouncer said.

Willie turned on the charm. Oh for fuck's sake, he said. We're in here every fucking night.

With that he made to sail past the bouncer, but the latter, taken aback, recovered himself enough to point to Dickie and say, I haven't seen *him* before.

Immediately Dickie took a step backwards, and began insisting the others go on without him. But Willie had already drawn himself up to his full height (not in itself terribly imposing) and was angrily informing the bouncer that he, Dickie, was his cousin from Norway, who, in the throes of a rare and possibly terminal brain disorder, had come to Ireland, having heard of the famous Irish hospitality. And I must say you are really letting the side down, he said. He turned to Dickie, and unspooled a looping sing-song of vaguely Scandinavian noises. He then looked at Dickie expectantly. After a moment, Dickie, weakly, emitted some noises of his own. With a frown Willie turned back to the bouncer. He says this is making his brain disorder act up, he chastened.

The bouncer looked elsewhere and, chewing his gum, removed the hand. The boys proceeded inside. Heart thumping, Dickie peeped about him, feeling like he'd been smuggled across a border in a pickup truck. He found himself in rather an ordinary-looking lounge, with the same chintzy banquettes and wood panelling one might find in the pubs at home. Though what had he expected? Boys in sequinned shorts riding swans? Oiled catamites fondling leather-clad bikers in billows of dry ice and rainbows?

No. Instead, there were men, that was all: some young, some old, some handsome, some not, some flamboyant, some – most – nondescript, chatting amiably over pints of Guinness. The tiniest twinge of disappointment swiftly disappeared under a wave of relief. This was a world he could handle. He turned to Willie and nodded at the bar. I'll get these. What will you have?

Oh Christ, we're not staying down here, Willie said. In Jurassic Park? We're going upstairs.

Dickie hadn't noticed the stairs, in a far corner. That was where the noise was coming from. With a sinking heart he trooped after him, into a loudening thud of techno, and a miasma of dry ice, sweat, smoke, and other, unplaceable odours.

He had seen rather a lot of this boy, Willie, over his first two years. Everybody saw a lot of Willie; Willie, in a way that struck Dickie as strange in someone so odd and so ugly, wanted to be seen. He was forever promenading about Front Square or holding forth on the ramp to the Arts Block – he never seemed to have any lectures to go to. But his main theatre for self-display was the Historical Society, known as the Hist, one of the university's two venerable debating clubs. (The other was the Philosophical Society, known as the Phil.) These clubs were the stomping ground of a certain Trinity 'type', and originally Dickie had steered clear; he had quite enough of their peacocking in the everyday run of things without deliberately subjecting himself to more. They frequently invited very prestigious guests to speak, however, and one night Dickie, early in the spring of his first year, had gone along to see a politician he'd read about. He'd stayed for the debate after – it was impossible to leave – and ever since, the Hist's weekly meetings had been a guilty pleasure. *Guilty* because his instincts had been entirely correct – the Hist was absolutely awash with Hooray Henrys, as his father called them. (He also called them West Brits, Queers and Quentins, Oxford rejects; as an ardent republican, his father had deep reservations about Dickie attending Trinity, or at least, felt he *ought* to have deep reservations.) Yet attending the Wednesday night debates, in a huge, grey, Gothic building, Dickie felt . . . bewitched, it was not too strong a word.

Here, distilled and formalized beneath the high ceiling of the Chamber, was college as he had imagined it. The boys wore dinner jackets, the (few) girls evening dresses. All were brilliant speakers – urbane, unflappable, flipping effortlessly from crystal-clear précis of what must have been whole shelf-loads of information, to witty putdowns and badinage which flew back and forth across the floor without cease. Everyone was so knowledgeable, so elegant, and yet so indifferent to their knowledge, their elegance; Dickie thrilled at the faint tang of godlessness that came with the public school accents and the ferocious, ubiquitous mockery, revelled in the certainty that the spectacle would be incomprehensible, simply incomprehensible, to the people at home.

And Willie was, of all these prodigious young men, the most prodigious. He knew the most, he was the funniest. He spoke in a melodious, bell-like voice that was at once sonorous and gently self-deprecating, just as his speeches, studded with quotations, allusions, Latin aphorisms, were somehow both learned and bashful, so the force and brilliance of them hit you only gradually; it was like drinking lightning, very slowly, from a wine glass. In this setting, even his ugliness took on a new light; it gave him a kind of aristocratic bearing, a seriousness and authority, as if beauty and such fripperies were beneath him.

The motion that night, the first night, was *That this House should have children.* The previous speaker, an Indian boy, had spoken with such eloquence and passion about the economic rise of his homeland, where even in the poorest of slums the arrival of a new child was a sign of hope, that Dickie, greatly moved, had felt certain this was the winning argument and the last word on the matter.

Then Willie got up.

He spent a certain amount of time literally clearing his throat, paging through his notes with an air of bemusement, as if he hadn't been expecting to speak. When he did speak, his tone was conversational, off the cuff, at least in the beginning. He invoked someone called Malthus, and talked about a Malthusian trap; then he said that it wasn't so much a trap as a mirage, and that Malthus himself was a straw man for religious conservatives. (Yes! thought Dickie, though also, Who was Malthus? What is a straw man?) His honourable friends, he said, gesturing across the divide to the opposing side, had said repeatedly that having children was a fundamental right. But the idea of a right was no more than a fairy tale the rich told themselves so they could sleep easy in their enormous Tudor mansions. (Everyone laughed at this bit, for reasons Dickie didn't know.) The poor have rights! he extolled with bitter mockery. They don't have homes, but they have rights! They don't have food to eat, but they have rights! You can rest easy, because they, off in their slums, have rights, enshrined in law!

The boy's voice dripped with anger. The audience cheered. But then he became quieter, wistful. Alas, rights are – as indeed people say of children themselves – only ever on loan to us. Where they become sufficiently inconvenient to the powerful, those rights can be revoked in an instant. And that's in Hants! he said, to more mystifying laughter. Elsewhere, for instance in the slums of India my learned friend – gesturing across the aisle again – has explored so thoroughly, those rights may better be considered as another mirage—

At this the Indian boy on the opposing team shouted that he'd clearly spent too long in the desert, if he was suffering from all these mirages.

Willie replied that he hadn't wanted to say it, but he'd found his honourable friend's argument something of a desert, during which he had fantasized or hallucinated that he was in a bar well-stocked with beer and earplugs, to which the first man responded that it seemed highly unlikely the speaker would be having children anyway, rights or no; that everyone knew what kind of bar the speaker preferred, and for that matter, what kind of plug, which drew jeers and hoots from the crowd. Willie waited quite unperturbed until there was relative calm again, and then responded that his honourable friend's interest in the well-being of the children in the slums of India was easy to understand, given that a ready supply of child labour was necessary for his father's factories in Bangalore, which in turn – as shouts and hoots began to rise again – was necessary to pay for his honourable friend's very own Tudor mansion currently under construction, as we have seen in the latest issue of *Tatler*, next door to his father's, in Brockenhurst, Hants – Hants! he exclaimed, and again, as a kind of rallying cry, Hants! – and here the house descended into anarchy, with the moderator banging his gavel and crying, Order! Order! with an enormous grin on his chops, while the honourable friend pointed at Willie and spluttered what were probably threats but remained inaudible in the din, while Willie himself took advantage of the pause in proceedings to take the daintiest of sips from his glass of water –

Dickie – who had understood so little of what had been said – clapped his hands in delight: he felt like he had at the circus as a little boy, watching the fire-eater, the knife-thrower, the girl standing atop a racing pony, marvelling that such skill was possible. Yes, here was adult life at last, in all its theatre and cruelty.

At the reception afterwards he clutched a glass of caustic white wine that was allegedly home-made by one of the members. Nearby, the Indian boy was holding forth to a small crowd, feigning nonchalance, as if being made a fool of had been part of his plan. A guy with an English accent came over to Dickie for no reason and started talking to him about the Lib Dems. Then Willie passed by, and, with a daring that surprised him, Dickie excused himself from his conversation and leaned out to tap him on the arm.

I just wanted to say, Dickie said, stammering as the new confidence instantly disappeared – I just wanted to say well done. The boy's blue eyes stared back at him like rare iridescent insects under glass. All of his intelligence was there in his gaze; it was intimidating, and yet, Dickie felt excited by it, and excited that intelligence could make him feel like that.

The boy took the compliment with a rather perfunctory nod and made to move on.

We met before, Dickie blurted. In Front Square. You told me about wasps.

About *wasps*? The boy gazed at him in mystification.

Or bees, it was, Dickie corrected himself. Bees, yes.

Bees? the boy repeated, in the same tone of incredulity.

Yes, their, ah, mating habits, Dickie said unhappily.

Oh yes, I remember now, the boy said. But it was clear that he didn't; it was clear that he had no idea who Dickie was. Certainly he did not seem to feel they had anything more to say to one another. Someone else came along, to whom he started talking without introducing Dickie, who slunk to the door and out to wait for his bus in the cold.

He knew there was some element to Willie that he hadn't understood, something that sat alongside but wasn't quite his intelligence. He'd heard the jibes of the other boys, of course, but he didn't make the connection. At home, everyone called everyone a faggot; if you dropped your pencil in class you were a faggot, if you ate the wrong biscuits. Dickie had been called a faggot since he was ten years old, but no one actually thought that he *was* a faggot, or that anyone else in the town was. The existence of homosexuals had to his mind the same somewhat liminal quality of the bands in the videos on MTV: he did not doubt that they were real, ontologically speaking, but he was confident that their world and his would never, ever meet.

He couldn't remember the exact moment he discovered Willie was one – was gay, a gay; maybe there was no exact moment, maybe the knowledge seeped into him by a kind of cultural osmosis. Once he saw it, he realized it was obvious; Willie was quite open about it, though Dickie didn't know who he did it with, if anyone. He was so ugly that it was hard to conceive of anyone being sufficiently attracted to sleep with him, quite aside from the impossibility of imagining a man loving a man.

After the discovery, he found that he thought differently of Willie. Not in a bad way; he wasn't repelled by him. Instead he felt a kind of pity, as if it was a crippling weakness. Dickie's own cleverness had often seemed a similar burden at home. It made Willie less daunting, such that Dickie could even imagine them being friends. As he continued to attend the debates, as he observed Willie perorating on the ramp, he pictured himself joining in with some ingenious aperçu of his own, Willie turning to him in pleased surprise. He didn't, of course. To Willie he remained just one of the anonymous spods in the benches, waiting to be dazzled by his wit.

But then at the end of Second Year he'd got Schol, and his Rooms, and one autumn morning shortly after the beginning of Third Year, while Dickie was outside rummaging in his pocket for his keys, the door to his building opened and Willie appeared. Oh, it's you, he said.

Yes, Dickie said pathetically. Despite his imaginary friendship with him, he still found Willie's intelligence had a chilling effect on his own, so he came across as being even duller than he in fact was.

Do you live here? Willie said, jabbing a thumb backwards, and then, before Dickie could answer nonchalantly, *Yes – do you?* he added, Awful hole, isn't it.

Above them was one of those perfect autumn skies that graced the city only rarely, a brilliant, cloudless silver-blue against which the trees' golden-red foliage glowed as if lit from within; around them, fallen leaves circled over the cobbles in sudden rushes, like debutantes whirled on the roguish arms of the wind.

What room are you in? I'm on the second floor.

Dickie said he was on the top floor, and Willie said that room was the haunted one. I'm quite serious, he said. You know this is regarded as being the most haunted building in Ireland.

Dickie said he hadn't noticed anything unusual, though as he spoke he remembered the scorch marks on the rug. Possibly to ward off ghosts? Or a witches' sabbat? A very small one?

Well, if you get a scare late at night, feel free to call down to mine, Willie said.

Have you got a supply of crucifixes? Dickie said.

No, but I have a double bed, said Willie.

Dickie spluttered, turned it into a laugh, to show he got the joke, that he wasn't a prude. It didn't mean anything, he knew, it was just the kind of outrageous remark Willie specialized in. He smiled, and climbed past him to the door, saying, as he went inside, that he would keep that in mind.

The upper floor of the Butterfly was different to downstairs; very different. He made his way across a dance floor populated by men most of whom had their shirts off, revealing tanned, muscular, hairless chests which rubbed wetly against Dickie as he passed. The walls were black. The air was dense with chemicals, wobbling with lubricious electronic music over which a woman's voice chanted, *Ass! Ass! Give me ass!* Dickie kept his eyes fixed on the back of Willie's head until they arrived at a table. Next to them, two men were kissing vigorously; Dickie could see their tongues, like meat-coloured slugs wrestling each other; and now an eye opened, and one of the men was staring right at him – hurriedly he turned in his seat. *I want to fist you in the ass!* Quiet here tonight, Willie remarked.

The other boy from the Hist and the waistcoated stranger reappeared with four pints of Guinness; they sat down and a conversation ensued, only snatches of which Dickie could hear, but which seemed to be about people they knew who'd had syphilis. As he drank his pint Dickie began to relax. This place was a kind of circus too, he thought, a chaotic circus with all of the acts on at once. Everybody was on show, at pains to impress each other. That he had no stake in the performance made him feel left out, but also oddly empowered, and even, once again, a little sorry for the denizens cavorting around him, people more reviled than he was. He decided to treat the evening as an anthropological exercise, and looked around him with a carefully neutral expression. There were women here too, he realized; they were the ones who looked like men. There were also men who were dressed as women, but not in the same way: these were exaggeratedly buxom, gaudily made up, like freakish dolls. He didn't understand why someone would want to look like that, or who could possibly desire something so obviously false. It seemed a kind of elaborate private joke – of the sort that had so often thrown him in his first months at Trinity, whereby people said things that they didn't mean in order to suggest what they did. But instead of just what they said, here it was what people did too – how they dressed, and spoke, and moved.

Willie seemed to know everyone. A steady stream of people – of men – came over to speak to him; they all took the time to ask Dickie's name, and how he knew Willie, and so on. Everyone's so friendly here, he remarked to Willie.

Yes, we don't get fresh meat coming through that often, Willie replied. If you play your cards right you could be flavour of the month right up to Christmas. He laughed, seeing Dickie's expression.

Joking, he said, patting his thigh. It's a nice bar for a late pint, that's all.

A man with cropped, bleach-blond hair and heavily mascaraed eyes plonked himself down on the banquette beside them and began gabbing to Willie. Dickie took the opportunity to put on his coat. It was time to leave. But first he really needed to go the toilet; he didn't think he could make it back to his Rooms.

To get there, he had to negotiate the dance floor again. Without Willie to guide him, the journey was very different. Sweaty bodies smeared him; he was jostled, he was grabbed; a half-naked man jumped in front of him and began thrusting his pelvis at him with his hands behind his head, while at the same moment someone whispered into his ear, he couldn't make out what – it might not have been a word at all, just a wet squelch. Now he was seeing their true colours, he thought grimly. He shook off an arm, stepped free of the dry ice, pushed through the door and followed the sign down a hallway, past a staircase, and through another door marked *Gents*.

The stench was the first thing that hit him: a sharp chemical odour that overlaid the usual toilet stink. Then the cries – a man's cries, plaintive, desperate. They were coming from one of the cubicles. Dickie wondered if he should alert security – it sounded as if someone were being violently attacked. Yet several other men were at the urinals and paying no attention. Then the baying man exclaimed, at the top of his lungs, Fuck me! Fuck my man-pussy! and the toilet door thudded repeatedly and it became all too clear, even to Dickie, what was happening. A flower of shame unfurled inside him, pushing up through his body to blossom hotly in his head; at the same time, anger, that *he* was the one to feel ashamed, here in the house of the shameless! He forced himself to piss quicker – cupping his hands to shield his privates, staring doggedly into the clotted trough of the urinal. It seemed to take for ever. Finishing at last, he stumbled backward, pulled up his zip, then hurried out without washing his hands.

Then, in the hallway between the door to the Gents and the door back to the bar, he paused. He wanted more than anything to leave, but he couldn't bear the thought of crossing the dance floor again. A wave of repulsion surged through him. What was he doing here? Why had he come? How had he let himself fall in with such low company?

A little window gave on to the street below. Dickie pressed his face against it and with blurry eyes gazed down on the city. How beautiful it was! How he envied the ordinary people going about their evening! How happy he would be when he was back among them! Once he was out, he vowed he would never return to this place – never even walk on this side of the street. And he'd never again so much as speak to Willie Laughton, whose fault all of this was!

But how would he get out? How could he leave the pub without being

seen? What if someone recognized him? In an instant, the question bal-
looned into a full-scale horror. What if someone from home was passing
as he came out the door? And went back and told his father? The idea
was so horrific that it blotted out everything else. Already it seemed he
could feel his father's disgust – his incomprehension, his shame – and
he knew that he would rather die than face that, literally die. And yet, at
the same moment he had the sudden, impossible idea that if he looked
out the window again, he would see his father appear – see him march
down the street, storm past the bouncer, stride upstairs and burst through
that door right there to take Dickie by the hand and, pushing the dance-
floor lechers out of the way, bring him safely back outside . . .

Behind him the door to the Gents opened and a voice said, That was
a bit much.

Was he talking to Dickie? He turned around. A fellow in a GAA jersey was there before him, scratching his head. I mean, each to his own,
like, he said. But . . . I don't know, *Fuck my man-pussy*?

He spoke with a thick accent that Dickie supposed must be Kerry, as
he was wearing the county colours. He was a little taller than Dickie, and
a couple of years older; he had a broad, open face, brown eyes, and
short, neat, dark hair. It's Dublin all over, he said. You can't go for a
slash without some lad shouting in your ear about his tool-hole.

Dickie laughed in spite of himself.

Where you from yourself? the young man said. Dickie told him the
name of his town. I know it! he said, with a smile of recognition. What's
the name of that pub on the square – Coady's, is it? Now that's a great
spot. He gave a little shake of the head. It's a long way from Coady's we
are here, boy. Good luck, anyhow.

He passed on, then at the door to the dance floor paused and said
to Dickie, Here, do you fancy getting out of here and having a pint
somewhere else? Like, no bother if you don't, but I can't take any
more of this.

Dickie grinned and said, You'd need a drink after this place all right.

Great! Here, I've just to go and get my jacket. See you outside in a minute? My name's Sean, by the way. The young man gave Dickie his hand to shake and then disappeared into the crowd.

Through the cavorting, sweat-sheened bodies, Dickie could see Willie prattling away at his table. He didn't feel like saying goodbye.

Instead, tucking down his head, he charged through the dance floor, then down the stairs, through the front bar, with its deceptive air of normality, and out. He didn't stop when he got to the street, but turned briskly and decisively from the door and started walking. He kept going for twenty yards or so, then stopped in front of a shop selling musical instruments.

Pretending to examine their wares, he glanced surreptitiously back down the street. It was impossible to be sure, but he didn't think he'd been seen leaving. He felt a surge of exhilaration. He had escaped! If he went back to his Rooms now, it would be like it had never happened. But what about Sean? Was he just going to abandon him? A country man like himself, that everybody probably called a sheepshagger too?

A light rain was falling. From under the awning, he looked again in the direction of the pub. He still felt exposed, too close to the bright double doors. He bit his lip. Could he walk back down the street, peep in as he passed and see if there was any sign of him? No, he didn't want to do that. There was nothing for it, then; he would have to go home. Typical that he should finally make a friend and lose him within a minute, he thought glumly. But then, just as he was about to move off, he saw Sean emerge from the door! And the look on his face as he stared searchingly left, then right – the confusion, the resignation – quite melted Dickie's heart. He smiled, waved; Sean caught sight of him, smiled in answer, and broke into a jog till he had reached him at his window full of violins and ukuleles.

There you are, Sean said.

Here I am, Dickie said.

They idled up the street. Sean told Dickie about his own home town, and Dickie nodded along happily. After the sensory torment of the Butterfly, the night seemed cool and charmed. Sean was easy to talk to: he had an upright quality, a kind of straightforward decency that radiated through everything he said and did. For the first time in his life, Dickie had a sudden urge to discuss GAA. To sit and drink a pint and talk about Gaelic Games – he literally could not imagine anything he wanted to do more. Although actually, Sean said, they were near enough to his flat. They could just go back there if Dickie wanted; Sean had cans in his fridge.

He looked at Dickie amiably. What do you think?

Oh, Dickie said.

They were at the foot of a little bridge that crossed the canal. The rain had died away, the last light was fading from the sky. The two men stopped there, and looked at one another. And in that moment Dickie learned something. This thing about *looking into someone's eyes*. If you're talking about making a connection, the term is quite misleading. He looked into people's eyes all the time. What's really happening in these moments is that you find yourself looking *at* their eyes – that is, the gaze stops at the eye itself, arrested by the beauty of it; and their gaze does the same at yours; and the two gazes and your souls behind them skate off each other, swirl over each other, like mercury on mercury, so that standing quite still you feel yourself spin out of control, around and around, like a car aquaplaning, until you come to rest again, and you show no sign at all that anything of note has happened, except to permit yourself perhaps a little smile.

Sean's flat was not all that near, really; it was in Rathmines, close to Dickie's old digs, and similarly dilapidated within. Peeling wallpaper in the hall – dismal floral stuff that looked a hundred years old; a spiked hoop with an unlit candle under it protruding from the wall, that Dickie took at first to be some sort of Gothic basketball hoop, and then realized was a representation of the Crown of Thorns. When Sean unlocked his apartment door and ushered him in, however, he had the fleeting impression of somewhere spare and clean. No more than that though: then Sean spun around and pushed him against the door and kissed him.

Dickie did not know what to do. It struck him that he hadn't washed his hands earlier – he really ought to do it now before anything else. But he was pinned there and couldn't get free. Sean had closed his eyes, so out of decorum he closed his too. That made things easier. Purely on the level of sensation, the kiss was not unpleasant. Sean's mouth tasted of alcohol and was a bit too forceful, but his warmth, the warmth of a living body, was agreeable, and so was his scent, of soap and shaving cream and supermarket deodorant; his arms were strong and smooth, while his jaw, by contrast, was softly rough with stubble. None of these things were bad in themselves and so – at the same time that a voice in his head screamed, *What are you doing?* – Dickie had the feeling that this could not be wrong, or not wholly so. Still he didn't run his hands under his shirt, though he wanted to – over his muscles, his nipples – he didn't say anything stupid like *I love you*; it was a relief in a sense when Sean pulled away and then said, as if nothing had happened, Do you want a can?

Oh yes, please, Dickie said. As Sean moved off, he looked around the room. It was a kitchen with a living room attached, or the other way around he supposed. There was a table with a bench and two chairs, then a couch and an armchair in reasonable repair, facing a big TV. At the fridge, Sean took out two cans of Carlsberg and threw one to Dickie. Dickie began to ask whether he lived here on his own, but Sean, rather than sit on the couch, had disappeared through a door.

After a moment, Dickie followed, and found himself in another room, darker, with drawn curtains and a stuffy or musky odour to the air. There was little in it, besides a stack of boxes and a rumpled bed, and Sean, who stood at the end of this bed, with the scant light that came through the curtains falling on his shoulders. He took a long pull on his beer, then unbuttoned his fly and took out his penis, which was erect, and very large; though maybe it was just that Dickie had never seen one in real life before, or not like that, i.e. erect, other than his own, obviously; and Sean stayed like that, staring at Dickie, lifting his beer to his lips with one hand and with the other stroking his penis, which resembled, Dickie thought, absurdly he supposed, a guard dog, straining at the leash, something fierce and hostile, held in check by someone whose intentions were unclear. But then, what were his own intentions? Why had he come here?

Come on, so, Sean said. Something in the way he said it made Dickie realize that he was much drunker than he'd seemed till now. How had Dickie not noticed before? He was just about keeping it together, but he was steaming, steaming. Simply standing there was causing him some effort.

Do you know, Dickie said quietly, I actually ought to get back. I've an essay—

Get onto the bed, Sean interrupted, and the tone of command woke something in Dickie that had been absent hitherto: obediently he climbed onto the grimy sheets. Take off your clothes and turn over, Sean said. Again, Dickie did what he was told; his Superdry shirt, his expensive, not quite right jeans, the underwear his mother had bought for him in Dunnes.

Sean stripped too. He was even more handsome naked; being naked suited him, while Dickie had always felt his body unclothed as a kind of outrage, a writhing white worm discovered beneath a rock. And yet here was a man kissing it – kissing his shoulders, his neck, hot breath crashing like waves in Dickie's ear, successive waves in a sea of desire. Dickie craned his head round to kiss him back but the mouth pulled away. Had he done something wrong? Again, he began to turn but this time a brawny hand grabbed his head and pushed it down into the pillow. Wait, Dickie said, I'm new at this – then he gasped. A searing pain ripped through him. He bit down: it was all he could do; he felt like a chainsaw was ripping up his bowels, while the brawny arms pinioned him, and over him and around him the man hissed and gasped and rocked and thrust, relentlessly, again and again – he tried to ask him to slow down, but the hands were crushing his head down into the pillow – he couldn't see anything, could hardly breathe, could only feel the pain, and the other man's body enveloping his – it was like being caught in a machine, like a child crawling inside the casing of a machine and finding itself trapped there – yet his body was responding, it was shaking, as though it was undergoing something his mind had barely grasped, and then the machine became an animal, and reared back, and roared, and with both hands raised Dickie's shoulders up, then dashed them down again, and then shuddered, and collapsed on top of him.

For a time they lay in the darkness. The man's arm was wrapped around his body, but his hand hung loose. Dickie thought he must be asleep, and tried to stop his trembling so it wouldn't wake him. Pain burned through him, and only seemed to worsen as the shock subsided. But also, deep in the darkness, he felt within him a little glow; and as Sean began to snore he thought of where they might go for breakfast in the morning, and what they might talk about, and then how he might show him his Rooms, his bed, where this time he would take the lead, be gentle, and slow . . .

He must have fallen asleep himself, because when he opened his eyes again the room was darker still. Something was rustling over to the side; simultaneously he realized he was alone in the bed. He propped himself up on his elbows. Sean was getting dressed in the darkness.

What's going on? Dickie said.

I've to go to work, Sean replied shortly.

Now? Dickie said. What time is it? Sean didn't reply. He tugged on his trousers, then cursed – he'd knocked over a can that he'd left by the bed last night, Dickie could hear beer glugging out and seeping, with a hiss, into the carpet. Here, he said, swinging himself out of bed, let me—

No, Sean said, and when Dickie reached down to right the can, *No!* he cried again and with one hand flipped Dickie back onto the bed: where he lay prone, like a bug, staring at Sean, who was staring back at him with blazing eyes.

What are you looking at? he said.

Dickie's own eyes had adjusted to the darkness now, but it took him a moment to understand what he was seeing. Then in the instant he understood, he saw too that he must not show it. Nothing, he whispered, lowering his head as if to unsee, or show he was unseeing, the badged cap, the blue shirt, the yellow number on the navy epaulette. But it was too late.

What are you looking at? Sean said quietly, then exploded in a bellow, Don't look at me! Don't you ever look at me!

And he sprang forward and beat his fists on Dickie's head. I'm sorry! Dickie heard himself squeal. I'm sorry! But the fists kept coming down like hammers and the great hulking body pressed him down, just as he had last night. If you ever – if you ever – he was roaring. He had turned Dickie's head so his fist fell on his face, though it felt too heavy to be a fist, more like a rock, trying to smash through to the other side of Dickie's skull. Dickie scrabbled desperately at the sheets – the man lost his grip on him, stood up to reposition himself on the bed – Dickie managed to slide off the mattress to the floor, where he found his underpants. But before he could put his trousers on Sean jumped off the bed and knocked him to the ground – kicking him and stamping on him and calling him all kinds of horrible names – till he somehow writhed clear and clambered across the bed to drag himself out the bedroom door then through the kitchen, where he was confronted by three doors. Which one had he come in? He heard Sean coming – he tried a door at random and saw the Crown of Thorns and the staircase, and he ran out and half-tumbled down it, pulling the trousers, which were caught on his ankle, after him, and then weeping and gasping, grabbed at the door to the street, which thank God opened—

And he ran, in his underwear, without looking back, down the deserted pitch-black 4 a.m. street, his eyes filled with blood, his ears ringing with Sean's clattering footsteps, while a mocking voice inside his head told him, *You are free, you are free, you are free.*

He didn't think Sean had followed him; still, when he got back to his Rooms he locked the door, just in case. He fell on the floor and lay there for a while, sobbing. Then he pulled himself together, took a deep breath, examined himself. There was no real harm done; nothing seemed to be broken. The bruising would go down in a few days, the cuts would heal. It hurt when he went to the toilet but that was to be expected. He was a bit concerned about his left eye, which he couldn't see out of. But the right eye was untouched. All in all, it could have been worse, he thought.

He tried to understand what had happened – to see it from Sean's point of view. Clearly he was angry because he thought that Dickie would betray his secret – he thought Dickie was no different to one of the 'regulars' in the bar, disloyal, amoral, untrustworthy. Really it was a crossed wire more than anything else. And Dickie had been there with Willie after all. He wished Sean had let him explain! He wished he could tell him he wasn't like that! (*But wasn't he?* a voice inside him asked.) Well, it was over now. There was no sense in dwelling on it. Best just to put it behind him.

That's when he discovered that he didn't have his wallet.

He went around the room a hundred times but couldn't find it. It must have fallen out of his pocket, either on the way home or in Sean's apartment. Panic engulfed him again. The wallet had his Trinity ID card in it, with his name and his student number. Could Sean use it to find him? Could he be out there right now, scouring the campus for him? He squeezed his eyes tight shut, tried to picture the card. As far as he remembered it didn't have his address on it. But would that stop him? Sean was a guard, tracking people down was his speciality! What if he questioned Dickie's lecturers, found out about Schol? Then a new wave of dread broke over him. Dickie had told him the name of his town! It would be so easy to find him there, and if he wasn't there to find his father, tell him what Dickie had done, tell everyone what he had done! He had only wanted to have a drink, but Dickie had tempted him, tricked him! Dickie would have said anything, to be kissed, to be held! A man he barely knew, he wanted to have sex with him, fuck him, be fucked in the arse! Dickie Barnes, of Goldenhill, Old Road! He saw Sean storm the streets of the town, hollering it over and over. He put a blanket over his head, he put his head between his knees and screamed silently. Then once again he took a deep breath.

He would have to go. To England, maybe, that was where people went, wasn't it? (*People like you*, hissed the voice in his head.) He had an uncle there, maybe he could transfer to an English university. Yes, that was what he would do. When it felt safe he would start to make enquiries. For now though the best thing was to lie low. Stay put, get a sense of Sean's movements; then once he knew the coast was clear he could work out his own next move. It wouldn't be too difficult. He would skip today's lectures. He had food – cornflakes; he had run out of milk, but there was tap water. His pains were already starting to recede. As soon as the sun came up things would start to get better. It would have to come up soon, wouldn't it? Logically? Until then he decided he would sit by the window and keep a lookout through a crack in the curtains. But it was tricky. There was undergrowth in the square below, where in the darkness it would be easy for someone to hide and watch him. He was so tired that he kept nodding off, even when he took the chair away and stood instead of sitting. There was a hum coming from somewhere. It was so loud! Clearly someone in one of the rooms downstairs had a generator, or it was the electricity in the wires, something like that? But it might be a police sweep – some machine they had to look through walls – so he went to hide in the wardrobe, though of course that meant he couldn't keep watch! Then once he had worked out how to do it, the two things, i.e. be at the window and in the wardrobe, he noticed something else: the room had a tendency to loom, or to lean, rather. He didn't think it had anything to do with Sean, so probably nothing to worry about. Only that it kept leaning into him, just hard enough for him to feel the pressure, and breathing, not loud, just so as to be sure he heard it – a room, leaning, breathing into him.

Stop it, he said.

And it pulled back. But still was there. And he was in it. How could he be in it, and feel it leaning on him? He remembered what Willie had said, that the building was haunted. But a room itself could not be a ghost, as it had never been alive. Unless he was the ghost? But when he pulled at the cuts on his eye they bled, meaning he was alive, therefore not a ghost. Perhaps he'd misheard when they said *the building was haunted*, perhaps they'd said *the building haunted*, i.e. had itself become a ghost. Perhaps that was why the previous resident had made the fire on the floor, to keep it away, the room. Also because it was cold, incredibly cold. Maybe he could light a fire? But if someone called the fire brigade they would bring the police too, that was procedure: it would lead Sean straight to him. He should have stayed in Sean's flat, he saw that now. If he had stayed and taken his punishment, none of this would be happening. When he ran he had made everything much worse. Could he go back? he wondered. If he showed he was sorry – that he'd already punished himself – or at least tried to explain the mistake? Yes, that was the best course of action. He started to put on his clothes in the dark. Now he'd made the decision he felt better. The hum was still there but when he went into the living room it was the heater, it must have switched itself on, or he had switched it on and forgotten about it. He pulled on his trousers, smiling at how he had carried them home, bundled in his arms. The fabric chafed against his legs as if the skin was red raw. He had left his coat in Sean's, so he put on an extra sweater. He didn't feel so cold now, though it occurred to him that it was very late to go out, or very early, rather, and of course Sean had been leaving for work, that was the whole issue – still, he could go back to the flat and wait outside? He started to move the furniture away from the door – how did that get there? – when it occurred to him that he must look disgusting. He decided to go and clean himself up. The hum from the heater was also coming from the bedroom, which was odd, and when he switched on the light and went to the mirror –

Sean was looking back at him! He must have got in through the window! (Or was he there all along!) Dickie had only a split-second to take in the look of absolute hatred on his face and to understand that it was too late to be sorry or to make amends, and then the man pulled him backwards in a headlock and flung him to the floor. With both hands he pounded at Dickie's face, and when Dickie brought his hands up to cover his eyes he jammed his cock into Dickie's bottom and the fists and the cock and the cock and the fists pounded, pounded, pounded at the door, and a voice he knew from somewhere said, Hello?

Daylight. He got up from the floor. It was streaked with blood. Hello? the voice said again. Who was it? He could almost remember but not quite, which annoyed him. He dragged the armchair away from the door and pressed his eye to the crack, but he couldn't see anything. Are you all right in there? the voice said. I'm in the room below. I thought I heard, ah . . .

Dickie didn't reply at first, in case it was a trick, but then it struck him that the person might complain to the college about the noise and he would lose his room. So he opened the door to apologize.

Willie stood outside. Of course! How could he not have guessed it? Sean had sent him, he was working for Sean, had been all along. It didn't matter, he was ready to give up. He held up his hands, he smiled. It's all right, he said, though he could barely hear himself over the hum.

But Willie didn't smile back. He didn't move, he didn't speak.

He was looking at Dickie.

Christ, he said.

IV

The grey squirrel is not native to Ireland. The species was introduced to the country just over a century ago, when a dozen arrived in a wicker hamper at Castle Forbes as a wedding present from the Duke of Buckingham. After the wedding breakfast, one of the daughters of the family opened the hamper on the lawn of the estate; the squirrels hopped out and scurried away into the woods. From there, like some fable of colonialism, they have spread through almost the entire country. The native red squirrel, *Sciurus vulgaris*, meanwhile, has almost vanished.

The greys carry a virus, squirrelpox. They are immune to it, but the reds are not. It gives them lesions around their mouths so they can't eat; after a week it's killed them. The only way to save the reds from extinction is to exterminate the pox-carrying greys.

For Victor this has become something like a moral crusade. Before Imelda complained, he liked to stalk the woods at dusk with a thermal-imaging camera fitted to his gun, looking for *the invaders*. Since then he's switched to traps; he checks them in the evening, returning with a sack which he empties into an old beer cooler.

Dickie has asked Victor to stop the cull. PJ doesn't like it; in truth, Dickie doesn't like it either. But Victor refuses. He's sorry that the boy is upset, he says. But if he quits now, it will reverse the effects of the work he's done so far.

He is not sorry, Dickie knows. He hasn't said it in so many words, but it's been clear for some time that Victor doesn't think PJ should be here. Whether it's because he thinks it's dangerous, or that the boy is slowing them down, Dickie doesn't know. He finds it hard to believe Victor has any serious interest in safety; as for delays, spending time with his son is one of Dickie's main reasons for doing the work, so as far as he's concerned, they're not in any hurry. He mollifies Victor by pointing out that PJ will be around much less now the summer holidays are over, and manages to extract a promise at least to stop cooking the squirrels in front of him. Then he goes back to PJ and once again goes through why the cull is not actually a bad thing.

The boy looks disconsolately at his shoes. Why can't they all just live together? he blurts.

At 5 p.m. on Friday, water appears at the bottom of the hole. By evening, they're baling out three buckets of water for every one of soil. PJ, dirt-smeared in his school uniform, films the two men from the side, his eyes alight, as if they've uncovered some buried treasure. With his auger, Victor goes down another foot. Then the digging is done. That's the hard part over with, Victor says. We're on our way now.

The next day he drives to Limerick to pick up some special clay for the well, leaving Dickie and PJ with the job of checking his squirrel traps. He has drawn them a map in biro, a medieval tableau of earthworks, rock formations, stands of trees, inscribed on the back of a takeaway menu. You'll need this too, he says, holding out a hammer.

The woods are silent. No birdsong, no buzzing, no rustles in the undergrowth: the only signs of life are their own, their breathing, their heartbeats, which in the void seem alien and somehow unholy.

Isn't there one around here?

PJ looks down at the map. Which ones are the sycamores?

Give us a look at that, Dickie says. He scratches his head. Hmm.

Around them the forest is a sea of emerald and dusty-brown, refracting itself into an endless network of arbours and copses and corridors like a silent, vegetal hall of mirrors. Dickie wonders if his son knows where they're going at all, or if he knows but doesn't want to get there.

On his phone, four missed calls from his father. No message. *He said you were supposed to come and see him.*

I found it! PJ exclaims. He dashes towards a tree with a biscuit box sitting in a cleft. Careful, Dickie says, automatically. But PJ has already stopped a little distance away, suddenly fearful of what he will find.

This trap is empty, though. So is the next. The boy begins to relax. Light lances through the green birdless canopy, falls upon them in thin brilliant stripes as if cleaving them in two. *Komorebi* is the Japanese word for the kind of light you see in a forest. PJ told him that.

Do you ever come out this far? When you're playing with Nev?

Sometimes. Once I saw a red squirrel.

You did?

Yeah, I tried to get a picture, but it ran off.

Oh, that's right, I remember. Well, there'll be lots more if Victor's plan works out, won't there? He doesn't reply. What's this your game is with Nev?

Just a game. The boy scuffs along for several yards, humming to himself. Then, People aren't always who they say they are, are they, Dad.

Dickie feels himself stumble, though he doesn't stumble, feels his breath catch, though it doesn't catch. Who does PJ mean? Nev? Victor? Himself?

Well, he says, in his most equable Dad-voice. It's important to trust people. If you possibly can. You can't be naive, obviously, but . . .

What does *naive* mean?

Easy to take advantage of.

Take advantage of?

Right, you know, if someone wants to – that is, if they want you to do something – who is it that you don't think is who they say?

No one, PJ says lightly. Hey, that must be the weird tree!

That is what Victor has called it on the map: WIERD TREE. His picture shows a black triangle in the trunk, like a door. In reality it is a deep gouge or gash, shaped like a witch's hat, with a twisting point. A black, treacly substance oozes from it onto to the ground. There is something horrific about it, as if it is pulling up evil from deep in the earth. Yet the tree is alive, with new leaves at the ends of its branches.

There's the trap! PJ exclaims, darting past the injured tree to reach up a tall beech with a box in a cleft.

This time it's not empty.

A grey squirrel is crouched at the back of the cage. She is utterly still, as if she thinks they will not see her. The black orbs of her eyes gleam, gathering together all the light of the forest into two pristine points.

She's fat, isn't she, Dad?

She's going to have babies, Dickie says, then wishes he hadn't, suddenly remembering what the point of this is. He offers the sack to PJ. Do you want to do the honours?

The boy doesn't move, seems to dwindle in some incalculable way. Dickie sighs. You understand why we have to do this?

PJ swallows. He is staring at the squirrel in the cage.

The babies will have pox, the pox will kill the baby reds. If she has her babies, everything will get worse.

But it's not her fault, PJ says in a shaky voice.

What?

It's not her fault she has pox.

No, it's not her fault. It's nobody's fault. It's just nature. But if we don't kill the greys, then the reds will die. And they'll die out completely. You see? You're killing them by not taking action.

He rests the cage into the sack, reaches in to undo the latch. The boy covers his face with his hands. But he has to understand, sometimes doing what is right means having to make hard choices. It's the whole reason they're out here, so he can teach him these tough lessons.

Lessons. For a moment he is back in the summer garden, among the lilies and azaleas, fists swinging fruitlessly through the air, his father dancing in front of him, always somehow out of reach.

He sighs again. Tell you what, he says. He sets the sack down on the ground and lifts out the cage and opens the door. The squirrel remains in a huddle at the back. He picks it up again and shakes it gently. Finally the squirrel tumbles out and dashes, with her load, her mother-load, zigzagging through the trees. Till she is gone.

In the evening they cook frankfurters over the fire. Victor is still off on his travels. The full moon hangs over them as if set to drop down into the clearing. Hey, Dad, did you know baby squirrels are called kittens?

No, I didn't.

PJ returns to his phone. Did you know – oh, this is gross – baby squirrels pee and poo into their mother's mouth, and she carries it outside so predators don't smell their nest. That is so disgusting.

That's parenting, Dickie says.

In his hand his own phone comes to life. It flashes urgently, silently, <<DAD>>. Then goes dark.

Their nest is called a drey, PJ reads. It's made of twigs and sticks and then lined with moss, bark, grass, and leaves.

Is that right, Dickie says. *Tell him you gambled it.*

It's usually built in the fork of a tall tree, but sometimes it's in the attic of a house.

Tell him there was a mechanic injured and you paid him off. Tell him you sourced a special import for a client and the buyer only took cash.

It says here that they're only born twice a year, the boy says. Once in the spring and once at the end of the summer.

The end of summer, the end of everything. *Tell him the squirrels ran away with it. Tell him you don't know what happened to it. It's a mystery, tell him, a total mystery.*

V

That autumn – the autumn of his accident, as it was known – he would walk, when he was able, in the woods. In the mornings, usually; sometimes in the evening too. When he was little he hadn't much liked the woods. They were too big, too dark, too confusing; he was never sure he would find his way home. Now all the things that had bothered him before – the loneliness, the silence, the maze-like impenetrability – seemed like blessings. He liked that no one could see him, no one could find him; he walked a little further every day, over red and gold leaves that scattered the ground like drops of flame, fallen from the sun.

When he wasn't out walking he mostly stayed in his room. It pained him to see the sorrow in his parents' eyes whenever they looked at him – pained him and shamed him. Their kindness made him feel wretched, opened a fresh wound of dishonesty. They didn't suspect his story, as far as he could tell – he did look as if he had been hit by a car, which besides was exactly the kind of thing they expected to happen in the big city. His skittishness, too, could plausibly be ascribed to shock, though when he woke screaming in the middle of the night, he wondered guiltily, after the terror subsided, what they had heard.

One day, he was helping his mother in the garden – where an early frost had caused 'chaos', as she termed it, though this seemed to entail not much more than carrying seedlings from the patio into the greenhouse – when he noticed her looking at him from the far side of the lawn. The sunlight was cold but very bright; she had been making an adjustment to the roses on the pergola, but now her hands, in their green gloves, were down at her sides, and she was watching him coolly, as if she were studying one of her recalcitrant peonies. Dickie had been back for two weeks, and today was the first day he could honestly say he felt better. He had slept through the night, and this morning his limbs had felt less like molten lead. But when he saw her look at him, though her eyes were half-lost in the shadows under the brim of her hat, the dread came bubbling up again. Perhaps she saw that too; she didn't take her gaze away. Then she said quietly – his mother was always quiet – You know, Dickie, that we will love you no matter what.

And Dickie had had to hurry inside and lock himself in the bathroom, where he crouched on the ground and beat at his head with his fists.

The days were long and lonely and the time went by only very slowly. The house was quiet – he suspected his parents had asked people not to call. Even Frank kept a discreet distance, which was a mercy; in his battered condition, he found his brother's height and strength and athletic ease unbearable.

The one solace during this interminable epoch was his nightly conversation with Willie. It began with a postcard. The message in its entirety consisted of the words *Back in action?* On the reverse was a picture of a man exposing himself to a flock of sheep. For days Dickie had tried to write back, but his mind was too foggy. Then one evening his mother came into his room, carrying the phone. She looked startled. It's someone from the Vatican, she whispered.

After that they'd spoken every night. It was curious: since his accident – he had already got in the habit of calling it that himself – Dickie could hardly bear to speak to anyone. Even telling his mother what he wanted for breakfast was agony. Yet somehow with Willie he couldn't stop.

Obviously he didn't have any news. And though Willie kept pressing him, he didn't want to talk about what had happened – couldn't talk about it, without finding himself back in it, back on the floor of that flat. Even if you won't tell me, you should go to the police, Willie said; it's important to have it on the record. To that Dickie just laughed. Perhaps on some perverse level he drew pleasure from it too – having a secret, having something, someone, Willie knew nothing about; Willie, who knew everything, everyone.

No, instead he found himself telling him about the town. He told him about his school, where three different teachers were now being investigated for child abuse, and about the old silver mine in the hills where teenagers would go and drink. He told him about the universal obsession with Gaelic football, the hysteria that would surround the most trivial matches, even though the team hadn't won anything in almost thirty years. He told him the town was slowly emptying out, that the farms were too small to make a full-time living; he told him that instead of *Hello*, people here greeted each other with *Well*, pronounced in a tone of resignation, as in, *Well, that's the end of that*, or *Well, I hope you're happy*, as though every conversation were taking place in the aftermath of some catastrophic defeat.

He realized he'd never talked about the town to someone from outside. He felt a little guilty running it down, but only a little. It *was* cramped and monotonous, the people *were* small-minded, judgemental. Describing it to Willie, he wondered how he'd ever felt intimidated by it, or cared what anyone here thought of him.

Willie loved these stories. He laughed so much that sometimes Dickie wondered if he was humouring him. But the laughter sounded genuine. And the stories were funny: he felt different when he told them – witty, fluent, expansive. It did not seem strange to him that someone should like this person. He imagined Willie in the mouldy foyer of House 24, standing *contrapposto* at the payphone at the foot of the stairs, his braying laugh showing all of his yellow, bockety teeth; and he wished, momentarily, to be back there with him.

Though Dickie did most of the talking, he made some discoveries about his friend. He was from a country town too, though he had lived there only intermittently. He was the youngest in his family, ten years behind his closest sibling; his parents weren't really interested in having another child – that was how he put it – and had sent him to boarding school in Sussex when he was four. His mother and father were both English, he explained; they had moved to 'the Republic' decades ago, but they only watched BBC, and only read the British press, and avoided as much as was humanly possible any encounter with the country they actually lived in. They reminded Dickie in a strange way of his father, who, though he'd always been a republican, and sang rebel songs, and told the boys stories about the wickedness of the British, had with time grown ever more baronial. Latterly he'd started wearing blazers and waistcoats, combing back his hair; he loved to tell people the history of the estate – 'the estate', 'the land', 'the grounds', he loved to speak these words – though the manor itself where their lordships once lived had been burned down long before he was born, and the house he'd actually bought was built on its foundations in the 1970s by a haulier; the forest was the only part of the original estate that remained. Still, he would stand on his porch, in a wax jacket ordered from London, and look out over his 'demesne'. *Not bad for a lad from Piggery Lane.* (He sounds like a riot, Willie said. I'd love to meet him. He would *hate* you, Dickie said. The townsfolk would hate him too – he'd told him that when Willie had mentioned coming to visit. He took a secret pleasure in telling him how disliked he would be here. But Willie didn't seem to feel the slights of people he had never met.)

When he was sixteen Willie had been expelled: caught smuggling, he said mysteriously. He had never gone back to school. Instead, he'd spent his time in the local library, reading everything, he said, literally everything they had. The Koran, *Woman's Own*, Robert Ludlum, the lot. This was where he'd developed his fearsome arsenal of knowledge and his sense of morality as essentially herd-driven and unthinking. I also collected some whizzo knitting patterns, he said.

But how did you not go back to school? Dickie said. I just didn't, Willie said. It sounded like his parents simply hadn't got around to putting him in a new one. They left him to his own devices, with no plan in mind for, or even particular interest in, his future.

Dickie found that incredible. For as long as he could remember he had been marked down to join his father and then succeed him as the head of the family business.

And what if you don't want to? Willie said.

What do you mean?

I mean, what if you don't want to spend the rest of your life in your home town selling cars?

This was not a question that Dickie had ever asked himself. Selling cars had made the family what it was, had taken his father from a childhood slum to a sprawling estate on the edge of town. Maurice could recite every detail of every model of VW going back almost fifty years, from the split-screen window on the early T2s to the notorious heater core in the '92 Jetta. The way he saw it, the family business and the nation's history were intertwined. When he started out – he would tell the boys – driving a Volks was a serious political statement. No self-respecting Englishman would ever buy a VW. A German-made car, created by the Nazis, endorsed by Hitler himself? No: the Volkswagen was the *rebel's* car, the *republican's* car. And although neither the manufacturer nor the dealers cared to stress the Nazi angle today, he still saw himself as an outlaw, an insurrectionist, building his own maverick empire.

Dickie had never felt quite the same way about cars; he'd been regularly travel-sick as a child. Still, he'd always assumed that on graduating he would be returning home to join his father in the dealership. It had simply never crossed his mind to do otherwise.

Now for the first time he wondered. On his walks in the woods he tried to picture what it might be like to do something different, be someone different.

After the cold snap that caused such chaos in his mother's garden the forest floor had turned white with frost, and crunched grudgingly under his boots. His leg hurt when he put weight on it, and the cold made the cuts on his face sting, but in the grey light of November the woods were even more beautiful than before. White leaves sparkled on the ground, like sequins fallen from a gown; the birds called to each other with a note of urgency, as if they were late for an appointment. There was an air of departure, of Nature clearing out for the winter. It felt like everything was too busy to pay any attention to him and he felt a great sense of relief; also because it heralded a deeper emptiness, a deeper silence.

One afternoon he was out among the trees, not thinking of the garage or the future, but of matters closer to hand, namely his return to Dublin. His mother wanted him to stay home till the New Year. Christmas was not far off, there was no sense in going back before then, she said. She had a point. There were only a handful of weeks left to the term, and everybody would be up to their eyes in essays; then there was the fact that every time he thought of the city he quaked, literally quaked, and every wound and bruise and lesion seemed to unheal itself in an instant and sing out with pain. But Willie said that it was important to face down his fears. The longer he stayed away, the harder it would be to come back. He didn't want to give up his Rooms, did he? Everything he'd worked so hard to achieve?

He was woken from his thoughts by a movement overhead. Something was looking down at him from a tree. Amid the sparse remaining leaves, he saw a flash of red fur and two black eyes. Its tail arched elegantly over it, like the plume from an old-fashioned ladies' hat; but it held its front paws clasped together rather unctuously, like a country priest greeting a parishioner. Dickie bowed back, ever so slightly; the squirrel cocked its head. Its features were sharp and intelligent; it looked like it wanted to tell him something. But then a voice called out, and suddenly it was gone, without Dickie ever seeing where, or even how.

He was at the edge of a clearing. His brother was standing in the doorway of the old shed. Lately their father had decided it was an ice house, 'probably Victorian'; he kept making noises about having historians come out to survey it. For the time being, though, its main purpose was to hide Frank's hash-smoking. Come in for a minute, he said. I've just skinned up.

Dickie did so, reluctantly. Frank sat down again on the dirt floor, with his back against the wall; Dickie sat against the wall opposite and watched him spark up and disappear momentarily into a cloud of densely fragrant smoke. He let out a prolonged sigh, as if granted relief after long suffering, though what could Frank have to suffer?

Then he passed the joint to Dickie, who pulled on it cursorily in the interests of politeness. He didn't like hash, it made him feel dull and treacly. He didn't like the shed, or ice house, either; it was damp and cold, and Dickie couldn't understand why, on a clear bright day, in the beautiful surroundings of the forest, his brother would want to be in here.

They continued to pass the joint back and forth without talking for a few minutes, and then, to allay the creeping feelings of panic that Dickie could sense unfurling within him, he said, The old base, eh? I didn't know you still used it.

Ah yeah, Frank said, not looking at him. Just when I want to get my head together.

Yes, they hadn't talked much since he'd come back, but Dickie was dimly aware that some catastrophe had occurred recently; Frank had missed a point or a goal or something in a football match and been dropped from the team. Obviously this was being treated like it was the end of the world. Frank's usual Tigger-ish disposition had given way to feelings of what he probably imagined to be despair, i.e. a lot of performative sighing, elegiac bollock-scratching, etc. Dad was involved too, somehow; Frank hadn't been working at the garage, and whenever Dickie came into a room with the two of them in it he got the strong sense that he had interrupted a fight. He hadn't asked about it. Frank and Dad were constantly jockeying and jousting with each other. They thought it was because they were so different, but in fact it was because they were the same.

Anyway, that explained why Frank was skulking out here in the shed like a tramp – he was 're-evaluating'. He'd probably seen someone do it on *Hollyoaks*. His brother's life often reminded him of a soap opera written in crayon.

Frank took a last tug on the roach, squinted at it disapprovingly and squashed it on the floor, then without pausing he took out his rolling papers and started work on another. I suppose you'll be heading back to Dublin soon enough, he said. Dickie made no response. He was feeling quite woozy now, despite trying not to inhale. Frank licked the side of a Rizla and laid it flat on his lap. He picked up his pouch of tobacco, then set it down again. Do you ever think about the future?

The future? Dickie repeated.

Like I know the plan is for you to finish college and come back and work for Dad. But if you ever changed your mind . . .

It took a moment for the words to penetrate. Then Dickie sat up. Why would I change it?

Well, you know, Frank said. His eyes flicked up to Dickie, as if for assistance. Like if you decided you wanted to stay on up in Dublin, do something else. If you ever did.

Dickie looked at him. What are you talking about?

I don't know, Frank said. I just meant with your brain and all. You might have other jobs in mind. Or you might want to keep studying. Instead of coming back here. And me – you know, I've been working in the garage a bit, and I know cars, and all, so it might make more sense even, for me to take over. When the time comes.

He couldn't understand what Frank was trying to say. The plan had always been that he would come back to take over the garage, always. Their father had made the decision years ago. Unless— Has *Dad* said this? he asked. Is this something Dad's thinking about?

No, Frank said, wagging his head dolefully. But everyone else does.

Dickie sat back, nodded to himself. Of course everyone said it. Everyone liked Frank, they would all enjoy chatting to him in the forecourt, in the pub after work. The fact remained that Frank did not have a business brain. He was a disaster with figures. He couldn't type. He was terrible with money – Dickie couldn't count the number of times he'd lost his ATM card. Furthermore, until now he had never expressed any interest in managing the garage. He'd never expressed lasting interest in anything besides playing Gaelic. This was another of his whims, that was all.

That's an interesting idea, he said. But you're so good in sales. I wouldn't even have thought you'd want to get stuck with all the back-office—

I don't want to be your employee all my life! Frank's voice rose sharply, then dropped again. I don't want to spend my life as your little brother.

Dickie was thrown: he hadn't known this was how Frank saw things. It gave him a certain amount of pleasure. It isn't up to us, though, is it? he said piously. It's Dad's decision.

But if we both agreed, Frank said. If we went to him together, told him that this was how we wanted to do it?

Dickie said nothing to this. For a moment, Frank devoted himself to gluing his joint together. I just feel like I need to start having some idea what my future's going to look like, he said. We wouldn't have to tell Dad now. But just so we knew ourselves that this was what we were going to do.

But we don't know ourselves, Dickie said. He got to his feet, and added, with a trace of rebuke, I don't see why you'd assume I wanted to stay in Dublin. After what happened to me.

They spoke no more about it. From then on, he treated his brother with a new wariness. It bothered him that he didn't know why Frank had changed course. Why should he suddenly want to run the family business? Was it an act of rebellion against their father? Was someone whispering in his ear?

Willie said the real mystery was why Dickie had committed to spending the rest of his life selling hatchbacks to shitkickers in some godforsaken backwater.

You've never even been here, Dickie retaliated.

That's what *you* called it, Willie said. You told me it was a death sentence!

He wouldn't let it go; he kept bringing it up, every time they spoke on the phone, pushing at him in the same tone he used in his debates. That's *genuinely* what you want to do? You're going to come back here, slave away on your degree for two more years, and then bury yourself for the rest of your life in a provincial car dealership?

It's actually a very lucrative franchise, Dickie said gruffly.

Willie crowed in delight. For weeks to come, whenever Dickie asked him a question – What's the time? What does 'deconstruction' mean? What's the capital of Chad? – the response came back, *It's actually a very lucrative franchise*.

But he didn't *know*: he didn't know Maurice Barnes, didn't know the business, didn't see what it meant that he had chosen Dickie to take over. When all was said and done, his father recognized his superior gifts: his father knew that he was the right man for the job. How could Willie understand that? His parents didn't care what he did; they didn't even care enough to keep him at school.

So he didn't try to explain. Instead, he told him he missed him. I can't wait to see you again, he said. The reason he said it was so Willie would stop asking questions. But as he spoke the words, he realized they were true.

VI

Victor is back from Limerick. At the site, they unload sacks from his van. The sacks are heavy. Lined up by the hole, they look like body bags about to be tossed in a mass grave. What is this stuff? PJ says, peering into one. It is full of blue powder. Bentonite clay, Victor says.

When they finished digging the hole, Victor had produced a long, plastic pipe from his van. He cut slits into the bottom third of it using a circular saw; these 'gills', as he called them, would allow water to flow in, but not dirt or rocks. Then he fed the pipe down into the hole, and filled up the space around it with gravel, three feet deep, to the water line. Now they will fill the rest of the hole with the blue clay. In the moisture of the soil, it will solidify and seal the well, so no contaminants from the ground can leach down into the water.

At first it looks to Dickie like there are far more bags than they'll need. But then they start pouring in the clay and it seems just to disappear. He thinks again how being up above it all the time, you never really get a feel for how much ground there is in the ground, how much earth there is to the earth, what it takes for us to have something to walk on.

In the end they don't have enough. Cursing, Victor goes off to find a signal so he can call his man in Limerick. Dickie and PJ sit on the log. What happens once the rest of the clay comes? PJ asks.

Then we're almost there, Dickie says. Victor wants to fit an electric pump and hook it up to a water tank. But a hand pump would do us for now. Then we're done, pretty much.

And the Bunker's almost finished too, PJ says, not looking at him.

The basics, anyway, Dickie agrees.

And then we go back to the house, PJ says. Everything goes back to normal.

Right, only now we'll have a survival shelter. He hesitates, trying to read the boy's mood. There'll be more bits and pieces to do, he says. We can come down at the weekends, keep tipping away at it? He nudges him conspiratorially. Though you've probably had enough digging to last you a lifetime!

PJ doesn't speak, just stares at his shoes.

It's a relief when Victor comes back with the news that it could be a week before his man in Limerick has the clay in stock again. In the meantime, he has a new project. First, he covers the exterior walls of the Bunker with chicken wire. Next, he takes twigs and branches from the forest floor, and begins to weave them into it. What's that for? Dickie says. Insulation?

Camouflage, Victor says.

Camouflage? Dickie laughs.

Leaves along the sides, Victor says, and the roof we can seed with grass. Then you'll have the whole place invisible.

Wait till they hear in the town I've an invisible Bunker, Dickie says humorously. People will be saying I've gone off the deep end altogether.

Well, if they do say it, you and me know why, Victor says, turning his back to thread a leafy tree limb into the wire.

Why's that, so?

Because they're scared.

PJ looks at Dickie a split-second before he's ready with a reassuring smile. Who's scared, Dad?

Victor turns to them both, swollen muscles pushing through his mud-spattered shirt. People aren't stupid, he says. They can see what's coming. But they're too scared to do anything about it. Instead all they can think is to pretend it's not happening. Keep going, like everything's normal. Pour on more fuel, to show there's no fire. But the day will come when they won't be able to deny it any longer. They'll go to the supermarket and find the shelves are empty. They'll turn on the TV to get the news, but there won't be any news. No more power, no more internet, no more water when they turn on the tap. All that stuff is gone, it's over! And what'll they do then? Then they'll come crying to the ones they laughed at. They'll come with their hands out to the ones who had the sense to prepare. To you. But you won't be home. You'll be here, invisible, where they can't find you. Because you've prepared for that too.

Around him and behind him, the wind strikes up, the treetops go swish-swish, swish-swish; evening arrives, in the sudden, surprise-attack way it's been doing all week as autumn takes hold, seeming to bloom from the air in dark-blue clouds that soak into it moment by moment until it is drenched, the air, the day, it is saturated in deep blue, like the blue clay dust that fills the well, immersing bodies, trees, the van, the tents, then slowly sealing them up within it.

You're talking about worst-case scenarios, Dickie says, aware of PJ's eyes on him. Obviously they'll step in before it gets that bad. The government, I mean. Mitigate the worst effects.

Victor laughs. Do you see anyone doing any mitigating? Do you see anyone doing a fucking thing?

Yes, yes, Dickie says, gesturing to the boy: he doesn't need to hear all this. You don't need to give us the whole sales pitch. We're only doing this for the bit of fun. A place the kids and their pals can camp out, that's all we're looking to do.

Victor stares at him like they have come to a fork in the road. It's not enough to build it, Dickie. You need to be ready to protect it. Survival is a zero-sum game.

What does that mean, Dad? PJ whispers. Dickie waves the question away. Shouldn't you go and check your traps? he asks Victor pointedly.

Say in five years the you-know-what hits the fan, Victor says, ignoring him. A drought, a flood, whatever it is. Harvests fail, then the next year they fail again. Suddenly what you're looking at in Europe is a famine. That might not be what they're calling it on the news, but that's what it is. It's worse in Ireland because we're a little island that imports half its food.

Now you've been wise. You've stocked up enough to feed your family for a year and please God that'll get you out the other end of it. There you are sitting at home, patting yourself on the back and thinking that things could be worse, when the neighbours come knocking on your door. You want to help them. Of course you do. You're a good man, Dickie Barnes, everyone knows it. But food to feed your family for a year is only enough to feed two families for six months. And that's just the beginning. Then the doorbell goes again. More neighbours, more friends. Three families, four. You bring them in too, you can feed everybody for four months, for three months. But what happens the next time the bell rings? How many families live within five miles of here, would you say? Ten? Twenty? A hundred? Do you see what I'm driving at?

And when you decide you can't feed any more, what happens then? When you stop answering your door, what do you think they do, the starving people, on your doorstep? You think they're just going to turn around and go home? You think just because they're your friends and neighbours it'll all stay peaceful and respectful? You think Myanmar and South Sudan weren't all how-d'ye-do and Tidy Towns before they started hacking each other to pieces?

That's why they say, begging your pardon, when the *shit* hits. It's *shit*. Everything's going to get covered in it. Everything's going to stink. Your neighbour's not your neighbour any more. He's not someone you borrow a power hose from and talk to about the match. He's someone taking the food meant for your children. He's competition for limited resources. Everyone will be in need, everyone will be under pressure, they will do things they never believed they could do, and that's before we talk about the others who will come, strangers—

Stop, Dickie mutters.

What others, Dad? PJ is huddled up against him now, clinging to him like he's five years old again. Victor is a luminous ghost in the oceanic forest night, some phosphorescent lascar crawled out of the shipwrecked Bunker.

None of this is set in stone, Dickie blurts. His voice is high and querulous. He does not sound much, to his own ears, like the rational one, the measured one, the one who has retained a sense of proportion. It's all in the future, none of it might ever happen.

It might not, Victor agrees. I hope to God it doesn't. But if it does, you'd better be ready.

With that, taking his hammer, he turns and is gone. PJ, at Dickie's side, lets out a curious sound, a gasp, sort of a *hoosh*. Dickie closes his eyes, opens them again. It doesn't seem to make much difference.

He's angry with Victor for dragging up all this stuff in front of the boy. After her class project on climate change, Cass couldn't sleep for a month. She stayed up making lists of all the local animals that had gone extinct. He'd catch her looking at him with rings under her eyes. *Are we the bad guys?*

PJ is different: he knows more about it than Cass – than Dickie too, most likely; maybe he's better able to separate the facts from the hyperbole. He does a good impression of the YouTube preppers when Victor's not around (*Meet your new best friend – your tarp.*) He seems to treat their predictions as ghost stories, the kind you might tell around a campfire; which in a way they are, ghost stories from the future.

After Victor's tirade he goes back to gathering branches and adding them to the Bunker's new mantle. It's only after nightfall he asks, as if in passing, Is Victor right, Dad? Are we going to die?

Everyone dies in the end.

No, I mean the way he says. From starving. Or burning.

No. No. They'll fix it. People will cotton on in the end. They always do.

Do you know every year there's more flights? Like more people taking planes? Still?

Is that right?

We did it in school. And more coal burned.

Dickie takes a deep breath. I suppose in the end you can't let yourself think about it too much. I mean, you can only be responsible for what you do yourself.

Is that why we're building the Bunker?

We're building it so we have somewhere we can all be together.

Where the people can't find us?

Shh. Go to sleep.

As a teen, Dickie had been obsessed with the end of the world. Nuclear attack, inferno, killer bees; for a long time, he took it for granted that he would end his days in an internment camp, cholera-ridden, watching the smoking ruins of the razed world through a scrim of barbed wire.

His father told Dickie he'd better snap out of it. A pessimist will never be a great salesman, he said. The salesman *believes* in the future. The future is good, that's your number one message! Who's going to shell out twenty grand on a new car if he thinks the sky's about to fall on his head?

At the time, Dickie thought this was pretty vacuous. He knew about history, he knew what it looked like. But his father was right; as Dickie grew older, his outlook lightened. Or at least, he was too busy to think of global devastation.

Periodically, though, these thoughts of annihilation would return. As a student, after his accident, he would wake up screaming, imagining boots were kicking down the door. That went on for months. It came back even worse when Imelda was pregnant with Cass. Now he had something to lose. He couldn't just climb out the window and run. He couldn't take an overdose or put a plastic bag over his head, couldn't simply *let* himself be annihilated. He would have to fight, he would have to try to protect them, even though he knew it was impossible to win. You couldn't protect the people you loved – that was the lesson of history, and it struck him therefore that to love someone meant to be opened up to a radically heightened level of suffering. He said *I love you* to his wife and it felt like a curse, an invitation to Fate to swerve a fuel truck head-on into her, to send a stray spark shooting from the fireplace to her dressing gown. He saw her screaming, her poor terrified face beneath his, as she writhed in flames on the living-room carpet. And the child too! Though she hadn't yet been born, she was there too. All night he listened to her scream in his head – he couldn't sleep from it, he just lay there and sobbed, because he knew he couldn't protect her, couldn't protect her *enough* –

But he must have slept, because he woke to find Imelda looking at him. Her eyes rolled white in the darkness, her hand was clamped over her mouth. What had he said?

She wouldn't tell him, or couldn't; she would not let him comfort her, would not lay her head down even until he went to sleep in the nursery, as she called it, though at that point it was just another empty room.

Fantasies like this, fantasies of disaster, of annihilation, being over-whelmed, dissolving, were not uncommon – that's what he was told. Strange as it may sound, they can actually be an attempt to find relief.

Relief! He'd laughed out loud, there in the doctor's surgery.

As I say, it's counterintuitive. But if you think about it. In the face of a natural disaster, for instance, your own situation becomes insignificant. Your responsibility to act, your being as a person even, all of that is lifted from you. That's an attractive idea for some people. Hence these fantasies.

But I'm not talking about fantasies. This is history – not just history, the news, today's news.

Maybe so. But these are events far away in time or in space, unlikely to affect us here.

Unlikely to affect us *yet*.

The doctor shrugged accommodatingly. The computer screen showed Dickie's vital signs. A cement mixer juddered in the distance; they were extending the practice.

Why would somebody want that? To have their being . . . what you said.

The doctor shifted his weight in his chair. It could be in response to a personal trauma. Something that they hadn't come to terms with. One might look at your own situation, obviously . . .

Respectfully, doctor, I didn't come here to talk about my family.

But is it possible, with the child on the way, things might be—

That is not what I came here to talk to you about. I'd prefer to stick to the—

—might be coming to a head?

No. Instead of this personal – if you'd just stick to the specific issue—

I can't find any physical cause for the symptoms you describe, Dickie. I can't find anything there. That's why I'm suggesting it might be helpful to look behind the scenes a little bit. The past remains with us, in all kinds of unexpected ways. If we haven't made peace with it, it will come back again and again.

You're talking about ghosts?

I meant in our bodies. As pain, physical pain, mental pain. Why do you say ghosts?

I just meant . . . sorry, I misheard.

Do you think of it often? What happened?

Dickie? Why do you say ghosts?

VII

It was February when Frank announced that he was coming up to the city if Dickie was around for a pint.

Oh, you have to bring me! Willie said, clapping his hands together. Dickie hadn't the slightest intention of bringing him, and told him so bluntly. But Willie kept at him. Frank, the buccaneer, the football hero, the bane of Dickie's childhood, the explanation of *everything*? He had to meet him, simply had to. Tell him I'm your pal, he said.

What else would I tell him? Dickie answered neutrally, taking secret pleasure in the momentary anguish that flickered across Willie's face.

They had got into the habit, the bad habit, of sleeping in one another's beds, particularly if they'd been out dancing, which they had been, last night; but they didn't do anything, it didn't mean anything, Dickie reasoned, other than that he didn't like to sleep on his own. He still hadn't told Willie the full story of what happened last autumn, but he made it known that he held him partly to blame; it was Willie who'd brought him to the Butterfly, after all, with the clear intention of seducing him. Willie denied this, but Dickie knew he felt guilty, and he used it to keep him in check.

He needed to have some way to restrain him. Willie was so clever! It wasn't just that you couldn't trust what he said; he was so persuasive that when he was around you couldn't trust *yourself*. Last week in the Hist, speaking against the motion *That Progress has failed us* – so many of the debates lately had had a *fin de siècle* theme – he had given a speech that revolved around the story of a girl from a remote Amazon tribe in the 1960s, who, on falling ill, had been brought downriver by her father in a kayak to the city. With no map, no common language, he'd somehow managed to make his way to the hospital, from where she was airlifted to New York and, after many false starts, successfully treated.

Now in itself, Willie had said, that's progress. Modern medicine and air travel save a life that wouldn't otherwise have been saved. But progress isn't just about stopping bad things from happening. It's about creating the conditions for *new* things to happen – things that otherwise wouldn't have happened, would never even have been imagined. The girl who didn't die went on to be a scientist, and pioneered the photovoltaic material used to make solar panels – basing it on a kind of quartzite from which her tribe traditionally made its ceremonial objects. Because she didn't die, the world now gets 10 per cent of its energy from the sun, pollution-free.

Who, listening to that story – he said – could maintain that progress had failed? Isn't it truer to say that progress needs failure? That progress is what humans *do with* failure? Failure, bad news, dark times – these are its fuel. In the same way that little girl turned her illness into light for a whole planet, progress takes failure and turns it into the future.

It was a brilliant speech, even by Willie's standards. People had tears in their eyes. Afterwards, Dickie was staggered – the word was not too strong – to learn that due to a miscommunication, up until an hour before the debate Willie had been under the impression he was on the opposing side.

But all of those facts and statistics he'd reeled off?

I made them up, Willie said.

The tribe? The girl, who became a scientist?

I made her up too, Willie said.

Dickie still struggled. It just didn't compute. But you spoke so *passionately*, he said. It felt like you really *believed*.

Willie, lying beside him, grinned satanically up at the ceiling. That's how you win, he said.

They met Frank in the Stag's Head. The pub at that time was an outpost of the Hist: surrounded by Trinity types, Frank, with his lacquered hair, shiny shirt, good shoes, stuck out like a sore thumb.

There was a girl with him. Dickie remembered her vaguely from the previous summer; she used to turn up at Goldenhill from time to time for excruciating family dinners. Willie was very taken with her. She's a goddess! he said afterwards. And she was, objectively speaking, very beautiful: blonde, with intensely green eyes, and high cheekbones which had been heavily accented with make-up. Still, to Dickie the beauty seemed impersonal, somehow; it didn't have anything of herself in it, and she wore it a little over-anxiously, like a piece of very expensive jewellery that had been rented only for the evening.

She sat at his brother's side, with her thigh-boots and her sequinned top and her own countrified notion of cool; she was stiff with them at first, as if she thought they were making fun of her, which they weren't, yet, though obviously they were planning to later; and Frank was stiff too, clearly anxious that she be at ease. After a couple of drinks, though, she came to life. She had an accent that could strip paint, but she was clever, and quick – quicker and cleverer than Frank, who tried to tease her, but was obviously, and hopelessly, in her thrall. As she spoke, her personality flooded her face, and she became all the more radiant.

Dickie trod gently with them. He addressed them, flatteringly, as a pair, as if Imelda was as familiar to him, or unfamiliar, as Frank. What brought them to the city? he wanted to know. Frank told him they were going to a concert the following night, an act Dickie had never heard of. You should have said, he told them, you could have stayed with me. But no, Frank had booked a room in a 'top' hotel in Temple Bar. Clearly he wanted to impress her, and Dickie realized that he too was intended as part of some display of sophistication. He duly gave them some brunch suggestions, which Frank duly wrote down, as if they were always swapping restaurant tips. Although this one wouldn't know brunch if it bit her on the arse, Frank said, with rather a forced laugh. We had an argument on the way up because she didn't know what an aubergine was.

Not this again, the girl said.

And when I told her, Frank persisted, she didn't believe me. She told me there was no such thing as an aubergine. Tell her, Dickie. Tell her aubergines are real.

They're real, Dickie said.

Well, aren't you the smart pair, the girl said, folding her arms.

She much preferred Willie to Dickie. People generally did. It was one of the surprising things about him: he seemed so cerebral and snooty – he *was* so cerebral and snooty, and smug, and full of himself – and yet he could talk to anybody. Not in a banal or fake or patronizing way: within minutes, he'd find some point of connection and next thing he'd have their life story. On two separate occasions, Dickie had had to sit in a stationary cab because both the driver and Willie were crying after Willie winkled some tale of heartbreak out of him. This girl had an interest in fashion, as – it turned out – did Willie; before long, they were gabbing away, exchanging names which meant nothing whatever to Dickie.

Frank watched the girl, positively aglow. He looked at her, it struck Dickie, with the same kind of reverential joy that the townsfolk had watching him, as he doled out miracles on the pitch.

Now he caught himself, and blushed, and tried to pretend he hadn't been staring.

He's a gas fella that Willie, isn't he? A real character.

He's just a friend from debating, Dickie said. He nodded at the girl. You two have been together for a while. This was unlike Frank; he tended to be more the wild-oats type.

Ah, Dickie, Frank said, seeming relieved to be free to gaze at her again. I've never met anyone like her. Look at her! She's like a supermodel! But the place she's from, it's barely a hole in the ground. Nothing, not even a shop, only a Texaco that the pikeys keep robbing. Her father's some kind of a gangster, you should see him. He's obsessed with Dad! Keeps asking where he gets his blazers!

He shook his head again, while seeming on the point of bursting into laughter, then sighed. My fucking balls are blue with this one, Dickie. She's half a savage but she says she's saving herself for her wedding day.

I'm after forking out two hundred quid for this hotel, and if I don't get the ride off her tonight, I don't know what I'll do. I'll have to marry her or something. He turned his merry face to Dickie. Can you imagine what the old pair would say to that?

Is that the way you're thinking? he asked. Marrying her?

Ah, no, Frank said, and then, Well, maybe. I mean, why not? He sat up, looked at Dickie earnestly. I've been doing a lot of thinking, he said. I'm not like you. You're here in the city with your new friends, going to the fancy college, knowing all the cool places. You've got a whole life for yourself here. But me, I'm a homebird. I used to think I wanted to travel the world, when I was younger. (Dickie allowed himself a little smile at this.) But actually I reckon I'd be happy kicking around the old town the rest of my days. If I was with the right woman.

They both looked at the girl. She had flung back her head, her eyes tight shut, in peals of laughter; Willie, with tears in his eyes, was literally slapping his thigh.

The tumblers in Dickie's brain turned slowly, and the mystery of their conversation that afternoon in the shed, Frank's sudden interest in his future, began to click into place. Is that why you were asking about the garage that time?

Frank nodded. She got Mam talking one night and she took down a boxload of photographs of herself and Dad going on cruises. Like when VW would send them off to the Caribbean and Mauritius and all this.

I remember, Dickie said. He knew the photographs: Dad with his hair slicked back, a cocktail glass in his hand and a sunset behind him in every picture; their mother in a swimsuit, smoking, working on her tan. Children were not invited on the cruises; instead he and Frank used stay with an aunt, who had a dog they weren't allowed pet and who always boiled his breakfast egg the wrong way.

Well, Imelda thought those were the height of glamour, Frank said. The *height*. That's what got me thinking about taking over. But fuck it, I don't need to be the boss. I'd stay on as a salesman either. I'd do anything, frankly. I don't care.

Dickie mulled on this for a moment. Then he said, I've been thinking about that talk. I realized afterwards you might have had a point.

Was it true? Had it slowly been dawning on him that his life might lie elsewhere? Or did he only want to match the person in Frank's description of him at that moment: the quester, the cosmopolitan, the adventurer seeking out knowledge? He didn't know: but he found himself saying the words. I haven't decided what I want to do when I'm finished. But you're right, there's a big world out there.

Listen, don't turn your plans upside down for my sake, Frank said. God knows I'd probably make a mess of it anyway. Plus, what would Dad say?

He'd come around, Dickie said. I could talk to him. His voice in his ears sounded warm and generous, and in Frank's eyes he saw himself as he so rarely had – as a big brother, someone solid, quiet, who knew the score: the kind of man of whom Frank might say to his friends, He keeps his cards to his chest, but get him talking, boys, and I'll tell you what, he has the whole fucking thing sussed out.

She is a riot, Willie said that night, as they lay in bed. She told me her cousin had been arrested for stabbing a dog with a fork. She said very proudly that he'd been on the news. She also said a gypsy put a curse on her brother's 'digging hand' and that's why he was on disability.

He's talking about marrying her, Dickie said.

I'd marry her in a heartbeat, Willie said.

Oh yes? And what would you do on your wedding night?

I would rise to the occasion, Willie said grandly. He turned onto his back, looked up at the ceiling.

I can't see why you made such a fuss about him, though. I was expecting a he-man, a Cúchulainn type. I mean, he's perfectly nice. But he's pretty ordinary.

And you're so much more interesting, Dickie said. Necking pills with the same fifty queers three times a week. Deciding which bow tie to wear to your debate.

But he was teasing. There in Willie's room, with the electric heater glowing in the corner, the odious statue of Ganesh on the mantel that Dickie had made Willie buy because he thought it looked like the Junior Dean, and books piled everywhere, he felt powerful, that is, he felt light, and in charge, and free, and expansive: he felt the future – which for so long he'd thought of as immutable – he felt the future amorphous, ethereal, waiting for him to decide its shape. He turned, leaned over, kissed Willie on the lips. Willie looked back at him in surprise; it was a little like the look Frank had given him earlier, hope mixed with gratitude; and now he lifted his head from the pillow, and his face, his ugly, protuberant face, which was also beautiful, which Dickie thought he might love, came closer till it was all he could see. And he closed his eyes and they kissed.

Was that the best time? Had he ever been happier than in the months after Frank's first visit? Three months, a season of the self, split between spring and summer. A season with its own weather, alternating between blithe sunshine and rain, proper rain, that hammered down purposefully and relieved you of the duty to go outside; with its own music – Daft Punk and the Backstreet Boys, Willie singing Jacques Brel in the stuttering shower; its own food (*You've* never had *dim sum?*); its smells – poppers and latex, sandalwood and E45; its own tastes and aches and ecstasies.

Roughly half of this enchanted time Willie spent nursing a cold. He was surprisingly sickly, always coming down with bugs, stomach aches, lurgies. He claimed this battery of minor ailments stopped him from ever getting anything serious; his *mauvais santé de fer*, he called it, ill-health of iron.

He was full of paradoxes like this; the more Dickie got to know him, the more unfathomable he seemed. He was endlessly licentious, but never missed Sunday service in the Trinity chapel. He shunned on principle anything calling itself 'natural', but nature itself he adored: he had an endless enthusiasm for hikes in the freezing glens south of the city. He dismissed the music of Nirvana as pure affectation, but he wore spats.

He was bewilderingly eccentric, in speech, in dress, in his basic attitudes to life and society, but when Dickie asked why he liked him, he said, Because you are so strange.

One weekend he brought Dickie to the house he'd grown up in, an old stone manor in County Meath with countless mice and a broken dishwasher. His parents were elderly, and, other than some laborious conversations about cricket, left them to their own devices. There was an old wasps' nest in the room Dickie slept in, and the bedspread was littered with tiny, weightless corpses. They spent most of their time hoovering.

He knew Willie expected him to return the invitation, and was hurt that he didn't. But why would he want to take him back there? Dublin was their home. He felt like his life before belonged to someone else, someone he felt sorry for but had no desire to see again.

They spent countless nights in the Butterfly. He had been wary at first about returning, but Willie insisted he would be safe, and Dickie trusted him, trusted that nothing bad would happen when he was with him. He wasn't sure where this faith came from; he had felt the same way with Frank, growing up, he realized, though he didn't know what to do with this association. From there they began to explore the city's growing underground. Every time you looked, there were new bars, new club nights, opalescent with a kind of righteous decadence.

They had to be careful, of course: gay men were regularly attacked on the streets. But we don't look like faggots, Willie reassured him. You look like a nerd. I look like an oddball. Nobody imagines people like us ever have sex.

On the street, in the square, in the college bar, even in the Butterfly and at HAM, they acted as friends, no more. They limited their movements, refrained from touching each other; this public restraint made the moment they were finally alone together – often after elaborate excuses which doubled as private jokes – all the more incandescent.

Dickie had never especially liked having a body. No: he hated having a body. He wasn't keen on his face either, but considered it only a minor-key prelude to the crashing debacle beneath his clothes. Scrawny, bony, unexpectedly hairy, a compendium of bad things, his body was coterminous with his shame. It was the generator of his endless shameful thoughts and desires; at the same time, it stood, in its shamefulness, in the way of ever acting on those thoughts. Its inadequacies were countless; nevertheless, he had, over the years, dedicated untold hours to counting them. He usually started with his feet. His feet! With their freakishly long, almost prehensile toes, their proneness to fungal infections and scaling, their grotesque patches of hair on the upper part, his feet alone were so uniquely repulsive as to stifle all debate. From there, if further demonstration were needed, one proceeded via his lower legs, where more gratuitous hair adorned bone-white, scrawny calves, to his knobbly (of course) knees, and then, after the sprawl of his thighs, at once fat and puny, to the dismal necro-pudding of his bottom. This was just his lower half, which, leaving aside the unspeakable tragedy that was his penis, he thought by far the better one. A mind brought low by a body: that was his life in a nutshell.

But that was not how Willie saw it. I like your feet, he'd say, and suck at his toes. And my knees? Dickie said, but Willie would already have buried his head in Dickie's crotch, and Dickie could only yelp and laugh and lie back and let his body – his poor body! which had lived for so many years like an unloved dog chained in a basement – succumb to pleasure. It was like feeling the sun on his skin for the first time, like bathing in sunlight, being fucked by sunlight, fucked in every pore; and he would wonder, with the scattered remnants of his mind, why anyone ever did anything other than have sex.

After the pleasure, he sometimes hated Willie. It happened against his will, like he'd drunk a potion: he felt himself transforming, shrivelling, into a cold, sclerotic old hag. In those moments, he'd simultaneously hate Willie for loving him, and despise him for pretending to do so: though nothing so much as he despised and hated himself.

It wasn't exclusively post-coital, this self-hatred; it came when he was on his own too, came and engulfed him. It presented itself as clarity.

With all of the emotional candyfloss washed away, he saw the act, he saw what he had become, in pitiless detail. That word, *faggot*, that Willie threw around so carelessly – well, he would, wouldn't he? That's what Willie was, a faggot, and faggoting consisted of an essential unseriousness, a triviality, because having surrendered to their desires the faggots had been hollowed out by them, and made incapable of any serious role in the world of men.

In his mind, the poison of lucidity quickly spread, till it touched every part of his life here. From the neon falsity of the Butterfly it passed to the Hist. Once he had thought this a sacred place, where beneath the surface froth deep truths were forged. Now he could see it too was pretence, performance, clever boys trying to appear more than what they were; only here they used truth, justice, rights, instead of falsies and steroids. Clever boys like Willie, using facts about the real world to make it look like they cared about it, to make themselves look like serious people while they larked about and positioned themselves for fat jobs in law and the media.

The best time was therefore bound up in the worst time. He could no longer avoid what he was. He lay on his bed numb with self-hatred, wondering if he'd ruined his life already, if there was a way he could still get out of this and be normal. More than anything he wished he could go back in time and befriend a different boy – someone who would just be his pal, talk to him about tennis or obscure bands, walk beside him through the square in the sunshine as boys did, innocent and healthy and normal together.

He told this to Willie one night, to hurt him. Willie bowed his head. He never fought Dickie when he was in one of his moods. Then he said, I suppose that's what everybody wants, isn't it. To be like everybody else. But nobody is like everybody else. That's the one thing we have in common.

We're all different, but we all think everyone else is the same, he said. If they taught us that in school, I feel like the world would be a much happier place.

Dickie didn't reply. It seemed to him that when Willie spoke tenderly or lovingly, or tried to describe his emotions, his intelligence vanished, and he sounded like a Hallmark card. He didn't want reassurance, certainly not from Willie. He wanted to be home, and for the last three years never to have happened. Failing that, he wanted flagellation; he wanted punishment; he wanted someone to *knock some sense into him*, as his father would say; and once again he remembered the evenings in the garden, his mother's lilacs and azaleas, her luminous phlox and philadelphus a-dance around them, as he stood toe to toe with his father, taking his lesson, little pieces of him knocked away until there was nothing left but the pale shifting shadows on the grass.

One time only he saw Sean again. He – Dickie – was walking down O'Connell Street on a Saturday afternoon when he ran into some sort of demonstration going on outside the GPO. Not large: twenty or thirty people, a couple of banners. A man was speaking into a megaphone that rendered everything he said unintelligible. As Dickie threaded his way through the crowd, someone turned and pressed a flyer into his hand.

He was not in uniform; he was wearing an Aran sweater that made him look like a fisherman, or a tourist's idea of one. There was a strange delay as his eyes flickered over Dickie's face. Dickie found he couldn't move. Inside him, like the symptom of an illness you thought long gone, the terror of that night foamed up again. But only for an instant; it was all in an instant; then he lowered his eyes, continued on his way.

It wasn't until he got back to his Rooms, and closed the door, and locked it, that he remembered the flyer. He still had it, balled up in his fist, damp with cold sweat: he smoothed it out on the counter. A picture of a foetus, covered in blood, partially dismembered. He saw himself on the floor of Sean's flat, something that should never have been born.

But these moments were anomalies, outliers. It *was* the best time, that season of the self; for the most part he was happy, happier than he had ever been. Perhaps that was what made it hard to accept. He had always assumed happiness was for other people, for the plodders, the norms, the sleepwalkers, as the reward for their blinkered conformism. He felt like he'd been initiated into a secret cult – a group of people who outwardly looked like everybody else, but who concealed a miraculous secret: they were in love.

And then Frank came back.

It was all very dramatic: arriving in the middle of the night, pounding on the door. Willie said afterwards that Frank was one of those secret drama queens who put themselves across as regular Joes, yet whose lives seemed constantly to unfold at the level of opera.

Dickie had been in bed: he heard the commotion downstairs, and went to investigate. The elderly professor on the ground floor had opened the front door, and was remonstrating with him. I couldn't remember which room you were in, Frank said to Dickie when he saw him appear on the stairs.

Dickie thanked the professor, and apologized, and invited Frank upstairs. Still waking up, he was within a heartbeat of bringing him through Willie's door; he remembered just in time to lead him up the next flight of stairs to his own Rooms, which quite clearly hadn't been inhabited in a month; he had to open a window to chase away the musty smell, though it was lashing rain outside.

There was no need to worry: Frank was oblivious. Dickie had never seen him in such a state. He was out of breath, and seemed to be sweating, though it was hard to be sure as he was drenched with rain. He kept wandering around the room, head bent, as if he were looking for something he'd dropped on the floor, ignoring Dickie's injunctions to sit. He had a holdall on his shoulder, a light jacket, a fugitive appearance. I'm in the horrors, he said. The horrors, he repeated, and then, Do you mind if I smoke? He fumbled out a packet of Benson & Hedges. Dickie directed him to the window, but he lit up where he stood. Then he sat, finally, at the kitchen table. I'm fucked, he said.

He was so agitated it was hard to get anything more coherent from him, but finally the story came out.

It was the girl. Or rather, it was her father. He had made it known in unambiguous terms that he wanted them to get married.

Now? Dickie said. Why? Is she . . . she's not pregnant?

Frank shook his head, wiped his nose. No, he said. At least, not by me. He pressed his lips together. We've never had sex, Dickie. Imelda's a virgin.

Dickie wondered at this, but said only, In that case, why now? Why is he suddenly saying this now?

Frank covered his face with his hands, groaned into them. Do you remember last winter, when I'd been dropped from the team, and I was trying to figure out what to do – remember when we talked about the business that time? Well, I decided I'd go to London, with Dolly. Find investors, or whatever. She wasn't happy about that.

But you didn't go, Dickie said.

No, because Dad took me back into the garage. And the team took me back, and everything got sorted out. But Paddy Joe – Imelda's father – he's found out about it, and he's going spare.

She told her dad you were leaving her?

She told her brother. And he let it slip to Paddy Joe and now he's going mad thinking I'm about to do a runner to England.

But it was months ago, Dickie says.

I know.

And you didn't go.

I know, Dickie, I know! I'm not saying it makes any sense! You don't know this man, he's a fucking headcase! He said – I was in her house, with her brothers all standing around me in a ring, and he said to me, *You've had your finger in the pie* – those were his actual words, can you believe it?

Dickie couldn't believe it, not fully. It sounded like something from a Western. But he saw that he was afraid – Frank, who was never afraid.

What am I going to do? his brother said.

You don't want to marry her? Dickie said. The last time I saw you, you seemed to be considering it.

I'm nineteen! I'm fucking nineteen years old! I don't want to marry anyone!

Okay, okay, calm down, Dickie said. And have you spoken to Dad?

Frank's head dropped, his hands flopped onto his lap. Oh Dad. Dad thinks I've dug my own hole.

He hardly thinks that, Dickie said.

Oh, he dresses it up with his usual bullshit. *Be a man, act with honour, live by your decisions,* all this. But he wants to punish me. It's the same as when he'd catch me with a cigarette and make me smoke the whole box till I puked.

And marrying Imelda is the punishment, Dickie said.

Frank hung his head, still slick with rain. I don't mean it like that, he mumbled. It's just – it's just too early! I'm not ready!

Couldn't you . . . Dickie wasn't sure how seriously to take this; Frank did tend to blow things out of proportion. If you had to, couldn't you get engaged and . . . you know, you don't need to name a day right away. Would that be enough, I mean?

But Frank slowly shook his head. And he began to speak about the father again, this man that Dickie had never met. He sounded like something from a fairy tale, the terrifying giant with the ravishing daughter, his monstrousness in direct proportion to her beauty. I think he's killed people, Dickie. He's got these videos of his fights – there's one of them where this man, his eye . . . He shuddered. He beat her brothers half to death growing up. He killed her cat, Dickie! He killed Imelda's cat when it got pregnant! And the dog, and a horse. And she calls it the homeplace! Jesus, Dickie, the things that went on there!

All right, all right, Dickie said, raising his hands again for calm. Let's consider your options. You don't want to get married – for now. Dad won't help. What's left?

Frank took a moment to compose himself. Then, summoning his

energy, in a low voice he said, There's a marketing course. It's in Birmingham, two years. I figure if I sign up for that, it'll get me out of Dodge, give me time to think, work out the best thing to do. And the timing's perfect, it starts next week.

Next week? At last Dickie realized the meaning of the holdall. You mean you're going *now*? You're going to England *now*?

It's not safe for me here! Frank implored. He keeps showing up in his van, when I'm training, or at the garage, he parks up outside and just sits there!

Inside, Dickie felt a sudden, cold clutch of nausea. He tried to sound objective. So you're going to do exactly what he was afraid you'd do – that's your plan. You're going to do the thing you'd decided not to do, because he thinks you're going to do it.

Ah Jesus, my head's wrecked enough as it is! Frank protested.

Right, Dickie said. I'm trying to see the point of this, that's all.

Well, it would be useful for the business, Frank said. And I could pay for it myself, I've money saved. And it'd give things a chance to settle down a bit. Like, even if I just did the first year, it'd give everyone a chance to cool off. Then we could go at our own pace.

He related this in a measured tone, as if he was explaining it to himself, or reciting it for a test: but at the end his voice broke, and he looked up pleadingly at his brother: But I don't know! I don't know if that's right, or . . . What do you think, Dickie? What do you think I should do?

And Dickie knew that this was a pivotal moment: he could feel it, literally, the room swaying ever so gently up and down, as if it were balanced on a point – listing towards one future, then another.

He rose and went to put on the kettle again. As it boiled he fished a packet of Rich Tea out of the press. Inside he was thinking, If Frank goes to England he will never come back. Dickie knew his brother: he knew that whether he did part of the course or all of the course, whether he forgot the girl or didn't forget her, none of that mattered, because whatever his intentions, if he went to England he would undoubtedly get himself snarled up in exactly the same kind of situation over there. He'd save a cat from a tree and the owner would turn out to have two beautiful daughters and he'd fall in love with them both, or he'd join the local GAA team and meet a millionaire who was opening up a business in Dubai, or he'd anger a local drug dealer and assume a false identity, or he'd fall off a bridge, or fall into an inheritance – something, there would inevitably be something.

And many years from now, he would sit in the back office of the dealership, in a padded-out waistcoat or a filthy anorak, reminiscing about the old days, the beautiful wild girl – Imogen? Irene? – who'd captured his heart once, but it hadn't worked out. He'd clap Dickie's knee – dutiful Dickie, reliable Dickie, in his manager's chair, where he had been sitting for so many years – and he'd say, Well, it was probably for the best. Can you imagine the state this place would be in, if you'd stayed up in Dublin, and I was the one who took over!

Yes, Frank would go and never come back, and Dickie would end up in the dealership after all: that was what he saw, like a vision, when he opened the press for the teabags. And equally clearly he saw that he did not want to go back to the dealership. He did not any longer want that life.

And so he said from across the room, I suppose the thing to remember is, you're marrying her, not her family. He brought the mugs to the table and set them down. I mean, the father sounds like a nightmare. But once you were married he'd probably leave you alone. You'd never have to see him again if you didn't want to.

Frank took this in with a frown of confusion. It's not that I don't ever want to marry her, Dickie. But he wants me to marry her *now*. He wants us to get married *now*.

Well, in some ways that's hardly surprising, Dickie said matter-of-factly, pouring the milk. You have to admit, you're not the best at sticking to things. I mean, you're telling me here that you want to run off to England, when last time you told me you'd decided you wanted to stay. You can see why her father might be concerned.

Frank pressed his lips together, took out a cigarette and tapped it on the table.

And she, does she want to marry you?

I suppose, Frank conceded.

And if she were to come and tell you she was leaving you because she didn't want to wait to get married, what would you say? Or put it another way – what if she *didn't* want to marry you? If she told you she enjoyed being with you but she didn't see a future with you – would you be happy then?

Frank slowly wagged his poor fogged head. Dickie felt his spirits rise. How quickly the arguments came to his mind! How cleverly and persuasively his tongue parsed them! Yes, he had learned something after all from his time here in Trinity, from those nights at the Hist, watching the boys joust in their dinner jackets.

Don't feel tied down by the business if you want to get away, he said, as if it had just occurred to him. We can always go back to the original plan if need be. I'm sure I'd find some position for you later, as a salesman or something.

No, no . . . I don't want that, Frank said laboriously. I just . . . you don't think it seems very early to be settling down?

Dickie considered this. I think the real question is, he said, bringing a thoughtful finger to his chin, just as he had seen Willie do, do you *love* her?

I don't know, Frank said. I think so.

Well then, Dickie said.

And Frank had gone home, and there were many weeks that followed, during which he proposed to Imelda, and she said yes, and they began to plan for their wedding; and Dickie went back for the engagement party, and then the two of them visited Dublin again; and Frank thanked Dickie for his advice, and Dickie, seeing how happy his brother was, knew that it was for the best; and he and Willie went out and stayed in and drank and debated and, as the college year drew to a close, studied for exams and made their plans for the summer.

But in his memory afterwards, it seemed that he went directly from that conversation with Frank – washing the mugs out in the sink, telling him he could sleep on the couch for tonight – to standing in the good room at home, with Willie, red-eyed, somehow there in front of him; not months, not days, but an instant only, from that midnight conversation to now, as if the squalid papered walls of his Rooms had fallen away, while his brother was still sitting at the table, drinking his tea, to reveal a world from which Frank was already gone, lay buried in the churchyard, and Dickie, drenched, blasted, annihilated, stood in the parlour, a cloth still covering the mirror, with Willie facing him accusingly, asking the same question Dickie had asked of Frank an instant, a lifetime before, *Do you love her?* The same words twisted up, splintered, charred, like the wreck of the car they had pulled out of the field outside Naancross. Dickie had seen it go by; he had been in the garden with his mother and heard her cry out, as if a sword had run her through; he turned to her first, then to see what she was looking at, and there it was, going by on a trailer, mangled, incinerated, but still recognizably Frank's car. His mother had dropped to the ground, she had covered her head with her hands, as you might in an air raid, though the bomb had already hit, the sword found its mark. It was worse than seeing his body somehow, though he couldn't explain why. He couldn't explain anything, that whole time was confusion, sightlessness, like crawling through a metal pipe, in darkness, while outside someone beat the walls with iron bars. But somewhere in there, yes, he had proposed to Imelda. He had fallen in love with her, now they were engaged.

Were you even going to tell me? Willie's voice trembled, his protuberant face pale as death. His backpack still sat on his shoulder. A friend from Dublin, Dickie had called to nobody when he found him at the door.

You shouldn't be here, Dickie said.

So you're really doing this, Willie said. Or perhaps it was, Why are you doing this? It didn't matter. Dickie checked his phone. He had new duties now, a million and one arrangements to make.

You laughed at her, Willie said. You called her Tinker Bell!

Dickie did not want to hear what that old self had done. You wouldn't understand, he said.

I do understand! Willie cried, agonized. You think it was your fault, you think it should have been you that died and not your brother!

Don't talk about my brother! His voice was like a whipcrack. Willie flinched. His face, white and wounded, looked up at him helplessly, his open mouth a weal. He had come to persuade Dickie, just as Dickie had persuaded Frank. But he was wasting his time.

Of course it should have been him. No one said it – there was no need, it was obvious. He had stood in Frank's bedroom and watched his father weep over the coffin, his tears falling onto Frank's waxy, reconstructed face – watched as he brought his fingers up and put them on his son's lips; he seemed to stagger, if you can stagger standing still; while Dickie hung back in the shadows, warm and clammy from what he'd been doing in Dublin, still feeling it on him, clinging to him, like a skin, a sin-skin. His uncle, back from England, beside him, shaking his head, saying, This will kill your father. Kill him.

Why is that your fault? What has that got to do with you?

Everything, everything to do with him. He was the one meant to take over the garage. That had always been the plan. But he had tried to escape it. He had tried to push Frank into his place.

You didn't push him, you didn't push anyone! You told him what he wanted to hear! You wanted him to be who he was! Good! Noble! True to himself, to his girl!

Only because it suited him. Only so he could continue his sordid pursuits in Dublin. He had known that what they were doing was evil. He'd pretended otherwise, but he'd known. *Contra naturam*, against nature – he remembered it from long ago, when he was a holy boy who knew such things, though he hadn't understood then what it meant. It was a very specific, very pernicious kind of evil, because it unwound, undid, the natural things it touched. Who was more natural than Frank, with his sports and his cars, his beautiful girlfriend with her sequinned dress? Dickie had tried to use his brother's very naturalness to cloak his own perversity. Now everything had unspooled in a black mess, like the ribbon pulled from a cassette. It was his fault: it didn't matter that he hadn't known it would happen.

Or did he know? Somewhere deep down, had he foreseen this? Was it conceivable that he had brought this about deliberately, a final, spiteful act against the brother he'd always envied? Whose life he had always craved? The idea was too horrific to contemplate: yet it remained there inside his head over the endless succession of unsleeping nights, the hours upon hours of blank unfillable life he found himself burdened with now in the grieving house – acres of it, of wakefulness, when it was the last thing he wanted, as if all the unused time that would have been Frank's had been dumped on him as a punishment. *Did you do this on purpose? Did you do this to destroy him?* Hour after hour he lay there, twisting under the silent interrogation – until one night, delirious with tiredness, he rose and went to Frank's room. It was what he'd always done as a little boy whenever he'd had a bad dream or fears of monsters. Only when he saw her looking at him from the bed did he remember that she was there. He waited for her to spring at him, pluck his eyes out, shrieking the accusations that resounded inside his head day and night, *You did this!* He hoped, he prayed she'd speak the words.

But she said only, Did I wake you up?

It's okay, he said. I wasn't sleeping.

She lay back down, turned away from him. He went to sit at the end of the bed. She sobbed quietly under the covers. The sound brought him a strange peace, as if she were doing it for both of them. And when at last she slept, he stayed awake for both of them, he could be exhausted for both of them. Beneath the greenish ceiling stars he felt exhausted, bereft, and only that. Not evil, not accused. The night after he went back, and the night after that, and every night, at two, three, four in the morning, when he heard her cry out. They didn't speak, he would just sit there with her, he with his howling skull, she weeping or lying in silence, wearing the same unwashed dress she had since the funeral. He felt like he had left the real world and entered another, like he was meeting a spirit in the forest who had nothing to do with the day, the person that he met in the kitchen, in the garden, with rings around her eyes. He sat, he laid his hand on her side. In the darkness she was like the reflection that he could bear to see. She took his hand and put it in her hair. He lay beside her in his brother's bed, and she pressed her lips to his forehead, and sometimes he slept. They were the same: they fit together, like the shrapnel of a car and the ruin of a garage: she was the only person he could bear to be near. A new terror seized him, at the thought of her leaving, but it was a pleasant terror, because it made no sense that she could go. It made no sense not to kiss the tears from her cheeks, then to kiss her mouth. Those reservations were part of a world that was past. They were no longer who they were. When she took off her dress her beauty lay in fragments around her like the shards of a broken vase. And his thoughts, his cleverness, lay buried in the woods, stored against a winter that would never appear again.

That's when it had come to him, what he had to do. He had wanted Frank to take his place: now he would take Frank's. It was the best, the only way to atone. Not only would he be Frank – *he would be the Frank that Frank himself was not*. Once he had decided that, everything was easy. When she told him she was pregnant that only proved he was on the right track. What was more natural? It cost him nothing to jettison his old plans, his old self. The way was clear now. Perhaps it was clear for the first time in his life. He asked her to marry him and she said yes.

Do you think you're in any fit state to make this kind of a decision? Willie said. Can't you see how insane this is? He placed his hands on his shoulders. His eyes swam behind his thick glasses. He crashed his car, Dickie. It's natural you feel guilty. But it isn't your fault!

Expressionlessly, Dickie took his hands away. Still he persisted. This isn't you, he said. The person I know would not just discard someone like this. You're not well, Dickie. None of this makes sense. Do you think you can hide from the truth? Is that what you're trying to do? You will hide from the truth for the rest of your life?

But what did Willie know about truth? What did he know about family, duty? He thought of Willie's parents, the air of benign indifference prevailing in their mouse-infested home.

I'm changing it, he told him. I'm changing the truth.

That doesn't make any sense!

Please, don't keep arguing with me, Dickie told him. My parents need me, my fiancée needs me.

Your *fiancée*! Willie laughed, bitterly, violently. Can you not even hear what a joke that is?

No one had laughed in this house in weeks, it struck Dickie, not even bitterly.

A clock ticked on the mantelpiece, nestled among the family photos: Frank a little boy, a teenager, a man. When Willie spoke again it was softer. Are you really going to do this? he said. Leave everything you have behind? Leave behind the person that loves you?

Dickie must have sat down at some point, because now he stood up; Willie, too, stood, and took Dickie's hands in his, as if they were there on the altar. Dickie, he whispered; he couldn't speak. Tears were running down his face, his poor ugly face. Dickie, he croaked. Come back to Dublin. Bring her with you, your . . . wife. We don't have to ever touch again. Or speak, we don't ever need to speak if you don't want to. Just be near, be near me.

Yes, it was sad, Dickie was sad to see him reduced like this. Once his talking lost its power, once you saw through it, there was really little left to him. He may have shed a tear too, as he stood there, watching Willie cry. But in the silence, he felt his heart lift, for he knew that this was the end.

VIII

One morning they wake up and find that the weather has changed. Overnight, the heat that blanketed them for so long has lifted and taken itself elsewhere. In its place is a freshness that Dickie recognizes as the beginnings of autumn, which, though it is the prelude to winter, has always felt to him the time of year when the world is new. He walks with PJ through the gorgeous dying forest, a shifting mosaic of reds and golds, taking in air that seems to sparkle with some knowing magic. They make their way around the circuit, no longer needing the map, releasing greys from the traps when they find them, and Dickie feels – he, a middle-aged man! A father of two! – he feels a-daze with this forest magic, this sparkling air. Beside him, his son chatters on about exoskeletons, space anomalies, what daimon he'd like to have. The leaves fall down around them, Dickie's veins brim full of ecstatic energy, as if he is a boy again, or a boy for the first time.

When they come back to the clearing, they find Victor lugging fresh bags of Bentonite out of the van. You're back, Dickie says. I am, Victor says. Back a good hour now. He continues to unload the van. It is hard to read his expression but it seems that he is smiling to himself. How did you get on? Dickie says. Oh good, good, Victor says tonelessly. We'll have her up and running before the end of the day, please God. Again the sly smile. He goes back to the van, effortlessly lifts another sack and sets it down by its brethren under a tree. Then he says, Your father was here looking for you.

The ecstasy of a moment ago instantly drains away. Here? he says. He was here?

You just missed him, Victor says. He checks his watch. Twenty minutes or so ago.

You saw him? Dickie says. You were talking to him?

Oh I did, Victor says. Again the secretive smile, as if he is amused at Dickie's plight.

Dickie looks forlornly at the Bunker, the two stark un-netted walls, the absurd thought coming to him that if they'd finished their camouflage his father might never have found them. What did he say?

Victor makes a choking noise, a repetitive hiss accompanied by shaking shoulders. It takes Dickie a moment to realize it's laughter. He didn't say much, Victor says. He hisses and chokes merrily for another moment, before he elaborates. He was stamping around the site making a speech, he says, and didn't he plant his foot in that pot of sealant there – Victor points to the tub, now sitting innocently on the tree stump – then he went and took a header into the tent. Now Victor points to the tent, which is, Dickie notices, sagging precariously.

Oh dear, Dickie says. Is he all right?

His shoes aren't all right, Victor says, bright red with laughter. They're suede, he says.

Oh dear, Dickie says again. I'd better call him, he says.

Is something wrong, Dad? PJ says.

No, no. He makes a weak attempt at a smile, then walks a little way out of the clearing, where he weaves about the undergrowth, holding his phone out in front of him just as he had the dowsing rods, till at last he's lit on a signal.

His father answers on the first ring. What the hell kind of bloody game do you think you're playing at? he says. What do you think you're doing, dragging me down to search you out in your bloody fort or whatever it is?

Dickie starts to apologize, but his father steamrolls over him. I have limited time here, Dickie, I have limited time and you have me running around the woods after you, because you can't even do me the courtesy of returning my calls. Is it hiding out from me you are?

By Jesus, I saw more of you when I was away in Portugal than I do now I'm home!

His anger crackles out of the phone to surround Dickie like a force field. Well, you have me now, Dickie says neutrally. What can I do for you?

What can you do for me? the voice jeers back. You can get in here and explain these bloody accounts!

At that word, a chill shoots through Dickie, like the sun has gone out overhead. He starts making vague, explanatory noises. Spreadsheet, upgrade, quarterlies, data transfer, he hears himself reciting these words, sees them spiral up into the forest air like mythical birds, nonsense creatures.

Again his father cuts him off. I don't want a whole lot of bloody talk, Dickie. I want to know why these numbers don't add up. Now if you have any interest in digging yourself out of the hole you're in, you'll be at my office at nine sharp tomorrow morning, and you'll explain to me and Big Mike and the accountant why the books are light by fifty fucking grand!

The line goes dead as Dickie is saying he'll be there. He is alone again in the green leaves and the hush.

Tell him you gave it to a friend whose child was dying of leukaemia. Tell him you invested in a top-secret new motoring technology.

On the way back to the clearing, he sees Victor's rifle, laid casually against the bole of an oak tree. He stops, picks it up. Victor never leaves it lying around. He never leaves it loaded. But here it is, with two cartridges in the breech. He pauses, for a long time, considering what this might mean.

Dad!

The voice comes from the clearing, urgent, imperative. Dad, come quick!

He sets down the rifle, hurries in the direction of the voice. In the clearing, he finds the boy at the well. He is hauling the pump up and down. Water, silver water bright as morning, is coursing from the spout. Dad, look! he says. He turns to Dickie with an expression of pure joy, the kind he used have on Christmas morning, when he still believed in Santa Claus.

It works? As he says it Dickie realizes that he never believed it would. Water gushes in answer from the pump. Behind, Victor looks on with an air of quiet satisfaction. It works, he says.

He ought to go back to the house tonight and prepare himself for the morning. But PJ would have to come too, and after the meeting who knows when they'll be out here together again. So instead he spends the evening sitting on the log with his son, drinking well water from plastic mugs as violet light floods the clearing.

Though they have achieved their goal, PJ isn't feeling retrospective. He tells Dickie the pros and cons of the different kinds of water tank, how if Victor can get the generator going they'll be able to heat poly-tunnels, farm vegetables, maybe enough to run a small surplus. As he talks, Dickie thinks over his strategy. Best maybe just to deny every-thing. Don't know why it's missing. Don't remember that withdrawal. With all that was going on, things got so confused. Play dumb, go in there and act like a thick.

Will his father believe him? No. What happens next will depend on how angry he's feeling.

He doesn't think there's any way he'll sleep but he must because he starts awake in the darkness. Unzipping the tent, he sees the first winding-sheet-grey flickers of dawn amid the gloom. He'd better leave now if he wants to be on time. He scrambles out of the tent, tugs on his clothes, sets off through the forest. It isn't far back to the house, but in the twilight he keeps losing his way, charging into briars and brambles. It should be getting lighter but somehow it's not. He starts to panic a little at the absurdity of the situation, looks at his watch to see how late he will be. Something dark thumps against his face – like a soft fist, or a sack of feathers fallen from the sky. Searching the undergrowth his eye is caught by a glint – two glints, two bright globes of black. Then he ducks, just in time as a streak of grey launches itself at him. He tries to swipe it away, its claws rake his hands, he hears it squeal somewhere below him, then more vengeful squeals among the briars. Head lowered, he charges away, blundering through the thicket, shielding his face, unable to see where he's going.

He comes out in a clearing. In the centre of it is a man. He is hunched over, arms wrapped round his knees, and – no. The darkness recedes a little more, and he sees it is not a man. It is the weird tree with the witch's-hat gouge in its side. He looks down to see if the blackness is still seeping out of it. But the gash is covered with a kind of bandage, in fact the whole tree appears to be wrapped in cloth. Has someone been out here? He spins around, sees only trees. Then looks again into the clearing.

This time there really is a man. A guard.

Well, he says. Didn't expect to be seeing me again, did you?

Is this some kind of . . .? Dickie looks pointlessly left and right. Tries to speak, nothing comes out.

You thought you covered your tracks, didn't you, the guard says. I told you I would find you. We've been watching you for a long time.

I can explain, Dickie gasps, thinking, *How long?*

You took it all, didn't you, the guard says.

I was going to give it back!

It's too late for that. He draws a baton from his holster, shiny and black. He shakes his head. My God, he says. Your own brother.

What? Dickie says. And he realizes: it was all part of the trap, to draw him out, going back years, they all knew—

There is a hum coming from somewhere. Do you recognize this man? The guard reaching down, lifts with his baton the shroud over what Dickie had thought was the tree. No! Dickie cries. The hum loudens – billowing up in their millions flies swarm into his face – but through the cloud, through the grey pre-dawn he sees—

Jesus, Dickie.

He is back in his own bed. Imelda is seated at his side, looking down at him. Drink, she says.

He cranes his neck with difficulty, takes a sip from the glass she offers, crashes back onto the pillow. A moment later he jolts up again, retches violently, and again.

What happened? he whispers when he is able.

This happened, she says, pointing to the bucket that sits by the bed. Puking your ring. Do you not remember?

Effortfully, he casts his mind back, to be met by brief, horrific images that explode like squibs inside his head. He sees himself bolt from the tent and into the undergrowth just as a cascade of vomit spurts out of his mouth – on the far side of the clearing, Victor, naked, ashen-faced, kneeling on the nettles, emitting gruesome, slobbering noises, like a monster devouring a corpse – while water, bright silver water, courses from the pump –

PJ, he gasps.

He's here, she says. He's fine.

He sinks again onto his pillow, looks up at her looking down at him. A memory comes unbidden, of his mother sat just where she is now, surveying his measles, waiting for the thermometer. That makes him think of something else – he checks his watch, sits up rapidly, attempts to swing himself out of the bed. Imelda places a hand on his chest, pushes him back. Hold on a minute there, she says. Where do you think you're going?

I've to go and see my father, he says.

No, no, she says.

I'll be late, he says. I've a meeting.

That was two days ago, she says.

He looks at her incredulously. Two days?

Do you not remember? she says again.

He casts his mind back again but finds only the carnage at the campsite.

Behind her, morning light pours through the split in the curtains, like the silver water spouting so joyously from the pump. The thought makes his stomach roil, he lurches towards the bucket again. I think there was a bug, he says, lifting his head. A bug in the water.

She presses her lips together, looks away.

It'll pass soon enough, he says, then quakes as another wave of cramp roils through him.

Imelda shakes her head. I can't take any more of this, Dickie, she says. I just can't.

It's over now, he says, we're finished. The woods, I mean. The well.

She wipes her eyes with the back of her hand. As it falls again he takes it, strokes it with his thumb. He is wearing clean pyjamas that she must have put on him. It was just something to keep the boy entertained, he says softly. She looks down at his hand on hers. She seems on the point of saying something, but doesn't say it.

What does he want to talk to you about? she says.

Who? he says.

Your father.

Oh, he says.

He called when you didn't show up, she says. He was angry.

I'll talk to him, he says.

You will?

Yes, he says. It'll be all right.

I just want things to be back to normal, she says. God help me, I never thought I'd say that.

I'll talk to him, he says again.

She gets up, asks if he wants his laptop. It's fine, he tells her. She sighs, looks about the room. I always thought we should have got a TV for this room, she says forlornly. We still can, he says. The point is there for it. We could put it on the dresser.

That dresser's a bloody eyesore, she says.

Maybe we could look at changing those wardrobes, he says. Then you could get rid of the dresser and mount the TV on the wall.

Mmm. She pauses a moment, in the centre of the room, and they both look at the space where the new wardrobes might be.

Then dipping her head she says, Is it about Ryszard?

Is what about Ryszard?

That Maurice wants to talk to you.

Gosh, he says. I don't know. I wouldn't think so.

You were saying his name while you were out.

Maurice?

Ryszard.

I was?

Yes.

Dickie thinks this over. Ryszard. Huh. God, I don't know. I was having some pretty strange dreams.

Right, she says. Will I bring you a cup of tea?

Maybe in an hour or so, he says. Thanks.

She closes the door. He lies back on the bed, gazes up at the white ceiling.

Tell him you had to pay a gang protection. Tell him you got addicted to drugs.

Tell him – tell him . . .

Dickie shuts his eyes.

IX

Ryszard: who knew if that was even his real name? Nothing on his CV checked out. Of his references, one was a wrong number, another for a bodyshop in the north of England that had recently gone out of business. There were details purportedly for a garage in Poland, which Dickie called just to see, but whoever it was that answered (an old man, it sounded like) he spoke no English. Ryszard, Dickie said, Ryszard, Ryszard, till the man got tired of him and hung up.

He couldn't give an account of where he had come from – his own English was weak, or so he made it appear – nor was it clear why he had come here. What was clear was that he was desperate. He'd do anything, he said. He was a good mechanic, but he would sweep floors if he had to. He offered to work one week full-time for free; after that Dickie could make up his mind.

Dickie was desperate too. The workshop was the only part of the business bringing in any money. Demand for repairs was through the roof; it was the one upside of the collapse in sales. His father always said there were two types of mechanic, lifers and leavers: he was against hiring the latter, as frequently being more trouble than they were worth. This boy was clearly not a lifer. But they were short-staffed and Dickie thought he might get a month or two out of him before he disappeared. So he took him on.

He was young, twenty-five at the most. His eyes were black and shining, his hair too, curly, black and gleaming. He was a good worker, skilled with his hands, and smart, willing to stand back from a problem and figure it out. He often had a grease stain on his lower lip from resting a finger there while he pondered. He worked hard, and was willing to stay late. This was a major advantage – the older mechanics had wives and families they wanted to get back to, and downed tools on the stroke of five. And they were dour, sullen, mealy-mouthed; that had always been the culture at the garage. His father said he didn't hire them to be his friends. Lately they had been worse than ever, muttering under their breath whenever Dickie went by. They knew what was going on – the whole town did; they worried, with good cause, that they'd soon be out of a job, backlog or no.

But Ryszard didn't know anything of the dealership's recent history, and even if he found out, it was not in his nature to badmouth. Good morning, boss-man, he would call every morning as Dickie passed through on his way to the office. He was often the first to arrive; sometimes Dickie would take his cup of tea onto the shop floor and watch him work, in the bright blue overalls that had not yet succumbed to the ambient mire. We have some real shitheaps here today, boss-man, he would say, shaking his head. Look at rust on this thing, Christ, is fucking horror show. Just keep at it, Dickie would tell him soberly, but inside it gladdened him to know there was one person working there who didn't hate him.

Not long after he started, things began to go missing. Not big things: a monkey wrench, a battery, a torch. A couple of the mechanics complained there was money gone from their wallets. Ever since your man started here, Phil the foreman said. You know what your father always said, he reminded Dickie.

Dickie did know. Petty theft had to be stamped out immediately. Mechanics are one step away from criminals at the best of times. If you don't keep a tight rein on them, they'll have the eye out of your head. That was what his father said. But he said so many things. And Dickie was so sick of listening. 'Retirement' to his father meant hanging around the office, offering his opinion on any and all aspects of the business. Part of the reason Dickie had so much trouble with the mechanics was that they still regarded him as a caretaker, keeping the seat warm until 'the gaffer' came back from his sabbatical to set the business to rights.

Most of his father's thoughts revolved around what did and what didn't say *Barnes*. The local GAA team said *Barnes* – figuratively, but also literally, as they were being sponsored by the garage. Sunroofs said *Barnes*; so did complimentary golf umbrellas and out-of-the-box thinking. Electric cars didn't say *Barnes*. Fuel efficiency didn't say *Barnes*. In fact, a lot of the innovations Dickie wanted to bring in turned out not to say *Barnes*. Though it had been his plan for him since Dickie was a child, his father still seemed unconvinced that Dickie was the right man for the job. The problem with Dickie, he would say to anyone who'd listen – customers, reps, mechanics – was that he didn't understand *people*. He didn't like pushing them to do things. What Dickie didn't understand was that people *want* to be pushed! They want to do things they shouldn't! Dickie doesn't see that. He doesn't understand *transgression*. Dickie was always a *good* boy. He was always happy following the rules. He doesn't see that people hate the rules! Under the surface, people dream of blasting through the rules! That's why they buy big, fast cars! Even if they'll never go up to 150 mph – they tell themselves that some day they might! They might!

Frank knew that, he would conclude. That boy never saw a rule but he was lepping up and down on it!

Frank knew cars, Frank knew people. As soon as Frank died, his father did a U-turn. Frank, the idler, the wastrel, the dosser, became a saint, while Dickie was now to be disdained, as if having lived entailed something underhand.

And Dickie took it without demur, because he thought the same thing.

Even after he moved to Portugal, the old man stuck his oar in. He called constantly; whenever he was back in Ireland, he'd always 'run into' one or other of the reps on his way home. It wasn't till the recession bit that he went quiet. He no longer asked to see the sales figures. If the business was mentioned to him, he'd come out with some sanctimonious line to the effect that all he could do was lay the foundations – it was for the next generation to build on them.

So, when Phil brought his accusations against Ryszard, it was above all the opportunity to ignore his father's wisdom that inclined Dickie to be lenient. He told Phil to keep an eye on him for now. We're understaffed, he said. Let's give him the benefit of the doubt.

Then Nuala Eglantine, who had brought in her Fiesta with a loose steering rod, brought it back shortly after collection with a 'rumble', which was traced to a missing catalytic converter. It was Phil himself who had made the discovery, but he didn't report it to Dickie until two more cars had been returned to the garage with the same issue, a few weeks after being left in for repairs.

What can have happened to them? Dickie said.

Phil had a sagging silvery moustache that gave him a misleadingly sleepy expression. He'd been with the garage from the very beginning. Maybe as a consequence Dickie had always found him the surliest of the workshop staff, whether because he didn't like taking orders from Maurice's son, or he resented Maurice for getting out and retiring to Portugal while he was stuck here.

These are all cars your Polish friend was working on, he said.

He'd brought the logbook with him; he pushed it across the table. Dickie picked it up and leafed through it, feeling Phil's sleepy eyes on him.

You're sure it was him, then? Dickie said. It wasn't . . . someone else, trying to get him in trouble? The other mechanics didn't like the boy, he knew, because he was foreign, because he was young and good-looking and the female customers noticed him, because they thought that Dickie favoured him.

Phil remained impassive, as if he hadn't heard.

What do you think we should do?

Phil crossed his arms in front of him. He was your hire, he said. So I thought I'd leave it up to you.

Dickie understood. It was always Phil who hired the mechanics; but Ryszard had come, with his dubious CV, to Dickie, and Dickie had taken him on, and Phil had added that to his long list of grievances.

He sent Phil away, spent the rest of the day pondering the situation. Ryszard was still in the workshop when he left the office, and called out to him, as was his habit, Cheerio, boss-man, see you next morning!

Dickie didn't reply. From beyond the lifts, he saw the boy look after him with the same troubled expression PJ had when his report card arrived. He was so young! Young, alone in a strange land, foolish and desperate enough, maybe, to carry out a crime for which he'd almost definitely get caught. Maybe he'd heard the business was on its last legs, and he'd hit on this as a way of making some extra cash before it went to the wall.

Dickie hated firing people. Whoever it was, he always felt sorry for them for being the type of person who'd done whatever they'd done. In this case, the obviousness of the theft, the ease with which he'd been discovered – didn't it point to a fundamental innocence in the boy? Didn't it show the very opposite of a criminal nature?

He made up his mind to speak to him the next day and hear what he had to say. If he owned up, maybe there was still a use for him here. If Dickie thought he was lying, he'd hand him his notice. They had got through most of the backlog now.

Before that happened, however, there was a fresh complaint. From Alistair Healy this time: he arrived at the garage before the doors were even open, hammering on the glass with the heel of his hand.

It was the same story again. He had left his car in for a pre-NCT check-up. When he'd gone to do the test, they'd told him the converter was missing.

Alistair Healy had a shop on Main Street that sold tat for the tourists – T-shirts, bodhráns made in China, leprechaun beards that sprang from the walls like a fungus. His wife, a Thai woman acquired in mysterious circumstances, had run off late last year; since then he'd developed a vindictive streak.

Dickie did not know him well, but had always considered their relationship, composed in the main of nods exchanged on the street, as a cordial one. Today, though, he was furious. He seemed to think Dickie had taken the converter from the car himself. Ye Barneses with your airs and graces, he roared. And all ye are is a bunch of crooks!

People said that kind of thing to Dickie now. Probably the worst aspect of the slow, agonizing death of the family business was finding out just how many of the townsfolk were enjoying it – how many of them, for all these years, had hated the Barneses in silence.

Dickie didn't think Alistair would go to the guards. He'd had a bad relationship with them since they'd caught him burning rubbish on his land. Still, Dickie had to offer him free rustproofing to get rid of him.

When he brought him to the office the boy denied everything, of course. As Dickie spoke, hearing his father's words resound in his own voice – *criminal, policy, will not be tolerated*, etc. – he sat not listening, his red lips pouting, the black gaze resting on his shoes. Asked if he had anything to add in his defence, he said only, His car is piece of shit.

Dickie folded his hands. He knew he had to fire him. But he found he couldn't do it. Maybe it was the malice in Alistair Healy's voice, his jabbing finger. Or maybe it was the way the boy sagged in the chair, his eyes full of self-recrimination, as if this were only the latest of a long list of missteps, miscalculations. He sighed, and told him that this was his final warning.

Before he'd finished speaking, Ryszard had bounced up off the chair, positively alight. He thanked Dickie profusely, and he swore up and down that (although he'd never admitted doing anything wrong) from hereon in he would be an exemplary employee. I do anything for you, boss-man, anything.

Yes, yes, Dickie said, rising from his desk to open the door, half delighted with this reaction, and half feeling already that he'd made the wrong decision. Ryszard turned to go, but in the threshold turned again. He reached out and took Dickie's hand and held it. I mean it, he said. I do anything.

Dickie was too surprised to respond. He just stood there, as Ryszard's dark eyes, with their curiously liquid appearance, like pools slowly turning, gazed into his. Then, smiling benignly, the boy gave his hand one last squeeze and, whistling, took his leave. Dickie withdrew behind his computer, at which he pretended to stare. His head was full of falling masonry and burning timber, a house on fire.

Dickie had been good for so long.

It hadn't even been difficult, once he'd made the decision. After Frank died, everything had fallen to him. His father was overcome with grief, his mother terminally ill. Who else could steer the ship? And so dependable Dickie was born – steadfast Dickie, capable Dickie, the Dickie who kept his head; while his previous self, his college self, with his neuroses and his desires, his clammy illicit flowerings, was shuffled offstage, to hunger and crave in oblivion.

In the early years, he kept waiting to get caught. He still had the terrifying thought that Sean would appear one day on Main Street; whenever he saw a garda car he'd get heart palpitations. But nobody questioned him. Nobody even seemed to remember the old Dickie. The people of the town took him as they found him – a successful local businessman, married to a beauty, with a young family to provide for. And that was who he was, he reminded himself; that was who he was.

Not difficult to be this new man: he could never have imagined, growing up, how easy it would be. Oh, the details were hard, of course. Running a business was hard. Raising a family was hard. He got so tired when the kids were small that sometimes he'd fall asleep on his feet. Yet sleepwalking was possible now as it had never seemed before. The world was made with this kind of life in mind, he came to realize. The world was a machine designed to sustain and perpetuate this kind of life – adult life, normal life. It wasn't like college, when every moment bristled with pathways, alternatives, strangers and confusion. Everything was linear, everything made sense, the future appeared before him like a railway track, moment by moment, day by day, carrying him onwards without his needing to do a thing.

What surprised him was how happy it made him. Dancing to Shakira with Cass and her Barbies. Balancing rocks on a log with her, laughing when the pile fell over. Sitting in the showroom, having 'picnics' together in the new Passat, the new Jetta, reading *My Little Pony* books from the library, eating Oreos, watching the town pass by outside. He did not sleepwalk through these moments. Every pleasure civilization had to offer suddenly seemed a paltry thing, compared to this – sitting in a stationary car with his daughter, going nowhere. Then PJ was born, and the happiness only grew. Where was it even coming from? Some aquifer within him, invisible till now, that the children had found a way to tap into. Reading *Spot* again, reading *That's Not My Dinosaur*. In the woods now there were two squirrels ranged against the hunter, one red, one grey.

And Imelda? Was she happy? He often wondered what kind of life she would have had without him – if she'd left town after Frank died, if he hadn't 'rescued' her. Maybe she'd have gone to Dublin, done some modelling, married a society type – a barrister, a TV chef, a business-man with a helicopter who'd set her up with a little boutique in Ranelagh where she could sit and drink chai tea and look at Instagram. More likely she'd have ended up with some good-time Charlie, lavish with gifts in the early days, savage when the money began to run out. A drinker who'd throw punches on Sundays when his hangovers were bad. The kids locked in the bathroom for safety. Bailiffs, barring orders. She had no sense that way, for everyday life. When he got engaged to her, she'd never had a bank account. Even after he set one up for her, she didn't trust it. She'd go to the ATM, take out all the money over two or three days; he'd find it stuffed down the couch in wads, or taped under the sink.

Did she love him? Did he love her? When he tried to remember how they'd first come together he found everything shrouded in hissing clouds of trauma. He could only recall the two of them clutching each other, crying. Was that love? It had seemed to him simply that without her he would die. Then she was pregnant, and it made him feel better to take care of her – absolved. When he came out of the church on their wedding day it was like he had started all over again. But what did she feel? After that day she never saw her father again, her brothers either. Even Rose, whom she'd been so close to, she seemed to turn against.

Those first years were the hardest. Her education was minimal. She believed the earth revolved around the equator, that Jews were born with an extra finger. She had a plethora of saints she prayed to, and different iterations of the Virgin Mary – Our Lady of Lourdes, Our Lady of Fatima, Our Lady of Perpetual Succour – for different complaints. Angels, too, who flitted in and out of our universe, and were courted with certain crystals available by mail order. That is: he was often lonely. But that only undergirded his sense of duty. What is love, only duty, absolution?

Yet he desired her too. Her beauty was otherworldly, being in her presence was like entering a fairy tale, even when she was mopping the floor or throwing dishes. When he slept with Willie, it had been like they were exploring a forbidden country, a forbidden territory they had trespassed onto together. When he slept with Imelda she *was* the country. He would see himself, as he touched her, stealing ashore from a black sea onto a midnight beach, a whole unbounded alien country waiting before him impassively.

They bought Goldenhill from his father – there was some complicated tax reason whereby it made more sense to do it that way. She didn't want to go back there, but he talked her round. She drifted away from angels, religion, got interested in home furnishings. At the school gate she befriended other mothers and reinvented herself as well-to-do. The mothers were all ten years older than her and made of materialism a kind of private language, displaying their acquisitions to each other like bees doing a waggle dance.

She spent money furiously, compulsively. It was as if she didn't quite believe in it and had to spend it to prove to herself it was real – which in turn made her worry that it was all gone, so she had to spend more to prove that it wasn't. They were rich now, but she never seemed able to accept it, that this was her life. Instead, wealth was a disguise that had to be continually renewed.

He didn't mind. He liked that he could give her what she wanted. She in turn provided him with an endless supply of fresh wants. It was a new way of communicating that satisfied both without necessitating closeness. Every situation presented itself in terms of something they needed to buy. Spending became the fuel that powered the illusion, the great machine that carried them, all of them, away from the past.

Sometimes, with a jolt, he'd snap awake – find himself looking at his life from the outside, as you might at the Facebook of a long-lost friend, years telescoped into a series of images, at once banal and incomprehensible. But even at these moments of vertiginous re-emergence, when he saw himself and wondered who he was – did it matter? The boys who'd huffed WD40 and done doughnuts in the mountains, the girls he'd see every weekend passed out on the floor of Paparazzi's now had earnest conversations with him about their shed refurbs or the right colours for a north-facing room. Wasn't that just adult life?

In all those years, he had never slipped, never stumbled. The same willpower that had kept him kneeling by his bed, aged eight, for a full Rosary every night, now kept him on the right track, kept him a family man, kept the old, perverse Dickie, if he still existed, banished so deep inside himself he could no longer be heard.

Which was ironic, because the old Dickie would have seen what was coming. The old Dickie was always ready for things to fall apart. The new Dickie didn't think that way. He believed in the future as something that would always work out in his favour, a series of incremental improvements he was due automatically, like phone upgrades.

The crash blindsided him. At first though he thought they could weather it. They had savings – the garage had been making so much money even they couldn't spend it all. For a time, amid the repossessions and closures, they gallantly kept up appearances – holidays, appliances, serious discussions of an indoor sauna. Imelda went up to Dublin and told him gleefully what mighty bargains there were in the sales this year.

But the crash was persistent. The second year was worse than the first. Every day was a succession of attacks, little erosions, nibbling away at them. A class trip, an electricity bill, a burst pipe. Payments on a table they'd bought six months before. You have to have a good table, he'd agreed with Imelda at the time, it's the foundation of the whole house.

At work sales were through the floor. He tried everything to lift them – discounts, add-ons, extended warranties, trifectas of deals worth thousands. None of it made any difference. He kept telling himself things were bound to improve. But they didn't. It was impossible to hide it from the family any longer. They cut back on their spending. That seemed like enough, for a little while. But things continued to get worse, over months, then years. Imelda sold her jewellery. She went on the internet trying to teach herself how to darn socks. He found crumpled-up drafts of cover letters she'd written for jobs, almost illegible even with spellcheck and autocorrect. He wanted to help her but he knew she would be embarrassed, and he was ashamed to have put her in that position. Anyway, there were no jobs.

The kids began to suffer. Out of nowhere PJ started having asthma attacks. Cass stopped seeing her friends. Then she started drinking, in shitty pubs in town. Imelda told him to ask his father for a loan. You have to, she said. She was angry – of course she was angry. She'd spent her childhood telling the debt collectors that her daddy wasn't home. Dickie was supposed to take her away from that. That was the whole point of Dickie, to be rich, to be clever, to know things, to anticipate events like this. Now the lifeboat was sinking, the coach turning back into a pumpkin. Soon the atmosphere in the house grew so toxic that he simply couldn't bear coming home. Instead he worked late. Though that was toxic too, make no mistake. That was hell, the business, the sinking ship – hell. The whole industry dissolving, the safe bet he'd made crocked, tanked.

He found himself wishing Maurice Barnes Motors would go under.

Just to have it done, once and for all. Declare bankruptcy, get a job delivering pizzas. People he knew answering the door, keeping their faces carefully controlled as they saw who it was. Wondering whether or not to give him a tip. That or emigrate with the family, to England, America, Australia. Thousands of others had left already. The drive into town was cluttered with For Sale signs, little farms that could no longer pay for themselves.

But he couldn't ever bring himself to pull the plug. If he really tried, if he went flat out, he found they could always eke out another few weeks. And that's what he did. Pleaded with the bank to restructure the debt. Pleaded with suppliers to take back the fleet, to change the terms. Pleaded with corporate to pay early for next year's cars, at a discount that was suicidal. Looked for mergers, potential buyers, deals that almost but never quite came through. For years! Years, putting on his suit and tie and going to sit at his desk, not moving from his chair, staring at the phone that didn't ring. The salesmen out on the forecourt trying to stay out of his line of sight. Polishing the cars over and over. Tensing every time he came out of the office, for fear the moment had finally come, and he was going to clap his hands and gather them round and tell them the business was done and they were out of a job. So he didn't come out of the office. Sat there with the air conditioning switched off in summer, the heat off in winter, saving pennies.

It was only in the evening that he felt a measure of peace – when the shift ended and everyone had gone home and he could sit with the lights out and let dusk settle over him.

Alone in the darkness he would wonder if he'd chosen the wrong path.

Tonight, though, he wasn't thinking about any of that. Tonight he was thinking of Ryszard, the electricity that passed through him when the boy's hand took his. Outside, the darkness fell like soft noiseless rain, on his computer the screensaver languorously extended itself and retracted again. He let his eyes fall closed, let his fantasies unfold, boys with black eyes and gleaming wet black hair.

Then, with a start, he looked up. Phil was standing in the doorway. Oh, Dickie said, blushing, as if Phil might know what had been going through his mind. The older man was impassive. I'm heading home, he said.

Right, Dickie said. Normally Phil didn't feel the need to inform him. *He's* still here, the mechanic said.

Who would that be, Phil? Dickie said, though he knew.

Phil rolled his eyes. Your friend. The Pole. He's finishing putting shocks in Delaney's campervan. So he says anyway. Will I run him?

Dickie, without looking at him, his attention drawn by a document on his desk, replied, Hmm? No, no, Phil, I'll be here another little while. I'll throw him out if he's not done by then.

Phil harrumphed, and lumbered off. Dickie listened to his footsteps fade away to nothing, to be replaced by a roaring silence. He sat motionless at his desk, time itself seeming to fizz and pop, to strain against the staid succession of moments—

All done, boss-man, he said.

His voice was soft; his muscular arm was raised, propped against the door frame. In his ears Dickie heard the sound of his own heartbeat, his own breathing, the tick of the clock, infinitely slow. The boy's eyes flashed across the desk to him with a strange expression, at once piercing and pliant, like a hunter intent on surrendering to his prey. Ah, oh, Dickie said. Right, very good.

Anything else I can do for you tonight? the boy said.

His eyes levelled onto Dickie's and held them. And Dickie realized that this could come true, his fantasy – that it could happen, that it *was* happening – and all he had to do now was to rise from the desk and go to him. The air shivered, time, space, pitched up and waited, suspended . . .

From out of their picture frame his family looked at him, as they were years ago in the Christmas fairground. And suddenly the electricity deserted him. No, no, he said. You can head home.

Ryszard seemed surprised. You sure?

Dickie – so heavy now he thought he might sink into the earth – Dickie said, Sure. And then, You head off home now.

And the boy turned around without another word. His fingers left inky prints on the white lintel.

Left on his own, Dickie didn't feel virtuous, elevated, even relieved. Instead the crushing weight on him only seemed to grow. For what purpose did it serve, renouncing sin, being good? Would it make his family happier to see him when he got home? Would it make a single thing about their situation better or easier? Was it even good, to be true to an illusion?

He felt utterly spent, as if whatever inner fuel had been keeping him going until now had finally run out. Outside the sky had grown completely dark. He lowered his head to the desk and laid it there. If he'd had a gun, this was the moment he would have put it in his mouth. But at the same time that he thought this, he knew it wasn't true. He was steady Dickie, dependable Dickie: there was no way out of that.

He raised his head, took his jacket down from the coat hook. He turned to the computer, dismissed the screensaver, started closing down his work.

And then, in his inbox, he saw an email from Willie.

In all those years, he had never sought him out – never called, never texted, never even looked up his name. He'd wanted to – a hundred thousand times he'd come within an inch of it. So much time had gone by, he'd tell himself, what was the harm?

But he never did it, because he knew it would be unbearable. It would be literally unbearable even for a moment to glimpse him in the present, in the life that Dickie might have lived alongside him. Better to stay in the dark, not knowing if he was alive or dead.

He had imagined sometimes – often he'd dreamed it – that Willie wrote to *him*; but he knew that would never happen. Not the way they'd parted. Willie had been very clear. If you change your mind, I want you to know it will be too late, he had said. Then he'd walked down the driveway without looking back. His little rucksack on, his expensive, old-fashioned shoes. The slenderness of his frame newly apparent against the trees, the big country sky. A boy, a weakling, like Dickie. Gone for ever, for ever.

And yet here he was in Dickie's inbox, his name in bold, subject header *Hi*.

Dickie drew a deep, rattling, uncertain breath. He put his hand on the mouse and opened the message.

Hello, it began. *Forgive me for writing out of the blue like this. I wanted to let you know something about what I've been doing lately, and to ask for your help. You might have heard that I'm running for the Seanad. The campaign is in full swing – you can see some pictures here! – and we're feeling confident. But . . .*

Dickie read on for another couple of lines before he realized it had not been written to him. It was a mailshot, a mass communication. They must have got his address from some petition or other – Cass had used to send him lots of them. His heart sank, the despairing weight came back. But only for a moment. Then he laughed, and read on.

Willie was a barrister. He still lived in Dublin, and had campaigned on a number of environmental and social issues – housing, air pollution, water, LGBT rights. There was a picture set into the text, showing him outside the Four Courts in his robes. He had lost all his hair, and no longer wore glasses: he was broader both in face and body, almost to the point of chubbiness. Dickie might have walked past him on the street – but for the look in his eyes, the sly, impish intelligence that was just as he remembered it. Now he was running for office.

After the original jolt and then the disappointment, Dickie found he was happy to have news of his friend. It felt, amid the prevailing darkness, like a good thing, a ray of light. Having been given this pass by Fate, he felt he would not be transgressing by looking a little further. He knew now that he could take it.

He clicked on the link at the foot of the message and found himself looking at Willie's campaign website. There were interviews with news media, with blogs and vlogs and tiny obscure journals; there were contributions to message boards going back a decade, on a wide variety of topics: conservation, speed bumps, glyphosate, marriage equality. There were photographs, hundreds of them, of Willie with colleagues and family and friends, of Willie campaigning, of holidays he'd been on, breakfasts he'd eaten. On the Pride march, in a rainbow-coloured suit. In the Butterfly, wearing a Santa hat, pantomiming shock as a drag queen planted a kiss on his cheek – he was *out and proud*, according to his Twitter profile.

Searching further, Dickie was able to find out quite a lot about his life. He lived in a Georgian house in the north inner city, extensively renovated. He liked to eat breakfast in a little Italian café around the corner. He had a wine cellar and reviewed wine occasionally for a magazine. He hosted monthly salons with writers and artists. He ran in the park in the summertime, in the winter by the sea.

He was alone.

There were faces that recurred in the pictures, though none for long. A burly man was the most constant, a heavy-set, glowering type, but after a while Dickie wondered if he might not be some sort of minder. Then in a recent interview, the reporter asked if there was a special someone? And Willie said simply, No. The accompanying photograph showed him in his living room – not the grand reception room, but the smaller, cosier one he called his 'inglenook'. On his mantelpiece was the statue of Ganesh that they had bought on Francis Street together.

Not that that meant anything. Dickie didn't take it to mean anything. It simply reminded him of those times. It simply made him think how strange it was that they hadn't reconnected over the years. Reaching out, touching base – everybody was constantly reaching and touching. He was probably the one person from Willie's past who'd remained out of contact! Suddenly it seemed ridiculous to have kept silent. Willie had probably been waiting to hear from him. Maybe he'd even sent him the email deliberately, masquerading as junk, in the hope of a response!

With a surge of elation, Dickie began to write a message back to him, saying how funny it had been to find him in his inbox, how crazy it was they hadn't spoken in so long. The words came easily; it was easy to be blithe, to be carefree, to speak truly and from the heart, when you knew you would never hit Send.

But he didn't retreat into silence either. In the days that followed, he set up a fake Twitter account and followed Willie, liking his tweets and occasionally responding with something banal. When Willie replied to one of these tweets – no words, just a smiley face – he felt overcome by joy.

He longed at that point to reveal himself. Instead, from that account and some other fake accounts, he began to send him messages. These were whimsical at first, but increasingly he found them becoming sexual in tone, what he would like to do to him and so on – he remembered what Willie liked doing and having done. He sent pictures purporting to be of his dick, though it was really just random dicks from the internet. Then one night, staying late, he sent a picture of his own dick, taken in the staff toilet. As soon as it left his phone he was consumed by dread of some terrible repercussion. Hurriedly he tucked himself in and zipped up his trousers; then he stood in the door, looking out at nothing, flushed a deep plum, or so it felt to him, a grotesquely phallic colour. He closed his eyes, clutched the door frame on either side. What was he doing? What was he doing with his life? Who are you? he whispered out loud.

Opening his eyes, he saw Phil in front of him in his overalls, looking surprised. It's me, Phil said. Phil.

Oh, Dickie said. Oh yes, of course.

Enough, he thought. Was he going to ruin his life all over again? He deleted his fake accounts, resolved never to contact Willie again. The past was the past.

It was not long after that he received word of a conference in Dublin. Partly a crisis meeting, the rep told him, but mostly to give the dealers a bit of a lift. There would be a few speeches from various bigwigs. Then dinner, drinks and entertainment until the small hours. The manufacturers were covering everything, hotel included. Bring the missus, he said.

That's generous, Dickie said.

It's the least they can do, the rep said. In your father's day, now, a night's stay in Dublin would only be the start of it. By God, we lived in those days, so we did.

It made no sense to think of it as fate. Dublin was only a couple of hours away, he could have driven up any time if he'd wanted to. Yet it appeared to him as an alignment of the stars. The email that had been sent 'by mistake', and now this? It seemed clear that he and Willie were meant to meet again – though for what purpose he didn't know.

This time, he resolved, there would be no more deception. He would tell Willie about the email, tell him that he was coming to Dublin, ask him if he wanted to meet.

He started writing him a letter. He didn't hold back. He talked about the tragedy that had engulfed the family. Willie never understood what it had done to him. He had died too – that's what it had felt like. That was why he'd left without even a note, why he hadn't answered the phone for a month, why he hadn't told him about the crash, or the funeral, or the engagement. He couldn't, that was the long and the short of it. The grief of losing Frank, of losing Willie, of losing himself was too much for him to put into words. It was too much – that was all.

He wrote it all out, everything he should have said so many years before. He was as truthful as he could be. But once again, when the time came, he couldn't send it. A letter wouldn't work. Willie would see his name and rip it right up. He had one chance. He needed to see him in person. For that he would have to be clever, lure him in. Once they were together in a room – then he could start being honest.

The first thing he did was to set up another online persona. This time it was a Brazilian man in his early thirties called David Silva. Unlike the previous aliases, Silva was real. He was from São Paulo, but lived in Barcelona, where he worked as a designer. If you looked him up, the profile picture on his social media showed a dark, bearded man with eyes that seemed at once warm and forbidding. He was intermittently active online, always in Spanish or Portuguese.

Dickie created an email address under his name, and as David Silva he wrote to Willie, briefly introducing himself and telling him that he was coming to Dublin and interested in Georgian architecture. He knew that Willie was something of an expert – did he have any recommendations?

An hour went by, another and another. He couldn't eat, he couldn't stop looking at his phone. In part he hoped that Willie wouldn't write back. Then, just as Dickie arrived home for dinner, his phone beeped.

This time the message was real – it was for him, that is, for David Silva. The response was short but generous. He wouldn't call himself an expert, he said, but he did have some favourites, which he listed, with links. He told him to check out the Marsh library too. Enjoy your trip!

The next move was crucial. He had made contact, the key now was to sustain it. Dickie had been devising a question about conservation strategies in Dublin, something only an architect might ask, or someone with a professional interest in the area. He had worked long and hard on this question, spending a lot of time on forums and Wikis. The temptation was to send it straight away, but he made himself wait until dinner was over and the kids had gone to their rooms.

Again he had to wait for a reply. He got so tense in that time that he drank a fifth of gin and didn't feel it. But then it arrived. Again, it was brief, but open; it closed with a question about the legislation in Silva's own city of Barcelona.

The conference was two weeks away. Dickie hardly slept that whole time. Every element of life suddenly seemed impossibly contingent: he felt as if he were playing some vast, metaphysical chess game, with invisible pieces. He kept up his correspondence with Willie. He told Willie his own city was actually in Brazil; he said he was part of the conservation group hoping to bring the changes similar to the ones Willie had achieved in Dublin. He worked hard to make the emails seem spontaneous, written hastily in a few spare minutes at work. He liked being David Silva, more so than the other aliases: he liked developing characteristic mistakes in David's grammar, his preference for short, terse sentences without verbs, interspersed with capitals. He imagined Willie googling David Silva, seeing the handsome smiling Latin face.

Sometimes, not often, he would seem to wake and look down at what he was doing, intricate and unintelligible as a dream. Surely there was an easier way of getting Willie in a room? Find out his schedule, go along to one of his events, pretend he'd just run into him by chance? But he knew that wouldn't work, wouldn't take. It had to be a proper *meeting*; the circumstances needed to be just right. And in itself, the plotting was not unenjoyable. It was fun to use his brain for something other than sales; it was fun to flirt, after all this time, to be interesting, a person someone else might desire.

The days passed in a strange blend of tension and elation. Meanwhile his life, his actual life, seemed to recede into a shadowy hinterland beyond his phone. He resolved only to write and read his correspondence at work, yet even when he came home the children appeared translucent somehow. He stayed late in the office most nights, but he didn't see Ryszard again. Since Dickie's rebuff, the boy had kept himself to the workshop. He too had become translucent.

There were no more than a handful of emails over a couple of weeks. Still, they had got to a point where it would be quite natural of David Silva to ask Willie if he wanted to meet for a coffee or a drink, during his brief stay. Yet Dickie couldn't bring himself to do it. As the time drew nearer he began to consider more deeply the moment when they came face to face – when he stopped being David Silva, and revealed himself. What would Willie *say*? When he looked up and saw Dickie there, what would he say, what would he do? Would he laugh? Would he fall silent? Would he turn on his heel and walk away? If he did, would Dickie run after him, grab his shoulder, say, Please, listen to me? I just wanted to say sorry, he would say. I know, I know it's too late. I still wanted to say it. And Willie would look down at the ground, blinking quickly, then he would reach his arms out to Dickie and they would hold each other. He would smell the same, after all these years. Or he would listen, white-faced, and then say flatly, Now, you've said it, and continue on his way. Or maybe he would be neither forgiving nor hostile, it would be polite, awkward, they would have nothing to say to each other, and after five minutes, Willie would say gently that he had better be getting along.

Or what if he was angry? If he knew Dickie had tricked him into meeting, he might be angry, violent, even! If he struck him, Dickie decided, he would not defend himself. In his mind's eye he saw Willie throw a punch, in a modish, anonymous hotel room, and then, immediately, as if awaking from a spell, clutching at himself in horror, moving to comfort the stricken form on the bed, crying out, I love you, I never stopped loving you!

It could be any of these outcomes, or none; there was no way to tell.

And then the rain came.

At first it seemed no more than a heavy shower – it was the season for them. But the fallen rain didn't clear. Instead it pooled on the street, like a mob discharged from a football match, milling about with nothing to do. Within hours there were lakelets and lagoons in the town square. By mid-afternoon cars were stranded in the knee-high water. Dickie went home early, spent the evening staring out the window, imagining, beyond the ghostly reflection of his face, sheets of precipitation descending on the forest.

It'll be the end of your trip if that keeps up, Imelda said.

That was just what he was thinking, but hearing her say it enraged him. Why's that? he said.

How would you make it up to Dublin through that? she said, nodding at the window. They'll probably cancel it.

He knew that now of all times he needed to keep a calm head, avoid arousing suspicion. But he couldn't do it. Why would they cancel it? he said, hearing his voice rise. There's no flood in Dublin. You think they're going to shut down the whole country because it's raining here? Do you think this fucking kip is the whole world?

Imelda did not reply, merely left the room, as if she were too dignified to stoop to his level – as if it weren't also her level, as if she hadn't invented this level, as if she hadn't dug it out with her talons over twenty fucking years!

The next morning – the day of the conference – the river had burst its banks. Half the roads were impassable. The schools were closed, the garage too, the kids were hanging around the house. PJ asked Dickie if he wanted to watch a film – he didn't. Cass wafted about in a cloud of stale smoke and alcohol, like a derelict ghost. Are you at a loose end? he asked her with false pleasantness. Have you thought of perhaps studying for your exams?

All of them just hanging around! He felt like he was under observation. He retreated to the study, checked his phone. Three days ago, David Silva had finally asked Willie if he'd like to meet while he was in Dublin. Willie had replied, Sounds good – let's talk closer to the time. That was positive, wasn't it? Non-committal but not a refusal. After that he'd held off from writing to him again. He didn't want to seem too eager; also, he didn't like the idea of doing it from the house. Instead he'd planned to email him when he got on the road, when he'd be alone and had time to think it out properly. But now – with the rain teeming outside – this precaution seemed unnecessary. Why wait? What difference did it make where the message was sent from? The arrangement was pretty much made anyway, why not just sign off on it?

Why don't you come to my hotel? he wrote. Around 8?

As soon as he'd hit Send he knew it was too much. Immediately he sent another: For a drink. But this second message only underlined the ambiguity of the first. Fuck! He was ruining it! For an hour he paced the house like a tiger, circling back endlessly to check his phone where it lay, like a tiny black slab in some Lilliputian graveyard. Nothing. Nothing, nothing. What the fuck had he been thinking?

Hey, Dad?

I'm in the middle of something here, buddy.

He could feel PJ hover. Because Dickie was blatantly just standing there looking at his phone.

He closed the app, switched off the phone. What is it?

Could you just show me again how to do equations?

Dickie took a deep breath. Sure, he said.

By the time he was leaving for Dublin, the town was on the news; the TV showed footage taken from a helicopter of dirty water swirling around the streets. See you tomorrow! he called in a sing-song voice. His family looked back at him like he was out of his mind.

He arrived in Dublin with no memory of the journey. Already it was home, his family, that seemed like another life. And the hotel, the conference, these composed a kind of Purgatory, a weird, interstitial space between one world and the next, filled with peripheral figures from the past, the kind of marginal acquaintances that turn up in dreams – reps, fellow dealers, opaque industry types he'd last seen at a Christmas party three years ago, or eight, or twenty. Some of them had been at his wedding, some were themselves the sons of men who'd been at his wedding. All of them asked about his father, told him funny things that his father had said or done at events such as this.

After an hour of mingling, someone went up to the podium and began to speak. Surreptitiously Dickie checked his phone. He told himself to stay calm. If it didn't happen now, it would happen some other time. Yet it felt as if this *had* to be the time. Purely because he could not go on as he was, no, not for a single day more.

The speeches ended, drinks were served, he had the same conversations again with different people – different men, there were almost no women here. He began to get an intense feeling of claustrophobia. The event seemed ever more inconsequential, meaningless, and yet, at the same time, inescapable, as if it were a prison designed just for him, a prison of complimentary canapés and Prosecco, each empty exchange with a red-faced good-humoured car dealer nailing him back down into who he was – as if he had come this far, this close to regaining his own life, only so he could be shown, could be made to understand, how impossible that was. The refugee who makes his way through the desert, over the ocean, to the border, only to see a wall that rises as far as the eye can see. He excused himself again, went to the bathroom, stared at the screen of the phone as if he could will a reply to appear. He longed just to tell him! But he knew Willie, knew him still; knew this was not the right tactic.

We finished our work at last! David Silva wrote. If you're free I would love to buy you a beer to say thanks for the advice?

He sent it and he waited. He stood there in the cubicle for he didn't know how long. Periodically, the urinals flushed themselves outside his door, a jerking, hissing sound, like the bells of some profane clock. Far away he seemed to see Willie mulling over his message, sensing something was off, deciding no.

Then the reply came. Hi David sorry I can't make it to ur hotel. I will be meeting shortly with some friends in this pub – prob not staying long but be great to say hi if u make it over

The link was to the Butterfly.

Dickie's hotel was in the docklands, a mile away from the pub, but he couldn't bear the thought of a taxi – too quick, too decisive. He set off on foot, imagining, as he walked, exactly what he would say. He was ready to plead, abase himself. He thought he would tell Willie everything he had written in his unsent letter. But now in his head it sounded thin, self-serving. Or maybe just mad. *I have died, I died too.*

You weren't too dead to find a wife, Willie said, in his imagination.

I did it for love, Dickie said. He shrugged ingenuously. I did it all for love. Maybe I was wrong.

People are always saying they do things for love, Willie said. The worst crimes in the world, they'll use love to justify it.

I loved you, Dickie said. Willie said nothing.

He walked along the river and over a bridge. His route took him through a back entrance into the grounds of Trinity. There were new buildings everywhere, with obtuse designs – deliberate acts of modernity that struggled against the university's aura of pastness, the plush heaviness, like a brocade of pure time, that covered everything and held it in suspension. As he walked along the path by the cricket pitch, the faces that appeared out of the darkness looked the same as the ones he had known in his time here – as if they had never left, stayed here, for ever young.

He passed the building where he had lived in Rooms, and Willie in Rooms beneath him, and then the two of them in Rooms together: he had the strangest impression that if he called at the door he would find them both there, unchanged. He saw himself setting out that evening in October twenty years before, a spring in his step, a man embracing his destiny; and as he continued on, over the wet cobblestones that glistened in the rain, he and the boy he had been seemed to merge into each other, and the urgency, the vitality he'd felt that night surged up within him anew. He'd thought then that it belonged to the city, a quickening that transmitted itself up to him from the pavement, down to him from the shops and signs and street lights; he realized now it was youth, the sense of possibility and exhilarating unmadeness that is youth. And now it had returned to him from the past, impelling him onward, out through Front Gate, across College Green, along Dame Street, to the junction with George's Street.

Then he came to a stop. He had turned the corner, he could see the doors of the pub, still a decadent purple, across the street. But his courage had failed him.

He remembered that too now, the wave of nausea that had always hit him at just this point. Night after night, he had walked up and down outside the pub, trying to work up the courage to go in. Maybe he never would have found it, if Willie hadn't chanced upon him, scooped him up and bustled him through the door.

Tonight, though, Willie was not here to usher him inside, and Dickie felt exactly as meagre and scrawny, as baffled and lost, as he had been that night. It was as if whatever confidence he might have gained in those twenty years, whatever sureness of himself or sense of himself as a man, had suddenly blown away in the breeze, a suit of armour made of dandelion clocks.

He stood outside the music shop – it was a restaurant now – and gathered himself. A few doors down, people, men and women, walked in and out of the pub. Chatting, laughing, sauntering up to the entrance, greeting the doorman with a word, or a kiss; there was no furtiveness, no backward glance, no fear of being spotted or attacked. No shame. It was like a utopia. That was the world now: he had seen it on his phone: everything was allowed now, everybody was available for everything, all the time. Is that what he'd be doing himself, if he'd chosen that path? Everything? He remembered something Willie had noted of him once – that he liked being desired, preferred to be desired than to actually fuck. Once he'd established that someone wanted him, Willie said, Dickie was satisfied. You're like a woman that way, he said.

The memory of the insight made him smile, made him desirous of the mind that conceived it. And like a dandelion clock taken up by the breeze, he found himself carried inside.

He experienced a moment of euphoria, followed by a blaze of intense self-consciousness. He made a beeline for the bar, clung on to the curved wood, his ears ringing with the clamour of voices and his own pounding heart. The barman came over. There you are now, Dickie, he said with a sly smile. Dickie froze. How? The barman laughed, pointed to his chest. With a groan Dickie saw he was still wearing his name-tag from the conference. He blushed deeply, ordered a drink, took off the tag.

His pint arrived. He turned his back on the bar to survey the room. He had known this part of the pub as Jurassic Park, but it struck him that most of the men here were younger than him. They were broader, too, than in his time, stronger, more muscular; or they were skinnier, waifish, with eyeliner and statement haircuts, long lashes and delicate hand gestures. They were men who did not have to disguise themselves when they left the bar, who did not have to worry about re-inserting themselves into normality. This was normality.

He couldn't see Willie anywhere. He took out his phone, but there were no messages. Cass and PJ looked back at him from the lock screen: hurriedly he put it away.

Casting off from the bar, he began to make his way through the room, examining the faces in a way that he tried to make non-sexual, general, like a tourist taking in local details, rather than someone scouting for a hook-up. Most did not seem to see him at all, though he knew that they had checked him out as soon as he came through the door. It was coming back to him, the hierarchical nature of this place, each allotted to their particular box. Back then, with Willie, it hadn't bothered him, because their box was the best one. They were young; everybody wanted them. He was in a different box now, one everybody here recognized: a dad up from the country for the night. Men like that had come here in those days, too; you could spot them a mile off, cowering at the bar, hunched in obvious terror over their *Evening Herald*. In the end, they usually found somebody to cop off with; there were people who liked that air of furtiveness and guilt, and knew furthermore that such men, while sexually inept, were always very grateful and could be relied upon to buy the drinks.

Holding his pint a little up and ahead of him, like a lamp, he insinuated his way through the bodies. A man with silver eyeshadow stopped him and asked if he wanted to see his paintings. Before Dickie could reply he produced his phone, showed him a series of grotesque portraits of celebrities – Tom Hanks, Kanye West, just about recognizable. There seemed to be no end to them; after a minute he excused himself as politely as he could. You think you're too good for me? the painter said scathingly. Have you looked in a mirror lately?

Dickie trudged away. He wondered if Willie might be on the upper level. He made his way glumly to the stairs. Flashing lights and crunching techno emanated from above. Suddenly Dickie felt exhausted – by the bristling personalities, the rampant selfhood. Still, he had come this far. He took a deep breath, prepared himself to brave the dance floor.

And then he saw him. Downstairs, in a corner he had already checked a moment earlier. Dickie knew what he looked like now from the pictures, of course; yet no picture could have prepared him for seeing him for real. Nothing could have prepared him.

He was chatting to a man – a boy, really. His bald head shone, and his tight T-shirt displayed a powerful upper body. Yes, he had changed. Dickie had never even seen him in a T-shirt, let alone with muscles. Yet the way he threw his hands around as he spoke, the way his mouth, his perfect bow lips moved, the spark he had, the mischievous intelligence, the cocksureness and kindness and glee, visible from twenty feet away – all was just as Dickie had known it twenty years before. All was as he had known and loved it. As he looked at him, he felt a profound sense of warmth and peace, like nothing he had ever experienced before. It was like seeing someone who'd come back to life; it was like seeing (say it!) Frank – as if he'd never gone away, as if that horrendous lifelong wound had merely been a misunderstanding.

For a long moment, Dickie just stood there, beholding him – the word didn't sound too grand – swathed in this feeling of blessedness. Then Willie looked up. What happened next was so quick and confused as to barely make sense, but of that he was sure – Willie looked at him, he saw him. Then, in the same instant, it semed, two firm hands fell on Dickie's shoulders – grabbed him, yanked him around, and propelled him at speed back through the bar, with barely time to glimpse the startled faces of the crowd as he hurtled through it. Next thing he was bundled out of the door and onto the street. Sorry, pal, said a voice in his ear. Regulars only.

The purple door closed. Dickie found himself alone on the city street, hunched over like he'd been winded, struggling to piece together his thoughts. What had happened? Why had he been thrown out? He got to his feet, stumbled away to a shuttered shopfront, stood there replaying in his head the moment before he was seized, that split-second of contact when Willie's eyes lit on his. He had seen him, he had recognized him, Dickie knew he had. Had he been expecting him even, had he known all along? But then?

He glanced back down the street. At the door of the pub the bouncer laughed with a couple of boys in fairy wings. Dickie took out his phone, wrote Willie a message: **Please come outside**. He didn't expect an answer, and none came. For five minutes he waited, watching the door. Then he turned and walked away.

Only then, when it was lost, did he realize how much he had staked on the moment. For years, for decades, he had been hoping for it, dreaming of it, the time when they would be reunited – feeding himself minuscule doses of a world that could never be. If he hadn't come here tonight, he could have carried on with it for the rest of his life. Now it was over.

He walked without knowing where he was going. In the indifferent eyes of the strangers he passed he saw himself as Willie must have seen him – a spectre emerged from the rainy evening, searching for the time it had lost. A sorrowful creature of endless need: a dad up from the country.

He found himself, somehow, back at the hotel. The idea of returning to the party, seeing the dealers, was unbearable. Even staying in his room was too much. He packed his bag, left without checking out.

Only when he was on the road did the scale of what had just happened, and what hadn't happened, finally hit him. The stars swam before his eyes, unpinned from their constellations, the lights of the city floated unmoored from the street lamps. Agonizing pains shot through his chest. He pulled over, sat there a moment, panting, clutching his breast. Again and again he saw Willie's eyes light on him and fall away. He started the car, panting, and drove with one hand on the wheel, the other pressed to his heart. On the motorway he drove in the fast lane, racing the black sky that roiled overhead, waiting for the moment when Death would seize the wheel from him, tug him sideways into the wall to die in flames just as Frank had.

He had forgotten about the flood. The rain had stopped for now, but the roads were waterlogged and stank of sewage. He crept through a labyrinth of diversions, past empty houses and abandoned cars. He realized he couldn't go home – couldn't face the explanations he would have to give, did not know what he might do with this coil of rage corkscrewing up into his brain. Why hadn't he thought of that till now? He cursed himself, cursed the silent, dripping town. Then knocking down a couple of emergency signs as he went, he took the car in the direction of the square.

The garage was in darkness. He could sleep in his office, he thought, head home tomorrow as if just returned from the hotel. He got out of the car, stepped into a puddle that went halfway up his shin. He swore, splashed to the door, let himself in. In his office he took off his socks, opened the closet where he kept a change of clothes. Then he heard a sound – something falling.

He left the office, went to the workshop. On the far side, Ryszard stood looking at him. He had a wrench in his hand, his eyes were molten black, his lips too in the unlit workshop seemed black. He looked at Dickie, Dickie looked at him. The air seemed to ring, like every atom had been set abuzz. A gate somewhere opened, his state was altered in some unaccountable way. He began to speak, but nothing came. Ryszard gazed silently at him through the darkness, and when Dickie looked away he could feel the gaze hanging there still, hanging there in space between them, burning in the air. It held him there, it pinned him to him, so when he turned to go he had not really gone, just the outward appearance of him. His outward appearance, utterly weightless, walking away, merely an illusion.

He returned to the office, switched on the desk lamp. From the bottom drawer he took out the spare socks, put them on. Feeling like a puppet, or a figure in a pantomime. None of this was real. Went to the closet, took down the pair of trousers. Unbuttoned the trousers he had on and slid them down.

Now Ryszard was in the doorway. The wrench was in his hand still. His face was expressionless, immobile. Dickie thought idly he might kill him. Dickie had one leg in and one leg out of the wet trousers. Their eyes met, the air buzzed, the molten bridge contracted suddenly, pulling them together. They did not speak. Ryszard's hand was on his prick, which was hard, so hard! Ryszard's mouth was on his. Tearing off their clothes. Running his tongue over the boy's chest, tasting sweat and grease and particles of blasted metal. It was like a mouthful of contaminated water after a month in the desert. In the desert, in the heat, in the sand, a renegade saint wandering amid the stunted trees! Please, his voice moaned in Dickie's ear. Dickie took him by the shoulders and spun him around. The boy planted his feet wide apart, gripped either end of the desk, and for an instant Dickie recoiled: on his bare buttocks were tattooed, in capitals, the words YOUR NAME. He didn't understand – the Gothic lettering made it look sinister, as if it were a warning of some kind. But then Ryszard moaned again, whimpered, and wiggled his arse, and Dickie, succumbing to the moment, gripped his tattooed cheeks and plunged into him. Yes! Plunged! No lube, no condom, none of the scruples of twenty years ago, the averted eyes and the prim redirecting hand – no, he plunged with abandon, wallowing in him, revelling in him! And watching himself doing it, watching himself love with abandon, from a lonely little bunker within. Tears brimmed over his eyelids and fell down onto the boy's back, and he remembered his father's tears falling onto Frank's face as he lay in his coffin. But he didn't stop thrusting, instead he thrust harder than ever, till the boy screamed, and he came, so hard he thought he was having a seizure; pleasure and pain were indistinguishable, one huge tidal wave that swept through his brain and flooded it, collapsed it. He slumped forward onto the desk. After a little while Ryszard crawled out from under him and put his arm around him and asked why he was sad.

No reason, Dickie said.

He realized Ryszard was somehow still clutching the wrench. He wondered again whether the boy intended to murder him, either in order to rob the garage, or simply as something amusing. It did not frighten him to think this. Killing or fucking seemed at the same vertiginous pitch, a literal knife-edge poised high, high in the black vault of the night. As if all this were happening in mid-air, remote from every other part of his life and at the same time with the potential to destroy all of it. Very quickly he found he was aroused again and he pushed the boy onto his knees.

After that he went home. When she woke he told Imelda that he had some paperwork he needed to do first thing, and that was why he'd come back from Dublin early.

From then on he fucked Ryszard every night. There was no arrangement, no conversation or explication of what they were doing. Often they didn't even say hello. This fact alone, the decadence of it, made him dizzy with lust. At the same time it made what they were doing, alone in the deserted, underwater town, so unreal that he felt buffered somehow from the consequences. Why should there be consequences? Why shouldn't there just be pleasure? That's what the boy wanted, that's what the boy was *for*. Do me, he commanded, and Dickie did. He gorged himself, stuffed himself with sex. He gave himself over to a vicious circular desire that even as it sated itself hungered for more, and took more, and desired more. He sank himself up to the hilt in Ryszard's beauty, in his youth, in the sheer carnal abundance of him. Yet even as he groaned and pummelled and exhorted, beneath the noise of the burning spinning wheel of desire and gratification he was always conscious of a lack; there was always a moment when deep within he told himself, This is not what you want.

And he supposed he thought that because his pleasure was incomplete, he wouldn't be punished for it.

The boy had been sleeping in the workshop – that was how he'd surprised Dickie, that first night. Until he got paid he didn't have any money for rent, he said. He'd got hold of Phil's keys and made copies; he showed Dickie the cubbyhole in one of the storage cupboards where he'd made a kind of nest. Where had he slept before he started working here? Where had he been, before he arrived in town? Where did he come from? But whenever he asked him anything, Ryszard grew coy. Is that why you brought me here, to talk about my grandmother's recipes? he would say, stroking Dickie's cock till it throbbed.

He was right: it wasn't love, it was lust. It was supposed to be sordid. Why dress it up as something else? Why pretend he didn't like the grime, the ephemerality, the transactional nature of it? They were just using each other's bodies, that was part of the thrill, wasn't it?

Ryszard didn't care about Dickie. It was unclear if he even cared about himself. He treated his body as throwaway, a plaything that he didn't mind getting damaged. He was always ready to fuck any time, the fucks were always full-throated, filthy, orgiastic. Once they did it in the cubbyhole, and almost got caught when Phil returned for his reading glasses. (The flood had receded by then and life in the town restarted – Dickie barely noticed.) Mostly they stayed in the office – that was a part of it too, the fantasy. Dickie was the boss-man, after all. And his father wasn't dead, Dickie couldn't fuck the boy on his actual grave, so this would have to do. (Yes, this thought shocked him too: the affair – ludicrous word – had opened up some hatch within himself from which all kinds of black imaginings came fluttering out, like bats.)

No one found out about them; no one, he was fairly sure, even suspected. He'd been hiding things his whole life, after all. In fact, his deception made him more attentive at home, more focused on whatever role he was playing at that moment, so he could even persuade himself that, considered in the round, his infidelity was good for everyone.

No, it was Ryszard who presented the problem. Small things at first. Cigarette breaks that took the piss. Sloppy work, insolence. Tardiness – this was almost impossible to understand, given that he was actually in the workshop until shortly before it opened. He delighted in provoking Phil. One time he made him so angry the foreman literally took off his cap and threw it on the ground, something Dickie had never seen outside of cartoons. When Phil complained, Dickie told him they couldn't afford to fire him. In the aftermath of the flood, they discovered that a lot of people had believed their cars to be waterproof. Now the garage had a long, lucrative backlog of shot electrics and ruined brakes.

He said he'd talk to the boy. He followed Phil back to the shop floor. And there was Ryszard, poised like a ballerina, one hand on his jutting hips, a smirk on his perfect bow lips. Inviolable. I swear to God, Dickie! Phil exclaimed. It's him or me! Behind him, Ryszard winked at Dickie, thrust his tongue into his cheek. And Dickie got a cold feeling in the pit of his stomach.

He brought Ryszard to the office. The boy put his hand on Dickie's hand. Dickie took his away. We have to be careful, he told him. The boy just pouted as if he didn't see the point of this. Are you ashamed of me? he said. Of course not, Dickie said soothingly, though he knew Ryszard did not need to be soothed, was doing this only to see how far Dickie could be pushed. You are bored of me then, the boy said, pouting again.

It was true that the initial thrill had worn off – quicker than he'd expected. Perhaps it meant that he was a family man after all, he reflected. Perhaps what he'd thought of as his 'true self', the untaken path, was only the residue of a youthful phase. Though they still had sex, he found himself seized by a new anxiety, even as he was in the act. The more he thrust, the deeper he saw himself burrow into a morass from which, at a certain point, it would be impossible to escape. Ryszard's cries, as loud and as full-throated as ever, seemed to have acquired a stagey quality, as if he were mocking Dickie, mocking the idea that Dickie could elicit such cries: or maybe it had been there all along, and he was only hearing it now.

Things started to go missing again. A wallet, a watch, tools. Items customers had left in their cars, a satnav, a dog harness, a pashmina throw. The electric fan from Dickie's own office. Again Dickie confronted him. Ryszard professed ignorance. You have to stop, Dickie told him, trying to sound authoritative and not pleading.

Then Brian Coady, the publican, came in. He'd left his car in with a knock in the engine. Now the knock was gone but there was a roar instead. He was no expert, but it sounded like a problem with the catalytic converter.

Dickie, when he heard this, feigned outrage, but secretly he was relieved. By now the anxiety of the relationship had dwarfed the pleasure; he had been looking for a way out, and here it was. Ryszard couldn't expect him to cover for this. Maybe that was why he had done it.

He summoned the boy to the office. He padded in, radiating louche, careless menace, like an animal on two legs, a tiger in a hat and a frock coat. Dickie closed the door behind him, then, putting on his gravest face, told him without preamble that he had no option but to let him go.

Ryszard was quite amenable. Dickie had anticipated a furious protestation of innocence, but it didn't come. This stoical acceptance led him to conclude that he was right to think of the stolen converter as a deliberate provocation, calculated to bring things to an end. It also released within him a flood of the old warmth – 'old', though their affair had lasted less than a month – for this beautiful boy who had driven Willie out of his head. He reached across the desk, gripped Ryszard's hand in his. I'll always be here for you, he said. If you come back through town, let me know.

This didn't have the effect he intended. The boy seemed puzzled. Come back? he said. From where?

Well, Dickie said slowly. You will have to leave town, obviously.

Now the boy looked surprised, as if this had never occurred to him.

Dickie, feeling absurd, began to explain. You can't stay here. It's only a matter of time before the police come round about these thefts.

The police don't scare me, Dickie, the boy said, as if to reassure him, then added, Not as much as they scare you.

Why would they scare me? Dickie said, keeping his voice neutral, while an icy tide of dread slowly climbed through him. I haven't done anything wrong.

Then why are you scared? Ryszard said. He smiled at Dickie, as if they were two friends arguing about nothing. Dickie did not return the smile: he kept his movements to a minimum, tried to keep his thoughts focused; he felt as if he were defusing a bomb.

If you don't have a job here, he said slowly, there's no reason to stay.

And to his relief, Ryszard uncrossed his legs and nodded. You are right, he said. I'll give you a reference, Dickie said. If you're looking for a job somewhere else. Ryszard did not reply for a moment, just nodded. But Dickie, he said, to get out of town, set up again elsewhere, while I have no job, this will not be easy. You can't just send me away!

You'll get your full month's pay, Dickie said. The boy cocked his head, smiled. The penny dropped – fool. Right, of course, Dickie said. He opened his wallet, took out what he had; went to the cash reserve he kept hidden in the filing cabinet. Close to €800, all told. He handed it across the table.

But Ryszard did not pick it up. He pressed his lips together, like a teacher whose star pupil has answered a question wrongly. Gently he advised Dickie that that would not be enough. How much would be enough? Dickie said. The ice had risen to his skull, freezing his jaw, his teeth, the cavities of his sinuses.

Ryszard named a figure that was many multiples of the sum on the table. Dickie started to laugh. I don't have that kind of money, he said. Ryszard nodded again, stoically. It's not easy for me to leave here, Dickie, he said. It's not easy for me to leave *you*.

I know that, Dickie said, no longer laughing.

I gave myself to you. I have never been with a man before.

Yes, Dickie said. He couldn't tell how much of this was pretence and how much genuine, or rather, how much of the pretence he was expected to go along with. He felt like he was walking into a trap, but had no idea where it lay. The sky could be the trap, the pale daytime moon over the car lot.

Look, Dickie, Ryszard said. He put his phone on the table, pushed it towards him. Dickie picked it up and looked at it.

He – or somebody – had recorded everything, even the very first time. The shots were from high up, as if from a camera hidden near the ceiling. How small and inconsequential, how bleak and foreshortened their trysts appeared, in this light, in this resolution, from this angle, on the tiny screen of the phone. Why? Dickie murmured, though the answer was already quite clear. Ryszard smiled again across the table, his bright dark smile, his raven's-wing eyes. So I will remember you, Dickie.

He gave him a week to get the money. Dickie spent the first part of it on the couch, watching televised golf. He told Imelda he had flu. Inside he cycled endlessly through plans and counter-plans. He would defy Ryszard, refuse to pay him a penny, let him do with his films as he pleased. He would fight him, he would kidnap him, he would have him beaten up. He would follow him out of work and kill him. He would go to the guards and say he was being blackmailed. He would confess everything to his father and beg for a loan. He would move the family overnight to another country, under another name. He would commit suicide, by rope, by poison, by overdose, by exhaust fumes. He would flee alone, begin another life, send money anonymously to Imelda every month; later, write long handwritten letters to his children, with no return address. *You have been my greatest joy, my greatest achievement.* He went through these and other absurd scenarios, knowing they were merely so much scenery on the way to the only possible destination: he would take the money from the company accounts and pay Ryszard off.

The withdrawal was easy to arrange, easy to disguise; so easy, so logical compared to the other, more baroque options, that Dickie could persuade himself that it *was*, in truth, a business expense, that he was buying a product to solve a problem. On Friday, he returned to work, brought the boy to his office. Wordlessly, he pushed the envelope across the desk. Ryszard took it and stowed it inside his jacket. You're a good man, Dickie, he said. And then he was gone.

There was no reason that anyone would ever find out. Most likely the business would fold shortly; even if it didn't, Dickie had kept the books himself since letting the accountant go last year, and no one else looked at them. His father had given up once the recession hit. Dickie supposed that losses didn't say *Barnes*.

X

He keeps throwing up long after the well water has left his body. At last his insides settle down, but he is weak as a child. He feels depleted – not just that, but roughed up, battered, like he's been chastened by some huge, chaotic, elemental force. Nature has cast him out, sent him back here.

Imelda brings him tea, food when his stomach can handle it, mops his brow. Later PJ comes in to show him the pictures of the Bunker, which he's arranged into a slideshow: they watch it expand and solidify as if by itself. For some reason the water hasn't affected him at all; Imelda rang the doctor, but he told her there was no need to bring him in. Now he wants to know when they can go back to the campsite.

When he looks out the window Dickie sees the clothes he wore in the woods fluttering in the wind, along with what must be last night's bed-sheets. The colours are so bright in the garden, in the woods, and the country beyond; and the faces of his wife and son too come to him with a fullness and definition he has not noticed in them before. Everything seems radiant with itself, and at the same time distant somehow, as if it were receding from him – moving away in time, while he stays where he is. This must be what it feels like to be dying, he thinks; the world remains around you, like a lover who does not want to hurt you by leaving, but in spirit it's already gone, taking with it the meaning of everything you shared. In truth it is already transforming into a future you will never be part of; and you realize only then that it has been transforming all of this time, throughout your whole life, and you with it; and that, in fact, is life, though you never knew, and now it is over.

He calls his father, leaves a message to apologize for missing the meeting and to say he will come to see him in the morning. There is no response.

The next day, though his limbs still feel like water, he gets out of bed and puts on his suit. Imelda asks if he wants breakfast. She asks if he wants her to drive him into town. No need, he tells her. I won't be long.

He has made a decision. Or maybe the sickness has made it for him. Either way, the idea of more lying, more pretending, is too exhausting to bear. He is going to tell the truth.

In the driveway the sunlight is impossibly bright. His hand shakes as he's unlocking the car. As he approaches the garage, panic flares up within him, the terror of an animal afraid for its life. Morning, Dickie! says the postman. Morning, Dickie! says the greengrocer, say Paddy Last and Doris Cannon. Morning, he says back. It feels like the light is passing through him. It feels like he is already well on the way to being nothing at all. He pushes through the door. There he is now, says Emer Gilhooley. Well, says Dickie. Just here for a word with himself.

The truth, so. Father, meet your son.

But his father isn't there. Nor is the IT specialist, or the accountant. Instead, he finds only Big Mike, wadded up behind his desk, like a spider gathered in the corner of its web.

There he is now, Big Mike says.

Well, Mike, Dickie says. He looks around the room, superficially familiar but fundamentally altered in some unplaceable way.

What can I do you for, Dickie? Big Mike says.

Just came in for a word with himself, Dickie says.

If it's your dad you mean, Dickie, I'm sorry to say you've missed him, Big Mike says.

He's out? Dickie says. I can call in later.

He's on his way back to Portugal, Big Mike says. He left this morning.

Portugal? Dickie feels like he's back in his fever dream.

There was some sort of hoo-ha at his golf club, Big Mike says. Someone's made an offer for the site. They're having a meeting to discuss it.

Did he say when he'd be back?

No, Big Mike says. I didn't get the sense he had any plans to come back, not in the short term anyhow.

Oh, Dickie says. And did he mention . . . me?

Well now, Dickie, he mentioned you a lot, Big Mike says. He sits back in the chair, swivels his corpulence a little to the left, a little to the right. When you didn't show up for that meeting on Tuesday, he had a fair bit to say about you, all right.

I was sick, Dickie says.

Right, Big Mike says. The thing is he had the accountant here, the IT guy, you know, to go through these discrepancies in the books. When you didn't show, he took it as a kind of a personal slap in the face.

He was angry?

I'm not going to lie, Dickie. There was talk of filing suit, police, all that.

Police?

You haven't spoken to him?

He won't answer his phone, Dickie says faintly.

Big Mike nods, as if this is what he expected. The way he sees it, he was offering you a lifeline and you threw it back in his face.

A lifeline?

His plan was to bring you back on board, that was the point of the meeting. Once you'd come in and explained yourself and got these snarl-ups in the accounts out of the way, he wanted you back in the reins.

I didn't realize, Dickie says slowly.

That's what everyone wants, Mike says, and smiles.

But look – he pats the papers on either side of him – don't worry yourself over it. I'll have a word with him, tell him you're ready to talk, we'll round up the accountant and whoever else and we'll hash out this money issue once and for all. As soon as that's cleared up, you'll be back in the driver's seat. And I can get back to my farm.

He looks brightly across the desk at Dickie.

Great, Dickie says tightly.

Big Mike stays looking at him for a moment. Then he says, Unless, of course, you prefer to leave things sit.

Leave them sit?

Leave them as they are, Big Mike says.

I'm not sure I follow, Dickie says.

Well, Dickie, I'll tell you how I see it, Big Mike says. Your father has got his teeth into these discrepancies, this hole as he calls it. But personally I wonder what the point is raking over the past. Any big company's going to have a bit of quicksand down in the files somewhere. That's just business. There are some problems it's not worth the trouble of fixing. It could be you and I both feel it's a historical issue that's best left where it is. In the past.

And where would that leave us? If we both felt that way?

In that latter situation, Dickie, I'd give your father my professional opinion that it wasn't worth the trouble. We should be focused on getting the business back on track. I feel your father with a bit of persuasion will see the sense in that.

Big Mike regards him benignly. A pen flips between his fingers.

And then, Dickie says.

We simply continue with the current arrangement. You still have a non-executive role. You still get paid.

And you?

I stay on as CEO.

His eyes are slate-blue and unreadable. He puts down the pen, folds his hands together again.

You stay on permanently, you mean, Dickie says.

Right. And I can see how that might stick in your throat, Dickie. In that case we drop that idea, and instead we get your dad back here and we all put our heads together and we do our damnedest to find out what happened to that missing money. Who knows, there may well be a simple explanation, once you shine a light on it.

At the same time . . . Mike swivels his chair again, looks up at the ceiling. You and me go back a long way, Dickie, I feel like I know you pretty well. I remember when you were up there in Dublin, in Trinity College, with the best of the best. I wonder what kind of life you might have had, if you hadn't of been dragged back here. Maybe this is one of those situations where you stop and ask yourself, Well, hold on here, do I *want* this position back? Or is this one of those door-closes-a-window-opens situations?

Dickie doesn't say anything to this.

Big Mike puts his elbows on the desk, leans in confidentially. I'll be honest with you, Dickie, I need this job like a hole in the head. I've plenty to be doing without taking on a business of this size. But if I'm in a position where I'm able to help your father out, and do you a favour too – it gives me genuine pleasure, to be able to do that.

Very noble of you, Mike.

He rocks back, smiles nostalgically. I've always admired your family, Dickie. The Barneses. I remember the first time I saw you, do you believe that? Maurice was dropping you off at school in that beautiful sedan he had – it was red, about the size of a gunboat. You and Frank came climbing out of it, like princes visiting the colonies. You were different, a different kind of people, I could see it even then. Skiing holidays, cruises, walking around the place in clothes you'd bought in New York City. Even with what happened Frank, God rest him. Awful as it was, when I seen you come out of the church, all of you in black, there was a glamour to it, you know? I thought to myself, There's something about this family. Watch these fellas, Mike, pay attention now. This is how you do it.

XI

Of course, in the eyes of the world it is a disaster. To be kicked out of the family business – to lose the job he'd been groomed for since he was a child! He doesn't know how he's going to explain it to Imelda. Still, as he steps back onto the street, Dickie feels like jumping for joy. His father is gone. The missing money will stay an unsolved mystery in a ledger on a drive. And Dickie's secrets too will remain buried in the past.

The sun falls on his face; the breeze lifts, it seems to blow through him, as if he were a tree, an infinity of rustling leaves. The town – the humdrum little town, with its hanging baskets and window boxes, its shrine to Our Lady and concatenation of pubs – gleams with a rain-bright innocence. He almost lost it, he thinks. He almost lost everything. He tried to reignite his dreams and he nearly burned the whole house down. Well, no more of that. Nothing could be worth that.

He walks away from the garage without knowing where he's going, plotting how he can be a better husband, a better father, a better man. For starters, he will take the family on holidays. He can use the last of his savings, find a destination not even Cass will be able to resist. Somewhere eco-friendly, some farm in Italy where you pet llamas and pick grapes. And then, when they get home, he can think about work, figure out what to try next. Maybe he could start again at the garage, work his way up. Or something new? He has contacts, a reputation still. Leasing? Or get away from cars altogether?

That's for the future. Today he should celebrate.

On a whim he calls in to Toomey's bakery, studies the cakes under the glass counter. There is a magnificent Victoria sponge, but he thinks

Imelda would be more impressed by the chocolate torte. He can already hear her ask him, suspiciously, What's the occasion? And he will tell her, Quit the garage. She'll freak out. But she'll be pleased, in the end, he knows it.

He selects the torte. Nora Toomey sighs and hisses and grunts as she lifts it out from under the glass, as though she's hefting girders. He has never understood how you can spend all day surrounded by cakes and remain in such misery. She places the torte in a box and begins to tape it up. Because it has many elaborate creamy layers, this is a slow, painstaking business. As he stands there rocking on his heels, the little bell over the door jingles merrily – making the old woman wince – and in walks Victor and asks Nora for a breakfast roll. I'm serving this gentleman first, she tells him, pointing to Dickie as if she'd never seen him before in her life. Take your time, Victor says.

The glacial cake-boxing resumes. Victor clears his throat, shuffles his feet. Dickie is confused. Somehow he had not envisaged Victor in his new life. For a moment he grins glassily at nothing. Then finally he turns to him. Well, Victor?

Well is fuckin' right, says Victor. That fuckin' thing nearly done for me.

Nora glowers at him over the counter. Dickie struggles to take his meaning.

E. coli, Victor says.

Excuse me? Dickie says.

In the water, Victor says. Spent the last three days on the jacks. I near shat myself inside out.

Behind the counter Nora lets out a hiss. Begging your pardon, Victor says.

She hands Dickie his box with pursed lips. He pays her, wonders if he can extricate himself without further conversation, then notices Victor is carrying his gun under his arm. I had to bring the van in to the garage, Victor says morosely. I bollixed up the suspension coming out of the woods that time.

A scud-missile of memory: Victor driving the van through the forest, hitting trees, lurching over ruts, the juddering exacerbating the riot in Dickie's bowels until—

Oh, Dickie says.

Left it with your lads just now, Victor says. Be a couple of days. He pays for his breakfast roll, then turns for the door. Thought I might see you up there, he says, in a way that to Dickie seems pointed. Has he been looking for him?

They go outside, stand for a moment on the footpath. Dickie doesn't especially want to continue the conversation, which can only lead to the status of the Bunker, but he feels at least partly responsible for the van. You'll need a lift home, so, he says. Aye, Victor says. Right, Dickie says.

They proceed in silence to Dickie's car, and then drive in silence.

Sorry I didn't call you, Dickie says eventually. I had a few things to take care of.

Victor chews his roll impassively and keeps his eyes on the road, as if he knows what Dickie is going to say, and is refusing to give him any excuse not to say it.

Finally he bites the bullet. About the Bunker, he says. I've been thinking.

Victor shakes his head. She'll not fly, Dickie.

What won't fly? Dickie says, surprised. You mean the Bunker?

No, Victor says obscurely. He stares out the window, takes another bite from his breakfast roll.

Why not? Dickie says, while feeling like he oughtn't. The water?

The water's only the start of it, Victor says. Again he does not elaborate. Dickie is irritated. But he does not let himself be drawn in. He leaves the new road, heads into the bogland. The fields are brownish and grazed down to stubble: here and there moth-eaten sheep stare out at the car with eyes that bear a family resemblance to Victor's.

It doesn't matter anyway, he says. The fact is I've decided not to proceed any further with the build. He pauses, tries to interpret Victor's chewing. I just had a meeting with Big Mike, he goes on. About the dealership. I'm standing down as chief executive for now, so – so—

He breaks off. The point of this was supposed to be that he would no longer have time to work on the Bunker. But he can't remember how this made sense. So I'll be starting a new job, he declares. The details are to be decided, but that's what I'll be focusing on.

Right, says Victor.

You might not think that makes much sense, Dickie says, after everything we've been saying about, ah, the future—

Right, here, Victor says urgently, and the tyres screech as Dickie swings the car around. They rattle up a lane and come to a stop by a tiny cottage. It is stained with damp and might be taken for a ruin only that it has eight or nine CCTV cameras attached to the wall, aimed in every conceivable direction, the road, the trees, the sky. A television aerial lies forlornly on the ground like a symbol of something. The windows of the house have been covered with black fabric.

For a moment they sit there in silence. Heat mounts inside the car, even with the windows open.

This is your house, isn't it? Dickie asks. Oh ah, Victor says. The silence resumes.

I'll pay you for your work, of course, Dickie says. He turns to Victor with a desperate smile. I do appreciate all the effort you've put in.

Victor doesn't speak, or move, just continues to chew on his foul-smelling sandwich, his glassy inhuman eyes fixed on the horizon. I'll need to pick up my gear, he says at last.

Right – right – of course, Dickie says. Whenever is convenient.

There's a fair lot of gear, Victor says. I won't have the van back till Thursday, he notes.

Do you want to go over and get it now? Dickie says.

Victor shrugs, chews. But then he says, I don't like the thought of it just sitting there in the woods.

Fine, Dickie says, starting the car. This is the last time, he tells himself. After today, it will be done.

He decides to call home first to put the cake in the fridge. Otherwise it will be sitting in the car for hours while they pack up Victor's equipment.

He's hoping he can get in and out undetected, but as soon as he pulls into the driveway PJ comes out to greet him.

Stick that in the fridge, there's a good lad, Dickie says, handing him the cake box.

What is it? Is it cake?

Yes, it's cake.

Why are we getting cake?

We just are, Dickie says. Come on now, off you go, I'm in a hurry.

PJ turns away, but then turns back. Is that Victor in the car? Are you going back to the Bunker?

We're just picking up a few bits and pieces.

I can help if you want? PJ says.

We're only staying a minute, Dickie says, but then gives up. Oh God, come and help, so. But put away the cake first. And don't tell your mother.

PJ goes inside with the cake. Dickie gets in the car and drives back towards the ghost estate.

As he parks up and they set off into the wilderness again, his mood lifts. Green light falls in dapples around them. He turns to Victor, stomping resolutely through the bracken and asks him, in a half-teasing way, why he's lost his faith in the Bunker.

This, for starters, Victor says. He stomps his foot. This fuckin' road.

A road? says Dickie. It's a dirt track. Barely even that. Leave it a week and it'll be covered in weeds.

A road or a track or whatever you want to call it, someone's been along it and someone will be along it again, Victor says. The site where we have it is too exposed.

It's in the middle of a wood, Dickie says.

It's too exposed, Victor repeats. I never liked it and it was only the convenience of having it half-built already made me put the well there. And look where that got us, he adds.

It's academic now, I suppose, Dickie says.

They arrive at the clearing. PJ, coming on foot from the house, has got there before them, and is examining his seedlings to see if they've grown. Victor does not greet him. He pulls up a cable, winds it back into its reel. Then he goes to the well head and begins to unscrew the hand pump. Everything he does seems aimed at Dickie.

So what would you do? Dickie says. Scrap the whole thing?

That's what we're doing, isn't it.

If we weren't. If we were continuing on with it.

Start over, Victor says. Go further out. He straightens, scans the impassive face of the treeline. Up there maybe. He points to a brake of yellow sycamores, with more sycamores rising behind them. Find a new aquifer. Dig a new well. Leave no tracks. This time no one knows where you are.

I don't think that's even our land any more, Dickie says. Victor shrugs.

Dickie scans the sycamores. Further out, he thinks. For one ecstatic second, he feels himself swept up in the forest, distributed through it. Passing from tree to tree, a spirit.

You mean start all over again? PJ says.

Hush for a minute, Dickie says.

You'd keep this here, Victor says, patting the well head like you would a good dog. But as a decoy. Then you could rig up a tripwire on the approach maybe. Or in the doorway. Either way, you're watching from up here – he traces an arc with his finger from the Bunker to the sycamores. So anyone coming in has got his back to you – totally exposed.

Who's exposed? PJ says. Exposed to what?

Stop interrupting, Dickie tells him.

You could go underground, even, Victor says, staring into the hill.

But you didn't want to use trucks, Dickie reminds him. And you'd need a digger for that, at the very least.

Where there's a will, there's a way, Victor says. You could make it bigger in that case.

Could you set up a Faraday cage? He remembers Victor mentioning this before. If we had the space?

What's a Faraday cage? says PJ.

For an EMP? Victor says.

What's an EMP?

PJ, says Dickie.

Electromagnetic pulse, Victor says. From a nuclear bomb exploding mid-air.

Why would a nuclear bomb explode mid-air—

PJ, Jesus Christ!

Are we starting a new bunker?

You're not starting anything, Dickie says. You've got schoolwork to do. The boy's face falls. Dickie looks at Victor. Victor looks at Dickie. Then Dickie's phone begins to ring. It's Imelda. He answers but the signal is bad. All he gets are querulous fragments, phonemes of complaint embedded in static. He hangs up, but she calls again, and the same thing happens. Fuck, he says, then glances at PJ to see if he heard, which of course he did. I'll just run back and have a quick word with your mother, he says. Tell her where we are.

I'll come back too, PJ says.

No, you stay, Dickie says.

There isn't really anything to—

Stay, he says. You two lads will be all right here, I'll only be a minute.

He doesn't want to have a whole long rigmarole with Imelda, but of course that's what it turns into. She asks what happened at the meeting. He tells her it was nothing – at this point he has almost forgotten about it. But that just leads to more questions. Why did Maurice make such a ruckus about him coming in, if it was nothing? Did he say when Dickie might start work again? So Dickie has to explain that his father wasn't actually there, that he had left this morning.

He's gone? Without even saying goodbye? She is shocked, and that's before he gets to telling her that he won't be going back to work at the garage for the foreseeable future. What does that mean, the foreseeable future? It means never, he says, losing his temper. Never.

At this she just starts to cry. Dickie withers inside. He puts his arm around her, blathers a few vague words meant as consolation. He wishes that she would just take his word that this is a victory, not a defeat, that the future which to her at this moment appears dark and frightening is in actuality awash with light and possibility. He begins to get frustrated, being pushed back into this box where he has to evade and utter half-truths. Finally, he disengages, tells her he needs to get back to Victor. Victor? she repeats, eyes narrowing. He tries to explain that Victor's there because they're striking camp, they're literally shutting it down, but she won't listen, keeps castigating him, and before long, there in the pristine kitchen with his fresh start and his vows to be better, he finds himself snapping back at her, until in the midst of the frenzy she stops — freezes. Where's PJ? she says.

I left him down there, he says.

On his own?

Victor's there, he says.

After that there is no talking to her. She is screaming, she is throwing things — she throws the beautiful chocolate torte! That is Imelda in a nutshell, you try to make her happy and she seizes on one tiny little detail she doesn't like and uses it to immolate everything. He begins to clean up the mess, but she chases him away, tells him to go and find his son and get him away from that freak of nature.

He stamps back across the meadow, his good mood ruined, his fresh start in disarray, ready to give PJ an earful for leaving the cake out on the counter. That's when it comes to him. A voice, a soft counselling voice. *Further out*, it says.

Further out, he thinks, and in his mind's eye he sees the yellow sycamores.

Imelda was wrong to worry. The forest is quiet and peaceful. He arrives at the clearing to find Victor and PJ squatting side by side, working together on something. PJ has his back to him; Victor is addressing him in a steady, clear voice. Instructing him. Drawing closer, Dickie sees something glint in his hand, and over the boy's shoulder he catches a glimpse of something red. Now PJ turns his head and looks up at his father. Dickie recoils. The boy's face is alabaster white, with an expression of exhausted horror. On the tarp before him Dickie sees a tiny carcass. A gooey string of guts issues from its middle; two black globes gleam at Dickie, bright and agonized.

Showing the young lad here how to field-dress a squirrel, Victor says.

His bland eyes address the trees to either side of Dickie. The bloody knife gleams in his hand. That's enough for now, Dickie says. He reaches out a hand to the boy. It's okay, he says. PJ stares at Dickie deathly pale, as if he is about to pass out. Slowly he gets to his feet, but he doesn't take Dickie's hand. Instead he keeps looking at him, or past him, with the same unreadable expression – revulsion, horror, something else too – incredulity? Realization? Then, with his back very straight and his hands held wide by his sides, he walks out of the clearing in the direction of the house.

Dickie watches till he has disappeared from view. Then he hears Victor say behind him, The car's loaded up if you want to drop me back.

And Dickie, still looking but now only at trees, the implacable facade of the trees, says, What were you saying about going further out?

AGE OF LONELINESS

I

CASS

The lecturer has piercings all over and writes their name as *jj*, two small j's. Beside you as jj tells Junior Freshman Introduction to the Novel about complicity Elaine is on her MacBook updating her Instagram. She has a piercing too now, a septum ring, when she gets drunk it skews off to one side so it looks like a big metal booger.

Junior is so patronizing, Elaine says. And why is it *Freshman*? Why isn't it Fresh*woman*? Or Fresh*person*?

And who says we have to be fresh? you say. What if we're stale? It should be Staleperson. Age-Nonspecific Staleperson.

I'm serious, Elaine says.

I know, you say.

From the lectern jj says, We must ask ourselves, is language racist?

They've got a happy hour in the frozen yoghurt place, Elaine says.

Outside the sky is tin-coloured, the wind seizes Elaine's hair and tosses it up so she looks for a moment like Medusa, a beautiful Medusa surrounded by golden snakes. She laughs, scoops the strands away from her face. Crazy weather! she says. You turn down the tunnel to the street but she hangs back. Let's see if the others want to come, she says.

You eat at the frozen yoghurt place and/or the Thai noodle bar around the corner almost every day, because the cooker in your house doesn't work. The dishwasher doesn't work either. The washing machine worked briefly, then stopped. The heater in the kitchen gives off a powerful smell of burning hair but no actual heat; sometimes the house gets so cold that you think it must be haunted, that there's no way it could be this cold naturally. What's it going to be like in the winter? you wonder.

I actually don't notice it? Elaine says, though she is still wearing her coat and earmuffs. Anyway, she reasons, we're hardly ever here.

It's true: there are so many parties and 'balls' in these first weeks that you almost never get home before 3 a.m. Instead the days and nights seem to roll into one sleepless blur of strangers and free wine. The girls have fringes and bangles and vintage coats, the boys have memes and conspiracy theories and talk about their music software. How intimidating it would be to come here on your own, to have to account for yourself over and over. But you are not on your own; you are with Elaine. The first thing she did on your first day was to point to Front Arch, which is actually a little arch set inside a big arch, and tell you it looked like a vulva.

In Front Square you dally through the Freshers' Week stands and smile enigmatically at the recruiters clamouring for your attention. You are new, you are in demand. The world is a garden of flowers turning their faces towards you. You join the Literature Society, the Sci-fi Society, the Japanese Culture Appreciation Society, Players, and go to their inaugural events – or don't, instead meet a bunch of people on the way in and form a new plan on the spot to go elsewhere. You meet other students from your course and have breathless, over-excited conversations with them that flurry into the air like cherry-flavoured vape smoke. By the third night you are greeting them like long-lost friends: Kit from London, Sophie from Vienna, Zack from New Mexico. You've got to be careful who you talk to in the first weeks, Elaine says. Otherwise you'll find yourself stuck with, like, a German theology student with armpit hair for the rest of the year. But so far she is confident that you are speaking to the right people.

You don't tell them where you're from. You wonder if you weren't there would Elaine make up a lie. But when someone asks how the two of you know each other, she will take your hand and swing it and tell them, Cass is my oldest friend. And she'll reach out to caress your hair. Isn't she beautiful? she'll ask, with a note of challenge, and everyone will turn in surprise to look at you.

Sometimes though you stay in. One night you watch an entire season of *Friends*, curled up together under a duvet to stay warm. Another time the two of you redecorate the bathroom with paint you find under the stairs. The paint is bright pink. I feel like I'm in an intestine, Elaine says.

One night for fun you both join a dating app to look at the freakshow, as she calls it, and spend four hours hilariously, agonizingly, swiping your way together through at least a hundred available boys.

Look at the size of that guy's biceps! Wow, he is super-proud of those.

Ugh, that hat.

Rapist.

Clown.

Serial killer.

Another rapist.

I like his dog, though.

Of course you like his dog. He's using the dog to distract you from his rapeyness.

Dweeb.

Garden gnome come to life and now working in finance.

All of this guy's pictures he's wearing pink, if he was standing in our bathroom he would be invisible.

OMG, *that* is literally the most terrifying man I've ever seen.

Have my own business with van – great, perfect for disposing of your body.

Have my own bone saw.

Have my own alibi.

That's a nice dog, though. I would actually date that dog.

Me too, they should have an app for available dogs.

It's like a never-ending sleepover. It's like those nights when you would stay up messaging each other only now it's in person for real. Your fingertips burn from the ice-cream tub. Whenever you think that this is your life now your heart bangs against your chest like you're on a rollercoaster.

She tells you things about herself you never knew. For example, when she was thirteen, she became obsessed with body hair. Every morning she would get up an hour before her parents and wax her arms. She did this for months, then one day she set the microwave wrong and gave herself a second-degree burn. Look, she says, and shows you the scar. How have you never seen it? Another time she got second-degree burns was when she spent fourteen hours in her garden wearing nothing but shea butter. It was because of you, she says. I saw you in church and you'd just come back from the Dordogne, and you had this beautiful all-over tan? Me? you say. It was before I knew you, she says. You are shocked. You don't even remember going to the Dordogne. You don't remember the time before you knew her.

When he was drinking, she says, her dad used to hit her mam. They'd fight because she thought he was cheating on her. Sometimes he'd walk out. Other times – pow.

You don't know what to say. He always seemed so nice, you tell her. Like – he's always been nice to me.

He probably wants to fuck you, Elaine says, and reaches for the remote.

Some of the country girls go home at the weekends to 'get away from the rat race'. You both agree that this is totally the wrong attitude. You've spent your whole lives trying to escape your town. Now you're going back every Friday to use the tumble dryer?

Anyway, it's not that bad here. Even if it was, Elaine says, she'd still take a rat race over a warzone.

Her parents are fighting; she thinks her dad might be cheating again.

At least cheating is normal, you say. My dad's quit his job so he can turn the Bunker into some kind of prepper man-cave.

What bunker? Our Bunker? Elaine says.

Yeah, you say.

WTF, she says.

You show her the pictures PJ has sent you. He says it's in case there's an apocalypse, you tell her, so the family has a place to go.

Random, Elaine says.

I don't care if there's ten apocalypses, you tell Elaine. I'm not going back there.

The light of the city is pale, silver blue – sea light. Your house lies under a flight path, and the air resounds with a constant low boom like a slow-motion explosion. The street is composed exclusively of cottages just like yours, and so is the next street, and so is the next and the next. There are no trees. One morning you find a leaf on your doorstep, and you look up and down the road trying to figure out where it came from.

I don't miss them, you say. But it must have been so weird for, like, my dad? He'd never even been to Dublin before, he didn't know anybody here. Didn't even have a phone! It must have been like being catapulted into outer space!

You imagine him young and lonely in the treeless streets, wishing that he was home. Maybe that was how he had his accident – daydreaming that he was calling in to Crossan's dairy for milk, not noticing the traffic as he stepped off the kerb.

On the way to Dublin he kept talking about the past, like when you were this perfect little person, before you went bad. He acted like the last two years simply hadn't happened, like you had gone straight from doing your climate change project with him in the kitchen to here, now, your new life at Trinity. To listen to him you would think that he was the one who had made it all happen, though you know for a fact Granddad is paying the rent.

He basically told me he wished he'd never had children, you tell Elaine. He said there was nothing for me at home any more, like in so many words.

He's probably still angry about you passing out at that dinner, Elaine says. As if it's nothing to do with him that his daughter is an alcoholic.

You like hearing Elaine say that he ruined everything, that everything that's wrong with you is his fault. When he calls you don't answer, send him a message later saying you're really busy.

There are two hundred people studying English. By now you've met nearly a quarter of them.

There is a girl called Chan with a tongue piercing that she runs constantly against her teeth in lectures, making a sound like a rattlesnake.

There is a boy called Darl with no appreciable personality traits who is nevertheless working on a collection of autobiographical essays.

There is a person called Kit who identifies neither as a girl nor as a boy and calls you Castaneda, for your chestnut hair and *because you are a traveller into the beyond*.

Boys these days have looked at so much porn they're warped by it, a girl called Kady says in your Feminism seminar. They're either terrified of actual women, or else they see us as kind of 3-D porn simulators where they can do all the stuff they've seen online.

Elaine agrees. I'm so over men, she says. Or she says, I haven't *personally* experienced abuse? I'm just sick of the whole male thing.

But then other times when you're on your own she'll say, Can you imagine *licking* a *vagina*?

*

There's a boy, Caleb, who has a tattoo that reads I MYSELF AM WAR and who works part-time at a vegan café called Hella Beans. Caleb makes things up and 'reports' them on his Twitter. For instance, he'll say that he knows a guy who works at the Westin hotel, who told him homeless people are booking rooms there when they've finished begging for the night. They make so much money they won't stay anywhere less than four-star. Some of them actually fly into Dublin from their homes in affluent parts of England.

What's the point of that? Elaine says.

Because then all these online racists start re-tweeting it, Caleb says. And the next thing you know they're saying it back to you. He looks at his phone and laughs. People are so stupid, he says. He refreshes his feed. Just watch.

One night Imelda rings you up to tell you Sarah Jane Hinchy got a late acceptance to MIT.

What does that mean? she says.

Another time she calls with the news that your old English teacher Ms Ogle is in hospital. Apparently she was in a car accident, but she came out of it unharmed, so she lit a candle in her bedroom to thank Our Lady for saving her and the curtains caught light and her house burned down.

Elaine listens without reaction as you pass on these bulletins. When you ask if she thinks the two of you should visit the teacher in hospital, she says, Frankly, I'd be happy not to hear about anyone from that place ever again.

Except me, right? you say jokingly. Elaine doesn't answer.

Except me, right?
Except me, right?
Except me, right?

But the next day she tells the story to the others. We were so obsessed with her, she says. She had all these catchphrases, remember, Cass?

Mellifluous, you say. *Memorious. Abundance. You girls are the future!*

Oh my God, Elaine says, with a laugh. Then this one time she was out sick and the substitute teacher was this super-hot poet and me and Cass both totally lezzed out over her. Didn't we, Cass?

You don't say anything: you can feel heat climbing your cheeks, up to your ears.

Like we were such kids we didn't even realize it was happening, Elaine says. It was just, suddenly we both decided we really really wanted to be poets? I would have jumped in a volcano for her, she says. Then, with a sudden sobriety, she adds, But she preferred Cass.

She did not, you protest. Why do you think that? Because she gave me a prize for that stupid poem?

It was obvious, Elaine says. Everyone could see it.

I couldn't see it, you say.

You never notice when people like you, Elaine says. And for a moment it seems she holds your gaze, and the college, your friends, drop away: like she has fixed you on the point of a spear.

Do you write poems? Kit says to you.

No, you say.

The dating app is full of codes and symbols.

A unicorn is a girl who is open for hook-ups with couples.

Ethically non-monogamous means you're already in a relationship but it's not cheating.

143 means I love you.

Cosplay latex cishet mermaid open-minded polyamory no-strings bears hedgehogs WAKAH

How do people know all that about themselves? Like, how do they know all the stuff they're into?

Elaine seems confused by the question. How would you not know? she says. How would you not know what you were into?

Like, say if you'd never seen a burned person. Would you know you were into them? Or would it be like, one day you see a burned person, and you're turned on, and after that you're always looking around for burned people, so you can hook up with them?

Yes, Elaine says, and then, That's a bad example.

It's just a part of being modern, she says. Like, it just means you don't have to accept what society presents you and that's that. You can choose. Try things out.

Right, you say.

It's just the modern world, she says again.

You imagine being modern: someone unafraid, unabashed, browsing the endless midnight warehouse of desire, its shelves piled high to the roof, to pick out the package that is uniquely and comprehensively you.

Professor Davis wears a gown, his hair is like ancient candyfloss. He is supposed to be teaching you *The Faerie Queen* but instead has spent two full lectures on proper punctuation. The modern generation seems to believe, he says, goggling down at you sardonically from his podium, that incoherence is a virtue. And any sort of clarity is a kind of fascism. He pronounces it *fass-ism*. No wonder you are so confused about yourselves, he says sadly.

Darl calls him the Grammar Nazi. You joke that he is having a secret affair with jj, an S&M relationship where they take turns to tie each other up and yell pronouns at each other. He she her him! Ze zir bun tree!

Caleb thinks Professor Davis has a point. Why should you get to make up your own rules of grammar? What if everyone did that? It would be chaos.

In Chinese they don't even have pronouns, Kit says. They seem to get by okay.

But what if I suddenly decide I don't want to be objectified in people's sentences any more, Caleb says. So I don't let anybody call me *you*? Or *him*? Only *Caleb* or *I*.

Why is all this such a big deal to you? Elaine says.

I'm sorry, you're objectifying me, Caleb says. The correct way to phrase your last remark is, *Why is this such a big deal to* I?

That guy is such an idiot, Melissa says, when Caleb has gone off to band practice.

He's hot though, Sophie says.

On the way to Dublin, Dad said, You're lucky, your generation doesn't hide things the way mine did.

What sort of things? you said. But Dad didn't seem to hear.

I have to tell you something, she says that night in the bar. Her green eyes fix you seriously. Something big.

Your heart thrums like hearts are surely not supposed to. Oh yeah? you say.

She takes a deep breath. I'm changing my settings, she says. From boys, to boys and girls.

She watches you take this in, you watch yourself take it in, mouth ajar, the whole of you vibrating like you're a tuning fork that's just been struck against the universe.

Oh wow, you say.

I wanted you to know before anyone else, she says. Because you're my best friend, and I know you'll understand.

I do, you say, or you try to say, but the words get crushed at the back of your throat. A smile is rising through you, there are tears leaking out of your eyes, and now your heartbeats come so fast they're a blur, like your heart is a hummingbird with flickering wings crashing around inside your chest. That's great, you say, that's really great.

And when you leave the bar she takes your hand and you run together across the moonlit square, spiriting over the cobblestones like nymphs, ethereal and beautiful. In your journal later you write *noctilucent gibbous* and *The She* which is or are the fairy creatures that haunt the land according to Aunt Rose but the name makes them sound like some magical omnipresent Girl and you can feel her around you, her moon-shine skin and her dark night-starred body.

In the morning you wake early and watch the dawn gather around you. You imagine it as a bowstring and you as an arrow, drawn back in the tightening light until at last you are fired from your bed. Today is the day! No more messing around! It must be today! You put on your leggings with an irresistible sense of purpose, go to seek her out, to tell her exactly how you feel.

Prostitute.

Hat.

That hat's insane. It's like a satellite dish.

Dog – I can't believe girls are pulling this dog shit too.

Trashy.

Yes! God, put some clothes on!

Her too. So much boob!

Her boobs are pretty amazing. Although I don't think they're real.

I don't think *she's* real. I'm starting to wonder if *anyone* on this is real.

The undatable ones are real.

You get up to see if the ice cream has thawed. After the ice cream you will tell her. From the couch you hear her say, No way, that guy Caleb is on this.

In the pictures he's wearing a rainbow-coloured Afro and Groucho Marx glasses. He lists his hobbies as suicide ideation and bocce ball. Such a dick, Elaine says, and then, I'm going to match him just to fuck with his head.

At the Poetry Society's magazine launch the wine comes in plastic glasses. Caleb says it tastes like petrol. Yeah, Elaine says, olden-days petrol when it still had lead in it. You're not missing anything, she says, and pats your hand.

On a dais a girl is reading a poem inspired by *an affair with an older man that I later realized was abusive.*

To her right on a table the trays of radiant liquid call to you, like a choir, a choir of your best friends that sings to you so beautifully and doesn't understand why you won't come.

I was a flower, the girl says. You were a botanist. I was an hour. You were a horologist.

Jesus Christ, Caleb says.

You should do something like that, Cass, Elaine says. I bet they'd print it.

They print anything, Caleb says.

Beside you her fingers interlaced with his.

There are days that simply don't *happen*, even when you're in them. The buildings are papier mâché, the people are extras, you feel like you're trapped in a filler episode. Throw coffee in someone's face, wave your tits at the lecturer, jump in front of a car – by tomorrow it will all be forgotten. But in the moment it is endless, like crawling through the desert.

Though you never want to see them again, still sometimes you can't help thinking of home, imagining what they might be doing there right now. You see Mam yelling at Dad to come and change the TV channel for her because she's just done her nails and can't pick up the remote and it's stuck on some programme Dad's recording about genocide. Upstairs, PJ blasting Space Nazis or making a biosphere out of Lego. Beyond, in the darkness, the swoosh and silence of the trees, the fucking trees.

One evening as you're leaving the library you get a call from Elaine. You're not coming back now, are you? she says. It's a question that is undoubtedly loaded, but you can't figure out how. Then she explains that she's making dinner for Caleb. It's our two-week anniversary, she says.

Oh, you say.

Obviously I'm not saying don't come home! she says. But, like, if you could give us some privacy for even a couple of hours.

No, of course, you say.

Sorry, I know it's short notice, she says.

No no, not at all, you say. Two weeks!

Yeah, she says.

You feel a sting at the suggestion that you have been intruding on their privacy. Also you wonder how she can possibly cook dinner, given that none of the appliances work. But you won't say any of that to her, because you are the one who always understands. But what will you do now, Cass? When you are tired with nowhere to go?

The answer is surprisingly simple. This whole time you've been at college you haven't had a drink. After you fell at Granddad's dinner Elaine made you promise. But it was only ever to humour her, wasn't it, not because you thought it was something you needed to do. She isn't here now and anyway who cares.

Night has fallen, faces bob over the drizzle-slicked cobblestones of Front Square with their phones held before them; if you half-close your eyes they look like will-o'-the-wisps – a community of will-o'-the-wisps, leading each other into the nth level of confusion and errancy. Open them again and you see a couple of people you know walking the same way, and you hurry over to join them. They're going to the Hist, though, not the bar. Someone is speaking about climate change. Come along! they say.

Dad was always telling you about the debating societies at Trinity and the *brilliant crack* he'd had there. Maybe that was why in Freshers' Week you didn't join either of them. If it ever gets to the point where we have nothing better to do than go to a fucking debate we might as well just drop out, Elaine said. But now you follow the others into a grand hall that's like something out of *Lord of the Rings*. On a stage a group of students in actual black tie, looking super-pleased with themselves. A big crowd has gathered; there isn't room for the three of you to sit together, so you tell your friends you'll come find them afterwards. It doesn't matter, they weren't actually your friends. Who are your friends, really? You tell yourself to shut up, suck it up, all you have to do is sit here and that's another two hours killed without drinking. By the time you get home maybe she and Caleb will have gone to bed. You'll still have to listen to them having sex though weirdly that's not as bad as making conversation with them.

Around you everyone is talking and laughing. You take out your phone and scroll through it. You think inadvertently of Dad, try to picture him sitting here on the bench in a dinner jacket. But nothing comes: it is impossible to imagine that part of his life.

The speaker is a politician, very bald with a shiny head and thick glasses. You used to follow him during your environmental phase but you've never seen him in real life before. He fumbles around with his papers for a while and then looks up. It's nice to be back here, he says. When I was in college I used to be a regular speaker at the Hist debates. I learned a lot about how to irritate people.

Everyone laughs at this and you find yourself smiling. His lips are weirdly pretty.

I'm here to talk to you about climate change, he says, which is another something that really irritates people. It irritates us because it makes us feel guilty. It makes us feel like everything we do is bad, that *we* are bad. And that's a real problem. If there's one thing I've discovered in my time as a campaigner, it's that blaming people is absolutely the worst way to motivate them. Make someone ashamed to their core, tell them that their very being is inimical to life and the best thing they could do for the planet is die, then ask if they want to make a donation?

Everyone laughs again.

So climate change remains this curious phenomenon that we're all aware of yet simultaneously manage never to think about. We know the terrible things that are happening to the world, our world. We know the terrifying statistics – an area of forest the size of New York City cut down every single day, seventy-seven per cent of insect life destroyed, ten consecutive years setting new records for the highest temperature in history. We know about the billions of plants and animals that have already been killed by pollution and habitat destruction, the rising seas, the melting ice, desertification – we know all that. And yet we continue *not* to do anything to stop it, because the things that are *causing* it, the things we're doing that are making it worse – building buildings, taking planes, driving cars, eating meat, buying stuff, *having children*! – these are the very things that make us *us*. So we seem to be faced with an impossible dilemma: if we don't want to be killed by climate change, we have to *stop* being ourselves. You can see why people aren't exactly rushing to man the barricades. The thought of addressing it actually seems in some ways *worse* to us than being killed by it. Or put it another way, the thought of no longer being ourselves is harder for us to get our head around than the thought of being dead.

So how can we get our head around it? I'm going to propose tonight that one path towards a solution lies in a radical rethinking of what we mean by 'us'. By really looking hard at these things we think make us ourselves. Those two words, in fact, give you the gist of the argument. 'Things' and 'selves'. What do 'things' have to do with 'selves'? How can a thing make you a self? Before people had things, were they not selves? When you were born, when you first came into the world, with no iPhone, no car, no Nikes or Adidas or in fact running shoes of any sort – did your parents think you were incomplete? We have a faulty baby here? No. They thought you were perfect. You were stark naked without even the power of speech, and they thought you were the acme of beauty and perfection.

But that's not how *we* think of ourselves, is it? That's not how we're encouraged to see ourselves. Instead, we're taught to think of ourselves as flawed, inadequate, incomplete. Different in some way that is repugnant, that is unacceptable. We're taught that if we don't hide that difference away, we're going to be alone. Unloved. And so we learn to cover ourselves up, with products, labels, masks of one kind or another. Clothes, goods, sports teams, belief systems, politics, nationalism – things from outside that we use to represent who we are. I'm the guy who's a Marxist, I'm the guy with the fancy watch, I'm the guy from *this* place not *that*. When you look at me, that's what I want you to see. Still different to you, but in an understandable, categorizable way.

Back when I was a student here, twenty years ago, I was a master at this kind of cover-up. You wouldn't have guessed that from talking to me. I was out, which was not so common at that point. People thought I was brave, and in a way that was quite true. This was a time when gay men, or men who looked gay or were suspected of being gay, regularly got beaten up. Nevertheless, my bravery was built on a foundation of fear. Because what really scared me wasn't that people would see I was *gay*. It was that they would see I was *me*. Even if they *hated* me as a gay man – or a Trinity type, or a Protestant, or whatever it might be – that was far, far better than that they should see the real me, who I believed was repulsive, shameful, unlovable. So my sexuality became a tool I used to distract attention away from myself.

And for a long time it worked, the persona worked. I was a champion debater. I was known and loved, or at least known, all over campus, I was a fixture on the gay scene. I was primed for a lucrative career at the bar, making iconoclastic noises while getting filthy rich. I had it all figured out. What ruined it? No, not hate crimes, not prejudice, the opposite. Yes. I fell in love.

I fell in love with a man, another student here, and it didn't work out. For lots of reasons. I don't need to go into them. We were young, it shouldn't have been a big deal anyway. Not at this time of your life, right? Isn't that what you're always told? But it was a big deal, and afterwards, I was devastated. I dropped out of college, I was – well, imagine the worst place that a person can be, and that was me.

The man pauses, he bows his head. The light shines off it into the darkness. The hall is totally silent. I can't tell you how strange it is to be back here, he says. That's the past, isn't it. You think it's behind you, then one day you walk into a room and it's there waiting for you.

The point is that after this relationship ended, I felt like I had nothing. I looked at my life and there was nothing there that I believed in. My debates, persuading people about things I didn't care about, my persona as a hilarious queer with fourteen pairs of Louboutins, the games, the masks, the whole carefully curated illusion – it just didn't work any more. None of that could get me through this. If I was going to live – if I was going to stay alive another day – I realized I had to let the world in. I had to be part of something real, and to do that I had to let people see me as I was. The thought of it horrified me, because the truth of myself horrified me. It was like coming out again, only a million times harder. But I didn't have a choice.

I joined a walking group. I'd always loved nature, but I'd kept it a closely guarded secret. Just the idea of being seen in an anorak! But I started going out with this group every Sunday. Sometimes during the week too. They were mostly retirees, and really there was no point me trying to impress them with my repartee because half of them had hearing aids. But there we were in the Wicklow mountains and it was . . . sublime. Just me and the world, feeling that the world was good, and people were good. And to cut a long story short, that's when I started getting interested in the environment, the countryside, the city too, how we can preserve it. And that's when I started to see just how huge and terrifying the problems are that we're facing.

At the risk of sounding narcissistic, it strikes me that the point we're at with climate change is not so different to the point I was at after my bad break-up. That is to say, we're at a moment where either we make a serious change to the way we live, or we destroy ourselves. The science is not ambiguous. If we don't face up to reality, we're not going to make it. And to face up to reality we first need to set aside all of these inventions and disguises we've been so busy accumulating. We need to take off our masks.

And that's hard, after a lifetime of hiding away, it's existentially hard, take it from me. But once you do it, the world is transformed. Once you take off your mask, it's like all the other masks become transparent, and you can see that beneath our individual quirks and weirdnesses, we're the same. We are the same *in being different*, in feeling bad about being different. Or to put it another way, we are all different expressions of the same vulnerability and need. That's what binds us together. And once we recognize it, once we see ourselves as a community of difference, the differences themselves no longer define us. That's when we can start to work together and things can change.

Maybe that sounds hippyish or fanciful. The sad truth is that right now, at the worst possible moment, we're being deluged in new ways to hide. So let me be clear. Togetherness is crucial, if we're to tackle something as total as climate change. Banging your own little drum, demanding everyone look at your mask, be it a consumer status symbol or one of sexuality or race or religious belief or whatever else, that will do no good. Division will do no good. You may gain some attention for your particular subgroup, there may even be minor accommodations made. But you are moving the deckchairs on a sinking ship, diversity deckchairs. Global apocalypse is not interested in your identity politics or who you pray to or what side of the border you live on. Cis, trans, black, white, scientist, artist, basketball player, priest – every stripe of person, every colour and creed, we are all going to be hit by this hammer. And that is another fact that unites us. We are all alive together in this sliver of time in which the human race decides whether or not it will come to an end. As the poet says, We must love one another, or die. And from bitter experience I know that you can't love when you're wearing a mask.

So, as a first but crucial step towards fighting climate change, I'm going to invite each of you to make contact with your neighbour. As an expression of our shared identity as humans living in this moment in time, which differentiates us from all the humans who have come before – as an expression of our hereness, if I could ask everybody to turn to their right, and place a hand on their neighbour's left arm. Trigger warning, if you don't like touching or being touched. Just ease into it, you might find you actually quite enjoy it – yes, that's it, you don't have to speak, just turn to your right –

He looks around the room, filled now with a rustling. You feel a soft hand land on your left forearm as you lay your own hand on the left sleeve of a dark-green puffa jacket: then to your surprise the jacket's owner's right hand falls upon yours. You look up to tell them they're doing it wrong: and find a pair of bright blue eyes looking back at you.

Her eyes are blue, her hair is too: it falls in oily blue-black waves to just above her shoulder, putting you in mind of an operative at a mermaid canteen. Her skin is pasty and she has a smattering of acne on one side of her chin.

She put her hand on yours *because I am sitting at the edge of the aisle, so I have no person at my right side*, she explained to you in an accent that turned out to be German. She is from Dortmund, here on Erasmus, studying to be a priest. *She's exactly the person that Elaine warned you about*: that is why you have stayed to talk to her after the lecture has ended.

Now the two of you are outside, sitting on the stone steps of another grand building whose purpose you do not know. Merle – that is her name – is giving her opinions of various things, with a conspicuously un-Irish candour. Some of this candour is charming, for instance when she notes that the moonlight on the cobblestones is very beautiful – an observation, it saddens you to realize, that no one you know, including yourself, would ever make out loud. Some of it is irritating, like when she tells you that she was surprised to meet you at the talk, because *when I see you at the lecture theatre, you are always hanging around with the 'in crowd'*. She adds finger-quotes here, like, in fact, a priest. But you are always at the edges, she reflects, possibly in mitigation. Then she reaches into her rucksack, plunging in all the way to her shoulder. Would you like an apple? she says. And you take it and tacitly forgive her for her previous comments, because anyone who doesn't know it is uncool to have an apple in your rucksack is not to be feared but pitied. The rucksack is also uncool. You have never noticed her at your lectures.

People can surprise you, you say through a mouthful of apple.

Yes, she says, and then, During this talk, you were crying.

Oh yeah, you say. It just reminded me of my dad.

He is dead, your father?

No, you say. I mean, not as such.

She looks at you blankly. Then she says, I think I have misunderstood?

No, I just mean, we used to be really into that stuff, for a while. He still is, but.

That stuff – you mean planet earth?

Well, yeah, whatever, you say. It makes me think of him. That's all. To change the subject, you ask why she came to Ireland, and she tells you about reading Heinrich Böll's diary of his time living on the west coast. In Germany, this is a very famous book, she says. Many people have come here because of it. But Ireland is very changed from his description. There is a lot of pollution, bad traffic, shops selling the junk food.

You shrug, though you find this observation annoying.

People don't seem to care, she says.

People care, you say. They just don't want to show it.

Why would they hide what they care about?

I don't know, you say. Because of what he said in the lecture. Being scared. Wanting to look normal.

Why is it normal to have pollution? she says. Or traffic jams? Or—

Maybe they're afraid that if they show they care about it someone will take it away, you blurt. Maybe this is a country where for centuries if you cared about anything someone would come and take it away.

Oh, she says.

It's not fucking Germany, okay?

Okay, she says quietly.

Anyway, this is just the city, you say. If you go out to where I'm from, it *is* green. My back yard is a forest. And it's beautiful.

Clouds pass across the moon. A group in wizard hats traipse noisily over the square. You are trembling. Beside you, the girl clears her throat. You have freaked her out, now she's going to run for it.

But instead she says, Would you perhaps like to go for a beer somewhere?

Can you be attracted to someone who is not attractive? Even with her

512

coat on you can tell the girl is pudgy and you think you can get a faint whiff of BO. And yet when you look at her looking at you all kinds of words come into your head – words like *minge*.

Okay, you say. The both of you stand up. She is casting about her for somewhere to put her apple core when your phone begins to ring.

Oh, wait a sec, you say.

I just keep putting myself out there! I keep putting myself out there, and then letting myself get hurt! Her face crinkles up and a fresh wave of tears bursts forth. Why am I such an idiot! she sobs. What is wrong with me?

Shh. You smooth her hair back, her golden hair. She wipes her eyes, huddles her body up against yours. Why is it so cold? she whispers. Is it always this cold in here?

Caleb and Elaine, in their two weeks together, had never discussed seeing other people. Elaine had assumed they were exclusive. Caleb apparently believed the opposite. In the course of their anniversary dinner, it emerged that for the duration of their relationship he has also been having sex with a girl from his Physics class. He told Elaine that he wasn't sure but he thought she might be up for a threesome.

You came straight away. Merle had looked crestfallen: her head dropped, her lank unclean hair dipped around her face. You said you would call her but you could tell she didn't believe you. You left her there with the apple core in her hand. It was nice to meet you, you said, departing.

And it was, it had been: you had felt, talking to her, like a veil had been lifted, like something was beginning. But in the taxi home you found, in the midst of your alarm, a strange sense of imminence; and when you entered the house and found Elaine prostrate on the couch, and you turned her over and she looked up with her face pink and bloated, tears spilling laterally in opposite directions towards her ears, for a moment you seemed to see again that same glimmer of a veil being lifted and you felt a shimmer of excitement, of something about to begin.

I'm so sick of guys! she exclaims now, but half-laughing this time.

They're incapable of love, she says.

Her head rests between your thighs, her golden hair spilling over your lap. Her hand rises like a flower from the soil and splays its petals to caress you. Thanks for coming back, she says softly.

It's okay, you say. I wasn't doing anything. She nods; her fingers brush your cheek, as if it were you who was crying. Her eyes starbright. You're my most beautiful friend, she whispers.

And for a moment the two of you are silent, stroking each other's cheek, brushing away tears that are not there. Her gaze on yours, nothing between you, she is here, you are here, and beneath your gaze her hereness resolves, deepens, like a veil has lifted delivering her up to you, and though she doesn't move she seems at the same time to unfurl, to fluoresce, and her liquid lips part and her liquid mouth is ajar and seems to call yours down upon it, stroke stroke goes her thumb on your cheek, stroke stroke goes your thumb by her liquid incarnadine mouth, and her head is on your lap and within your lap is a sea, a sea that is balanced on a point, and if that point should shift if it took a single touch it would spill out of you and drench the whole world

You move your hips just slightly just ever so slightly as if to tell her that's all it will take just one touch

the sea poised there on its point ready to flood the world soak it in rainbows

just a single touch to release it that's all she would need to do

that's all it would need just

just that

DICKIE

You become pure presence. You are diffused among the trees, in the ground, the air, the water. You wake every morning in a clearing damp with dew, leaves glistening around you, ferns and bushes still vigorously growing, reaching out of themselves: all is changing continuously, and yet you feel outside of time, released from it, living instead in a single verdant moment. Every day the earth seems new, you too are new.

You see, what you felt on the footpath outside the showroom was only the beginning. It's out here, among the trees, on your third day or your fourth or your fifth (you quickly lose any sense of the calendar) that you realize the truth. There is no need for you to return to the garage, to work your way back up the ladder, to regain your father's trust. That life is behind you. The story is over, the debt is paid, the darkness of those years dispelled. And the person that remains, the man here in the woods – is you.

The first task of your new life is to seek out a fresh site: trekking back and forth taking levels, hacking away at the weeds and brambles to disclose the forest's secret topography, its hidden slopes and hollows. You work side by side, stripped to the waist; you get sunburned through the trees and through the clouds. At last Victor settles on a spot. To you it doesn't look like anything until he shows you: it offers a clear sight of the Bunker and of the track but can't be seen from either. Even as you stand there looking, you can't understand how that's possible. It's like magic, you think; like an enchantment that has been waiting there in the land.

The Hide: that is what you call this new construction. The greater part of it will be underground, with windows or portholes just above ground level, like a birdwatcher's hide. But it puts you in mind too of the hide of an animal, as if you were wrapping yourselves in a beast's pelt. The Bunker was limited by its existing walls, which you did not want to disturb. Here you can have as much as space as you manage to excavate. The plan is to dig a rectangular hole big enough to fit a shipping container. Cover it with soil, let the undergrowth return, no one will ever find it.

It strikes you that Victor can *see* things that other people don't. Maybe it's because of the strange alignment of his eyes: he doesn't look *at*, but past, or beyond. He sees a road where there are only ferns and thickets, he sees a hill where the land to you appears flat, he sees water where you see only parched earth. He looks at the muddy gash you've scraped out amid the knee-deep weeds and sees a citadel, and, inside it, you and your family together. When he sets to work on it it's as if he's merely painting colour onto something that is already, invisibly there.

In the morning you drive PJ to school. You must come down and look at the dig later, you say. It's going great guns.

He keeps his eyes fixed on his phone.

There'll be a lot more space, you say. You'll have a room to yourself. And Cass. You should come down and have a look.

Again, he does not reply. At the school gates he says, Maybe Mam should bring me in tomorrow.

You miss him around the place. At the same time, the work goes quicker without him there – without you having to worry about him falling into something, or off something, or on top of something. It is easier to talk too. The Siege of Leningrad, the Great Leap Forward, the Famine in this very country, on this very ground. People digging up graves to eat corpses. Now imagine the whole world like that, Victor says. Billions of people on the brink of starvation, who'll do anything to survive? It'll make the Holocaust look like fuckin' Ladies Day at Ascot.

You find these stories oddly consoling – cosy, even, like listening to the rain fall from a warm bed. It's as if for you the shit has already hit, the flood, the famine, whatever shape it takes. Outside, the world has drowned, and the desolation swaddles you like a blanket.

Most evenings, once you've finished eating you head together into the trees. Another advantage of PJ's departure is that the squirrel cull can resume. Victor has upgraded his rifle with a silencer, so the noise won't reach Imelda, and with a thermal-imaging scope, so you can hunt after sundown.

He gives it to you to put to your eye: out of the darkness, you see animals blaze forth as lurid orange-pink-yellow blobs of life. You find this disquieting at first. Their light is so bright, so small amid the vastness of the surrounding dark.

It's only later that the thought occurs to you of a major disadvantage to hunting at night. What if it's not a grey? you say. What if it's a red? How would you know?

There are no reds, Victor says.

Initially you're back and forth to the house a couple of times a day, to pick up bits and pieces and fill up on water. Once Victor has made his repairs and the well is useable, your visits become more irregular. In fact before very long stepping out of the forest and going into the house comes to feel weirdly like playing a video game. You watch the walls and furniture track past you, you watch your hands float through space, reaching up in front of you and grasping things in the cupboards which then follow the hands down through the air. When PJ appears or Imelda it's with the same sudden, bewildering luminosity as the squirrels in the heat vision scope. Similarly, on your way back into the woods you experience the strange dissonance you used get as a boy, when after switching off your computer you'd find the movements and colours and cues of the game world still imprinted vestigially on the real. But it lasts only a few minutes and then you forget.

Victor has bleached the pipes, and the well is safe to use. Safer than what's coming out of the fuckin' tap at home, anyway, he says. If it tastes a little different, that's because it's not full of fluoride and whatever else the government's putting in it. Certainly you have never felt better. Though on occasion as well as feeling wonderful you *also* feel dizzy, confused, feverish. Ever since the bug in the water. An odd sense – how would you put this? – that something (or someone) is living inside you.

At the hardware store people don't recognize you, shy away from you. It's the beard, Gertie McDowell explains to you, waving her hand in front of her face. Not just that, it's the whole . . . what would you call it, that look.

Sitting in the van on Main Street afterwards you watch the townsfolk go by. Rhona Gaffney waddling along with a shopping bag full of frozen quiches. Antony O'Connor at the traffic lights, scratching his balls.

Look at them, Victor says. Who of them has a single thing they can offer? Who of them is anything but a pure bloody drain on resources?

They are like toddlers, he says, toddlers crying for their bottle.

They're not *bad*, you say.

Victor turns to you, his eyes gazing ironically at the dashboard to your right, the murky depths of the van on your left. You think these people believe in anything? You think there's a single principle they wouldn't drop if it meant ten minutes off their commute?

He points out the window. What about that? he says.

The dark wall of the deserted convent looms over the van. Baskets of bright flowers have been hung along it at intervals.

In the centre of this town, he says. Women locked up from girlhood until the day they dropped dead. And nary a word spoken against it.

That was before, you say. Things have changed.

They change, Victor says, and then they change back.

People know what's going on, he says. People are capable of anything.

Maybe every era has an atrocity woven into its fabric. Maybe every society is complicit in terrible things and only afterwards gets around to pretending they didn't know. When the kids ask, tell them that no one meant any harm.

On the walls of the shopfronts, on Fegan's butchers and Extreme Internet and Wickham's Elegant Antiques, you can still make out the tidemarks from the flood. A once-in-a-century event – that's what you were told. Then came the drought, and that was once-in-a-century too. Maybe that's how it will go – instead of one definitive cataclysm, a series of 'anomalies', each time lasting longer, with the stretches of what you call normal life becoming further and further apart, until one day it dawns on you that this *is* normal life now – the flooding, the empty shelves, the candlelight, the networks down, the impassable streets, the sewage in your living room, schools closed, work closed, because what use is work now? Selling cars, selling golf holidays, selling apps to deliver coffee to your desk, all those things are gone, all the invisible people you never met but spent your days talking to on the phone or tweeting or emailing or messaging, they are gone too, and instead you spend the day crossing and recrossing the same ground, the sinking besieged ground of home . . .

And the prospect fills you with a kind of joy.

The world, the fallen world, will fall away. The toxicity that you were part of, that you made them be part of too, will be gone. The four of you will be *de-worlded*: no more schools, news, internet: instead only the straight reality of the four walls around you, the sky overhead, the food you have grown from the soil.

Now if Cass says, When you heard the warnings, what did you do? you will reply, I built this.

One night after a video of a man showing you how to grow micro-vegetables a video comes on of a man telling you about signals embedded in social media to turn children trans and after that a video comes on of a man talking about phones. People think their phone is their best friend, he says. Well, guess what?

The next day Victor goes into town and comes back with a pair of walkie-talkies. Perfect for short-range comms, he says. These'll still work when the networks go down.

It makes sense, you say. Especially when the phone signal out here is so bad.

He holds up a Ziploc bag containing his phone. I've wanted to do this for a long time, he says. He puts the bag on the log then hits it with the hammer. It is the same hammer he used on the squirrels. He hits it over and over. Finally he lifts the bag. It's full of broken pieces of glass and plastic. Try eavesdropping on that, he says with an air of triumph.

He hands the hammer to you. Oh, you say.

You won't regret it, Victor says.

Yes, you say. You see the point of it, certainly. At the same time, what if one of the kids wants to call?

But they don't call, Victor says.

He shrugs, picks up a spirit level. Up to you, he says, and ambles off into the bushes. You take out your phone and put it on the log and look at it. You keep thinking of the squirrels and the sack and the hammer. It's not alive, you tell yourself. It's not your family. You wouldn't be cutting yourself off. If anything you'd be doing the opposite. How many thousands of hours have you wasted staring into it? Consuming illusions?

You raise the hammer over your head, just to see what it will feel like. It feels thrilling, intoxicating. The sheer craziness of it makes you want to do it. You adjust the phone on the log so it is laid out in front of you like a sacrifice. Are you going to do this? With a surge of exhilaration you think that you might – you actually might!

And then the phone begins to ring.

Of course if you're about to destroy it you should just destroy it, regardless of it ringing. But that is not what you do.

The number is unfamiliar. You pick up. Hello?

Hello, boss-man, the voice says. It's been a long time.

IMELDA

The rushes at the lake's edge high as your head The lane crowded with hawthorn blossoms The meadow behind the ruined abbey where the jackdaws line up on that one tree

The old haunts are just as they were Unchanged As if they have been waiting for you to return The thought makes you dizzy like the years are rising up over you Waves crashing against a sea wall higher and higher

He puts his hand on yours What are you thinking he says His voice is low and gentle

I used come here before you say

And you never thought you would come again did you Now here you are

You meet in the daytime when PJ is at school

If Dickie asks though he never does you tell him you are going for a drive It seems less of a lie that way for driving is what you do out towards the hills the forest the lakeshore waiting for the moment when from some plain little turn-off or lay-by you will see in the mirror Mike's car appear behind yours His lights flashing up Hello

And then following you along winding byways you haven't been down in years not knowing exactly where you are going Feeling like you are sewing the thread of yourself into the green hills Your heart racing your mind turning turning

Till you come out in a valley or on the crest of a hill in a blinding chorus of sun The gods of love Flashing up at you Hello

And in the light you both slow down to a stop

*

The first time you only talked About Dickie furthermore as though to prove it was all in innocence

I am worried about him you said He is behaving strangely you said Mike raised his eyebrows like he hadn't noticed like it wasn't the talk of the whole town

It's that garage you said It's his whole life and he's cut off from it now and it's plain to see he doesn't know what to do

There's plenty of things he could do he said A man of Dickie's intelligence

Oh yes he says he'll do this and do that but he's at sea it's plain as can be It wasn't just a job for him He gave up everything for that place everything

Hmm he said frowning tapping his head

The two of you sat side by side in his car looking out at the lake

If there was a place could be found for him you said Something he could do in there

And Mike heaved a sigh I'd love to Imelda believe me The thing of it is though that I don't call the shots I'm only a whatdoyoucall caretaker It's Maurice who makes the decisions and Maurice unfortunately at the moment is not well-disposed towards Dickie

Nor towards me either Not these days

No he shook his head No Imelda that's not true He has no grudge against you You're only an innocent bystander It's Dickie has brought this down on himself

And you got a shock at that The way he put it Is it that bad you said and he made a sort of a grimace

It's not great he said I'll be honest with you But listen to me Imelda I promise you this While I'm in there I'll see to it you're looked after You've no need to worry while I'm in that garage nor Dickie either

Thank you Mike I do appreciate it you said and you opened the door and went back to your own car as though that was the only reason you'd come out to see him Started the engine but then turned it off again and climbed back out and went back to him and leaned in the window

How come you're so good to us you said just to see what he'd say

He was quiet a long spell

There were some hard times when I was a boy he said And the Barneses were very generous to us I never forgot it he said I swore some day I'd pay them back

Yes Just like you he grew up without a penny His father was a drinker Used beat us with his rosary beads he says And I'll tell you it was divil and all Our Lady or any of the rest of them bothered to do about it

Sometimes the chain broke he says and the four of us had to go scuttling around the floor trying to gather up the beads With my father roaring down at us all the while trying to kick us stamp on us It was comical in its way I suppose he says But in his eyes there is only sadness

You couldn't blame him he says Them times would drive anyone to drink Working as a day labourer Castrating pigs and emptying septic tanks Christ Is that how any man imagines his life will be And never enough money to feed us for all that

You are at the edge of a yellow wood Birds are singing The world seems abundant with riches

Trapped in a hovel in Piggery Lane he says My sister and I used drink mud he says We were that hungry sometimes we'd get jars of water and mix in mud and drink it We thought it had vitamins in it It's a wonder we didn't each die of typhus he says and he laughs Though his sister did die you happen to know though it was years later and not typhus but leukaemia

But you say only Piggery Lane that's where Maurice grew up

It is he says But he got out

You got out you say

He looks at you with his grey-blue eyes He smiles Sometimes I wonder he says

There was one winter he says and we had nothing to eat Just nothing for days on end He laughs again To think back on it now it seems impossible like another country but that's how it was And my father there was no sign of him and my mam sent us out to knock on people's doors for milk or teabags whatever they might have I'll never forget he says He looks out at the bright leaves The shame of it

Yes No you did not forget that either Going out on the beg In the van crying A few tears were no harm Daddy thought Bruises though were too much Bruises scared people They might start asking questions or call the guards

On streets you'd never been before you and Lar hand in hand while Daddy and the boys waited round the corner in the van If they ask you inside go Daddy said If you're inside they'll have to give you something

Strangers' gates Strangers' houses The clamour of strangers' televisions behind the net curtains Getting up on tippy-toes to press the doorbell Your heart in your mouth yet you never thought of turning back for scary as it was nothing was as bad as the thought of returning to the van empty-handed How old was Daddy then Not old Not as old as you are now But he seemed like all the monsters from all the fairy tales rolled into one a wolf a devil a troll a witch a haunted castle a sea a mountain

Though also sometimes a roly-poly jolly giant who'd let you bounce on his tummy If you could only work out how to make him happy

And so you rang the bell

The people in those houses Mike says and he shakes his head God knows looking back I'm sure they had it hard themselves but Jesus they'd make you feel this small

Yes people the people the ghost of their faces twitching at the living-room curtain or there above you in a glimpse before the door slammed

Shouting from inside Don't open it it's the tinkers Dogs barking Stones thrown Men standing there grim-faced telling you not to come back here

Or inviting you in

Touching your arm Stroking your hair Well aren't you the pretty miss Come inside and tell my fortune I've a cupboard full of good things Your brother can wait out here

Only ever giving you their garbage Sour milk Scraps Black bags of clothes that didn't fit any of you a broken toaster a radio-controlled car with the aerial broken off Maybe you can make something of that

In the back of the van Daddy scrabbling through it would roar like he'd been gored by a bull Throw it out the window as you were driving home stick his head out to swear at the car horns honking behind

I remember very clearly going up the Barneses' driveway Mike said They were decent Whenever we'd call to the house Maurice always made sure we'd get something Dickie was in my class of course

He closes his eyes tight

I'd rather have died Imelda that's the truth seven years old I remember it clearly saying to myself I wish I could die right now rather than knock on this door

He looks down as if gathering himself and when he raises his head he is smiling again

Compared to those days we're on the pig's back he says Even with our ups and downs

But when you've been through something like that he says You never really feel like it's over

And he turns to you looks directly at you Do you he says

You tell him things you never told anyone

The stories come pouring out of you like a dam has burst From him too stories Then somehow they join together into a river

You tell yourself it isn't wrong because he's helping Dickie though you don't believe it

You tell yourself that it is not he making your heart rise up and fly away it's the blackbirds it's the forget-me-nots it's the rye grass brushing up against the old stone wall

A pine-tree air freshener dangling from the mirror St Christopher medal stuck to the dashboard

Afterwards you drive away in separate directions

And Dickie?

You find yourself trying so hard to be nice to him that one day you give yourself a nosebleed Any time you have to talk to him for more than five minutes you think you will either punch him or scream

It's like he's the one cheating You don't understand it The rage

He's growing a beard I see Geraldine says It's a new look what would you call it the woodsman look Palaeo

You don't know You don't look He comes in like some beast-man out of the mountains tries to make conversation You must come down and see what we've done he says or We must go up one of these days and see Cass Smelling like Victor Dirt on his hands like he's been digging a grave *Doing the dirt* you think A wave of horror rises up in you and it takes everything you have to smile like a mam in a TV ad and say I'll just go and check on the oven

You ought to be worried about him but there isn't room in your head Your mind is like one big pile of Jenga bricks and if it gets one good prod the whole thing will come tumbling down.

Sometimes you do genuinely go for a drive just yourself as if that will make the other times less of a lie

In the Touareg you can drive for ever and stay cool Drive out to the edge of town and beyond it into the country the yellow hills sloping up to meet the blue sky Oak trees on the crest At the crossroads a shuttered pub a blackened sign Guinness Time the country gazes back at you like a mirror with nothing in it

The last time you were here it was winter Cass was a baby Burbling in a snowsuit in the car seat behind you You'd wanted to see had they

Could they really have They could And they had You'd known straight away without even needing to stop the car Something about the colour of the garbage in the yard You'd known they were gone even before you saw the notice slapped on the door

Today the garbage is gone the shell of the car the mattresses all that The yard is paved over The sheds knocked The walls painted white You would think you had got the wrong place only that Noeleen still has her gnomes lined up next door

As you are looking a man comes out in a singlet with biceps like melons Foreign-looking Fierce Scowling left and right Then a little girl dances from the house after him and he breaks into a smile

She is blonde isn't that funny You've half a mind to get out and tell her you were once a little blonde girl in that very same house

And when you grew up you married a prince and now you live in a castle with horses and bluebirds

The cottage is otherwise Weeds coming out the windows Branches poking through the roof Poor Rose She would be living there yet if she could Smoking and listening to the radio amidst the dandelions and the mice

You reach the turn for Naancross You wait there Another empty cross-roads in the ticking sunshine

Then you turn the car around Go back the way you came

I love Joan he says I always will love Joan But she is from a different world to me

Someone who hasn't been there could never understand he says If you've never seen your father beat your mother with a plunger how you could ever understand

Now I like the fine things as much as anyone he says More maybe But at the end of the day they don't mean that to me Snapping his fingers That's not what I was praying for when I hid up in my room When I ran down the street buck naked to escape him That wasn't what I dreamed of What money I have now what wealth what nice things if I'd had them then God knows I'd have piled them up in front of him Take them they're yours I'd have said Only please

Please

He sinks his head in his hands A grown man

You lift it up again push your lips against his Your tears flow down his cheeks You put your head to his The hair falls around the two of you like a curtain Hello you say Hello

CASS

Today is the day! No more messing around! That's how every morning starts. The pattern is well established by now. You wake up telling yourself *it has to be* today, that you're *definitely* going to do it today; then you spend the next sixteen hours trying and failing to summon the courage.

If you could skip ahead to the end of the day and see that it hadn't happened, that wouldn't be so bad. But no, you have to live through each moment one by one, a succession of vertiginous cliff-edges that you charge towards then at the last second shy away from. On and on, up and down, the exhausting flux of emotions locked tight inside you, like a rollercoaster in a prison.

Does Elaine have any inkling? You thought that night on the couch that you were on the brink of something, and when you revisit it in your head, which you do twenty thousand times a day, you still think, you're almost *sure*, you were. But then why would she show no sign of it afterwards? Is she still waiting for you to make a move? Is she punishing you for not making one? Has she lost interest? Or did you imagine it all?

If there *is* something there, then this is undeniably your best-ever chance. Since she broke up with Caleb, she's sworn off dating, to the point of deleting all the apps from her phone. At lectures, she sits with you in the front row, wearing reading glasses and a forbidding expression. At home in the evening, she sits beside you on the couch holding a heavy book about gender while looking at her WhatsApp. Your job is to tell her how impressive her new regime is, and to ply her with ice cream; she has already put on a couple of pounds, which you find almost unbearably erotic.

For the moment, she is all yours, but you need to act swiftly before someone else appears on the horizon. If only you could know! If only she'd give you some kind of a sign!

But nothing becomes clear, and the cowardly part of you tells you that by confessing you risk losing everything, while what you have with her now – where you hide your feelings but get to share her life – may be the best you can hope for. Stay quiet, it tells you, and there's no reason why you shouldn't go on like this the whole way through college.

As the weeks go by, though, something changes. *You* change. You find yourself getting annoyed with her, exasperated, snappish. Little things you barely noticed before begin to infuriate you. The way she leaves her food in the fridge and her dishes in the sink until they literally grow mould. The way she complains relentlessly about her father, his dishonesty, his violence, then meets him in town and lets him buy her earrings. The way she takes up Twitter causes (military rule in Egypt, non-Mexicans wearing sombreros) and then forgets them the next day. How *weird* she is. Sometimes you wonder if there is a single thing she does that is not in the interest of making somebody, somewhere, like her. She buys trending books and carries them around and abandons them without ever having opened them. She asks you if her jumper is too non-non-binary. One morning, not much after 7 a.m., you come upon her at the kitchen table, eating carrot sticks and gazing expressionlessly at her laptop, as on the screen a girl with a ball gag in her mouth is fucked simultaneously by two men.

You're concerned. It's nothing new for you to be disgusted with yourself. You're used to that, you're fine with that. But the disgust seems to be spreading outwards to absorb Elaine too. Now when she tells people that she has a peanut allergy, you interrupt to say you've seen her eat literally thousands of peanuts, and gloat as she stammers and backtracks and says that it comes and goes. You ask her to *stop fucking telling people* you're a recovering alcoholic. You argue with her, you contradict her, you bait her, even as a voice inside you goes, *Stop! You're ruining everything!*

Quickly the toxicity spreads from Elaine to everything else. One night you are in a club with a group of your friends. The music is loud, they have used computers to make the singers' voices sound like those smoothies that come in a tube, sugar masquerading as fruit, something edgeless pretending to be good for you. By the cigarette machine, Elaine in her reading glasses is deep in conversation with a boy. You're on a banquette drinking a cocktail that cost €18. The girl beside you is talking about climate change. Specifically, she's saying that she intends to travel as widely and see as many places as she can in the next few years, because sooner or later long-haul flights are going to be banned.

You tell the girl that that is the most monstrously stupid and selfish thing you've ever heard. It's like saying you want to hunt elephants because some day they'll be extinct, you tell her.

I'm not talking about hunting elephants, the girl says. I'm talking about seeing the world. I have one life. I want to see as much of the world as I can.

You're killing the world, you say. You're killing the world because you don't want to be bored.

What's the story with your friend? the girl says to Elaine, who has arrived back.

The city itself becomes toxic. The only animals you see are pigeons and whatever's been run over outside your house. Walking in to college one morning, you meet a group of schoolchildren being led into the park. Before we touch the trees, the teacher says, let's all put on our latex gloves.

*

In a taxi one night the driver tells you that he's heard for a fact that so-called refugees are staying at the Westbury hotel.

You go to class and discuss famous poems. The poems are full of swans, gorse, blackberries, leopards, elderflowers, mountains, orchards, moonlight, wolves, nightingales, cherry blossoms, bog oak, lily-pads, honeybees. Even the brand-new ones are jam-packed with nature. It's like the poets are not living in the same world as you.

You put up your hand and say isn't it weird that poets just keep going around noticing nature and not ever noticing that nature is shrinking? To read these poems you would think the world was as full of nature as it ever was even though in the last forty years so many animals and habitats have been wiped out. How come they don't notice that? How come they don't notice everything that's been annihilated? If they're so into noticing things?

I look around and all I see is the world being ruined. If poems were true they'd just be about walking through a giant graveyard or a garbage dump. The only place you find nature is in poems, it's total bullshit. Even the sensitive people are fucking liars, you say.

No, you don't, you sit there in silence like always.

You start skipping classes and just walking around instead. You are not looking specifically for things that will make you feel angry/sad/freaked out, but that's what you find. You make notes on your phone, so you don't look like you're trying to be a writer, just someone staring at a screen, like everybody else.

You go to buy a refill pad and on your way out of the shop you're snagged by a magazine you recognize from home. You wonder if Dad has got this issue: you imagine it sitting on the side table by the front door in its cellophane wrapper with the label D BARNES, or resting on the wing of the armchair, or shuffled with the other magazines and newspapers and paraphernalia into a pile on the island that Mam's always threatening to throw out the bloody lot of. But he cancelled all his subscriptions when the trouble began so you suppose not.

You leaf through it, begin to read an article about species die-off. A scientist is quoted saying that though many people call the current era the Anthropocene, which means the Age of Humans, he thinks with the widespread extinctions a better name for it would be Eremocene.

As you read, something hits you – a rancid odour, febrile, like meat left to rot. You turn and see the odour is coming from a person, a man. He is wearing a black leather coat that reaches almost down to the floor and underneath it black leather trousers and a black T-shirt or vest with a low neck that reveals clammy white gooseflesh and an upside-down pentacle. He has black storm-trooper boots and black fingerless gloves that are more like gauntlets, with studs on the back. He has long black curly hair, but it is dyed you can tell, and sits back on his head so the top part of his skull is naked, it may indeed be a wig. He is old. And just as you are telling yourself that it's not a crime to stink, to walk around the city in stinking black leather, even though you are old, you realize what he is doing. He is standing at the section for children's magazines, all rainbow colours and airbrushed happy anthropomorphic animals. He is staring through the different titles, methodically selecting one of each, one *PAW Patrol*, one *CBeebies*, one *Octonauts*, one *Dora the Explorer*, which he adds to a bundle he has already gathered to his pentagrammed chest.

Maybe he is planning to visit the children's hospital.

Maybe his nephews and nieces are coming to see him hundreds and hundreds of them.

You go home and sit on the toilet and cry.

We need to talk, Elaine says.

You pause, startled, in the doorway. She is sitting on the couch with her reading glasses on. She pats the cushion for you to come and sit.

We can't keep going like this, she says.

Like what? you say, innocently.

This, she says. She points above, around. In this *lugubrious atmosphere*.

I don't find it lugubrious, you say.

I know that after my break-up with Caleb I was traumatized, she says. And I worried that maybe I was bringing you down. But I feel like I'm over that now. I'm ready to move on. You still seem depressed. Even though you didn't break up with anybody.

Me, depressed? you say. I'm not depressed. Why would you think that?

She looks at you coolly. Lugubriousness is pouring from you like a bleak, invisible gas. It seems sometimes like you haven't really embraced being in Dublin, she says.

Really? you say.

You talk about the past a lot, she says. You talk about home, your family.

I talk about them critically, you say. I talk about the things there I don't like.

I feel like you're looking backward all the time, Elaine says. I sometimes wonder if being with me is stopping you from making new connections.

I'm looking forward, you say, trying to choose your words carefully while inside your head a huge mushroom cloud of dread ascends. It's just you aren't around the times I'm looking forward. When I'm with you I probably do look back a bit, out of habit. But I can stop? That's no problem. Just tell me when I'm doing it and I'll stop.

Again a long measured look from Elaine, intensified by the reading glasses. I just don't want you to be unhappy, she says.

I'm not unhappy, you say. I mean, I knew you were unhappy after you broke up with Caleb, so I've been quiet, you know, out of sympathy. But if you've moved on, then I'm ready to have fun!

Really? Elaine says, squinting at you.

Absolutely, you say, nodding. A hundred per cent.

Okay, she says. Well, in that case we should do something *big*. Like, to reset the narrative. For instance, I was thinking, maybe we should have a party.

Here? you say.

Yeah, she says. Like a housewarming.

Wow, you say. Every vacuous, posturing phoney you know right here in your house, inescapable.

That's such a great idea, you say.

Awesome! she exclaims, clasping her hands together. I was thinking maybe this weekend? Like, Friday night?

You wonder if this whole conversation wasn't something she planned beforehand to stop you saying no. But there is nothing you can do about that now.

Perfect, you say. Friday night.

DICKIE

Silence. The phone sits lifelessly in your hand. Or maybe you are the lifeless one, maybe you have been sitting here like a rock for a thousand years. Maidens plant garlands on you in spring, the action of the rain has made the shape of almost human features, the shape of eyes, a nose, a mouth unspeaking.

You were a fool to think he had gone away. Nothing goes away any more. Everything leaves its trace now, everything you do remains with you, hangs over you, building and building in a cloud of invisible poison till it has choked the life out of the very air you breathe. Your history.

Back at the site, Victor is waist deep in the hole, labouring in a wife-beater as if it's still the height of summer, though already the insects are thinning out and the early-morning cold lingers into the day, clinging to the opened earth like a shroud. Without speaking you pick up your shovel and set to work beside him.

Got that hammer, he says after a while.

Hmm? Oh yes, yes, you say. Didn't use it in the end.

Oh ah, he says indifferently.

Yes, right as I was about to, ah, I got a call. It was funny, because you'd said that no one ever calls.

Victor grunts, digs. Then, grudgingly, The kids?

No, just a chap I know. Having a bit of money trouble.

Looking for a loan, is it?

Something like that.

A friend, did you say?

A friend, yes. Or, we were friends at one time. I explained the situation with the garage. Told him I wasn't exactly flush myself.

How'd that go down?

He didn't like it, you admit. He got a bit . . . he's a bit . . .

Victor pauses, wipes his nose, rests his hand on the handle of the shovel. Putting the screws on, is he.

Oh no, I don't mean like that.

Victor says nothing. He is leaned on his shovel amid the heaped earth, watching you.

I might go to the bank tomorrow, you say, see if I can sort something out. I'd hate to leave him in the lurch.

You pick up your shovel and get back to work, pretending you don't feel Victor's gaze on you. I'm sure it will be fine, you say.

You told him the truth: you don't have access to that kind of money any more. You can make all the threats you want, you told him. Those days are gone. That's all there is to it.

You have till the end of the week, he said.

You're not listening to me. I can't get you your money! I can't get it! You can.

How? Where? Tell me!

That's not my problem, Dickie.

It is your problem! You need to find somebody else.

I don't need anybody else. Listen to me, Dickie. Friday night.

It's not enough time!

I call again Friday morning, give you the meeting place. When I have the money, then I will destroy the recordings. I promise.

You said that the last time. That's just what you said the last time!

I'm sorry, Dickie. My girlfriend, she's pregnant. You know how it is.

How do I know this is the end? How do I know you'll really do it this time?

But he only repeated, Friday night.

*

In the morning you go to the house. You find PJ in the kitchen.

Ah oh! No school today? A panicked thought occurs to you. It's not Saturday, is it?

It's an in-service day, the boy responds laconically. He sits at the table tapping at his phone. An empty cereal bowl sits in front of him; it gives the impression of having been there for some time.

Want to take your dishes over to the dishwasher?

Without replying, the boy gets up and sets the bowl on his plate and his cup in the bowl and carries them across the room one-handed, so he can continue to type on his phone.

What you up to there? Chatting to a pal?

The boy nods without looking at you.

Is it beyond you to speak in words?

PJ rolls his eyes, says stiff-armed, *Yes-I-am-chatting-to-a-pal.*

You're a real fucking wiseguy, aren't you?

The boy freezes, whites of his eyes showing. You shouldn't have said that. But Jesus, his capacity to generate conflict out of thin air! As if there wasn't enough trouble in the world! Hey, you say, changing your tone, I'm going into town in a few minutes, want to come along?

He doesn't reply. His eyes flick up to yours, trying to figure out what you want him to say.

We can get an ice cream, see if there's any new games in the shop?

Okay, he says neutrally, attending to his phone again.

Good man, you say. Ten minutes, all right? Is your mother about?

I think she's in there, he says, waving at the living room.

You don't go in there. Instead, you go up to the bedroom, in search of your suit. But that is where you find her, lying on the bed in her robe, on top of the covers. Oh, you say, excuse me, as though you had come into the wrong room.

She doesn't reply. She must be asleep. You take your suit from the wardrobe and go into the bathroom, hang it on the rail to take out the creases. You turn on the shower, but before you can get in your phone sounds. **Look Dickie, we're famous!** The link takes you to a porn site. In the centre is a black square, over it the title, *My Irish lover takes me hard*. You wipe steam off the touchscreen, press Play.

The clip seems to explode in your head without your actually seeing it. Instead it's like you've been catapulted thirteen seconds into the future. So you have to watch it again. This time you definitely see.

A man in a shirt, trousers pooled around his ankles, has another man bent before him over a desk. The man on the desk cries out obscenities, exhorts the other man. The other man does not speak, but he is emitting a low constant sound that oscillates between a gurgle and a wheeze. Both men have their heads turned so from this angle their faces can't be seen. From *this* angle; in *this* clip. A warning. Already it has been viewed eighty-eight times.

In the mirror you have almost disappeared behind the steam. You open your mouth wide, try to pull in air, like a fish. Then you stumble out of the bathroom and downstairs. It's not until you step outside that you realize you're not wearing your shoes. You turn around and go back inside.

The shoes are under the bed. You crouch down to retrieve them and find yourself looking into Imelda's eyes. She is fully made up, mascara, smoky eyeshadow, bright red lipstick. The violent green of her irises is offset by the limpness of her body. She looks like she has been kidnapped from a ball, drugged and deposited here. She gazes at you unblinking – no, not at you, *through* you.

Just grabbing my shoes, you hear yourself say – that is, you feel your mouth moving, your tongue thrusting against your palate.

Has she seen it? Has she seen the clip? She couldn't have, could she? Could she?

You sit at the end of the bed with your back to her and put your shoes on, then leave the room.

Find yourself in the car. The engine already running. Hear a voice from behind you. Dad? A boy is standing on the step. I'm coming too, right?

Did you ask him to come? Why would you do that?

Oh yeah, of course, hop in.

Beside you the boy is talking about games. You can't feel your fingers on the wheel. A car is coming in the opposite direction, you feel a sweat break out as it approaches. Blue Passat, it's Aidan Balfe. You sold him that car, threw in a sunroof. You raise a hand as you pass him.

He does not wave back. His bulging eyes fix on yours. *Eighty-eight views*, you think. The boy hasn't noticed. What's this stuff on the floor? he says.

Just something Victor was working on.

He is quiet for a moment, then he says, Dad?

Yes, son?

He has asked you something but oddly when you turn he is not in the passenger seat: that is, you cannot see him, though you can still hear his voice speaking. You don't want to alarm him, so you smile and nod as if nothing is wrong.

Park the car on the square. You still have to stop yourself from pulling in to the garage. As you get out Mrs Borrodale bustles by you. Good *morning*, Dickie, she says. The way she says it strikes you as odd, as if she might be concealing something. Across the street a boy with freakishly large ears stares at you, now there can be no doubt about that, he is staring at you! You bow your head, inhale through your nostrils, till your heart slows down.

Dad?

Gosh, I'm not with it at all today, am I. You grin at him. He smiles back uneasily.

I've to pop in to Gerry in the bank, you say. Why don't you head on down to the shop, I'll be with you in a few minutes.

Once he's gone you get back into the car, check yourself in the mirror. The suit is not new but still looks the part. A good suit will pay for itself, that's what your father always says. Take a deep breath. Across the street is the showroom. A spindly young man stands amid the gleaming cars looking at his phone – who is he, is he new? Is Big Mike taking on salesmen?

Don't think of that now. Eyes on the prize. Friday night. When you hand over the money, he will take down the video. In fact, once you *get* the money, he might be persuaded to take it down. Then all this will be over. Really it's such a short time between going into the bank and getting the money that it's basically over now! Rejoice! You put your best foot forward

. . . .
. . . .

find yourself back on the square. Telephone wires, grey clouds, angles, bookie's sign with cartoon horses. PJ holding your hand, looking down at you fearfully. Not just him either, everyone on the footpath has stopped to stare – gazing in a kind of horror as if you have just hatched out of a chrysalis. Have you? Check – no, you're still in the suit. A streak of dust on your thigh, you brush that off. All right, you say, with a wave. Just lost my footing. All good. You climb back up, get into the car. PJ does the same. We never got your game, you say. The boy just looks at you.

PJ

Here's something you've been thinking about lately: when things come back, very often they come back different, like they come back weird or wrong.

The best example of course would be *Pet Sematary*, which you watched in the bowling alley one time with Zargham on Zargham's brother's phone, where this family's cat gets run over and they bury it in this weird graveyard and then it magically comes back from the dead except now it's evil and attacks everybody but for some reason they don't 100 per cent get the message so then when their son dies they bury him there too and basically that goes even worse than it did with the cat. The moral of the film is that you can technically bring things back but it's a lot of trouble and at the end of the day you will probably wish you hadn't. Ghosts, similar situation, like it's different because nobody actually asks ghosts to come back, they just come back, but the point is that they act so insane when they do it's impossible to imagine that they were ever people. You could even sort of say it about oil, in fact that's what got you thinking about it because you were doing it in Geography about how oil is formed from tiny sea creatures from 150 million years ago, like plankton that were swimming around during the Jurassic, so in a way it's the total *Pet Sematary* thing of at first you pull it out of the ground and think *Fantastic this solves all my problems* but then after a while everyone realizes whoa, wait a sec, this miracle substance is actually annihilating the entire planet, which obviously the original plankton wouldn't have tried to do anything like that before someone decided to resurrect them.

So the big question then is how far gone something has to be before bringing it back becomes a bad idea.

Some people might say that the key problem is with coming back from the dead specifically. Because obviously death is a pretty serious step with all kinds of long-term effects that you're not going to just shake off. But lately you've noticed it with other things too, that even though they never actually died, when they came back from where they'd gone they were still completely changed. For example: when Cian Conlon lost his rabbit Oisin during the massive storm, and Fiach O'Connor found it a few days later, in his dad's boat in his dad's boatshed, and he knew straight away it was Oisin from Cian Conlon's posters, still, though it looked exactly the same, maybe slightly thinner, it acted like a completely different rabbit. It huddled in a corner of its hutch, it stared at you in this quite freaky unsettling way, it had developed this menacing snakelike kind of hiss. Till the question became unavoidable as Cian Conlon asked on his YouTube channel, Is this actually the same rabbit?

Because while the rational answer is like Cian Conlon's dad says, Yes, definitely, let's hear no more debate over that bloody rabbit, and although when you mentioned *Pet Sematary* to him Cian Conlon said he was pretty confident the rabbit hadn't died and come back to life, the fact is Cian Conlon's brother is scared of it and won't go into the kitchen after bedtime, because that's where they keep Oisin's hutch now, and he says it's not the same.

And you wonder if that would be the case for e.g. a person too, like say if there was a person who had gone somewhere – or maybe they hadn't even gone somewhere, say they were still nearby but something had happened to them so they were different – how different would they have to be for it to become a very bad idea to try to bring them back? Like, is it that things are just supposed to go their own way and you basically can't do anything to stop them and if you do it'll just make everything way worse? Or is it worth taking the risk? Sometimes? If you could still sort of see the person they were and you thought maybe there was still enough time, if you knew what to do or say?

One person whose take you'd be interested in getting on this would be Zargham. In the bowling alley when you watched it together you remember Zargham had some interesting ideas about *Pet Sematary*, e.g. how you could maybe use it *deliberately* to create an evil army of cats/ other creatures? He'd be able to tell you straight away whether this plan you're figuring out could work, and if not he'd help you come up with a new one.

But Zargham himself is different, has come back different. Since you returned to school after the summer break he doesn't talk about the things he talked about before (Nerf guns, Roblox, how to make a mech suit) and if you try he gets this weird look in his eyes and storms off. He's put fluorescent laces in his shoes and he's been trying to get people to call him Tyler, which you don't understand, Zargham is such a brilliant name, you personally would love a name that begins with a Z, and you've pointed out to him more than once how high its Scrabble score is, or would be if people's names were allowed in Scrabble. But he doesn't want to hear it, or not from you anyway. Instead he's hanging around with Dave Okinwale and Pete Barron, who have also done the fluorescent laces thing, which you have to admit looks pretty cool.

So that's why you're sitting here on a bench in the yard on your own, watching a seagull stick its beak in an empty bag of Hunky Dorys, trying to figure out whether your plan is a good one or if it's even a plan at all.

But not on your own, because when you glance up at the school clock to see how much break is left you find yourself looking instead at the pointed, smirking face of Julian Webb.

What's going on with your dad? Julian Webb says.

Hmm? you say. Lately you've become very good at this. Hmm? As in, Dad? That name does ring a bell, let me just check my records . . .

He came into our shop, Julian Webb says. The stink off him! Jesus. His bony face screws up.

Oh yeah, you say. Well, see, he's working on this project in the woods . . .

He's lost the plot, Nev says, materializing ghoulishly at Julian's side. He's gone nutso.

You let this go, you know Nev's still angry over the whole sister-fucking thing.

He had this dwarf with him, Julian Webb says with a gleam in his eye now, rolling his jaws together in enjoyment like a praying mantis.

Yeah, that's our builder, you say, as if this is a normal conversation instead of you walking into a mantis trap. He's not actually a dwarf, he just has bad posture.

Julian grins and says something you don't catch but Nev hisses with laughter behind him and it's the hiss that launches you off your bench.

You quickly realize that you're no good at fighting. The moves you've seen in *Avengers* and practised so diligently in the back garden for some reason don't seem to work in real life. Almost immediately you find yourself in a headlock getting punched. Then Mr Kennedy appears, exclaiming, Boys, boys! and pulls you apart. He makes the two of you shake hands. The bell goes for class. When the teacher's out of earshot, Julian says to you, You're going to wind up in the mental home, just like your nutjob dad.

IMELDA

Hello stranger Maisie says Long time no see

Someone's got a spring in her step says Geraldine

And a bloom to her cheek says Roisin

It must be this new probiotic yoghurt you tell them

It's not that Geraldine says I know well what it is

You freeze

It's that you have Cass gone she says You've your life back I told you

You sit down Bojangles is hopping You shouldn't have come you think

We were just talking about Big Mike Roisin tells you

Joan's finally had enough Una says She's off to her sister's that's what I heard Ten bob says she'll not be back

About bloody time Roisin says He does the dirt and she's still there cooking him his fry every morning

Why now Maisie says Isn't your one long gone The maid Hasn't he mended his ways

Once a cheater always a cheater Roisin says It must have dawned on her at last

He's up the swanny in that case Geraldine says She'll clean him out leave him naked as the day he was born

Oh him Una says It won't be long till he finds some other mug to sponge off

Everyone knows the cut of his jib by now Roisin says Who'd be fool enough to throw their lot in with him?

You'd be surprised Maisie says No shortage of fools
No fool like an old fool Geraldine says

I don't understand Do you want to stop is that it

No you say Speaking the word almost crushes you

Then why not he says What's wrong with two people who care about each other being together

You have only ever been with Dickie you don't tell him that You only say that it has to be right You don't want your first time together to be in a car in a field

A hotel he says Somewhere far off The next county You say nothing A hotel seems worse even than a car you don't know why Or how about this he says and he starts to tell you about a house he has on the edge of the woods In the half-built estate You can't believe your ears It's not a hundred per cent finished he says But there's power A bit of furniture It's the showhouse he says while you're getting a cold dank feeling like you've sunk into a pond wondering did he bring her there the housekeeper Were they right the girls Are you only the next one The mug The fool

I hate those old woods you tell him Anyway that's where Dickie's building his whatever-it-is Let's just leave it for now you say Then reach for the door to go back to your car

Wait says Mike wait He lets out a sigh Do you not think this is real he says Is that it

It's not that you say

I don't know if I can do it you say I don't know if I can be with someone else then go home and lay down beside Dickie I'm not like you you say

Mike considers this then says Well if he's off running around the woods most likely you won't be laying down beside him at all

That's not what you meant How can he not see it I should get back you say We'll talk about it some other time

Wait Imelda Again he reaches after you

Joan's going out of town he says Her sister's not well She's going to stay with her

Why don't you come over to the house some night he says I'll make you dinner Whatever you want

You can stay for an hour or you can stay for the night We can be together or not as you like Bring Dickie even And we'll all play Scrabble if that's what you want we'll do that

Crows in the cornfield black yellow blue

His hand on your arm he says gently I want you to be part of my life Imelda Whatever way feels right to you We can go as fast or as slow as you like I just want to be near you

What do you think he says

You pause for a moment still facing away I can't leave PJ on his own

Couldn't Dickie look after him Mike says

Now you turn to him Oh right you say I'll tell him to be sure he's around to babysit so I can go and have my affair

Mike flinches Well PJ will be grand on his own for one night What is he twelve?

Turning away again Don't tell me how to run my home you say

From behind you you hear him sigh Okay he says Well you're right anyway Time to be getting back

You don't hear from him for the rest of the day Usually he sends a message late in the evening to say he is thinking of you or just an X Tonight nothing You tell yourself it's for the best but keep picking up your phone In the middle of the night even just to see Sometimes messages get delayed But no

Funny how soon you get used to it how quickly you come to rely on it A few kind words A single letter even Take them away and you feel like you're falling apart

It's for the best you tell yourself it's for the best

Then next morning as you're making breakfast PJ asks if he can stay over in Zargham's house on Friday

The radio jabbers on about tax or traffic You stand there with your back to him stirring the porridge

You feel his eyes on you It seems like the whole world is gathered behind you waiting to hear what you will say You keep stirring Hmm? you say

Can I stay over in Zargham's?

I thought you weren't getting on with Zargham

Oh yeah we repaired our friendship

Didn't he change his name

No that was just a temporary thing Anyway we're doing this project together on crustaceans We need to finish it this weekend

Hmm you say again expressionlessly

I'm in love with you Imelda

Gazing into the porridge still you say Would you need me to drive you over

No his mam will pick us up after school

So she'll be there They'll be there his parents

Of course Mam obviously

The world gathered behind you gathered above you Balanced on a pinpoint

Let me think about it you say

It's never too late to start again Clara Langan says You're never too old to find love

The model designer and actress was thirty-seven when she met dashing London restaurateur Brian Boles after divorcing two years before from her childhood sweetheart Richie Nagle following his affair with his wellness advisor

It was hard to come back from that and put my trust in someone the beauty confirms She talks openly about the heartbreak of her marriage ending It nearly ended me with it she says

But now with Brian blue skies have returned

I'm not the type to go out and start dating left and right she says I didn't think I'd ever be able to feel that way again But with Brian it's like his love has woken the love in me He's brought out the passionate person I thought was gone She laughs I feel like I'm eighteen again!

At Naancross you can still see where the flowers had been

After the crash someone tied a bouquet to the telephone pole It used drive you mad Every time you went out there the flowers had withered more till they were ragged Black You would have pulled them down but they were too high up Whoever did it must have come out there with a ladder

And on the telephone pole you can still see it Not the bouquet of course but the plastic tie that held it and now it's the only way you can tell you're in the right place

You used to come out here all the time In the weeks after he died Climb out Frank's bedroom window and walk however many miles Sometimes it was the middle of the night Dickie never knew You'd squeeze through the straggling brambles Go on your hands and knees feeling around on the dark ground

Can I help you?

A man has come out of the blue shipping container that is the office He stands there looking at you with his hands on his hips

Oh you say rising to your feet I thought I dropped something that's all

You smile brightly Glister your beauty at him Why not do him too Imelda in his shipping container Why not do everyone

The man pushes the cap back off his forehead scratches his scalp He is young in his twenties with a beard Are you wanting to rent a bike he says

Oh no you say Just looking around

He appears puzzled at this Looks around himself at the empty car park the rack of mountain bikes

A man died here once you explain My true love I used come out here to look for his ghost I was only a girl then I married his brother We were both sick with grief Out of our heads with it He is a good man We were happy or getting by anyway Then something changed

No

I used to have a friend lived here That's what you say When this was a field

He looks at you quizzically You realize this does not sound quite right

It was a long time ago you say

You point to the racks of bikes Busy? you say

Not busy enough he says

Nice day all the same

They say we'll have rain the man says

Do they

He nods soberly On firm ground at last Storms they say Friday night

Huh you say

Well you say

Good luck now he says

He waits there while you get back in the car

You start the engine Eye the tarmac wistfully as you pull out

You had never found anything anyway Probably the glass all melted when the car burned And his blood that you'd imagined went into the soil to feed the trees and grass It probably didn't It probably turned straight to steam

But the plastic that'll be there on that pole when you're all dead and gone Isn't that what the kids are always telling you Use it once then it's hanging around for a thousand years Time doesn't do what you think it will does it

You get your turn But they don't tell you that's all it is a turn a moment Everything explodes you're nothing but feelings Your life begins at last You think it will all be like that Then the moment passes

The moment passes but you stay in the shape you were then In the life that's come out of the things that you did The remainder of that girl you used be that is gone

They don't tell you How could they How could anyone make any sense of that

A little way down the road you pull in again

Take out your phone and send a message to Mike: **Friday night x**

CASS

As you walk up Dame Street there is still light at the base of the darkening sky. The city is coming to life again after the office crowd have gone home: a queue has formed outside the falafel place, another at the theatre across the road where green-haired school kids with plaid miniskirts and holes in their stockings are waiting for some emo band. Elaine is all a-flutter. Can you believe this is our first time going to the Butterfly? she says. Like, isn't that insane? She keeps telling you how it's *legendary* and *an underground institution*, meaning it will be full of intimidating people judging you for wearing the wrong clothes or looking too cis or too femme or something wrong anyhow because that's what it's like every time you go out in Dublin. You smile, try to make yourself feel excited. Elaine's phone is blowing up with messages from the people who are already there, who are trying to get there, who are so jealous you will be there! Are you there? We're almost there! We'll see you there in like three minutes! She turns to you and beams. She is so happy! And for a moment you are happy too.

It's your third night out in a row, part of your ongoing mission to prove you're not lugubrious. You have followed her to the legendary places and the brand-new pop-up places literally no one knows about, though when you got there it seemed pretty clear lots of people did know, and you drank your Diet Coke and laughed at the jokes you couldn't hear and feigned interest in the boys who came to chat you up.

Tonight when you get inside it's full of ordinary people and just looks like a regular pub and for a split-second you think that everything might actually be fine. But then you hear the beats coming from overhead.

With a sinking heart you follow Elaine up the stairs, then lose her almost immediately in the sea of faces.

I hate these fucking places, Caleb says. Everyone's so self-congratulatory. Acting like they're Che Guevara because they're wearing their mam's earrings? He looks around at the crowd and scowls. I bet you a million euro that when they're not here performing their *category*, ninety per cent of these people work for some tech firm that runs on tax evasion and Chinese labour camps.

Chan raises an eyebrow at you. Caleb's cranky because he's trying to get this Nazi over to speak at the Hist, but they won't let him.

He's not a Nazi, Caleb protests. He's trying to stop Europe committing cultural suicide. It's fucking bullshit.

Why did you come here? you ask him. If diversity bothers you so much?

Someone told me they're doing free mojitos, he says.

He leaves you to go to the bar. I heard they basically did have a Nazi at the Hist last week, Chan says. This guy who was supposed to talk about the environment and instead he went on this tirade about how gender identity doesn't exist and gay people are just pretending?

The music thumps and zaps. How can anybody like this? Chan is telling you about a Pokémon outfit she's making for a cosplay event; you gaze into the crowd, searching for Elaine among the bright happy faces. *I can't go on like this*, you think.

Caleb arrives back. He hands you a glass, then notes your surprise. Didn't you want one?

She's a recovering alcoholic, you ass, Chan hoots.

Oh right, Caleb says. I forgot. I'll drink it.

It's fine, you say. It's just something Elaine likes to tell people.

Just holding the drink makes you feel better. Kit comes over with Edelle, who says she has to write a story for her writing workshop from the point of view of a man, what should she do? Imagine it's a woman, Kit begins, but then change it so he keeps punching people! And thinking about sex, Chan says. And worrying his truck is small, you say. And obsessing about his mother, Edelle says. And buying speakers on Amazon, you say. And worrying he's going bald, Kit says.

And at the end he drives his truck into the sea?

Yes! Classic end for a story. He drives into the sea.

And then he punches it!

You are laughing, you think to yourself maybe it's going to be a good night after all, and then Elaine appears at your side. You'll never guess who's here! she says. jj!

What's jj doing here?

Who's jj? says Edelle, who's taking Russian.

They're one of our English professors, Chan says. So incredible.

So incredibly *phoney*, Caleb says.

Elaine catches your eye, giggles. I did something crazy, she says. I told them about the party and I asked them if they'd come. And they said maybe! She bursts out laughing.

You smile at her glassily.

You're having a party? Edelle says.

Tomorrow, Elaine says. It's on Facebook. She does a little jig. jj's coming to my house! I'm so happy!

That's so great, you say. You lift the glass to your lips and drink drink drink till you have swallowed yourself and the whole of the night.

II

DICKIE

Late that night he posts another clip. There are three now. This new one is a close-up of a fuzzy, flabby jowl, shuttling back and forth over a disembodied member. Eight seconds long, impossible to recognize you from it. Yet as you lie in the cold darkness all you can think of is the people who might recognize you nevertheless, the people who might see it, which over the torturous unsleeping hours turns into a list of everybody you've ever met – the Mayor, the head of the Chamber of Commerce, the chairman of the Golf Club, the parish priest, the school principal, the management of VW Ireland, the Trinity Alumni Association, Nora Toomey in the cake shop, Dinny Clarke in the fishing shop, the dads of the U10 GAA squad, the boy in the petrol station, the girls in the bank, the old ladies at their Veneration, the butcher, the baker, the candlestick maker. Your father, your wife. The children.

Christ, the children.

You keep having dreams in which they're disintegrating: pieces dropping from their faces, limbs falling off, while you run around frantically after them, trying to pick up noses, lips, arms, and stick them back on, like some nightmarish game. In others you watch helplessly as they are submerged in an invisible tide, eyes bulging, white with panic, not understanding that they're drowning.

You have tried calling Ryszard, you have sent him messages begging him to take the videos down. But he won't pick up, he won't reply. Tomorrow when he calls with the drop-off point you can ask him directly, but you already know what he'll say. First the money.

And you don't have the money.

You've tried everything you can think of – remortgaging the house, selling the car. But your desperation wards people away. The bank manager keeps his eyes turned carefully to his screen, taps on his keyboard, tells you he'll need more documentation. Buyers sit in the car, turn over the engine, admire the upholstery, then look back at your twitching, ice-white face. Even your father avoids you, your increasingly urgent messages, almost as if he and Ryszard were working together, from opposite poles, to teach you a lesson.

PTZSCHEEERRRRR The chainsaw roars, golden dust flurrying up into the air.

Can you stop that, please?

Victor stops, stands there motionless like an automaton set to standby. Or you presume it's Victor; he's wearing goggles and a face mask, so it could theoretically be someone else. Soft white sawdust showers your good shoes – you are still in your suit, hunkered in a clearing in the forest.

Sorry, you say. I'm trying to think. Though you don't think, do you, simply grind your hands into your jaws. The day is advancing, time tensing around you. Every moment brings you closer to the moment he will call and you will have to tell him the truth. And then? And then? And then?

Victor peels off the mask. Did you sort things out with your friend?

You have just been in to Big Mike to see if there was anything that could be done at his end. A loan, if he could organize a loan, from the company account.

And?

He told me . . . he told me . . . You pause. You know what Big Mike told you. Yet you can't seem to lay a hand to it. It sits in front of you, bulky but invisible, like furniture covered by a sheet.

Maybe it's time to tell your friend where to go, Victor says.

Yes . . . You laugh weakly, steal a glance over to him. He has turned away to his pile of sawn logs.

I suppose the problem there is . . . the thing about it is that he . . .

He lifts the logs, deposits them on a larger pile.

There are some decisions I made in the past. Things I'm not proud of. Which my friend, which this person would have, have evidence of.

Victor is on his hands and knees, fiddling with a truss. He makes no sign of hearing. Still it feels good just to say it out loud.

Pictures, you say. Recordings.

You sigh conclusively. That's the problem, you say.

Wouldn't make any difference anyway.

You start, look up. Pardon?

Fella like that, even if you got him his money, as soon as he had it spent he'd be back looking for more. He'll keep coming back sure as eggs, till everything's cleaned out.

He pulls his mask back on, lowers the goggles. Only one way to deal with people like that, he says. He yanks the cord. With a scream the blade descends again into the helpless pale wood.

CASS

The morning of the party you're woken by the sound of the hoover. It's Elaine, cleaning the living room for the first time since you moved in. She's already mopped the floor of the kitchen, and she's strewn fairy lights over the broken washing machine, the broken dishwasher, the broken microwave, so it looks like a kind of magical garbage dump. You help her bag up the vast collection of takeaway cartons, scrub down the bathroom.

It takes a while because it hasn't been done in so long and because Elaine keeps stopping to post before-and-after pictures. Still, working side by side like this is surprisingly enjoyable. It reminds you of studying together back at home, up in Elaine's room, one of you lying on the bed, one of you on the laptop going, *Guess what Harry Styles's favourite food is bread, that's mine too!* or reading out inspirational quotes from the girls on the Miss Universe Ireland website.

Oh yeah! Elaine laughs when you tell her this.

It's funny how something boring can be fun, you say. Like, even doing homework, it was always such a laugh, wasn't it? When we were together.

Yeah, she says. She catches your eye, gives you a look you don't quite understand: with a sudden rush you wonder is this the moment? Should you tell her now? But you're having such a nice time that you don't want to spoil it. And she's already turned her attention back to her feed. People are really liking our aprons, she says.

*

When the cleaning is done the two of you go to the supermarket and wrestle slabs of beer into the trolley. A red-faced man with a protruding belly stops to help you. His trolley is also full of slabs of beer: in fact, most of the people in the supermarket are buying slabs of beer.

Are you going to be okay with this? Elaine says as you wait at the checkout.

With what? you say.

She doesn't reply. You turn to look at her. I don't know, she says. Buying alcohol. Having all this alcohol in the house.

Of course, you say.

It's not like I'm a real alcoholic, you say.

Again she gives you a curious look.

I'm not, you say.

You did used to drink a lot, she says. And you had to have your stomach pumped.

That was one time, you say.

Okay, she says. As long as you feel you're being honest with yourself.

Today, in the developed world, the great threat to political order is that people will pay attention to their surroundings. Thus, even slaves have access to entertainment. You could even say we are paid in entertainment. The novel was the first instance of what in the twenty-first century has become a vast and proliferating entertainment industry, an almost infinite machine designed to distract us and disempower us. We are presented with a virtual world powered, literally, by the incineration of the real.

Cass? Quick word?

You turn desperately but everyone else has already drained out of the seminar room.

Don't worry, it's nothing bad, they say.

They are sitting at the desk still. They've coloured their hair: it is red now, cinnamon. Unwillingly you take a couple of steps back towards them.

As you may or may not know, I'm advisor to *St Botolph's*, they say.

That's the college poetry magazine. And I wondered if you have any work you might like to submit.

You don't say anything. You look at the floor.

I heard that you write – am I mistaken?

You shrug, mumble something, you don't even know what.

Anyway. They spread their hands. If you do, we'd love to see it. That's all.

You nod. Your face is blazing. You turn for the door.

Cass.

You turn back the minimum amount possible.

If you ever want to talk to someone. I'm here. There are people here. I don't want my students ever to feel that they're on their own.

You nod again, hurry out of the room before you burst into flames.

Outside the Arts Block you meet the German girl. You have been avoiding her ever since that night on the steps, but you're so preoccupied that on the ramp now you literally run into her. She is wearing an oatmeal-coloured cardigan and carrying a rucksack on her back, a different one, enormous. You did not call me, she says, getting straight to the point and immediately making you angry, because you are already stressed enough without being guilt-tripped. But you just tell her you're sorry, that you've been busy. That's all right, she says, Merle says. She tells you the man you heard speak at the Hist is suing the government for accelerating climate change. It probably won't work, she says, but I have heard there is an Irish saying, that even though a candle is not very bright, it is better to light one than if you do not light any candle at all, and then you are complaining because it is too dark.

Have I got this right? she says, suddenly looking doubtful.

A hundred per cent, you say. In the daylight her skin is unexpectedly pale and translucent, her blue eyes are surprisingly bright. Merle means blackbird, you looked it up. You feel like you should invite her to the party, though you wonder what Elaine will make of her, with her eco-activism and her thermal leggings.

But she won't be here tonight. I am going to visit a grave, she says. Oh wow, you say. Can't compete with that. Yes, it is very famous, she nods. It is very old, with the tunnels inside a hill? Like a passage grave? you say. Yes! she says, lighting up. She tells you the name of the passage grave. That's in my county! you say. You have visited it many times, with your dad, on countless class trips. You say you wish she'd told you before, then you could have given her some ideas for places to stay, good pubs nearby. She looks at you for a moment, clearly about to say that if you had called her, as you promised, then she would have said. But for once she manages to keep it to herself. It will be nice to be back in the nature, she says instead, and hops the rucksack up on her shoulders. Well, she says, I must be going. You can't help laughing. *I must be going*, is that something they teach you in school in Germany? you say. Because it's not something people actually say. She smiles at you, and you watch her make her way past the Hub and the 1937 and then into the square and out of sight.

It's funny, she seems like a loser, but she acts like she doesn't know or care she's a loser, which makes you wonder whether she is, in fact, a loser. And for a moment a part of you wishes you could go with her.

PJ

If anyone asked you about it you'd have to say so far your plan is going great. The sleepover idea was risky, often Mam wants to ring the other person's parents to make sure it's all right but this time she hardly even asked any questions. Zargham was a good choice because Zargham's mam's accent is so hard to understand that Mam always avoids talking to her if she can. She avoids talking to you too at the moment so the truth is you could probably have said you wanted to stay two nights and she would have said okay. There's a small question mark in your mind about Cass. She hasn't written back yet to any of your messages. But she never writes back, you didn't expect her to write back, that's the whole reason you're going all the way to Dublin to talk to her, so that's all basically fine.

What's bugging you still is whether there should be a plan at all. Like whether you're going down the wrong track, interfering when it would be better to just drop it, so that even if the plan succeeds, it might make things even worse. How could things get worse would be one response to this but no doubt that's exactly what the guys were thinking in the movie when they buried their kid in the Pet Sematary.

But you have to do something, you can't not do something.

Morning classes seem to go on for ever. It's impossible to concentrate, you keep coming up with new potential flaws in your plan. What if the bus breaks down on the way to Dublin and the driver says, Everybody had better just call their parents to come and pick them up? Or what if your mam finds your spare inhaler and thinks it's your regular inhaler and drives over to Zargham's house to give it to you? Or she decides she wants to make some traditional Iranian food and rings Zargham's mam for recipes?

That's why, though, you haven't said anything to him before, now when you see Zargham crossing the yard with Pete Barron at break you call out to him, Yo, Zargham! Zargham stops, winces. Oh shoot, I mean Tyler, you say. Sorry. Zargham looks embarrassed. Pete Barron is watching you with a smirk, the kind of smirk that wants you to see it and to imagine what lies behind it. You ignore it, ignore Pete, say directly to Zargham, Can I talk to you for a second?

Pete Barron's smirk widens into a grin, as if you had just bent over and split your pants. I'm going to the shop, Zargham mumbles. Right, you say. I just wanted to run something by you about this plan I'm, uh, planning. You blush, aware how infantile and lame that sounds, even though this is a real plan involving genuine deception and risk. Pete is laughing out loud now. Maybe when I come back, Zargham says. Okay, you say, and then, Or I could go to the shop with you?

But he and Pete are already walking away. Down by the school gates they meet Dave Okinwale and Rory Coyle.

You tell yourself it's highly unlikely that Mam will want to make Iranian food. Particularly if nobody's home, you add. But no sooner have you dispatched one worry than another appears to take its place, e.g. what if you find Cass and *she's* turned weird? Or you? What if *you* come back weird and wrong?

The bus stops outside the chip shop across the street ten minutes after the end of school. You take everything you need from your locker at lunch break, so when the final bell rings, you're ready to go. There are always loads of boys milling around the chip shop, so you won't look suspicious to anyone passing by.

But at the gate somebody grabs your arm. It's Julian Webb. Not so fast, he says.

You turn to him, surprised. His pointy white teeth glisten at you. What? you say.

It's payback time, Julian Webb says.

Payback, echoes Nev, bobbing at Julian's elbow. Simon 'Splat' Slattery looms behind them. What's he doing here?

I don't have time for this, you say, and start to walk off but Splat blocks your path and Julian grabs your arm again. That's not how this works, Julian says. You leave when we say you can leave.

Cars ebb up and down the street. The clock above the newsagent's says five to four.

I have to go, you say. I need to be somewhere.

You should have thought of that before you disrespected me, Julian says.

And me, Nev says.

Three minutes to four. You have to get that bus, you have to. But when you make to leave, Splat grabs your rucksack, and Julian laughs and says, Are you running home to get bummed by your—

Look, you interrupt him, this'll have to wait.

Julian looks disconcerted. I told you, you don't get to—

Whatever, you say, raising your voice. Do all this on Monday. Bully me then. I don't care. But right now, I'm going. Goodbye.

With that you push Splat aside and walk across the street to the bus stop.

From the school gate the boys look back at you, confused. They talk among themselves, before finally resolving to follow you over the street. But it's too late, the bus is here. Now if they want to beat you up they'll have to pay for a ticket.

Where are you even going? Julian Webb asks in dismay from the pavement.

Straight to hell, you tell him.

This bus is for Dublin, the driver says.

Right, yeah, that's what I meant, you say. You pay for your ticket and take your seat, give the boys the finger as you pull out into the street.

IMELDA

You'd booked yourself in to Beauteeze At the last minute you rang up to cancel

You'd picked out a few things you might wear You don't even look at them

You wrote a message I can't do this I just can't I'm sorry 4give me xxxxx It sits on your phone unsent

In the big window the blue sky lightens darkens lightens Shadows appear and melt away again The whole house like a giant clock and you waiting inside it paralysed still in your pyjamas

Nothing has to happen That is what you have agreed A quick bite to eat All perfectly above board Maybe probably you'll leave it at that Just be friends you think

But then you think of his sad eyes his warm hands *For the first time I feel someone truly knows me* he told you

You wish you could talk to the girls! You wish you could tell them Say Lookit girls here's the story Big Mike's invited me over to have it off with him now will I go to his house or will I not?

Leave the rights and the wrongs out of it Tell them what it's like to be held again to be desired How you feel his wanting you like an electric charge That it lights everything up like a house that has lain empty and now is all ablaze But how afterwards it's worse than before because now the darkness knows it is darkness the emptiness knows it's emptiness the poor house knows there's nobody home

But they would say back to her Well Imelda what do *you* want?

If only he'd call or he'd write Tell you something romantic

then just as you're thinking it the phone beeps with a message You lunge for it but it's only from Geraldine on the Tidy Towns girls' group chat

Well you'll never guess who I've just seen on Main Street she says

Who? says Maisie

Who??? says Roisin

See for yourself Geraldine says and posts a video clip that shows a blonde woman from behind Branded jeans Coat from Penneys Walking past the butcher's Young you can tell and right there before she types another word your stomach cinches up like a bag full of ice

Who's that supposed to be? Are we supposed to be able to recognize them from their arse?

You recognize her but you don't say a thing Bite your lip hope and pray you're wrong

I'll tell you will I? Geraldine says She loves a bit of drama

Oh Jesus come on so Roisin says

Isn't it Augustina Geraldine says The Comerfords' old nanny or housekeeper or whatever it was that Big Mike was sticking it into Marching up and down Main Street like a royal visit

She's back? Maisie says What's she doing showing her face around here?

I suppose she needs a new job Roisin says

A job! Maisie crows Yes indeed Homewrecker Wanted Apply Within!

I'll tell you girls if I'd taken her picture from the front you wouldn't be asking me that

Pregnant??? write Roisin and Maisie in unison

Five months if she's a day Big as a house

You think Mike knows?

If he doesn't yet he will soon That's my guess anyway

It couldn't be his Maisie says Could it? What'll Joan make of that?

Lucky for Mike she's out of town Roisin says

Luck has nothing to do with it Geraldine says This one's had it planned all along I bet Now she's playing her ace

Looking for money?

What else would she be doing parading up and down Main Street She's making sure everybody sees her is what it is Showing Mike how much trouble she can make for him The chickens have come home to roost He's had his fun now it's time to pay up

No more than he deserves Roisin says Filleann an feall ar an bhfeallaire

A pang in your chest *Stay quiet* a voice urges inside you but you write He's not a bad man he just made a mistake

You know better than anyone what kind of a man he is Imelda Geraldine says and your heart lurches sideways The way he sneaky-snaked his way into your garage she goes on Elbowed out poor Dickie

Maurice asked him you reply Anyway it's only temporary

Temporary my eye Geraldine says He won't stop there Next thing you know he'll be inviting Maurice over for Christmas dinner He'll be one of the family You'll never see rid of him Till he's his mitts on everything that's yours

As long as the nanny plays ball Maisie says

She'll play ball if the price is right Geraldine says

I have to go you say and you switch off your phone put your head in your hands

She means nothing to me Imelda Those were his very words *It was a mistake She is gone I will never see her again*

But now she has come back

Back and with a child in her belly But maybe not his But why else would she have come And what if he sees it and realizes it was not a mistake at all but what he wanted A new family Start again Off to Brazil Goodbye for ever

Maybe he's with her now Maybe he's brought her out to the house by the woods

You switch your phone on again Nothing Should you call him Send him a message Not about her something sensual Thinking of you Can't wait for tonight But then No you think Isn't this the sign you've been waiting for Doesn't it prove once and for all this is wrong Enough Too much Go back to your old message *I cannot* Then the phone rings and you lunge

Imelda Barnes? a woman's voice says

Yes you say slowly

Hmmph the woman says as if she doesn't believe you and then Your aunt is very sick

My aunt? you say

Yes your aunt The woman's accent is foreign Hostile There is the sound of keys on a keyboard Maura Brennan?

Rose!

Hello? the woman says

I'm here you say Yes that's Is she all right

No she has unfortunately had a stroke

A stroke? Everything is spinning Is she going to be okay?

No That's why I'm calling you If you want to see her you better come now

Then satisfied Have a nice day And she hangs up

You gather your coat your keys your heart breaking for Rose that this day you have dreaded so long might have finally come Yet at the same moment thinking *But what about the dinner?* An image coming into your mind then of the Brazilian girl with Mike's hands on her round belly in the house in the woods and you think *Please let her die some other night*

God forgive me! you say out loud

DICKIE

He hasn't called. It's after six now. For hours you've been sitting here, standing here, in one of the few places in the clearing with a semi-reliable signal. You're starting to wonder if it was just a wind-up. Yes! Just a prank! He never meant any of it, he won't call at all!

Yet you know that he will. And when he does? What will you tell him then? Admit you don't have his money? Throw yourself on his mercy?

Victor thinks this is the wrong tack. Victor says you need to take a firm hand.

What do you mean?

I mean, you and me talk to this fellow, and we set him to rights.

For a moment, you just goggle at him. Set him to rights?

He gazes back at you expressionlessly through the woodsmoke.

You mean, I tell him I have his money, and then we go along to meet him and . . .

Victor is silent.

I don't want any trouble, you say. Any more than we have already.

Some would say he's asking for it.

He promised this would be the last time, you say.

There's been a time before?

You don't answer. Instead you say, Anyway, we don't know where he wants to meet. It could be somewhere in the open. Can't just start throwing punches.

You do like the idea of going to meet him, though – talking to him, reasoning with him. Face to face, he might be more amenable to giving you more time, to seeing sense, mightn't he?

Victor says nothing to this, sits back against the log, whittling a twig with his penknife.

But what if he's angry that you showed up without the money? That you lied? What if he wants to punish you? Panic courses through you, a churn of fragmentary, pornographic images. You can't let your family see them – you can't!

Victor raises his eyes. Above the canopy the sky has swirled up with blue-black clouds. They're giving rain for tonight, he says equably.

All day he has been sitting on his log, listening or not listening while you argue with yourself, like God importuned by some unfortunate Israelite. He barely speaks – maybe that is what gives you the irrational sense that the answer is contained within him, that he knows what to do, what will happen.

Could I ask him to meet without the money? you say. Tell him the truth, say we need to talk?

Victor gets up. You want a hotdog from the van?

You shake your head. You haven't eaten all day, the very thought of eating seems like something from the distant past.

The moment he leaves the clearing, your phone sounds. Not a call, but a message.

dropoff tonite 10pm no early no later in this following locate:

You read his directions distractedly. **Take new road out of town . . . second right turn after bridge . . . empty houses . . .** You stop, frown, begin again. But your confusion only grows.

There is a woods . . . walk five minutes . . .

You rub your eyes. You must be getting something wrong. At the end of the message he has given a link with GPS coordinates. You click on it, watch the map slowly assemble itself on the screen.

Around you the trees shake, as if a giant is trying to wrench the forest up by the roots.

The phone is showing the very spot you're in.

A mistake – you've done it wrong, it's just showing you your own location. You erase the coordinates, close the app, start again. But no. Here you are, by the Hide, a blue pin in the green blank of the forest. And here is the drop-off, a glowing red point, fifty metres due south. You take your bearings, though you already know what you will see. You look down the slope at the dark oblong just about visible in the dark. And through the leaves it looks back at you.

an old stone shed with the tin roof

Why would he do that? Why here? What's he trying to tell you?

You are pacing back and forth through the clearing. The campfire gives everything a chiaroscuro, medieval feel, a deep and tenebrous uncertainty. Victor sits impassive in its midst, smoke drifting up from his fingers.

It's got to be part of his plan, you say. Some kind of a trick. But what? What's he at? What does it mean?

Victor shrugs. Maybe it doesn't mean anything.

How could it not mean anything, you say, scathingly. Out of the whole county he picks our Bunker for his drop-off, and it doesn't mean anything?

Your mind is racing. How did he find it? Did he follow you? Has he planted cameras here too?

Maybe he doesn't know, Victor says.

Doesn't know?

Doesn't know it's your land. Doesn't know it's your Bunker.

How could he not know? Your voice rises querulously, almost hysterical. At the same time the thought comes to you, how would he know?

Did you ever bring him here? Victor says.

You shake your head.

But he lives in the town?

He used to, you reply reluctantly. For a little while. You think he found it on his own? He doesn't know we're here? Or is it a trap?

Victor puffs on his rollie. It could be that he's checked out the site, he says, and he's seen us working, and he's come up with some sort of way to use it against us.

He looks at the dog end, flicks it into the flames. But from what you've told me, this lad's a chancer. He doesn't have a grand plan. He's making it up as he goes.

Look at it from his point of view, he says. He's left town months ago. He's not been back since. He's racking his brains trying to think of a nice, out-of-the-way spot someone could leave a bag full of cash. Then he thinks of it – that old shed in the middle of the woods. Perfect. He should come back to check it first, make sure it's the way he remembers. But that's not our boy. And so he makes a serious mistake.

He levels his gaze at you. Smoke wafts around him as if he's risen up out of the earth.

He trespasses on a local man's land, he says, where two hunters are doing pest control with legally held firearms. It's late, it's dark. He's hiding in the undergrowth.

You wait, as if you don't know the outcome. Victor brings his hands together, and then apart. A tragic accident, he says.

You don't speak – you can't speak; nor can you look away from the splayed gaze, the eyes that angle off into other dimensions, leaving between them a space of pure emptiness, a terrible place of darkness, where you seem to see yourself, ungrounded, null.

I don't want to hurt anyone, you say faintly.

Of course not, Victor says. But it's the same as with the squirrels. If you don't do something, the situation will only get worse.

It's not the same, you say. He's a human being.

Sure everyone's a human being, once you go down that road, Victor says.

You break away from him. Maybe it's a mistake, you say. Maybe the coordinates are wrong. I'll call him.

But Ryszard doesn't pick up. And into the silence Victor speaks.

I'm not saying it's a sign, Dickie. But isn't this the whole reason you're out here? Because you knew that sooner or later someone would appear and try to do your family harm. And you wanted a place you could defend them.

Darkness fills the sky like rising water. Dying leaves quiver tremulously on the bone-grey branches. My God, you whisper to yourself. My God.

CASS

It's not even dark yet and the party is in full swing. You were still getting ready but then Edelle's butoh workshop got cancelled at the last minute so she came straight here and brought her whole class with her, still in their leotards. Already there are so many people in your house that for the first time it's actually almost warm. Music thumps from the speakers, the beer you brought from the supermarket is almost gone from the fridge, a boy crouches on your coffee table in a surfer pose. Great party! That's what everyone is saying. And it *is* a great party. You don't know who 90 per cent of these people are. But no one could come here and call the atmosphere lugubrious.

Only Elaine doesn't look like she's enjoying it. She stands in a large ring of Players types, not even pretending to listen to what they're saying; every time the doorbell goes, her head whips round to see who it is, only to turn back, crestfallen, as the wrong person crosses the threshold.

You know she is waiting for jj. And you, watching from across the room, are waiting too, experiencing the same feelings in reverse, like a mirror image. As hope flames up in her eyes, your heart plummets, as disappointment returns you breathe again, reprieved.

All of your wise resolutions – about just being honest with her, telling her how you feel, being ready to let go if that's what she wants – have vanished. Who were you kidding? The idea of letting go of her is unbearable. So, consequently, is the idea of being honest. Instead you are back behind your mask, doing the best you can to make it look like you personally are having a fantastic (non-lugubrious, unobsessed) time, while getting yourself in position to comfort her once she accepts that jj's not going to come. She'll be drunk and vulnerable; maybe she'll cry in your lap again.

But if jj does come, what then? Will you just stand here in this same corner, watching forlornly while Elaine ploughs through the bodies to greet them? Look on helplessly as she takes their coat, exclaiming laughingly, *You made it!* then, *Come and have a drink* and leading them away to the kitchen? And then will you follow them there, and moon around in the background, as your housemate plies the professor with questions, all sorts of complicated, considered enquiries she has about literature, and gender, and patriarchy, and then listens intently to their responses, glowing like a Chinese lantern, not even noticing you're lurking by the door, spying like a creep, though maybe she does, because when you're distracted momentarily by something in the other room, you turn back to find you can't see them any more – they're not in the kitchen, and they're not in the living room, and they're not in the yard with the smokers, and so you check the living room again, around and around, your own little circle of agony, though you know it is too late, too late . . .

And even if they don't come: you think you'll be off the hook? Think, Cass! If it's not tonight, it'll be some other night! If it's not jj, it'll be someone else! What is the world but a shadowy army of Elaine's potential lovers? You need to DO something! You need to ACT! You need to stop being such a pathetic, unlovable coward, and make your move, TONIGHT! NOW!

The boy beside you is taking a can of beer from a bag and sees you looking. Want one? he asks. You nod. Crack it open and chug it back in one go. It bubbles through you like magic lemonade. Instantly you feel like you've filled up with superpowers. The boy laughs and hands you another. Bet you can't do two in a row, he says.

Okay, you think. Okay, okay.

You find her in the living room with Kit. You insinuate your way into their conversation. In-*sinew*-ate, like a sinew, a slithery cable of flesh. Or *in-sin-you-ate*, like sinning, then eating. Eating with someone you're not married to? Or eating the someone? Not marrying them and then killing and eating them?

They have stopped speaking and are looking at you.

Can I talk to you for a second? you say to Elaine.

You pull her away to huddle at the bottom of the stairwell. Great party, you say. You smile at her. It's going really well.

Yeah, Elaine says, and then, What's up?

What? you say.

You said you wanted to talk to me, she says.

Oh right! you laugh. It's funny, on the one hand you can't believe you're actually finally doing this, and on the other you feel totally relaxed about it, because you know you're going to say it this time and you know it will work out! You feel almost like you've already said it and Elaine's like, *OMG at last, I've been waiting so long—*

So what is it? she says. Her eyes move distractedly to the door and then back.

Oh nothing, really, you say. Just checking in.

I was in the middle of a conversation, Elaine says.

Right, you say, me too. I mean, earlier.

Are you feeling all right? Elaine says.

Who, me?

You're acting weird, she says. Then her eyes narrow. Are you drunk?

No, you say. Listen—

You are, she says, you're fucking plastered.

I had a can, you admit.

You had more than one, she says.

It doesn't matter, you say. Listen. I have to tell you something.

She presses her lips, looks at you with laser eyes. Your heart is beating so hard, like someone's just stuck it brand new into your chest.

Well? she says.

I was just thinking how amazing it is that we're actually here, in college together, throwing a cool party. When we used to be, like, little nerds together in school in this tiny town. We've come a long way, is what I mean.

Yeah. I'm going back to Kit now, okay?

No, wait, you say. There's something I need to tell you—

You can tell me later! You can tell me any time! We literally live together!

She turns to go. Impulsively you reach out and grab her dress. She wheels around with a frosty expression. The dress is new. The fabric is thin in your hand.

Sorry, you say. It's important.

Elaine waits. The air is wavering. The boy with the beer had a friend with a joint and the joint has just hit you. You try to focus. Maybe if you had another drink? That makes you think of something, suddenly you crease up laughing. Remember that barman in the Drain that fancied you and he'd always give us these insane shots?

Is that what you brought me over here to tell me? Elaine says.

No – no. You calm your giggles, gather yourself. How to begin. Well, remember at home when we met that weird Russian guy—

Elaine rolls her eyes. Cass, I'm at a *party*!

So?

So stop asking me to remember things from, like, the past!

No, but—

Ever since we got here you've been going *on* and *on* about home! The shitty pubs! The teachers! The *haybarns*! I came here to get away from that stuff! She breaks off as the doorbell goes behind her. It's not jj, you say, as she turns to look.

What? she snaps. Who said anything about jj?

No one, you say.

She narrows her eyes. You're not sure how this has gone quite as wrong as it has. Maybe we should talk about it another time, you say.

Elaine sighs. I'm really starting to wonder if we're good for each other, she says.

You gape at her. Your heart is thumping anew. What do you mean?

I mean, I wonder if we're holding each other back. If this relationship belongs to an earlier part of our lives.

You start to speak, but you don't know what to say. Your eyes are prickling, you search for words but everything keeps slipping away from you. I'm sorry. I won't talk about home – I didn't realize –

Elaine gazes impassively back at you. All the alcohol you have drunk, which you have been drinking all day, swims up to your head, and pitches about like a lurching black sea, you think you might cry, no, you think you might throw up, but through the chaos a desperate imperative voice rises telling you, *Fix this! Fix this!* So although now is the exact wrong time to tell her, you begin to say it anyway: The thing is, I . . . I . . .

But the expression on her face has changed. Her eyes widen, her nostrils flare. At the same time, you become aware of a commotion in the living room. Near the front door, which is open, you see people laughing – some jeering, some bemused – and now, through the crowd emerges—

What the actual fuck, Elaine says.

It's your brother. It's PJ. You stare, wondering if you're dreaming. He sees you, and he waves, then checks himself, peers at you uncertainly, at your smeared face, and you feel a thunderhead of shame break in your chest.

Elaine turns to you, hands on her hips, incandescent. I don't know what he's doing here! you hear yourself quail. This wasn't my idea!

She throws up her hands, turns away in disgust. Fuck! Fuck! Launching yourself across the room, an arrow at last, you grab PJ by the shoulders. What are you doing here? you shriek. You can't be here!

He begins to squeak an explanation, but you don't wait for it: you spin him round and propel him back out onto the street. You close the door behind you. What are you doing here? you repeat. You can't just burst in on people!

I tried to call, he insists. You never answer!

Because I don't want to talk!

It's an emergency! he squeaks, and he starts gabbling about Dad and guns and squirrels and bunkers, on and on and on in an incomprehensible torrent till you raise your voice and shout out, Stop!

He flinches, looks up at you. He seems smaller, here in the city. Your anger has merged with your nausea, and between your legs a queasy pain throbs.

What are you doing here? Does Mam know you're here?

The torrent starts up again, Dad, bank, car, fall – you shake him. You're not listening to me! You can't be here! You can't just come here! Don't you get that?

I'm really worried about him!

What do you expect me to do about it?

He bows his head. I thought you could talk to him, he mumbles.

To Dad?

He listens to you.

Ha! You can't help laughing at this, as into your head comes the image of Dad's horrified face looking down at you as you lie on the floor of the ballroom of Burke's hotel, weirdness seeping out of you for all the guests to see. Behind you the door opens. Is this a joke? Elaine says. Do you think this is funny?

It's fine, you say. I'm dealing with it.

He can't stay, she says.

He's not staying, you assure her. Just give me a minute, okay?

It's not a kids' party, she says. People are already putting this on Twitter.

He's going! you repeat.

Elaine looks down the street. No one is in sight. You and your fucking family, she says, and closes the door.

You look at PJ, standing there obliviously like he's waiting to be picked up from football practice, and you feel a fresh burn of rage. Didn't you hear her? you say. You have to go!

He looks up at you uncomprehending. He's supposed to be smart but he's so fucking gormless! Look! you say. I don't care about Dad's midlife crisis, or whatever it is! Do you understand that? I don't care about the garage! That's not my life any more! Now please, would you please just fucking go!

Finally he rises to his feet, cheeks pinkening. He's about to make another speech, but you cut him off. That way, you tell him, taking him by the shoulders and spinning him round. Follow the tram tracks. That takes you to the bus station. Goodbye.

You don't wait to see him start walking. Instead you leave him there, like a dog that won't shoo, and you march back inside and slam the door behind you. In the kitchen you take somebody's can from the fridge and you open it and you drink it. When the doorbell goes you're terrified he's come back, but it's a bunch of new people so you go out into the living room.

What was that all about? Darl says.

Hmm? you say.

Was that your brother?

Oh yeah, you laugh.

What was he doing here? Darl says. I thought you lived down the country.

Yeah, he's such a freak, you say.

Darl frowns.

It's fine, you say. You drink from your can and smile. The conversation moves on. In another minute or two it's as if P J was never there at all.

Checking your phone you see that he did in fact message you that he was coming. You just didn't get that he meant now. You thought it was just a general intention to visit at some point. It doesn't matter anyway.

Elaine waves at you from across the room. She's smiling, she wants you to come over. She doesn't seem angry about what happened. Probably she's impressed that you dealt with it so quickly. Maybe it was a good thing, even, because it distracted her from what happened earlier.

She is talking to a boy with black hair and blue eyes. You recognize him from college, you think he does History. This is my friend that I was telling you about, she says to him. The boy smiles at you, he starts telling you about this guy who does parodies of famous rappers. You laugh. But you are not actually hearing him. Something is buzzing around in your head. Squirrels: you feel like he told you Dad was *shooting* squirrels. You don't remember him saying it, and yet there it is, in your mind. Dozens of squirrels – that's the image you have – their bodies lying around the forest.

It seems impossible. Dad won't even put down mousetraps unless they're the humane kind. You must have imagined it, you tell yourself sternly, and redirect your attention to the boy and his memes. But the squirrels keep appearing – scurrying through the undergrowth of your mind in their stop–start staccato way, pausing on their haunches to survey you; and with them come thoughts of PJ, stumbling away down the street with his backpack, and for an instant a clammy hand seems to grasp your heart.

He'll be fine, you tell yourself, the Luas goes straight to the bus station. What did he expect you to do, anyway? Organize an intervention? Wave a magic wand and make Mam and Dad love each other again? Did he think you'd just drop everything and rush home and make it all better?

Is that what he thought?

Is that why he wanted to see you? Because he thought he could persuade you?

Is that why he came all the way up here, to the city, on his own?

Check this out, the boy is saying, and he takes out his phone and splays his finger and thumb across the screen. Let me see too, Elaine says, huddling against the boy's shoulder.

Turning slightly away you take out your phone and send a message, **Did u get to bus?**

On the boy's phone a man in a white T-shirt in his car is going *ehhhh ehhhh ehhhh Mom's spaghetti*.

That's so funny! Elaine says. The boy smiles at Elaine, and then at you. You smile back at him. The message remains unread. Still smiling, you turn away slightly, call PJ, lift the phone to your ear. It goes straight to voicemail, is it off, has he switched his phone off? Or is he ignoring you? Or? Give me a ring back when you get this, you murmur. Elaine shoots you a look, but the boy hasn't noticed. You've got to see his Lil Wayne, he says. As he hunts around on his phone, he says, So are you guys from Dublin? Elaine answers and he nods. All the sound people are from somewhere else, he says. You take a deep breath but nothing happens, nothing's going in. So you know each other well? he says. Elaine looks at you the way she does when someone else is looking at her looking at you. You could say that, she says. We did almost get in a three-way once, didn't we, Cass? Her hand closes around yours.

Don't touch me, you say.

She starts. The boy with the videos looks confused. You are confused too. The words just came out, you don't know where from. But suddenly you're overcome by revulsion, like you're looking in a mirror and your reflection is rotting. You okay, babe? Elaine asks. You don't know what to say back. Except you do. I hate you, you say. I fucking hate you, you say. By *you* of course you mean *yourself*, in the mirror, but there's no time to explain that. Your hand is still in hers, you tug it free, then you turn and you run.

Next thing you know you're outside, looking down the street as if he might still be there, as if all this time he has been walking on the spot, trusting that you would reappear. But he's not. No one is there, only the blank faces of the houses arranged in a line, a hundred houses on one side, another hundred on the other, and beyond this street another street, and beyond that another and another and another, streets and streets and streets of houses and houses and houses, with people in each of them you know nothing about, have never laid eyes on. You're in the city now. If you wanted to find someone, even someone you loved, you wouldn't know where to begin. And when you start running you have no idea where you're running to.

IMELDA

She is waxy pale shrunken More even than before One side of her mouth droops and spit leaks out the side Her eyes are scared She has had a second stroke we believe the nurse says

You sit down by the bed Rose you say It's me Imelda

Hal hal she whispers Ba Ba Ba

There are three big hairs sprouting from her chin It's a disgrace she should be left looking like that you tell the nurse A disgrace You root in your bag to see have you tweezers You know you do but you can't find them

The nurse puts her soft hand on your shoulder She's in no pain she says gently

You try to ask her has the priest been in but the words won't come I'll give you a few minutes on your own she says and closes the door softly behind her

You take her hand Now that you're alone with her you don't know what to say You have a dreadful feeling that it's you did this That you made her sick with your carry-on Though you know it's not that But simply that she is old Old A fragment of the past Like a blue jewel of glass lying unfound in a field Her face so lined Her eyes that do not recognize anything My God Time What it does You could weep from morning to night and it would not be enough

Sof she gasps Ka

Rose you whisper as if she might hear you Rose as she was The Rose of the past As if she might hear you and take you back there to her cottage Back to your house Back to those terrible days Daddy drunk and fighting Mammy screeching like a bat The boys knocking lumps off each other The police pulling up The house flashing in the blue light You would give anything to go back to it anything

Fl Fo she whispers Fan

You fold her hand in yours Kiss it With your eyes closed press it to your cheek

Frank she says

You look up

A watery eye looks back at you

On the wall in the corner from the switched-off TV a red dot in the black glass glows like an ember

Frank is here she says

The door opens A man comes in

From the past Everything comes back

For a moment you don't recognize him He could be anybody A man in an anorak thinnish balding If you saw him on the street you'd walk right past him Then in an instant it changes you know him and it's as if you'd been living side by side for all this time Or like no time has passed at all that just as you wished you are a girl again The two of you throwing sticks in the stream

You rise to your feet you throw your arms around him

Where have you been you say

Daddy told them you were dead

Dead? you say

Cancer he says like Mammy

I was not so sure he says I did not know if I believed it

But I didn't think you'd want to hear from the likes of us anyway he says Not now you were wed

The likes of you? you say You were my family

Lar looks down at the floor

I wrote you a letter one time he says Did you not get it?

You shake your head you cannot speak

I paid a man to write it he says He must of never sent it at all

They had gone to England All of them Daddy Lar Christy JohnJoe Golly There was trouble again with the Finlay boys and after that they had to go Back to Doncaster stripping cars for parts selling scrap metal always talking about coming home Never returning

That was why you left? you say Because of the Finlays?

His eyes are blue and kind The longer you look at him the more he is as he was Through the worn face the boy in him shining out plain as day As if time's gone backwards

How is Dickie he says Is he still in the garage

Oh you say and you wave your hand Don't talk to me

But I've two children you say You take out your phone and show him pictures The girl is up in college in Dublin you say Cassandra is her name

Is that so he says Well well One of our lot up in college in Dublin Can you beat that

You feel aglow He was always the best of them Lar

You? you say Have you kids?

He sucks on his teeth Naw he says

JohnJoe has a couple down in Chester and Golly has a whole brood in Oz though he's separated from the wife there

Marriage is hard you say It's not for everyone

I done a spell in prison he says And when I got out Daddy had took a turn I went back to mind him I suppose I never left

You stayed with him you say thinking *After everything he did*

He needed someone to take care of him he says He shrugs He needed someone

You say no more You want to ask him you can't But he says it anyway

He died he says Six months ago about the time of them terrible floods You had them here too

He died you repeat

A curtain seems to fall in the room or is it inside you It was the drink did for him he says He stayed at it even after he lost both the legs

He shows you a picture on his own phone A wispy white face set into a shapeless mound of pink The lines of rage smoothed out into fat like he'd sunk into quicksand Hands like claws clutching the arms of his wheelchair

I never touch the stuff now myself he says

The two of you fall silent Rose wheezes on the bed The switched-off TV hums And you are back in that little house where Daddy had loomed over everything like the sky and you lived in his moods the sunshine the frost the storms Now the sky is gone the weather is gone

Lar's arms are around you

I wish someone had of told me you croak into his shoulder

He pats your back He hands you a tissue from the box by the bed

Did he ever talk about me Did he ever mention me at all

He lets out a heavy sigh

Bad things you say

Lar frowns Choosing his words He didn't think you should of married Dickie he says

And despite your heartache you can't help but laugh You can say that again

It was hard on him he says

You pull away Wipe your eyes Hard on *him*?

I suppose he never thought you would go through with it he says That you would defy him

I suppose he had expectations he says looking at his folded hands

That I'd take care of him you say Wait on him the rest of his days

That you would always be his little girl Lar says

Your eyes burn For a moment you think the grief will crush you Till it becomes anger That's easier And he couldn't see past that you say Right up to the end Couldn't bring himself to even admit I was alive

You know what he was like he says He was a proud man Never would admit he was wrong

Yes And everyone around him had to pay the price Mammy the boys Lar that's had the life sucked out of him It would have been you His little girl If not for the baby it would have been you Picking up his beer cans plumping his pillows Boiling his vests The rest of your life

But quick as it came the rage leaves you What's the use What's the sense going back into it now He's dead Let all that misery be dead with him

Rose gurgles hacks up phlegm her eyes are closed Koll she says Curl

I am glad I saw you here he says I hoped I would

Though you thought I was dead

He smiles looks at his hands A dot on one A blue tattoo of a cross How did you know to come you say How did you know that Rose was sick Was it the nursing home called you too *Though why would they call him?* you think

How did you even know she was here you say

And Lar looks up the smile drops away nervous He starts to say something then stops Presses his lips together

What is it you say

Lar sighs reaches up tousles his thinning hair Then leans forward elbows on his knees pulls at his face Imelda he says You know Rose would have her flashes See things before they happen

Well these last few years I've started getting the same thing

It was in prison I started getting them he says and he touches his head Flashes he says

I see you say Your heart sinking

First it's headaches They go on for days sometimes I can barely get up off the floor then at the end of them He trails off His foot hops on the floor At the end of them

He screws up his eyes tugging at his hair Do you remember the Finlays long ago When they came to our house And that huge black dog come up outside staring in at the hall

We seen it outside Eyes big as saucers I never forgot it the look of it Well I been seeing him again In these flashes The selfsame dog I swear to Jesus

I didn't know what it meant only that it was nothing good And after a while I thought to come back here Look for Rose Ask her if she seen it too If she knows Then I find her like this

The nylon curtain stirs though the window is shut Beside you the old woman languishes burbles nonsense Surl soll soll

So it's true It has come for her She is dying

You must have got an awful shock you say

At least I seen her before the end he says That dog done me a favour there

And now I seen you too he says I never forgot you Imelda all those years No matter what they said

I always thought of you I always prayed for you You can always count on me I am your brother still

He smiles His eyes blue bright His face so chipped and worn away A smell of drink off him that would knock you down The boy that stood beside you throwing sticks into the stream That for years was your only friend

He never escaped from Daddy's house Is there still with the ghosts and demons

Thank you you say and put your arms around him

In the sickroom so quiet Only the hum of the lights And the old lady babbling with the last of her breath Sarl Skral skrol

Skirls she whispers

Those poor little skirls

And when you look there are tears on her cheeks

PJ

Here's a fact about the universe, maybe the number one fact: it's impossible to comprehend how much it doesn't care about us. It's not just that it doesn't care about Life. It doesn't even care about *matter*. Everything we think of as everything – starlight, marshmallows, frogs, basketball, electricity, every single person who ever lived and died, all the stuff there is and all the energy – that's only a minuscule fraction of the universe. The rest of it is darkness – dark energy, dark matter, which are just words scientists use for 'we don't know what this is'. What we call the universe is basically a microscopic speck on this giant incomprehensible darkness, like a piece of lint on an XXXXXXXXXXXL-size sweater, and life is like a nano-sized speck on that speck.

So when you think about it who cares about saving it, or anything in it, because basically none of it was ever even supposed to be there. Cass was right about that.

But you still don't see why she had to yell at you. You don't see why she had to *kick you out of her house*. She'd told you before that you could come down any time and stay, she *told* you that, even if she says now that she didn't. How were you supposed to know she was having a party? What did she think you were going to do, start demanding jelly and ice cream?

Though what did you think *she* was going to do? Throw down everything and come back home with you there and then? Jump off the bus and run into the woods and find Dad and say I love you and everything would be all right? Like in a cartoon where someone gets a bump on the head and loses their memory then they get another bump and it all comes back, he'd just be okay again? Seriously, what kind of plan is that, only a child would ever have thought it would work, only an idiot, you're just such an idiot, *idiot* you say to yourself out loud then see some guy look round at you and you lower your eyes and hurry on.

The thing is, you're not 100 per cent positive where you're hurrying to. You were concentrating so hard on just getting away and not looking back and letting her see you cry that you didn't pay all that much attention to what direction you were going. And now you're not super-sure where you are. She said something about tram tracks, and when you look at Google Maps you can see, Yes, follow those tram tracks and they will absolutely take you all the way to the bus station. For some reason however you are not on the street with the tram tracks. You're on a different street, with bags of garbage and stacks of pallets and shuttered buildings, and though Google Maps says the next street on the right will take you down to the tram tracks, when you get to it, it's not really a street so much as an alley. And the garbage is piled so high you can't actually see if it will take you anywhere.

Hmm. You look around, wondering if there's someone you could ask. There's a guy skulking in a doorway, hidden beneath his hood. You decide not to bother him. It's not really a directions kind of *place*, that's the problem. You check Google Maps again. The best option seems to be to go left. You'd be moving away from the tracks, but at least it has lights.

You hurry down that street, then the next, then another one, and you think you're making progress till you turn a corner and find yourself back on the first street with the pallets. You look at Google Maps in dismay, and it makes this metallic bonking noise, like, *I have no idea what you've done here, PJ.* But there's no time to figure it out, the skulking guy, who is not happy to see you again, has emerged from his doorway, so you hurry away again, remembering as you go something you read about bees, how the pesticide the farmers use on plants contains a neurotoxin that destroys their memory so they forget their way home, can't make it back to the hive where they live, and that's why they're dying out. *When they looked in the hives they found them not full of dead bees, but mysteriously empty.* Maybe that's what happened to Cass, you think.

Maybe air pollution in the city has damaged her brain and now she's forgotten her home. Though really you know it started way before she came here. Just as you're thinking this your phone pings. Well, well, Cass again, Miss Toxic Environment, Miss Neonicotinoid – she keeps calling, probably to threaten you some more, well she can go—

EARTH TO PJ COME IN PJ

Wait a second, it's not Cass.

CALLING ALL PJS, R U OUT THERE?

Ethan? Wow what are the chances! You write back, **Hey!!!!**

:) HEY DUDE BEEN A WILE!!!! JUST THOT ID CHECK IN!!!!! U GOOD?

This is so crazy! In an instant the gloom overhanging you evaporates and though at the back of your mind there's something you feel like you're not quite remembering it's blocked out by the excitement of getting to write this message and imagining how surprised he's going to be: **Guess where I am!!!!**

EAGLES NEST???

Dublin!!!!!

WOAH WHAT??? 4 REAL?

Yes!!!!

U YANKIN MY CHAIN???

No!!!! I'm really here!!!!!

A stream of emojis follows – Smiley Face, Sunglasses, Mind Blown – and as the messages fly in you feel like you're filling up with sweets, you laugh at the phone screen there in the bleak darkened street.

WHAT R U DOING HERE? R U WITH UR PARENTS?

No I came down myself, you write back with a touch of pride.

OMG DID U FINALLY RUN AWAY???!!!!

Ha ha No it's just for tonight I told them I was staying with a friend

LOL THEY DONT EVEN KNOW WHERE YOU ARE?

No

LOL THATS SO FUNNY

U SHUD OF TOLD ME I CUD OF SHOWD U AROUD!!!!

Yeah you say, **Had sum stuff 2 take care of,** though the truth is you didn't even think of contacting him, you haven't been in touch with him at all since that time his phone got hacked. You feel slightly bad about this, but he doesn't seem pissed off.

WHERE R U?? LETS MEET UP NOW!!!

Great! you say but then Except I have to go in a few minutes

UR LEAVING?!!!!!!

Yeah I have to go and get the bus

:(but then BUT U TOLD UR PARENTS U WERE STAYING WITH A FRIEND

Right

SO Y U LEAVING? UR PARENTS DONT EXPECT U BACK TILL 2MORO

You're so surprised you stop dead on the street. He's right! You're not supposed to come home tonight. You're supposed to be staying the night at Zargham's! How did you not see it?

The problem is – you now realize – that the plan cut from getting to Cass's house straight to the next scene, with the two of you in the Bunker, talking with Dad and him looking around with an I-just-got-my-memory-back type expression, and everything being fixed and everyone being so happy that no one including you thinks to ask questions like, *Shouldn't you be at your friend's?* Now you'll have to tell Mam Zargham was sick or something, though then if she meets his mam she's bound to ask if he's better and Zargham's mam will be like *Excuse me?* and then SHIT this is a real freaking mess BALLS—

Y DONT U COME AND STAY WITH ME???!!!

Wow, you write. That'd be great but

SRSLY!!! THERS A SPARE BED WE CAN GET PIZZA U CAN SEE MY DADS NEW CAR

Pizza?

AND IVE GOT A LOAD OF MAGIC TG DOUBLES 2 GIVE U

You'd forgotten about those doubles. Seeing as you've come all this way . . . It wouldn't be any trouble? you write.

LOL NO WAY MY MOMS DYING 2 MEET U IVE TOLD HER ALL
ABOUT U 2MORO ILL SHOW U D BEST SHOPS N WE CAN GO SEE
BLACK DAWN

The movie? It's out?

:) IT'S BEEN OUT FOR 2 WEEKS IVE SEEN IT TWICE ALREADY!!!!

Holy shit! That's awesome!

RIGHT??? ;) STAY WHERE U R IM GOING TO COME GET YOU RIGHT
NOW!!!!

Wait I'll try and find a street sign

NO NEED!!! U STILL HAVE D APP ON YOUR PHONE!!!

App?

REMMEMBER?? WHEN U WERE COMIN DOWN B4
D FREINDFINDER APP IN CASE U GOT LOST

Oh yeah! You'd totally forgotten about that.

I CAN SEE U EXCATLY WERE U R
UR SO NEAR MY HOUSE!!!!
STAY THER I'LL NBE THERE IN 5

Great!!!

You put your phone in your pocket, and park yourself under a street light to wait. Ethan is coming! It's a good thing too actually because at this point you have no idea where you are. Seems to be some kind of warehouse district, warehouses and deserted parking yards, a few minutes ago you might have found it on the sinister side? But now the broken glass sparkles in the gutter, the abandoned factory is a friend you just haven't met yet. It's like you've discovered the city's secret identity: though everything looks the same it's like it's all winking at you, glittering at you secretly from under its drab disguise.

While you wait another call comes in from Cass. You decline with a mocking laugh. This is going to be way better than her lame party. You imagine yourself telling everyone at school you've already been to the *Black Dawn* movie. *Oh yeah, I saw it up in Dublin* (slight pause, indifferent voice) . . . *in IMAX*. What's great too is not only is it more fun to stay with Ethan, i.e. than executing your plan, but it's also more honest, because you told Mam you were staying with a friend and now you are, just a different friend.

It's just such an amazing coincidence! You haven't spoken to Ethan in months and he gets in touch just as you're about to leave town! Fifteen minutes later and you'd already have been on your way back to Crazyland. Now instead you're going to eat pizza and get the *Magic: The Gathering* doubles including Deathrite Shaman and see his dad's car and the baby marmoset too, that is if there's time, though as you wait there leaning against the newly comfortable and non-intimidating broken street lamp you wonder to yourself could you actually stay in town for tomorrow night too? At the very back of your mind meanwhile a new thought is forming though you haven't fully acknowledged it yet, which is, why go back at all? Why not run away for real? Ask Ethan if you can relaunch your old plan, stay with him for a week or two, see if that lures Dad out of the woods. If not – if not maybe it's time to start exploring new horizons. Again you see yourself in the mirror sunglasses, looking out over the Manhattan skyline, Elaine at your side in a swimsuit, she's sorry about the party, it was Cass who turned her against you, *Your sister never told me how mature you are for your age*, she murmurs in your ear, and you're like, *I don't have a sister.*

Then in the midst of all these happy thoughts you start to get a strange prickly feeling. You look up and see a car driving down the street. Nothing weird about that, even though it's the first car to appear while you've been standing here. But this car is driving slowly, very slowly, the way you might if you were looking for somebody. You wonder if it could be Ethan, but from this distance it doesn't look like the kind of car Ethan's dad would drive. Suddenly the street seems fractionally less magical. You take out your phone, send Ethan a message: U on ur way??

Instantly the message comes back, JUST AROUND D CORNER :) and you feel relieved. The slow-moving car meanwhile has come to a halt halfway up the block, and that's reassuring too, probably it's just a delivery man, although no one gets out of the car. Maybe he's lost too, and he's stopped to check the address on his phone? You can't really see anything, because of the lights. His lights are shining right at you, it gives you the feeling he's looking at you. Like he's probably not, you're probably just being paranoid because the street's so deserted, it's just this dumb feeling, still you turn your back on him. As soon as you do though you realize this isn't an ideal solution because on the one hand if he (?) gets out of the car you want to know about it, also because you need to keep an eye out for Ethan, who, though you keep forgetting it, you've never actually met before so you don't 100 per cent know what he looks like except from the photos in his profile, and the same goes for him and you. It's pretty unlikely he'd actually walk past you, seeing as you're the only person on the street, but still. You risk a quick glance over your shoulder. There's no sign of him, just the car, its white lights. When you turn back though, someone's appeared at the other end of the street. Ethan! Even as you think it, you know it's not him: it's a woman in a long coat. Somehow, seeing another person brings home just how freaky it's been waiting here on your own. You find yourself leaving your lamp post, making your way down the street towards the woman. New plan: you're going to ask her for directions to the tram tracks and follow them into the city centre. As you walk you write Ethan (where is he?) a message, telling him you're going to wait somewhere else and he can come and meet you there—

But then you stop. Now that you're closer, you see that the lady's not a lady at all. It's a man – an old man, like Granddad's age, but with black curly hair down to his shoulders, like an olden-days king. He's wearing a long black coat that reaches right down to his feet and almost looks more like a cloak than a coat, and he is tremendously pale, like underground pale, larva pale, so if you were describing him to someone you would have to say with the best will in the world he'd be in the same ballpark looks-wise as e.g. Death, Voldemort, that sort of person. Basically exactly who you do not want to encounter when you're on your own on a creepy deserted street. You forget about asking for directions but you have to keep walking, you can't change direction now, that would look too weird. Another message pings in from Ethan, **ARRIVING DONT LEAVE!!!**

with a GIF of a camel on a skateboard and then another message, **STAY THERE.** So now you don't know what to do because Ethan is obviously super-close but the weirdo is even closer, moving in this very eerie glid-ing kind of way, less like a camel on a skateboard than a bride going up the aisle, an ancient old-man bride in black clutching, instead of flowers, a (WTF) *My Little Pony* comic, and *staring* at you intensely from his side of the street – staring the way your parents always told you is not polite to do, and you feel your cheeks burn which is annoying because why should *you* be blushing if he's the one being rude, why should you be ashamed, it's all back to front, and suddenly you are angry, like angry at this fucking weirdo, but angry at Ethan too for being late, and at Cass for ruining your plan, and Mam and Dad for wrecking their marriage, and Zargham and Nev and Julian Webb and whoever else, there are so many people to be angry at, though as well as angry and maybe more so you're scared, because there is no one around to help, no house even whose door you can knock on, and as he draws nearer you see he's even older than you thought, his bloodshot eyes with big pouches under them that he's covered up with powder, so much powder it looks like his face is turning to dust, and you get a smell, that is, a stench, that grows fouler with every footstep, and for some reason makes you think of the squirrel under your knife spilling its tiny guts into the forest floor, you feel your throat closing up, your lungs begin to burn, furtively as you can you tap another mes-sage to Ethan onto your phone, **wer TF r u**, hit Send—

And from very close by you hear, *Beep.*

You look at the old man. The old man looks at you. His face breaks into a smile. For a moment you can't move, only stare, open-mouthed. Then you run.

Immediately an engine roars to life at the top of the street. From behind you hear a voice call out, then a car hurtling closer, a door opening – more voices, louder, you duck down an alley, stumbling over garbage, piled up high, it's a dead end! And now car lights flood you, shouts and calls again, but you see in the new light there's a way out, behind the garbage bags, you run on – and there are the tracks! There are the tram tracks! You race towards them, a car pulls out in front of you, you dodge around it, jump onto the tracks, there is a roar, the blare of a horn as a tram surges by you, and you run, you run, you run, till you find yourself – how close it was all this time! – somewhere you recognize. It's the street with the department store where you bought shoes with Mam before Granddad's big dinner. It's thronged with people, all walking around like everything's normal. Scanning the crowd you can't see the old man, but though your lungs are burning it doesn't seem safe to stop. You turn down a side street, and you've only gone a few steps when from out of the shadows something jumps out at you – a face, smiling, yellow, familiar –

Pikachu!

And you push through the door into the video-game shop.

There is low music, a guy behind the counter looking at his phone. He glances up at you, nods. You nod back, trying to suppress your wheezing. Head to the back of the shop, fumble through your rucksack for the Ventolin and inhale. Feel your lungs unlock, the dancing sparks lift from before your eyes.

Through the window people are going by, ordinary people chatting and laughing or listening to headphones, carrying shopping bags, schoolbags, briefcases.

You go to the racks of games, flick through the titles you know so well, thinking, *What just happened?*

Did you dream it? Did you imagine it all?

You take out your phone again. Nothing. You bite your lip, wonder if you should send Ethan a message. Or should you not, should you absolutely not.

Just as you're thinking it over, the phone starts to ring. It's Dad! You remind yourself you're supposed to be in Zargham's, but as you answer – Hey, Dad? – you hear your voice shake and you know that if he asks the right question you'll probably tell him where you are and what happened, and he'll get straight in the car and come and get you.

But it must be a pocket call, because all that comes from the other end is silence, a strange staticky silence, like the night itself breathing down the line. Hello? you say. Somewhere in the background there's the sound of voices – Hello? Dad? – then they are gone again and it's back to the hissing not-quite-silence, the sound of black trees, pine-needle soil, the dark unknowable universe swirling like sharks around you. You hang up, feeling worse now than if he hadn't called at all. You wish you hadn't lied to Mam! You wish someone in the world knew where you were!

Then it hits you. Someone does know.

REMMEMBER?? WHEN U WERE COMIN DOWN B4

The app he told you to download **SO I NO WHERE TO FIND U** It's still there on your phone.

I CAN SEE U EXCATLY WERE U R

And if it's running now that means—

You turn to look at the door—

as a hand comes down on your shoulder.

DICKIE

Perfect, Victor mutters, and hands you the rifle. You fumble it into position, line it up, press your eye to the sights. You see? he says.

The darkness presses around you, packs the air. Victor climbs out of the Hide, strides through the undergrowth to the Bunker door, hunkers down and squints at you where you kneel in the wet earth. And by ten it'll be pitch dark, he calls. He'll not see a thing.

'He' means Ryszard. Sometimes he'll refer to him as 'this boyo', 'this buachaill', 'your friend'. But mostly it is 'he', 'him'. It takes you a while to realize that he doesn't actually know Ryszard's name. Nor does he know Ryszard's background, his motivation, the nature of your relationship with him, beyond the scant details you gave him; he has no interest in him, except as an adversary to be bested. Why is he doing this? He hasn't mentioned money, it doesn't seem even to have occurred to him. Is it out of loyalty to you? Or does he see it simply as an extension of his original brief? Another demonstration of his future-proofing solutions?

He stoops down, arranges some fronds at the edge of the Hide, rises up to survey it. Perfect, he says again, and then, Really, it couldn't have turned out better.

And you? Why are you doing this? Do you really think you're going to go through with it? Every minute you feel weaker, less resolved, your hands flimsy and powerless as the wet leaves piled around you, your body damp and adrift in the autumn mist. Intermittently, as if you've just thought of them, you pitch ideas up from the trench, like *Of course, we don't need to actually shoot*, or *Once we've thrown a scare into him, that should be enough*; Victor accepts these graciously, without allowing them to distract him from his preparation. You don't know if you believe them yourself; you have a suspicion that it no longer matters what you believe, that the story has taken on a life of its own and will follow its path to the end, with or without you.

How did it come to this? You look back at the past and you can't tell where exactly you went wrong. Was it a single misstep? When you reached for Ryszard in the empty garage? The night in your musty Rooms when you told Frank to do the honourable thing? Or is it everything? Your years raising a family, running a business, your little loves, your thwarted desires, your whole innocuous life, has it all been leading up to this moment? And if it has, what does that make you?

One thing we haven't thought about, Victor says, is accomplices. He tramps over to the far side of the clearing. Is this lad going to have someone with him? Because if he is, we should have two different positions. He turns to you. What do you think?

He told me he had a girlfriend, you remember. He said she was pregnant. That's why he wanted the money.

Yeah, they've all got a fuckin' sob story, Victor says. He holds out his finger and thumb and draws a bead on the Bunker. Not likely he'll be bringing her out here then, if she's up the spout. As for a backup – I reckon no, not with this fella. He just wants to get in and get out, as fast as he can, with as much as he can. He thinks it'll be an easy take. But it won't, will it.

No, I suppose it won't.

By God it won't, either.

There is silence for a moment. When you speak, your voice sounds faint, the hissing of wind in the leaves. Do you think that you can do a bad thing and still be a good person?

How's that?

If you do something evil, do you think that means that you were evil all along?

Victor wipes his nose. You can't be too hard on yourself, he says. In a war no one says killing a man is evil, do they?

We're not in a war.

It's nothing but war, Victor says. It's never not been war. Here, I've to get something from the van. Back in a minute. You might as well get up out of that and stretch your legs for a bit. We'll be sat there a while tonight.

He shuffles back to the clearing and away. He needs a break from your snivelling. And you need a break too. He is right, your legs are aching. But you don't want to move. How long has it been since you kneeled? Knelt? It reminds you of going to Mass when you were a child, gazing up in wonderment at the Cross behind the altar, the magical figure hanging from it who with his impenetrable sorrow and effortless miracles seemed to you to represent the mysteries of adult life. You would pray then, for all your little wishes. An A+ in the spelling test. A new Subbuteo team. Tallness. To beat Frank. In return I promise I will never sin again.

You have been to Mass since, of course. You were at Mass last week. But how long since you prayed? Prayed and expected to be answered? Or even listened to?

Now in the place of the Cross is the Bunker. You can still just about see it, sepulchral in the gloom. When the kids were little this was their squirrel house. A sign on the door saying HQ NO ADOLTS. You were the hunter with the shotgun who would always be foiled. They'd knock you to the ground, pile onto you. We're killing you! Cass would shriek, her brother squeaking in echo, Killing! And you would roll and roar upon the forest floor, and think what a wonderful way that would be to die.

And now on that same ground, in that same sacred space, a man will die for real. You will kill a man for real, a man you once loved, on the loved ground where you played with your children.

It's a high price to pay, isn't it. Taking a life.

Victor, beside you in the trench, his hand on your shoulder.

I've been so stupid, you whisper.

Loneliness can make people do terrible things, he says. When you set out on this road, you never thought for an instant you would be this lonely, did you?

Tears run down your cheeks; he brushes them away with the backs of his fingers. So lonely for so long, he says. Being your brother's ghost! What a way to live your life.

He turns you to look at him. His eyes are very clear and bright.

You don't have to do this, Dickie, he says. There is another way.

You gaze at him, half-hopeful, half-dreading.

Tell the truth. Let it all come out. Admit what you did—

You let out a groan that rises from your bowels.

Admit what you did, he persists. Tell Maurice, tell Imelda, tell the kids.

You sink your head, cover your eyes with your hands.

What's the alternative? Kill a man? You want the kids to have a killer for a father? You think you can do something like that and stay the same?

Your eyes, your ears too, you raise your voice in a wail so you won't hear him. But you hear him anyway. Is this how you'd want your children to live? Hiding themselves away, for shame of who they are? In a million years, is that what you would want for them? Dickie – he prises the hands away from your eyes – Dickie, I won't lie, it will be horrible. For them and for you. They will be hurt, they will be traumatized. They will not understand. They will leave you.

He leans in to you, whispers, But they will come back.

The trees are spinning around you, like an out-of-control carousel, and his face is snatched up with them to become a blur. But his voice comes to you clear and composed. Your children love you, he says. They'll find a way to understand. Imelda too, even her. That is what love is. It is bigger than facts. It is bigger than the sum of what you have done. You can be done with that false life, take the good things with you. Start again.

You only have to trust in the people who love you, he says. You only have to open your heart up to love.

He smiles. Though it seems impossible his wayward eyes somehow look straight into yours; and his hand rises again to caress your cheek.

You take a deep breath, let his soft lips fall softly on yours, let your heavy eyelids close.

Then open them again.

Victor has entered the clearing. Something is in his hand.

This is for you, he says. He passes you the object, wrapped in a plastic bag.

Ordered it off the dark web, he says. They sent it to me in fifty separate fuckin' packages. Just got the last one yesterday. Lucky for you.

You take it out of the bag. It is long, heavy, metal, black. A cylinder with appendages, a mutated cousin of something you recognize.

Had to put it together meself, Victor says. Looks a bit weird but it shoots true. Tried it out on the crows in me back field. Go on, give it a go.

It's all right, you say. You run your hand along the barrel. You can feel energy humming through it, just as you did with the wire hangers when you were dowsing for water. As if it is full of spirits, as if spirits are descending from the dark sky to fill it.

There is a rattling sound. Victor is looking down at his outstretched palm. He has something there: you think it is teeth at first, his country teeth. Then he loads them into his rifle.

Who was that you were talking to? he says.

No one, you say. You crack open your gun to receive the shells.

IMELDA

By the time you leave the nursing home the sky has darkened Rain on the way they said and you didn't believe it but now over the car park you see big black clouds hanging and more packing in like a crowd before a match and that same air of waiting And in your heart for a moment you feel a cold pang remembering Poor Lar he is not right in the head You asked him had he somewhere to stay You could put him up till he goes back to England But he shrugged it off Said he had it sorted You didn't ask again It was all too much wasn't it Going back into that madness

Shush enough leave it

You take a deep breath Get in the car check yourself in the mirror One thing's for certain you're in no fit state for dinner Your face all puffed out from crying In a ratty old hoody and jeans because you didn't have time to get changed You wonder should you just call him and put it off till again but then as you're sitting there figuring it out the phone rings in your hand and it's him Mike

Listen he says I'm sorry but something's come up A breech birth on the farm I've to go out there now with the vet I'm very sorry

You look at the gathering clouds The first thing in your head of course the girl the housekeeper But you keep your voice light Another time so you say Who knows Maybe it's for the best

I'm not calling it off Mike says anxiously Only that I'll be late It won't take more than an hour if you don't mind hanging on

I've got the dinner mostly cooked he says and he laughs For what it's worth

You're sure? you ask him

Sure as can be he says Tell you what I'll leave the door on the latch for you and if you like just come on over pour yourself a glass of wine and I'll be back before you know it

Okay you say thinking wouldn't that be best To get out of the mad-house of your family your past for a few hours at least I'm only in a hoody you say

Well I'll be covered head to toe in cow shite he says So we'll be quite the pair

You laugh despite yourself Everything all right there? he asks You sound a bit off

Oh you say dabbing at your eyes Nothing major Just a funny sort of a day

But starting the car you think determinedly of the night ahead and already you feel a bit better

Dusk is falling in the meadows as you drive back towards town The trees shuttle black by the window and beyond them the blue ghosts of the mountains appear and disappear When you were little Daddy would point up to them and tell you he'd buried a chest of gold coins there If there's ever a time I'm not here to take care of you I'll send you word where that chest is You go and dig it up you'll be right till I'm back

But then he'd be gone and he never did tell you where it was

And then after the wedding you never saw him again

The sky darkens The dark deepens The road is empty with only you on it and the trees In the green-black light it's like driving underwater As if a river had seized you was bearing you off Leaves and tendrils rubbing against you The wash of the stones beneath you Creatures peering at you through the murk

He'd come to bring you to the church

You were in Rose's cottage The bridesmaids swirling around you The woman from the salon standing back God is my witness I have never seen a more beautiful bride She wanted to take a picture she could use in her ads You were looking out the window at the sun Then came the knock at the door

There on the step was Daddy in a morning suit Behind him in the yard a car a Jaguar Vintage The colour of blood with ribbons on the bonnet He wanted to take you Aren't you my only daughter?

You looked to Rose but she was at that moment out of sight Hidden somewhere in the bustle Or hiding Maurice is sending a car you said

It's a father's job Daddy said I talked to Maurice He agrees with me Come on now or you'll be late

Did you believe him Did you even care You were thinking only of the church So you lifted the hem of your frilly white dress and stepped over the mud to the car He held the door open for you as you squeezed into the seat packing your wedding train around you and he closed the door again

That car God knows where he got it The seats were leather the dashboard walnut but the heating was broken so he couldn't turn it off though the sun was beating down Splitting the stones He had the windows open Still you were sweating in your dress The radio playing the Dubliners The Road to God Knows Where He had a can of beer tucked between his knees He pretended he didn't hear when you asked him not to smoke When you were a little way from the cottage he said So you're going to go ahead with this

You turned You looked at him His eyes were fixed on the road You should have known then He never watched where he was going But you just said Yes

A hiss broke from him Have you lost your mind he said His brother? Frank's own brother?

It's none of your business you said You had been through all this a thousand times Is this the right thing all that And had heard Frank's voice like God's speaking inside your head *Go to the church That's where I'll see you* So you were going

You heard a gulp You thought he might be crying Did you ever even love him he said Did you love him at all

Dickie? you said

Frank! he said Frank! Have you forgotten his name already

And something snapped inside you Oh Frank Frank I'm sick hearing about him Why didn't you marry him yourself if you were that gone on him

Then you lurched forward as he slammed on the brakes You were on some little boreen in the middle of nowhere His face turned to you pushing out of the heat like a sea monster from the waves and when he spoke it was in a low gurgling voice like he was mashing himself to pieces in his rage You're a cold vicious little creature he said You always were

And he started the car again with his face set and his jaw grinding away as if he was chewing scrap metal You sat back into your dream thinking only of the church

But was that where you were going? What way is this you said He didn't answer Just took a drink from his can and you got a feeling at the pit of your stomach You asked him again Is this the way to the church?

We're not going to the church he said shortly and now a wave ran through you

I'm not letting you go through with this he said You're not in your right mind You started screaming

I'm taking you to England he said till we get you back to yourself again

It's for your own good he bellowed I won't let you disgrace me

There was more He had it all planned The ferry The boys following with your things in the van But you barely heard You were frantic You had to get to that church You tried the door but he'd locked it You begged You pleaded You even tried to grab the wheel he pushed you back That fellow has bewitched you he roared Can you not see what he is Taking up with his own brother's woman and poor Frank not cold in the ground It is unholy A mockery And all the money and riches in the world will not make it right

You fell silent Stunned

You'll thank me he said In a few months you will see this for the madness it is and you will thank me

You sat there in silence sweating into your dress Then you thought of something and you laughed

That shook him You let him drive on You laughed softly to yourself

What's funny he said

In a few months I'm going to have a baby you said

He didn't say anything You wouldn't think he'd heard you Only very slowly the car drew to a halt

The boreen was full of elderflowers that came pressing through the windows Bees buzzed Nobody was around for miles His face turned towards you once more and you felt almost sorry for him because you had won Defeated him with your treacherous woman's body

I'm pregnant you said

He blackened It was like a storm about to break The air getting thick and tight You knew there was nothing you could do to stop it even if you'd wanted to

But still he saw a glimmer of light Is it Frank's?

You just laughed again That's when he hit you

Yes his princess his angel his untouched beauty He hit you with the can of beer Your head snapped sideways It felt like your eye had burst But from the other eye you saw him twist his belly round in the seat so he could get at you properly His hands came at you shovelling the lacy veil aside so he could reach your throat I'll kill you by Christ You knew he'd do it You would die here among the flowers

Only at that moment a tractor came puttering around the bend and a little farmer in a flat cap asked from the cab were you having difficulties

Well full credit to him he was never caught short for a lie Oh says he Wasn't it a bee got in there under her veil

A bee says the farmer

Can you believe it Daddy says She is to be married this very morning up in the town Only now this bee has gone and stung her beautiful face

God works in mysterious ways said the farmer But you are headed the wrong way for the town

Is that so said Daddy

Yes the farmer said and he pointed back down the road and told them the right way to go

Thank you indeed Daddy said

You're most welcome the farmer said And congratulations to you both With that he waved as if in goodbye Though he didn't leave but stayed there watching till Daddy had started the car again and turned it around

You drove on together in silence

Coming into town the streets were empty as if every living soul was in there in that church

Daddy pulled up at the gate He sat there a moment You wondered would he come in after all after everything But then he spoke

Listen to me now he said His mouth was downturned His yellowed eyes were sour and heavy These are the last words I will say to you

I would curse you both he said Only you've done that for yourselves already

So I'll just tell you how it will go

You will lose everything

Your house and your land The ground under your feet Your child inside you Everything you have will vanish away On the side of the road you'll be begging strangers for pennies Maybe then you'll understand what it is that you've done

A cunt like you with your airs and ways You think how you can act as you please But there are some things the world will not abide Marrying that man You'd be better off putting your head in a noose and that's the God's truth

You let him finish then lowered your veil stepped out of the car The dress had remained white by a miracle You heard him start the engine drive off You didn't look back You went up to the church door Alone

If he'd known your plan he might have gone easier on you Maybe you should have explained What a fool to think you'd forgotten Frank When Frank was all you thought of For months going to his grave Speaking to his ghost Readying yourself for this moment Daddy could have wrung your neck it wouldn't have stopped you getting here Where you knew he'd be waiting inside Standing there sparkling and see-through Twinkling at you like something off the TV Raised up out of the ground in the suit he was buried in Handsome unspoiled A hand reached out ready to take you to heaven

But you opened the door and it was only Dickie there waiting

Dickie green at the gills who could blame him What must he have thought He must have known though he never let on Came home every night to make dinner Tipped away at the nursery Brought you catalogues for the new house Asked your opinion What d'you think of these curtains Or should we get blinds How do you feel about parquet floors You with holes in your shoes from the walk to Naancross Dirt under your nails from scrabbling at the ground Should we get a washer-dryer combo or are separate units better

Trying to reel you back in to earth Must have supposed some day you'd be in your right mind again

Waited for you at the altar while Daddy left never to return Just as Frank had

Damn it! you exclaim out loud alone in the car because now everything has blurred up again Drive and cry That's all you ever do these days You are going to look like shit for Mike Absolute shit If you'd thought of bringing a bit of lipstick even

But here's the turn for your own house coming up You told yourself you would not go back there Not to have to tell him more lies But he's probably down in his fort and if you keep it quick change your top at least Put on a skirt Decent knickers If you're going to do this you might as well do it right So you switch on the indicator though there is no one on the road and take the turn-off A quick stop that is all Then you're not thinking of any of this stuff any more Daddy Frank Dickie any of that

Tonight is about the future You've had enough past frankly to last you a lifetime

CASS

It's warm on the bus and your seat is right over the engine and you keep wanting to doze off, but every time your eyes close you instantly jerk awake again, seized by a terror that he has gone, and you have to stop yourself reaching out and grabbing him to be sure he's really there. This must be what it's like being a parent, constantly worrying your kids will be annihilated the moment you look away. That must be why they're all so insane.

You ran all the way to the bus station. The bus hadn't boarded yet, but you couldn't find him in the crowd waiting at the barrier. Anyway you knew he wasn't there. You ran back down the tracks, back through the streets, up and down, up and down, through the sea of wrong faces, in a panic that was simultaneously curdling into despair. Till you stopped, feeling more alone than you ever had in your life, at a cross-roads, took a deep breath, tried to put yourself in his shoes. What would he do, where would he go? That's when you saw the game shop – appearing to you like a gift, a shimmering holy grail, right across the street. When you went up to him he nearly jumped out of his skin. You grabbed him with both hands, like he was a lucky leprechaun that might disappear.

He didn't seem especially pleased to see you, which you supposed was fair enough. You yelled at him again, you knew you shouldn't but you were just so freaked out. You walked him to the bus station to make sure he got on the bus, then you bought a ticket for yourself too to make sure he didn't get off it again.

Since then he hasn't spoken much. You asked about Dad hunting the squirrels, but he didn't want to talk about it. He seemed embarrassed, like he regretted making a fuss. Now he gazes out the window, looking somehow unlike himself – older, sadder, his cheeks hollower, his mouth bunched up, like someone's just handed him all of his adult worries for the rest of his life.

There's a house on the way back that has signs posted in the lawn about barcodes and chemtrails and a big one that says UFOs ARE REAL – PROOF WITHIN ADMISSION FREE. Coming home from Dublin you'd always see it and PJ would ask Dad if you could stop and he'd always say, Next time. Now you watch out to see if you can spot it, you're half-tempted to suggest you get out and take a look. Just to cheer him up a bit? But it's dark outside so you might already have passed it. Anyway, the proof probably isn't anything if it's just sitting in some guy's back yard.

Your phone bleeps. Elaine has posted another picture from the party. Your feed is full of them – full of Elaine, laughing and smiling, smiling and laughing. In the latest someone has given her a tiara. It makes her look like the winner of one of those beauty competitions you used to look at together in her room, the girls who had overcome adversity to become brand ambassadors, queens of the universe. She hasn't messaged to ask you where you are. What would she say if she knew you were on your way home? It would confirm everything she thought about you. Maybe you were the adversity all along, and now she has overcome you.

The tiara picture already has fifty likes. You hit Mute. Then, gently, without rancour or regret, you hit Unfollow.

From beside you, but without looking at you, PJ says, are you going to tell Mam?

Tell her what?

That I came to Dublin.

Is that what you think? That I'm coming back to tell on you?

He doesn't reply to this.

Well, anyway, I'm not going to, you say.

So why are you coming back?

Uh, because you gatecrashed my party then got lost in the city?

No, I mean, what will you tell Mam?

Oh. You hadn't thought of this. I'll tell her I had to pick up a book or something, you say. She won't ask. I bet she won't even notice. You know what she's like.

You *don't* know what she's like, he says. She's different. They both are. And again you see the bunched-up mouth and the haggard grown-up face.

Stop worrying, you say. It's going to be okay.

Your phone sounds again and a new picture appears. This time it's not of Elaine. Instead, a blue-haired girl is grinning manically as she climbs out of a dark hole in a low hill, guarded by oblong stones.

Who's that? PJ says, looking over your shoulder.

No one, you say, and then, Just this girl from college.

Is that the passage grave?

Yeah, she was visiting it today. Merle.

What?

That's her name.

Along with many pictures, taken from the inside and out of the burial mound, Merle has written a very long text about the astronomical knowledge of the ancients, who have constructed the tomb so that on the darkest day of the year the sun's rays will fall through a shaft in the roof and strike its heart with their light. This is the very powerful metaphor of rebirth, she says.

She should go to the other one, PJ says. The one where there's no tourists.

Yeah, you say.

Seriously, he says. That one is way better.

He's right: and it strikes you now that you could actually bring her there, tomorrow, if you wanted. You could meet up with her and show her the sights, invite her back to the house, even. You picture her at your dinner table, Mam and Dad struggling to reconfigure themselves around her oatmeal cardigans, her Germanic candour. You begin to write to her,

Hey guess what! Then you pause, and return your gaze to the window, the dark country fleeting so mysteriously by.

Here's the thing: ever since you got on the bus, you've been feeling weirdly happy.

You know that once you get home everything will go arseways. You will remember how utterly fucked up Mam and Dad's relationship is, not to mention what they're like with you. Mam will talk and talk and talk, and you will feel besieged and overshadowed and diminished. You will feel Dad simultaneously judging you and also inviting pity and you won't know which is worse. Immediately it'll come back to you why you started hating him: because he taught you to be upright and wholesome and good and you found out you could not be those things; because he wants you, needs you, to be his little girl still, when you have become loathsome, crawling, ugly and perverse. Because you know that if he knew the truth he would love you anyway and somehow that is unbearable to you.

Yes: once you start thinking about it, you can see just what a nightmare this trip is going to be. Still the bus rolls on and the twilight lengthens and you just feel happier and happier.

Your eyelids are drooping again. Heat swarms around you, with beckoning words *memorious minge merle* . . . Before you drift off you check your phone. You're making good time.

We'll be home by ten, you say.

III

Dickie   Stay calm, he says. Don't shoot till you have a clear sight of him. Don't shoot till you know.

That makes sense. But the gun *wants* to shoot. You can feel it straining against your fingers, like a dog tugging at its lead. Sensing the moment arrive.

Beside you Victor stands stock-still with the rifle raised to his shoulder – finger on the trigger, eye pressed to the sights. He has been like that, unmoving, hardly speaking, for an hour, while you fidget and quiver beside him. Damp clings to you thick as moss. Above you, around you, darkness falls through the trees, rises up from the ground. That is the only sound to be heard, the hush of the falling dark.

And then a branch snaps. Reflexively, Victor cocks the rifle – your nerves jolt, your mind floods with panic –

He uncocks again. Nothing, he says.

You gasp, heart hammering between your ears.

You have been terrified so long you are wearied by it. Terror has become indistinguishable from boredom, a kind of tumultuous numbness. If only the shit could hit now! If only there could be a tsunami, a firestorm, some Ragnarok that would engulf the world! To suffer, to die en masse, in innocence – somehow that seems better than one person being killed, seems better for everybody.

You check your phone. It is almost ten.

What if he doesn't come?

He'll come, Victor says, keeping his eye to the gun sights.

But what if it's not tonight? Ten was just the time he gave

you for the drop-off. It doesn't mean he'll be here to pick it up. Maybe he won't come till tomorrow, you think. Maybe he won't come till many years later, and you can grow old here in the forest, kneeling in a hole in the earth.

This fella doesn't want to stick around, Victor says. He'll grab his money, and then he'll be off like a hot snot.

Right, you say, your little squib of hope dying instantly into the darkness. Victor sees, misunderstands. But we won't let him, Dickie.

No, you say.

He peers at you through the mustering gloom. There's no other way, he says. You know there's no other way.

Yes, you say. You know this. You just have to toughen up. *Toughen up!* You hiss it to yourself. Imagining yourself surrounded by azaleas, in the garden, your father slapping your ear.

Thunder rumbles overhead, so loud that Victor lowers the rifle and looks up. A moment later the deluge begins, hitting the leaves with a sound like a thousand machine guns opening fire.

Within a minute, you are drenched. The ground around your feet begins to fill up with water. How plausible is it that we're out here in weather like this? you say.

Victor looks at you in mystification. Plausible? he says.

We're hunting squirrels and he wanders into our path, isn't that the story? But who'd be hunting out here in the middle of a storm?

We don't have to use it if you don't want, he says. We don't have to have a story at all. We can always just bury him here.

Something about that word – *bury* – strikes home as nothing else has. Maybe because the sound and feel of your shovel in the soil has become so familiar. Nightmarish images flood your mind, unaskable questions. What if someone finds out? What if it's *not enough*? What if you bury him, and still he comes back? You close your eyes, take a deep breath. Then you say quietly, If we go through with this. Can you promise me the children will never see those recordings? Can you guarantee it?

Victor considers this. He is barely visible in the rain and darkness. Well, I'm not saying it'll *guarantee* it, he says at last. You say this lad's got films on his phone, then fuck knows who he's given them to. A hundred people could have them. A thousand people could have them. It's the twenty-first century, the entire fuckin' planet could have seen them for all I know. Now I'm betting we'll put an end to the whole business tonight. But if you wanted to *guarantee* they didn't see anything – it'd be the kids you'd need to shoot, not your man.

You stare back at him in horror. Then covering your mouth with one hand, you scramble out of the trench and into the trees.

Imelda You pull up at the top of the driveway but instead of going in and changing your clothes you don't get out of the car You just sit there

The house is in darkness Nobody home Even with a storm on the way And though you wanted to avoid him the longer you stare at those black windows the angrier they make you That he is not even there for you to have to lie to That inside the hour you will be with Big Mike and he doesn't even know let alone try to stop you He is out in the woods with his troll and you with your father dead and Rose dying and on your way to another man's arms and he has driven you to it and does he even care?

Well to hell with him To hell with make-up too Big Mike will take you as you are You turn the key in the ignition The lights flare up against the house The engine roars You reverse at speed but hit a potted plant FUCK and you turn the engine off again and fling open the door so roughly it rebounds against your knee and pain shoots through your leg and you beat your fists on the steering wheel and scream out loud alone in the car *I can't do this!*

You can't You just can't go and be with someone else and come home and pretend nothing's wrong when everything's wrong

And there and then you decide if you're going to cheat on him you're going to bloody well tell him first He's bloody well going to know about it You take out your phone but get voicemail So much the better You will go right down into the woods Confront him in his warren Tell him to his face that his marriage is ending and it's his fault

You go inside for a torch but Dickie must have them all down there And when you open the back door to look out Wondering could you find your way in the dark At that instant like it's been waiting for you there's a rumble of thunder directly overhead and a second later rain comes down in torrents like it's the end of the world But if he thinks that's going to stop you he's got another thing coming You charge out as you are Don't even bring a coat Slam the door behind you

The instant you step out you're soaked Rain comes at you in waves The ground's already turning into marsh Your shoes keep sinking so you reach down pull them off throw them back in the direction of the house and march barefoot over the field towards the woods You're going to let him have it Both barrels

Just as you reach the treeline your phone beeps with a message from Big Mike **Darling Still delayed See you before long** ♥ ♥ ♥ ♥ ♥ ♥ You leave it open ready to show Dickie See this? *Darling* that's what he calls me Look at all those hearts Six

Both barrels Dickie Barnes By Jesus if you knew what was coming

PJ   Whoa, says Cass.

Yeah, you say.

Out of nowhere the rain's come hammering down so thick that you can barely see through the windows. Even the cars that sluice by are almost hidden, all you can see are their lights, pale and fizzing like disintegrating moons.

We're going to get drenched if we walk back from town, Cass says. She turns to you. Will I just call Mam? Do you reckon she'd come pick us up?

I think she's out, you say. I think she has Tidy Towns.

What about Dad? Do you want to call Dad?

You make a show of considering this, then say, We could ask the driver to let us out up ahead and then go through the woods? It'd be way quicker.

Rain thunders against the roof. Cass looks reluctant.

I know a short cut, you say.

I know a short cut, she retorts. I *invented* the short cut. It's just it's pitch dark.

We have our phones? you say, then as she's still wavering, Red car–blue car?

She presses her lips together. You both look out into the streaming night. A car passes by, and another, but it's impossible to make out their colours.

Okay, okay, Cass says, throwing up her hands. Go and ask the driver.

Augustina   The mattress in the corner is stained with black mould. A bag sits on it containing everything you own. The smell of damp here is overpowering. You have been gone for months but the house feels like it has been empty for years, a ruin from long ago. A tree is pushing through the roof of the house next door. Like the forest is taking it back, bit by bit.

What you looking at? Ryszard says, coming up behind you.

The woods, you say, pointing at the window, though there is nothing to see.

How he ever thought anyone would want to live here, you say.

Mmm. He is not listening. His hands rest on your hips, then slide up to your breasts.

Don't, you say. He keeps going. I can't, you say. Not in this place.

You fucked me in this place, he says. And you fucked him.

You turn to look at him. His eyes, his lips, glister blackly at you through the gloom. He says these things to see what you will do. He doesn't really care, he is not the jealous type.

Mike kept you here after his wife found out. It was different then. The mattress had no mould, it had sheets, Egyptian cotton he told you. How long were you here? Weeks? Months? Time stopped making sense, each day was the same. He brought you every luxury. Takeout every night, every possible cream and lotion for the shower. But the water flipped hot and cold like someone with a fever, and he didn't like you going outside in case you might be seen.

You felt like you were seen anyway, in the daytime on your own. Like someone was watching from the trees. You never told him, he said he didn't like crazy types. He was going to leave his wife for you, he said, he was just waiting for the right moment. Then over time he stopped coming. Day after day, night after night, alone looking into these woods. One night a car pulled up outside. You thought someone had come to kill you. Went to look anyway out of sheer boredom. Saw a beautiful man taking machine parts from the boot of his car. When he left town for good you left with him. You should never have come back.

I hate it here, you say.

After tonight you'll never see it again, he says. He picks up his coat. Stay there. Don't go outside.

Just like Mike used to say, you think. But you say only, How long will you be gone?

He shrugs. All I have to do is grab the money, he says. Then he squeezes your hips and whispers in your ear, *Then we are rich*.

Sometimes he feels like a house that no one has ever lived in. Shiny and enticing but not quite finished. Trees waiting under the floor to take over the off-white rooms.

He turns the light out as he leaves. Only then do you see his torch on the table. How could he go without it in this rain? He is more nervous than he lets on, you think. You run to the door, scan the face of the woods, but you can't see him. You return inside, sit in the dark. Crazy, this whole plan is crazy. And you are crazy too, to fall in love with him, to get pregnant with his child. Crazy ever to come back here.

Dickie You run into the trees as far as you are able before you have to stop and tug down your trousers. You throw up into the darkness at the same time as you void your bowels. You cry too. Everything is coming out of you tonight. You wipe yourself with a paper tissue, dither over what to do with it, finally push it into the undergrowth. Then, jaggedly sucking in air, you rise to your feet.

Emptied out, you find yourself calmer. Your panic has left you along with everything else. You see that Victor is right: this is the only way. Yes, it's insane. To be out here, in the dark, with a gun, waiting to kill someone – to *kill* them, in cold blood, it is insane, absurd, horrific. But how much of life is insane, when you think about it? Civilization itself is insane, it's insane to continue as normal when the world is burning alive. So leave that aside, leave all thoughts of right and wrong, of fate, Furies, penance, atonement. See the problem for what it is. Then it becomes quite simple. Someone is trying to take something from you; this is how you stop him. In all likelihood you will succeed. In all likelihood Ryszard will die, and there will be no consequences. No dogged pipe-smoking inspector will appear on your doorstep, no echoing heartbeat will pound from the forest to wake you from your sleep. You will not be racked by guilt, your children will not sense any difference in you, you will not be estranged, exiled. The fact is that people do terrible things every day and the world goes on, they commit atrocities, and then resume their ordinary humdrum lives. In real terms a death is practically non-existent. It's simply a case of seeing that, of seeing things as they are.

With this eerie clarity, that is akin to weightlessness, you start to make your way back. But what is the way back? In the light of the phone all you can see are trees, skeletal white and eye-socket black, teeming around you thick as the rain.

Dickie! The walkie-talkie, clipped to your jacket, erupts in a fizz of noise. *It's almost ten! Where are you?*

I don't know, you say. The blackness has suddenly grown hot, you feel sweaty, clammy, as if you were indoors, in a crowd.

You must be close, the walkie-talkie reasons. *Shine your torch till I see if I can see you.*

You raise the phone, bring it in a circle.

Anything? you say.

Hello? you say. Victor? But there is no response.

You stumble forwards in what seems like the right direction. The trees, slick with rain, press in on you, as though herding you. Between them, in the torchlight, you seem to see – you see –

Hello? you say again. Hello?

You take a breath. Don't worry about what you see. It's just a matter of retracing your steps. Realistically, you can't have come far. *Realistically*. Yes! That's what you need to focus on. You lift your hand to your eyes, make a concentrated effort to see it. It is real, the gun it holds is real. The moon is real. The trees are real.

Ghosts are not real. The faces are not real.

Imelda   Then you step into the trees and instantly it's as if the world's been scrubbed away leaving only the rain and the dark How could he think this grass was greener How could he desert you for this

Or is Geraldine right Has it just come time Does marriage have a sell-by date like everything else

That's what she said Not that long ago but before all this You were all in Bojangles together Girls listen to me she said If you had the chance to go back in time knowing what you know now Would you do it again Leaving the kids out of it would any woman in their right mind marry her husband again?

Well that had you all stumped Even Una Dwan who'd usually offer some sort of perspective

It was Roisin who spoke up in the end You remember it how you were surprised The one who was having so much fun since Martin left her Swingle Having a ball Still it was she who said now: But you can't go back in time

How's that Geraldine said

You can't go back in time she said Isn't that the whole point of it Marriage I mean That's why you do it Because you can't go back You can only go forward So you're making a vow you'll go forward together Stay together even though you'll change get sick get old That's the vow

A vow you think now Yes And imagine yourself confronting Dickie *You made a vow On our wedding day You made a vow!*

But you can't remember what the vow was

You must have said it too You remember standing there in front of the priest But you were so out of it You barely knew what was happening

It's impossible to think in this rain You can't even tell if you're going the right way There's a track or a trail you know but you can't see it and then Something stabs you right in the eye

A tree branch it must be You crash back into wet leaves Your eye burns like it's on fire The same one as then That day the wedding and as you pick yourself up and stumble forward again a little voice in your head laughs and says Maybe you're gone back in time after all Imelda Maybe you've got your wish

Ridiculous But the pain's the same too Like it's been in there waiting all this time to return You remember squinting out of it from the top table trying to spot Frank like if you looked hard enough you could make him appear

And then being led out by the hand by the man you'd just married The band playing the first dance Wonderwall Across the room you saw yourself in the mirror wrapped up in gauze A white drift of sadness A ghost Dickie with his hands on your hips The guests grinning at you from every side and their smiles were a wonderwall closing you in and Dickie's arms were a wall and the new house was a wall and the stack of gifts was a wall and all of those walls were toppling in on you and you felt like you were being buried alive

And at the back of the room you thought you saw Daddy there with a leer on his chops raising a glass as if to say Well girleen are you satisfied Are you happy now

Cass The bus pulls in and hisses to a stop. Across the road you see the lane that leads up to the unfinished houses and the track you used take to the Bunker and you get a rush of excitement, *I'm back! I'm back!* But as soon you step down onto the roadside it's immediately clear you've made a mistake. The wind pounds you, the rain hits you in freezing slaps like you're out on the open sea with waves coming over the deck. You turn to PJ, whose teeth are already chattering. Let's just stay on the bus – you have to shout over the storm. We can get a taxi from town. What? he yells back. *Back on the bus!* you repeat, pointing. But already the bus is pulling away and vanishing into the rain.

Nothing else for it. Hugging yourself, you hurry over the empty road. After he crosses, though, PJ stops. What is it? you say.

He doesn't reply. Rain explodes on the asphalt. It's so cold it feels like little splinters of ice.

I'm not so sure this is a good idea, he says.

What are you talking about? The short cut?

He looks back unhappily. Something is clearly bothering him, but he won't say what it is. He just keeps looking back and forth from the woods to your face with a troubled expression. Then he asks if you've seen *Pet Sematary*.

What the fuck? you say. He starts in on a confusing speech about things coming back when they're not meant to – something like that, you can't really follow, it's hard to hear and the rain is like someone is literally continuously emptying a bathtub of water over you. But we never had any pets, you tell him, trying to hold on to your patience. Look, let's just get moving. At least in the woods we'll have some cover.

You continue up the lane. Reluctantly, PJ trudges after you. As you near the ghost estate, you see something: a light in one of the houses. I didn't know there were people living there, you say.

Yeah, PJ says.

Yeah, there are, or . . .?

He doesn't reply: he is walking in the other direction, over to the track. Now it's you who wants to hold back. Maybe you could knock on their door? Take shelter until the rain has eased? But at that moment the light goes out and something about it gives you the chills and you follow PJ as he splashes away into the brambles.

Big Mike Cantwell House on your left like a grey ghost coming out of the trees. Creaghan's Stores closed. The forest in the distance, a black sprawl. Phone mast on the hill rising over it. Harder and harder to see anything with this rain.

In your left pocket two grand in cash, in the back seat a bolt gun from the farm. You're not going to hurt her. But you need to be firm.

Your father used to say you can never trust a woman: it was a whatdoyoucall with him, an article of faith. The biggest joke God ever played was to create women's bodies then put women's brains into them, that's what he said. Like leaving a poisoner in charge of a sweetshop. She never seemed like the tricky type. But look at this. Doesn't even tell you she's back, just shows up on the fucking main street, you have to hear it from your foreman. *I seen that old housekeeper of yours is in the family way.* With a smirk on him.

Mind games, that's the way they operate. She knew it'd get back to you. Planning to come out of the woodwork once she had you nice and rattled. But she won't be expecting you tonight. Hasn't made her move yet, you'll get the jump on her.

Past the Barnes place. Not far now. Watch for the turn. Here we go.

You park halfway up the lane, sit there a minute. The lights are out in the house, but you know she's in there. It'd be just like the brass neck of her to put herself up in your own bloody private property while she's back in town to put the squeeze on you. When you had her living there she did nothing but complain about it. Too damp, too cold, nothing working. Didn't like the woods. What brought her back? She'll say it's for money but you'll bet anything she's heard about you and Imelda. They can never bear to imagine you with someone else. Naturally jealous. Even the good-looking ones – especially them. It's all fun and games at the start then for the rest of eternity they're wheeling over you like vultures.

You haven't been out this way in months – not since she ran off. Too depressing, looking at these houses. You used to be here every day, calling in to her with this and that. She had this green T-shirt she wore – Little Miss Innocent. That's when you first noticed her, really noticed her that is. Wearing that T-shirt, doing the ironing. Something about her bare arms moving back and forth through the cloud of steam, the green eyes coming up to meet yours then dropping back down. Getting into your head so you couldn't think straight.

You told her you'd run away with her. She didn't want to go back to Brazil. Okay, Thailand, then. Patagonia, Costa Rica. I don't give a fuck so long as it's warm and no one can find us. Madness, of course. You say these things in the heat of the moment. Though at the same time, why not? If the market hadn't tanked you could have sold these gaffs. Cleaned out the accounts, slowly, over six months say. Then one day you're gone. Could have spent the rest of your days playing golf, drinking pina coladas. Instead you're stuck here in Joan's fucking spiderweb.

Enough. Stay focused. If word gets out of that baby it'll be like a bomb gone off, doesn't matter whose it is. You can say goodnight to Imelda, Joan, the garage too most likely. Yes, she has it all worked out.

You check your phone, send Imelda a quick text. **Almost there Darling Can't wait.** Then you grab the bolt gun and get out of the car.

Little Miss Innocent – what a joke. If a man had a notion what was going on inside a woman's head he'd run a mile, that's what your father always said.

May he rot.

Dickie   But the faces are not unhappy. They are laughing, they are pleased. It is all going terribly well. The band has begun to play the first bars. You look around for Imelda.

Dickie! crackles the walkie-talkie. J*esus, boy, where the fuck are you?*

At the wedding, you say softly.

What? I can't hear you, what?

You smile to the guests, the pink glazed faces, the dealers among them that your father thought it politic to invite, the Nolans of Banaher, the Tighes of Rathcoole; you give a little wave, making your way through the sweltering ballroom to the floor for the first dance.

Yes, a real success, you think. A shame of course that Paddy Joe couldn't come. People wondered about it, no doubt. No father of the bride? You wondered yourself. *But it's one less speech!* you told them. And it was undeniably for the best. You'd taken enough of a chance as it stood, God knows.

Your mother begged you not to do it this way. Why not have something small, she'd said. Why all this show? But you had insisted. It had to be grand, it had to be at the same scale as Frank's. You didn't want it to feel like a consolation prize. *We are going to find joy in this tragedy* – that's what you told her. *We owe it to Frank.*

And you were right, weren't you? Though for a time, you knew, people hadn't been sure. On the street corners, in the pubs, at the petrol station, shouting to each other over the pumps as they filled up their cars, the townsfolk had debated whether this was the right thing. But now they were all behind it, behind *you*, Dickie, rooting for you, as in times past they had rooted for Frank on the football pitch. The Barnes boy had come good, they told each other. He had stepped up, just as he did with the garage; he'd put his notions behind him, done right by his family in the face of great sorrow. And now wasn't he marrying the most beautiful girl in the four provinces?

It was the kind of story that gave everyone a lift. And so they had filled the church, they had sung the hymns and wept at th vows, and at the end they lined up at the door – more of them even than there had been at the funeral – to shake your hand. Freed from the burden of condolence, the embarrassment of its insufficiency, they had looked you in the eye as if seeing you for the first time. Good man, Dickie, they said. *Maith an fear.* Good man.

The only dampener was the bee sting; she was still wearing the veil. At the same time, was it the worst thing? It suggested a hint of sorrow remaining beneath the surface; it silenced any voices that might otherwise have found the celebrations unseemly, *too* joyous. In Imelda's veiled face, anyone who wanted to could divine the pain you had suffered, what it had taken you to get here.

Now, as the music played and you led Imelda onto the floor, you breathed a sigh of relief. You were on the home stretch; you had pulled it off. For the first time in a long time (in a lifetime?) you felt you were standing on solid ground. You turned to her and smiled. But when you placed your hands on her hips, she started, and pulled back. You asked, in a murmur, if she was all right. She stared at you a moment, as if she didn't know who you were. Then, lifting the folds of the dress clear of the floor, she turned and rushed away.

Perhaps you should have expected something like this. She'd been so strange all day, and throughout the speeches, you'd had a sense of agitation, a growing, unaccountable desperation brewing beneath the veil. Her head strained this way and that, searching for something, someone: her father, you thought. Now, as she sped away, you wondered had she finally found him in the crowd. But she continued through the door of the reception room and out of sight.

The guests were too surprised even to react. The music stopped, the band gaped incredulously at the space from which she had disappeared. And you, with a fixed smile on your face, floundered there on the dance floor, alone in the circling disco lights, not knowing what to do. For a moment it appeared everything might collapse. It seemed you could see the cracks, sprinting over the floor, up the walls, the guests starting to blink and check themselves, as though waking from a dream. Then your eyes fell on your mother, watching impassively from the top table, and with a burst of inspiration you went to her and took her hand.

She was clad that day in grey, the furthest she would budge from her mourning: stone-grey, like a statue, and her face too was that of a statue. Not a word, not a flicker of movement, that whole day long, as if she feared the merest tremor of life would send grief exploding through the bones of her face to destroy her. Yet she rose from her chair as if this had been the plan all along. Her fingers were pliant in your hand, and cold, like living marble. The band struck up again; the two of you danced together to the moronic music. The guests took in the spectacle with fond smiles, and applause, and flashing cameras: as if this was the first dance after all, as if they thought she truly was Imelda, or it didn't matter that she was not Imelda, that she was your bereaved mother, expressionlessly waltzing over the parquet. They believed in you, you realized – believed in the person that they'd encountered here tonight, in the transformation they had witnessed, the odd, awkward boy into the likeness of his brother. They had accepted you as one of their own, and anything that might shake that acceptance they would simply refuse to see. That was what it meant to belong.

It was a measure of your success, of the night's success, and yet – here at your moment of triumph – you felt a chill steal over you, eerily akin to that horrible sense you'd have in college when, working on an essay, you pressed the wrong key and accidentally wiped it; and the more you thought it couldn't possibly just be gone, the more it wasn't there. But what was wiped here? What had you lost? As the song reached its climax, and the guests' voices joined in with the chorus, you searched and searched and failed to find an answer: there was only this cold persisting sensation of being *exposed*, in a way that you didn't recall ever feeling before, as though certain protections, magic spells that had shielded you all your life without your knowing, were suddenly gone, and you found yourself alone, nameless, lost amid strangers.

The song drew to a close, the crowd erupted in a cheer; your mother broke away from your arms and in a bitter rasp said, *Go to your wife, Dickie, for the love of God.*

You stumbled away from her; someone thrust a pint into your hand, but you didn't drink, for fear it would pass right through you. In the heat everyone looked strange and horrific, sweat shining from their jowls; the jostle of bodies was like a midnight forest, bone-white and grave-black, that pitched forward, blocked and receded, as if steering you down a secret path . . .

Dickie, Dickie, come in, Victor's voice sizzles from the walkie-talkie. *Dickie, are you there?*

Yes, you say falteringly. Yes, I'm here.

Where? Where are you?

You look around. Wind charges through the clearing, the trees bow to you, sorcerers at a black Mass. The ballroom, the guests, the pint in your hand, all that is gone.

But the path is there still.

I'm close, you say. I'm on my way.

Imelda   You ran Shame burning in your eye Dress clinging to your back in the heat Ran as fast as your legs would carry you out of the reception room with its columns and dark wood through the hall up the grand staircase Not knowing where you were going till you came to your room Flung yourself through the door Slammed it behind you

The bridal suite of Burke's hotel It was the grandest room you'd ever been in Everything gold with a coat of arms Champagne in a bucket on a little table to itself More gifts piled up on the dresser Cookware dinner plates crystal linen bedsheets The rest of your life stacked in a pyramid and tied with ribbons

You went to the window raised the blind Looked out the window there was nothing to see The last of your hope gently ebbed away And as you stood there you wondered how you'd ever believed it All that you'd lived for A child's dream a fairy tale

The truth was that Frank had not been a great one for showing up at the best of times Alive Hale and hearty Those poor under-10s he'd leave hanging around in the rain waiting for him to coach them And weddings Definitely not his thing Couldn't hardly even speak about his own without five pints inside him and a line of coke

Yes it was always going to be a long shot you saw that now

From below came the faraway sound of music laughter and as you listened something did return to you then A story you'd heard once About a traveller who finds his way inside a mountain to a magical feast Beautiful people dancing laughing all that Decked out in gold Join us they say glad to see him and he does Has a brilliant time thinks it will never end Till it ends he wakes up on the hill in the morning Goes home to his home but it's a hundred years later there's no one That's all gone his family his life

What is there left to do but to disappear

You put on the TV lay down on the bed The presenter off that show advertising hair extensions

England after all maybe A fallen woman in a shelter in Cricklewood A witch drinking cider in rags behind the station

Tomorrow you said out loud

Then the door opened and he was standing there

PJ   Things are always coming back. Birds. Comets. Leaves on the trees.

Yeah, that's true.

Rebirth, she says. That's the whole nature thing.

Yes, good point, you say. I forgot about that.

You know she's trying to cheer you up, but it's not working You've got this feeling like in a movie when someone's going down the stairs in the dark to a basement and you're watching thinking no one would ever do that but now the someone is yo and you just keep going down. Around you the woods yawn like a mouth packed with a million teeth, the way the black wet leaves glisten and drip in the torchlight make you think again of squirrel guts, like the whole forest is covered in them. You wish you could just turn back! But you know Cass would laugh if you said it and also there is someone (who?) in the sex house so you can't so you keep going.

I'd forgotten how fucked up the signal is here, Cass says, looking at her phone. I get it for a second, then it vanishes.

Dad says it's spirits.

Spirits?

Yeah, he says spirits control the signal.

She doesn't say anything to that. She looks up and around at the crashing night. Where are we?

I think we're going the right way, you say.

You think? Cass says. What happened to the track?

This is the track, you say. It must just have got a bit over-grown. Though actually you're starting to wonder whether it is in fact the track or even *a* track, because right now you don't recognize anything. It's like the forest has rearranged itself or even that it's a completely different forest, though of course that's impossible.

We're not lost, are we?

It's just because of the storm, you tell her.

Thunder crashes overhead again, the rain hammers down KKKSSCCCCCHHHHH. You wonder if you did turn around would you even be able to find your way back to the road, is there even a road left to find.

Then through the clamour comes a clear, bell-like *ping*. A moment later: Oh my God, Cass says.

What is it?

Nothing. It's just – they're publishing my poem.

What?

I just got an email. She laughs. In a forest in the middle of the night, how random is that.

You wrote a poem? you say.

It's just for this tiny college magazine, she says. It's no big deal.

It's going to be in a magazine? you say. An actual magazine? Made of paper?

It's not one anybody reads, she says.

Wow, you say. Maybe you're going to be famous!

She laughs again and tells you that when she's a millionaire poet living in a big mansion you'll be welcome to stay with her any time. Then she holds up her hand. Wait, she says. Did you hear something?

No, you say, but then you wonder. Like what?

I don't know, she says. Like rustling, she says. Like someone moving through the trees.

Isn't that just the sound the rain makes? you say.

She doesn't reply.

And the two of you stand and stare into the dark, listening.

Augustina   With the lights out the house seems smaller, a tiny thing in the grip of the storm. The walls shake, the wind is like a great hand, pounding its palm on the roof – no, wait. There really is a pounding. You run out to the hall, see a shape in the glass.

Augustina! Open the door!

But it is not Ryszard's shape. And the voice is not his voice.

I can see you! Open the fucking door!

You switch the light off again, run back to the kitchen. How is he here? Why?

The hand thuds on the door again. Then the sound of jingling and an intestinal metallic slurp as he tries a key in the door.

Leave me alone! you scream from the back of the hall.

He is in the house now. He is at the foot of the stairs. He switches on the light. Leave *you* alone? You're in my fucking house! He takes a step towards you, and another. You shrink back into the kitchen. I'm sorry, you gabble. I'm not staying.

No one asked you to come back here! Mike bellows.

I'm not staying, you repeat. I'm leaving now. I just had to ge something. You can't tell if he even hears you. His eyes are black, deathly. Please, you cry. I'm pregnant.

But that only makes him worse. Pregnant? he repeats. Pregnant? And he starts to shout, words that make no sense, money, main street, *black male* – he looms over you, roaring like a bear, you sob, you wrap your hands around your belly. Then he tips backwards as an arm appears around his throat. Ryszard, dripping rain, clings to his back, punches him in the head. Mike reaches over his shoulder to claw at Ryszard's eyes, totters backwards to crush him against the door frame. The light goes on again, off again.

Imelda   Dickie came to you He knelt at your side Can I look? he said And he drew back the veil Colours lights seared like hot irons into your eye In the mirror you saw yourself red raw and swollen

That's not from a bee is it he said

Who did this to you Was it him

You didn't reply Who he him what did it matter You turned to the wall

He stepped away went to the champagne bucket Took an ice cube wrapped it in a handkerchief put it to your eye His hands were gentle Hold it there he said and you did You lay there and felt the cold bite into your skin

While Dickie sat down on the bed beside you Put his elbows on his knees his head in his hands As you watched his shoulders began to shake What have I done he said

Without the veil you could see him clearly for the first time He was the first thing you'd seen clearly in a while in fact And as he sat there you could see that he was a ghost too That Frank had gone and left him here like you Life done but still wandering the earth

That he'd thought tonight would change things That he'd expected something to happen Some transformation or transportation just as you had But here you were it was only the two of you in a room

You would have liked to comfort him He was so sad But what could you say What solace has a ghost for another ghost So you sat and watched him cry and somewhere at the back of your mind you remembered your mother telling you when you were a little girl of the secrets between a woman and a man that you would find out on your wedding night And you wondered if she meant that there was nothing simply nothing That was the secret No spells No magic Just two people in a room seeing for the first time life stretching on ahead of them endlessly And you lay back closed your eyes thought would God only let you die here

That's when you felt it

Cass

The forest is a sea of goblins, slapping you, snagging you, jabbing you, grabbing at your arms and ankles. You run until you can't any more. Then you stop, panting, raise your phone. PJ's face stares back at you, pale, dripping rain. You turn the phone light on the trees surrounding. Every direction shows the same indistinct mass. Well now we're really lost, you say. You shine the light on PJ again. Why'd you run?

Why did *you* run? he counters.

I was following you!

I thought I saw something, he confesses.

Was it a cat? you say. Was it a resurrected zombie cat?

He lowers his eyes, presses his lips together.

So where are we?

He ponders, then snaps his fingers. If we see what side of the trees the moss is growing on, I think that's north.

You think it is? Or it is?

It's north, he says, it's definitely north.

You both look at the nearest trees but they either have no moss or there's moss on every side.

Fuck this forest, you say. PJ concedes that it actually doesn't matter because he doesn't know what direction the house is in anyway.

Dickie   Walking in the darkness. Paths split and split again. You choose without thinking, they are all leading to the same spot.

Dickie, goes the walkie-talkie. *Dickie, I think we've got company.*

You raise the gun sights to your eye. Through the heat vision scope everything is doubly dark, as if all life has been removed from the planet. In the future this is what the world will look like all the time. Darkness illuminated only by enemies.

Augustina   Behind you the house is silent once more. Mike's keys are in the ignition. You turn the car around, take it back towards the road. Everything you own in the bag on the back seat, two grand in cash in your left pocket.

Imelda   The first time you thought you'd imagined it

Then it came again like knocking on a door

Dickie! you said

He raised his head from his lamenting You took his hands and you placed them on your belly

Feel you said

And on his knees by the bedside he looked up at you mouth open

There she is you said That's her

And she You knew it was a she She kicked and kicked like she'd just figured it out Hello Hello Here I am Hello

PJ   This is ridiculous, she says, and opens up her keypad.

What are you doing? you say.

Calling Dad, she says.

Your blood runs cold. You can't! you exclaim.

This place is freaking me out! she yells back. You lunge for the phone but she dodges you, shoves you away. What the fuck! she shouts. Stop being such a child! You come at her again but she pushes you back, just like when you were little kids. She's still taller and stronger. So all you can do is watch from a distance, hating her, while she crouches defensively with the phone pressed to her ear.

Imelda   For a long moment you stayed like that him kneeling before you your hands on his hands on your belly like it was the whole world which it was as far as she was concerned

And at the same time you felt the world re-gather around you or you re-gather in it because you knew from now on things would have to be different There was no more time for lamenting No time to be sorrowful ghosts You would have to be solid flesh and blood right here The two of you together You knew he knew it too We're in it now you said I suppose we are that he said There's no getting round it You laughed He laughed with you put his ear to your tummy the feast inside the mountain

And that was the vow you realize Then There That long moment *We're in it* Two people that had ought to be dead and buried Now here you were in a room in a town together alive That's what the baby was telling you as she thumped around in your womb Alive she was saying This is a miracle I will keep kicking until you get it

Dickie   Suddenly amid the rain you hear a sound, a familiar sound that it takes you a few seconds nevertheless to recognize. Christ! You never set the phone to silent! You scramble a hand into your pocket and dig it out and then see <<CASS>>

And for a long moment you are frozen. You watch the phone glow in your palm, on and off: at the back of your mind the dim form of a memory stirs in response, when she was so small she would fit in your hand and you felt her heart beat against your palm.

Imelda   And then from nowhere your phone beeps with a message Must be Dickie He is thinking the same thing as you Do you remember the time Yes It made me realize Me too Do you think we can Yes We can try Stay where you are so I'm coming back

But no **Almost there Darling Can't wait**

638

Big Mike You had forgotten him You come to a stop there in the forest

Dickie   Then Victor's voice crackles from the walkie-talkie again: *Dickie! I see him! I have a visual!*
          You silence the phone, put it back in your pocket.

PJ   Cass takes the phone from her ear, moves on into the trees without looking back at you.

Imelda   You start to reply But can't think what to say You can hardly go over to him with your eye all swollen up anyway Just leave it for now till you get back to the house Leave it till you've got Dickie out of these woods that's the main thing for now It's not right to be out in weather like this Bunker or no

Cass   You press on into the forest. It's utterly black, even with the torches: like walking into dark matter.

Imelda   No he has not been right for a while Not himself Things have been changing so much Maybe it would be good for him to talk to someone Una might know a good person Tomorrow you'll call her Yes you think and call Lar while you're at it Tell him to come stay Insist this time There's plenty of room What will the girls make of him Your true origins Maybe Roisin will take a shine He can tell her her fortune You will meet a black dog
          And in the instant your smile drops away You come to a halt there in the woods
          As if you could see it in the shadows As if it was stood there for real right in front of you
          That you thought had come for Rose
          Staring at you with eyes like saucers

Dickie   A visual, no. But you hear something, or think you do. And when you raise the scope – isn't that? In the distance, but drawing closer?

J   It's so dark you can hardly make her out now, a shadow among shadows. The staircase feeling of earlier has gone. You're in the basement now. And she must feel the same, because her voice comes thinly out of the dark: Tell me some science.

Science?

One of your weird facts, tell me one of those. I need distraction.

Okay, you say. Any particular area of science?

Anything.

You think for a moment. How about this: did you know that there are more bacterial cells in your body than human cells?

Seriously?

Way more. You have five hundred different species of bacteria just in your intestine. There's enough bacteria inside you to fill a two-litre bottle. Scientists believe some human genes originally came from bacteria.

Well that's disgusting, she says.

Yeah, you say. But when you think about it, it's also pretty interesting. People get so hung up on are they this kind of person or that. But if you have ten times more not-human cells than human cells, then, in a way, you're not even *you*.

It kind of takes the pressure off, you say. I feel like if people knew they were mostly bacteria it would solve a lot of problems.

Cass laughs. *You're* definitely you, she says. Whatever about the bacteria. You're you, a hundred per cent. She shakes her head: and for a moment you get this surge of happiness, there in the wind and the rain, as if somehow the future will actually be okay in spite of everything.

Then Cass says, Hey, look! Isn't that that weird tree?

Imelda   And without knowing why you start to run Fast as you can Running to Dickie just like at the wedding you ran from him But the ground is treacherous Roots and brush grab at your feet Branches spike you slap you stab you jab you The darkness itself pushes you back like it's trying to stop you getting to him like it doesn't want you to get there in time But in time for what? In time for *what?*

Cass   Oh yeah, he says. We must have been going in the right direction after all.

Dickie   Yes, it is – a figure! Red, white and gold, how hot, how bright, in the inky darkness! Promethean! What a thing life is!

Imelda   Just like in a dream the harder you run the less it feels like you're getting anywhere But you keep going You know he's there That you're close

Dickie   *He's almost here! Are you in position?* Yes, you are in position. Yes, you are ready. You have been ready for a long time – you see that now.

Imelda   Dickie! you cry But your words are smothered in the rain

PJ   Now ahead of you at last you see the Bunker.

Doesn't look like there's anyone there, Cass says. I guess we can take shelter for a minute.

And something shrills up inside you, a numb terror.

Cass, you whisper. But how could you begin to describe it.

Dickie   You raise your rifle. You take a deep breath. Every day people have to do things that are ugly, even wrong. Sometimes you have to make sacrifices for the ones that you love. Sometimes what you give up is the best part of yourself.

Imelda   So you run harder again Faster again As if you could run back into the past Take your veil again Dry his eyes again Lie down together again on the bed

Cass   PJ stops and turns to you, arms down by his side, eyes round, and whispers, I'm sorry I made you miss your party.

Dickie   The world is how it is. That's not your fault. You can only think about your family. Do your best to protect them from the worst of it. And when the world breaks through – make sure that they don't suffer.

Imelda   Put his hands on your hands on your belly and tell him again This is the world now It will be how we make it

Dickie	*There's two of them! Do you see?* Yes, you see their torches flash in and out through the thickets. But you remain calm – you have never felt so calm.
Cass	Whisper back to him, I'm glad you did – I'm glad I found you.
Dickie	Kneel down, resting your elbow on your thigh, the gun to your shoulder. Remind yourself why you are doing this.
PJ	A click from somewhere – a glint of light –
Imelda	It's not too late We can start again
Cass	Grey squirrel! you cry and you grab your brother's hand –

It is for love. You are doing this for love.

ACKNOWLEDGEMENTS

Thank you: Hermione Thompson, Mitzi Angel, Simon Prosser, Natasha Fairweather, Matthew Marland, Milo Walls, Mary Chamberlain, Yasmin McDonald, Sarah Bannan, Ailbhe Reddy, Ciaran O'Neill, Hannah Lennon, Christopher and Kathleen Murray, Christian Dupont and the Burns Library at Boston College.

Thanks to the Arts Council of Ireland for their financial support.

Thanks to Joe Nugent and Annemarie Lawless for their friendship and stories.

To Miriam and Parker: my love and gratitude always.

SKIPPY DIES

PAUL MURRAY

Ruprecht Van Doren is an overweight, adolescent genius whose hobbies include very difficult maths and the Search for Extra-Terrestrial Intelligence. Daniel 'Skippy' Juster is his roommate. Nobody at Seabrook College for Boys pays either of them much attention. But when Skippy falls for Lori, the frisbee-playing siren from the girls' school next door, suddenly all kinds of people start taking an interest – including Carl, part-time drug-dealer and official school psychopath . . .

A tragicomedy of epic proportions, *Skippy Dies* is a dazzling, uproarious love letter to the pain, joy and occasional beauty of adolescence, and an unforgettable meditation on the cruelty of a world always happy to sacrifice its weakest members.

'That rare thing, a comic epic . . . Murray is a brilliant comic writer, but also humane and touching'

David Nicholls, *Guardian*

'A tragicomic tour de force . . . I loved *Skippy Dies*'

Ali Smith, *Times Literary Supplement*

'A triumph . . . Brimful of wit and narrative energy'

Sunday Times